Praise for *The Avram 1*

"My favorite book of 1998—by far—is *The Avram Davidson Treasury*. Davidson was beyond question one of the unjustly neglected writers of the twentieth century, an author of immense talent and the most formidable erudition who died alone and in poverty. I met him long, long ago when I was too young and too badly read to understand what an honor Fate had vouchsafed me. About twenty years later I glimpsed him as I walked swiftly by the open door of a hotel room: that patriarchal face, those knowing eyes, at once cynical and devout. For two days I wracked my brain, certain I had seen a great man while utterly ignorant of the identity of the great man I had seen. At last it came to me.

"What more can I tell you? That he was one of the very few to serve in both World War II (Pacific Theater) and the Five Day War? That magic streamed from his heart into the hearts of his readers? How about this: I sent him a pocket knife with which to peel his apple shortly before he died; and he wrote 'My Boy Friend's Name Is Jello,' 'The Golem,' 'Help! I Am Dr. Morris Goldpepper,' 'Or All the Seas with Oysters,' 'Ogre in the Vly,' 'The Woman Who Thought She Could Read,' 'The Sources of the Nile,' 'Goslin Day,' 'Polly Charms, the Sleeping Woman,' 'Manatee Gal, Won't You Come Out Tonight,' and 'The Slovo Stove.' All those wonderful stories are in this book, with many others and a raft of introductions; and if all that isn't enough, there is a foreword by Robert Silverberg and afterwords by Ray Bradbury and Harlan Ellison."

—Gene Wolfe

"Avram Davidson (1923–1993) was one of the most original and charming writers of our time. So, it almost goes without saying, he was generally neglected and undervalued during much of his career. . . . Grasping fruitlessly for comparisons, his admirers have likened Davidson to Saki, Chesterton, John Collier, Lafcadio Hearn, Kipling, even I. B. Singer and S. J. Perelman. And you can see what they mean. I would add that he frequently reminds me of the *New Yorker* writer Joseph Mitchell: two similarly brilliant stylists with a compassionate interest in bohemians, losers, immigrant culture, New York, oddities, con artists, crackpot inventors, and the passing of humane, small-scale neighborhood life."

—Michael Dirda, *The Washington Post Book World*

"A great and truly wondrous collection . . . The book contains the cream of Davidson's short stories, which means it is an anthology no serious student of short fantasy can afford to miss. This is how to do it if you be interested in horror, science fiction, Faerie, or diving into forms untried and altogether new. This is how it's done."

—Gahan Wilson

"*The Avram Davidson Treasury*, with its generous selection, all-star story introductions, and characteristic Davidsonian unpredictability, was the most surprising and enlightening retrospective of the year."

—*Locus*

"Of all writers (except, perhaps, Kipling), the most likely to insert the marvellous into the everyday."

—Guy Davenport

"Avram's ear for weird ways of talking was wonderful."

—Ursula K. Le Guin

"The best by a giant in the field."

—*Toronto Star*

"A king's ransom of short fiction from one of America's least-known masters of the form . . . These stories are as important and vital as those by Updike and Cheever."

—*Des Moines Register*

The

AVRAM DAVIDSON

Treasury

A TRIBUTE COLLECTION

EDITED BY

Robert Silverberg
&
Grania Davis

TOR®

A TOM DOHERTY ASSOCIATES BOOK
NEW YORK

THE AVRAM DAVIDSON TREASURY

Copyright © 1998 by Grania Davis

This book is printed on acid-free paper.

Edited by Teresa Nielsen Hayden

Design by Judith Stagnitto Abbate

A Tor Book
Published by Tom Doherty Associates, LLC
175 Fifth Avenue
New York, NY 10010

www.tor.com

Tor® is a registered trademark of Tom Doherty Associates, LLC.

Library of Congress Cataloging-in-Publication Data

Davidson, Avram.
The Avram Davidson treasury : a tribute collection / edited
by Robert Silverberg & Grania Davis.
p.   cm.
"A Tom Doherty Associates book."
ISBN 0-312-86729-8 (hc)
ISBN 0-312-86731-X (pbk)
1. Science fiction, American. I. Silverberg, Robert.
II. Davis, Grania. III. Title.
PS3554.A924A6 1998
813'.54—dc21
                                                98-23556
                                                CIP

First Hardcover Edition: October 1998
First Trade Paperback Edition: September 1999

Printed in the United States of America

0   9   8   7   6   5   4   3   2   1

To Puff, Herman, and Mudge
Who Made Us Laugh
and
To Seth Davis, Dr. Stephen Davis, and Ethan Davidson
The Mighty Copy-Shop Crew

Contents

THE EIGHTIES AND NINETIES

Foreword

OH, AVRAM, AVRAM, WHAT A WONDER YOU WERE!

Robert Silverberg

H<small>E WAS A SMALLISH</small>, rumpled, bearded man who had the look of a rabbi for some down-at-the-heels inner-city Orthodox congregation. He had a rabbi's arcane erudition, a rabbi's insight into human foibles, a rabbi's twinkling avuncular charm, a rabbi's amiable self-mocking modesty; and, of course, a rabbi's profound faith in Judaism, at least until, to my amazement if not his own, he gave up all his obsessive observance of the myriad Jewish rules and regulations and converted late in life to an exotic Japanese cult called Tenrikyo. He was also one of the finest short-story writers ever to use the English language, as the fortunate readers of this book are about to discover, or to rediscover, whichever is the case.

I can't remember when or precisely where I met him, though it had to have been in New York City somewhere between 1956 and 1961. During those years I lived in a spacious and pleasant apartment on the fourth floor of a building on Manhattan's Upper West Side, and I distinctly recall Avram's coming to visit me on a Friday night—the eve of the Jewish Sabbath—when, as I had forgotten at the time, it is forbidden for Orthodox Jews to perform any sort of mechanical labor. The prohibition extends even unto pressing a button to summon an elevator; and so Avram diligently walked up the four flights of stairs to my apartment that evening, and walked down again when he left, which struck me—Jewish also, but not particularly observant—as a charming but bizarre adherence to Talmudic dogma.

But I think we must have met even before that, for why would I have invited an utter stranger to my apartment? I can't tell you where that first Davidson-Silverberg encounter took place, though my memory for such things normally is extraordinarily precise. And, oddly, considering the rare precision of Avram's own memory, he came to forget the details of our first meeting also, as I know from the evidence of a letter from him dated July 17, 1971, in which Avram wrote, apropos of nothing in particular, "We—you and I—first met in an apt in Mannahattoe; but *whose*? Fit would help you to recall, you had been talking about a story you'd just then written, '. . . and on this planet the people have no sexual parts, they're all built like dolls. . . .' Hey! a great title! 'All Built Like Dolls.' But you can have it if you like."

I quote this not only to illustrate that Avram was capable of forgetting things occasionally too, but also to demonstrate certain notable idiosyncracies of the man and of his style. Consider his use of the archaic term "Mannahattoe" for "Manhattan"—the original uncorrupted Native American name for that island in New York Harbor, which the Dutch twisted into the form used today, and which Avram of course knew, paying me the compliment of expecting that I would know it too. (I did.) Note also his genial colloquialism "Fit" for "If it," and the borrowing from his friend and colleague Philip K. Dick in his use of "apt" for "apartment," and the generosity implicit in his offering me, without strings, the story title he had plucked from my account of my own recent story. (A story of which, by the way, I have no recollection whatever; but all this was close to forty years ago, and there are a lot of stories I wrote then that I no longer remember, nor do I want to.)

Anyway, I definitely did meet Avram in New York City somewhere in the 1950s, and thereafter we maintained a pleasant acquaintanceship for decades. We were not precisely close friends, with all the intimate sharing of woes and triumphs and confessions that that term implies in my mind, but certainly we were friends of some sort, and beyond doubt we maintained a warm collegial relationship, fellow toilers in the vineyard of letters, always ready to exchange tidbits of professional information with each other or to query each other on some point of esoteric knowledge. (I quote from a typical letter from him, under date of Dec 8 1984: "As I know that you have a complete collection of EVERYTHING, and that there is nothing you like better than LOOKING THINGS UP to please a friend, so I am asking you, please, to find out: Who wrote the *Galaxy* 'Bookshelf' review column in #6 vol. 39. . . .")

In the days when we both lived in New York, we saw each other most frequently at the monthly gatherings of the local science-fiction-writer's organization, a pleasant casual group called the Hydra Club, or at parties held at various writers' homes, such as at the one in (I believe) 1961, given by Daniel Keyes of "Flowers for Algernon" fame, at which Avram proudly introduced us to his (literally) blushing teenage bride Grania, with whom I would sustain a friendship extending decades beyond her marriage to Avram, and who is now my esteemed co-editor on this project. And often we would meet and break booze together at some science-fiction convention, where Avram was always a welcome sight to see, since he was in the habit of carrying a bag of excellent New York bagels around with him to distribute to his friends. (One time, also, he had a pocketful of coproliths—fossilized dinosaur turds—which he distributed similarly to those he knew would appreciate them. I cherish mine to this day.)

Avram entered New York s-f social circles with an instantly lofty literary reputation. Since 1946 his work had been appearing in places like *Orthodox Jewish Life Magazine*, but we knew nothing of that. However, his first professionally published story, "My Boy Friend's Name Is Jello" (*Fantasy & Science Fiction*, July 1954), though only a few pages long, announced immediately that a quirky, utterly original writer, as distinctive in his way as Ray Bradbury was in his, had arrived in our field. The following year the same magazine offered the similarly brief and similarly impressive "The Golem," and then, in 1956 and 1957 and 1958, came a whole flurry of concise and brilliant little Davidson tales in nearly all the science-fiction magazines at once.

The New York s-f community, which at that time included (if you count its suburban branch in Milford, Pennsylvania) virtually all the movers and shakers of the field, was awed and captivated by the prolific performance of the kindly, charming, formidably learned, and rather peculiar little man who had taken up residence in its midst. He was, at the same time, contributing dazzling mystery stories to the premier mystery magazine of the day, *Ellery Queen's*. Plainly there was a prodigious writer here. The author of "Help! I Am Dr. Morris Goldpepper" (*Galaxy*, July 1957)—that's the one about the Jewish dentist who sends messages back from an alien planet, where he is being held captive, via dental fixtures—could be nothing other than a genius. The author of "Or All the Seas With Oysters" (*Galaxy*, May 1958), the story of alien residents of Earth who disguise themselves as safety pins in their pupal form and become coat-hangers when they reach the larval stage, must surely be a man of distinctly original mind. (So original, indeed, that he could conceive of pupas hatching into larvae, a stunning reversal of the usual order of things.) Not that the only thing he wrote was high whimsy; for there was the dark and brooding "Now Let Us Sleep" (*Venture*, September 1957) and the sinister Dunsanyesque fantasy "Dagon" (*Fantasy & Science Fiction*, October 1959) and the quietly passionate "Or the Grasses Grow" (*Fantasy & Science Fiction*, November 1958) and ever so much more.

So we clustered around this curious little man at our parties and got to know him, and when his stories appeared we bought the magazines that contained them and read them; and our appreciation, and even love, for his work and for him knew no bounds. He was courtly and droll. He was witty. He was lovable. He could be, to be sure, a little odd and cranky at times (though not nearly as much as he would come to be, decades later, in his eccentric and cantankerous old age), but we understood that geniuses were entitled to be odd and cranky. And that he was a genius we had no doubt. Ray Bradbury, in an introduction to a collection of Davidson short stories that was published in 1971, spoke of his work in the same breath as that of Rudyard Kipling, Saki, John Collier, and G. K. Chesterton, and no one who knows Avram's work well would call Bradbury guilty of hyperbole in that.

Even though Avram had seemed to materialize among us like a stranger from another world, there in the mid-1950s, it turned out that he was in fact a New Yorker like the rest of us. (Well, not strictly like the rest of us, because Avram wasn't really like anyone else at all, and the fact that he came from the suburban city of Yonkers rather than from one of the five boroughs of New York City disqualified him as a true New Yorker for a city boy like me.) Indeed he had been active in New York science-fiction fandom in his teens—co-founder, no less, of the Yonkers Science Fiction League. (I find the concept of

a teenage Avram Davidson as difficult to comprehend as the concept of the
Yonkers Science Fiction League, but so be it.) Exactly where he had been living
immediately before his debut in the science fiction magazines, I was never sure,
though he did once admit to having served in the Israeli Army at the time of
Israel's independence in 1948; certainly he gave the impression of one who was
returning to New York after prolonged absence in exotic parts. In one of his
infrequent autobiographical pieces he revealed this much:

> Well, I was born in Yonkers, New York in 1923, and I attended the
> public school system there and some short time at New York Uni-
> versity. Then I went into the Navy at the end of 1942 and stayed there
> until the beginning of 1946. Most of that time was spent at various air
> stations in Florida; I was attached to the 5th Marine regiment, was in
> the South Pacific, and then in China. Came back, went back to school
> a little bit, but never took any degrees; and in fact never was on campus
> again until I was a visiting instructor or writer many decades later.

Born in 1923—that means he was only thirty-five or so when I first met
him at that unspecified party at an indeterminable time in the late 1950s. Which
is hard to believe now, because I think of thirty-five-year-olds these days as
barely postgraduate, and Avram, circa 1958, bearded and rotund and profes-
sorial, seemed to be at least sixty years old. (Beards were uncommon things
then.) Of course, I was only twenty-something myself, then, and *everybody* in
science fiction except Harlan Ellison seemed sixty years old or thereabouts to
me. But Avram always looked older than his years; he went on looking a
perpetual sixty for the next quarter of a century, and then, I guess, as his health
gave way in his not very happy later years, he began finally to look older than
that.

He led a complicated life. For a couple of years, from 1962 to 1964, he was
the dazzlingly idiosyncratic editor of *Fantasy & Science Fiction*, and many a
wondrously oddball story did he purchase and usher into print during that
time. Then he went off with Grania to Mexico, and lived in a place called
Amecameca, the name of which fascinated me for its repetitive rhythm, and in
Belize, formerly British Honduras, for a time after that, before settling for a
prolonged period in California. Somewhere along the way he and Grania split
up, though in an extremely amicable way; she remarried, Avram never did, and
for years thereafter Avram functioned as a kind of auxiliary uncle in the California household of Grania and her second husband, Dr. Stephen Davis. In
1980 or thereabouts he gravitated northward to the Seattle region, where he
spent the last years of his life, the years of the diminishing career and the
increasing financial problems and the series of strokes and the ever more querulous, embittered letters to old friends. (Which, nevertheless, were inevitably
marked with flashes of the old Avram wit and charm.)

His career as a writer was, I think, more checkered than it needed to be.
He had, as I hope I've made clear, the respect and admiration and downright
awe of most of his colleagues; and he was not without acclaim among readers,
either. "Or All the Seas with Oysters" won the Hugo award in 1958 for the

best short s-f story of the previous year; "The Necessity of His Condition" (*Ellery Queen's Mystery Magazine*, April, 1957) won the 1957 Ellery Queen Award; "The Affair at Lahore Cantonment" (*Ellery Queen's Mystery Magazine,* June 1961) took the Edgar Award of the Mystery Writers of America; the World Fantasy Convention gave him its Howard trophy in 1976 for his short story collection *The Enquiries of Dr. Esterhazy,* and again in 1979 for his short story "Naples," and once more in 1986 for Lifetime Achievement, an award that has also been given to the likes of Italo Calvino, Ray Bradbury, Jorge Luis Borges, and Roald Dahl.

But there is more to a professional writing career than winning awards and the respect of your peers. Avram remained close to the poverty line for most of his adult life. This was due, in part, to the resolutely individual nature of his work: His recondite and often abstruse fictions, bedded as they often were in quaint and curious lore known to few other than he, were not the stuff of best-sellers, nor did the increasingly hermetic style of his later writings endear him to vast audiences in search of casual entertainment. Beyond that, though, lay an utter indifference to commercial publishing values that encouraged him to follow his artistic star wherever it led, even if that meant abandoning a promising trilogy of novels one or two thirds of the way along, leaving hopeful readers forever frustrated. Nor was he as congenial in his business dealings as he was in his conversations with his colleagues. There was a subtext of toughness in Avram not always apparent at superficial glance—remember, this mild and bookish and rabbinical little man served with the Marines in the Pacific during World War II, and then saw action in the Arab-Israeli War of 1948—and, as the economic hardships of his adult life turned him increasingly testy, he became exceedingly difficult and troublesome to deal with, thereby making the problems of his professional life even worse.

Be that as it may. Avram is dead, now—he died near Seattle, weary and poor, just after his seventieth birthday—but his work lives on, free at last of the shroud of rancor that he wove around it in his final years. The stories are magical and wondrous. It will be your great privilege to read them; or, if that is the case, to read them once again. You will want to seek out the best of his novels afterward—*The Phoenix and the Mirror* and *The Island Under the Earth* and *Peregrine: Primus.* They will be hard to find; they will be worth the search. We are all of us one-of-a-kind writers, really, but Avram was more one-of-a-kind than most. How lucky for us that he passed this way; how good it is to have the best of his stories available once more.

—ROBERT SILVERBERG
September, 1995

Foreword

STARSHIP AVRAM: A WRITERS'
MEMORIAL PARTY

GRANIA DAVIS

AVRAM DAVIDSON: APRIL 23, 1923–MAY 8, 1993

AVRAM DAVIDSON'S REMARKABLE WRITING career spanned nearly half a century. He lived and wrote enough for many lifetimes—he was writing letters to beloved friends on the day he passed away in May 1993. He discovered "magical realism" before the term was invented, and his later works of imaginative fiction are as strong and inventive as the powerful stories of his youth.

He wrote intensely, and published over two hundred works of short fiction. Many stories are award winners or award nominees, or were included in "Best of . . ." anthologies. The score stands at:

Five World Fantasy Award nominations, and three awards (Best Short Fiction, Best Collection, and Life Achievement).

Seven Nebula nominations, covering *all* categories. (The Nebula is awarded by one's colleagues in the Science Fiction and Fantasy Writers of America.)

Two Edgar nominations and one award, for Best Short Mystery Story, from his fellow Mystery Writers of America.

The Ellery Queen Award for Best Short Mystery Story.

Appearances in nearly fifty (count 'em!) "Best Of . . ." anthologies.

(And a partridge in a pear tree. . . .)

Yet many of these acclaimed stories have never appeared in an Avram Davidson collection, or have fallen out of print and are rare and hard to find.

Avram once wrote, "A labor which might have made Hercules pause is persuading a publisher to issue a collection of short stories. At the first suggestion of it they whine, whimper, climb trees, and go seek their homes in the rocks like the aunts." (Preface to *Strange Seas and Shores*, Doubleday, 1971.)

But here they are—or at least some of them, gathered into a wonderful, whiz-bang volume. Ask your bookseller for more.

Avram Davidson has always been a writers' writer—the author that other authors choose when they want a warm, witty, literate read. This became strikingly clear when we sent invitations to his friends and colleagues, requesting introductions to their favorite Avram Davidson stories—a sort of Writers' Memorial Party. The response was exciting, as you will see. Many stories in this book were award winners or nominees; most of them appeared in one or more "Best of . . ." anthologies; and all of them were picked by a respected author of imaginative fiction as a beloved favorite.

I want to thank all the authors who wrote introductions, and pass along Avram's advice to you:

A million schoolmams, male and female, have taught us as if teaching geometry or other holy writ, that a story must have a beginning, a middle, and an end. And, of course, a story has. The beginning of a story is where it begins, the middle of a story is where it middens, and the end of a story is where it ends. This is exemplified by the one book found even in homes where the mom and the dad have provided no Bible, namely the telephone book. It begins at A and it ends at Z and it middens at or about L. It is the story or song of the Tenth Sister, Elemenope, the Muse of the Alphabet. Characters? *Look* at all those characters! Plots? Plots? As many as you like. From Abbott Plott to Zygmunt Plotz. (Afterword to *The Best of Avram Davidson*, Doubleday, 1979.)

This book has been the cooperative effort of Avram Davidson's friends, and mine. I owe thanks and gratitude to every one—you are *each* a treasure. To Robert Silverberg, my esteemed co-editor, and to Teresa Nielsen Hayden, our Tor editor, who was with us from the start. To every friend who wrote an introduction—and especially to every friend who *offered* to write an introduction, even after the book was filled. To my dear husband, Dr. Stephen L. Davis, and my fine sons Ethan Davidson and Seth Davis (Avram Davidson's son and godson), who made countless field-trips to the dreaded copy-shop. To Darrell Schweitzer and George Scithers at Owlswick Literary Agency, who persevered, and to Peter Crowther and Stewart Wieck, who got our ball rolling. Many thanks to author Sr. Richard Gibbons, who kept it together, and to Davidson bibliographers extraordinaire, Richard Grant, who saved so much, and *vajra* Henry Wessells. To those who listened patiently, tracked down information, offered help and ideas, encouragement, kindness and love in so many ways—you know who you are.

Thanks most of all to the readers, who are about to embark on an adventure. You are in for some laughs and verbal thrills, and your mind will be bent in many directions. Please remember that some of the stories were written decades ago, when language customs were different—like those wonderful old black-and-white *noir* films, where all the women are called "babe." Fasten your seat belts, hold onto your hats, and don't forget to send postcards home.

STARSHIP AVRAM TAKING OFF—BON VOYAGE.

YOURSLY YOURS (AS AVRAM OFTEN SAID),

GRANIA DAVIS (THE "IRON KREPLACH"),
1998, SAN RAFAEL, CALIFORNIA, AND KAHUKU,
    HAWAII

Acknowledgments

"The Affair at Lahore Cantonment" first appeared in *Ellery Queen's Mystery Magazine*, June 1961

"And Don't Forget the One Red Rose" first appeared in *Playboy*, September 1975

"Author, Author" first appeared in *The Magazine of Fantasy and Science Fiction*, July 1959

"Crazy Old Lady" first appeared in *Ellery Queen's Mystery Magazine*, March 1976

"Dagon" first appeared in *The Magazine of Fantasy and Science Fiction*, October 1959

"Full Chicken Richness" first appeared in *The Last Wave*, vol. 1, October 1983

"The Golem" first appeared in *The Magazine of Fantasy and Science Fiction*, July 1958

"Goobers" first appeared in *Swank*, November 1965

"Goslin Day" first appeared in *Orbit 6*, 1970, ed. Damon Knight

"Hark! Was That the Squeal of an Angry Throat?" first appeared in *Fantastic*, December 1977

"Help! I Am Dr. Morris Goldpepper" first appeared in *Galaxy*, July 1957

"The Hills Behind Hollywood High" (with Grania Davis) first appeared in *The Magazine of Fantasy and Science Fiction*, April 1983

"The House the Blakeneys Built" first appeared in *The Magazine of Fantasy and Science Fiction*, January 1965

"The Last Wizard" first appeared in *Ellery Queen's Mystery Magazine*, December 1972

"Manatee Gal, Won't You Come Out Tonight" first appeared (as "Manatee Gal, Ain't You Coming Out Tonight") in *The Magazine of Fantasy and Science Fiction*, April 1977

"My Boy Friend's Name Is Jello" first appeared in *The Magazine of Fantasy and Science Fiction*, July 1954

"Naples" first appeared in *Shadows*, ed. Charles L. Grant (Doubleday, 1978)

"The Necessity of His Condition" first appeared in *Ellery Queen's Mystery Magazine*, April 1957

"Now Let Us Sleep" first appeared in *Venture Science Fiction*, September 1957

"Ogre in the Vly" first appeared (as "The Ogre") in *Worlds of If*, July 1959

"Or All the Seas with Oysters" first appeared in *Galaxy*, May 1958

"Or the Grasses Grow" first appeared in *The Magazine of Fantasy and Science Fiction*, November 1958

"Polly Charms, The Sleeping Woman" first appeared in *The Magazine of Fantasy and Science Fiction*, February 1975

"The Power of Every Root" first appeared in *The Magazine of Fantasy and Science Fiction*, October 1967

"The Price of a Charm; or, The Lineaments of Gratified Desire" first appeared (as "Price of a Charm") in *Ellery Queen's Mystery Magazine*, December 1963

"Revenge of the Cat-Lady" first appeared in *The Magazine of Fantasy and Science Fiction*, January 1985 (1,700 words)

"Revolver" first appeared in *Ellery Queen's Mystery Magazine*, October 1962

"Sacheverell" first appeared in *The Magazine of Fantasy and Science Fiction*, March 1964

"Selectra Six-Ten" first appeared in *The Magazine of Fantasy and Science Fiction*, October 1970

"The Slovo Stove" first appeared in *Universe 15*, ed. Terry Carr (Doubleday, 1985)

"The Sources of the Nile" first appeared in *The Magazine of Fantasy and Science Fiction*, January 1961

"The Spook-Box of Theodore Delafont De Brooks" first appeared in *Tomorrow*, July 1993

"Take Wooden Indians" first appeared in *Galaxy*, June 1959

"The Tail-Tied Kings" first appeared in *Galaxy*, April 1962

"Where Do You Live, Queen Esther?" first appeared in *Ellery Queen's Mystery Magazine*, March 1961

"While You're Up" first appeared in *The Magazine of Fantasy and Science Fiction*, November 1988

"The Woman Who Thought She Could Read" first appeared in *The Magazine of Fantasy and Science Fiction*, January 1959

"Yellow Rome; or, Vergil and the Vestal Virgin" first appeared in *Weird Tales*, no. 305, Winter 1992–1993

THE FIFTIES

My Boy Friend's Name Is Jello

INTRODUCTION BY ROBERT SILVERBERG

This little story was the science-fiction world's introduction to the art of Avram Davidson. It occupied just four pages of the July, 1954 issue of The Magazine of Fantasy and Science Fiction, *which then was an elegant and fastidious publication edited by the elegant and fastidious Anthony Boucher, a connoisseur of fine wines and opera and mystery stories and fantasy, and his colleague J. Francis McComas. Boucher's brief introduction to the story went like this:*

> *Avram Davidson, scholar and critic, has the most beautiful beard that has ever visited our office, and one of the most attractively wide-ranging minds, full of fascinating lore on arcane and unlikely subjects. For his first fiction outside of specialized Jewish publications, he takes his theme from an offtrail branch of folklore, the baffling rime-games sung by little girls, with distinctive and delightful results.*

Thus the new author was placed perfectly for us as he actually was: the bearded scholar with the wide-ranging off-beat mind. And Avram did the rest, with the dazzling opening paragraph that (while seeming to be bewilderingly diffuse) actually communicates a dozen different significant things about the narrator and his predicament, and then, deftly leading us onward through one circumlocution after another, depositing us less than two thousand words later at the sharply ironic final moment.

It was all there, right at the outset: the cunning narrative strategy, the mannered prose, the flourish of esoteric erudition, the sly wit, all done up in a four-page marvel of a story. Surely we all saw, right away, that a stream of further masterpieces would follow this introductory tidbit. Surely we did: surely. Oh, Avram, Avram, what a wonder you were!

MY BOY FRIEND'S NAME IS JELLO

FASHION, NOTHING BUT FASHION. Virus X having in the medical zodiac its course half i-run, the physician (I refuse to say "doctor" and, indeed, am tempted to use the more correct "apothecary")—the physician, I say, tells me I have Virus Y. No doubt in the Navy it would still be called Catarrhal Fever. They say that hardly anyone had appendicitis until Edward VII came down with it a few weeks before his coronation, and thus made it fashionable. He (the medical man) is dosing me with injections of some stuff that comes in vials. A few centuries ago he would have used herbal clysters.... Where did I read that old remedy for the quinsy ("putrescent sore throat," says my dictionary)? *Take seven weeds from seven meads and seven nails from seven steeds.* Oh dear, how my mind runs on. I must be feverish. An ague, no doubt.

Well, rather an ague than a pox. A pox is something one wishes on editors ... strange breed, editors. The females all have names like Lulu Ammabelle Smith or Minnie Lundquist Bloom, and the males have little horns growing out of their brows. They must all be Quakers, I suppose, for their letters invariably begin, "Dear Richard Roe" or "Dear John Doe," as if the word *mister* were a Vanity ... when they write at all, that is; and meanwhile Goodwife Moos calls weekly for the rent. If I ever have a son (than which nothing is more unlikely) who shows the slightest inclination of becoming a writer, I shall instantly prentice him to a fishmonger or a Master Chimney Sweep. Don't write about Sex, the editors say, and don't write about Religion, or about History. If, however, you *do* write about History, be sure to add Religion and Sex. If one sends in a story about a celibate atheist, however, do you think they'll buy it?

In front of the house two little girls are playing one of those clap-handie games. Right hand, left hand, cross hands on bosom, left hand, right hand ... it makes one dizzy to watch. And singing the while:

My *boy* friend's *name* is *Jel*lo,
He *comes* from *Cincinel*lo,
With a *pim*ple on his *nose*

And *three* fat toes;
And *that's* the *way* my *story* goes!

There is a pleasing surrealist quality to this which intrigues me. In general
I find little girls enchanting. What a shame they grow up to be *big* girls and
make our lives as miserable as we allow them, and oft-times more. Silly, nasty-
minded critics, trying to make poor Dodgson a monster of abnormality, simply
because he loved Alice and was capable of following her into Wonderland. I
suppose they would have preferred him to have taken a country curacy and
become another Pastor Quiverful. A perfectly normal and perfectly horrible
existence, and one which would have left us all still on *this* side of the looking
glass.

Whatever was in those vials doesn't seem to be helping me. I suppose old
Dover's famous Powders hadn't the slightest fatal effect on the germs, bacteria,
or virus (viri?), but at least they gave one a good old sweat (ipecac) and a mild,
non-habit-forming jag (opium). But they're old-fashioned now, and so there
we go again, round and round, one's train of thought like a Japanese waltzing
mouse. I used to know a Japanese who—now, stop that. Distract yourself. Talk
to the little girls . . .

Well, that was a pleasant interlude. We discussed (quite gravely, for I never
condescend to children) the inconveniences of being sick, the unpleasantness
of the heat; we agreed that a good rain would cool things off. Then their attention began to falter, and I lay back again. Miss Thurl may be in soon. Mrs.
Moos (perfect name, she lacks only the antlers) said, whilst bringing in the
bowl of slops which the medicine man allows me for victuals, said, My Sister
Is Coming Along Later And She's Going To Fix You Up Some Nice Flowers.
Miss Thurl, I do believe, spends most of her time fixing flowers. Weekends she
joins a confraternity of over-grown campfire girls and boys who go on hiking
trips, comes back sunburned and sweating and carrying specimen samples of
plant and lesser animal life. However, I must say for Miss Thurl that she is
quiet. Her brother-in-law, the bull-Moos, would be in here all the time if I
suffered it. He puts stupid quotations in other people's mouths. He will talk
about the weather and I will not utter a word, then he will say, Well, It's Like
You Say, It's Not The Heat But The Humidity.

Thinking of which, I notice a drop in the heat, and I see it is raining. That
should cool things off. How pleasant. A pity that it is washing away the marks
of the little girls' last game. They played this one on the sidewalk, with chalked-
out patterns and bits of stone and broken glass. They chanted and hopped back
and forth across the chalkmarks and shoved the bits of stone and glass—or
were they potshards—"potsie" from potshard, perhaps? I shall write a mon-
ograph, should I ever desire a Ph.D. I will compare the chalkmarks with Toltec
emblems and masons' marks and the signs which Hindoo holy men smear on
themselves with wood ashes and perfumed cow dung. All this passes for erudition.

I feel terrible, despite the cool rain. Perhaps without it, I should feel worse.

Miss Thurl was just here. A huge bowl of blossoms, arranged on the table across the room. Intricately arranged, I should say; but she put some extra touches to it, humming to herself. Something ever so faintly reminiscent about that tune, and vaguely disturbing. Then she made one of her rare remarks. She said that I needed a wife to take care of me. My blood ran cold. An icy sweat (to quote Catullus, that wretched Priapist), bedewed my limbs. I moaned. Miss Thurl at once departed, murmuring something about a cup of tea. If I weren't so weak I'd knot my bedsheets together and escape. But I am terribly feeble.

It's unmanly to weep....

Back she came, literally poured the tea down my throat. A curious taste it had. Sassafrass? Bergamot? Mandrake root? It is impossible to say how old Miss Thurl is. She wears her hair parted in the center and looped back. Ageless... ageless...

I thank whatever gods may be that Mr. Ahyellow came in just then. The other boarder (upstairs), a greengrocer, decent fellow, a bit short-tempered. He wished me soon well. He complained he had his own troubles, foot troubles... I scarcely listened, just chattered, hoping the Thurl would get her hence.... Toes... something about his toes. Swollen, three of them, quite painful. A bell tinkled in my brain. I asked him how he spelt his name. A-j-e-l-l-o. Curious, I never thought of that. Now, I wonder what he could have done to offend the little girls? Chased them from in front of his store, perhaps. There is a distinct reddish spot on his nose. By tomorrow he will have an American Beauty of a pimple.

Fortunately he and Miss Thurl went out together. I must think this through. I must remain cool. Aroint thee, thou mist of fever. This much is obvious: There are sorcerers about. Sorcer*esses,* I mean. The little ones made rain. And they laid a minor curse on poor Ajello. The elder one has struck me in the very vitals, however. If I had a cow it would doubtless be dry by this time. Should I struggle? Should I submit? Who knows what lies behind those moss-colored eyes, what thoughts inside the skull covered by those heavy tresses? Life with Mr. and Mrs. Moos is—even by itself—too frightful to contemplate. Why doesn't she lay her traps for Ajello? Why should I be selected as the milk-white victim for the Hymeneal sacrifice? Useless to question. Few men have escaped once the female cast the runes upon them. And the allopath has nothing in his little black bag, either, which can cure.

Blessed association of words! Allopath—Homeopath—*homoios,* the like, the same, *pathos,* feeling, suffering—*similia similibus curantur*—

The little girls are playing beneath my window once more, clapping hands and singing. Something about a boy friend named Tony, who eats macaroni, has a great big knife and a pretty little wife, and will always lead a happy life... that must be the butcher opposite; he's always kind to the children.... Strength, strength! The work of a moment to get two coins from my wallet and throw them down. What little girl could resist picking up a dime which fell in front of her? *"Cross my palm with silver, pretty gentleman!"*—eh? And now to tell them my tale...

I feel better already. I don't think I'll see Miss Thurl again for a while. She opened the door, the front door, and when the children had sung the new verse she slammed the door shut quite viciously.

It's too bad about Ajello, but every man for himself.

Listen to them singing away, bless their little hearts! I love little girls. Such sweet, innocent voices.

My *boy* friend will *soon* be *heal*thy.
He *shall* be *very* *wealthy.*
No *wo*man shall *harry*
Or *seek* to *marry;*
Two and *two* is *four,* and *one* to *carry!*

It will be pleasant to be wealthy, I hope. I must ask Ajello where Cincinello is.

The Golem

INTRODUCTION BY DAMON KNIGHT

"The Golem" was the second Avram Davidson story that sf readers ever saw. The first was "My Boy Friend's Name Is Jello," which appeared a few months before it in The Magazine of Fantasy & Science Fiction. *The title of "My Boy Friend's Name Is Jello" is memorable, but although I have read the story many times, I never remember anything else about it.*

One of my many theories about short stories is that their titles and first lines ought to be memorable, because if not memorable they will not be remembered, and if not remembered the stories will not be reprinted (because no one can find them). Well, according to this theory it's no wonder that "The Golem" is Davidson's most-reprinted story. It is full of memorable lines; if they were any more memorable than they are, the story would be just a bunch of quotations strung together, as someone said of Hamlet.

But really "The Golem" is memorable for a different reason: because it is a perfect story. I know this seems like gross hyperbole, but the statement has a literal meaning and is true. There isn't a word in "The Golem" that a sympathetic reader would want to change; one word more would be too many, one less would be too few. There is nothing labored about "The Golem," it does not falter or wamble; it flows like clear syrup down a tablecloth, and by the way it is very funny. One imagines that the author stared at it in a wild surprise.

He (the author) was twenty-nine or thirty years old, and he had almost forty years of creative triumphs ahead of him. He was then, I take it, living in San Francisco; Anthony Boucher, the editor of F&SF, said he had "the most beautiful beard that has ever visited this office." Later he moved to New York, where I once visited him in a ground-floor apartment with a china cabinet in which there was a half-eaten sandwich. Before that he had been a yeshiva student, a Navy corpsman, and a pioneer in Israel, where he tried to teach the herdsmen to milk their goats from the side, in order to keep the goat-shit out of the milk. (This is the way I remember it, but it may have been sheep.)

THE GOLEM

THE GRAY-FACED PERSON came along the street where old Mr. and Mrs. Gumbeiner lived. It was afternoon, it was autumn, the sun was warm and soothing to their ancient bones. Anyone who attended the movies in the twenties or the early thirties has seen that street a thousand times. Past these bungalows with their half-double roofs Edmund Lowe walked arm-in-arm with Leatrice Joy and Harold Lloyd was chased by Chinamen waving hatchets. Under these squamous palm trees Laurel kicked Hardy and Woolsey beat Wheeler upon the head with codfish. Across these pocket-handkerchief-sized lawns the juveniles of the Our Gang Comedies pursued one another and were pursued by angry fat men in golf knickers. On this same street—or perhaps on some other one of five hundred streets exactly like it.

Mrs. Gumbeiner indicated the gray-faced person to her husband.

"You think maybe he's got something the matter?" she asked. "He walks kind of funny, to me."

"Walks like a *golem*," Mr. Gumbeiner said indifferently.

The old woman was nettled.

"Oh, I don't know," she said. "*I* think he walks like your cousin Mendel."

The old man pursed his mouth angrily and chewed on his pipestem. The gray-faced person turned up the concrete path, walked up the steps to the porch, sat down in a chair. Old Mr. Gumbeiner ignored him. His wife stared at the stranger.

"Man comes in without a hello, goodbye, or howareyou, sits himself down and right away he's at home. . . . The chair is comfortable?" she asked. "Would you like maybe a glass tea?"

She turned to her husband.

"Say something, Gumbeiner!" she demanded. "What are you, made of wood?"

The old man smiled a slow, wicked, triumphant smile.

"Why should *I* say anything?" he asked the air. "Who am I? Nothing, that's who."

The stranger spoke. His voice was harsh and monotonous.

"When you learn who—or, rather, what—I am, the flesh will melt from your bones in terror." He bared porcelain teeth.

"Never mind about my bones!" the old woman cried. "You've got a lot of nerve talking about my bones!"

"You will quake with fear," said the stranger. Old Mrs. Gumbeiner said that she hoped he would live so long. She turned to her husband once again.

"Gumbeiner, when are you going to mow the lawn?"

"All mankind—" the stranger began.

"*Shah!* I'm talking to my husband. . . . He talks *eppis* kind of funny, Gumbeiner, no?"

"Probably a foreigner," Mr. Gumbeiner said, complacently.

"You think so?" Mrs. Gumbeiner glanced fleetingly at the stranger. "He's got a very bad color in his face, *nebbich*. I suppose he came to California for his health."

"Disease, pain, sorrow, love, grief—all are naught to—"

Mr. Gumbeiner cut in on the stranger's statement.

"Gall bladder," the old man said. "Guinzburg down at the *shule* looked exactly the same before his operation. Two professors they had in for him, and a private nurse day and night."

"I am not a human being!" the stranger said loudly.

"Three thousand seven hundred fifty dollars it cost his son, Guinzburg told me. 'For you, Poppa, nothing is too expensive—only get well,' the son told him."

"*I am not a human being!*"

"Ai, is that a son for you!" the old woman said, rocking her head. "A heart of gold, pure gold." She looked at the stranger. "All right, all right. I heard you the first time. Gumbeiner! I asked you a question. When are you going to cut the lawn?"

"On Wednesday, *odder* maybe Thursday, comes the Japaneser to the neighborhood. To cut lawns is *his* profession. *My* profession is to be a glazier—retired."

"Between me and all mankind is an inevitable hatred," the stranger said. "When I tell you what I am, the flesh will melt—"

"You said, you said already," Mr. Gumbeiner interrupted.

"In Chicago where the winters were as cold and bitter as the Czar of Russia's heart," the old woman intoned, "you had strength to carry the frames with the glass together day in and day out. But in California with the golden sun to mow the lawn when your wife asks, for this you have no strength. Do I call in the Japaneser to cook for you supper?"

"Thirty years Professor Allardyce spent perfecting his theories. Electronics, neuronics—"

"Listen, how educated he talks," Mr. Gumbeiner said, admiringly. "Maybe he goes to the University here?"

"If he goes to the University, maybe he knows Bud?" his wife suggested.

"Probably they're in the same class and he came to see him about the homework, no?"

"Certainly he must be in the same class. How many classes are there? Five *in ganzen:* Bud showed me on his program card." She counted off on her fingers. "Television Appreciation and Criticism, Small Boat Building, Social Adjustment, The American Dance... The American Dance—*nu,* Gumbeiner—"

"Contemporary Ceramics," her husband said, relishing the syllables. "A fine boy, Bud. A pleasure to have him for a boardner."

"After thirty years spent in these studies," the stranger, who had continued to speak unnoticed, went on, "he turned from the theoretical to the pragmatic. In ten years' time he had made the most titanic discovery in history: he made mankind, *all* mankind, superfluous: he made *me.*"

"What did Tillie write in her last letter?" asked the old man.

The old woman shrugged.

"What should she write? The same thing. Sidney was home from the Army, Naomi has a new boy friend—"

"*He made* ME!"

"Listen, Mr. Whatever-your-name-is," the old woman said; "maybe where you came from is different, but in *this* country you don't interrupt people the while they're talking. . . . Hey. Listen—what do you mean, he *made* you? What kind of talk is that?"

The stranger bared all his teeth again, exposing the too-pink gums.

"In his library, to which I had a more complete access after his sudden and as yet undiscovered death from entirely natural causes, I found a complete collection of stories about androids, from Shelley's *Frankenstein* through Capek's *R.U.R.* to Asimov's—"

"Frankenstein?" said the old man, with interest. "There used to be Frankenstein who had the soda-*wasser* place on Halstead Street: a Litvack, *nebbich.*"

"What are you talking?" Mrs. Gumbeiner demanded. "His name was Franken*thal,* and it wasn't on Halstead, it was on Roosevelt."

"—clearly shown that all mankind has an instinctive antipathy towards androids and there will be an inevitable struggle between them—"

"Of course, of course!" Old Mr. Gumbeiner clicked his teeth against his pipe. "I am always wrong, you are always right. How could you stand to be married to such a stupid person all this time?"

"I don't know," the old woman said. "Sometimes I wonder, myself. I think it must be his good looks." She began to laugh. Old Mr. Gumbeiner blinked, then began to smile, then took his wife's hand.

"Foolish old woman," the stranger said; "why do you laugh? Do you not know I have come to destroy you?"

"What!" old Mr. Gumbeiner shouted. "Close your mouth, you!" He darted from his chair and struck the stranger with the flat of his hand. The stranger's head struck against the porch pillar and bounced back.

"When you talk to my wife, talk respectable, you hear?"

Old Mrs. Gumbeiner, cheeks very pink, pushed her husband back in his chair. Then she leaned forward and examined the stranger's head. She clicked her tongue as she pulled aside a flap of gray, skin-like material.

"Gumbeiner, look! He's all springs and wires inside!"

"I *told* you he was a *golem*, but no, you wouldn't listen," the old man said.

"You said he *walked* like a *golem*."

"How could he walk like a *golem* unless he *was* one?"

"All right, all right. . . . You broke him, so now fix him."

"My grandfather, his light shines from Paradise, told me that when MoHaRaL—Moreynu Ha-Rav Löw—his memory for a blessing, made the *golem* in Prague, three hundred? four hundred years ago? he wrote on his forehead the Holy Name."

Smiling reminiscently, the old woman continued, "And the *golem* cut the rabbi's wood and brought his water and guarded the ghetto."

"And one time only he disobeyed the Rabbi Löw, and Rabbi Löw erased the *Shem Ha-Mephorash* from the *golem*'s forehead and the *golem* fell down like a dead one. And they put him up in the attic of the *shule* and he's still there today if the Communisten haven't sent him to Moscow. . . . This is not just a story," he said.

"*Avadda* not!" said the old woman.

"I myself have seen both the *shule* and the rabbi's grave," her husband said, conclusively.

"But I think this must be a different kind *golem*, Gumbeiner. See, on his forehead: nothing written."

"What's the matter, there's a law I can't write something there? Where is that lump clay Bud brought us from his class?"

The old man washed his hands, adjusted his little black skullcap, and slowly and carefully wrote four Hebrew letters on the gray forehead.

"Ezra the Scribe himself couldn't do better," the old woman said, admiringly. "Nothing happens," she observed, looking at the lifeless figure sprawled in the chair.

"Well, after all, am I Rabbi Löw?" her husband asked, deprecatingly. "No," he answered. He leaned over and examined the exposed mechanism. "This spring goes here . . . this wire comes with this one . . ." The figure moved. "But this one goes where? And this one?"

"Let be," said his wife. The figure sat up slowly and rolled its eyes loosely.

"Listen, Reb *Golem*," the old man said, wagging his finger. "Pay attention to what I say—you understand?"

"Understand . . ."

"If you want to stay here, you got to do like Mr. Gumbeiner says."

"Do-like-Mr.-Gumbeiner-says . . ."

"*That's* the way I like to hear a *golem* talk. Malka, give here the mirror from the pocketbook. Look, you see your face? You see on the forehead, what's written? If you don't do like Mr. Gumbeiner says, he'll wipe out what's written and you'll be no more alive."

"No-more-alive . . ."

"*That's* right. Now, listen. Under the porch you'll find a lawnmower. Take it. And cut the lawn. Then come back. Go."

"Go . . ." The figure shambled down the stairs. Presently the sound of the lawnmower whirred through the quiet air in the street just like the street where Jackie Cooper shed huge tears on Wallace Beery's shirt and Chester Conklin rolled his eyes at Marie Dressler.

"So what will you write to Tillie?" old Mr. Gumbeiner asked.

"What should I write?" old Mrs. Gumbeiner shrugged. "I'll write that the weather is lovely out here and that we are both, Blessed be the Name, in good health."

The old man nodded his head slowly, and they sat together on the front porch in the warm afternoon sun.

The Necessity of His Condition
INTRODUCTION BY POUL AND KAREN ANDERSON

We have remembered this story since we first read it, nearly forty years ago. Published in Ellery Queen's Mystery Magazine, *it won first prize in that periodical's 1957 contest, against strong competition.*

Like other early works of Avram Davidson's, already it showed what rich diversity was to come. Two of his fantasies had been set in the here-and-now, although their quirky originality made each of them sui generis. *But elsewhere had appeared elements less familiar—a larcenous antique dealer in Cyprus, a Casbah-smart youth with Agitprop training, a mesmerizer in eighteenth-century England. Always the thought and speech of the characters was authentic, fully within their given cultures, and yet those characters were always fully individual human beings. Later tales kept this far too rare quality. They explored more of today's world, other planets, the future, real and legendary epochs of the past. Invariably their landscapes, mental as well as physical, were vivid and utterly convincing. Much of this came through in the dialogue, for which Avram had an incredibly keen ear.*

"The Necessity of His Condition" is set in an antebellum border state. With a few strokes he gives a town, in it a history, economy, and population as various, in both good and evil, as any real community's. Every true tragedy is profoundly moral. Avram bore a deep sympathy for the weak and oppressed. Here, in an almost biblical fashion, the unrighteous has digged a pit for another, and fallen therein.

THE NECESSITY OF HIS CONDITION

SHOLTO HILL WAS MOSTLY residential property, but it had its commercial district in the shape of Persimmon Street and Rampart Street, the latter named after some long-forgotten barricade stormed and destroyed by Benedict Arnold (wearing a British uniform and eaten with bitterness and perverted pride). Persimmon Street, running up-slope, entered the middle of Rampart at right angles, and went no farther. This section, with its red brick houses and shops, its warehouses and offices, was called The T, and it smelled of tobacco and potatoes and molasses and goober peas and dried fish and beer and cheap cookshop food and (the spit-and-whittle humorists claimed) old man Bailiss' office, where the windows were never opened—never had *been* opened, they said, never were *made* to be opened. Any smell off the street or farms or stables that found its way up to Bailiss' office was imprisoned there for life, they said. Old man Bailiss knew what they said, knew pretty much everything that went on anywhere; but he purely didn't care. He didn't have to, they said.

J. Bailiss, Attorney-at-Law (his worn old sign said), had a large practice and little competition. James Bailiss, Broker (his newer, but by no means new, sign), did an extensive business; again, with little competition. The premises of the latter business were located, not in The T, but in a white-washed stone structure with thick doors and barred windows, down in The Bottom—as it was called—near the river, the canal, and the railroad line.

James Bailiss, Broker, was not received socially. Nobody expected that bothered him much. Nothing bothered old man Bailiss much—Bailiss, with his old white hat and his old black coat and his old cowhide shoes that looked old even when they were new—turned old on the shoemaker's last (the spit-and-whittle crowd claimed) directly they heard whose feet they were destined for.

It was about twenty-five years earlier, in 1825, that an advertisement—the first of its kind—appeared in the local newspaper.

"*Take Notice!* (it began). James Bailiss, having lately purchased the old arsenal building on Canal Street, will henceforth operate it as a Negro Depot. He will at all times be found ready to purchase all good and likely young Negroes at the Highest Price. He will also attend to Selling Negroes on Com-

THE NECESSITY OF HIS CONDITION | 39

mission. Said Broker also gives Notice that those who have Slaves rendered
unfit for labor by yaws, scrofula, chronic consumption, rheumatism, & C., may
dispose of them to him on reasonable terms.''

Editor Winstanley tried to dissuade him, he said later. "Folks," he told
him, "won't like this. This has never been said out open before," the editor
pointed out. Bailiss smiled. He was already middle-aged, had a shiny red face
and long mousy hair. His smile wasn't a very wide one.

"Then I reckon I must be the pioneer," he said. "This isn't a big plantation
State, it never will be. I've give the matter right much thought. I reckon it just
won't pay for anyone to own more than half a dozen slaves in these parts. But
they will multiply, you can't stop it. I've seen it in my lawwork, seen many a
planter broke for debts he's gone into to buy field hands—signed notes against
his next crop, or maybe even his next three crops. Then maybe the crop is so
good that the price of cotton goes way down and he can't meet his notes, so
he loses his lands *and* his slaves. If the price of cotton should happen to be
high enough for him to pay for the slaves he's bought, then, like a dumned
fool"—Bailiss never swore—"why, he signs notes for a few more. Pretty soon
things get so bad you can't *give* slaves away round here. So a man has a dozen
of them eating their heads off and not even earning grocery bills. No, Mr.
Winstanley; slaves must be sold south and southwest, where the new lands are
being opened up, where the big plantations are."

Editor Winstanley wagged his head. "I know," he said, "I know. But folks
don't like to say things like that out loud. The slave trade is looked down on.
You know that. It's a necessary evil, that's how it's regarded, like a—well . . ."
He lowered his voice. "Nothing personal, but . . . like a sporting house. Nothing personal, now, Mr. Bailiss."

The attorney-broker smiled again. "Slavery has the sanction of the law. It
is a necessary part of the domestic economy, just like cotton. Why, suppose I
should say, 'I love my cotton, I'll only sell it locally'? People'd think I was just
crazy. Slaves have become a surplus product in the Border States and they must
be disposed of where they are not produced in numbers sufficient to meet the
local needs. You print that advertisement. Folks may not ask me to dinner, but
they'll sell to me, see if they won't."

The notice did, as predicted, outrage public opinion. Old Marsta and Old
Missis vowed no Negro of *theirs* would ever be sold "down the River." But
somehow the broker's "jail"—as it was called—kept pretty full, though its
boarders changed. Old man Bailiss had his agents out buying and his agents
out selling. Sometimes he acted as agent for firms whose headquarters were in
Natchez or New Orleans. He entered into silent partnerships with gentlemen
of good family who wanted a quick return on capital, and who got it, but who
still, it was needless to say, did not dine with him or take his hand publicly.
There was talk, on and off, that the Bar Association was planning action not
favorable to Bailiss for things connected with the legal side of his trade. It all
came to nought.

"Mr. Bailiss," young Ned Wickerson remarked to him one day in the old
man's office, "whoever said that 'a man who defends himself has a fool for a
client' never had the pleasure of your acquaintance."

"Thank you, boy."

"Consequently," the young man continued, "I've advised Sam Worth not to go into court if we can manage to settle out of it."

"First part of your advice is good, but there's nothing to settle."

"There's a matter of $635 to settle, Mr. Bailiss." Wickerson had been practicing for two years, but he still had freckles on his nose. He took a paper out of his wallet and put it in front of them. "There's this to settle."

The old man pushed his glasses down his nose and picked up the paper. He scanned it, lips moving silently. "Why, this is all correct," he said. "Hmm. To be sure. 'Received of Samuel Worth of Worth's Crossing, Lemuel County, the sum of $600 cash in full payment for a Negro named Dominick Swift, commonly called Domino, aged thirty-six years and of bright complexion, which Negro I warrant sound in mind and body and a slave for life and the title I will forever defend. James Bailiss, Rutland, Lemuel County.' Mmm. All correct. And anyway, what do you mean, six hundred and *thirty-five* dollars?"

"Medical and burial expenses. Domino died last week."

"Died, now, did he? Sho. Too bad. Well, all men are mortal."

"I'm afraid my client doesn't take much comfort from your philosophy. Says he didn't get two days' work out of Domino. Says he whipped him, first off, for laziness, but when the doctor—Dr. Sloan, that was—examined him, Doctor said he had a consumption. Died right quickly."

"Negroes *are* liable to quick consumptions. Wish they was a medicine for it. On the other hand, they seldom get malaria or yella fever. Providence."

He cut off a slice of twist, shoved it in his cheek, then offered twist and knife to Wickerson, who shook his head.

"As I say, we'd rather settle out of court. If you'll refund the purchase price we won't press for the other expenses. What do you say?"

Bailiss looked around the dirty, dusty office. There was a case of law books with broken bindings against the north wall. The south wall had a daguerreotype of John C. Calhoun hanging crookedly on it. The single dim window was in the east wall, and the west wall was pierced by a door whose lower panels had been scarred and splintered by two generations of shoes and boots kicking it open. "Why, I say no, o' course."

Wickerson frowned. "If you lose, you know, you'll have to pay *my* costs as well."

"I don't expect I'll lose," the old man said.

"Why, of course you'll lose," the young man insisted, although he did not sound convinced. "Dr. Sloan will testify that it was *not* 'a quick consumption.' He says it was a long-standing case of Negro tuberculosis. And you warranted the man sound."

"Beats me how them doctors think up long words like that," Bailiss said placidly. "Inter'sting point of law just come up down in N'Orleans, Ned. One of my agents was writing me. Negro brakeman had his legs crushed in a accident, man who rented him to the railroad sued, railroad pleaded 'negligence of his fellow-servant'—in this case, the engineer."

"Seems like an unassailable defense." The younger lawyer was interested despite himself. "What happened?"

"Let's see if I can recollect the Court's words." This was mere modesty. Old man Bailiss' memory was famous on all matters concerning the slave codes. "Mmm. Yes. Court said: 'The slave status has removed this man from the normal fellow-servant category. He is fettered fast by the most stern bonds our laws take note of. He cannot with impunity desert his post though danger plainly threatens, nor can he reprove free men for their bad management or neglect of duty, for the necessity of his condition is upon him.' Awarded the owner—Creole man name of Le Tour—awarded him $1300."

"It seems right, put like that. But now, Dr. Sloan—"

"Now, Neddy. Domino was carefully examined by *my* Doctor, old Fred Pierce—"

"Why, Pierce hasn't drawn a sober breath in twenty years! He gets only slaves for his patients."

"Well, I reckon that makes him what they call a specialist, then. No, Ned, don't go to court. You have no case. My jailer will testify, too, that Domino was sound when I sold him. It must of been that whipping sickened him."

Wickerson rose. "Will you make *partial* restitution, then?" The old man shook his head. His long hair was streaked with gray, but the face under it was still ruddy. "You *know* Domino was sick," Wickerson said. "I've spoken to old Miss Whitford's man, Micah, the blacksmith, who was doing some work in your jail awhile back. He told me that he heard Domino coughing, saw him spitting blood, saw you watching him, saw you give him some rum and molasses, heard you say, 'Better not cough till I've sold you, Dom, else I'll have to sell you south where they don't coddle Negroes.' This was just before you *did* sell him—to my client."

The old man's eyes narrowed. "I'd say Micah talks over-much for a black man, even one of old Miss Whitford's—a high and mighty lady that doesn't care to know me on the street. But you forget one mighty important thing, Mr. Wickerson!" His voice rose. He pointed his finger. "It makes no difference what Micah heard! Micah is property! Just like my horse is property! And property can't testify! Do you claim to be a lawyer? Don't you know that a slave can't inherit—can't bequeath—can't marry nor give in marriage—can neither sue nor prosecute—and that it's a basic principle of the law that a slave can never testify in court except against another slave?"

Wickerson, his lips pressed tightly together, moved to the door, kicked it open, scattering a knot of idlers who stood around listening eagerly, and strode away. The old man brushed through them.

"And you'd better tell Sam Worth not to come bothering me, either!" Bailiss shouted at Wickerson's back. "I know how to take care of trash like him!" He turned furiously to the gaping and grinning loungers.

"Get away from here, you mud-sills!" He was almost squeaking in his rage.

"I reckon you don't own the sidewalks," they muttered. "I reckon every white man in this state is as good as any other white man," they said; but they gave way before him. The old man stamped back into his office and slammed the door.

. . .

It was Bailiss' custom to have his supper in his own house, a two-story building just past the end of the sidewalk on Rampart Street; but tonight he felt disinclined to return there with no one but rheumaticky old Edie, his housekeeper-cook, for company. He got on his horse and rode down toward the cheerful bustle of the Phoenix Hotel. Just as he was about to go in, Sam Worth came out. Worth was a barrel-shaped man with thick short arms and thick bandy legs. He stood directly in front of Bailiss, breathing whiskey fumes.

"So you won't settle?" he growled. His wife, a stout woman taller than her husband, got down from their wagon and took him by the arm.

"Come away, now, Sam," she urged.

"You'd better step aside," Bailiss said.

"I hear you been making threats against me," Worth said.

"Yes, and I'll carry them out, too, if you bother me!"

A group quickly gathered, but Mrs. Worth pulled her husband away, pushed him toward the wagon; and Bailiss went inside. The buzz of talk dropped for a moment as he entered, stopped, then resumed in a lower register. He cast around for a familiar face, undecided where to sit; but it seemed to him that all faces were turned away. Finally he recognized the bald head and bent shoulders of Dr. Pierce, who was slumped at a side table by himself, muttering into a glass. Bailiss sat down heavily across from him, with a sigh. Dr. Pierce looked up.

"A graduate of the University of Virginia," the doctor said. His eyes were dull.

"At it again?" Bailiss looked around for a waiter. Dr. Pierce finished what was in his glass.

"Says he'll horsewhip you on sight," he muttered.

"Who says?" Bailiss was surprised.

"Major Jack Moran."

Bailiss laughed. The Major was a tottery veteran of the War of 1812 who rode stiffly about on an aged white mare. "What for?" he asked.

"Talk is going around you Mentioned A Lady's Name." Pierce beckoned, and at once a waiter, whose eye old man Bailiss had not managed to catch, appeared with a full glass. Bailiss caught his sleeve as the waiter was about to go and ordered his meal. The doctor drank. "Major Jack says, impossible to Call You Out—can't appear on Field of Honor with slave trader—so instead will whip you on sight." His voice gurgled in the glass.

Bailiss smiled crookedly. "I reckon I needn't be afraid of him. He's old enough to be my daddy. A lady's name? What lady? Maybe he means a lady who lives in a big old house that's falling apart, an old lady who lives on what her Negro blacksmith makes?"

Dr. Pierce made a noise of assent. He put down his glass. Bailiss looked around the dining room, but as fast as he met anyone's eyes, the eyes glanced away. The doctor cleared his throat.

"Talk is going around you expressed a dislike for said Negro. Talk is that the lady has said she is going to manumit him to make sure you won't buy him if she dies."

Bailiss stared. "Manumit him? She can't do that unless she posts a bond of a thousand dollars to guarantee that he leaves the state within ninety days after being freed. She must know that free Negroes aren't allowed to stay on after manumission. And where would she get a thousand dollars? And what would she live on if Micah is sent away? That old lady hasn't got good sense!"

"No," Pierce agreed, staring at the glass. "She is old and not too bright and she's got too much pride on too little money, but it's a sis"—his tongue stumbled—"a singular thing: there's hardly a person in this town, white or black or half-breed Injun, that doesn't *love* that certain old lady. Except you. And *nobody* in town loves *you*. Also a singular thing: here we are—"

The doctor's teeth clicked against the glass. He set it down, swallowed. His eyes were yellow in the corners, and he looked at Bailiss steadily, save for a slight trembling of his hands and head. "Here we are, heading just as certain as can be towards splitting the Union and having war with the Yankees—all over slavery—tied to it hand and foot—willing to die for it—economy bound up in it—sure in our own hearts that nature and justice and religion are for it—and yet, singular thing: nobody likes slave traders. Nobody likes them."

"Tell me something new." Bailiss drew his arms back to make room for his dinner. He ate noisily and with good appetite.

"Another thing," the doctor hunched forward in his seat, "that hasn't added to your current popularity is this business of Domino. In this, I feel, you made a mistake. *Caveat emptor* or not, you should've sold him farther away from here, much farther away, down to the rice fields somewhere, where his death would have been just a statistic in the overseer's annual report. Folks feel you've cheated Sam Worth. He's not one of your rich absentee owners who sits in town and lets some cheese-paring Yankee drive his Negroes. He only owns four or five, he and his boy work right alongside them in the field, pace them row for row."

Bailiss grunted, sopped up gravy.

"You've been defying public opinion for years now. There might come a time when you'd want good will. My advice to you—after all, your agent only paid $100 for Domino—is to settle with Worth for five hundred."

Bailiss wiped his mouth on his sleeve. He reached for his hat, put it on, left money on the table, and got up.

"Shoemaker, stick to your last," he said. Dr. Pierce shrugged. "Make that glass the final one. I want you at the jail tomorrow, early, so we can get the catalogue ready for the big sale next week. Hear?" the old man walked out, paying no attention to the looks or comments his passage caused.

On his horse Bailiss hesitated. The night was rather warm, with a hint of damp in the air. He decided to ride around for a while in the hope of finding a breeze stirring. As the horse ambled along from one pool of yellow gaslight to another he ran through in his mind some phrases for inclusion in his catalogue. *Phyllis, prime woman, aged 25, can cook, sew, do fine ironing...*

When he had first begun in the trade, three out of every five Negroes had been named Cuffee, Cudjoe, or Quash. He'd heard these were days of the week in some African dialect. There was talk that the African slave trade might be legalized again; that would be a fine thing. But, sho, there was always such talk, on and off.

The clang of a hammer on an anvil reminded him that he was close to Black Micah's forge. As he rounded the corner he saw Sam Worth's bandy-legged figure outlined against the light. One of the horses was unhitched from his wagon and awaited the shoe Micah was preparing for it.

A sudden determination came to Bailiss: he would settle with Worth about Domino. He hardly bothered to analyze his motives. Partly because his dinner was resting well and he felt comfortable and unexpectedly benevolent, partly because of some vague notion it would be the popular thing to do and popularity was a good thing to have before and during a big sale, he made up his mind to offer Worth $300—well, maybe he would go as high as $350, but no more; a man had to make *some*thing out of a trade.

As he rode slowly up to the forge and stopped, the blacksmith paused in his hammering and looked out. Worth turned around. In the sudden silence Bailiss heard another horse approaching.

"I've come to settle with you," the slave trader said. Worth looked up at him, his eyes bloodshot. In a low, ugly voice Worth cussed him, and reached his hand toward his rear pocket. It was obvious to Bailiss what Worth intended, so the slave trader quickly drew his own pistol and fired. His horse reared, a woman screamed—did *two* women scream? Without his meaning it, the other barrel of his pistol went off just as Worth fell.

"Fo' gawdsake don't kill me, Mister Bailiss!" Micah cried. "Are you all right, Miss Elizabeth?" he cried. Worth's wife and Miss Whitford suddenly appeared from the darkness on the other side of the wagon. They knelt beside Worth.

Bailiss felt a numbing blow on his wrist, dropped his empty pistol, was struck again, and half fell, was half dragged, from his horse. A woman screamed again, men ran up—where had they all come from? Bailiss, pinned in the grip of someone he couldn't see, stood dazed.

"You infernal scoundrel, you shot that man in cold blood!" Old Major Jack Moran dismounted from his horse and flourished the riding crop with which he had struck Bailiss on the wrist.

"I never—he cussed me—he reached for his pistol—I only defended myself!"

Worth's wife looked up, tears streaking her heavy face.

"He had no pistol," she said. "I made him leave it home."

"You said, 'I've come to get you,' and you shot him point-blank!" The old Major's voice trumpeted.

"He tried to shoot Miss Whitford too!" someone said. Other voices added that Captain Carter, the High Sheriff's chief deputy, was coming. Bodies pressed against Bailiss, faces glared at him, fists were waved before him.

"It wasn't like that at all!" he cried.

Deputy Carter came up on the gallop, flung the reins of his black mare to eager outthrust hands, jumped off, and walked over to Worth.

"How was it, then?" a scornful voice asked Bailiss.

"I rode up . . . I says, 'I've come to settle with you' . . . He cussed at me, low and mean, and he reached for his hip pocket."

In every face he saw disbelief.

"Major Jack's an old man," Bailiss faltered. "He heard it wrong. He—"

"Heard it good enough to hang you!"

Bailiss looked desperately around. Carter rose from his knees and the crowd parted. "Sam's dead, ma'am," he said. "I'm sorry." Mrs. Worth's only reply was a low moan. The crowd growled. Captain Carter turned and faced Bailiss, whose eyes looked at him for a brief second, then turned frantically away. And then Bailiss began to speak anxiously—so anxiously that his words came out a babble. His arms were pinioned and he could not point, but he thrust his head toward the forge where the blacksmith was still standing—standing silently.

"Micah," Bailiss stuttered. "Ask Micah!"

Micah saw it, he wanted to say—wanted to shout it. *Micah was next to Worth, Micah heard what I really said, he's younger than the Major, his hearing is good, he saw Worth reach . . .*

Captain Carter placed his hand on Bailiss and spoke, but Bailiss did not hear him. The whole night had suddenly fallen silent for him, except for his own voice, saying something (it seemed long ago) to young lawyer Wickerson.

"It makes no difference what Micah saw! It makes no difference what Micah heard! Micah is property! . . . And property can't testify!"

They tied Bailiss' hands and heaved him onto his horse.

"He is fettered fast by the most stern bonds our laws take note of . . . can't inherit—can't bequeath . . . can neither sue nor prosecute—"

Bailiss turned his head as they started to ride away. He looked at Micah and their eyes met. Micah knew.

". . . it's basic principle of the law that a slave can never testify in court except against another slave."

Someone held the reins of old man Bailiss' horse. From now on he moved only as others directed. The lights around the forge receded. Darkness surrounded him. The necessity of his condition was upon him.

Help! I Am Dr. Morris Goldpepper

INTRODUCTION BY F. GWYNPLAINE MacINTYRE

Where I come from in northern Australia, there's a type of eucalyptus tree that's called a blue gum. In Avram Davidson's story "Help! I Am Dr. Morris Goldpepper," you'll meet some blue gums of a very different sort.

One of the hallmarks of a first-rate storyteller is that he or she (or it) can begin with the most outlandish premise—something utterly unbelievable—and upon this framework craft a narrative which is so thoroughly plausible that it compels our belief.

"Help! I Am Dr. Morris Goldpepper" offers a uniquely Avramesque premise: Namely, the planet Earth has been invaded by hostile aliens, and the only thing that can save mankind form this dread interstellar menace is the American Dental Association.

Clearly, this story takes place in an alternate universe, in which dentists are selfless dedicated artisans who have pledged themselves to the betterment of humanity. In real life, of course, dentists are a bunch of sadistic ghouls who enjoy torturing innocent people by shoving pneumatic drills into our bicuspids. Even after the drilling has stopped, and the screams turn to silence, dentists continue their reign of sadism by inflicting psychological torture upon us: They try to make us feel guilty for neglecting to floss.

Sorry, Avram, but if the ultimate battle between Good and Evil amounts to an Armageddon between the dentists and the blood-sucking extraterrestrial slime-monsters, I know which side I'm cheering for . . . and it isn't the dentists.

Rinse, please.

ONE

FOUR OF THE MEN, Weinroth, McAllister, Danbourge and Smith, sat at the table under the cold blue lighting tubes. One of them, Rorke, was in a corner speaking quietly into a telephone, and one, Fadderman, stood staring out the window at the lights of the city. One, Hansen, had yet to arrive.

Fadderman spoke without turning his head. He was the oldest of those present—the Big Seven, as they were often called.

"Lights," he said. "So many lights. Down here." He waved his hand toward the city. "Up there." He gestured toward the sky. "Even with our much-vaunted knowledge, what," he asked, "do we know?" He turned his head. "Perhaps this is too big for us. In the light of the problem, can we really hope to accomplish anything?"

Heavy-set Danbourge frowned grimly. "We have received the suffrage of our fellow-scientists, Doctor. We can but try."

Lithe, handsome McAllister, the youngest officer of the Association, nodded. "The problem is certainly not worse than that which faced our late, great colleague, the immortal Morton." He pointed to a picture on the panneled wall. "And we all know what *he* accomplished."

Fadderman went over and took his hand. "Your words fill me with courage."

McAllister flushed with pleasure.

"I am an old man," Fadderman added falteringly. "Forgive my lack of spirit, Doctor." He sat down, sighed, shook his head slowly. Weinroth, burly and red-haired, patted him gently on the back. Natty, silvery-haired little Smith smiled at him consolingly.

A buzzer sounded. Rorke hung up the telephone, flipped a switch on the wall intercom. "Headquarters here," he said crisply.

"Dr. Carl T. Hansen has arrived," a voice informed him.

"Bring him up at once," he directed. "And, Nickerson—"

"Yes, Dr. Rorke?"

"Let no one else into the building. *No* one."

They sat in silence. After a moment or two, they heard the approach of the elevator, heard the doors slide open, slide shut, heard the elevator descend. Heavy, steady footsteps approached; knuckles rapped on the opaque glass door.

Rorke went over to the door, said, "A conscientious and diligent scientist—"

"—must remain a continual student," a deep voice finished the quotation.

Rorke unlocked the door, peered out into the corridor, admitted Hansen, locked the door.

"I would have been here sooner, but another emergency interposed," Hansen said. "A certain political figure—ethics prevent my being more specific—suffered an oral hemorrhage following an altercation with a woman who shall be nameless, but, boy, did she pack a wallop! A so-called *Specialist*, gentlemen, with offices on Park Avenue, had been, as he called it, 'applying pressure' with a gauze pad. I merely used a little Gelfoam as a coagulant agent and the hemorrhage stopped almost at once. When will the public learn, eh, gentlemen?"

Faint smiles played upon the faces of the assembled scientists. Hansen took his seat. Rorke bent down and lifted two tape-recording devices to the table, set them both in motion. The faces of the men became serious, grim.

"This is an emergency session of the Steering Committee of the Executive Committee of the American Dental Association," Rorke said, "called to discuss measures of dealing with the case of Dr. Morris Goldpepper. One tape will be deposited in the vaults of the Chase Manhattan Bank in New York; the other will be similarly secured in the vaults of the Wells Fargo and Union Trust Company Bank in San Francisco. Present at this session are Doctors Rorke, Weinroth and Smith—President, First and Second Vice-presidents, respectively—Fadderman, Past President, McAllister, Public Information, Danbourge, Legal, and Hansen, Policy."

He looked around at the set, tense faces.

"Doctors," he went on, "I think I may well say that humanity is, as of this moment, face to face with a great danger, and it is a bitter jest that it is not to the engineers or the astronomers, not to medicine nor yet to nuclear nor any other kind of physics, that humanity must now look for salvation—but to the members of the dental profession!"

His voice rose. "Yes—to the practitioners of what has become perhaps the least regarded of all the learned sciences! It is indeed ironical. We may at this juncture consider the comments of the now deceased Professor Earnest Hooton, the Harvard anthropologist, who observed with a sorrow which did him credit that his famed University, instead of assisting its Dental School as it ought, treated it—and I quote his exact words—'Like a yellow dog.' " His voice trembled.

McAllister's clean-cut face flushed an angry red. Weinroth growled. Danbourge's fist hit the table and stayed there, clenched. Fadderman gave a soft, broken sigh.

"But enough of this. We are not jealous, nor are we vindictive," President

Rorke went on. "We are confident that History, 'with its long tomorrow,' will show how, at this danger-fraught point, the humble and little thought-of followers of dental science recognized and sized up the situation and stood shoulder to shoulder on the ramparts!"

He wiped his brow with a paper tissue. "And now I will call upon our beloved Past President, Dr. Samuel I. Fadderman, to begin our review of the incredible circumstances which have brought us here tonight. Dr. Fadderman? If you please . . ."

The well-known Elder Statesman of the A.D.A. nodded his head slowly. He made a little cage of his fingers and pursed and then unpursed his lips. At length he spoke in a soft and gentle voice.

"My first comment, brethren, is that I ask for compassion. *Morris Goldpepper is not to blame!*

"Let me tell you a few words about him. Goldpepper the Scientist needs no introduction. Who has not read, for instance, his 'The Bilateral Vertical Stroke and Its Influence on the Pattern of Occlusion' or his 'Treatment, Planning, Assemblage and Cementation of a 14-Unit Fixed Bridge'—to name only two? But I shall speak about Goldpepper the Man. He is forty-six years of age and served with honor in the United States Navy Dental Corps during the Second World War. He has been a widower since shortly after the conclusion of that conflict. Rae—the late Mrs. Goldpepper, may she rest in peace—often used to say, 'Morry, if I go first, promise me you'll marry again,' but he passed it off with a joke; and, as you know, he never did.

"They had one child, a daughter, Suzanne, a very sweet girl, now married to a Dr. Sheldon Fingerhut, D.D.S. I need not tell you, brethren, how proud our colleague was when his only child married this very fine young member of our profession. The Fingerhuts are now located on Unbalupi, one of the Micronesian islands forming part of the United States Trust Territory, where Dr. Sheldon is teaching dental hygiene, sanitation and prosthesis to the natives thereof."

Dr. Hansen asked, "Are they aware of—"

"The son-in-law knows something of the matter," the older man said. "He has not seen fit to inform his wife, who is in a delicate condition and expects shortly to be confined. At his suggestion, I have been writing—or, rather, typing—letters purporting to come from her father, on his stationery, with the excuse that he badly singed his fingers on a Bunsen burner whilst annealing a new-type hinge for dentures and consequently cannot hold his pen." He sipped from a glass of water.

"Despite his great scientific accomplishments," Dr. Fadderman went on, "Morry had an impractical streak in him. Often I used to call on him at his bachelor apartment in the Hotel Davenport on West End Avenue, where he moved following his daughter's marriage, and I would find him immersed in reading matter of an escapist kind—tales of crocodile hunters on the Malayan Peninsula, or magazines dealing with interplanetary warfare, or collections of short stories about vampires and werewolves and similar superstitious creations.

" 'Morry,' I said reproachfully, 'what a way to spend your off-hours. Is it worth it? Is it healthy? You would do much better, believe me, to frequent the pool or the handball court at the Y. Or,' I pointed out to him, 'if you want to read, why ignore the rich treasures of literature: Shakespeare, Ruskin, Elbert Hubbard, Edna Ferber, and so on? Why retreat to these immature-type fantasies?' At first he only smiled and quoted the saying, 'Each to his or her own taste.' "

The silence which followed was broken by young Dr. McAllister. "You say," he said, " 'at first.' "

Old Dr. Fadderman snapped out of his revery. "Yes, yes. But eventually he confessed the truth to me. He withheld nothing."

The assembled dental scientists then learned that the same Dr. Morris Goldpepper, who had been awarded not once but three successive times the unique honor of the Dr. Alexander Peabody Medal for New Achievements in Dental Prosthesis, was obsessed with the idea that *there was sentient life on other worlds—that it would shortly be possible to reach these other worlds— and that he himself desired to be among those who went.*

" 'Do you realize, Sam?' he asked me," reported Fadderman. " 'Do you realize that, in a very short time, it will no longer be a question of fuel or even of metallurgy? That submarines capable of cruising for weeks and months without surfacing foretell the possibility of traveling through airless space? The chief problem has now come down to finding how to build a take-off platform capable of withstanding a thrust of several million pounds.' And his eyes glowed."

Dr. Fadderman had inquired, with good-natured sarcasm, how the other man expected this would involve *him*. The answer was as follows: Any interplanetary expedition would find it just as necessary to take along a dentist as to take along a physician, and that he—Dr. Goldpepper—intended to be that dentist!

Dr. Weinroth's hand slapped the table with a bang. "By thunder, I say the man had courage!"

Dr. Rorke looked at him with icy reproof. "I should be obliged," he said stiffly, "if there would be no further emotional outbursts."

Dr. Weinroth's face fell. "I beg the Committee's pardon, Mr. President," he said.

Dr. Rorke nodded graciously, indicated by a gesture of his hand that Dr. Fadderman had permission to continue speaking. The old man took a letter from his pocket and placed it on the table.

"This came to me like a bolt from the blue beyond. It is dated November 8 of last year. Skipping the formal salutation, it reads: 'At last I stand silent upon the peak in Darien'—a literary reference, gentlemen, to Cortez's alleged discovery of the Pacific Ocean; actually it was Balboa—'my great dream is about to be realized. Before long, I shall be back to tell you about it, but just exactly when, I am not able to say. History is being made! Long live Science! Very sincerely yours, Morris Goldpepper, D.D.S.' "

He passed the letter around the table.

Dr. Smith asked, "What did you do on receiving this communication, Doctor?"

Dr. Fadderman had at once taken a taxi to West End Avenue. The desk clerk at the hotel courteously informed him that the man he sought had left on a vacation of short but not exactly specified duration. No further information was known. Dr. Fadderman's first thought was that his younger friend had gotten some sort of position with a Government project which he was not free to discuss, and his own patriotism and sense of duty naturally prevented him from making inquiries.

"But I began, for the first time," the Elder Statesman of American Dentistry said, "to read up on the subject of space travel. I wondered how a man 46 years of age could possibly hope to be selected over younger men."

Dr. Danbourge spoke for the first time. "Size," he said. "Every ounce would count in a spaceship and Morris was a pretty little guy."

"But with the heart of a lion," Dr. Weinroth said softly. "Miles and miles and miles of heart."

The other men nodded their agreement to this tribute.

But as time went on and the year drew to its close and he heard no word from his friend, Dr. Fadderman began to worry. Finally, when he received a letter from the Fingerhuts, saying that *they* had not been hearing either, he took action.

He realized it was not likely that the Government would have made plans to include a dentist in this supposed project without communicating with the A.D.A. and he inquired of the current President, Dr. Rorke, if he had any knowledge of such a project, or of the whereabouts of the missing man. The answer to both questions was no. But on learning the reasons for Dr. Fadderman's concern, he communicated with Col. Lemnel Coggins, head of the USAF's Dental Corps.

Col. Coggins informed him that no one of Dr. Goldpepper's name or description was or had been affiliated with any such project, and that, in fact, any such project was still—as he put it—"still on the drawing-board."

Drs. Rorke and Fadderman, great as was their concern, hesitated to report Dr. Goldpepper missing. He had, after all, paid rent on apartment, office and laboratory, well in advance. He was a mature man, of very considerable intelligence, and one who presumably knew what he was doing.

"It is at this point," said Dr. Danbourge, "that I enter the picture. On the 11th of January, I had a call from a Dr. Milton Wilson, who has an office on East 19th Street, with a small laboratory adjoining, where he does prosthetic work. He told me, with a good deal of hesitation, that something exceedingly odd had come up, and he asked me if I knew where Dr. Morris Goldpepper was . . ."

The morning of the 11th of January, an elderly man with a curious foreign accent came into Dr. Wilson's office, gave the name of Smith and complained about an upper plate. It did not feel comfortable, Mr. Smith said, and it irritated the roof of his mouth. There was a certain reluctance on his part to allow Dr.

Wilson to examine his mouth. This was understandable, because the interior of his mouth was blue. The gums were entirely edentulous, very hard, almost horny. The plate itself—

"Here is the plate," Dr. Danbourge said, placing it on the table. "Dr. Wilson supplied him with another. You will observe the perforations on the upper, or palatal, surface. They had been covered with a thin layer of gum arabic, which naturally soon wore almost entirely off, with the result that the roof of the mouth became irritated. Now this is so very unusual that Dr. Wilson—as soon as his patient, the so-called Mr. Smith, was gone—broke open the weirdly made plate to find why the perforations had been made. In my capacity as head of the Association's Legal Department," Dr. Danbourge stated, "I have come across some extraordinary occurrences, but nothing like *this*."

This was a small piece of a white, flexible substance, covered with tiny black lines. Danbourge picked up a large magnifying glass.

"You may examine these objects, Doctors," he said, "but it will save your eyesight if I read to you from an enlarged photostatic copy of this last one. The nature of the material, the method of writing, or of reducing the writing to such size all are unknown to us. It may be something on the order of microfilm. But that is not important. The important thing is the *content* of the writing—the *portent* of the writing.

"Not since Dr. Morton, the young Boston dentist, realized the uses of sulphuric ether as an anesthetic has any member of our noble profession discovered anything of even remotely similar importance; and perhaps not before, either."

He drew his spectacles from their case and began to read aloud.

TWO

Despite the fact that our great profession lacks the glamour and public adulation of the practice of medicine, and even the druggists—not having a Hippocratic Oath—can preen themselves on their so-called Oath of Maimonides (though, believe me, the great Maimonides had no more to do with it than Morris Goldpepper, D.D.S.), no one can charge us with not having as high a standard of ethics and professional conduct as physicians and surgeons, M.D. Nor do I hesitate for one single moment to include prostheticians not holding the degree of Doctor of Dental Surgery or Doctor of Dental Medicine, whose work is so vital and essential.

When the records of our civilization are balanced, then—but perhaps not before—the real importance of dental science will be appreciated. Now it is merely valued at the moment of toothache.

It is only with a heavy heart that I undertake deliberately to produce inferior work, and with the confidence that all those to whom the standards of oral surgery and dental prosthetics are dear will understand the very unusual circumstances which have prompted me to so to do. And, understanding, will forgive. No one can hold the standards of our profession higher or more sacred than I.

It must be admitted that I was not very amused on a certain occasion when my cousin, Nathaniel Pomerance, introduced me to an engineering contractor with these words, "You two should have a lot in common—you both build bridges," and uttered a foolish laugh. But I venture to say that this was one of the truest words ever spoken in questionable jest.

Humility is one thing, false pride another. Those who know anything of modern dentistry at all know of the Goldpepper Bridge and the Goldpepper Crown. It is I, Dr. Morris Goldpepper, inventor of both, and perfector of the Semi-retractable Clasp which bears my name, who writes these words you see before you. Nothing further should be needful by way of identification. And now to my report.

On the first of November, a day of evil import forever in the personal calendar of the unhappy wretch who writes these lines, not even knowing for sure if they will ever be read—but what else can I do?—shortly after 5:00 P.M., my laboratory door was knocked on. I found there a curious-looking man of shriveled and weazened appearance. He asked if I was Dr. Morris Goldpepper, "the famous perfector of the Semi-retractable Clasp," and I pleaded guilty to the flattering impeachment.

The man had a foreign-sounding accent, or—I thought—it may be that he had an impediment in his speech. Might he see me, was his next question. I hesitated.

It has happened to me before, and to most other practitioners—a stranger comes and, before you know it, he is slandering some perfectly respectable D.D.S. or D.M.D. The dentist pulled a healthy tooth—the dentist took such and such a huge sum of money for new plates—they don't fit him, he suffers great anguish—he's a poor man, the dentist won't do anything—*et cetera, ad infinitum nauseamque.* In short, a nut, a crank, a crackpot.

But while I was hesitating, the man yawned, did not courteously cover his mouth with his hand, and I observed to my astonishment that the interior of his mouth was an odd shade of blue!

Bemused by this singular departure from normalcy, I allowed him to enter. Then I wondered what to say, since he himself was saying nothing, but he looked around the lab with interest. "State your business" would be too brusque, and "Why is your mouth blue?" would be too gauche. An impasse.

Whilst holding up a large-scale model of the Goldpepper Cap (not yet perfected—will it ever be? Alas, who knows?) this curious individual said, "I know all about you, Dentist Goldpepper. A great scientist, you are. A man of powerful imagination, you are. One who rebels against narrow horizons and yearns to soar to wide and distant worlds, you are."

All I could think of to say was, "And what can I do for *you*?"

It was all so true; every single word he said was true. In my vanity was my downfall. I was tricked like the crow with the cheese in the ancient fable of Aesop.

The man proceeded to tell me, frankly enough, that he was a denizen of another planet. He had *two hearts,* would you believe it? And, consequently, two circulatory systems. Two pulses—one in each arm, one slow, the other fast.

It reminded me of the situation in Philadelphia some years ago when there were two telephone systems—if you had only a Bell phone, you couldn't call anyone who had only a Keystone phone.

The interior of his mouth was blue and so was the inside of his eyelids. He said his world had three moons.

You may imagine my emotions at hearing that my long-felt dream to communicate with otherworldly forms of sentient life was at last realized! And to think that they had singled out *not* the President of the United States, *not* the Director-General of the U.N., but *me,* Morris Goldpepper, D.D.S.! Could human happiness ask for more, was my unspoken question. I laughed softly to myself and I thought, What would my cousin Nathaniel Pomerance say *now?* I was like wax in this extraterrestrial person's hands (he had six distinct and articulate digits on each one), and I easily agreed to say nothing to anyone until the question of diplomatic recognition could be arranged on a higher echelon.

"Non-recognition *has* its advantages, Goldpepper Dental Surgeon," he said with a slight smile. "No passport for your visit, you will need."

Well! A personal invitation to visit Proxima Centauri Gamma, or whatever the planet's name is! But I felt constrained to look this gift-horse just a little closer in the mouth. How is it that they came inviting *me,* not, let us say, Oppenheimer? Well?

"Of his gifts not in need, we are, Surgical Goldpepper. We have passed as far beyond nuclear power as you have beyond wind power. We can span the Universe—*but in dentistry, like children still,* we are. Come and inspect our faculties of your science, Great Goldpepper. If you say, 'This: Yes,' then it will be yes. If you direct, 'This: No,' then it will be no. In respect to the science of dentistry, our Edison and our Columbus, you will be."

I asked when we would leave and he said in eight days. I asked how long the trip would take. For a moment, I was baffled when he said it would take no longer than to walk the equivalent of the length of the lab floor. Then he revealed his meaning to me: Teleportation! Of course. No spaceship needed.

My next emotion was a brief disappointment at not being able to see the blazing stars in black outer space. But, after all, one ought not be greedy at such a time.

I cannot point out too strongly that at no time did I accept or agree to accept any payment or gratuity for this trip. I looked upon it in the same light as the work I have done for various clinics.

"Should I take along books? Equipment? What?" I asked my (so-to-speak) guide.

He shook his head. Only my presence was desired on the first trip. A visit of inspection. Very well.

On the morning of Nov. 8th, I wrote a brief note to my old and dear friend, Dr. Samuel Fadderman, the senior mentor of American Dentistry [on hearing these words, the Elder Statesman sobbed softly into his cupped hands], and in the afternoon, so excited and enthralled that I noticed no more of my destination than that it was north of the Washington Market, I accompanied my guide to a business building in the aforesaid area.

He led me into a darkened room. He clicked a switch. There was a humming noise, a feeling first of heaviness, then of weightlessness, and then an odd sort of light came on.

I was no longer on the familiar planet of my birth! I was on an unknown world!

Over my head, the three moons of this far-off globe sailed majestically through a sky wherein I could note unfamiliar constellations. The thought occurred to me that poets on this planet would have to find another rhyme, inasmuch as *moons* (plural form) does not go with *June* (singular form). One satellite was a pale yellow, one was brown, and the third was a creamy pink. Not knowing the names of these lunary orbs in their native tongue, I decided to call them Vanilla, Chocolate and Strawberry.

Whilst my mind was filled with these droll fancies, I felt a tug at my sleeve, where my guide was holding it. He gestured and I followed.

"Now," I thought to myself, "he will bring me before the President of their Galactic Council, or whatever he is called," and I stood obediently within a circle marked on the surface of the platform whereon we stood.

In a moment, we were teleported to an inside room somewhere, and there I gazed about me in stupefaction, not to say astonishment. My eyes discerned the forms of Bunsen burners, Baldor lathes, casting machines and ovens, denture trays, dental stone, plaster, shellac trays, wires of teeth, and all the necessary equipment of a fully equipped dental prosthetic laboratory.

My surprise at the progress made by these people in the science at which they were allegedly still children was soon mitigated by the realization that all the items had been made on Earth.

As I was looking and examining, a door opened and several people entered. Their faces were a pale blue, and I realized suddenly that my guide must be wearing makeup to conceal his original complexion. They spoke together in their native dialect; then one of them, with a rod of some kind in his hand, turned to me. He opened his mouth. I perceived his gums were bare.

"Dentical person," he said, "make me teeth."

I turned in some perplexity to my guide. "I understood you to say my first visit would be one of inspection only."

Everyone laughed, and I observed that all were equally toothless.

The man in the chair poked me rudely with his rod or staff. "Talk not! Make teeth!"

Fuming with a well-justified degree of indignation, I protested at such a gross breach of the laws of common hospitality. Then, casting concealment to the winds, these people informed me as follows:

Their race is entirely toothless in the adult stage. They are an older race than ours and are born looking ancient and wrinkled. It is only comparatively recently that they have established contact with Earth, and in order that they should not appear conspicuous, and in order to be able to eat our food, they realized that they must be supplied with artificial teeth.

My so-called guide, false friend, my enticer and/or kidnaper, to give him his due, had gotten fitted at a dentist's in New York and cunningly enquired who was the leading man in the field. Alas for fame! The man answered without a second of hesitation, "That is no other one than Morris Goldpepper, D.D.S., perfector of the Semi-retractable Clasp."

First this unscrupulous extraterrestrial procured the equipment, then he procured *me*.

"Do I understand that you purport that I assist you in a plan to thwart and otherwise circumvent the immigration laws of the United States?" was my enquiry.

The man in the chair poked me with his rod again. "You understand! So now make teeth!"

What a proposition to make to a law-abiding, patriotic American citizen by birth! What a demand to exact of a war veteran, a taxpayer and one who has been three times on jury duty since 1946 alone (People vs. Garrity, People vs. Vanderdam, and Lipschutz vs. Krazy-Kut Kool Kaps, Inc.)! My whole being revolted. I spoke coldly to them, informing them that the situation was contrary to my conception of dental ethics. But to no avail.

My treacherous dragoman drew a revolver from his pocket. "Our weapons understand, you do not. Primitive Earth weapons, yes. So proceed with manufacture, Imprisoned Goldpepper."

I went hot and cold. Not, I beg of you to understand, with fear, but with humiliation. *Imprisoned Goldpepper!* The phrase, with all the connotations it implied, rang in my ears.

I bowed my head and a phrase from the literary work "Sampson Agonistes" (studied as a student in the College of the City of New York) rang through my mind: Eyeless in Gaza, grinding corn . . . Oh, blind, blind, amidst the blaze of noon . . .

But even in this hour of mental agony, an agony which has scarcely abated to speak of, I had the first glimmering of the idea which I hope will enable me to warn Earth.

Without a word, but only a scornful glance to show these blue-complected individuals how well I appreciated that their so-called advanced science was a mere veneer over the base metal of their boorishness, I set to work. I made the preliminary impressions and study casts, using an impression tray with oval floor form, the best suited for taking impressions of edentulous ridges.

And so began the days of my slavery.

Confined as I am here, there is neither day nor night, but an unremitting succession of frenum trims, post dams, boxing in, pouring up, festoon carving, fixing sprue channels, and all the innumerable details of dental prosthetic work. No one assists me. No one converses with me, save in brusque barks relevant to the work at hand. My food consists of liqueous and gelatinous substances such as might be expected would form the diet of a toothless race.

Oh, I am sick of the sight of their blue skins, bluer mouths and horny ridges! I am sick of my slavish serfdom!

I have been given material to keep records and am writing this in expectation of later reducing it in size by the method here employed, and of thereinafter inserting copies between the palatal and occlusual surfaces of the plates. It will be necessary to make such plates imperfect, so that the wearers will be obliged to go to dentists on Earth for repairs, because it is not always practical for them to teleport—in fact, I believe they can only do it on the 8th day of every third month. Naturally, I cannot do this to every plate, for they might become suspicious.

You may well imagine how it goes against my grain to produce defective work, but I have no other choice. Twice they have brought me fresh dental supplies, which is how I calculate their teleporting cycle. I have my wristwatch with me and thus I am enabled to reckon the passing of time.

What their exact purpose is in going to Earth, I do not know. My growing suspicion is that their much-vaunted superior science is a fraud and that their only superiority lies in the ability to teleport. One curious item may give a clue: They have questioned me regarding the Old Age Assistance programs of the several States. As I have said, they all *look* old.

Can it be that elsewhere on this planet there is imprisoned some poor devil of a terrestrial printer or engraver, toiling under duress to produce forged birth certificates and other means of identification, to the fell purpose of allowing these aliens to live at ease at the financial expense of the already overburdened U.S. taxpayer?

To whom shall I address my plea for help? To the Federal Government? But it has no official or even unofficial knowledge that this otherworldly race exists. The F.B.I.? But does teleporting under false pretenses to another planet constitute kidnaping across State lines?

It seems the only thing I can do is to implore whichever dental practitioner reads these lines to communicate at once with the American Dental Association. I throw myself upon the mercy of my fellow professional men.

Dentists and Dental Prostheticians! Beware of men with blue mouths and horny, edentulous ridges! Do not be deceived by flattery and false promises! Remember the fate of that most miserable of men, Morris Goldpepper, D.D.S., and, in his horrible predicament, help, oh, help him!

THREE

A long silence followed the reading of this document. At length it was broken by Dr. Hansen.

"That brave man," he said in a husky voice. "That brave little man."

"Poor Morris," said Dr. Danbourge. "Think of him imprisoned on a far-off planet, slaving like a convict in a salt mine, so to speak, making false teeth for these inhuman aliens, sending these messages to us across the trackless void.

It's pitiful, and yet, Doctors, it is also a tribute to the indomitable spirit of Man!"

Dr. Weinroth moved his huge hands. "I'd like to get ahold of just one of those blue bastards," he growled.

Dr. Rorke cleared his throat. All present looked at their President respectfully and eagerly.

"I need hardly tell you, Doctors," he said crisply, "that the A.D.A. is a highly conservative organization. We do not go about things lightly. One such message we might ignore, but there have been eleven reported, all identical with the first. Even eleven such messages we might perhaps not consider, but when they come from a prominent scientist of the stature of Dr. Morris Goldpepper—

"Handwriting experts have pronounced this to be *his* handwriting beyond cavil of a doubt. Here"—he delved into a box—"are the eleven plates in question. Can any of you look at these clean lines and deny that they are the work of the incomparable Goldpepper?"

The six other men looked at the objects, shook their heads.

"Beautiful," murmured Dr. Smith, "even in their broken state. Poems in plastic! M. G. *couldn't* produce bad work if he tried!"

Dr. Rorke continued. "Each report confirmed that the person who brought in the plate had a blue mouth and edentulous ridges, just as the message states. Each blue-mouthed patient exhibited the outward appearance of old age. *And,* gentlemen, of those eleven, no less than *eight* were reported from the State of California. Do you realize what that means? California offers the highest amount of financial assistance to the elderly! Goldpepper's surmise was right!"

Dr. Hansen leaned forward. "In addition, our reports show that five of those eight are leaders in the fight against fluoridation of drinking water! It is my carefully considered belief that there is something in their physical makeup, evolved on another planet, which cannot tolerate fluorine even in minute quantities, because they certainly—being already toothless—wouldn't be concerned with the prevention of decay."

Young Dr. McCallister took the floor. "We have checked with dental supply houses and detail men in the New York metropolitan area and we found that large quantities of prosthetic supplies have been delivered to an otherwise unknown outfit—called the Echs Export Company—located not far north of the Washington Market! There is every reason to believe that this is the place Dr. Goldpepper mentioned. One of our men went there, found present only one man, in appearance an *old* man. Our representative feigned deafness, thus obliging this person to open his mouth and talk loudly. Doctors, he reports that this person *has a blue mouth!*"

There was a deep intake of breath around the table.

Dr. Rorke leaned forward and snapped off the tape recorders. "This next is off the record. It is obvious, Doctors, that no ordinary methods will suffice to settle this case, to ensure the return of our unfortunate colleague, or to secure the withdrawal of these extraterrestrial individuals from our nation and planet. I cannot, of course, officially endorse what might be termed 'strong-arm' methods. At the same time, I feel that our adversaries are not entitled to polite treatment. And obviously the usual channels of law enforcement are completely closed to us.

"Therefore—and remember, no word of this must pass outside our circle—therefore I have communicated something of this matter to Mr. Albert Annapollo, the well-known waterfront figure, who not long ago inaugurated the splendid Longshoremen's Dental Health Plan. Mr. Annapollo is a somewhat rough person, but he is nonetheless a *loyal* American. . . .

"We know now the Achilles heel of these alien creatures. It is fluorine. We know also how to identify them. And I think we may shortly be able to announce results. Meanwhile—" he drew a slip of paper from his pocket—"it is already the first of the month in that quarter when the dental supplies are due to be transported—or teleported, as Dr. Goldpepper terms it—to their distant destination. A large shipment is waiting to be delivered from the warehouses of a certain wholesaler to the premises of the Echs Exporting Company. I have had copies of this made and wrapped around each three-ounce bottle of Ellenbogen's Denture Stik-Phast. I presume it meets with your approval."

He handed it to Dr. Hansen, who, as the others present nodded in grimly emphatic approval, read it aloud.

"*From The American Dental Association, representing over 45,000 registered dentists in the United States and its Territories, to Dr. Morris Goldpepper, wherever you may be: DO NOT DESPAIR! We are intent upon your rescue! We will bend every effort to this end! We shall fight the good fight!*

"*Have courage, Dr. Morris Goldpepper! You shall return!*"

Now Let Us Sleep

INTRODUCTION BY GREGORY BENFORD

When "*Now Let Us Sleep*" first appeared it excited a fine reaction. The dark issues it confronts lie deep within us. Since its publication, we have learned much about our origins, our connections to the other primates, and implications for our own lot in the universe.

Consider the chimpanzees. We separated from them genetically about six million years ago and differ by less than two percent in our DNA. We've patched together, from field observation and evolutionary logic, a picture of how they— and we—evolved our social behaviors.

The issues of this story arise from a conflict between Avram's clear, liberal sympathies and the nagging knowledge that maybe our core natures conflict. This is dismaying news indeed.

Let me sketch some of the perspectives from a scientific view, to outline the problems.

Chimpanzees move in small groups, disliking outsiders, breeding mostly within their modest circle of a few dozen. This meant that any genetic trait that emerged could pass swiftly into all the members, through inbreeding. If it helped the band survive, the rough rub of chance would select for that band's survival.

But the trait had to be undiluted. A troop of especially good rock throwers would get swallowed up if they joined a company of several hundred, their genetic heritage watered down.

What to do? Striking a balance between the accidents of genetics in small groups, and the stability of large groups—that was the trick, we believe.

Some lucky troop might have genetic traits that fit the next challenge handed out by the ever-altering world. They did well. With some out-breeding, that trait got spread into other bands. Down through the strainer of time, others picked up the trait. It spread.

So small bands held fast to their eccentric traits, and some prospered. Evolutionary jumps happened faster in small, semi-isolated bands which out-bred slightly. They kept their genetic assets in one small basket, the troop. The price was steep: a strong preference for their own tiny lot.

This would lead to a species that hated crowds, strangers, general alienness. Nature, then, did not produce a natural liberal.

Bands of less than ten were too vulnerable to disease or predators; a few losses and the group failed. Too many, and they lost the concentration of close breeding. They were intensely loyal to their group, identifying each other in the dark by smell.

Because they had many common genes, altruistic actions were common. This meant even heroism—for even if the hero died, his shared genes were passed on through his relatives.

So it was actually helpful to develop smoldering animosity to outsiders, an immediate sense of their wrongness.

Even if strangers could pass the tests of difference in appearances, manner, smell, grooming—even then, culture could amplify the effects. Newcomers with different language or dress, or habits and posture, would seem repulsive. Anything that served to distinguish a band would keep hatreds high.

Each small genetic ensemble would then be driven by natural selection to stress the noninherited differences—even arbitrary ones, dimly connected to survival fitness—and so they evolved culture. Diversity in their tribal intricacies avoided genetic watering down. They heeded the ancient call of aloof, wary tribalism.

Does this chimp scenario fit us? Some resemblances are striking.

After all, we still resemble the common chimps and pygmy chimps. We're just bigger and with less hair, walking upright. The visible differences between us and chimps were far less than, say, between Great Danes and Chihuahuas. Yet dogs interbreed. We and chimps do not.

In nature, genocide occurs in wolves and chimps alike. Murder is widespread. (Further afield, ducks and orangutans rape, ants have organized warfare and slave raids. The Walt Disney world never existed.) Chimps in the field have at least as good a chance of being murdered as did humans.

Of all the hallowed human hallmarks—speech, art, technology, and the rest—the one that comes most obviously from animal ancestors is genocide. Human tribes may well have evolved as a group defense—clubbiness against clubs.

Luckily, today's worldwide instantaneous communication blurs distinctions between Us and Them, blunting the deep impulse to genocide.

Our biological baggage of dark behaviors includes delight in torture, and easy exterminations of other species for short-term gain. Against such Darwinian imperatives, willed to us by vast time, we can muster only our intuitive values.

Avram knew this, and so framed his story as a quiet affirmation of solidarity with the Other. A noble sentiment, and one which may well have eventual positive effects upon our own evolution. For we cannot go on as super-chimps, pacing restlessly upon a shrinking globe.

Still less can we think of the galaxy itself as a great veldt, ready for our primate passions. We need something more. Art and artifice, fiction among them, are our ways of confronting our troubling selves.

A PINK-SKINNED YOUNG CADET ran past Harper, laughing and shouting and firing his stungun. The wind veered about, throwing the thick scent of the Yahoos into the faces of the men, who whooped loudly to show their revulsion.

"I got three!" the chicken cadet yelped at Harper. "Did you see me pop those two together? Boy, what a stink they have!"

Harper looked at the sweating kid, muttered, "You don't smell so sweet yourself," but the cadet didn't wait to hear. All the men were running now, running in a ragged semi-circle with the intention of driving the Yahoos before them, to hold them at bay at the foot of the gaunt cliff a quarter-mile off.

The Yahoos loped awkwardly over the rough terrain, moaning and grunting grotesquely, their naked bodies bent low. A few hundred feet ahead one of them stumbled and fell, his arms and legs flying out as he hit the ground, twitched, and lay still.

A bald-headed passenger laughed triumphantly, paused to kick the Yahoo, and trotted on. Harper kneeled beside the fallen Primitive, felt for a pulse in the hairy wrist. It seemed slow and feeble, but then, no one actually knew what the normal pulse-beat should be. And—except for Harper—no one seemed to give a damn.

Maybe it was because he was the grandson of Barret Harper, the great naturalist—back on Earth, of course. It seemed as if man could be fond of nature only on the planet of man's origin, whose ways he knew so well. Elsewhere, it was too strange and alien—you subdued it, or you adjusted to it, or you were perhaps even content with it. But you almost never *cared* about the flora or fauna of the new planets. No one had the feeling for living things that an earth-born had.

The men were shouting more loudly now, but Harper didn't lift his head to see why. He put his hand to the shaggy gray chest. The heart was still beating, but very slowly and irregularly. Someone stood beside him.

"He'll come out of it in an hour or so," the voice of the purser said. "Come on—you'll miss all the fun—you should see how they act when they're cornered! They kick out and throw sand and"—he laughed at the thought—"they weep great big tears, and go, *'Oof! Oof!'* "

Harper said, "An ordinary man *would* come out of it in an hour or so. But I think their metabolism is different.... Look at all the bones lying around."

The purser spat. "Well, don't that prove they're not human, when they won't even bury their dead? ... *Oh,* oh!—look at that!" He swore.

Harper got to his feet. Cries of dismay and disappointment went up from the men.

"What's wrong?" Harper asked.

The purser pointed. The men had stopped running, were gathering together and gesturing. "Who's the damn fool who planned this drive?" the purser asked, angrily. "He picked the wrong cliff! The damned Yahoos *nest* in that one! Look at them climb, will you—" He took aim, fired the stungun. A figure scrabbling up the side of the rock threw up its arms and fell, bounding from rock to rock until it hit the ground. "*That* one will never come out of it!" the purser said, with satisfaction.

But this was the last casualty. The other Yahoos made their way to safety in the caves and crevices. No one followed them. In those narrow, stinking confines a Yahoo was as good as a man, there was no room to aim a stungun, and the Yahoos had rocks and clubs and their own sharp teeth. The men began straggling back.

"This one a she?" The purser pushed at the body with his foot, let it fall back with an annoyed grunt as soon as he determined its sex. "There'll be Hell to pay in the hold if there's more than two convicts to a she." He shook his head and swore.

Two lighters came skimming down from the big ship to load up.

"Coming back to the launch?" the purser asked. He had a red shiny face. Harper had always thought him a rather decent fellow—before. The purser had no way of knowing what was in Harper's mind; he smiled at him and said, "We might as well get on back, the fun's over now."

Harper came to a sudden decision. "What're the chances of my taking a souvenir back with me? This big fellow, here, for example?"

The purser seemed doubtful. "Well, I dunno, Mr. Harper. We're only supposed to take females aboard, and unload *them* as soon as the convicts are finished with their fun." He leered. Harper, suppressing a strong urge to hit him right in the middle of his apple-red face, put his hand in his pocket. The purser understood, looked away as Harper slipped a bill into the breast pocket of his uniform.

"I guess it can be arranged. See, the Commissioner-General on Selopé III wants one for his private zoo. Tell you what: We'll take one for him and one for you—I'll tell the supercargo it's a spare. But if one croaks, the C-G has to get the other. Okay?"

At Harper's nod the purser took a tag out of his pocket, tied it around the Yahoo's wrist, waved his cap to the lighter as it came near. "Although why anybody'd *want* one of these beats me," he said, cheerfully. "They're dirtier than animals. I mean, a pig or a horse'll use the same corner of the enclosure, but these things'll dirty anywhere. Still, if you *want* one—" He shrugged.

As soon as the lighter had picked up the limp form (the pulse was still fluttering feebly) Harper and the purser went back to the passenger launch. As they made a swift ascent to the big ship the purser gestured to the two lighters. "That's going to be a mighty slow trip *those* two craft will make back up," he remarked.

Harper innocently asked why. The purser chuckled. The coxswain laughed.

"The freight-crewmen want to make their points before the convicts. *That's* why."

The chicken cadet, his face flushed a deeper pink than usual, tried to sound knowing. "How about that, purser? Is it pretty good stuff?"

The other passengers wiped their perspiring faces, leaned forward eagerly. The purser said, "Well, rank has its privileges, but that's one I figure I can do without."

His listeners guffawed, but more than one looked down toward the lighters and then avoided other eyes when he looked back again.

Barnum's Planet (named, as was the custom then, after the skipper who'd first sighted it) was a total waste, economically speaking. It was almost all water and the water supported only a few repulsive-looking species of no discernible value. The only sizable piece of land—known, inevitably, as Barnumland, since no one else coveted the honor—was gaunt and bleak, devoid alike of useful minerals or arable soil. Its ecology seemed dependent on a sort of fly: A creature rather like a lizard ate the flies and the Yahoos ate the lizards. If something died at sea and washed ashore, the Yahoos ate that, too. What the flies ate no one knew, but their larvae ate the Yahoos, dead.

They were small, hairy, stunted creatures whose speech—if speech it was— seemed confined to moans and clicks and grunts. They wore no clothing, made no artifacts, did not know the use of fire. Taken away captive, they soon languished and died. Of all the primitives discovered by man, they were the most primitive. They might have been left alone on their useless planet to kill lizards with tree branches forever—except for one thing.

Barnum's Planet lay equidistant between Coulter's System and the Selopés, and it was a long, long voyage either way. Passengers grew restless, crews grew mutinous, convicts rebellious. Gradually the practice developed of stopping on Barnum's Planet "to let off steam"—archaic expression, but although the nature of the machinery man used had changed since it was coined, man's nature hadn't.

And, of course, no one *owned* Barnum's Planet, so no one cared what happened there.

Which was just too bad for the Yahoos.

It took some time for Harper to settle the paperwork concerning his "souvenir," but finally he was given a baggage check for "One Yahoo, male, live," and hurried down to the freight deck. He hoped it would be still alive.

Pandemonium met his ears as he stepped out of the elevator. A rhythmical chanting shout came from the convict hold. "Hear that?" one of the duty officers asked him, taking the cargo chit. Harper asked what the men were yelling. "I wouldn't care to use the words," the officer said. He was a paunchy, gray-haired man, one who probably loved to tell his grandchildren about his "adventures." This was one he wouldn't tell them.

"I don't like this part of the detail," the officer went on. "Never did, never will. Those creatures *seem human to me*—stupid as they are. And if they're *not* human," he asked, "then how can we sink low enough to bring their females up for the convicts?"

The lighters grated on the landing. The noise must have penetrated to the convict hold, because all semblance of words vanished from the shouting. It became a mad cry, louder and louder.

"Here's your pet," the gray-haired officer said. "Still out, I see . . . I'll let you have a baggage-carrier. Just give it to a steward when you're done with it." He had to raise his voice to be heard over the frenzied howling from the hold.

The ship's surgeon was out having tea at the captain's table. The duty medical officer was annoyed. "What, another one? We're not veterinarians, you know . . . Well, wheel him in. My intern is working on the other one . . . *whew!*" He held his nose and hastily left.

The intern, a pale young man with close-cropped dark hair, looked up from the pressure-spray he had just used to give an injection to the specimen Yahoo selected for the Commissioner-General of Selopé III. He smiled faintly.

"Junior will have company, I see. . . . Any others?"

Harper shook his head. The intern went on, "This should be interesting. The young one seems to be in shock. I gave him two cc's of anthidar sulfate, and I see I'd better do the same for yours. Then . . . Well, I guess there's still nothing like serum albumen, is there? But you'd better help me strap them down. If they come to, there's a cell back aft we can put them in, until I can get some cages rigged up." He shot the stimulant into the flaccid arm of Harper's Yahoo.

"Whoever named these beasties knew his Swift," the young medico said. "You ever read that old book, *Gulliver's Travels?*"

Harper nodded.

"Old Swift went mad, didn't he? He hated humanity, they all seemed like Yahoos to him. . . . In a way I don't blame him. I think that's why everybody despises these Primitives: They seem like caricatures of ourselves. Personally, I look forward to finding out a lot about them, their metabolism and so on. . . . What's *your* interest?"

He asked the question casually, but shot a keen look as he did so. Harper shrugged. "I hardly know, exactly. It's not a scientific one, because I'm a businessman." He hesitated. "You ever hear or read about the Tasmanians?"

The intern shook his head. He thrust a needle into a vein in the younger Yahoo's arm, prepared to let the serum flow in. "If they lived on Earth, I wouldn't know. Never was there. I'm a third generation Coulterboy, myself."

Harper said, "Tasmania is an island south of Australia. The natives were the most primitive people known to Earth. They were almost all wiped out by the settlers, but one of them succeeded in moving the survivors to a smaller island. And then a curious thing happened."

Looking up from the older Primitive, the intern asked what that was.

"The Tasmanians—the few that were left—decided that they'd had it. They refused to breed. And in a few more years they were all dead. . . . I read about them when I was just a kid. Somehow, it moved me very much. Things like that *did*—the dodo, the great auk, the quagga, the Tasmanians. I've never been able to get it out of my mind. When I began hearing about the Yahoos, it seemed to me that they were like the old Tasmanians. Only there are no settlers on Barnumland."

The intern nodded. "But that won't help our hairy friends here a hell of a lot. Of course no one knows how many of them there are—or ever were. But I've been comparing the figures in the log as to how many females are caught and taken aboard." He looked directly at Harper. "And on every trip there are less by far."

Harper bowed his head. He nodded. The intern's voice went on: "The thing is, Barnum's Planet is no one's responsibility. If the Yahoos could be used for labor, they'd be exploited according to a careful system. But as it is, no one cares. If half of them die from being stungunned, no one cares. If the lighter crews don't bother to actually land the females—if any of the wretched creatures are still *alive* when the convicts are done—but just dump them out from twenty feet up, why, again: no one cares. Mr. Harper?"

Their eyes met. Harper said, "Yes?"

"Don't misunderstand me. . . . I've got a career here. I'm not jeopardizing it to save the poor Yahoos—but if *you* are interested—if you think you've got any influence—and if you want to try to do anything—" He paused. "Why, now is the time to start. Because after another few stopovers there aren't going to *be* any Yahoos. No more than there are any Tasmanians."

Selopé III was called "The Autumn Planet" by the poets. At least, the P.R. picture-tapes always referred to it as "Selopé III, The Autumn Planet of the poets," but no one knew who the poets were. It was true that the Commission Territory, at least, did have the climate of an almost-perpetual early New England November. Barnumland had been dry and warm. The Commissioner-General put the two Yahoos in a heated cage as large as the room Harper occupied at his company's bachelor executive quarters.

"Here, boy," the C-G said, holding out a piece of fruit. He made a chirping noise. The two Yahoos huddled together in a far corner.

"They don't seem very bright," he said, sadly. "All my *other* animals eat out of my hand." He was very proud of his private zoo, the only one in the Territory. On Sundays he allowed the public to visit it.

Sighing, Harper repeated that the Yahoos were Primitives, not animals. But, seeing the C-G was still doubtful, he changed his tactics. He told the C-G about the great zoos on Earth, where the animals went loose in large enclosures rather than being caged up. The C-G nodded thoughtfully. Harper told him of the English dukes who—generation after ducal generation—preserved the last herd of wild White Cattle in a park on their estate.

The C-G stroked his chin. "Yes, yes," he said. "I see your point," he said. He sighed gustily. "Can't be done," he said.

"But why not, sir?" Harper cried.

It was simple. "No money. Who's to pay? The Exchequer-Commissioner is weeping blood trying to get the budget through Council. If he adds a penny more— No, young fellow. I'll do what *I* can: I'll feed these two, here. But that's all I can do."

Trying to pull all the strings he could reach, Harper approached the Executive-Fiscal and the Procurator-General, the President-in-Council, the Territorial Advocate, the Chairman of the Board of Travel. But no one could do anything. Barnum's Planet, it was carefully explained to him, remained No Man's Land only because no man presumed to give any orders concerning it. If any government did, this would be a Presumption of Authority. And then every other government would feel obliged to deny that presumption and issue a claim of its own.

There was a peace on now—a rather tense, uneasy one. And it wasn't going to be disturbed for Harper's Yahoos. Human, were they? Perhaps. But who cared? As for morality, Harper didn't even bother to mention the word. It would have meant as little as chivalry.

Meanwhile, he was learning something of the Yahoos' language. Slowly and arduously, he gained their confidence. They would shyly take food from him. He persuaded the C-G to knock down a wall and enlarge their quarters. The official was a kindly old man, and he seemed to grow fond of the stooped, shaggy, splay-footed Primitives. And after a while he decided that they were smarter than animals.

"Put some clothes on 'em, Harper," he directed. "If they're people, let 'em start acting like people. They're too big to go around naked."

So, eventually, washed and dressed, Junior and Senior were introduced to Civilization via 3-D, and the program was taped and shown everywhere.

Would you like a cigarette, Junior? Here, let me light it for you. Give Junior a glass of water, Senior. Let's see you take off your slippers, fellows, and put them on again. And now do what I say in your own language . . .

But if Harper thought that might change public opinion, he thought wrong. Seals perform, too, don't they? And so do monkeys. They talk? Parrots talk better. And anyway, who cared to be bothered about animals *or* Primitives? They were okay for fun, but that was all.

And the reports from Barnumland showed fewer and fewer Yahoos each time.

Then one night two drunken crewmen climbed over the fence and went carousing in the C-G's zoo. Before they left, they broke the vapor-light tubes, and in the morning Junior and Senior were found dead from the poisonous fumes.

That was Sunday morning. By Sunday afternoon Harper was drunk, and getting drunker. The men who knocked on his door got no answer. They went in anyway. He was slouched, red-eyed, over the table.

"People," he muttered. "Tell you they were *human!*" he shouted.

"Yes, Mr. Harper, we know that," said a young man, pale, with close-cropped dark hair.

Harper peered at him, boozily. "Know you," he said. "Thir' gen'ration Coulterboy. Go 'way. Spoi' your c'reer. Whaffor? Smelly ol' Yahoo?" The young medico nodded to his companion, who took a small flask from his pocket, opened it. They held it under Harper's nose by main force. He gasped and struggled, but they held on, and in a few minutes he was sober.

"That's rough stuff," he said, coughing and shaking his head. "But—thanks, Dr. Hill. Your ship in? Or are you stopping over?"

The former intern shrugged. "I've left the ships," he said. "I don't have to worry about spoiling my new career. This is my superior, Dr. Anscomb."

Anscomb was also young, and, like most men from Coulter's System, pale. He said, "I understand you can speak the Yahoos' language."

Harper winced. "What good's that now? They're dead, poor little bastards."

Anscomb nodded. "I'm sorry about that, believe me. Those fumes are so quick. . . . But there are still a few alive on Barnum's Planet who can be saved. The Joint Board for Research is interested. Are you?"

It had taken Harper fifteen years to work up to a room of this size and quality in bachelor executives' quarters. He looked around it. He picked up the letter which had come yesterday. ". . . neglected your work and become a joke . . . unless you accept a transfer and reduction in grade . . ." He nodded slowly, putting down the letter. "I guess I've already made my choice. What are your plans?"

Harper, Hill, and Anscomb sat on a hummock on the north coast of Barnumland, just out of rock-throwing range of the gaunt escarpment of the cliff which rose before them. Behind them a tall fence had been erected. The only Yahoos still alive were "nesting" in the caves of the cliff. Harper spoke into the amplifier again. His voice was hoarse as he forced it into the clicks and moans of the Primitives' tongue.

Hill stirred restlessly. "Are you sure that means. *'Here is food. Here is water'*—and not, *'Come down and let us eat you'*? I think I can almost say it myself by now."

Shifting and stretching, Anscomb said, "It's been two days. Unless they've determined to commit race suicide a bit more abruptly than your ancient Tasmanians—" He stopped as Harper's fingers closed tightly on his arm.

There was a movement on the cliff. A shadow. A pebble clattered. Then a wrinkled face peered fearfully over a ledge. Slowly, and with many stops and hesitations, a figure came down the face of the cliff. It was an old she. Her withered and pendulous dugs flapped against her sagging belly as she made the final jump to the ground, and—her back to the wall of rock—faced them.

"Here is food," Harper repeated softly. "Here is water." The old woman sighed. She plodded wearily across the ground, paused, shaking with fear, and then flung herself down at the food and the water.

"The Joint Board for Research has just won the first round," Hill said. Anscomb nodded. He jerked his thumb upward. Hill looked.

Another head appeared at the cliff. Then another. And another. They watched. The crone got up, water dripping from her dewlaps. She turned to the cliff. "Come down," she cried. "Here is food and water. Do not die. Come down and eat and drink." Slowly, her tribes-people did so. There were thirty of them.

Harper asked, "Where are the others?"

The crone held out her dried and leathery breasts to him. "Where are those who have sucked? Where are those your brothers took away?" She uttered a single shrill wail; then was silent.

But she wept—and Harper wept with her.

"I'll guess we'll swing it all right," Hill said. Anscomb nodded. "Pity there's so few of them. I was afraid we'd have to use gas to get at them. Might have lost several that way."

Neither of them wept.

For the first time since ships had come to their world, Yahoos *walked* aboard one. They came hesitantly and fearfully, but Harper had told them that they were going to a new home and they believed him. He told them that they were going to a place of much food and water, where no one would hunt them down. He continued to talk until the ship was on its way, and the last Primitive had fallen asleep under the dimmed-out vapor-tube lights. Then he staggered to his cabin and fell asleep himself. He slept for thirty hours.

He had something to eat when he awoke, then strolled down to the hold where the Primitives were. He grimaced, remembering his trip to the hold of the other ship to collect Senior, and the frenzied howling of the convicts awaiting the females. At the entrance to the hold he met Dr. Hill, greeted him.

"I'm afraid some of the Yahoos are sick," Hill said. "But Dr. Anscomb is treating them. The others have been moved to this compartment here."

Harper stared. "Sick? How can they be sick? What from? And how many?"

Dr. Hill said, "It appears to be Virulent Plague. . . . Fifteen of them are down with it. You've *had* all six shots, haven't you? Good. Nothing to worry—"

Harper felt the cold steal over him. He stared at the pale young physician. "No one can enter or leave any system or planet without having had all six shots for Virulent Plague," he said slowly. "So if we are all immune, how could the Primitives have gotten it? And how is it that only fifteen have it? Exactly half of them. What about the other fifteen, Dr. Hill? *Are they the control group for your experiment?*"

Dr. Hill looked at him calmly. "As a matter of fact, yes. I hope you'll be reasonable. Those were the only terms the Joint Board for Research would agree to. After all, not even convicts will volunteer for experiments in Virulent Plague."

Harper nodded. He felt frozen. After a moment he asked, "Can Anscomb do anything to pull them through?"

Dr. Hill raised his eyebrows. "Perhaps. We've got something we wanted to try. And at any rate, the reports should provide additional data on the sub-ject. We must take the long-range view."

Harper nodded. "I suppose you're right," he said.

By noon all fifteen were dead.

"Well, that means an uneven control group," Dr. Anscomb complained. "Seven against eight. Still, that's not *too* bad. And it can't be helped. We'll start tomorrow."

"Virulent Plague again?" Harper asked.

Anscomb and Hill shook their heads. "Dehydration," the latter said. "And after that, there's a new treatment for burns we're anxious to try. . . . It's a shame, when you think of the Yahoos being killed off by the thousands, year after year, *uselessly*. Like the dodo. We came along just in time—thanks to you, Harper."

He gazed at them. "*Quis custodiet ipsos custodes?*" he asked. They looked at him, politely blank. "I'd forgotten. Doctors don't study Latin any more, do they? An old proverb. It means: 'Who shall guard the guards themselves?' . . . Will you excuse me, Doctors?"

Harper let himself into the compartment. "I come," he greeted the fifteen.

"We see," they responded. The old woman asked how their brothers and sisters were "in the other cave."

"They are well. . . . Have you eaten, have you drunk? Yes? Then let us sleep," Harper said.

The old woman seemed doubtful. "Is it time? The light still shines." She pointed to it. Harper looked at her. She had been so afraid. But she had trusted him. Suddenly he bent over and kissed her. She gaped.

"Now the light goes out," Harper said. He slipped off a shoe and shattered the vapor tube. He groped in the dark for the air-switch, turned it off. Then he sat down. He had brought them here, and if they had to die, it was only fitting that he should share their fate. There no longer seemed any place for the helpless, or for those who cared about them.

"Now let us sleep," he said.

Or the Grasses Grow

INTRODUCTION BY ALAN DEAN FOSTER

Ever cut a diamond? Talk to a diamond-cutter sometime. They'll tell you that, sure, size matters—but by itself it doesn't make a good gem. Color's important, too. The whiter a stone, the purer and more transparent, the more valuable it is. And after color, clarity. Look at a diamond under a jeweler's loupe or, better still, beneath a 'scope. Imperfections stand out, and some of them shout, disrupting the play of light inside the crystal. Dispersion, it's called.

Anybody can take an idea, throw it at the reader, wrap a few quotes and exclamation points and adjectives around it, and call it a story. Might even be a big idea, flashy and impressive at first read. But dig into most stories and it won't take long to find the imperfections and discolorations.

Take a small idea, now, and hone it perfectly, so that there are no wasted words, no endless and unnecessary expository phrases, no participles dangling off the edges of otherwise well-cut sentences. That's much more difficult to do. Most writers achieve modest results with grandiose effects. In this regard, fantasy fiction is particularly guilty. Flying horses, gigantic djinn, sorcerers throwing lightning bolts at one another—effective at first, but after a while reduced to a kind of literary mendacity.

But a bunch of guys sitting around talking about their lives—ordinary people, with everyday problems. How do you reach out and grab the reader with that? How do you travel from a discussion of personal problems to a conclusion that stops a reader dead in his or her tracks, maybe just a little out of breath?

The same way an old diamond-cutter takes a tiny lump of dull, misshapen, milky crystal and turns it into an ornament that dazzles and overpowers the eye, that's how. Avram Davidson was a master shaper of small stories. "Or the Grasses Grow" is a prime example of his ability to, well, facet, what at first appears to be a small idea, and turn it into something brilliant.

ABOUT HALFWAY ALONG THE narrow and ill-paved county road
between Crosby and Spanish Flats (all dips and hollows shimmering falsely
like water in the heat till you get right up close to them), the road to Tickisall
Agency branches off. No pretense of concrete or macadam—or even grading—
deceives the chance or rare purposeful traveller. Federal, State, and County
governments have better things to do with their money: Tickisall pays no taxes,
and its handful of residents have only recently (and most grudgingly) been
accorded the vote.

The sunbaked earth is cracked and riven. A few dirty sheep and a handful
of scrub cows share its scanty herbage with an occasional swaybacked horse
or stunted burro. Here and there a gaunt automobile rests in the thin shadow
of a board shack, and a child, startled doubtless by the smooth sound of a
strange motor, runs like a lizard through the dusty wastes to hide, and then to
peer. Melon vines dried past all hope of fruit lie in patches next to whispery,
tindery cornstalks.

And in the midst of all this, next to the only spring which never goes dry,
are the only painted buildings, the only decent buildings in the area. In the
middle of the green lawn is a pole with the flag, and right behind the pole, over
the front door, the sign:

U.S. BUREAU OF INDIAN AFFAIRS.
TICKISALL AGENCY
OFFICE OF THE SUPERINTENDENT

There were already a few Indians gathering around that afternoon, the
women in cotton-print dresses, the men in overalls. There would soon be more.
This was scheduled as the last day for the Tickisall Agency and Reservation.
Congress had passed the bill, the President had signed it, the Director of the
Bureau of Indian Affairs had issued the order. It was supposed to be a great
day for the Tickisall Nation—only the Tickisalls, what was left of them, didn't
seem to think so. Not a man or woman of them spoke. Not a child whimpered.
Not a dog barked.

Before Uncle Fox-head sat a basket with four different kinds of clay, and next to the basket was a medicine gourd full of water. The old man rolled the clay between his moistened palms, singing in a low voice. Then he washed his hands and sprinkled them with pollen. Then he took up the prayer-sticks, made of juniper—(once there had been juniper trees on the reservation, once there had been many trees)—and painted with the signs of Thunder, Sun, Moon, Rain, Lightning. There were feathers tied to the sticks—once there had been birds, too . . .

> *Oh, People-of-The-Hidden Places,*
> *Oh, take our message to The Hidden Places,*
> *Swiftly, swiftly, now . . .*

the old man chanted, shaking the medicine-sticks.

> *Oh, you, Swift Ones, People-with-no-legs,*
> *Take our message to The-People-with-no-bodies,*
> *Swiftly, swiftly, now . . .*

The old man's skin was like a cracked, worn moccasin. With his turkey-claw hand he took up the gourd rattle, shook it: West, South, Up, Down, East, North.

> *Oh, People-of-the-hollow Earth,*
> *Take our message to the hollow Earth,*
> *Take our song to our Fathers and Mothers,*
> *Take our cry to the Spirit People,*
> *Take and go, take and go,*
> *Swiftly, swiftly, now . . .*

The snakes rippled across the ground and were gone, one by one. The old man's sister's son helped him back to his sheepskin, spread in the shade, where he half-sat, half-lay, panting.

His great-nephews, Billy Cottonwood and Sam Quarterhorse, were talking together in English. "There was a fellow in my outfit," Cottonwood said, "a fellow from West Virginia, name of Corrothers. Said his grandmother claimed she could charm away warts. So I said my great-uncle claimed he could make snakes. And they all laughed fit to kill, and said, 'Chief, when you try a snow-job, it turns into a blizzard!' . . . Old Corrothers," he reflected. "We were pretty good buddies. Maybe I'll go to West Virginia and look him up. I could hitch, maybe."

Quarterhorse said, "Yeah, you can go to West Virginia, and I can go to L.A.—but what about the others? Where *they* going to go if Washington refuses to act?"

The fond smile of recollection left his cousin's lean, brown face. "I don't know," he said. "I be damned and go to Hell, if I know." And then the old pick-up came rattling and coughing up to the house, and Sam said, "Here's Newton."

Newton Quarterhorse, his brother Sam, and Billy Cottonwood, were the only three Tickisalls who had passed the physical and gone into the Army. There weren't a lot of others who were of conscripting age (or any other age, for that matter), and those whom TB didn't keep out, other ailments active or passive did. Once there had been trees on the Reservation, and birds, and deer, and healthy men.

The wash-faded Army suntans had been clean and fresh as always when Newt set out for Crosby, but they were dusty and sweaty now. He took a piece of wet burlap out and removed a few bottles from it. "Open these, Sam, will you, while I wash," he said. "Cokes for us, strawberry pop for the old people . . . How's Uncle Fox-head?"

Billy grunted. "Playing at making medicine snakes again. Do you suppose if we believed he could, he could?"

Newt shrugged. "So. Well, maybe if the telegrams don't do any good, the snakes will. And I'm damned sure they won't do no worse. That son of a bitch at the Western Union office," he said, looking out over the drought-bitten land. " 'Sending a smoke-signal to the Great White Father again, Sitting Bull?' he says, smirking and sneering. I told him, 'You just take the money and send the wire.' They looked at me like coyotes looking at a sick calf." Abruptly, he turned away and went to dip his handkerchief in the bucket. Water was hard come by.

The lip of the bottle clicked against one of Uncle Fox-head's few teeth. He drank noisily, then licked his lips. "Today we drink the white man's sweet water," he said. "What will we drink tomorrow?" No one said anything. "I will tell you, then," he continued. "Unless the white men relent, we will drink the bitter waters of The Hollow Places. They are bitter, but they are strong and good." He waved his withered hand in a semi-circle. "All this will go," he said, "and the Fathers and Mothers of The People will return and lead us to our old home inside the Earth." His sister's son, who had never learned English nor gone to school, moaned. "Unless the white men relent," said the old man.

"They never have," said Cottonwood, in Tickisall. In English, he said, "What will he do when he sees that nothing happens tomorrow except that we get kicked the Hell out of here?"

Newt said, "Die, I suppose . . . which might not be a bad idea. For all of us."

His brother turned and looked at him. "If you're planning Quarterhorse's Last Stand, forget about it. There aren't twenty rounds of ammunition on the whole reservation."

Billy Cottonwood raised his head. "We could maybe move in with the Apahoya," he suggested. "They're just as dirt-poor as we are, but there's more of them, and I guess they'll hold on to their land awhile yet." His cousins shook their heads. "Well, not for us. But the others . . . Look, I spoke to Joe Feather Cloud that last time I was at the Apahoya Agency. If we give him the truck and the sheep, he'll take care of Uncle Fox-head."

Sam Quarterhorse said he supposed that was the best thing. "For the old

man, I mean. I made up *my* mind. I'm going to L.A. and pass for Colored."
He stopped.

They waited till the new shiny automobile had gone by towards the
Agency in a cloud of dust. Newt said, "The buzzards are gathering." Then he
asked, "How come, Sam?"

"Because I'm tired of being an Indian. It has no present and no future. I
can't be a white, they won't have me—the best I could hope for would be that
they laugh: 'How, Big Chief'—'Hi, Blanket-bottom.' Yeah, I *could* pass for a
Mexican as far as my looks go, only the Mexes won't have me, either. But the
Colored will. And there's millions and millions of them—whatever price they
pay for it, they never have to feel lonely. And they've got a fine, bitter contempt
for the whites that I can use a lot of. 'Pecks,' they call them. I don't know
where they got the name from, but, Damn! it sure fits them. They've been
pecking away at us for over a hundred years."

They talked on some more, and all the while the dust never settled in the
road. They watched the whole tribe, what there was of it, go by towards the
Agency—in old trucks, in buckboards, on horses, on foot. And after some
time, they loaded up the pick-up and followed.

The Indians sat all over the grass in front of the Agency, and for once no one
bothered to chase them off. They just sat, silent, waiting. A group of men from
Crosby and Spanish Flats were talking to the Superintendent; there were maps
in their hands. The cousins went up to them; the white men looked out of the
corners of their eyes, confidence still tempered—but only a bit—by wariness.

"Mr. Jenkins," Newt said to one, "most of this is your doing and you
know how I feel about it—"

"You better not make any trouble, Quarterhorse," said another townsman.

Jenkins said, "Let the boy have his say."

"—but I know you'll give me a straight answer. What's going to be done
here?"

Jenkins was a leathery little man, burnt almost as dark as an Indian. He
looked at him, not unkindly, through the spectacles which magnified his blue
eyes. "Why, you know, son, there's nothing personal in all this. The land
belongs to them that can hold it and use it. It was made to be used. You
people've had your chance, Lord knows— Well, no speeches. You see, here
on the map, where this here dotted line is? The county is putting through a
new road to connect with a new highway the state's going to construct. There'll
be a lot of traffic through here, and this Agency ought to make a fine motel.

"And right along *here*—" his blunt finger traced, "—there's going to be
the main irrigation canal. There'll be branches all through the Reservation.
I reckon we can raise some mighty fine alfalfa. Fatten some mighty fine cattle . . . I always thought, son, you'd be good with stock, if you had some good
stock to work with. Not these worthless scrubs. If you want a job—"

One of the men cleared his sinus cavities with an ugly sound, and spat.
"Are you out of your mind, Jenk? Here we been workin for years ta git these
Indyins outa here, and you tryin ta make um stay . . ."

The Superintendent was a tall, fat, soft man with a loose smile. He said ingratiatingly, "Mr. Jenkins realizes, as I'm sure you do too, Mr. Waldo, that the policy of the United States government is, and always has been—except for the unfortunate period when John Collier was in charge of the Bureau of Indian Affairs—man may have *meant* well, but Lord! hopeless sentimentalist—well, our policy has always been: Prepare the Indian to join the general community. Get him off the reservation. Turn the tribal lands over to the *Individual*. And it's been done with other tribes, and now, finally, it's being done with this one." He beamed.

Newt gritted his teeth. Then he said, "And the result was always the same—as soon as the tribal lands were given to the individual red man they damn quick passed into the hand of the individual white man. That's what happened with other tribes, and now, finally, it's being done with this one. Don't you *know*, Mr. Scott, that we can't adapt ourselves to the system of individual land-ownership? That we just aren't strong enough by ourselves to hold onto real estate? That—"

"Root, hog, er die," said Mr. Waldo.

"Are men *hogs*?" Newt cried.

Waldo said, at large, "*Told* ya he w's a trouble-maker." Then, bringing his long, rough, red face next to Newt's, he said, "Listen, Indyin, you and all y'r stinkin relatives are through. If Jenkins is damnfool enough ta hire ya, that's his look-out. But if he don't, you better stay far, far away, because nobody likes ya, nobody wants ya, and now that the Guvermint in Worshennon is finely come ta their sentces, nobody is goin ta protec ya—you and y'r mangy cows and y'r smutty-nosed sheep and y'r blankets—"

Newt's face showed his feelings, but before he could voice them, Billy Cottonwood broke in. "Mr. Scott," he said, "we sent a telegram to Washington, asking to halt the break-up of the Reservation."

Scott smiled his sucaryl smile. "Well, that's your privilege as a citizen."

Cottonwood spoke on. He mentioned the provisions of the bill passed by Congress, authorizing the Commissioner of Indian Affairs to liquidate, at his discretion, all reservations including less than one hundred residents, and to divide the land among them.

"Mr. Scott, when the Treaty of Juniper Butte was made between the United States and the Tickisalls," Cottonwood said, "there were thousands of us. That treaty was to be kept 'as long as the sun shall rise or the grasses grow.' The Government pledged itself to send us doctors—it didn't, and we died like flies. It pledged to send us seed and cattle; it sent us no seed and we had to eat the few hundred head of stock-yard cast-offs they did send us, to keep from starving. The Government was to keep our land safe for us forever, in a sacred trust—and in every generation they've taken away more and more. Mr. Scott—Mr. Jenkins, Mr. Waldo, and all you other gentlemen—you knew, didn't you, when you were kind enough to loan us money—or rather, to give us credit at the stores, when this drought started—you knew that this bill was up before Congress, didn't you?"

No one answered him. "You knew that it would pass, and that turning our lands over to us wouldn't mean a darned thing, didn't you? That we already owed so much money that our creditors would take all our land? Mr. Scott, how can the Government let this happen to us? It made a treaty with us to keep our lands safe for us 'as long as the sun rises or the grasses grow.' Has the sun stopped rising? Has the grass stopped growing? We believed in you—we kept our part of the treaty. Mr. Scott, won't you wire Washington—won't you other gentlemen do the same? To stop this thing that's being done to us? It's almost a hundred years now since we made treaty, and we've always hoped. Now we've only got till midnight to hope. Unless—?"

But the Superintendent said, No, he couldn't do that. And Jenkins shook his head, and said, sorry; it was really all for the best. Waldo shrugged, produced a packet of legal papers. "I've been deppatized to serve all these," he said. "Soons the land's all passed over ta individj'l ownership—which is 12 P.M. tonight. But if you give me y'r word (whatever that's worth) not ta make no trouble, why, guess it c'n wait till morning. Yo go back ta y'r shacks and I'll be round, come morning. We'll sleep over with Scott f'r tonight."

Sam Quarterhorse said, "We won't make any trouble, no. Not much use in that. But we'll wait right here. It's still possible we'll hear from Washington before midnight."

The Superintendent's house was quite comfortable. Logs (cut by Indian labor from the last of the Reservation's trees) blazed in the big fireplace (built by Indian labor). A wealth of rugs (woven by Indians in the Agency school) decorated walls and floor. The card-game had been on for some time when they heard the first woman start to wail. Waldo looked up nervously. Jenkins glanced at the clock. "Twelve midnight," he said. "Well, that's it. All over but the details. Took almost a hundred years, but it'll be worth it."

Another woman took up the keening. It swelled to a chorus of heartbreak, then died away. Waldo picked up his cards, then put them down again. An old man's voice had begun a chant. Someone took it up—then another. Drums joined it, and rattles. Scott said, "That was old Fox-head who started that just now. They're singing the death-song. They'll go on till morning."

Waldo swore. Then he laughed. "Let'm," he said. "It's their last morning."

Jenkins woke up first. Waldo stirred to wakefulness as he heard the other dressing. "What time is it?" he asked.

"Don't know," Jenkins said. "But it feels to me like gettin-up time. . . . You hear them go just a while back? No? Don't know how you could miss it. Singing got real loud—seemed like a whole lot of new voices joined in. Then they all got up and moved off. Wonder where they went . . . I'm going to have a look around outside." He switched on his flash-light and left the house. In another minute Waldo joined him, knocking on Scott's door as he passed.

The ashes of the fire still smoldered, making a dull red glow. It was very cold. Jenkins said, "Look here, Waldo—look." Waldo followed the flash-light's beam, said he didn't see anything. "It's the grass . . . it was green last night. It's all dead and brown now. Look at it . . ."

Waldo shivered. "Makes no difference. We'll get it green again. The land's ours now."

Scott joined them, his overcoat hugging his ears. "Why is it so cold?" he asked. "What's happened to the clock? Who was tinkering with the clock? It's past eight by the clock—it ought to be light by now. Where did all the Tickisalls go to? What's happening? There's something in the air—I don't like the feel of it. I'm sorry I ever agreed to work with you, no matter what you paid me—"

Waldo said, roughly, nervously, "Shut up. Some damned Indyin sneaked in and must of fiddled with the clock. Hell with um. Govermint's on *our* side now. Soons it's daylight we'll clear um all out of here f'r good."

Shivering in the bitter cold, uneasy for reasons they only dimly perceived, the three white men huddled together alone in the dark by the dying fire, and waited for the sun to rise.

And waited . . . and waited . . . and waited. . . .

Or All the Seas with Oysters

INTRODUCTION BY GUY DAVENPORT

This story has for thirty years had a double life. As a text it has been extensively anthologized and admired as one of Avram's best and most beguiling. It has also entered urban folklore, told as an anecdote by people who have never read it or heard of Avram Davidson. Newspaper columnists like to recount its crazily plausible concept that safety pins are the pupae and coat hangers the larvae of bicycles. In some plagiarisms that turn up regularly in Creative Writing classes, paper clips (more familiar to young unmarried writers) become the pupal stage. A colleague once told me he had a genius among his students, giving a garbled version of this story as evidence. The student, it turned out, had not read Avram but admitted that he had taken the idea from the academic air. Avram himself did a brisk business in setting the record straight with letters to newspapers and magazines.

The story had its first inception when Avram once noticed two bicycles, male and female, seemingly abandoned by a path in a woody park, and heard, from behind nearby bushes, the bikes' owners involved in mutual esteem. But he knew his Samuel Butler, whose Erewhon *has in its chapters called "The Book of the Machines" the theory that the evolution of things occurs at a faster rate than that of organisms. Hence Avram's title, from the Sherlock Holmes story "The Adventure of the Dying Detective," in which Holmes, feigning dementia, raves that any unchecked species is programmed by natural law to fill all available biological space. "I cannot think why the whole bed of the ocean is not one solid mass of oysters, so prolific the creatures seem."*

Avram's bike-shop owners Oscar the sensualist and Ferd the intellectual are an urban Don Giovanni and Samuel Butler. Their conjunction and the tension between them might have turned up in an H. G. Wells fantasy, and he might have tapped the demonic undertones as well as Avram has, but, though he is of all writers (except, perhaps, Kipling) the most likely to insert the marvellous into the everyday, he could not have managed Avram's deft transformation of an American ordinariness into so sinister a fable of man and his losing battle with the machine.

OR ALL THE SEAS WITH OYSTERS

WHEN THE MAN CAME in to the F & O Bike Shop, Oscar greeted him with a hearty "Hi, there!" Then, as he looked closer at the middle-aged visitor with the eyeglasses and business suit, his forehead creased and he began to snap his thick fingers.

"Oh, say, I know you," he muttered. "Mr.—um—name's on the tip of my tongue, doggone it . . ." Oscar was a barrel-chested fellow. He had orange hair.

"Why, sure you do," the man said. There was a Lion's emblem in his lapel. "Remember, you sold me a girl's bicycle with gears, for my daughter? We got to talking about that red French racing bike your partner was working on—"

Oscar slapped his big hand down on the cash register. He raised his head and rolled his eyes up. "Mr. Whatney!" Mr. Whatney beamed. "Oh, *sure*. Gee, how could I forget? And we went across the street afterward and had a couple a beers. Well, how you *been*, Mr. Whatney? I guess the bike—it was an English model, wasn't it? Yeah. It must of given satisfaction or you would of been back, huh?"

Mr. Whatney said the bicycle was fine, just fine. Then he said, "I understand there's been a change, though. You're all by yourself now. Your partner . . ."

Oscar looked down, pushed his lower lip out, nodded. "You heard, huh? Ee-up. I'm all by myself now. Over three months now."

The partnership had come to an end three months ago, but it had been faltering long before them. Ferd liked books, long-playing records and high-level conversation, Oscar liked beer, bowling and women. Any women. Any time.

The shop was located near the park; it did a big trade in renting bicycles to picnickers. If a woman was barely old enough to be *called* a woman, and not quite old enough to be called an *old* woman, or if she was anywhere in between, and if she was alone, Oscar would ask, "How does that machine feel to you? All right?"

"Why . . . I guess so."

Taking another bicycle, Oscar would say, "Well, I'll just ride along a little bit with you, to make sure. Be right back, Ferd." Ferd always nodded gloomily. He knew that Oscar would not be right back. Later, Oscar would say, "Hope you made out in the shop as good as I did in the park."

"Leaving me all alone here all that time," Ferd grumbled.

And Oscar usually flared up. "Okay, then, next time *you* go and leave *me* stay here. See if I begrudge you a little fun." But he knew, of course, that Ferd—tall, thin, pop-eyed Ferd—would never go. "Do you good," Oscar said, slapping his sternum. "Put hair on your chest."

Ferd muttered that he had all the hair on his chest that he needed. He would glance down covertly at his lower arms; they were thick with long black hair, though his upper arms were slick and white. It was already like that when he was in high school, and some of the others would laugh at him—call him "Ferdie the Birdie." They knew it bothered him, but they did it anyway. How was it possible—he wondered then; he still did now—for people deliberately to hurt someone else who hadn't hurt them? How was it possible?

He worried over other things. All the time.

"The Communists—" He shook his head over the newspaper. Oscar offered an advice about the Communists in two short words. Or it might be capital punishment. "Oh, what a terrible thing if an innocent man was to be executed," Fred moaned. Oscar said that was the guy's tough luck.

"Hand me that tire-iron," Oscar said.

And Ferd worried even about other people's minor concerns. Like the time the couple came in with the tandem and the baby-basket on it. Free air was all they took; then the woman decided to change the diaper and one of the safety pins broke.

"Why are there never any safety pins?" the woman fretted, rummaging here and rummaging there. "There are *never* any safety pins."

Ferd made sympathetic noises, went to see if he had any; but, though he was sure there'd been some in the office, he couldn't find them. So they drove off with one side of the diaper tied in a clumsy knot.

At lunch, Ferd said it was too bad about the safety pins. Oscar dug his teeth into a sandwich, tugged, tore, chewed, swallowed. Ferd liked to experiment with sandwich spreads—the one he liked most was cream-cheese, olives, anchovy and avocado, mashed up with a little mayonnaise—but Oscar always had the same pink luncheon-meat.

"It must be difficult with a baby." Ferd nibbled. "Not just traveling, but raising it."

Oscar said, "Jeez, there's drugstores in every block, and if you can't read, you can at least reckernize them."

"Drugstores? Oh, to buy safety pins, you mean."

"Yeah. Safety pins."

"But . . . you know . . . it's true . . . there's never any safety pins when you look."

Oscar uncapped his beer, rinsed the first mouthful around. "Aha! Always plenny of clothes hangers, though. Throw 'em out every month, next month same closet's full of 'm again. Now whatcha wanna do in your spare time, you invent a device which it'll make safety pins outa clothes hangers."

Ferd nodded abstractedly. "But in my spare time I'm working on the French racer . . ." It was a beautiful machine, light, low-slung, swift, red and shining. You felt like a bird when you rode it. But, good as it was, Ferd knew he could make it better. He showed it to everybody who came in the place until his interest slackened.

Nature was his latest hobby, or, rather, reading about Nature. Some kids had wandered by from the park one day with tin cans in which they had put salamanders and toads, and they proudly showed them to Ferd. After that, the work on the red racer slowed down and he spent his spare time on natural history books.

"Mimicry!" he cried to Oscar. "A wonderful thing!"

Oscar looked up interestedly from the bowling scores in the paper. "I seen Edie Adams on TV the other night, doing her imitation of Marilyn Monroe. Boy, oh, boy."

Ferd was irritated, shook his head. "Not that kind of mimicry. I mean how insects and arachnids will mimic the shapes of leaves and twigs and so on, to escape being eaten by birds or other insects and arachnids."

A scowl of disbelief passed over Oscar's heavy face. "You mean they change their *shapes*? What you giving me?"

"Oh, it's true. Sometimes the mimicry is for aggressive purposes, though— like a South African turtle that looks like a rock and so the fish swim up to it and then it catches them: Or that spider in Sumatra. When it lies on its back, it looks like a bird dropping. Catches butterflies that way."

Oscar laughed, a disgusted and incredulous noise. It died away as he turned back to the bowling scores. One hand groped at his pocket, came away, scratched absently at the orange thicket under the shirt, then went patting his hip pocket.

"Where's that pencil?" he muttered, got up, stomped into the office, pulled open drawers. His loud cry of "Hey!" brought Ferd into the tiny room.

"What's the matter?" Ferd asked.

Oscar pointed to a drawer. "Remember that time you claimed there were no safety pins here? Look—whole gahdamn drawer is full of 'em."

Ferd stared, scratched his head, said feebly that he was certain he'd looked there before . . .

A contralto voice from outside asked, "Anybody here?"

Oscar at once forgot the desk and its contents, called, "Be right with you," and was gone. Ferd followed him slowly.

There was a young woman in the shop, a rather massively built young woman, with muscular calves and a deep chest. She was pointing out the seat of her bicycle to Oscar, who was saying "Uh-huh" and looking more at her than at anything else. "It's just a little too far forward ("Uh-huh"), as you can see. A wrench is all I need ("Uh-huh"). It was silly of me to forget my tools."

Oscar repeated, "Uh-huh" automatically, then snapped to. "Fix it in a jiffy," he said, and—despite her insistence that she could do it herself—he did fix it. Though not quite in a jiffy. He refused money. He prolonged the conversation as long as he could.

"Well, thank *you*," the young woman said. "And now I've got to go."

"That machine feel all right to you now?"

"Perfectly. Thanks—"

"Tell you what, I'll just ride along with you a little bit, just—"

Pear-shaped notes of laughter lifted the young woman's bosom. "Oh, you couldn't keep up with me! My machine is a *racer!*"

The moment he saw Oscar's eye flit to the corner, Ferd knew what he had in mind. He stepped forward. His cry of "No" was drowned out by his partner's loud, "Well, I guess this racer here can keep up with yours!"

The young woman giggled richly, said, well, they would see about that, and was off. Oscar, ignoring Ferd's outstretched hand, jumped on the French bike and was gone. Ferd stood in the doorway, watching the two figures, hunched over their handlebars, vanish down the road into the park. He went slowly back inside.

It was almost evening before Oscar returned, sweaty but smiling. Smiling broadly. "Hey, what a babe!" he cried. He wagged his head, he whistle, he made gestures, nosies like escaping steam. "Boy, oh, boy, what an afternoon!"

"Give me the bike," Ferd demanded.

Oscar said, yeah, sure; turned it over to him and went to wash. Ferd looked at the machine. The red enamel was covered with dust; there was mud spattered and dirt and bits of dried grass. It seemed soiled—degraded. He had felt like a swift bird when he rode it . . .

Oscar came out wet and beaming. He gave a cry of dismay, ran over.

"Stand away," said Ferd, gesturing with the knife. He slashed the tires, the seat and seat cover, again and again.

"You crazy?" Oscar yelled. "You outa your mind? Ferd, no, don't, Ferd—"

Ferd cut the spokes, bent them, twisted them. He took the heaviest hammer and pounded the frame into shapelessness, and then he kept on pounding till his breath was gasping.

"You're not only crazy," Oscar said bitterly, "you're rotten jealous. You can go to hell." He stomped away.

Ferd, feeling sick and stiff, locked up, went slowly home. He had no taste for reading, turned out the light and fell into bed, where he lay awake for hours, listening to the rustling noises of the night and thinking hot, twisted thoughts.

They didn't speak to each other for days after that, except for the necessities of the work. The wreckage of the French racer lay behind the shop. For about two weeks, neither wanted to go out back where he'd have to see it.

One morning Ferd arrived to be greeted by his partner, who began to shake his head in astonishment even before he started speaking. "How did you *do* it, how did you *do* it, Ferd? Jeez, what a beautiful job—I gotta hand it to you—no more hard feelings, huh, Ferd?"

Ferd took his hand. "Sure, sure. But what are you talking about?"

Oscar led him out back. There was the red racer, all in one piece, not a mark or scratch on it, its enamel bright as ever. Ferd gaped. He squatted down and examined it. It *was* his machine. Every change, every improvement he had made, was there.

He straightened up slowly. "Regeneration . . ."

"Huh? What say?" Oscar asked. Then, "Hey, kiddo, you're all white. Whad you do, stay up all night and didn't get no sleep? Come on in and siddown. But I still don't see how you done it."

Inside, Ferd sat down. He wet his lips. He said, "Oscar—listen—"

"Yeah?"

"Oscar. You know what regeneration is? No? Listen. Some kinds of lizards, you grab them by the tail, the tail breaks off and they grow a new one. If a lobster loses a claw, it regenerates another one. Some kinds of worms— and hydras and starfish—you cut them into pieces, each piece will grow back the missing parts. Salamanders can regenerate lost hands, and frogs can grow legs back."

"No kidding, Ferd. But, uh, I mean: Nature. Very interesting. But to get back to the bike now—how'd you manage to fix it so good?"

"I never touched it. It regenerated. Like a newt. Or a lobster."

Oscar considered this. He lowered his head, looked up at Ferd from under his eyebrows. "Well, now, Ferd . . . Look . . . How come all broke bikes don't do that?"

"This isn't an ordinary bike. I mean it isn't a real bike." Catching Oscar's look, he shouted, "Well, it's *true!*"

The shout changed Oscar's attitude from bafflement to incredulity. He got up. "So for the sake of argument, let's say all that stuff about the bugs and the eels or whatever the hell you were talking about is true. But they're alive. A bike ain't." He looked down triumphantly.

Ferd shook his leg from side to side, looked at it. "A crystal isn't, either, but a broken crystal can regenerate itself if the conditions are right. Oscar, go see if the safety pins are still in the desk. Please, Oscar?"

He listened as Oscar, muttering, pulled the desk drawers out, rummaged in them, slammed them shut, tramped back.

"Naa," he said. "All gone. Like that lady said that time, and you said, there never are any safety pins when you want 'em. They disap—Ferd? What're—"

Ferd jerked open the closet door, jumped back as a shoal of clothes hangers clattered out.

"And like *you* say," Ferd said with a twist of his mouth, "on the other hand, there are always plenty of clothes hangers. There weren't any here before."

Oscar shrugged. "I don't see what you're getting at. But anybody could of got in here and took the pins and left the hangers. *I* could of—but I didn't. Or *you* could of. Maybe—" He narrowed his eyes. "Maybe you walked in your sleep and done it. You better see a doctor. Jeez, you look rotten."

Ferd went back and sat down, put his head in his hands. "I feel rotten. I'm scared, Oscar. Scared of what?" He breathed noisily. "I'll tell you. Like I explained before, about how things that live in the wild places, they mimic other things there. Twigs, leaves . . . toads that look like rocks. Well, suppose there are ... things ... that live in people places. Cities. Houses. These things could imitate—well, other kinds of things you find in people places—"

"*People* places, for crise sake!"

"Maybe they're a different kind of life-form. Maybe they get their nourishment out of the elements in the air. You know what safety pins *are*—these other kinds of them? Oscar, the safety pins are the pupa-forms and then they, like, *hatch*. Into the larval-forms. Which look just like coat hangers. They feel like them, even, but they're not. Oscar, they're not, not really, not really, not ..."

He began to cry into his hands. Oscar looked at him. He shook his head.

After a minute, Ferd controlled himself somewhat. He snuffled. "All these bicycles the cops find, and they hold them waiting for owners to show up, and then we buy them at the sale because no owners show up because there aren't any, and the same with the ones the kids are always trying to sell us, and they say they just found them, and they really did because they were never made in a factory. They grew. They grow. You smash them and throw them away, they regenerate."

Oscar turned to someone who wasn't there and waggled his head. "Hoo, boy," he said. Then, to Ferd: "You mean one day there's a safety pin and the next day instead there's a coat hanger?"

Ferd said, "One day there's a cocoon; the next day there's a moth. One day there's an egg; the next day there's a chicken. But with ... these it doesn't happen in the open daytime where you can see it. But at night, Oscar—at night you can *hear* it happening. All the little noises in the night-time, Oscar—"

Oscar said, "Then how come we ain't up to our belly-button in bikes? If I had a bike for every coat hanger—"

But Ferd had considered that, too. If every codfish egg, he explained, or every oyster spawn grew to maturity, a man could walk across the ocean on the backs of all the codfish or oysters there'd be. So many died, so many were eaten by predatory creatures, that Nature had to produce a maximum in order to allow a minimum to arrive at maturity. And Oscar's question was: then who, uh, eats the, uh, coat hangers?

Ferd's eyes focused through wall, buildings, park, more buildings, to the horizon. "You got to get the picture. I'm not talking about real pins or hangers. I got a name for the others—'false friends,' I call them. In high school French, we had to watch out for French words that looked like English words, but really were different. '*Faux amis*,' they call them. False friends. Pseudo-pins. Pseudo-hangers ... Who eats them? I don't know for sure. Pseudo-vacuum cleaners, maybe?"

His partner, with a loud groan, slapped his hands against his thighs. He said, "Ferd, Ferd, for crise sake. You know what's the trouble with you? You talk about oysters, but you forgot what they're good for. You forgot there's two kinds of people in the world. Close up them books, them bug books and French books. Get out, mingle, meet people. Soak up some brew. You know what? The next time Norma—that's this broad's name with the racing bike— the next time she comes here, *you* take the red racer and *you* go out in the woods with her. I won't mind. And I don't think she will, either. Not *too* much."

But Ferd said no. "I never want to touch the red racer again. I'm afraid of it."

At this, Oscar pulled him to his feet, dragged him protestingly out to the back and forced him to get on the French machine. "Only way to conquer your fear of it!"

Ferd started off, white-faced, wobbling. And in a moment was on the ground, rolling and thrashing, screaming.

Oscar pulled him away from the machine.

"It threw me!" Ferd yelled. "It tried to kill me! Look—blood!"

His partner said it was a bump that threw him—it was his own fear. The blood? A broken spoke. Grazed his cheek. And he insisted Ferd get on the bicycle again, to conquer his fear.

But Ferd had grown hysterical. He shouted that no man was safe—that mankind had to be warned. It took Oscar a long time to pacify him and to get him to go home and into bed.

He didn't tell all this to Mr. Whatney, of course. He merely said that his partner had gotten fed up with the bicycle business.

"It don't pay to worry and try to change the world," he pointed out. "I always say take things the way they are. If you can't lick 'em, join 'em."

Mr. Whatney said that was his philosophy, exactly. He asked how things were, since.

"Well . . . not *too* bad. I'm engaged, you know. Name's Norma. Crazy about bicycles. Everything considered, things aren't bad at all. More work, yes, but I can do things all my own way, so. . . ."

Mr. Whatney nodded. He glanced around the shop. "I see they're still making drop-frame bikes," he said, "though, with so many women wearing slacks, I wonder they bother."

Oscar said, "Well, I dunno. I kinda like it that way. Ever stop to think that bicycles are like people? I mean, of all the machines in the world, only bikes come male and female."

Mr. Whatney gave a little giggle, said that was *right,* he had never thought of it like that before. Then Oscar asked if Mr. Whatney had anything in particular in mind—not that he wasn't always welcome.

"Well, I wanted to look over what you've got. My boy's birthday is coming up—"

Oscar nodded sagely. "Now here's a job," he said, "which you can't get it in any other place but here. Specialty of the house. Combines the best features of the French racer and the American standard, but it's made right here, and it comes in three models—Junior, Intermediate and Regular. Beautiful, ain't it?"

Mr. Whatney observed that, say, that might be just the ticket. "By the way," he asked, "what's become of the French racer, the red one, used to be here?"

Oscar's face twitched. Then it grew bland and innocent and he leaned over and nudged his customer. "Oh, *that* one. Old Frenchy? Why, I put *him* out to stud!"

And they laughed and they laughed, and after they told a few more stories they concluded the sale, and they had a few beers and they laughed some more. And then they said what a shame it was about Ferd, poor old Ferd, who had been found in his own closet with an unraveled coat hanger coiled tightly around his neck.

Take Wooden Indians

INTRODUCTION BY JOHN M. FORD

Attempting to write even a thousand words about a few thousand words is a spooky prospect. To go on at length about Davidson's concision rapidly starts to resemble a Bob & Ray routine:

BOB: *So these are the Niagara Falls?*
RAY: *Or, as some call them, the Falls of Niagara.*
BOB: *And this is all water passing over them?*
RAY: *Primarily water, yes, though the occasional barrel enters the flow.*

At some point in the perusal of this collection, the alert reader must twig to Davidson's apparently inexhaustible knowledge, worn as lightly as Astaire's black patent pumps. Volumes could be written about the twists and burrowings of Davidson's historical adventuring, and when they are, nobody will believe them.

But the knowledge isn't the important point, though it is the fletching on the clothyard shaft leading up to the point, which is what gets done with that knowledge. With the inevitability of glaciers, one comes to understand that the demise of the wooden advertising figure led to the billboard and the bumper sticker and the radio jingle, and thence to the television commercial, which (if that were not disaster enough) gave us the little triphammers inside the aching head, created by the same man who advertised Eisenhower into the White House, bringing us the McCarthy hearings, the Interstate Highway System, and, uh, what's his name, Ike's vice president. Against that, the Burma-Shave signs were just straws in a Great Plains twister.

Perhaps the most direct way to "say something" about Davidson's achievement is to look at what he didn't do—what he didn't, but others did.

Look for a moment at brother-in-law Walt. Forgive him, for that long at least, for being a little too much the postwar hustler-up-the-block, a man with dreams just as wide as the fenders of a used Studebaker, a Bilko demobilized before he could make sergeant. Recognize that there but for the grace of the woodcarver's chisel goes the story's hero.

Not could have been, was, in the consanguinity of the fiction magazines: you would not have had to turn many pages before finding Walters who, having earned the disfavor of their fellows by toiling alone on the garage time machine, take the blueprints of the two-stroke engine or the Zippo lighter or the Real Estate Investment Trust into the dark past, and retire in the fashion of an Eastern Potentate, or at least an August Belmont.

To be sure, these Walts Protagonistes would never walk away from their sisters (however often those sisters told them to stop playing with that war-surplus junk out back and take the job at Pump 'n' Wash).

Which points us down another turn in the crosstime subway, a tale-of-the-tale as might equally well have suited an editor's needs: the version in which the Wooden Indian Society, far from being a crowd of off-center joiners bent on fixing history's error with a Pure Vision and a case of forty-percent dynamite (not that we know anyone like that), but reasonable men driven forward by the good of humanity—as they see themselves in the story-that-is.

You can probably plot this one yourself. Alfred Nobel's invention certainly figures, as this would come from the school of No Climax Without a Corresponding Explosion. There would be a thrilling chase through gaslit Brooklyn, pursued by such and sundry, with Mr. Rat Nolan involved (for indeed there is always he) ostensibly for the cause of Fenian liberation but with his true allegiance in doubt till the end. All fuses would burn to Demuth's, and the vanishment of Dusty Benedict in the apocalyptic kaboom that stands in so eloquently for plot resolution. A wooden fly-figure of Dusty, chisel in its lowered hand, is erected on the site. If the author is in an ironical mood, Dusty watches the unveiling from a nearby alcove, and goes off whistling. Possibly a lady, not necessarily named Aura Lee, accompanies him, twirling a parasol. Did I forget to mention that the class system has exploded as well, without any naughty Bolshevism being required? Well, one does forget.

A good idea, that. Forget the other versions, for those writers are the waves of the sea. While we have only so much Davidson and no more, like the coast of Monterey, it is there in its length and breadth, let the waves do as they will.

TAKE WOODEN INDIANS

Down from the streets (morning air already gray and bitter with motor exhaust and industrial fumes), into the jampacked subway he passed. His clothes, though mildly incongruous in that unhappy throng, brought him no special measure of attention. Weary, wary, cynical, grim, displeasured indifference lying on each countenance like an oily film, the folk stared not so much at him as over and through him.

He fought to keep his feet, struggled to maintain his balance. This, merely the antechamber to everyday existence, was difficult enough. Add to it the need to be constantly on the lookout for the Wooden Indian Society and he felt he had reason to be tense and jumpy. "Benedict, a leading modern free-form sculptor in wood—" Ha!

Twice he had been aware that they had tailed him as far as Times Square. Twice he had lost them. A third time—

The man in the faintly funny-looking clothes (his name was Don Benedict, but some called him "Dusty") paused for a minute under one of the red-lettered wooden signs, took a quick look at the paper in his hand (more, it almost seemed, to reassure himself that it was still there than to scan the contents), did an about-face and started back the way he had come. By and by he came to a stairway which he ascended for five steps, then turned around and went down. At the bottom—

At the bottom of it all was Elwell, and Elwell was dead: not from the cough which had been tearing him apart for years, but dead of a slippery little patch of ice no bigger than a man's hand. Elwell, dying, with blood in the corners of his mouth, holding Don's hand in a grip which the younger man could feel the heat going out of.

"But it belongs to the WIS," Don had protested.

And Elwell: "No, Don, no—it belongs to me. I formed it. I proved it."

"They'll never allow—"

With a desperate, slow intensity, shaking his head, Elwell had explained. Reluctantly, Don agreed. It seemed to him that he was agreeing to no more than the first risk. But then, with Elwell dead, and the WIS turning against them both—first with coldness, then with clamor, then with a silent tenacity more disturbing than either—Don Benedict came to see that it was not only the beginning which was his, but that it was all his. Forevermore.

At the bottom of the stairs, he saw the man out of the corner of his eye, eye intent upon feet, feet pacing out the pattern. He stopped for a moment, intending only to turn. And stayed stopped. The man (it was Anders) took hold of his arm as if to urge him on.

"I'm coming with you, Benedict." Eyes burning, voice iron-hard.

"I'm going alone."

"You've betrayed the trust, used what belongs to all of us, used it for yourself alone. The WIS—"

As always, so now, the Wooden Indian Society undoing themselves: Anders, trembling with fury, unawarely released his grip. Don placed the cushion of his palm under Anders' chin, thrust forward and upward with all his strength. And at once, swift—but not forgetting himself, not breaking into a run—he finished what he had to do. Anders staggered back, arms flailing, feet failing at purchase; then Don, turning his head at the last, saw him fall, the electric lights glaring on the white-tiled walls.

His foot jarred, as always, missing the familiar flooring by an inch. He adjusted his gait to the flagstone pave of the alley. It stretched before him and behind him for twenty feet in either direction. There was no one in sight.

About halfway along, there was a deep recess, a bricked-up door, and here Don hid until he was quite sure that Anders was not coming through. There was never any certainty that the WIS had not pieced it together, spying—somehow—pieced it together, bit by bit. There was always that tension, even here—though less, much less. After all, if they did get through, it would no longer be him that they were primarily after. It would be Demuth's. And Demuth's could look out for themselves.

Waiting, ears alert, he recalled the last meeting of the WIS he had dared attend. Mac Donald, eyes blazing deep in their sockets, had broken into Derwentwater's measured phrases, thrust a shaking finger into Don's face.

"Do you call yourself a Preservationist? Yes or no? Stand up and be counted!"

Staunchly, he had faced him, had answered. "I consider myself a philosophical Preservationist. I do not believe in violent—"

Face convulsed, fists clenched in the air, *"Traitor! Traitor!"* Mac Donald had screamed.

Not yielding, Don started to speak, got no further than Elwell's name, when Mac Donald—and Anders, Gumpert, De Giovanetti, almost all of them, in fact—had drowned him out with their outcry, their threats. *How much had Demuth's paid him? How much had he sold out for?*

Demuth's! Don mouthed the name scornfully. As if he would touch their tainted money. He had learned, the hard way, that Elwell was right all along, that the WIS were fanatics who would shrink from nothing. Well, he wasn't doing any shrinking, either.

Don Benedict came out of the niche—Anders wasn't going to get through this time, that was clear—and walked on down the alley. In less than a minute, he came out into a courtyard where heaps of chips and sawdust lay on one side and heaps of hay on the other. A man in dung-smeared boots came out of the building to the left with a bucket of milk in his hand. He paused, squinted, tugged his tobacco-stained beard and put down the bucket.

"Hey, Dusty! Glad to see you," he greeted the newcomer. "You just get into town?"

"Ee-yup," said Don/Dusty. "How you, Swan?"

Swan said he was fine, and inquired about things up in Sairacuse.

"Capital," said Dusty. "Hay's bringing a fine price—"

Swan groaned, spat into the sawdust. "Good for dem, maybe. Not for me. I tink you been at de bottle, hey, Dusty? You look yumpy, like always, ven you yust come in."

"Bottle? I get little enough out of any bottle I buy. My damned brother-in-law" (it was true—he had forgotten about Walter; it would be nice if he never had to remember) "drinks my liquor, smokes my cigars, wears my shirts, and spends my money."

Swan groaned sympathetically, picked up the bucket. "Vy don't you kick him de hell out?"

Nice advice, would be a pleasure to take it. Of course, Mary wouldn't be able to stand it. Poor rabbity Mary.

"All I need is to get back to work. That'll fix me up." Don/Dusty waved, continued on his way across the yard and went into the doorway of the tall brick building to the right. Inside, it was cool and dark and smelled of wood and paint.

Dusty took a deep breath and began to smile.

He started up the stairs, ignoring the painted hand with outstretched finger and word *Office* on the first floor. By the time he reached the second floor, his smile was very broad. Softly, he began to sing "Aura Lee" and went in through the open door.

The big loft was dark; little light came in through the small and dirty windows, but at regular intervals a gas-jet flared. Dusty paused to greet his friends. Silently they stared down at him, peering from underneath the hands shading their eyes, stretching out their arms in wordless welcome, plumage blazing in a frenzy of colors.

"Hello, there, Tecumseh! How, Princess Redwing! Osceola, Pocahontas—"

A red-faced little man in a long striped apron trotted out into view, two tufts of snowy hair decorating his cheeks, a hat of folded newsprint on his head.

"Dusty, Dusty, I'm darned glad to see you!" he exclaimed.

"Hello, Charley Voles. How's everything at C. P. Hennaberry's?"

Charley shook his head. "Good *and* bad," he said. "Good *and* bad. Oscar snagged his hand on a nail moving some plunder at home and it festered up something terrible. We was feared it was going to mortify at first, but I guess he's on the mend at last. Can't work, though, no-o-o-o, can't work. And Hennery was too numerous with the drink, fell off the wagon again and I think he must still be in the Bridewell, unless'n maybe his sentence is up today. Meanwhile, the work is piling high. Thunderation, yes—fly-figures, rosebuds, pompeys, *two* Turks under orders—"

"*Two?*" Dusty paused with his arms half out of his coat sleeves, whistled.

Charley nodded proudly. "Gent in Chicago opening up a big emporium, two Turks *and* two Sir Walters. Only thing is—" his ruddy little face clouded— "gent is clamoring for delivery, says if he don't get 'em soon he'll order from Detroit. And you know what *that* means, Dusty: Let trade get away and it never comes back. Why, the poor Major is pulling his whiskers out worrying. 'Course, with you back in town—"

Dusty, tying his apron, pursed his lips. "Well, now, Charley—now you know, I never did fancy my work much on the special figures. I want to help Major Hennaberry all I can, but—" He shook his head doubtfully and started to lay out his tools.

Charley Voles tut-tutted. "Oscar and Hennery was working on the Turks when they was took sick or drunk. *I* had the top three of a Sir Walter done, but I had to leave off to handle a couple of prior orders on sachems. Now if you'll take on the sachems, I can finish the specials. How's that strike you?"

Dusty said it struck him fine. He strode over to the hydraulic elevator shaft and gave two piercing whistles.

"Boy!" he shouted. "Boy! Benny?"

A treble from the office floor inquired if that was him, Mr. Dusty, and said it would be right up. A noise of gasping and stomping from below indicated that someone else would be right up, too.

"I want some breakfast, Benny," Dusty said, tossing him a coin. "Here's a quarter of a dollar. Get me the usual—eggs, pancakes, sausages, toast, coffee and crullers. Get some beer for Mr. Voles. And you can keep the change. *Hello,* Major Hennaberry!"

The elevator cage surged slowly into view. First came Major Hennaberry's bald spot, then his custard-colored eyes, magenta nose and cheeks, pepper-and-salt whiskers, and, gradually, the Major himself, breathing noisily. In his hand he held a booklet of some sort.

Slowly and sybillantly, the Major moved forward, shook Dusty's hand.

"Don't know what's come over the American mechanic nowadays," he said at last, asthmatically. "Can't seem to keep himself safe, sober, or in the city limits, and acts as if Hell has let out for noon. . . . Got some lovely white pine for you, my boy, fresh up from the spar yards. Don't waste a minute—soon's you get outside of your victuals, commence work. Draw on the cashier if you want anything in advance of wages: a dollar, two dollars, even a half-eagle.

"Never had so many orders nor so few men to execute them since starting in business," the Major wheezed on. "Even had Rat Nolan on picket duty for me, combing South Street and the Bowery—offered him three dollars apiece for any carvers he could find. Nothing, couldn't find a one. It's the catalog that's done the boom, my lad. The power of advertising. Here—read it whilst you eat; be pleased to have your opinion."

Hissing and panting, he made his way back to the elevator, jerked the rope twice, slowly sank from sight.

Dusty turned to the old artisan. "Charley," he said, slowly, as if he hadn't quite determined his words, "hear anything about Demuth's?"

Charley made a face. "What would you want to hear about that ugly, pushy outfit?"

Changing, somewhat, his point of inquiry, Dusty asked, "Well, now, have you ever thought about the significance of the wooden Indian in American history?"

The old man scratched the left fluff of whisker. "By crimus, that's a high-toned sentence," he said, rather dubiously. "Hmm. Well, all's I can tell you—history, hey?—the steam engine was the makings of the show-figure trade, tobacco shop or otherwise. Certainly. All of us old-timers got our start down on South Street, carving figureheads for sailing craft. That was about the time old Hennaberry got his major's commission in the Mercantile Zouaves—you know, guarding New York City from the Mexicans. Yes, sir. But when the steam come *in*, figureheads went *out*. Well, 'twasn't the end of the world."

And he described how he and his fellow-artists had put their talents at the disposal of the show-figure trade, up to then a rather haphazard commerce. "History, hey? Well, I have had the idea it's sort of odd that as the live Indian gets scarcer, the wooden ones gets numerouser. But how come you to ask, Dusty?"

Carefully choosing his words, Dusty asked Charley to imagine a time in the far-off future when wooden Indians—show figures of any sort—were no longer being carved.

Had, in fact, suffered for so long a universal neglect that they had become quite rare. That gradually interest in the sachems revived, that men began to collect them as if they had been ancient marble statues, began to study all that could be learned about them.

That some of these collectors, calling themselves the Wooden Indian Society, had been consumed with grief at the thought of the debacle which overtook the figures they had grown to love. Had claimed to see in the decline and death of this native art a dividing line in American history.

"It was like, Charley, it was like this was the end of the old times altogether," Don went on, "the end of the Good Old Days, the final defeat of native crafts and native integrity by the new, evil forces of industrialism. And they thought about this and it turned them bitter and they began to brood. Until finally they began to plan how they could undo what had been done. They believed that if they could travel from their time to—to our time, like traveling from here to, say, Brooklyn—"

How much of this could Charley grasp? Perhaps better not to have tried.

Don/Dusty spoke more rapidly. "That if they could reach this time period, they could preserve the wooden Indian from destruction. And then the great change for the worse would never occur. The old days and the old ways would remain unchanged, or at least change slowly."

"You mean they got this idea that if they could change what happened to the wooden Indians, they could maybe change the course of American history?"

Dusty nodded.

Charley laughed. "Well, they were really crazy—I mean they would be, if there was to be such people, wouldn't they? Because there ain't no way—"

Dusty blinked. Then his face cleared. "No, of course there isn't. It was just a moody dark thought. . . . Ah, here comes Ben with my breakfast."

Charley lifted his beer off the laden tray, gestured his thanks, drank, put down the glass with a loud "Hah" of satisfaction. Then a sudden thought creased his face. "Now leave me ask you this, Dusty. Just what could ever happen to destroy such a well-established and necessary business as the show-figure business? Hmm?"

Dusty said that these people from the Wooden Indian Society, in this sort of dark thought he'd had, had looked into matters real thoroughly. And they came to believe very deeply, very strongly, that the thing which killed the wooden Indian, and in so doing had changed American history so terribly for the worst, had been the invention and marketing of an Indian made of cast-iron or zinc. An Indian which would have no life, no soul, no heart, no grace— but which would never wear out or need to be replaced.

And so it would sell—sell well enough to destroy the carvers' craft—but would destroy the people's love for the newer show figures at the same time.

Charley looked shocked. "Why, that'd be a terrible thing, Dusty—a thing which it'd cut a man to the heart! Cast-iron! Zinc! But I tell you what—if there ever was to be an outfit which'd do a thing like that, there'd be only one outfit that would. Demuth's. That's who. Ain't I right?"

Dusty lowered his head. In a low, choked voice, he said, "You're right."

Dusty propped the catalog against a short piece of pine, read as he ate.

"I don't know what it is," he said to old Charley, "but I have such an appetite here. I never eat breakfast at all when I'm—" He stopped, put a piece of sausage in his mouth, intently began to read.

We would respectfully solicit from the Public generally an inspection of our Large and Varied Assortment of WOODEN SHOW FIGURES *which we are constantly manufacturing for all classes of business, such as* SE-GAR STORES, WINES & LIQUORS, SHIP CHANDLERS, INSTRUMENT MAKERS, DRUGGISTS, YANKEE NOTIONS, UMBRELLA, CLOTHING, CHINA TEA STORES, GUNSMITHS, BUTCHERS, &C, &C. *Our Figures are both carved and painted in a manner which cannot be excelled, are durable and designed and executed in a highly artistic manner; and are furnished at noncompetitive low prices. We are constantly receiving orders for statues and emblematic signs, and can furnish same of any required design with promptness.*

The sausage was fresh and savory; so was the coffee. Dusty chewed and swallowed with relish, slowly turned the pages of the catalog.

OUR NUMBER *23. Fly-figure, male 5 ft. high, bundle of 20 in out-stretched hand (r.), usual colors. A nice staple type Show Figure no*

*moderate-sized bus. need feel ashamed to display. At rival establish-
ments,* UP TO *$75. C. P. Hennaberry's Price: $50 even (with war-
bonnet, $55).*

Note: Absolutely impos. to cite trade-in values *via* mails, as this depends on
age, size, condition of fig., also state of market @ time.

OUR NUMBER 24. *Same as above, with musket instead of tomahawk.*

OUR NUMBER 36. *Turk, male 6 ft. high, for shops which sell the fragrant
Ottoman weed, polychrome Turk holding long leaf betw. both hands,
choice of any two colors on turban.* A. C. P. HENNABERRY SPECIAL:
$165. *(with beard & long pipe, $5 extra).*

They went upstairs after Dusty had finished his breakfast, pausing on the
third (or second-hand figures) floor, to greet Otto and Larry.

Young Larry was still considered a learner and was not yet allowed to go
beyond replacing arms, hands, noses, and other extra parts.

Otto, to be sure, was a master carver, but Otto had several strikes against
him. In his youth, in his native Tyrol, Otto had studied sacred iconography;
in his maturity, in America, Otto had studied drinking. As a result, when he
was mellow, unless he was carefully supervised, his Indians had a certain saintly
quality to them, which made purchasers feel somehow guilty. And when, on
the other hand, Otto was sobering up, a definite measure of apocalyptic horror
invariably appeared in his sachems which frightened buyers away.

As a result, Otto was kept at doing extras—bundles of cigars, boxes of
cigars, bundles of tobacco leaf, coils of tobacco leaf, twists of the same, knives,
tomahawks, all to be held in the figures' hands—and at equally safe tasks like
stripping off old paint, sanding, repainting, finishing.

He nodded sadly, eyes bloodshot, to Dusty and Charley, as he applied
ochre and vermillion to a war bonnet. "Ho, Chesus," he groaned softly.

Up in the woodloft, they made an inspection of the spars. "Now you
needn't pick the ones I started, of course," Charley said. "Take fresh ones, if
you like. 'Course, all's I did was I drawn the outlines and just kind of chiseled
'em in. And put the holes in on top for the bolts."

Dusty stood back and squinted. "Oh, I guess they'll be all right, Charley,"
he said. "Well, let's get 'em downstairs."

This done, Charley went back to work on the Sir Walter, carefully chiseling
Virginia Tobacco in bas-relief on the cloak.

Dusty took up his axe and blocked out approximate spaces for the head,
the body down to the waist, roughly indicated the division of the legs and feet.
Then he inserted the iron bolt into the five-inch hole prepared for it, and tilted
back the spar so that the projecting part of the bolt rested on a support. When
he had finished head and trunk, he would elevate the lower part of the figures
in the same way.

Finally, finished with blocking out, he picked up mallet and chisel.

"I now strike a blow for liberty," he said.

Smiling happily, he began to chip away. The song he sang was "Aura Lee."

Don/Dusty Benedict let himself into his studio quietly—but not quietly enough. The sharp sound of a chair grating on the floor told him that his brother-in-law was upstairs. In another second, Walter told him so himself in an accent more richly Southern, probably, than when he had come North as a young boy.

"We're upstairs, Don."

"Thank you for the information," Don muttered.

"We're *upstairs,* Don."

"Yes, Walter. All right. I'm coming."

Walter welcomed him with a snort. "Why the hell do you always wear those damn cotton-pickin' clothes when you go away? Not that it matters. I only wish *I* could just take up and go whenever the spirit moves me. Where was it you went this time?"

"Syracuse," Don mumbled.

"Syracuse. America's new vacation land." Walter laughed, not pleasantly. "Don, you really expect me to believe you? Syracuse! Why not just say to me, frankly, 'I've got a woman'? That's all. I wouldn't say another word." He poured himself several drams of Don's Scotch.

Not much you wouldn't, Don thought. Aloud, "How are you, Mary?" His sister said that she was just fine, sighed, broke off the sigh almost at once, at her husband's sour look.

Walter said, "Roger Towns was up. Another sale for you, another commission for me. Believe me, I earned it—gave him a big talk on how the Museum of Modern Art was after your latest. So he asked me to use my influence. He'll be back—he'll take it. This rate, the Modern Art *will* be after you before long."

Don privately thought this unlikely, though anything was possible in this world of no values. He wasn't a "modern, free-form" artist, or, for that matter, any kind of artist at all. He was a craftsman—in a world which had no need for craftsmen.

"But *only*—" another one of the many qualities which made Walter highly easy to get along without: Walter was a finger-jabber—"but *only* if you finish the damned thing. About time, isn't it? I mean vacations are fine, but the bills . . ."

Don said, "Well, my affairs are in good hands—namely, yours."

Walter reared back. "If that's meant as a dig—! Listen, I can get something else to do any time I want. In fact, I'm looking into something else *now* that's damned promising. Firm sells Canadian stocks. Went down to see them yesterday. 'You're just the kind of man we're interested in, Mr. Swift,' they told me. 'With your vast experience and your knowledge of human nature. . . .' "

Walt scanned his brother-in-law's face, defying him to show signs of the complete disbelief he must have known Don felt. Don had long since stopped pretending to respond to these lies. He only ignored them—only put up with Walt at all—for his sister's sake. It was for her and the kids only that he ever came back.

"I'd like a drink," Don said, when Walt paused.

Dinner was as dinner always was. Walt talked almost constantly, mostly about Walt. Don found his mind wandering again to the Wooden Indian Society. Derwentwater, ending every speech with *"Delendo est Demuth's!"* Gumpert and his eternal "Just one stick of dynamite, Don, just one!" De Giovanetti growling, "Give us the Equation and we'll do it ourselves!"

Fools! They'd have to learn every name of those who had the hideous metal Indian in mind, conduct a massacre in Canal Street. Impossible. Absurd.

No, Elwell had been right. Not knowing just how the Preservationist work was to be done, he had nonetheless toiled for years to perfect a means to do it. Only when his work was done did he learn the full measure of WIS intransigence. And, after learning, had turned to Don.

"Take up the torch," he pleaded. "Make each sachem such a labor of love that posterity cannot help but preserve it."

And Don had tried. The craft had been in him and struggling to get out all the time, and he'd never realized it!

Slowly the sound of Walter's voice grew more impossible to ignore.

". . . and you'll need a new car, too. I can't drive that heap much longer. It's two years *old*, damn it!"

"I'd like a drink," Don said.

By the time Edgar Feld arrived, unexpectedly, Don had had quite a few drinks.

"I took the liberty not only of calling unheralded, but of bringing a friend, Mr. White," the art dealer said. He was a well-kept little man. Mr. White was thin and mild.

"Any friend of Edgar's is someone to be wary of," Don said. "Getchu a drink?"

Walt said he was sure they'd like to see the studio. There was plenty of time for drinks.

"Time?" Don muttered. "Whaddayu know about time?"

"Just step this way," Walt said loudly, giving his brother-in-law a deadly look. "We think, we rather think," he said, taking the wraps off the huge piece, "of calling this the Gemini—"

Don said genially that they had to call it *something* and that Gemini (he supposed) sounded better than Diseased Kidney.

Mr. White laughed.

Edgar Feld echoed the laugh, though not very heartily. "Mr. Benedict has the most modest, most deprecatory attitude toward his work of any modern artist—working in wood or in any other medium."

Mr. White said that was very commendable. He asked Don if he'd like a cigar.

"I would, indeed!" the modest artist assented. "Between cigarette smoke, gasoline and diesel fumes, the air is getting unfit to breathe nowadays. . . . So Edgar is conning you into modern art, hey, Whitey?"

"Ho, ho!" Edgar Feld chuckled hollowly.

"Nothing better than a good cigar." Don puffed his contentment.

White said, with diffidence, that he was only just beginning to learn about modern art. "I used to collect Americana," he explained.

Edgar Feld declared that Mr. White had formerly had a collection of wooden Indians. His tone indicated that, while this was not to be taken seriously, open mockery was uncalled for.

Don set down the glass he had brought along with him. No, White was hardly WIS material. He was safe. "Did you really? Any of Tom Millards, by any chance? Tom carved some of the sweetest fly-figures ever made."

Mr. White's face lit up. "Are you a wooden Indian buff, too?" he cried. "Why, yes, as a matter of fact, I had two of Millard's fly-figures, and one of his pompeys—"

Walt guffawed. "What are fly-figures and pompeys?"

"A fly-figure is a sachem with an outstretched arm," Don said. "A pompey is a black boy."

"A rosebud," Mr. White happily took up the theme, "is a squaw figure. A scout is one who's shading his eyes with one hand. Tom Millard, oh, yes! And I had some by John Cromwell, Nick Collins, Thomas V. Brooks, and Tom White—my namesake. Listen! Maybe you can tell me. Was Leopold Schwager a manufacturer or an artist?"

Don Benedict laughed scornfully. "Leopold Schwager was a junk-dealer! Bought old figures for five, ten dollars, puttied and painted 'em, sold 'em for twenty-five. Cobb!" he exclaimed suddenly. "You have any Cobbs, Mr. White?"

"Cobb of Canal Street? No, I always wanted one, but—"

Edgar Feld looked at Walter Swift, cleared his throat. "Now, Don—"

"Cobb of Canal Street," Don said loudly, "never used a mallet. No, sir. Drove the chisel with the palm of his hand. And then there was Charley Voles—"

Feld raised his voice above Don's. "Yes, we must talk about his fascinating though obsolete art sometime. Don't you want to step a little closer to the Gemini, Mr. White?"

"Yes, White, damn it, buy the damned Gemini so they'll quit bothering us and we can get back to *real* art," said Don.

And forget about Walter, Demuth's and the WIS, he said to himself.

Next morning, he tried to remember what had happened after that. White *had* taken the shapeless mass of wood Walt called Gemini. (What would he tell Roger Down, the private collector? Some good, whopping lie, depend on it.) He was sure he remembered White with his checkbook out. And then? A confused picture of White examining the polished surface, pointing at something—

Don Benedict badly wanted a cup of coffee. His room was just off the studio, and once there had been a hot-plate there, but Walt had ordered it removed on the grounds of danger. So now Don had to go up to Walt's apartment when he wanted a cup of coffee. That was how Walt liked everything to be: little brother coming to big brother. Well, there was no help for it. Don went upstairs, anticipating cold looks, curt remarks, at every step.

However, Walt was sweetness itself this morning. The coffee was ready; Walt had poured it even before Don entered the kitchen. After he finished his cup (made from unboiled water, powdered coffee, ice-cold milk) Walt urged another on him. Rather than speak, he took it.

Don knew, by the falsely jovial note of Walter's voice, that Something Was Up. He gulped the tepid slop and rose. "Thanks. See you later, Walter—"

But Walter reached out his hand and took him by the arm. "Let's talk about the Lost Dutchman Mine. ("The *what?*") The Spanish Treasure. ("I don't—") Spelled E-l-w-e-l-l," said Walter, with an air at once sly and triumphant.

Don sat down heavily.

"Don't know what I mean by those figures of speech? Odd. You did last night. Matter of fact, they were yours," said Walter, mouth pursed with mean amusement. He would refresh Don's memory. Last night, Mr. White had asked Don how he had come to have so much contemporary knowledge about the making of wooden Indians. Don had laughed. "An old prospector I befriended left me the map to the Lost Dutchman Mine," he had said, waving his glass. "To the Spanish Treasure."

When Mr. White, puzzled, asked what he meant, Don had said, "It's easy. You just walk around the horses." Now what, just exactly, had Don meant by that?

"I must have been drunk, Walter."

"Oh, yes, you were drunk, all right. But *in vino veritas* . . . Now I've been thinking it out very carefully, Don. It seems to me that 'the old desert rat' you spoke of must have been that fellow Elwell, who slipped on the ice two winters ago. The one you got to the hospital and visited regularly till he died. Am I right, Don? Am I?"

Don nodded miserably. "Damn liquor," he added.

"*Now* we're making progress," said Walt. "*Okay*. Now about this map to the mine. I know he left you that damn notebook. I know that. But I looked it over very carefully and it was just a lot of figures scribbled—equations, or what ever th' hell you call 'em. But it had something else in it, didn't it? Something you took out. We'll get to just what by and by. So—and it was right after that that you started going on these vacations of yours. Made me curious. Those funny clothes you wore."

Stiff and tight, Don sat in the bright, neat kitchen and watched the waters rise. There was nothing for him here and now, except for Mary and the children, and his love for them had been no more selfish than theirs for him. He had been glad when Walt first appeared, happy when they married, unhappy when Walt's real nature appeared, very pleased when the chance occurred to offer "a position" to his brother-in-law. The misgivings felt when a few people actually offered to buy the shapeless wooden things he had created almost aimlessly (he knowing that he was not a sculptor but a craftsman) vanished when he saw it was the perfect setup for keeping Mary and the kids supported.

Of course, after a while Don had been able to arrange the majority of the "sales." The waste of time involved in hacking out the wooden horrors which "private collectors" bought was deplorable. The whole system was dreadfully clumsy, but its sole purpose—to create a world in which Walter would be satisfied and Mary happy—was being fulfilled, at any rate.

Or had been.

What would happen now, with Walter on the verge of finding out everything?

"And Syracuse—what a cottonpickin' alibi! I figured you had a woman hid away for sure, wasting your time when you should have been working, so—well, I wanted to find out who she was, where she lived. That's why I always went through your pockets when you came back from these 'vacations'—"

"Walter, you didn't!"

But of course he knew damned well that Walter did. Had known for some time that Walter was doing it. Had acted accordingly. Instead of hiding the evidence, he had deliberately planted it, and in such a way that it couldn't possibly fail to add up to exactly one conclusion.

"What a lot of junk!" Walter jeered. "Like somebody swept the floor of an antique shop and dumped it all in your pocket. Ticket stubs with funny old printing, clippings from newspapers of years back—and all like that. *However*—" he jabbed a thick, triumphant finger at Don—"money is money, no matter how old it is. Right? *Damned* right! Old dollar bills, old gold pieces. Time after time. You weren't very cautious, old buddy. So now—just what *is* this 'Spanish Treasure' that you've been tapping? Let's have the details, son, or else I'll be mighty unhappy. And when I'm unhappy, Mary is too . . ."

That was very true, Don had realized for some time now. And if Mary couldn't protect herself, how could the youngsters escape?

"I'm tired of scraping along on ten per cent, you see, Don. I got that great old American ambition: I want to be in business for myself. And you are going to provide the capital. So—again, and for the last time—let's have the details."

Was this the time to tell him? And, hard upon the thought, the answer came: Yes, the time was now, time to tell the truth. At once his heart felt light, joyous; the heavy weight (long so terribly, constantly familiar) was removed from him.

"Mr. Elwell—the old gentleman who slipped on the ice; you were right about that, Walter—" Walter's face slipped into its familiar, smug smile. "Mr. Elwell was a math teacher at the high school down the block. Imagine it—a genius like him, pounding algebra into the heads of sullen children! But he didn't let it get him down, because that was just his living. What he mainly lived for were his space-time theorems. 'Elwell's Equations,' we called them—"

Walter snorted. "Don't tell me the old gimp was a time traveler and left you his time machine?"

"It wasn't a machine. It was only a—well, I guess it *was* a sort of map, after all. He tried to explain his theories to me, but I just couldn't understand them. It was kind of like chess problems—I never could understand *them,* either. So when we arranged that I was going to visit 1880, he wrote it all down for me. It's like a pattern. You go back and forth and up and down and after a while—"

"After a while you're in 1880?"

"That's right."

Walter's face had settled in odd lines. "I thought you were going to try not telling me what I'd figured out for myself," he said in the cutting exaggeration of his normally exaggerated Southern drawl. This was the first time he had used it on Don, though Don had heard it used often enough on Mary and the kids. "The map, and all those clues you were stupid enough to leave in your pockets, and the stupidest of all—carving your own squiggle signature into all those dozens of old wooden Indians. Think I can't add?"

"But that was Canal Street, 1880, and this is now," said Don in a carefully dismal-sounding voice. "I thought it was safe."

Walter looked at him. Walter—who had never earned an ethical dollar in his life, and had scarcely bothered to make a pretense of supporting his wife since Don's work had started to sell—asked, "All right, why 1880—and why wooden Indians?"

Don explained to him how he felt at ease there, how the air was fresher, the food tastier, how the Russians were a menace only to other Russians, how—and the sachems! What real, sincere pleasure and pride he got out of carving them.

They were *used!* Not like the silly modern stuff he turned out now, stuff whose value rested only on the fact that self-seekers like Edgar Feld were able to con critics and public into believing it was valuable.

Walt scarcely heard him. "But how much money can you make carving wooden Indians?"

"Not very much in modern terms. But you see, Walt—I invest."

And that was the bait in the trap he'd set and Walt rose to it and struck. "The market! Damn it to hell, of *course!*" The prospect of the (for once in his whole shoddy career) Absolutely Sure Thing, the Plunge which was certain to be a Killing, of moving where he could know without doubt what the next move would be, almost deprived Walter of breath.

"A tycoon," he gasped. "You could have been a tycoon and all you could think of was—"

Don said that he didn't want to be a tycoon. He just wanted to carve wooden—

"Why, I could make us better than tycoons! Kings! Emperors! One airplane—" He subsided after Don convinced him that Elwell's Equation could transport only the individual and what he had on or was carrying. "Lugers," he muttered. "Tommy-guns. If I'm a millionaire, I'll need bodyguards. Gould, Fisk, Morgan—they better watch out, that's all."

He slowly refocused on Don. "And *I'll* carry the map," he said.

He held out his hand. Slowly, as if with infinite misgivings, Don handed over to him the paper with Elwell's 1880 Equation.

Walter looked at it, lips moving, brows twisting, and Don recalled his own mystification when the old man had showed it to him.

"*. . . where* X *is one pace and* Y *is five-sixth of the hypotenuse of a right-angled triangle of which both arms are* X *in length . . .*"

"Well," said Walter, "now let's get down to business." He rose, went off toward the living room, returned in a minute. Following him was a man with the tense, set face of a fanatic. He looked at Don with burning eyes.

"Anders!" cried Don.

"Where is the Equation?" Anders demanded.

"Oh, *I* got that," Walter said.

He took it out, showed a glimpse, thrust it in his pocket. He stepped back, put a chair between him and the WIS man.

"Not so fast," he said. "I got it and I'm keeping it. At least for now. So let's talk business. Where's the cash?"

As Anders, breathing heavily, brought out the roll of bills, "Oh, Walter, what have you done?" Don moaned. "Don't throw me in the bramble-bush, Brer Wolf!"

"Here is the first part of it," said Anders, ignoring his former WIS associate. "For this you agree to return to Canal Street, 1880, and destroy—by whatever means are available—the infamous firm of Demuth's. In the unlikely case of their continuing in the business after the destruction—"

"They won't. Best goon job money can buy; leave it to me."

Anders hesitated.

Walter promptly said, "No, you can't come along. Don't ask again. Just him and me. I'll need him for bird-dogging. I'll get in touch when we come back. As agreed, I bring back copies of the New York papers showing that Demuth's was blown up or burned down. On your way."

With one single hate-filled glance, not unmixed with triumph, at Don, Anders withdrew. The door closed. Walter laughed.

"You aren't—" Don began.

"Not a chance. Think I'm crazy? Let him and his crackpot buddies whistle for their money. No doubt you are wondering how I put two and two in a vertical column and added, hey, Donny boy? Well, once I figured out that the 'Prospector' was Elwell, and saw the WIS membership card in your pocket, I remembered that he and you used to go to those WIS meetings together, and I got in touch with them. They practically told me the whole story, but I wanted confirmation from you. All right, on your feet. We've got a pea patch to tear up."

While Walt was shaving, Don and Mary had a few minutes together.

"Why don't you just go, Don?" she begged. "I mean for good—away where he can't find you—and stay there. Never mind about me or the children. We'll make out."

"But wouldn't he take it out on you and them?"

"I said don't worry about us and I mean it. He's not all bad, you know. Oh, he might be, for a while, but that's just because he never really adjusted to living up North. Maybe if we went back to his home town—he always talks about it—I mean he'd be different there—"

He listened unhappily to her losing her way between wanting him out of her misery and hoping that the unchangeable might change.

"Mary," he broke in, "you don't have to worry any more. I'm taking Walt along and setting him up—really setting him up. And listen—" he wrote a name and address on the back of her shopping list—"go see this man. I've been investing money with his firm and there's plenty to take care of you and the kids—even if things go wrong with Walt and me. This man will handle all your expenses."

She nodded, not speaking. They smiled, squeezed hands. There was no need for embrace or kiss-the-children.

Whistling "Dixie," Walter returned. "Let's go," he said.

"Good-by, Don," said Mary.

"Good-by, Mary," said Don.

That afternoon, Don Benedict and Walter Swift, after visits to a theatrical costumer and a numismatist, entered the Canal Street subway station. Those who have had commerce with that crossroads of lower Manhattan know how vast, how labyrinthine, it is. Only a few glances, less than idly curious, were given them as they paced through the late Mr. Elwell's mathematical map. No one was present when they passed beneath a red-lettered sign reading "Canarsie Line" and vanished away.

As soon as he felt the flagstones beneath his feet, Walter whirled around and looked back. Instead of the white-tiled corridor, he saw a wet stone wall. For a moment, he swore feebly. Then he laughed.

"A pocketful of long green and another of gold eagles!" he exclaimed. "What shall we try for first? Erie or New York Central Common? No—first I want to see this place where you work. Oh, yes, I *do*. Obstinacy will get you nowhere. Lead on."

Wishing eventually to introduce Walt into Hennaberry's, Don had first taken him out to Canal Street. Leopold Schwager's second-hand establishment was opposite, the sidewalk lined with superannuated sachems. Other establishments of the show-figure trade were within stonethrow, their signs, flags and figures making a brave display. Horsecars, cabs, drays, private carriages went clattering by.

Walter watched the passing scene with relish, leering at the women in what he evidently thought was the best 1880 masher's manner. Then he wrinkled his nose.

"Damn it all," he said, "I hadn't realized that the Hayes Administration smelled so powerfully of the horse. But I suppose *you* like it? Yes," he sneered, "you would. Well, enjoy it while you can. As soon as I manage to dig up some old plans, I propose to patent the internal combustion engine."

Don felt his skin go cold.

"John D. Rockefeller ought to be very, ver-ry interested," Walt said exultantly. "Why, five years from now, you won't know it's the same street . . . What're you pointing at?"

Don gestured to a scout-figure in full plumage outside a store whose awning was painted with the words, "*August Schwartz Segar Mfger Also Snuff, Plug, Cut Plug and Twist.*"

"One of mine," he said, pride mixed with growing resolve.

Walter grunted. "You won't have any time for that sort of thing any more; I'll need you myself. Besides—yes, why not? Introduce cigarette machinery. Start a great big advertising campaign, put a weed in the mouth of every American over the age of sixteen."

A drunken sailor lurched down the street singing "Sweet Ida Jane from Portland, Maine." Automatically, Don stepped aside to let him pass.

"But if you do that," he said, no longer doubting that Walter would if he could, "then there won't be any more—nobody will need—I mean my work—"

Walter said irritably, "I told you, you won't have the time to be piddling around with a mallet and chisel. And now let's see your wooden-Injun mine."

Acting as if he felt that nothing mattered any more, Don turned and led the way toward the brick building where C. E. Hennaberry, Show Figures and Emblematic Signs, did business. Ben the boy paused in his never-ending work of dusting the stock models to give a word and a wave in greeting. He stared at Walt.

In the back was the office, old Van Wart the clerk-cashier and old Considine the clerk-bookkeeper, on their high stools, bending over their books as usual. On the wall was a dirty photograph in a black-draped frame, with the legend "Hon. Wm. Marcy Tweed, Grand Sachem of the Columbian Order of St. Tammany" and underneath the portrait was the Major himself.

"So this is the place!" Walter declared, exaggerated Southern accent rolling richly. Major Hennaberry's friend, Col. Cox, sitting on the edge of the desk cutting himself a slice of twist, jumped as if stung by a minié-ball. His rather greasy sealskin cap slid over one eye.

"Get all kinds of people in here, don't you, Cephas?" he growled. "All's I got to say is: I was at Fredericksburg, I was at Shiloh, and all's I got to say is: the only good Rebel is a dead Rebel!"

The Major, as Don well knew, hated Rebels himself, with a fervor possible only to a Tammany Democrat whose profitable speculations in cotton futures had been interrupted for four long, lean years. Don also knew that the Major had a short way of dealing with partisans of the Lost Cause, or with anyone else who had cost or threatened to cost him money—if he could just be brought to the point.

The Major looked up now, his eye lighting coldly on Walter, who gazed around the not overly clean room with a curious stare. "Yes, sir, might I serve you, sir? Nice fly-figure, maybe? Can supply you with a Highlander holding simulated snuff-mill at a tear-down price; no extra charge for tam-o-shanter. Oh, Dusty. Glad to see you—"

"Dusty" mumbled an introduction. How quickly things had changed—though not in any way for the better—and how paradoxically: because he had refused the WIS demand to change the past by violence so that modernism would be held off indefinitely, he was now condemned to see modernism arrive almost at once. Unless, of course . . .

"Brother-in-law, eh?" said Major Hennaberry, beginning to wheeze. "Dusty's done some speaking about you. Mmph." He turned abruptly to Don/Dusty. "What's all this, my boy, that Charley Voles was telling me—Demuth's coming up with some devilish scheme to introduce cast-iron show figures?" Dusty started, a movement noted by the keen though bloodshot eyes of his sometime employer. "Then it *is* true? Terrible thing, unconscionable. Gave me the liver complaint afresh, directly I heard of it. Been on medicated wine ever since."

Walt turned angrily on his brother-in-law. "Who told you to open your damn cotton-pickin mouth?"

The Major's purplish lips parted, moved in something doubtless intended for a smile.

"Now, gents," he said, "let's not quarrel. What must be must be, eh?"

"*Now* you're talking," said Walt, and evidently not realizing that he and Hennaberry had quite separate things in mind, he added: "Things will be different, but you'll get used to them."

Watching the Major start to wheeze in an unreasoning attack of rage, Dusty knew catalytic action was needed. "How about a drink, Major?" he suggested. "A Rat Nolan special?"

Unpurpling quickly, now merely nodding and hissing, the Major called for Ben. He took a coin out of his change purse and said: "Run over to Cooney's barrelhouse and bring back some glasses and a pitcher of rum cocktail. And ask Cooney does he know where Nolan is. I got some business with him."

The boy left on the lope, and there was a short, tight silence. Then Col. Cox spoke, an anticipatory trickle already turning the corners of his mouth a wet brown. "I was at Island Number Ten, and I was at Kennesaw Mountain, and what I say is: the only good Rebel is a dead Rebel."

Walt grinned and said nothing until Ben came back with the drinks.

"Well, Scotch on the rocks it isn't," he said then, taking a brief sip, "but it's not bad."

He gave a brief indifferent glance at the shifty little man with Burnside whiskers who had come back with Ben, carrying the glasses.

"To science and invention!" cried Walt. "To progress!" He drained half his glass. His face turned green, then white. He started to slide sidewise and was caught by the little man in Burnsides.

"Easy does it, cully," said Mr. Rat Nolan, for it was he. "Dear, dear! I hope it's not a touch of this cholera morbus what's been so prevalent. Expect we'd better get him to a doctor, don't you, gents?"

Major Hennaberry said that there was not a doubt about it. He walked painfully over to the elevator shaft, whistled shrilly. "Charley?" he called. "Larry? Oscar? Otto? Hennery? Get down here directly!"

Dusty emerged from his surprise at how neatly it had happened. He reached into Walter's coat pocket and took out the paper with Elwell's Equation on it. Now he was safe, and so was Canal Street, 1880. As for what would happen when Walter recovered from his strange attack—well, they would see.

The staff came out of the elevator cage with interest written large and plain upon their faces. Ben had evidently found time from his errand to drop a few words. Major Hennaberry gestured toward Walter, reclining, gray-faced, against the solicitous Mr. Rat Nolan, who held him in a firm grip.

"Gent is took bad," the Major explained. "Couple of you go out and see if you can find a cab—Snow Ferguson or Blinky Poole or one of those shunsoaps—and tell them to drive up by the alley. No sense in lugging this poor gent out the front."

Franz, Larry and Charley nodded and went out.

Otto stared. "No more vooden Indians, if he gets his vay," he said dismally at last. "Ho, Chesus," he moaned.

Dusty began, "Major, this is all so—"

"Now don't be worriting about your brother-in-law," said Rat Nolan soothingly. "For Dr. Coyle is a sovereign hand at curing what ails all pasty-faced, consumptive types like this one."

Dusty said that he was sure of it. "Where is Dr. Coyle's office these days?" he asked.

Mr. Rat Nolan coughed lightly, gazed at a cobweb in a corner of the ceiling. "The southwest passage to Amoy by way of the Straits is what the Doc is recommending for his patients—and he insists on accompanying them to see they follows doctor's orders, such being the degree of his merciful and tender-loving care . . ."

Dusty nodded approvingly.

"Ah, he's a rare one," said R. Nolan with enthusiasm, "is Bully Coyle, master of the *Beriah Jaspers* of the Black Star Line! A rare one and a rum one, and the Shanghaiing would be a half-dead trade without 'm, for it does use up men. And they leave on the morning tide."

There was a noise of *clomp-clomp* and metal harness-pieces jingled in the alley. Charley, Larry and Hennery came in, followed by a furtive-looking cab-man with a great red hooked nose—Snow Ferguson, presumably, or Blinky Poole, or one of those shunsoaps.

"Ah, commerce, commerce," Rat Nolan sighed. "It waits upon no man's pleasure." He went through unconscious Walter's pockets with dispatch and divided the money into equal piles. From his own, he took a half-eagle which had been slightly scalloped and handed it to Dusty. "Share and share alike, and here's the regular fee. That's the spirit what made America great. Leave all them foreign monarchs beware . . . Give us a lift with the gent here, cullies . . ."

Charley took the head, Hennery and Otto the arms, while Larry and Ben held the feet. Holding the door open, the cabman observed, "Damfino-looking shoes this coffee-cooler's got on."

"Them's mine," said Rat Nolan instantly. "He'll climb the rigging better without 'em. Mind the door, cullies—don't damage the merchandise!"

Down the dim aisles the procession went, past the fly-figures, scout-figures, rosebuds, pompeys, Highlandmen, and Turks. The gas-jets flared, the shadows danced, the sachems scowled.

"If he comes to and shows fight," Major Hennaberry called, "give him a tap with the mallet, one of you!" He turned to Dusty, put a hand on his shoulder. "While I realize, my boy, that no man can be called to account for the actions of his brother-in-law in this Great Republic of ours, still I expect this will prove a lesson to you. From your silence, I preceive that you agree. Your sister now—hate to see a lady's tears—"

Dusty took a deep breath. The air smelled deliciously of fresh wood and paint. "She'll adjust," he said. Mary would be quite well off with the money from his investments. So there was no need, none at all, for his return. And if the WIS tried to follow him, to make more trouble, why—there was always Rat Nolan.

"Major Hennaberry, sir," he said vigorously, "we'll beat Demuth's yet. You remember what you said when the catalog came out, about the power of advertising? We'll run their metal monsters into the ground and put a wooden fly-figure on every street block in America!"

And they did.

Author, Author

INTRODUCTION BY MELISA MICHAELS

Avram Davidson was a giant of a man. He must have stood at least five feet five inches in his stocking feet, and all of it solid muscle. He never backed down from a challenge (except to change his typewriter ribbon, and surely it was a bold man's indifference to peril that led him to carry his typewriter to a friend who would change the ribbon cartridge for him). Avram was, to put it simply, a hero.

Those who say he was testy and irascible, who call him curmudgeon, who point to his impatience with editors as an example of his smallness and ordinariness, have perhaps never opposed the hideous fiends he did and never felt their sulphurous breath at that vulnerable junction where the fingertips meet the keyboard.

Avram doggedly defied a monstrous wickedness so powerful and depraved it would have sent a lesser man gibbering for the safety of a day job. "Author, Author" may have been written at a low point in this intrepid struggle: one can tell from the ambiguous ending that he very nearly despaired of conquering the loathsome creatures that, unobstructed, might transform even university libraries to best-seller racks. His tenacity sets an example for butlers and baronets everywhere.

AUTHOR, AUTHOR

Rodney stirrup had always taken care (taken *damned good* care! he often emphasized) not to get married; several former morganatic lady friends, however, frequently testified that the famous writer was Not A Very Nice Person. Perhaps even they might have felt sorry for him if they could have been with him that day at Boatwright Brothers, the publishers. And thereafter.

But then again, perhaps they might not.

Rodney stared at J. B. across the vast, glossy desk.

"With one hand you cut my throat," he protested; "And with the other hand you stab me in the back!"

A slightly pained look passed across Jeremy Boatwright's pink and wide-spread face, hesitated, and decided to stay. "Come now, Rodney . . . these professional phrases. . . . Really, there are no other choices left to us, owing, ah, to Conditions In The Trade."

Stirrup confounded conditions in the trade. "You reduce my royalties—I call that cutting my throat. And you demand a larger share in the secondary rights: reprints, paperbacks, television—I call that stabbing me in the back. If this continues I won't be able to keep my car. It is bad enough," he said, bitterly, "that I am confined to London in the winter. I *always* went to the South of France, the West Indies—or, at *least*, to Torquay. Next winter I shall not only shiver and cough in the damp, but I won't even be able to drive away for a week end. I'll have to go by train or bus—if you are good enough to leave me my fare. . . . You aren't giving up *your* car, are you?" he asked.

J. B. leaned his well-tailored elbows on the desk, bent forward. "Confidentially, old man, it's my wife's money that pays for it." Stirrup asked if it weren't true that Mrs. Boatwright's income was derived in large part from her stock in the publishing firm. J. B.'s face went stiff. "Let's leave Mrs. Boatwright out of this, shall we?" he proposed.

"But—"

"Why don't you mix yourself a drink? Sobriety always makes you surly."

Stirrup said he supposed he might as well. "It's my books that are paying for your booze," he observed gloomily.

"Look here—" The publisher flung out his plump hand. "You seem to think this is a special plot to defraud our writers, don't you?" Rodney shrugged. "Oh, my dear fellow!" Boatwright's voice was pained, pleading. "Do let me explain it to you. It is true that Rodney Stirrup, whom I have known since the days when he was still Ebenezer Quimby—" the writer shuddered— "is one of the world's top-ranking writers of the classical detection story. But what good's it do a man to be one of the world's top-ranking designers of carriage whips if no one is buying carriages? Have you *seen* the paperbacks coming out these days? Sex and slaughter." He tittered.

Stirrup angrily put down his drink. He suspected, strongly, that the bottle he'd poured it from was not the one proffered to better-selling writers. "I can show you—you should have read them yourself, dammit—my latest reviews."

Jeremy Boatwright shrugged away the latest reviews. "The reviewer gets his copies free; *our* only concern is with copies *sold*. Now, in the past, old man—" he made a church roof of his well-manicured fingers—"your books sold chiefly, and sold admittedly very well, to the American circulating libraries. Now, alas, the libraries are dying. Hundreds of them—thousands—are already dead. Dreadful pit-y. The people who used to take your books out now stay home and watch television instead. Eh?" He glanced, none too subtly, at his watch.

"Then why don't you sell more of my things to television? Eh?"

Boatwright said, Oh, but they *tried*. "Sometimes we succeed. But in order to equalize our losses, we—Boatwright Brothers—simply have to take a larger slice of your television and other secondary earnings. It's as simple as that."

Stirrup suggested that there was a simpler way: that Boatwright Brothers move to cheaper quarters, cut down on their plushy overhead and pass the savings on to their writers. J. B. smiled indulgently. "Oh, my dear fellow, how I wish we could. You've no idea how this place *bores* me—to say nothing of what dining out does to my poor liver. But we're not so lucky as you. A writer can pig it if he wants to, but we publishers, well, we simply are obliged to maintain the façade."

And, with a sigh, he changed the subject; began to explain to Stirrup why it was difficult nowadays to sell his writings. "You hit upon a good formula. A *very* good formula. But it's outmoded now. Almost all your stories begin the same way: a traveler's car breaks down on a lonely road across the moors, about dusk. Just over the hill is a large mansion, to which he is directed by a passing rustic. Correct? Well, large mansions are out of date. No one can afford them. The rustics are all home watching television and reading their newspapers. And another thing: your books have too many butlers in them, and too many noblemen. In actuality, butlers are dying off. (Mine died not long ago and we're having no luck in finding a replacement; they've all gone into the insurance business.) Things have *changed,* dear boy, and your books have failed to change with them. In effect, you are writing ghost stories." He smiled moistly. "Must you go quite so soon?" he asked, as Stirrup continued to sit.

Stirrup put down the empty glass and began to draw on his gloves. "Yes— unless you are planning to invite me to luncheon."

Boatwright said, "I'd love to. Unfortunately I have a prior engagement with Marie-Noëmi Valerien and her mother. You know, the fifteen-year-old French girl who wrote *Bon Soir, Jeunesse*. I understand she's finished another, and her publishers have treated her simply vilely, so—Where are you off to?"

"Out of town. Some old friends have a place in the country." The publisher inquired if they lived in a large mansion. "As a matter of fact," the writer said, not meeting his eye, "the big house is closed for the time being, and they are living in what used to be the gatekeeper's cottage. Very cosy little place," he added bitterly, remembering Nice, Cannes, Antibes. . . . "They raise poultry."

The publisher, Stirrup reflected, had no need to raise poultry at *his* country place—which was in the same county as his friends' rundown acreage. The Mill Race (a name, unknown to the local Typographical Society, bestowed by its current proprietor in fancied honor of an all but vanished ruin by an all but dried-up stream) was both well furnished and well kept. Once a year Stirrup was invited down for the long week end; no oftener. He felt no twinge at hearing of the demise of Boatwright's butler, Bloor, a large, pear-shaped man with prominent and red-rimmed eyes who had always treated him with insultingly cold politeness—a treatment he repaid by never tipping the man.

Jeremy Boatwright magnanimously walked Stirrup to the door. "Have a *pleasant* week end, old man. Perhaps taste will change; in the meanwhile, though, perhaps *you'll* consider changing. A psychological thriller about a couple who live in the gatekeeper's cottage and raise poultry—eh?"

Rodney Stirrup (he was a withered, short man, with a rufous nose) did think about it, and as a result he lost his way. There are many people who dislike to ask directions, and Stirrup was one of them. He was certain that if he continued to circle around he would find the needed landmarks and then be able to recognize the way from there. It grew late, then later, and he was willing to inquire, but there was no one in sight to ask.

And finally, just at dusk, his engine gave a reproachful cough and ceased to function. He had passed no cars and no people on this lonely side road, but still he couldn't leave his car standing in the middle of it. The car was small and light; steering and pushing, he got it off to the side.

"Damned devil wagon!" he said. Wasn't there a rule about lighting a red lantern and leaving it as a warning? Well, too bad; he had none. He looked around in the failing light, and almost—despite his vexation—almost smiled.

" 'A traveler's car breaks down on a lonely road about dusk. Just over a hill is a large mansion,' " he quoted. "Damn Boatwright anyway. 'Ghost stories!' " He sighed, thrust his hands into his pockets and started walking. Ahead of him was a slight rise in the road. "If only there were someone I could ask directions of," he fretted. "Even 'a passing rustic.' "

A man in a smock came plodding slowly over the rise. In that first moment of relief mingled with surprise, Stirrup wondered if the thought had really preceded the sight. Or if—

"I say, can you tell me where I can find a telephone?" he called out, walking quickly toward the figure, who had halted, open-mouthed, on seeing him. The rustic slowly hook his head.

"Televown?" he repeated, scratching his chin. "Nay, marster, ee wown't voind nâo devil's devoice loike that erebâouts."

Stirrup's annoyance at the answer was mixed with surprise at the yokel's costume and dialect. When had he last heard and seen anything like it? Or not heard and seen—read? If anyone had asked him, and found him in an honest mood, he should have said that such speech and garb had been nothing but literary conventions since the Education Acts had done their work. Why, he himself hadn't dared employ it since before the first World War. And the fellow didn't seem that old.

"Surely there must be a house somewhere along here." Reaching the top of the rise, he looked about. "There! That one!" About a quarter mile off, set back in grounds quickly being cloaked in coming night, was a large mansion.

The man in the smock seemed to shiver. "That gurt äouze? Ow, zur, daon't ee troy they'm. Ghowsties and bowgles. . . ." His voice died away into a mumble, and when Stirrup turned to him again, he was gone. Some village idiot, perhaps, unschooled because unschoolable. Well, it didn't matter. The house—

At first glance the house had seemed a mere dark huddle, but now there were lights. He made his way quickly ahead. A footman answered his knock. Self-consciously, Stirrup spoke the words he had so often written. "I'm afraid my car has broken down. May I use your telephone?" The footman asked—of course—if he might take his hat and coat. Feeling very odd, Stirrup let him. Then another man appeared. He was stout and tall and silver-haired.

"Had a breakdown? Too bad." Voices sounded and glasses clinked in the room he had left. It was warm. "My name is Blenkinsop," he said.

"Mine is Stirrup—Rodney Stirrup." Would Mr. Blenkinsop recognize— Evidently Mr. Blenkinsop did. He stared, his eyes wide.

"Rod-ney *Stir*rup?" he cried. *"The writer?"* His voice was like thunder.

Another man appeared. He was thin, with small white side whiskers— lamb chop rather than mutton chop. "My dear Blenkinsop, pray modulate your voice," he said. "Richards is telling a capital story. And whom have we here?"

"This gentleman, my dear Arbuthnot," said Blenkinsop in clear and even tones, "is Mr. Rodney Stirrup. The wri-ter. He's come *here!*"

"No!"

"Yes!"

"Oh, ho-ho-ho!" Mr. Arbuthnot laughed.

"Ah, ha-ha-ha!" Mr. Blenkinsop laughed.

Stirrup, first puzzled, grew annoyed. Young men, the kind who wear fuzzy beards and duffle coats, read *avant-garde* publications and live in attics where they entertain amoral young women, might understandably be moved to laugh at a writer of the Classical Detective Story. But there seemed no excuse at all for men older than himself, contemporaries of Hall Caine and Mrs. Belloc Lowndes and other all but forgotten literary figures, to laugh.

The two men stopped and looked at him, then at each other.

"I fear we must seem very boorish to you," Mr. Arbuthnot said. He looked very much like Gladstone, a picture of whom had hung in the home of Malachi Quimby, the Radical cobbler, Stirrup's long dead father. Something of the awe felt for his father had transferred itself to the Grand Old Man; and even now a remnant of it was left for Mr. Arbuthnot. "Pray accept my apologies," Mr. Arbuthnot said.

"Oh, don't mention it."

"The fact is," explained Blenkinsop, "that we are all of us very great followers of your books, Mr. Stirrup. It is the coincidence of meeting our favorite author, via a fortuitous accident, which provoked our untimely risability. Do excuse us."

Stirrup said that it was pleasant to realize he was not forgotten.

"Oh, not here," said Arbuthnot. "Never. Pray come and meet our friends."

"Do," urged Blenkinsop, leading the way. "Oh, no, indeed, we've not forgotten you. We have a little celebration tonight. We often do. . . . Right through this door, Mr. Stirrup."

The room to which they led him contained perhaps a dozen men, all distinguished in mien, all well on in years. They looked up as Stirrup entered. Glasses were in their hands, and cigars. Several of them were still chuckling, presumably at the "capital" story told by Richards, whichever one he was. A tall and heavy man, with a nose like the Duke of Wellington's, sipped from his glass and smacked his lips.

"Excellent, my dear Richards," he said.

"I thought you'd like it, Peebles," Richards said. He was a red-faced, husky-voiced, many-chinned man. "Whom have we here, Arbuthnot, Blenkinsop?"

Arbuthnot smiled on the right side of his face. Blenkinsop rubbed his hands. "This gentleman has had the ill chance to suffer a breakdown of his motorcar. I am sure—quite sure—that we shall endeavor to welcome him in a fitting manner. He is no ordinary guest. He is a well-known author."

There was a stir of interest. "He writes thrillers." Another stir. "He is none other than—" a dramatic pause—"*Mr. Rodney Stirrup!*"

The reaction was immense.

Three men jumped to their feet, one dropped a lit cigar, one snapped the stem of his wine glass, another crashed his fist into his palm.

"I told Mr. Stirrup—" Blenkinsop lifted his voice; the hum subsided— "that few writers, if any, have received the attention which we have given to the works through which his name became famous. We followed his tales of crime and detection very carefully here, I told him."

Peebles said, "You told him no more than the truth, Mr. Blenkinsop. Do us the honor, sir, of taking a glass of wine. This is a great occasion, indeed, Mr. Stirrup." He poured, proffered.

Stirrup drank. It was a good wine. He said so. The company smiled.

"We have kept a good cellar here, Mr. Stirrup," said Peebles. "It has been well attended to." Stirrup said that they must have a good butler, then. A good butler was hard to find, he said. Between the men there passed a look, a sort of spark. Mr. Peebles carefully put down his glass. It was empty. "How curious you should mention butlers," he said.

Stirrup said that it was not so curious, that he was, in a way, very fond of butlers, that he had put them to good use in his books. Then he turned, surprised. A noise very like a growl had come from a corner of the room where stood a little man with a red face and bristly white hair.

"Ye-e-es," said Mr. Peebles, in an odd tone of voice. "It is generally conceded, is it not, that you, Mr. Stirrup, were the very first man to employ a butler as the one who stands revealed, at story's end, as the murderer? That it is you who coined the phrase which so rapidly became a household word wherever the English tongue is spoken? I refer, of course, to: *'The butler did it.'*?"

Rather proudly, rather fondly, Stirrup nodded. "You are correct, sir."

"And in novel after novel, though the victims varied and the criminal methods changed, the murderer was almost invariably—a butler. Until finally you were paid the supreme compliment one writer can pay another—that of imitation. A line of thrillers long enough to reach from here to London—to say nothing of short stories, stage plays, music hall acts, movie and television dramas—each with a murderous butler, poured forth upon the world, Mr. Stirrup—beginning, if I am not mistaken, with Padraic, the butler of Ballydooly House, in *Murder By The Bogs*."

Stirrup was pleased. "Ah, do you remember Padraic? Dear me. Yes, that was my very first detective novel. Couldn't do it today, of course. Irish butlers are dreadfully passé, obsolete. De Valera and Irish Land Reform have extinguished the species, so to speak."

The red-faced little man dashed from his corner, seized a poker, and brandished it in Stirrup's face. "The truth is not in ye!" he shouted. "Ye lie, ye scribbling Sassenach!" Stirrup could not have said with any degree of accuracy if the brogue was that of Ulster, or Munster, or Leinster, or Connaught—the four provinces of Northern Ireland—but he recognized as being of sound British workmanship the heavy iron in the speaker's hand.

In a rather quavering tone, Stirrup demanded, "What is the meaning of this?"

"Allow me to introduce you," Peebles said, "to O'Donnell, for fifty years butler to Count Daniel Donavan of Castle Donavan. O'Donnell, put that away."

Still growling, O'Donnell obeyed. Stirrup, regaining his aplomb, said: "*Count?* Surely not. The peerage of Ireland, like other British peerages, contains countesses, but no counts. The husband of a countess is an earl."

"The count's toitle, sor," said O'Donnell, looking at him with an eye as cold and gray as Galway Bay in winter, "is a Papal toitle. Oi trust ye've no objections?"

Stirrup hastily said he had none, then retreated to the other side of a table. The man whose wine glass had snapped in his hand finished wiping port from his fingers with a monogrammed handkerchief, then spoke in mellowed, measured tones.

"We must, of course," he said, "make due allowances for Celtic—I do not say, West British—exuberance; but the matter now before us is too serious to permit any element of disorder to enter." There was a general murmur of agreement. "Gentlemen, I move that the doors be locked. Those in favor will signify by saying 'Aye.' The ayes have it."

He locked the doors and pocketed the key. "Thank you, Mr. Piggot," said Peebles.

"Mr. Arbuthnot," Stirrup said, loudly, "since I am here in response to your invitation, it is from you that I must demand an explanation for these actions."

Arbuthnot smiled his slant smile again. Peebles said, "All in good time. By the way," he inquired, "I trust you have no objections if I refer to you henceforth as the Accused? Protocol, you know, protocol."

Stirrup said that he objected very much. "Most vehemently. Of what am I accused?" he asked plaintively.

Peebles flung out his arm and pointed at him. "You are accused, sir," he cried, "of having for over thirty years pursued an infamous campaign of literary slander designed to bring into contempt and disrepute a profession the most ancient and honorable, dating back to Biblical days and specifically mentioned—I refer to Pharoah's chief butler—in the Book of Deuteronomy."

Knuckles were rapped on tables and the room rang with murmurs of, "Hear, hear!" and, "Oh, well said, sir!"

"Pardon me, Mr. Peebles," said Blenkinsop. "The Book of Genesis."

"Genesis? H'm, dear me, yes. You are correct. Thank you."

"Not at all, not at all. Deuteronomy is very much like Genesis."

Stirrup interrupted this feast of love. "I insist upon being informed what all this has to do with you, or with any of you except O'Donnell."

Peebles peered at him with narrowed, heavy-lidded eyes.

"Are you under the impression, Mr.—is Accused under the impression that our esteemed colleague, Mr. Phelim O'Donnell, is the only butler here?"

Stirrup licked dry lips with a dry tongue. "Why, ah, yes," he stammered. "Isn't he? Is there another?" A growl went round the circle, which drew in closer.

"No, sir, he is *not. I* was a butler. *We were all of us butlers!*"

A hoarse scream broke from Stirrup's mouth. He lunged for the open windows, but was tripped up by the watchful Piggot.

Peebles frowned. "Mr. Blenkinsop," he said, "will you be good enough to close the windows? Thank you. I must now warn the Accused against any further such outbursts. Yes, Accused, we were all of us, every one of us, members of that proud profession which you were the first to touch with the dusty brush of scorn. Now you must prepare to pay. Somehow, Mr. Stirrup, you have pushed aside what my former lady—the justly-famed Mme. Victoria Algernonovna Grabledsky, the theosophical authoress—used to call 'The Veil of Isis.' This room wherein you now stand is none other than the Great Pantry of the Butlers' Valhalla. Hence—"

"May it please the court," said Piggot, interrupting. "We find the Accused guilty as charged, and move to proceed with sentencing."

"*Help!*" Stirrup cried, struggling in O'Donnell's iron grasp. "*He-e-e-l-l-p!*"

Peebles said that would do him no good, that there was no one to help him. Then he looked around the room, rather helplessly. "Dear me," he said, a petulant note in his voice; "whatever shall I use for a black cap while I pronounce sentence?"

A silence fell, broken by Richards. "In what manner shall sentence be carried out?" he asked.

Piggot, his face bright, spoke up. "I must confess, Mr. Peebles, to a fondness for the sashweight attached by a thin steel wire to the works of a grandfather's clock," said Piggot; "as utilized (in the Accused's novel of detection, *Murder In The Fens*) by Murgatroyd, the butler at Fen House—who was, of course, really Sir Ethelred's scapegrace cousin, Percy, disguised by a wig and false paunch. I recall that when I was in the service of Lord Alfred Strathmorgan, his lordship read that meretricious work and thereafter was wont to prod me quite painfully in my abdominal region, and to inquire, with what I considered a misplaced jocularity, *if my paunch were real!* Yes, I favor the sashweight and the thin steel wire."

Peebles nodded, judiciously. "Your suggestion, Mr. Piggot, while by no means devoid of merit, has a—shall I say—a certain degree of violence, which I should regret having to utilize so long as an alternative—"

"*I* would like to ask the opinion of the gentlemen here assembled," said Blenkinsop, "as to what they would think of a swift-acting, exotic Indonesian poison which, being of vegetative origin, leaves no trace; to be introduced via a hollowed corkscrew into a bottle of Mouton Rothschild '12? Needless to say, I refer to the Accused's trashy novel *The Vintage Vengeance*. In that book the profligate Sir Athelny met his end at the hands of the butler, Bludsoe, whose old father's long-established wine and spirits business was ruined when the avaricious Sir Athelny cornered the world's supply of corks—thus occasioning the elder Bludsoe's death by apoplexy. The late Clemantina, Dowager Duchess of Sodor and Skye, who was quite fond of her glass of wine, used frequently to tease me by inquiring if I had opened her bottle with a corkscrew of similar design and purpose; and I am not loath to confess that this habit of Her Grace's annoyed me exceedingly."

"The court can well sympathize with you in that, Mr. Blenkinsop." The Great Pantry hummed with a murmur of accord.

Blenkinsop swallowed his chagrin at this memory, nodded his thanks for the court's sympathy, and then said smoothly, "Of course we could not *force* the Accused to drink without rather a messy scene, but I have hopes he would feel enough sense of *noblesse oblige* to quaff the fatal beverage Socraticlike, so to speak."

Stirrup wiped his mouth with his free hand. "While I should be delighted, under ordinary circumstances," he said, "to drink a bottle of Mouton Rothschild '12 I must inquire if you have on hand such an item as a swift-acting, exotic Indonesian poison, which, being of vegetative origin, leaves no trace? Frankly, I have neglected to bring mine."

A mutter of disappointment was followed by a further consultation of the assembled butlers, but no sooner had they begun when a shot rang out, there was a shattering of glass, and O'Donnell fell forward. Richards turned him over; there was a bullet hole in the exact center of his forehead. Everyone's eyes left Stirrup; his captor's grip perceptibly loosened. Stirrup broke away, snatched up the poker, smashed the window and, jumping forward onto the terrace, ran for his life.

He reached the road just in time to see the headlights of an automobile moving away. *"Help!"* he shouted. *"Help! Help!"*

The car went into reverse, came back to him. Two men emerged.

"Oh, a stranger," said the driver. He was a man with long gray hair, clad neatly, if unconventionally, in golf knickers, deerstalking cap, and smoking jacket.

"The most fantastic thing—" Stirrup gasped. "My life was threatened by the inhabitants of that house back there!"

The other man cried, "Ah, the scoundrels!" He wore a greasy regimental dinner jacket and a soft, squashed hat; he shook a clenched fist toward the house and slashed the air with his cane. Deep-set eyes blazed in a gaunt face. Then, abruptly, his expression changed to an ingratiating smile. "It is at a time like this, sir," he said to Stirrup, "that I am sure you must ask yourself, 'Are my loved ones adequately protected in case of mishap, misadventure, or un-toward occurrences affecting me?' Now, the Great South British Assurance Company, of which I happen to be an agent, has a policy—"

"Stop that, you fool!" said the driver. "Can't you ever remember all that's over with now?" He took a revolver from his pocket, and Stirrup—suddenly recalling the bullet in O'Donnell's head—trembled. But as the other man's face creased with disappointment and petulance, the driver said to Stirrup, "Pray do not be alarmed, sir. But in the matter of butlers one simply *must* be prepared with strong measures. *They* stop at nothing. Fancy threatening an innocent, inoffensive gentleman such as you! My motto, when confronted with butlers, is: 'St. George and no quarter'!"

A trifle nervously, Stirrup said, "If you could drive me to the nearest town—"

"All in good season, sir," the man answered, waving his weapon carelessly. "I was once tried for shooting my butler; did you know that? I am not ashamed; in fact, I glory in the deed. It was during the grouse season in Scotland. I'd caught the swine pilfering my cigars. I gave him a fair run before bringing him down, then claimed it was an accident." He chuckled richly. "Jury returned a verdict of Not Proven. You should've seen the face of the Procurator-Fiscal!"

"*I* was never even indicted," the man in the dirty regimentals and crushed hat observed, with no small amount of smugness. "When I discovered that *my* butler had been selling the wine to the local pub, I chased him with hounds through the Great Park. Would have caught him, too, only the cowardly blighter broke his neck falling from a tree which he had climbed in trying to escape. 'Death by misadventure' was all the coroner could say. Hah! But then these damnation taxes obliged me to sell the Great Park, and reduced me to a low insurance broker. *Me!*" He ground his teeth.

Scarcely knowing if he should believe these wild tales, Stirrup said, "You have all my sympathy. Now, my book, *The Vintage Vengeance*—to give you only a single example—brought me in twenty-one hundred pounds clear of taxes the year it was written; whereas last year—"

The driver of the car turned from his revolver. His brows, which were twisted into horny curves of hair at the ends, went up—up—up. "*You* wrote *The Vintage Vengeance? You* are that fellow Rodney Stirrup?"

Stirrup drew himself erect. It was recognition such as this which almost made up for treacherous publishers, ungrateful mistresses, and a declining public. "I am. Did you read it? Did you like it?"

"Read it? We read it twen-ty-sev-en times! We were par-*ti*cularly interested in the character of Sir Athelny Aylemore, the unfortunate victim: an excellently-delineated portrait of a great gentleman. But you will recall that Sir Athelny was a baronet. Now, baronets possess the only hereditary degree of knighthood, and hence should be accorded an infinite degree of respect. And yet we feel your book failed to show a correct amount of respect."

The other man scowled and cut at the air with his cane. "Not at all a correct amount of respect," he said.

"The butlers," Stirrup began, trying to shift the conversation.

Again the driver ground his teeth. "I'm prepared for *them!* See here—a cartridge clip with silver bullets. My gunsmith, Motherthwaite's of Bond Street, wriggled like an eel when I ordered them, and a similar set for shotguns, but in the end he had them made up for me. Lucky for him. Hah!" He snorted, aimed at an imaginary and refractory gunsmith, went *Poom!*, and—with an air wickedly self-pleased—blew imaginary smoke from the muzzle.

Stirrup gave a nervous swallow, then said, with a half-convulsive giggle, "My word, but there's a lot of superstition in this part of the country! That yokel in the smock—"

The driver rubbed the muzzle of his revolver against his smoking jacket. "Yokel in a smock? Why, that's Daft Alfie. He drowned in the mill pond about the time of the Maori War—or was it the Matabele? But they couldn't prove suicide, so he ended up in the churchyard instead of at the crossroads. So Daft Alf's been walking again, has he? Hah!"

His friend came forward, turned his feverishly-bright eyes on Stirrup. "Now, in *our* case," he said, "there was no doubt at all. Prior to crashing our car into the ferro-concrete abutment, we left in triplicate a note explaining that it was an act of protest against the Welfare State which had, through usurpatious taxation, reduced us to penury."

"And furthermore had made the people so improvident that they no longer even desired to purchase the insurance policies which we were obliged to sell. And we *insisted* upon crossroads burial as a further gesture of defiance. But the wretched authorities said it would be a violation of both the Inhumation and Highways Acts. So—"

Stirrup felt the numbness creeping up his legs. "Then you are—then you were—"

The man with the revolver said, "Forgive my boorishness. Yes: I, my dear fellow, was Sir Sholto Shadwell, of Shadwell-upon-Stour; and this was Sir Peregrine de Pall of Pall Mall, Hants., my partner in the insurance agency to which these degenerate times had driven us. We were well known. The venal press often said of us that in our frequent pranks and japes we resembled characters from the novels of Rodney Stirrup more than we did real people. They used to call us—"

"They used to call us 'The Batty Baronets,' " said Sir Peregrine; "though I can't think why!"

Their laughter rang out loud and mirthlessly as Sir Sholto snapped the safety catch off on his revolver and Sir Peregrine slid away the casing from his sword cane.

"It grows so damn tedious back at the Baronets' Valhalla," one of them muttered sulkily, as they closed in.

Rodney Stirrup, suppressing the instinct which rose in every cell of him to flee shrieking down the lonely road across the moors, raised his hand and eyebrows.

"One moment, gentlemen—or should I not rather phrase it, 'Sirs Baronet'?"

"*Hem.* You should, yes." Sir Sholto let his revolver sink a trifle. Sir Peregrine, prodding a turf with the point of the sword, nodded portentously.

Straining very hard, Stirrup managed to produce the lineaments of gratified desire in the form of a thankful smile. "I am *so* glad to have that point cleared up. Burke's Peerage was of no help at all, you know."

"None whatsoever. Certainly not. *Burke's,* pah!" Sir Peregrine spitted the turf. A trifle uncertainly, he asked, "You had some, ah, special reason—"

Never since that frenzied but glorious week at Monte in the year '27, when deadlines of novels from three publishers were pressing upon him, had Rodney Stirrup improvised so rapidly. "A very, very special reason. I *had* intended, in my next novel, due to appear on Boatwright's spring list, to urge the election of a certain number of baronets to the House of Lords, in a manner similar to that of representative Scottish peers. Such a proposal could not fail to be of benefit. ("Certainly not!" said Sir Sholto.) But then the question arises, how is such a one to be addressed? 'The honorable member' obviously won't do. ("Won't do at all!" said Sir Peregrine.) What, then? *You,* with that erudition which has always characterized your rank—" the two hereditary knights coughed modestly and fiddled their weapons with a certain measure of embarrassment—"have supplied the answer: 'Sir Baronet.' " Stirrup allowed the smile to vanish, an easy task, and sighed.

"Mphh. I notice your use of the past pluperfect. '*Had* intended.' Eh?"

With a horrible start Stirrup noticed, just beyond the headlights' brightness, the silent approach of a company of men. Temper obviously in no way improved by the hole in his forehead, O'Donnell scowled hideously.

Speaking very rapidly, Stirrup said in a loud voice, "I am not to blame. The reading public little realize the small extent to which writers are their own masters. My own attitude in regard to baronets and, ah, butlers, was of no importance at all. *It was my publisher!* He laughs at butlers. Despises baronets. I give you my word. Indeed, I would freely admit how richly I deserve the punishment an ignoble government has failed to mete out to me for the slanders I have written—but I really could not help it. I was bound hand and foot by contracts. How many times have I stood there with tears in my eyes. 'Another bad butler,' demanded Boatwright. 'Another silly baronet,' Boatwright insisted. What could I do?"

There was a long silence. Then Peebles stepped forward. "It was very wrong of you, sir," he said. "But your weakness is not altogether beyond exculpation."

"Not altogether, no," conceded Sir Sholto, twisting a lock of his long, gray hair. "The second Sir Sholto, outraged by the filthy treatment accorded the proffered manuscript of his experiences in the Peninsular Wars, was in the habit of toasting Napoleon for having once shot a publisher."

"And quite properly, Sir Sholto," said Peebles. "*And* quite rightly."

"Never would've been allowed if the Duke of Cumberland hadn't been cozened out of the crown by Salic Law," said Sir Peregrine, moodily.

Peebles stiffened. "While it is true that a mere valet has not the status of a butler, and equally true that His Royal Highness (later King Ernest of Hanover) was absolved of guilt for having caused the death of his personal gentleman—"

"Who was a foreigner anyway," Stirrup put in; "taking bread from the mouths of honest British men, and doubtless richly deserved his fate. . . ."

Butlers and baronets, once the matter was put in this light, nodded judiciously.

"Therefore," said Peebles, "I propose a joint convocation of both Houses, as it were, to deal with the case of the Infamous Publisher Boatwright."

"Bugger the bastard with a rusty sword, you mean? And then splatter his tripes with a silver bullet or two?"

Peebles said that that was the precise tenor of his meaning, and he much admired Sir Sholto's vigorous way of phrasing it.

"Mr. Boatwright is at his country place not far from here at this very moment," Rodney Stirrup quickly pointed out. "The Mill Race, Little Chitterlings, near Guilford." He held his breath.

Then, "*Fiat justicia!*" exclaimed Peebles.

And, "St. George, no quarter, and perish publishers!" cried the baronets.

There was a diffident cough, and a large, pear-shaped man with prominent and red-rimmed eyes stepped forward. He looked at Stirrup and Stirrup felt his hair follicles retreat.

"If I may take the liberty, gentlemen," he said, with an air both diffident and determined.

"Hullo, hullo, what's this?" Peebles queried. "A newcomer to our ranks. Pray, silence, gentlemen: a maiden speech."

"It is not without misgivings that I feel obliged to pause *en route* to the Butlers' Valhalla and raise a rather unpleasant matter," said the newcomer. "I am Bloor, late butler to Jeremy Boatwright. Not being conversant with the latter's business affairs, I can neither confirm nor deny Mr. Stirrup's charges. However, I feel it my duty to point out that while Mr. Stirrup was for many years an annual week end guest at The Mill Race (Little Chitterlings, near Guilford), *he invariably failed to tip the butler on taking his departure!*"

There was a chorus of sharp, hissing, indrawn breaths. Lips were curled, eyebrows raised.

"Not the thing, not the thing at all," said Sir Peregrine. "Shoot butlers, yes, certainly. But—fail to tip them on leaving? Not done, simply not done."

"A loathsome offense," said Arbuthnot.

"Despicable," Peebles declared.

Stirrup, trembling, cried, "It was the fault of my publisher in not allowing me a proper share of royalties." But this was ill received.

"Won't do, won't do at all." Sir Sholto shook his head. "Can't scrape out of it that way a second time. If one's income obliges one to dine on fish and chips in a garret, then *dine* on fish and chips in a garret—dressing for dinner first, I need hardly add. But unless one is prepared to tip the butler, one simply does not accept week end invitations. By gad," he said furiously, "a chap who would do that would shoot foxes!"

"Afoot," said Sir Peregrine.

Bloor said it was not that he wished to be vindictive. It was purely out of duty to his profession that he now made public the offense which had rankled—nay, festered—so long in his bosom.

"I see nothing else for it," said Peebles, heavily, "but that Mr. Rodney Stirrup must occupy the lesser guest room at Butlers' Valhalla until his unspeakable dereliction be atoned for."

("Man's a rank outsider," huffed Sir Sholto. "And to think I was about to ask him to shoot with us when the were grouse season starts!")

The lesser guest room! In a sudden flash of dim, but all-sufficient, light, Stirrup saw what his fate must be. Henceforth his life was one long week end. His room would be the one farthest from the bath, his mattress irrevocably lumpy. The shaving water would always be cold, the breakfast invariably already eaten no matter how early he arose. His portion at meals would be the gristle; his wine (choked with lees), the worst of the off-vintage years. The cigar box was forever to be empty, and the whisky locked away . . .

His spirits broke. He quailed.

For a brief moment he sought comfort in the fate awaiting Boatwright. Then despair closed in again, and the most dreadful thought occurred to him. Sir Sholto Shadwell's silver bullets: ghosts, werewolves (and were grouse), vampires, ghouls—yes. But would they work, he wondered, despairingly, *could* they really work, on a creature infinitely more evil and ungodly? Was there anything of any nature in any world at all which could kill a publisher?

Dagon

INTRODUCTION BY JOHN CLUTE

There are stories which tell us they are something significant, and there are stories whose greatness slides into the back of the mind, where they explode in a sudden nectar of meaning. "Dagon," which is a genuinely great tale, is one of the latter. The quietude it generates in the reader is what a waterbug might feel floating in the meniscus above a hungry pike. Like the waterbug, readers of "Dagon" (1959) will find the ultimate meaning of their tale beneath the surface of events.

It is not, perhaps, an easy surface to penetrate. The story is told in the first person, by an American military officer who has arrived in Peking with fellow officers on 12 October 1945 as part—it would seem—of a liaison team. In a seeming aside, he mentions the lotos, which when crushed into wine engenders forgetfulness, and the plural form of which—lotoi—reminds him of Pierre Loti, who had also arrived in Peking, forty-five years earlier, on 12 October. The narrator tells of his slow immersion in the underlife of the great, half-destroyed, smouldering city; of his admiring thoughts on the "mystery of fish . . . , growing old without aging and enjoying eternal growth without the softness of obesity"; of his meeting with a Chinese police officer whom he corrupts, buys a concubine from, and has killed; of his earning money by selling faked drugs to Chinese buyers hungry for virility; of his meeting a Chinese magician who does magic tricks with a goldfish caught in a bowl, and who seems to be his concubine's father-in-law; and of his final retreat into what might seem to be a lotos-eater's torpor.

What has actually "happened," within the element which has become his world, is that the narrator has taken on the role of Dagon, the half-fish god worshipped by the Philistines after they arrived in Canaan. But after he has sinned irrecoverably, the Chinese magician has magicked away his human parts, *transforming him into a great carplike goldfish in the bowl of hell. All he can see is "a flashing of gold," which is nothing but a mirror-effect, nothing but the gold scales of bondage which flash when he moves his fins. "But when I am still I cannot see it at all."*

Without seeming to say a word about itself, "Dagon" proves to be a tale—a labyrinth of a tale—about good and evil, usurpation (the narrator refers to himself as "porphyrogenitive"), hubris and punishment and hell. It is as vicious as the world of a fish, and wise. It is masterly. Like the best stories of Gene Wolfe—whose work resembles "Dagon" at times—it cannot be read. It can only be re-read.

Then the Lords of the Philistines gathered together to rejoice before Dagon their god, and behold, the image of Dagon was fallen upon its face to the ground, with both his face and his hands broken off, and only the fishy part of Dagon was left to him. . . .

THE OLD CHINESE, HALF-MAGICIAN, half-beggar, who made the bowl of goldfish vanish and appear again, this old man made me think of the Aztecs and the wheel. Or gunpowder. Gunpowder appeared in Western Europe and Western Europe conquered the world with it. Gunpowder had long ago been known in China and the Chinese made firecrackers with it. (They have since learned better.) When I was free, I heard men say more than once that the American Indians did not know the use of the wheel until Europeans introduced it. But I have seen a toy, pre-Conquest, fashioned from clay, which showed that the Aztecs knew the use of the wheel. They made toys of it. Firecrackers. Vanishing goldfish.

Noise.

Light and darkness.

The bright lotos blossoms in the dark mire. Lotos. Plural, lotoi? Loti? That is a coincidence. On October 12, 1900, Pierre Loti left at Taku the French naval vessel which had brought him to China, and proceeded to Peking. Part of that city was still smoking, Boxers and their victims were still lying in the ruins. On October 12, 1945, I left the American naval vessel which had brought me and my fellow officers to China, and proceeded to Peking—Peiping, as they called it then. I was not alone, the whole regiment came; the people turned out and hailed and glorified us. China, our friend and partner in the late great struggle. The traffic in women, narcotics, stolen goods, female children? Merely the nation's peculiar institution. Great is China, for there I was made manifest.

Old, old, old . . . crumbling temples, closed-off palaces, abandoned yamens. Mud-colored walls with plaster crumbling off them reached a few feet over a man's head and lined the alleys so that if a gate was closed all that could be seen was the rooftop of a one-story building or the upper lineage of a tree, and if a gate was open, a tall screen directly in front of it blocked the view except for tiny glimpses of flagstone-paved courtyards and plants in huge glazed pots. Rich and poor and in between and shabby genteel lived side by side, and there was no way of knowing if the old man in dun-colored rags who squatted by a piece of matting spread with tiny paper squares holding tinier heaps of tea or groups of four peanuts or ten watermelon seeds was as poor as he and his trade seemed, or had heaps of silver taels buried underneath the fourth tile from the corner near the stove. Things were seldom what they seemed. People feared to tempt powers spiritual or temporal or illegal by displays of well being, and the brick screens blocked both the gaze of the curious and the path of demons—demons can travel only in straight lines; it is the sons of men whose ways are devious.

Through these backways and byways I used to roam each day. I had certain hopes and expectations based on romantic tales read in adolescence, and was bound that the Cathayans should not disappoint. When these alleys led into commercial streets, as they did sooner or later, I sought what I sought there as well. It is not too difficult to gain a command of spoken Mandarin, which is the dialect of Peking. The throaty sound which distinguishes, for example, between *lee-dza*, peaches, and *lee'dza*, chestnuts, is soon mastered. The more southerly dialects have eleven or nineteen or some such fantastic number of inflections, but Pekingese has only four. Moreover, in the south it is hot and steamy and the women have flat noses.

In one of my wanderings I came to the ponds where the carp had been raised for the Imperial table in days gone by. Strange, it was, to realize that some of the great fish slowly passing up and down among the lily pads must have been fed from the bejeweled hands of Old Buddha herself—and that others, in all likelihood (huge they were, and vast), not only outdated the Dowager but may well have seen—like some strange, billowing shadow above the watersky—Ch'ien Lung the Great: he who deigned to "accept tribute" from Catherine of Russia—scattering rice cake like manna.

I mused upon the mystery of fish, their strange and mindless beauty, how—innocently evil—they prey upon each other, devouring the weaker and smaller without rage or shout or change of countenance. There, in the realm of water, which is also earth and air to them, the great fish passed up and down, growing old without aging and enjoying eternal growth without the softness of obesity. It was a world without morality, a world without choices, a world of eating and spawning and growing great. I envied the great fish, and (in other, smaller ponds) the lesser fish, darting and flashing and sparkling gold.

They speak of "the beast in man," and of "the law of the jungle." Might they not (so I reflected, strolling underneath a sky of clouds as blue and as white as the tiles and marble of the Altar of Heaven), might they not better speak of "the fish in man"? And of "the law of the sea"? The sea, from which they say we came . . . ?

Sometimes, but only out of sociability, I accompanied the other officers to the singsong houses. A man is a fool who cannot accommodate himself to his fellows enough to avoid discomfort. But my own tastes did not run to spilled beer and puddles of inferior tea and drink-thickened voices telling tales of prowess, nor to grinning lackeys in dirty robes or short sessions in rabbit warren rooms with bodies which moved and made sounds and asked for money but showed no other signs of sentient life.

Once, but once only, we visited the last of the Imperial barber-eunuchs, who had attended to the toilet of the Dowager's unfortunate nephew; a tall old man, this castrate, living alone with his poverty, he did for us what he would for any others who came with a few coins and a monstrous curiosity.

I mingled, also, officially and otherwise, with the European colony, none of whom had seen Europe for years, many of whom had been born in China. Such jolly Germans! Such cultured Italians! Such pleasant spoken, *çi-devant* Vichy, Frenchmen! How well dressed and well kept their women were, how anxious, even eager, to please, to prove their devotion to the now victorious cause—and to the young and potent and reasonably personable officers who represent it.

After many an afternoon so well spent, I would arise and take a ricksha to one of the city gates to be there at the sunset closing, and would observe how, when half the massy portal was swung shut, the traffic would increase and thicken and the sound of cries come from far down the road which led outside the city and a swollen stream pour and rush faster and faster—men and women on foot and clutching bundles, and carriers with sedan chairs, and families leading heavily laden ox-carts and horses, children with hair like manes, trotting women swollen in pregnancy, old women staggering on tiny-bound feet, infants clinging to their bent backs. The caravans alone did not increase their pace at this time. Slow, severe, and solemn, woolly, double-humped, padfooted, blunt, their long necks shaking strings of huge blue beads and bronze bells crudely cast at some distant forge in the Gobi or at the shore of Lop Nor, the camels came. By their sides were skullcapped Turkomen, or Buryat-Mongols with their hair in thick queues.

My eyes scanned every face and every form in all this, but I did not find what I looked for.

Then I would go and eat, while the gates swung shut and the loungers dispersed, murmuring and muttering of the *Bah Loo*, the said to be approaching slowly but steadily and as yet undefeated *Bah Loo*, the Communist Eighth Route Army; and the air grew dark and cold.

One afternoon I chose to visit some of the temples—not the well-frequented ones such as those of Heaven, Agriculture, Confucius, and the La-mas—the ones not on the tourist lists, not remarkable for historical monuments, not preserved (in a manner of speaking) by any of the governments which had held Peking since the days of "the great" Dr. Sun. In these places the progress of decay had gone on absolutely unchecked and the monks had long ago sold everything they could and the last fleck of paint had peeled from the idols. Here the clergy earned corn meal (rice in North China was a delicacy, not a staple) by renting out the courtyards for monthly fairs and charging stud fees for the services of their Pekingese dogs. Worshipers were few and elderly. Such, I imagine, must have been the temples in the last days of Rome while the Vandal and Goth equivalents of the Eighth Route Army made plans to invest the city at their leisure.

These ancients were pleased to see me and brought bowls of thin tea and offered to sell me dog-eared copies of pornographic works, poorly illustrated, which I declined.

Later, outside, in the street, there was an altercation between a huge and pock-marked ricksha "boy" and a Marine. I stepped up to restore order—could not have avoided it, since the crowd had already seen me—and met the Man in Black.

I do not mean a foreign priest.

The coolie was cuffed and sent his way by the Man in Black, and the Marine told to go elsewhere by me. The Man in Black seemed quite happy at my having come along—the incident could have gotten out of hand—and he stuck to me and walked with me and spoke to me loudly in poor English and I suffered it because of the face he would gain by having been seen with me. Of course, I knew what he was, and he must have known that I knew. I did not relish the idea of yet another pot of thin tea, but he all but elbowed me into his home.

Where my search ended.

The civil police in Peking were nothing, nothing at all. The Japanese Army had not left much for them to do, nor now did the Chinese Nationalist Army nor the U.S. Forces, MPs and SPs. So the Peking police force directed traffic and cuffed recalcitrant ricksha coolies and collected the pittance which inflation made nothing of.

Black is not a good color for uniforms, nor does it go well with a sallow skin.

She was not sallow.

I drank cup after cup of that vile, unsugared tea, just to see her pour it.

Her nose was not flat.

When he asked her to go and borrow money to buy some cakes, not knowing that I could understand, I managed to slip him money beneath the table: he was startled and embarrassed at this as well. After that, the advantage was even more mine.

She caught my glance and the color deepened in her cheeks. She went for the cakes.

He told me his account of woes, how his father (a street mountebank of some sort) had starved himself for years in order to buy him an appointment on the police force and how it had come to nothing at all, salary worth nothing, cumshaw little more. How he admired the Americans—which was more than I did myself. Gradually, with many diversions, circumlocutions, and euphuisms, he inquired about the chances of our doing some business.

Of course, I agreed.

She returned.

I stayed long; she lighted the peanut oil lamps and in the stove made a small fire of briquettes fashioned from coal dust and—I should judge, by a faint but definite odor—dung.

After that I came often, and we made plans; I named sums of money which caused his mouth to open—a sight to sell dentifrice, indeed. Then, when his impatience was becoming irritating, I told him the whole thing was off—military vigilance redoubled at the warehouses, so on. I made a convincing story.

He almost wept. He had debts, he had borrowed money (on his hopes) to pay them.

No one could have been more sympathetic than I.

I convinced him that I wished only to help him.

Then, over several dinner tables I told him that I was planning to take a concubine shortly. My schedule, naturally, would leave less time for these pleasant conversations and equally pleasant dinners. The woman was not selected yet, but this should not take long.

Finally, the suggestion came from *him*, as I had hoped it would, and I let him convince me. This was the only amusing part of the conversation.

I suppose he must have convinced *her*.

I paid him well enough.

There was the apartment to furnish, and other expenses, clothes for her, what have you. Expenses. So I was obliged to do some business after all. But not, of course, with *him*. The sulfa deal was dull enough, even at the price I got per tablet, but the thought of having sold the blood plasma as an elixir for aging Chinese vitality (masculine) was droll beyond words.

So my life began, my real life, for which the rest had been mere waiting and anticipation, and I feel the same was true of her. What had she known of living? He had bought her as I had bought her, but my teeth were not decayed, nor did I have to borrow money if I wanted cakes for tea.

In the end he became importunate and it was necessary to take steps to dispense with him. Each state has the sovereign right, indeed the duty, to protect its own existence; thus, if bishops plot against the Red governments or policemen against the Kuomintang government, the results are inevitable.

He had plotted against *me*.

The curious thing is that she seemed genuinely sorry to hear that he'd been shot, and as she seemed more beautiful in sorrow, I encouraged her. When she seemed disinclined to regard this as the right moment for love, I humbled her. In the end she came to accept this as she did to accept everything I did, as proper, simply because it was I who had done it.

I.

She was a world which I had created, and behold, it was very good.

My fellow officers continued, some of them, their joint excursions to the stews of Ch'ien Men. Others engaged in equally absurd projects, sponsoring impecunious students at the Protestant university, or underwriting the care of orphans at the local convent schools. I even accompanied my immediate superior to tea one afternoon and gravely heard the Anglican bishop discuss the moral regeneration of mankind, after which he told some capital stories which he had read in *Punch* several generations ago. With equal gravity I made a contribution to the old man's Worthy Cause of the moment. Afterwards she and I went out in my jeep and had the chief lama show us the image of a jinni said to be the superior of rhinoceros horn in the amorous pharmacopoeia, if one only indulged him in a rather high priced votive lamp which burned butter. The old Tibetan, in his sales talk, pointed out to us the "Passion Buddha's" four arms, with two of which he held the female figure, while feeding her with the other two; but neither this, nor the third thing he was doing, interested me as much as his head. It was a bull's head, huge, brutal, insensate, glaring. . . .

If I am to be a god, I will be such a god as this, I thought; part man and part . . . bull? No—but what? Part man and—

I took her home, that she might worship Me.

Afterwards, she burned the brass butter lamps before Me, and the sticks of incense.

I believe it was the following day that we saw the old Chinese. We were dining in a White Russian restaurant, and from the unusual excellence of the food and the way the others looked at Me I could sense that awareness of My true Nature, and Its approaching epiphany, was beginning to be felt.

The persimmons of Peking are not like the American persimmons; they are larger and flattened at each end. In order for the flavor to be at its best, the fruits must have begun to rot. The top is removed and cream is put on, heavy cream which has begun to turn sour. This is food fit for a god and I was the only one present who was eating it. The Russians thought that persimmons were only for the Chinese, and the Chinese did not eat cream.

There was an American at the next table, in the guise of an interfering angel, talking about famine relief. The fool did not realize that famine is itself a relief, better even than war, more selective in weeding out the unfit and reducing the surfeit of people from which swarming areas such as China and India are always suffering. I smiled as I heard him, and savored the contrast between the sweet and the sour on My spoon, and I heard her draw in her breath and I looked down and there was the old Chinese, in his smutty robe and with some object wrapped in grimed cloth next to him as he squatted on the floor. I heard her murmur something to him in Chinese; she greeted him, called him *lau-yay*—old master or sir—and something else which I knew I knew but could not place. The air was thick with cigarette smoke and cheap scent. The fool at the next table threw the old man some money and gestured him to begin.

His appearance was like that of any beggar, a wrinkled face, two or three brown teeth showing when he smiled in that fawning way. He unwrapped his bundle and it was an empty chinaware bowl and two wooden wands. He covered the bowl with cloth again, rapped it with wands, uncovered it, and there was a goldfish swimming. He covered, he rapped and rapped and whisked away the cloth and the bowl was gone. I darted My foot out to the place where it had been, but there was nothing there.

The American at the next table spread out a newspaper on the floor, the old man rolled his sleeves up his withered, scrannel, pallid-sallow arms; he spread the cloth, struck it with his sticks, and then removed it, showing a much larger bowl with the goldfish, on top of the newspaper. So it had not come from some recess in the floor, nor from his sleeve. I did not like to see anyone else exercising power; I spoke roughly to the old man, and he giggled nervously and gathered his things together. The fools opposite began to protest, I looked at them and their voices died away. I looked at *her*, to see if she would still presume to call him *old master;* but she was My creation and she laughed aloud at him and this pleased Me.

My powers increased; with drops of ink I could kill and I could make alive. The agents of the men of Yenan came to Me at night and I wrote things for them and they left offerings of money on the table.

Infinitely adaptive, I, polymorphous, porphyrogenitive, creating iniquity, transgression, and sin.

But sometimes at night, when they had left and we had gone to bed and I pretended to sleep as others, sometimes there was a noise of a faint rattling and I saw something in the room turning and flashing, like a flash of gold, and the shadows loomed like the shadow of an old man. And once it came to Me—the meaning of the Chinese words she had used once. They meant *father-in-law,* but I could not remember when she had used them, though distantly I knew she had no more husband. I awoke her and made her worship Me and I was infinitely godlike.

When was this? Long ago, perhaps. It seems that I do not remember as well as formerly. There is so little to remember of present life. I have withdrawn from the world. I do not really know where I now am. There is a wall of some sort, it extends everywhere I turn, it is white, often I press my lips against it. I have lips. I do not know if I have hands and feet, but I do not need them. The light, too, has an odd quality here. Sometimes I seem to be in a small place and at other times it seems larger. And in between these times something passes overhead and all goes dark and there is a noise like the beating of heavy staves and then it is as if I am nothing . . . no place . . . But then all is as before and there is light once more and I can move freely through the light, up and down; I can turn, and when I turn swiftly I can see a flashing of gold, of something gold, and this pleases and diverts Me.

But when I am still I cannot see it at all.

Ogre in the Vly

INTRODUCTION BY PETER S. BEAGLE

Having reached the stage of life where I am perfectly willing to believe anything *of academics, I take a special personal delight in this lesser-known tale of Avram's. Its libelous suggestion of the lengths to which a museum director might go to protect his career isn't, of course, the only reason that I'm so fond of this story. I love its central notion, which I find hauntingly credible, as so many of Avram's modest proposals and almost-theories so often are. (For further reference—not to mention a lifetime's worth of truly wondrous delight—get at any cost, financial or moral, a copy of* Adventures in Unhistory, *published by George Scithers' Owlswick Press in 1993.)*

And then there's the damn language *again. . . . It isn't so much that Professor Sanzmann endearingly says "Chairmany" for Germany, or "walley" for valley. It's that he refers to "the nexten walley," and to peasants who "huddle fearingly together," as he would if he were translating himself directly from the German as he goes along. Avram is never wrong about stuff like that, not even when the translation is from a language that doesn't exist. I know I keep saying it, but when it comes to pure sensitivity to the human use of words, the man has few peers and no equals.*

Without wishing to give away the kicker of the story-within-a-story that propels "The Ogre," let me say that in recent years similar speculations, developed at lumbering wide-screen length, have become something of a cottage industry. For poignancy and provocativeness, I'll back this small jewel of a tale against any of them.

OGRE IN THE VLY

WHEN THE MENACE OF Dr. Ludwig Sanzmann first arose, like a cloud no bigger than a man's hand, Dr. Fred B. Turbyfil, at twenty-seven, had been the youngest museum director in the country; and now at thirty-five he was still one of the youngest. Moreover, he had a confident, if precarious, hold on greater glories to come. High on the list of benefactors and patrons, Mr. Winfield Scott H. Godbody was an almost-dead (in more ways than one) certainty to will most of his substance to what would then become the Godbody Museum of Natural History: Dr. Fred B. Turbyfil, Director. The salary would be splendid, the expense account lavish and tax-free, and the Director would have ample time to finish his great work, at present entitled *Man Before the Dawn*—recondite, yet eminently readable. There were already seventeen chapters devoted to the Mousterian, or Neanderthal, Era alone. (It would be certain to sell forever to schools and libraries: a big book, firm in the grasp, profusely illustrated and done in so captivating a style that even a high school senior, picking it up unwarily in search of nudes, would be unable to extricate himself for hours.)

Mr. Godbody was a skeptic of the old-fashioned sort. "Where did Cain get his wife?" was a favorite cackle, accompanied by a nudge of his bony elbow. "Found any feathers from angels' wings yet?" was another.

He had pioneered in supplying cotton prints to flour millers for sacking. The brand name washed out, the figured cloth was then used for underwear and children's dresses by the thrifty farmers. This had made him a wealthy man, and increased his devotion to Science—the Science which had destroyed the cosmogony of the M.E. Church, South, and invented washable ink.

There was, at the moment, a minor hitch. Old Mr. Godbody affected to be shaken by the recent revelation of scandal in the anthropological hierarchy. From this respectable group, whose likenesses were known to every school child, long since having replaced Major and Minor Prophets alike in prestige and esteem, from this jolly little club—judgment falling like a bolt of thunder—the Piltdown Man had been expelled for cheating at cards. If Piltdown Man was a fake, he demanded querulously, why not all the rest? Java Man, Peiping Man, *Australopithecus tranvalensis*—all bone-scraps, plaster of Paris, and wishful thinking? In vain, Turbyfil assured him that competent scholars had been leery of H. Piltdown for years; ugly old Mr. Godbody testily replied, "Then why didn't you say so?" Having lost one faith in his youth, the textile print prince was reluctant to lose another in his old age. But Dr. Turbyfil trusted his patron's doubt was only a passing phase. His chief anxiety, a well-modulated one, was whether Mr. Godbody's health would carry him over the few weeks or months necessary to get past this crochet.

In sum, Dr. Turbyfil was about to reap the rewards of virtue and honest toil, and when he reflected on this (as he often did) it amused him to sing—a trifle off-key—a song from his childhood, called "Bringing in the Sheaves." Prior to his coming to Holden, the museum—an architectural gem of the purest late Chester A. Arthur—had been headed by a senile, though deserving, Democrat, who had been washed into office on the high tide of the Free Silver movement. *And* the museum itself! Dr. Turbyfil found that every worthless collection of unsalable junk in the state made its way thither. Postage stamps of the sort sold by the pound on Nassau Street, stuffed and moldering opossums, tinted photographs of wall-eyed pioneers, hand-painted "china," unclassified arrowheads by the gross, buttons from Confederate uniforms, legislative gavels, mounted fish, geological "specimens" collected by people with no faintest knowledge of geology, tomahawks—oh, there was no end to the stuff.

That is, there had been no end to the stuff until the appointment of Dr. Fred B. Turbyfil . . . the trash still continued to come in, of course: there was no tactful way of stopping that. There were still many people to whom it seemed, when Uncle Tatum died, that the natural thing to do with Uncle Tatum's "collection" was to ship it to the Holden Museum. Dr. Turbyfil had developed his own technique of handling such shipments. He had then arranged—at night—in as many showcases as might be needed, prominently labeled with the donors' names; then he had the works photographed. To the contributory family, a gracious letter of thanks. To their local newspaper, a copy of the letter. To both family and paper, a Manila envelope of glossy prints. And then, for Uncle Tatum's musty nonsense, tomahawks and all, the blessed oblivion of the cellars. ("We are recataloguing," Dr. T. explained to the few inquirers.)

(But you couldn't put Dr. Sanzmann in the cellar, could you?)

The letters of thanks were worded in phrases as unchanging as a Buddhist litany. They extolled the career of the dead pioneer, gave proper credit to the sense of public interest displayed by his heirs, and hoped that their concern for the Important Work of the Holden Museum would be shared by others. The liturgical response was seldom wanting, and took the form of a check, the amount of which was, as Dr. Turbyfil had lightly pointed out, Deductable From Income Tax. *Om mani padme hum!*

Ah, that was a day when they opened the Hall of Practical Science! The governor, the senior U.S. senator, university presidents, hillbilly singers, and other public figures—scores of them. There was a real oil pump that pumped real oil, and a genuine cotton gin that ginned genuine cotton. It was the machines which set the tone for the exhibits, but Dr. Turbyfil was proudest of the huge photographic montages, mounted to give a three-dimensional effect. There was one of Mr. Opie Slawson (Slawson Oil and Natural Gas) pointing to the oil pool on the cross section (in natural color) of a typical oiliferous area. There was another of Mr. Purvie Smith (P.S. Cotton and P.S. Food Products) watching his prize steers nuzzle cottonseed cake while replicas of the lean kine of Egypt stared hungrily at a clump of grass. There were others. And how the checks had come in! And continued to come!

(*But Doktor Philosoph. Ludwig Sanzmann was coming, too.*)

Months of preparation had gone into what was, after all, really just a prestige exhibit—the display of Bouche Perce Indian life before the Coming of the White Man. A huge semi-circular backdrop gave the illusion of distance. Buffalo grazed conveniently not too far away, and wild horses galloped along a hill crest. The primitive Bouche Perces ground corn, played games, scraped hides, wove weavings, put on war paint, rocked papooses, and received the non-socialized ministrations of the tribal medicine man. There were authentic wickiups, simulated campfires, and a bona fide buffalo skull.

The Bouche Perces (who were "Oil Indians") drove up in their Packards from miles around, and received such a boost in tribal pride that they shortly afterward filed suit for thirty million dollars against the Federal Government. (They were finally awarded a judgment of four million, most of which the Government deducted to cover the expense of itself in allowing the Bouche Perces to be swindled, cheated, and starved for the three generations preceding the discovery of oil.) The Tribal Council voted to make the museum the custodian of its ceremonial regalia, and Dr. Turbyfil received several honorary degrees and was made a member of learned societies. The only opposition to his efforts on behalf of American Indian culture came from the oldest (and only surviving pure-blood) Bouche Perce. Her name was Aunt Sally Weatherall, she was a prominent member of the Baptist Ladies Auxiliary, and she steadfastly refused his offer to be photographed with her in front of all them Heathen Reliets and Nekked Women. She also added that if her old granddaddy had ever caught any Bouche Perce a-weaving *Navaho* blankets like that huzzy in the pitcher, he'd of slit her wizzand.

The trouble was that Aunt Sally Weatherall *wouldn't* come, and Dr. Sanzmann *would*. Any minute now.

Dr. Turbyfil had been expecting this visit for years. Dr. Sanzmann had mentioned it at every meeting. Sometimes his tones were bright and arch, sometimes they were gloomy and foreboding and sometimes they were flat and brusque.

The two men had come to Holden within a few months of one another, Dr. Turbyfil from his two-year stay at the Museum of Natural Philosophy in Boston, and Professor Sanzmann from a meager living translating in New York, whither he had come as an exile from his native country. Sanzmann was politically quite pure, with no taint of either far right or near left; was, in fact, a Goethe scholar—and what can be purer than a Goethe scholar? He had a post at the local denominational university: Professor of Germanic *and* Oriental Languages, neatly skipping the questionable Slavs. Dr. Turbyfil was not an ungenerous man, and he was quite content to see Professor Sanzmann enjoy the full measure of linguistic success.

But Dr. Philosoph. Ludwig Sanzmann was also an amateur anthropologist, paleontologist, and general antiquarian: and this was enough to chill the blood of any museum director or even curator. Such amateurs are occupational hazards. They bring one smelly cow bone, and do it with a proud air of expectancy, fully anticipating the pronouncement of a new species of megatherium or brontosaurus. Although Dr. Sanzmann had not—so far—done *that,* he often put Turbyfil in mind of the verse,

"A little learning is a dangerous thing;
Drink deeply or touch not the Whozis Spring."

Ah, well, better to have it over with and done. It would be necessary to take a firm line, and then—finished! No more hints of precious secrets, world-shaking discoveries, carefully guarded treasures, and so on.

When the Professor arrived, Dr. Turbyfil ran his left hand rapidly across his waving brown hair—still thick, praise be!—smiled his famous warm and boyish smile, held his right hand out in welcome. But with horror he saw that Sanzmann had a cardboard carton with him. The worst! Oh, the things one has to put up with . . . ! If not Mr. Godbody, then Professor—

"My dear Dr. Turbyfil! I have looked forward to this our meeting for so long! I cannot tell you—" But, of course, he would. He shook the proffered hand, sat down, held the carton as if it contained wedding cake, took out a handkerchief, wiped his rosy face, and panted. Then he began to speak.

"Dr. Turbyfil!" The name assumed the qualities of an indictment. "What is that which they used always to tell us? Urmensch—Primal Man, that is—he was a stunted little cre-a-ture, like a chimpanzee with a molybdenum deficiency, and he—which is to say, *we*—grew larger and bigger and more so, until, with the help of the actuarial tables of the insurance companies, we have our present great size attained and life expectancy. And we, pres-u-mably, will greater grow yet.

"*But!*" (Dr. Turbyfil quivered.) "What then comes to pass? An anthropologist goes into an Apotheke—a druck-store, yes?—in Peiping—oh, a bea-u-tiful city, I have been there, I love it with all my heart!—he goes into a native Chinese pharmacy, and there what is it that he finds? He finds—amongst the dried dragon bones, powdered bats, tigers' gall, rhinoceros horn, and pickled serpents—two human-like gigantic molar teeths. And then, behold, for this is wonderful! The whole picture changes!"

Oh my, oh my! thought Dr. Turbyfil.

"Now Primal Man becomes huge, tremendous, like the Sons of Anak in the First Moses-Book. We must now posit for him ancestors like the great apes of your Edgar Burroughs-Rice. And how it is that we, his children, have shrunken! Pit-i-ful! Instead of the pigs becoming elephants, the elephants are becoming pigs!" Dr. Sanzmann clicked his tongue.

"But that is nothing! Nothing at all: Wherefore have I come to you now? To make known to you a something that is so much more startling. I must begin earlier than our own times. Charles the Fifth!"

~~Dr. Turbyfil quavered. "I beg your pardon?"~~

"Charles the Fifth of Hapsburg. In 1555 Charles the Emperor resigns, no, retires? Abdicates. His brother Ferdinand succeeds him as sovereign of the Hapsburg dominions, and Charles retreats himself to a monastery.

" 'With age, with cares, with maladies oppres't,

" 'He seeks the refuge of monastic rest—' "

"Ahhh, Professor *Sanzmann*," Dr. Turbyfil began, stopped, blinked.

"Yes—yes: I *di*-gress. Well. Charles and Ferdinand. A medallion is struck, Charles, one side—Ferdinand the other. And the date, 1555. Here is the medallion." Dr. Sanzmann reached into an inner pocket and pulled out a flat little box, such as jewelers use. He opened it.

Inside lay a blackened disk about the size of a silver dollar, and a piece of paper with two rubbings—the profiles of two men, Latin mottoes, and the date: 1555. Completely at sea, and feeling more and more sorry for himself, Dr. Turbyfil looked at his rosy-faced and gray-haired caller; made a small, bewildered gesture.

"Soon, soon, you will understand everything. Nineteen thirty. My vacations—I am still in Chair-many—I spend at Maldenhausen, a little rural hamlet in a walley. Then things are quiet. Ah, these Chairman walleys! So green, remote, enchanting, full of mysteries! I drink beer and wine, I smoke my pipe, and go on long walks in the countryside. And—since I am a scholar, and ever the dog returns to his womit—I spend also some time in the willage archives . . . Many interesting things . . . A child named Simon.

"In 1555 a child named Simon is stolen by an ogre."

Dr. Turbyfil pressed a fist to his forehead and moaned faintly. "Is—*what?*" he said, fretfully.

"Please. You see the hole in the medallion? The child Simon wore it about his neck on a thong. They were very reverend, these peasant people. An Imperial medallion, one wears it on one's bosom. A photostatic copy of the testimony." Professor Sanzmann opened the box, removed papers. Photostatic copies, indeed, were among them, but the language was a monkish Latin, and in Gothic lettering. Dr. Turbyfil felt his eyes begin to hurt him, closed them. Professor Sanzmann, dreadful man, spoke on. There were two witnesses, an old man of the name Sigismund, a boy called Lothar. It was winter. It was snow. The child Simon runs with his dog down the field. He shouts. He is afraid. Out of the snow behind him the ogre comes. He is just as they always knew ogres to be: huge, hairy, crooked, clad in skins, carrying a cudgel. Terrible.

"Lothar runs for help. The old man cannot run, so he stays. And prays. The ogre seizes up the child Simon and runs away with him, back into the fields, toward the hills, until the snow hides them.

"The people are aroused, they are fearful, but not surprised. This happens. There are wolves, there are bears, there are ogres. Such are the hazards of living on the remote farms."

Dr. Turbyfil shivered. A chill crept into his flesh. He rubbed his fingers to warm them. "Folklore," he croaked. "Old wives' tales."

Dr. Sanzmann waved his hands, then placed them on the photostats. "This is not the Brothers Grimm," he said. "These are contemporary accounts with eyewitnesses. I continue. The people go out in the storm, with dogs and pikes and even a few matchlocks; and since they huddle fearingly together and the snow has hid all footmarks, it is not a surprise that they do not find the child or the ogre's spoor. The dog, yes—but he is quite dead. Crushed. One tremendous blow. The next day they search, and then the next, and then no more. Perhaps in the spring they will find some bones for Christian burial . . .

"The child had been warned that if he went too far from home he would be stolen by an ogre. He *did* go too far from home, and he *was* stolen by an ogre. So. Fifteen sixty."

Dr. Turbyfil ventured a small smile. "The child has been dead for five years." He felt better now that he knew what was in the carton. He visualized the card which would never, certainly *never,* be typed! *"Bones of child devoured by ogre in 1555. Gift of Prof. Ludwig Sanzmann, Dr. Phil."*

The Goethe scholar swept on. "In 1560 the child Simon," he said, "is discovered trying to pilfer fowls from a farmyard in the nexten walley. He is naked, filthy, long-haired, lousy. He growls and cannot speak coherent speech. He fights. It is very sad."

The museum director agreed that it was very sad. (Then what *was* in the carton?)

"Child Simon is tied, he is delivered up to his parents, who must lock him in a room to keep him from escaping. Gradually he learns to speak again. And then comes to see him the Burgomeister, and the notary, and the priest, and the Baron, and I should imagine half the people of the district, and they ask him to tell his story, speaking ever the truth.

"The ogre (he says) carried him away very distantly and high up, to his cave, and there in his cave is his wife the ogress, and a small ogre, who is their child. At first Simon fears they will consume him, but no. He is brought to be a companion to the ogre child, who is ill. And children are adaptive, very adaptive. Simon plays with the ogre child, and the ogre brings back sheep and wenison and other foods. At first it is hard for Simon to eat the raw meat, so the ogress chews it soft for him—"

"Please!" Dr. Turbyfil held up a protesting hand, but Professor Sanzmann neither saw nor heard him. With gleaming eyes gazing into the distance he went on.

"It comes the spring. The ogre family sports in the forest, and Simon with him. Then comes again the autumn and winter and at last the ogre child dies. It is sad. The parents cannot believe it. They moan to him. They rock him in their arms. No use. They bury him finally beneath the cave floor. *Now* you will ask," he informed the glassy-eyed Turbyfil, "do they smear the body with red ocher as a symbol of life, of blood and flesh, as our scientists say? No. And why not? Because he is already smeared. All of them. All the time. They like it so. It is not early religion, it is early cosmetic, only."

He sighed. Dr. Turbyfil echoed it.

"And so, swiftly pass the years," Professor Sanzmann patted his hand on the empty air to indicate the passing years. "The old ogre is killed by a she-bear and then the ogress will not eat. She whimpers and clasps Simon to her,

~~and presently she grows cold and is dead. He is alone. The rest we know.~~ Simon grows up, marries, has children, dies. But there are no more ogres.

"Not ever.

"Naturally, I am fascinated. I ask the peasants, where is there a cave called the Cave of the Ogres? They look at me with slanting glances, but will not answer. I am patient. I come back each summer. Nineteen thirty-one. Nineteen thirty-two. Nineteen thirty-three. Everyone knows me. I give small presents to the children. By myself I wander in the hills and search for caves. Nineteen thirty-four. There is a cow-tending child in the high pastures. We are friends. I speak of a cave near there. This, I say, is called Cave of the Ogres. The child laughs. No, no, he says, for that is another cave: it is located thus and so.

"And I find it where he says. But I am circumspect. I wait another year. Then I come and I make my private excavations. And—I—find—this."

He threw open the carton and unwrapped from many layers of cotton wool something brown and bony, and he set it in front of Dr. Turbyfil.

"There was a fairly complete skeleton, but I took just the skull and jaw-bone. You recognize it at once, of course. And with it I found, as I expected, the medallion of Charles and Ferdinand. Simon had allowed them to bury it with the ogre child because he had been fond of it. It is all written in the photostatic paper copies . . . In 1936 the Nazis—"

Dr. Turbyfil stared at the skull. "No, no, no, no," he whispered. It was not a very large skull. "No, no, no," he whispered, staring at the receding forehead and massive chinless jaw, the bulging eye ridges.

"So, tell me now, sir museum director: Is this not a find more remarkable than big teeths in a Peiping herb shop?" His eyes seemed very young, and very bright.

Dr. Turbyfil thought rapidly. It needed just something like this to set the Sunday supplements and Mr. Godbody ablaze and ruin forever both his reputation and that of the Holden Museum. Years and years of work—the seventeen chapters on the Mousterian Era alone in *Man Before the Dawn*—the bequest from old Mr. Godbody—

Then the thought sprang fully-formed in his mind: Where there had been *one* skeleton, there must be others, unspoiled by absurd sixteenth-century paraphernalia—which had no business being there, anyway. He arose, placed a hand on Professor Sanzmann's shoulder.

"My friend," he said, in warm, golden, dulcet tones. "My friend, it will take some time before the Sanzmann Expedition of the Holden Museum will be ready to start. While you make the necessary personal preparations to lead us to the site of your truly astounding discovery, please oblige me by saying nothing about this to our—alas—unscholarly and often sensational press. Eh?"

Dr. Sanzmann's rosy face broke into a thousand wrinkles and tears of joy and gratitude rolled down his cheeks. Dr. Turbyfil generously pretended not to see.

"Imagine what a revolution this will produce," he said, as if he were thinking aloud. "Instead of being tidily extinct for fifty thousand years, our poor cousins survived into modern times. Fantastic! Our whole timetable will have to be rewritten . . ." His voice died away. His eyes focused on Professor Sanz-mann, nodding his head, sniffling happily, as he tied up his package.

"Incidentally, my dear Professor," he said: "before you leave I must show you some interesting potsherds that were dug up not a mile from here. You will be fascinated. Aztec influences! This way . . . mind the stairs. I am afraid our cellar is not very well arranged at present; we have been recataloguing . . . this fascinating collection formerly belonged to a pioneer figure, the late Mr. Tatum Tompkins."

Behind a small mountain of packing cases, Dr. Turbyfil dealt Professor Sanzmann a swift blow on the temple with one of Uncle Tatum's tomahawks. The sinister Continental scholar fell without a sound, his rosy lips opened upon an unuttered aspirate. Dr. Turbyfil made shift to bury him in the farthest corner of the cellar, and to pile upon his grave such a pyramid of uncatalogued horrors as need not, God and Godbody willing, be disturbed for several centuries.

Dusting his hands, and whistling—a trifle off-key—the hymn called "Bringing in the Sheaves," Dr. Turbyfil returned to the office above stairs. There he opened an atlas, looking at large-scale maps of Germany. A village named Maldenhausen, in a valley . . . (Where there had been *one* skeleton, there must be others, unspoiled by absurd sixteenth-century paraphernalia—which had no business being there.) His fingers skipped joyfully along the map, and in his mind's eye he saw himself already in those valleys, with their lovely names: Friedenthal, Johannesthal, Hochsthal, Neanderthal, Waldenthal . . . beautiful valleys! Green, remote, enchanting . . . full of mysteries.

The Woman Who Thought She Could Read

INTRODUCTION BY MARTHA SOUKUP

I happened on short science fiction and fantasy during heady times, the 1970s. Many of the great anthology series were publishing then: Orbit, Universe, New Dimensions, Dangerous Visions: *exciting books filled with stories by strong new voices. A walk to the library after school would reap an armful of stories by Lafferty, Delany, Wolfe, Wilhelm, Bishop, Piserchia, Effinger, Silverberg, Dozois, Russ, so many, too many to keep in your head. Fine voices, quirky, intelligent, and fresh: half of what I learned about science fiction and fantasy I learned from stories like theirs.*

But the hottest new voices couldn't top what Avram Davidson had done in a collection of short stories, written as much as two decades before they came along. Pocket Books issued a paperback edition of his 1962 collection Or All the Seas with Oysters *in 1976. The copy I bought then sits on the arm of my chair now. The story ending the book, in the place of honor, is "The Woman Who Thought She Could Read."*

The stories in that reprint taught me as much about what short stories could do as any book I'd read. I wondered then and wonder still: Why write a novel when you can make a few thousand words like "The Woman Who Thought She Could Read" this rich?

Davidson gives his characters voices as distinctive as his own. Their voices reveal things about them they don't know about themselves, from the narrator recollecting his boyhood. It seems there are more characters than there are, because Davidson creates in this story a warm, but unsentimental, sense of a community; and from the community a sense of a whole America of several generations ago, living and breathing and laughing and worrying, loving, screaming. The curious boy recalled by his adult self; the cheerful immigrant midwife and bean-reader Mrs. Grummick; friends and neighbors painted, some-

times, in strokes just a sentence or three long. He even tosses in vivid characters long dead before his story opens. It deepens the sense of ongoing community. Folks. You recognize them when he shows them to you.

So why write a whole novel? (Well, there are other reasons.) Other writers can say this much about a time and a place: the way that time and place create the people in them, the way those people (eccentrically, clumsily, caringly) create that time and place. Two nights ago I went to a Chekhov play; Chekhov could.

It is always worth remarking when a writer has done this. It is doubly worth remarking when he has done it with economy and grace.

Here is a story where Avram Davidson has, and has. Remark it.

THE WOMAN WHO THOUGHT SHE COULD READ

ABOUT A HUNDRED YEARS ago a man named Vanderhorn built the little house. He built it one and a half stories high, with attached and detached sheds snuggling around it as usual; and he covered it with clapboards cut at his own mill—he had a small sawmill down at the creek, Mr. Vanderhorn did. After that he lived in the little house with his daughter and her husband (being a widower man) and one day he died there. So the daughter and son-in-law, a Mr. Hooten or Wooten or whatever it was, they came into his money which he made out of musket stocks for the Civil War, and they built a big new house next to the old one, only further back from the street. This Mr. Wooten or Hooten or something like that, *he* didn't have any sons, either; and *his* son-in-law turned the sawmill into a buggy factory. Well, you know what happened to *that* business! Finally, a man named Carmichael, who made milk wagons and baggage carts and piewagons, he bought the whole Vanderhorn estate. He fixed up the big house and put in apartments, and finally he sold it to my father and went out of business. Moved away somewhere.

I was just a little boy when we moved in. My sister was a lot older. The *old* Vanderhorn house wasn't part of the property any more. A lady named Mrs. Grummick was living there and Mr. Carmichael had sold her all the property the width of her house from the street on back to the next lot which faced the street behind ours. I heard my father say it was one of the narrowest lots in the city, and it was separated from ours by a picket fence. In the front of the old house was an old weeping willow tree and a big lilac bush like a small tree. In back were a truck garden and a few flowerbeds. Mrs. Grummick's house was so near to our property that I could look right into her window, and one day I did, and she was sorting beans.

Mrs. Grummick looked out and smiled at me. She had one of those broad faces with high cheekbones, and when she smiled her little bright black eyes almost disappeared.

"Liddle boy, hello!" she said. I said Hello and went right on staring, and she went right on sorting her beans. On her head was a kerchief (you have to remember that this was before they became fashionable) and there was a tiny gold earring in each plump earlobe. The beans were in two crocks on the table and in a pile in front of her. She was moving them around and sorting them into little groups. There were more crocks on the shelves, and glass jars, and bundles of herbs and strings of onions and peppers and bunches of garlic all hanging around the room. I looked through the room and out the window facing the street and there was a sign in front of the little house, hanging on a sort of one-armed gallows. *Anastasia Grummick, Midwife,* it said.

"What's a midwife?" I asked her.

"Me," she said. And she went on pushing the beans around, lining them up in rows, taking some from one place and putting them in another.

"Have you got any children, Mrs. Grimmick?"

"One. I god one boy. *Big* boy." She laughed.

"Where is he?"

"I think he come home today. I *know* he come home today." Her head bobbed.

"How do you know?"

"I know because I know. He come home and I make a bean soup for him. You want go errand for me?"

"All right." She stood up and pulled a little change purse out of her apron pocket, and counted out some money and handed it to me out of the window.

"Tell butcher Mrs. Grummick want him to cut some meat for a bean soup. He knows. Mrs. Schloutz. And you ged iche-cream comb with nickel, for you."

I started to go, but she gave me another nickel. "Ged *two* iche-cream combs. I ead one, too." She laughed. "One, too. One, two, three—Oh, Englisht languish!" Then she went back to the table, put part of the beans back in the crocks, and swept the rest of them into her apron. I got the meat for her and ate my French vanilla and then went off to play.

A few hours later a taxicab stopped in front of the little gray house and a man got out of it. A big fellow. Of course, to a kid, all grownups are real big, but he was *very* big—tremendous, he was, across, but not so tall. Mrs. Grummick came to the door.

"Eddie!" she said. And they hugged and kissed, so I decided this was her son, even before he called her "Mom."

"Mom," he said, "do I smell bean soup?"

"Just for you I make it," she said.

He laughed. "You knew I was coming, huh? You been reading them old beans again, Mom?" And they went into the house together.

I went home, thinking. My mother was doing something over the washtub with a ball of bluing. "Mama," I said, "can a person read beans?"

"Did you take your milk of magnesia?" my mother asked. Just as if I hadn't spoken. "Did you?"

I decided to bluff it out. "Uh-huh," I said.

"Oh *no* you didn't. Get me a spoon."

"Well, why do you ask if you ain't going to believe me?"

"Open up," she ordered. "More. Swallow it. Take the rest. All of it. If you could see your face! Suppose it froze and stayed like that? Go and wash the spoon off."

Next morning Eddie was down in the far end of the garden with a hoe.

He had his shirt off. Talk about shoulders! Talk about arms! Talk about a chest! My mother was out in front of our house, which made her near Eddie's mother out in back of hers. Of course my mother had to know everybody's business.

"That your son, Mrs. Grummick?"

"My son, yes."

"What does he do for a living?"

"Rachel."

"No, I mean your *son* . . . what does he do. . . ."

"He rachel. All over country. I show you."

She showed us a picture of a man in trunks with a hood over his head. "The Masked Marvel! Wrestling's Greatest Mystery!" The shoulders, arms, and chest—they could only have been Eddie's. There were other pictures of him in bulging poses, with names like, oh, The Slav Slayer, Chief Thunderwing, Young Kehoe, and so on. Every month Eddie Grummick sent his mother another photograph. It was the only kind of letter he sent because she didn't know how to read English. Or any other language, for that matter.

Back in the vegetable patch Eddie started singing a very popular song at that time, called "I Faw Down And Go *Boom!*"

It was a hot summer that year, a long hot summer, and September was just as hot as July. One shimmering, blazing day Mrs. Grummick called my father over. He had his shirt off and was sitting under our tree in his BVD top. We were drinking lemonade.

"When I was a kid," he said, "we used to make lemonade with brown sugar and sell it in the streets. We used to call out

> *Brown lemonade*
> *Mixed in the shade*
> *Stirred by an old maid.*

"People used to think that was pretty funny."

Mrs. Grummick called out: "Hoo-hoo! Mister! Hoo-hoo!"

"Guess she wants *me*." my father said. He went across the lawn. "Yes ma'am . . ." he was saying. "Yes ma'am."

She asked, "You buy coal yed, mister?"

"*Coal?* Why, no-o-o . . . not *yet*. Looks like a pretty mild winter ahead, wouldn't you say?"

She pressed her lips together, closed her eyes and shook her head.

"No! Bedder you buy soon coal. Lots coal. Comes very soon bad wedder. Bad!"

My father scratched his head. "Why, you sound pretty certain, Mrs. Grummick, but—uh—"

"I *know*, mister. If I say id, if I tell you, I *know*."

Then I piped up and asked, "Did you read it in the beans, Mrs. Grummick?"

"Hey!" She looked at me, surprised. "How you know, liddle boy?"

My father said, "You mean you can tell a bad winter is coming from the *beans?*"

"Iss true. I know. I read id."

"*Well,* now, that's very interesting. Where I come from, used to be a man— a weather prophet, they called him—*he* used to predict the weather by studying skunk stripes. Said his grandfather'd learned it from the Indians. How wide this year, how wide last year. Never failed. So you use beans?"

So I pushed my oar in and I said, "I guess you don't have the kind of beans that the man gave Jack for the cow and he planted them and they were all different colors. Well, a beanstalk grew way way up and he climbed—"

Father said, "Now don't bother Mrs. Grummick, sonny," but she leaned over the fence and picked me up and set me down on her side of it.

"You, liddle boy, come in house and tell me. You, mister: buy coal."

Mrs. Grummick gave me a glass of milk from the nanny goat who lived in one of the sheds, and a piece of gingerbread, and I told her the story of Jack and the beanstalk. Here's a funny thing—she believed it. I'm sure she did. It wasn't even what the kids call Making Believe, it was just a pure and simple belief. Then she told *me* a story. This happened on the other side, in some backwoods section of Europe where she came from. In this place they used to teach the boys to read, but not the girls. They figured, what did they need it for? So one day there was this little girl, her brothers were all off in school and she was left at home sorting beans. She was supposed to pick out all the bad beans and the worms, and when she thought about it and about everything, she began to cry.

Suddenly the little girl looked up and there was this old woman. She asked the kid how come she was crying. Because all the boys can learn to read, but not me. Is *that* all? the old lady asked.

Don't cry, she said. *I'll* teach you how to read, only not in books, the old lady said. Let the *men* read books, books are new things, people could read before there were books. Books tell you what *was,* but you'll be able to tell you what's *going* to be. And this old lady taught the little girl how to read the beans instead of the books. And I kind of have a notion that Mrs. Grummick said something about how they once used to read *bones,* but maybe it was just her accent and she meant beans. . . .

And you know, it's a funny thing, but, now, if you look at dried beans, you'll notice how each one is maybe a little different shape or maybe the wrinkles are a little different. But I was thinking that, after all, an "A" is an "A" even if it's big or small or twisted or. . . .

But that was the story Mrs. Grummick told me. So it isn't remarkable, if she could believe *that* story, she could easily believe the Jack and the Beanstalk one. But the funny thing was, all that hot weather just vanished one day suddenly, and from October until almost April we had what you might call an ironbound winter. Terrible blizzards one right after another. The rivers were frozen and the canals were frozen and even the railroads weren't running and the roads were blocked more than they were open. And coal? Why, you just couldn't *get* coal. People were freezing to death right and left. But Mrs. Grummick's little house was always warm and it smelled real nice with all those herbs and dried flowers and stuff hanging around in it.

A few years later my sister got married. And after that, in the summertime, she and her husband Jim used to come back and visit with us. Jim and I used to play ball and we had a fine time—they didn't have any children, so they made much of me. I'll always remember those happy summers.

Well, you know, each summer, a few of the churches used to get together and charter a boat and run an excursion. All the young couples used to go, but my sister always made some excuse. See, she was always afraid of the water. This particular summer the same thing happened, but her friends urged her to come. My brother-in-law, he didn't care one way or the other. And then, with all the joking, someone said, Let's ask Mrs. Grummick to read it in the beans for us. It had gotten known, you see. Everybody laughed, and more for the fun of it than anything else, I suppose, they went over and spoke to her. She said that Sister and Jim could come inside, but there wasn't room for anybody else. So we watched through the window.

Mrs. Grummick spread her beans on the table and began to shove them around here and there with her fingers. Some she put to one side and the rest she little by little lined up in rows. Then she took from one row and added to another row and changed some around from one spot to another. And meanwhile, mind you, she was muttering to herself, for all the world like one of these old people who reads by putting his finger on each word and mumbling it. And what was the answer?

"Don't go by the water."

And that was all. Well, like I say, my sister was just looking for any excuse at all, and Jim didn't care. So the day of the excursion they went off on a picnic by car. I'd like to have gone, but I guess they sort of wanted to be by themselves a bit and Jim gave me a quarter and I went to the movies and bought ice-cream and soda.

I came out and the first thing I saw was a boy my own age, by the name of Bill Baumgardner, running down the street crying. His shirt was out and his nose was running and he kept up an awful grinding kind of howl. I called to him but he paid no attention. I still don't know where he was running from or where to and I guess maybe he didn't know either. Because he'd been told, by some old fool who should've known better, that the excursion boat had caught on fire, with his parents on it. The news swept through town and almost everybody with folks on the boat was soon in as bad a state as poor Billy.

First they said everybody was burned or drowned or trampled. Later on it turned out to be not that bad—but it was bad enough.

Oh, my folks were shook up, sure enough, but it's easier to be calm when you know it's not your own flesh and blood. I recall hearing the church clock striking six and my mother saying, "I'll never laugh at Mrs. Grummick again as long as I live." Well, she never did.

Almost everyone who had people on the boat went up the river to where it had finally been run ashore, or else they waited by the police station for news. There was a deaf lady on our street, I guess her daughter got tired of its being so dull at home and she'd lied to her mother, told her she was going riding in the country with a friend. So when the policeman came and told her— shouted at her they'd pulled out the girl's body, she didn't know what he was talking about. And when she finally understood she began to scream and scream and scream.

The policeman came over toward us and my mother said, "I'd better get over there," and she started out. He was just a young policeman and his face was pale. He held up his hand and shook his head. Mother stopped and he came over. I could hear how hard he was breathing. Then he mentioned Jim's name.

"Oh, no," my mother said, very quickly. "They didn't *go* on the boat." He started to say something and she interrupted him and said, "But I tell you, they didn't *go*—" and she looked around, kind of frantically, as if wishing someone would come and send the policeman away.

But no one did. We had to hear him out. It was Sister and Jim, all right. A big truck had gotten out of control ("—but they didn't go on the boat," my mother kept repeating, kind of stupidly. "They had this warning and so—") and smashed into their car. It fell off the road into the canal. The police were called right away and they came and pulled it out. ("Oh, *oh!* Then they're all *right!*" my mother cried. *Then* she was willing to understand.) But they weren't all right. They'd been drowned.

So we forgot about the deaf neighbor lady because my mother, poor thing, *she* got hysterical. My father and the policeman helped her inside and after a while she just lay there on the couch, kind of moaning. The door opened and in tiptoed Mrs. Grummick. She had her lower lip tucked in under her teeth and her eyes were wide and she was kind of rocking her head from side to side. In each hand she held a little bottle—smelling salts, maybe, and some kind of cordial. I was glad to see her and I think my father was. I *know* the policeman was, because he blew out his cheeks, nodded very quickly to my father, and went away.

Mother said, in a weak, thin voice: "They didn't go on the boat. They didn't go because they had a warning. That's why—" Then she saw Mrs. Grummick. The color came back to her face and she just leaped off the couch and tried to hit Mrs. Grummick, and she yelled at her in a hoarse voice I'd never heard and called her names—the kind of names I was just beginning to find out what they meant. I was, I think, more shocked and stunned to hear my mother use them than I was at the news that Sister and Jim were dead.

Well, my father threw his arms around her and kept her from reaching Mrs. Grummick and I remember I grabbed hold of one hand and how it tried to get away from me.

"You *knew!*" my mother shouted, struggling, her hair coming loose. "*You* knew! You read it there, you witch! And you didn't tell! You didn't tell! She'd be alive now if she'd gone on the boat. They weren't all killed, on the boat— But you didn't say a *word!*"

Mrs. Grummick's mouth opened and she started to speak. She was so mixed up, I guess, that she spoke in her own language, and my mother screamed at her.

My father turned his head around and said, "You'd better get out."

Mrs. Grummick made a funny kind of noise in her throat. Then she said, "But, Lady—mister—no—I tell you only what I see—I read there, *'Don't go by the water.'* I only can say what I see in front of me, only what I read. Nothing else. Maybe it mean one thing or maybe another. I only can read it. Please, lady—"

But we knew we'd lost them, and it was because of her.

"They ask *me,*" Mrs. Grummick said. "They *ask* me to read."

My mother kind of collapsed, sobbing. Father said, "Just get out of here. Just turn around and get out."

I heard a kid's voice saying, high, and kind of trembling, "We don't want you here, you old witch! *We hate you!*"

Well, it was *my* voice. And then her shoulders sagged and she looked for the first time like a real old woman. She turned around and shuffled away. At the door she stopped and half faced us. "I read no more," she said. "I never read more. Better not to know at all." And she went out.

Not long after the funeral we woke up one morning and the little house was empty. We never heard where the Grummicks went and it's only now that I begin to wonder about it and to think of it once again.

THE SIXTIES

Where Do You Live, Queen Esther?

INTRODUCTION BY KATE WILHELM

There is magic, indeed there is. Not in amulets or powders, not in rings with powers, or wells that grant wishes. The real magic is in words; the real magician is one who has mastered that magic. Avram was a magician. In a few words he opens the door to reveal another world, magic. Oh, my, but a woman your age shouldn't be working, the ladies said. No, no, I couldn't, really. *Magic. A revealed world. Or later:* "Another day. And everything is left to me. Every single thing . . . Don't take all morning with those few dishes." *Another world, narrower, meaner. And again:* Her thrust she hand into she bosom. . . . "You ugly old duppy! Me never fear no duppy, no, not me!"

Deftly, with enviable precision, savage wit, an undeceived eye and infallible ear Avram created his magic spell and in a very short story answered the question: "Where Do You Live, Queen Esther?" But more, by drawing us into his universe, his universe also entered us. It is now part of us. That is the enchantment of words woven by a master magician.

WHERE DO YOU LIVE, QUEEN ESTHER?

COLD, COLD, IT WAS, in the room where she lodged, so far from her work. The young people complained of the winter, and those born to the country—icy cold, it was, to them. So how could a foreign woman bear it, and not a young one? She had tried to find another job not so far (none were near). *Oh, my, but a woman your age shouldn't be working,* the ladies said. *No, no, I couldn't, really.* Kindly indeed. Thank you, mistress.

There was said to be hot water sometimes in the communal bathroom down the hall—the water in the tap in her room was so cold it burned like fire: so strange: hot/cold—but it was always too late when she arrived back from work. Whither she was bound now. Bound indeed.

A long wait on the bare street corner for the bus. Icy winds and no door-way, even, to shelter from the winds. In the buses—for there were two, and another wait for the second—if not warm, then not so cold. And at the end, a walk for many blocks. The mistress not up yet.

Mistress . . . Queen Esther thought about Mrs. Raidy, the woman of the house. At first her was startled by the word—to she it mean, a woman live with a man and no marriage lines. But then her grew to like it, Mrs. Raidy did. Like to hear, too, mention of *the Master* and *the young Master,* his brother.

Both of they at table. "That second bus," Queen Esther said, unwrapping her head. "He late again. Me think, just to fret I."

"Oh, a few minutes don't matter. Don't worry about it," the master, Mr. Raidy, said. He never called the maid by name, nor did the mistress, but the boy—

As now, looking up with a white line of milk along his upper lip, he smiled and asked. "Where do you live, Queen Esther?" It was a game they played often. His brother—quick glance at the clock, checking his watch, head half turned to pick up sounds from upstairs, said that he wasn't to bother "her" with his silly question. A pout came over the boy's face, but yielded to her quick reply.

"Me live in the Carver Rooms on Fig Street, near Burr."

His smile broadened. "Fig! That's a fun-ny name for a street. . . . But where do you live at home, Queen Esther? *I* know: Spahnish Mahn. And what you call a fig we call a bah-nah-nah. See, Freddy? *I* know."

The older one got up. "Be a goodboynow," he said, and vanished for the day.

The boy winked at her. "Queen Esther from Spanish Man, Santa Marianne, Bee-Double-You-Eye. But I really think it should be Spanish *Main,* Queen Esther." He put his head seriously to one side. "That's what they used to call the Caribbean Sea, you know."

And he fixed with his brooding, ugly little face her retreating back as she went down to the cellar to hang her coat and change her shoes.

"The sea surround we on three sides at Spanish Man," she said, returning.

"You should say, 'surrounds *us,*' Queen Esther. . . . You have a very funny accent, and you aren't very pretty."

Looking up from her preparations for the second breakfast, she smiled. "True *for* you, me lad."

"But then, neither am I. I look like my father. I'm *his* brother, not *hers,* you know. Do you go swimming much when you live at home, Queen Esther?"

She put up a fresh pot of coffee to drip and plugged in the toaster and set some butter to brown as she beat the eggs; and she told him of how they swim at Spanish Man on Santa Marianna, surrounded on three sides by the sea. It was the least of the Lesser Antilles. . . . She lived only part of her life in the land she worked in, the rest of the time—in fact, often at the same time—she heard, in the silence and cold of the mainland days and nights, the white surf beating on the white sands and the scuttling of the crabs beneath the breadfruit trees.

"I thought I would come down before you carried that heavy tray all the way upstairs," said the mistress, rubbing her troubled puffy eyes. Her name was Mrs. Eleanor Raidy—she was the master's wife—and her hair was teased up in curlers. She sat down with a grunt, sipped coffee, sighed. "What would I ever do without you?"

She surveyed the breakfast-in-progress. "I hope I'll be able to eat. And to retain. Some mornings . . ." she said darkly. Her eyes made the rounds once more. "There's no pineapple, I suppose?" she asked faintly. "Grated, with just a little powdered sugar? Don't go to any extra trouble," she added, as Queen Esther opened the icebox. "Rodney. *Rodney?* Why do I have to shout and—"

"Yes, El. What?"

"In *that* tone of voice? If it were for my pleasure, I'd say, Nothing. But I see your brother doesn't care if you eat or not. Half a bowl of—"

"I'm finished."

"You are not finished. Finish now."

"I'll be *late,* El. They're waiting for me."

"Then they'll wait. Rush out of here with an empty stomach and then fill up on some rubbish? No. Finish the cereal."

"But it's *cold.*"

"Who let it get cold? I'm not too sure at all I ought to let you go. This Harvey is older than you and he pals around with girls older than he is. Or maybe they just fix themselves up to look—eat. Did you *hear* what I say? Eat. Most disgusting sight I ever saw, lipstick, and the *clothes*? Don't let me catch you near them. They'll probably be rotten with disease in a few years." Silently, Queen Esther grated pineapple. "I don't like the idea of your going down to the Museum without adult supervision. Who knows what can happen? Last week a boy your age was crushed to death by a truck. Did you have a—*look* at me, young man, when I'm talking to you—did you have a movement?"

"Yes."

"Ugh. If looks could kill. I don't believe you. Go upstairs and—RodNEY!"

But Rodney had burst into tears and threw down his spoon and rushed from the room. Even as Mrs. Raidy, her mouth open with Shock, tried to catch the maid's eye, he slammed the door behind him and ran down the front steps.

The morning was proceeding as usual.

"And his brother leaves it all to me," Mrs. Raidy said, pursuing a piece of pineapple with her tongue. She breathed heavily. "I have you to thank, in part, I may as well say since we are on the subject, for the fact that he wakes up screaming in the middle of the night. I warned you. Didn't I warn you?"

Queen Esther demurred, said she had never spoken of it to the young master since that one time of the warning.

"One time was enough. What was that word? That name? From the superstitious story you were telling him when I interrupted. Guppy?"

"Duppy, mistress." It was simply a tale from the old slave days, Queen Esther reflected. A cruel Creole lady who went to the fields one night to meet she lover, and met a duppy instead. The slaves all heard, but were affrighted to go out; and to this day the pile of stones near Petty Morne is called The Grave of Mistress-Serve-She-Well. Mistress Raidy had suddenly appeared at the door, as Queen Esther finished the tale, startling Master Rodney.

"Why do you tell the child such stories?" she had demanded, very angry. "See, he's scared to death."

"*You* scared me, El, sneaking up like that."

Queen Esther hastened to try to distract them.

" 'Tis only a fancy of the old people. Me never fear no duppy—"

But she was not allowed to finish. The angry words scalded her. And she knew it was the end of any likelihood (never great) that she might be allowed to move her things into the little attic room, and save the hours of journeying through the cutting, searing cold.

Said the mistress, now, "Even the sound of it is stupid. . . . He didn't eat much breakfast." She glanced casually out the window at the frost-white ground. "You noticed that, I suppose."

Over the sound of the running water Queen Esther said, Yes. She added detergent to the water. He never did eat much breakfast—but she didn't say this out.

"No idea why, I suppose? No? Nobody's been feeding him anything—that you know of? No spicy West Indian messes, no chicken and rice with bay

leaves? Yes, yes, I know, not since that one time. All right. A word to the wise
is sufficient." Mrs. Raidy arose. A grimace passed over her face. "Another day.
And everything is left to me. Every single thing . . . Don't take all morning
with those few dishes."

Chicken and rice, with bay leaves and peppercorns. Queen Esther, thinking
about it now, relished the thought. Savory, yes. Old woman in the next yard
at home in Spanish Man, her cook it in an iron caldron. Gran'dame Hephsibah,
who had been born a slave and still said "wittles" and "vhiskey" . . . Very sage
woman. But, now, what was wrong with chicken and rice? The boy made a
good meal of it, too, before he sister-in-law had come back, unexpected and
early. Then shouts and tears and then a dash to the bathroom. "You've made
him sick with your nasty rubbish!" But, for true, it wasn't so.

Queen Esther was preparing to vacuum the rug on the second floor when
the mistress appeared at the door of the room. She dabbed at her eyes. "You
know, I'm not a religious person," she observed, "but I was just thinking: It's
a blessing the Good Lord didn't see fit to give me a child. You know why?
Because I would've thrown away my life on it just as I'm throwing it away on
my father-in-law's child. Can you imagine such a thing? A man fifty-two years
old, a widower, suddenly gets it into his head to take a wife half his age—"
She rattled away, winding up, "And so now they're both dead, and who has
to put up with the results of his being a nasty old goat? No . . . Look. See what
your fine young gentleman had hidden under the cushion of his bedroom
chair."

And she rifled the pages of a magazine. Queen Esther suppressed a smile.
It was only natural, she wanted to say. Young gentlemen liked young ladies.
Even up in this cold and frozen land—true, the boy was young. That's why it
was natural he only looked—and only at pictures.

"Oh, there's very little gets past *me*, I can assure you. Wait. When he gets
back. Museum trips. Dirty pictures. Friends from who knows where. No
more!"

Queen Esther finished the hall rugs, dusted, started to go in to vacuum the
guest room. Mrs. Raidy, she half observed in the mirror, was going downstairs.
Just as the mistress passed out of sight, she threw a glance upward. Queen
Esther only barely caught it. She frowned. A moment later a faint jar shook
the boards beneath her feet. The cellar door. Bad on its hinges. Queen Esther
started the vacuum cleaner; a sudden thought made her straighten up, reach for
the switch. For a moment she stood without moving. Then she propped the
cleaner, still buzzing, in a corner, and flitted down the steps.

There was, off the kitchen, a large broom closet, with a crack in the wall.
Queen Esther peered through the crack. Diagonally below in the cellar was an
old victrola and on it the maid had draped her coat and overcoat and scarf; next
to it were street shoes, not much less broken than the ones she wore around
the house.

Mistress Raidy stood next to the gramophone, her head lifted, listening.
The hum of the vacuum cleaner filtered through the house. With a quick nod
of her head, tight-lipped in concentration, the mistress began going through
the pockets of the worn garments. With little grunts of pleasurable vexation

she pulled out a half-pint bottle of fortified wine, some pieces of cassava cake. "That's all we need. A drunken maid. Mice. Roaches. *Oh,* yes." A smudged hektographed postal card announcing the Grand Annual Festivity of the St. Kitts and Nevis Wesleyan Benevolent Union, a tattered copy of Lucky Tiger Dream Book, a worn envelope . . .

Here she paused to dislodge a cornerless photograph of Queen Esther's brother Samuel in his coffin and to comment, "As handsome as his sister." There were receipts for international postal orders to Samuel's daughter Ada— "Send my money to foreign countries." A change purse with little enough in it, and a flat cigarette tin. This she picked at with nervous fingers, chipping a nail. Clicking her tongue, she got it open, found, with loathing large upon her face—

—a tiny dried frog—a *frog?*—a—surely *not!*—

"Oh!" she said, in a thin, jerky, disgusted voice. "Uh. *Uh!*" She threw the tin away from her, but the thing was bound with a scarlet thread and this caught in her chipped fingernail.

"—out of this *house!*" she raged, flapping her wrist, "and never set foot in it *again,* with her *filthy—ah!*" The thread snapped, the thing flew off and landed in a far corner. She turned to go and had one unsteady foot on the first step when she heard the noise behind her.

Later on, when Queen Esther counted them, she reckoned it as twenty-five steps from the broom closet to the bottom of the cellar stairs. At that moment, though, they seemed to last forever as the screams mounted in intensity, each one seeming to overtake the one before it without time or space for breath between. But they ceased as the maid clattered down the steps, almost tripping over the woman crouched at the bottom.

Queen Esther spared she no glance, then, but faced the thing advancing. Her thrust she hand into she bosom. "Poo!" her spat. "You ugly old duppy! Me never fear no duppy, no, not me!"

And her pulled out the powerful obeah prepared for she long ago by Gran'dame Hephsibah, that sagest of old women, half Ashanti, half Coromanti. The duppy growled and driveled and bared its worn-down stumps of filthy teeth, but retreated step by step as her came forward, chanting the words of power; till at last it was shriveled and bound once more in the scarlet thread and stowed safely away in the cigarette tin. *Ugly old duppy . . . !*

Mr. Raidy took the sudden death of his wife with stoical calm. His young brother very seldom has nightmares now, and eats heartily of the savory West Indian messes that Queen Esther prepares for all three of them. Hers is the little room in the attic; her chimney passes through one corner of it, and Queen Esther is warm, warm, warm.

The Sources of the Nile

INTRODUCTION BY GREGORY FEELEY

By 1960 Avram Davidson had developed his own peculiar mastery of the modern short story, and within ten years he would produce a novel of classic stature, but his work in the "novelette" form—that hybrid category, shorter than the novella that has enjoyed so distinguished a history in American literature yet essentially different from the brief compass of the short story—has been relatively little remarked. To be sure, the (much later) Limekiller and Eszterhazy stories are mostly novelettes, but they possess the peculiar status of stories that form parts of a sequence, and can moreover be seen as variations (in their different ways) on the Vergil Magus figure, which increasingly occupied the last decades of Davidson's life. The actual novelette, which can retain the concision and urgency of the short story while permitting more complex dramatic development, is a form that the early Davidson rarely used.

When "The Sources of the Nile" appeared in the January, 1961, issue of Fantasy & Science Fiction, *Davidson had written one previous novelette, the unorthodox time-travel fantasy "Take Wooden Indians," which* Galaxy *had published a year earlier. The two stories are essentially companion pieces: each is set in a contemporary Manhattan that is satirized with an acute eye; each offers an escape from the world of commercial philistinism into another time. But while the arcadia of "Take Wooden Indians" is the idealized small-town America of the nineteenth century, "The Sources of the Nile" looks rather to the future, a future in which one can escape the banalities of modern fashion only by embracing them. This paradox (the first of several) lies at the heart of Davidson's story, which is constructed of oppositions—something subtly different and more complex than the contrasts (between a rich past and an impoverished present, for example) that constitute Davidson's more usual dramatic method.*

Don Benedict, the sculptor of "Take Wooden Indians" who yearns to be an artisan laboring in the extinct craft of carving cigar-store Indians, is able to escape the horrors of the modern art world by way of the mysterious Elwell equations; but Bob Rosen, the struggling writer in "The Sources of the Nile," sees the commercial bonanza implicit in the Bensons' ability to predict fashions as a means of making his fortune. He is also besotted with the Bensons' daughter Kitty, with an erotic (and comical) urgency that foretokens his role as betrayed dupe. But Bob Rosen (whom we first see reading an arcane article on "The Demography of the Jackson Whites") is also enough of a scholar gypsy—though distracted by avarice and lust—to appreciate the Bensons for the wonder they are: the fascination they hold for him is also the fascination they hold for us.

This complexity of motivation—as well as the fact that the faithless Rosen has wronged his girlfriend Noreen as surely as she (later) wrongs him—gives the story a moral core (although one hesitates to apply so sober a term to a work of such comic energy) that is significantly knottier than most of Davidson's stories dealing with an artist at odds with the workaday world, in which the protagonist tends to get off rather easily (and women rather hard). Even Davidson's villain, the awful T. Pettys Shadwell ("the most despicable of living men"), seems no worse, save for his appalling style—the perforated business cards being an especially nice touch—than the executives who go baying after Peter Martens' secret, a pack among which Rosen finds himself. Davidson's exhilarating comedy, which begins with old Peter Martens cadging the drinks that will kill him and ends in utter defeat and desolation, is humor of the blackest hue.

Davidson considered himself weak in plot construction, and indeed many of his stories constitute a triumph of stylistic virtuosity over structure, but the architecture of "The Sources of the Nile" is nearly perfect. The story is free of expository baggage (compare "Take Wooden Indians," which betrays an occasionally unsure hand) and exceptionally close-knit: tiny droll elements (such as the talkative blonde in the bar) appear, seemingly as throwaway lines, then later prove crucial to the plot. Davidson's earlier short stories were largely miniatures, which often revolved around a single dramatic event; his later stories tended toward the picaresque. "The Sources of the Nile" is one of the few works in which Davidson combined the compression of his finest prose with genuine dramatic development.

Davidson's comic effects work in broad-seeming strokes that are actually quite deft. Joseph Tressling's fulsome assurances are almost fugal in form: the hearty declaration "What the great cheese-eating American public wants is a story of resolved conflict concerning young contemporary American couples earning more than ten thousand dollars a year" is immediately followed by the antiphonal "But nothing sordid, controversial, outré, or passé"; and variations are played upon both themes for another page, which reach a climax that is immediately capped by the sinister query: "You're not going to be one of those

hungry *writers, are you?" References to "the sources of the Nile" and the hack-
neyed wisdom that comes down from Robert R. Mac Ian are similarly sounded
like musical motifs.*

*But, as with all Davidson, it is the prose we finally remember. Rereading,
we note the tiny details: the colloquialisms from the heyday of British imperi-
alism that cluster about the aged Martens, or the various hangover cures that
Bob Rosen tries (they include the recipe Jeeves uses on Bertie Wooster). The title
of Rosen's best-known short story is taken from a passage in one of Lincoln's
letters, and even the horrid Shadwell makes a witty reference to* The Merchant
of Venice. *Peter Martens, "glaring at [Bob] with bloody eye," is both the Ancient Mariner and Dickens's Magwitch, bestowing a terrible legacy on a chance-
met young man. These baroque allusions are set against a series of sharp details
concerning life in the Manhattan business world: the issues of* Botteghe Oscure
*(a highbrow literary quarterly published in Rome until 1960), or the passing
references to* The Man in the Grey Flannel Suit *and the vogue for books about
Aku-Aku, which firmly set Davidson's tale in the late 1950s. The overheard
remarks by a hussy in a bar are a staple of Madison Avenue satires of this
period—see William Gaddis's* The Recognitions—*but whether Davidson observed this phenomenon himself or encountered it in books (and one should
never underestimate the breadth of Davidson's reading), he makes it seem au-
thentically of its time, unforced, and funny.*

*In "The Sources of the Nile" the future is presented, for perhaps the only
time in Davidson's work, as something other than a calamity. The (near-term)
changes it will bring—soup-bowl haircuts for men, etc.—are, to be sure, utterly
arbitrary, but the wealth awaiting those who espy them correctly gives the story
a prospective (rather than backward-looking) impulse that is finally cheering.
When we last see Bob Rosen, he has made the vanished Bensons his El Dorado,
whom he pursues with undiminished ardor like the man who chases the horizon
in the Stephen Crane poem. We want to cheer him on.*

THE SOURCES OF THE NILE

It was in the Rutherford office on Lexington that Bob Rosen met Peter ("Old Pete"—"Sneaky Pete"—"Poor Pete": take your pick) Martens for the first and almost last time. One of those tall, cool buildings on Lexington with the tall, cool office girls it was; and because Bob felt quite sure he wasn't and damned well never was going to be tall or cool enough for him to mean anything to them, he was able to sit back and just enjoy the scenery. Even the magazines on the table were cool: *Spectator, Botteghe Oscure,* and *Journal of the New York State Geographical Society.* He picked up the last and began to leaf through "Demographic Study of The Jackson Whites."

He was trying to make some sense out of a mass of statistics relating to albinism among that curious tribe (descended from Tuscorora Indians, Hessian deserters, London street women, and fugitive slaves), when one of the girls—delightfully tall, deliciously cool—came to usher him in to Tressling's office. He laid the magazine face down on the low table and followed her. The old man with the portfolio, who was the only other person waiting, got up just then, and Bob noticed the spot of blood in his eye as he passed by. They were prominent eyes, yellowed, reticulated with tiny red veins, and in the corner of one of them was a bright red blot. For a moment it made Rosen feel uneasy, but he had no time then to think about it.

"Delightful story," said Joe Tressling, referring to the piece which had gotten Rosen the interview, through his agent. The story had won first prize in a contest, and the agent had thought that Tressling . . . if Tressling . . . maybe Tressling . . .

"Of course, we can't touch it because of the theme," said Tressling.

"Why, what's wrong with the Civil War as a theme?" Rosen said.

Tressling smiled. "As far as Aunt Carrie's Country Cheese is concerned," he said, "the South *won* the Civil War. At least, it's not up to Us to tell Them differently. It might annoy Them. The North doesn't *care.* But write another story for us. The Aunt Carrie Hour is always on the lookout for new dramatic material."

"Like for instance?" Bob Rosen asked.

"What the great cheese-eating American public wants is a story of resolved conflict concerning young contemporary American couples earning over ten thousand dollars a year. But nothing sordid, controversial, outré, or passé."

Rosen was pleased to be able to see Joseph Tressling, who was the J. Oscar Rutherford Company's man in charge of scripts for the Aunt Carrie Hour. The *Mené Mené* of the short story was said that year to be on the wall, the magazines were dying like mayflies, and the sensible thing for anyone to do who hoped to make a living writing (he told himself) was to get into television. But he really didn't expect he was going to make the transition, and the realization that he didn't really know any contemporary Americans—young, old, married, single—who were earning over ten thousand dollars a year seemed to prophesy that he was never going to earn it himself.

"And nothing avant-garde," said Tressling.

The young woman returned and smiled a tall, cool smile at them. Tressling got up. So did Bob. "Mr. Martens is still outside," she murmured.

"Oh, I'm afraid I won't be able to see him today," said Joe Tressling. "Mr. Rosen has been so fascinating that the time seems to have run over, and then some. . . . Great old boy," he said, smiling at Bob and shaking his hand. "Really one of the veterans of advertising, you know. Used to write copy for Mrs. Winslow' Soothing Syrup. Tells some fascinating yarns. Too bad I haven't the time to listen. I expect to see you back here soon, Mr. Rosen," he said, still holding Bob's hand as they walked to the door, "with another one of your lovely stories. One that we can feel delighted to buy. No costume dramas, no foreign settings, nothing outré, passé, or avant-garde, and above all—nothing controversial or sordid. You're not going to be one of those *hungry* writers, are you?"

Even before he answered, Rosen observed Tressling's eyes dismiss him; and he resolved to start work immediately on an outré, controversial, sordid costume drama with a foreign setting, etc., if it killed him.

He made the wrong turn for the elevator and on coming back he came face to face with the old man. " 'Demography of the Jackson Whites'," the old man said, feigning amazement. "What do you care about those poor suckers for? They don't buy, they don't sell, they don't start fashion, they don't follow fashion. Just poach, fornicate, and produce oh-point-four hydrocephalic albinoes per hundred. Or something."

The elevator came and they got in together. The old man stared at him, his yellow-bloody eye like a fertilized egg. "Not that I blame them," he went on. "If I'd had any sense I'd've become a Jackson White instead of an advertising man. The least you can do," he said, without any transition, "is to buy me a drink. Since Truthful Tressling blames it onto you that he can't see me, the lying bugger. Why, for crying out loud!" he cried. "What I've got here in this little old portfolio—why, it's worth more to those men on Madison, Lexington, Park—if they only—"

"Let me buy you a drink," said Rosen, resignedly. The streets were hot, and he hoped the bar would be cool.

"A ball of Bushmill," said old Peter Martens.

The bar *was* cool. Bob had stopped listening to his guest's monologue about what he had in his little old portfolio (something about spotting fashion trends way in advance) and had begun talking about his own concerns. By and by the old man, who was experienced beyond the norm in not being listened to, had begun to listen to *him.*

"This was when everybody was reading Aku-Aku," Bob said. "So I thought for sure that mine would go over good because it was about Rapa Nui—Easter Island—and Peruvian blackbirders and hints of great legends of the past and all that."

"And?"

"And it didn't. The publisher, the only one who showed any interest at all, I mean, *that* publisher, he said *he* liked the writing but the public wouldn't buy it. He advised me to study carefully the other paperbacks on the stands. See what they're like, go thou and do likewise. So I did. You know the stuff. On even-numbered pages the heroine gets her brassiere ripped off while she cries, '*Yes! Yes! Now! Oh!*' "

He was not aware of signalling, but from time to time a hand appeared and renewed their glasses. Old Martens asked, "Does she cry 'rapturously'—or 'joyously'?"

"Rapturously *and* joyously. What's the matter, you think she's frigid?"

Martens perished the thought. At a nearby table a large blonde said, lugubriously, "You know, Harold, it's a lucky thing the Good Lord didn't give me any children or I would of wasted my life on them like I did on my rotten step-children." Martens asked what happened on the odd-numbered children.

"I mean, 'pages'," he corrected himself, after a moment.

The right side of Bob Rosen's face was going numb. The left side started tingling. He interrupted a little tune he was humming and said, "Oh, the equation is invariable: On odd-numbered pages the hero either clonks some bastard bloodily on the noggin with a roscoe, or kicks him in the collions and *then* clonks him, or else he's engaged—with his shirt off, you're not allowed to say what gives with the pants, which are so much more important: presumably they melt or something—he's engaged, shirtless, in arching his lean and muscular flanks over some bimbo, *not* the heroine, because these aren't her pages, some other female in whose pelvis he reads strange mysteries . . ." He was silent for a moment, brooding.

"How could it fail, then?" asked the old man, in his husky voice. "I've seen the public taste change, let me tell you, my boy, from *A Girl of the Limberlost* (which was so pure that nuns could read it) to stuff which makes stevedores blench: so I am moved to inquire, How could the work you are describing to me fail?"

The young man shrugged. "The nuns were making a come-back. Movies about nuns, books about nuns, nuns on TV, westerns. . . . So the publisher said public taste had changed, and could I maybe do him a life of St. Teresa?"

"Coo."

"So I spent three months doing a life of St. Teresa at a furious pace, and when I finished it turned out I'd done the wrong saint. The simple slob had no idea there was any more than one of the name, and I never thought to ask did he mean the Spanish St. Teresa or the French one? D'Avila or The Little Flower?"

"Saints preserve us. . . . Say, do you know that wonderful old Irish toast? 'Here's to the Council of Trent, that put the fasting on the meat and not on the drink'?"

Bob gestured to the barkeeper. "But I didn't understand why if one St. Teresa could be sold, the other one couldn't. So I tried another publisher, and all *he* said was, public taste had changed, and could I do him anything with a background of juvenile delinquency? After that I took a job for a while selling frozen custard in a penny arcade and all my friends said, BOB! You with *your* talent? How COULD you?"

The large blonde put down a jungle-green drink and looked at her companion. "What you mean, they love me? If they love me why are they going to Connecticut? You don't go to Connecticut if you love a person," she pointed out.

Old Martens cleared his throat. "My suggestion would be that you combine all three of your mysteriously unsalable novels. The hero sails on a Peruvian blackbirder to raid Easter Island, the inhabitants whereof he kicks in the collions, if male, or arches his loins over, if female; until he gets converted by a vision of both St. Teresas who tell him their life stories—as a result of which he takes a job selling frozen custard in a penny arcade in order to help the juvenile delinquents who frequent the place."

Bob grunted. "Depend on it, with my luck I would get it down just in time to see public taste change again. The publishers would want a pocket treasury of the McGuffey Readers, or else the memoirs of Constantine Porphyrogenitos. I could freeze my arse climbing the Himalayas only to descend, manuscript in hand, to find everybody on Publishers' Row vicariously donning goggles and spearing fish on the bottom of the Erythrean Sea. . . . Only thing is, I never was sure to what degree public taste changed by itself or how big a part the publishers play in changing it. . . ."

The air, cool though he knew it was, seemed to shimmer in front of him, and through the shimmer he saw Peter Martens sitting up straight and leaning over at him, his seamed and ancient face suddenly eager and alive. "And would you like to be sure?" old Martens asked. "Would you like to be able to know, really to *know*?"

"What? How?" Bob was startled. The old man's eye looked almost all blood by now.

"Because," Martens said, "*I* can tell you what. *I* can tell you how. Nobody else. Only *me*. And not just about books, about everything. Because—"

There was an odd sort of noise, like the distant sussuration of wind in dry grass, and Rosen looked around and he saw that a man was standing by them and laughing. This man wore a pale brown suit and had a pale brown complexion, he was very tall and very thin and had a very small head and slouched somewhat. He looked like a mantis, and a mustache like an inverted V was cropped out of the broad blue surface of his upper lip.

"Still dreaming your dreams, Martens?" this man asked, still wheezing his dry whispery laugh. "Gates of Horn, or Gates of Ivory?"

"Get the Hell away from me, Shadwell," said Martens.

Shadwell turned his tiny little head to Rosen and grinned. "He been telling you about how he worked on old Mrs. Winslow's Soothing Syrup Account? Too bad the Harrison Narcotics killed that business! He tell you how he worked on the old Sapolio account. The old Stanley Steamer account?" ("Shove off, Shadwell," Martens ordered, planting his elbows in the table and opening his mouth at Bob again.) "Or has he been muttering away like an old Zambezi hand who claims to know the location of the Elephants' Graveyard? Tell me, where is fashion bred?" he intoned. "In the bottle—or in Martens' head?"

Martens' head, thinly covered with yellowish-white hair, jerked in the direction of the new arrival. "This, my boy, is T. Pettys Shadwell, the most despicable of living men. He runs—out of his pocket, because no one will sell him a hat on credit—he runs a so-called market research business. Though who in blazes would hire him since Polly Adler went respectable beats the Hell out of me. I'm warning you, Shadwell," he said, "take off. I've had my fill of you. I'm not giving you any more information." And with a further graphic description of what else he would *not* give T. Pettys Shadwell if the latter was dying of thirst, he folded his arms and fell silent.

The most despicable of living men chuckled, poked a bone-thin hand into a pocket, plucked out a packet of white flaps of cardboard, one of which he tore along a perforated line and handed to Bob. "My card, sir. My operation, true, is not large, but it is Ever Growing. Don't take Mr. Martens too seriously. And don't buy him too many drinks. His health is not as good as it used to be—and then, it never was." And with a final laugh, like the rustling of dried corn-shucks, he angled away.

Martens sighed, lapped the last few dewy drops of Bushmill's off a molten ice-cube. "I live in mortal fear that some day I'll have the money to buy all the booze I want and wake up finding I have spilled the beans to that cockatrice who just walked out. Can you imagine anyone having business cards printed to be torn off of perforated pads? Keeps them from getting loose and wrinkled, is his reason. Such a man has no right, under natural or civil law, to live."

In the buzzing coolness of the barroom Bob Rosen tried to catch hold of a thought which was coyly hiding behind a corner in his mind. His mind otherwise, he felt, was lucid as never before. But somehow he lost the thought, found he was telling himself a funny story in French and—although he had never got more than an 80 in the course, back in high school—marvelled at the purity of his accent and then chuckled at the punch-line.

" 'Never mind about black neglijays,' " the stout blonde was saying. " 'If you want to keep your husband's affections,' I said to her, 'then listen to me—' "

The errant thought came trotting back for reasons of its own, and jumped into Bob's lap. " 'Spill the beans'?" he quoted, questioningly. "Spill *what* beans? To Shadwell, I mean."

"Most despicable of living men," said old Martens, mechanically. Then a most curious expression washed over his antique countenance: proud, cunning, fearful . . .

"Would you like to know the sources of the Nile?" he asked. "Would you?"

" 'Let him *go* to Maine,' I said. 'Let him paint rocks all day,' I said. 'Only for Heaven's sake, keep him the Hell off of Fire Island,' I said. And was I right, Harold?" demanded the large blonde.

Pete Martens was whispering something, Bob realized. By the look on his face it must have been important, so the young man tried to hear the words over the buzzing, and thought to himself in a fuddled fashion that they ought to be taken down on a steno pad, or something of that sort . . . *want to know, really know, where it begins and how, and how often?* But no; what do I know? For years I've been Clara the rotten step-mother, and now I'm Clara the rotten mother-in-law. *Are there such in every generation? Must be . . . known for years . . . known for years . . . only, Who?—and Where?—searched and sought, like Livingston and all the others searching and seeking, enduring privation, looking for the sources of the Nile . . .*

Someone, it must have been Clara, gave a long, shuddering cry; and then for a while there was nothing but the buzzing, buzzing, buzzing, in Bob Rosen's head; while old Martens lolled back in the chair, regarding him silently and sardonically with his blood-red eye, over which the lid slowly, slowly drooped: but old Martens never said a word more.

It was one genuine horror of a hangover, subsiding slowly under (or perhaps despite) every remedy Bob's aching brain could think of: black coffee, strong tea, chocolate milk, raw-egg-red-pepper-worcestershire sauce. At least, he thought gratefully after a while, he was spared the dry heaves. At least he had all the fixings in his apartment and didn't have to go out. It was a pivotal neighborhood, and he lived right in the pivot, a block where lox and bagels beat a slow retreat before the advance of hog maw and chitterlings on the one hand and *bodegas, comidas criollas,* on the other; swarms of noisy kids running between the trucks and buses, the jackhammers forever wounding the streets.

It took him a moment to realize that the noise he was hearing now was not the muffled echo of the drills, but a tapping on his door. Unsteadily, he tottered over and opened it. He would have been not in the least surprised to find a raven there, but instead it was a tall man, rather stooping, with a tiny head, hands folded mantis-like at his bosom.

After a few dry, futile clickings, Bob's throat essayed the name "Shadburn?"

"Shadwell," he was corrected, softly. "T. Pettys Shadwell . . . I'm afraid you're not well, Mr. Rosen . . ."

Bob clutched the doorpost, moaned softly. Shadwell's hands unfolded, revealed—not a smaller man at whom he'd been nibbling, but a paper bag, soon opened.

" . . . so I thought I'd take the liberty of bringing you some hot chicken broth."

It was gratefully warm, had both body and savor. Bob lapped at it, croaked his thanks. "Not at all, not-a-tall," Shadwell waved. "Glad to be of some small help." A silence fell, relieved only by weak, gulping noises. "Too bad about old Martens. Of course, he *was* old. Still, a shocking thing to happen to you. A stroke, I'm told. I, uh, trust the police gave you no trouble?"

A wave of mild strength seemed to flow into Bob from the hot broth. "No, they were very nice," he said. "The sergeant called me, 'Son.' They brought me back here."

"Ah." Shadwell was reflective. "He had no family. I know that for a fact."

"Mmm."

"But—assume he left a few dollars. Unlikely, but— And assume he'd willed the few dollars to someone or some charity, perhaps. Never mind. Doesn't concern us. He wouldn't bother to will his papers . . . scrapbooks of old copy he'd written, so forth. That's of no interest to people in general. Just be thrown out or burned. But it would be of interest to *me*. I mean, I've been in advertising all my life, you know. Oh, yes. Used to distribute handbills when I was a boy. Fact."

Bob tried to visualize T. Pettys Shadwell as a boy, failed, drank soup. "Good soup" he said. "Thanks. Very kind of you."

Shadwell urged him strongly not to mention it. He chuckled. "Old Pete used to lug around some of the darndest stuff in that portfolio of his," he said. "In fact, some of it referred to a scheme we were once trying to work out together. Nothing came of it, however, and the old fellow was inclined to be a bit testy about that, still—I believe you'd find it interesting. May I show you?"

Bob still felt rotten, but the death wish had departed. "Sure," he said. Shadwell looked around the room, then at Bob, expectantly. After a minute he said, "Where is it?" "Where is what?" "The portfolio. Old Martens'."

They stared at each other. The phone rang. With a wince and a groan, Bob answered. It was Noreen, a girl with pretensions to stagecraft and literature, with whom he had been furtively lecherous on an off-and-on basis, the off periods' commencements being signaled by the presence in Noreen's apartment of Noreen's mother, (knitting, middleclass morality and all) when Bob came, intent on venery.

"I've got a terrible hangover," he said, answering her first (guarded and conventional) question; "and the place is a mess."

"See what happens if I turn my back on you for a minute?" Noreen clucked, happily. "Luckily, I have neither work nor social obligations planned for the day, so I'll be right over."

Bob said, "Crazy!", hung up, and turned to face Shadwell, who had been nibbling the tips of his prehensile fingers. "Thanks for the soup," he said, in tones of some finality.

"But the portfolio?" "I haven't got it." "It was leaning against the old man's chair when I saw the two of you in the bar." "Then maybe it's still *in* the bar. Or in the hospital. Or maybe the cops have it. But—" "It isn't. They don't." "But *I* haven't got it. Honest, Mr. Shadwell, I appreciate the soup, but I don't know where the Hell—"

Shadwell rubbed his tiny, sharp mustache, like a Δ-mark pointing to his tiny, sharp nose. He rose. "This is really too bad. Those papers referring to the business old Peter and I had been mutually engaged in—really, I have as much right to them as . . . But look here. Perhaps he may have spoken to you about it. He always did when he'd been drinking and usually did even when he wasn't.

What he liked to refer to as, 'The sources of the Nile'? Hmm?" The phrase climbed the belfry and rang bells audible, or at least apparent, to Shadwell. He seemed to leap forward, long fingers resting on Bob's shoulders.

"You do know what I mean. Look. You: Are a writer. The old man's ideas aren't in your line. I: Am an advertising man. They are in my line. For the contents of his portfolio—as I've explained, they are rightfully mine—I will give: One thousand: Dollars. In fact: For the opportunity of merely *looking* through it: I will give: One *hundred*. Dollars."

As Bob reflected that his last check had been for $17.72 (Monegasque rights to a detective story), and as he heard these vasty sums bandied about, his eyes grew large, and he strove hard to recall what the Hell *had* happened to the portfolio—but in vain.

Shadwell's dry, whispery voice took on a pleading note. "I'm even willing to pay you for the privilege of discussing your conversation with the old f— the old gentleman. Here—" And he reached into his pocket. Bob wavered. Then he recalled that Noreen was even now on her way uptown and crosstown, doubtless bearing with her, as usual, in addition to her own taut charms, various tokens of exotic victualry to which she—turning her back on the veal chops and green peas of childhood and suburbia—was given: such as Shashlik makings, *lokoumi*, wines of the warm south, *baklava*, *provalone*, and other living witnesses to the glory that was Greece and the grandeur that was Rome.

Various hungers, thus stimulated, began to rise and clamor, and he steeled himself against Shadwell's possibly unethical and certainly inconveniently timed offers.

"Not now," he said. Then, throwing delicacy to the winds, "I'm expecting a girl friend. Beat it. Another time."

Annoyance and chagrin on Shadwell's small face, succeeded by an exceedingly disgusting leer. "Why, of *course*," he said. "Another time? Certainly. My card—" He hauled out the perforated pack. "I already got one," Bob said. "Goodbye."

He made haste to throw off the noisome clothes in which he had been first hot, then drunk, then comatose; to take a shower, comb his mouse-colored hair, shave the pink bristles whose odious tint alone prevented him from growing a beard, to spray and anoint himself with various nostra which T. Pettys Shadwell's more successful colleagues in advertising had convinced him (by a thousand ways, both blunt and subtle) were essential to his acceptance by good society; then to dress and await with unconcealed anticipation the advent of the unchaste Noreen.

She came, she kissed him, she prepared food for him: ancient duties of women, any neglect of which is a sure and certain sign of cultural decadence and retrogression. Then she read everything he had written since their last juncture, and here she had some fault to find.

"You waste too much time at the beginning, in description," she said, with the certainty possible to those who have never sold a single manuscript. "You've got to make your characters come *alive*—in the very first sentence."

" 'Marley was dead, to begin with,' " muttered Bob.

"What?" murmured Noreen, vaguely, feigning not to hear. Her eye, avoiding lover boy, lit on something else. "What's this?" she asked. "You have so much money you just leave it lying around? I thought you said you were broke." And Bob followed her pointing and encarnadined fingertip to where lay two crisp twenty-dollar bills, folded lengthwise, on the table next the door.

"Shadwell!" he said, instantly. And, in response to her arched brows (which would have looked much better unplucked, but who can what will away?), he said, "A real rat of a guy—a louse, a boor—who had some crumby proposal."

"And who also has," said Noreen, going straight to the heart of the matter, "money." Bob resolved never to introduce the two of them, if he could help it. "Anyway," she continued, laying aside Bob's manuscript, "now you can take me out somewhere." Feebly he argued the food then cooking; she turned off the gas and thrust the pots incontinently into the ice-box, rose, and indicated she was now ready to leave. He had other objections to leaving just then, which it would have been impolitic to mention, for in Noreen's scheme of morality each episode of passion was a sealed incident once it was over, and constituted no promise of any other yet to come.

With resignation tempered by the reflection that Shadwell's four sawbucks couldn't last forever, and that there was never so long-drawn-out an evening but would wind up eventually back in his apartment, Bob accompanied her out the door.

And so it was. The next day, following Noreen's departure in mid-morning, found Bob in excellent spirits but flat-broke. He was reviewing the possibilities of getting an advance from his agent, Stuart Emmanuel, a tiny, dapper man whose eyes behind double lenses were like great black shoebuttons, when the phone rang. ESP or no ESP, it was Stuart himself, with an invitation to lunch.

"I'm glad *some* of your clients are making money," said Bob, most ungraciously.

"Oh, it's not my money," said Stuart. "It's J. Oscar Rutherford's. One of his top men—no, it's not Joe Tressling, I know you saw him the day before yesterday, yes, I know nothing came of it, this is a different fellow altogether. Phillips Anhalt. I want you to come."

So Bob left yesterday's half-cooked chow in the ice-box and, very little loath, set out to meet Stuart and Phillips Anhalt, of whom he had never heard before. The first rendezvous was for a drink at a bar whose name also meant nothing to him, though as soon as he walked in he recognized it as the one where he had been the day before yesterday, and this made him uneasy—doubly so, for he had callously almost forgotten what had had happened there. The bartender, it was at once evident, had not. His wary glance at the three of them must have convinced him that they were reasonably good insurance risks, however, for he made no comment.

Anhalt was a middle-sized man with a rather sweet and slightly baffled face and iron-gray haircut *en brosse*. "I enjoyed your story very much," he told Bob—thus breaking in at once upon the shallow slumber of the little scold who boarded in Bob's Writer's Consciousness. Of *course* (it shrilled) I know *exactly* the one you mean, after all, I've written only *one* story in my entire *life* so *"your story"* is the only identification it needs. I liked your *novel*, Mr. Hemingway. I enjoyed your *play*, Mr. Kaufman.

Stuart Emmanuel, who knew the labyrinthine ways of writers' mind as he knew the figures in his bank statement, said smoothly, "I expect Mr. Anhalt refers to *Unvexed to the Sea."*

With firm politeness Mr. Anhalt disappointed this expectation. "I know that's the prize-winner," he said, "and I mean to read it, but the one I referred to was *The Green Wall."* Now, as it happened this very short little story had been bounced thirteen times before its purchase for a negligible sum by a low-grade salvage market of a magazine; but it was one of Bob's favorites. He smiled at Phillips Anhalt, Anhalt smiled at him, Stuart beamed and ordered drinks.

The waiter passed a folded slip of paper to Bob Rosen when he came with the popskull. "The lady left it," he said. "What lady?" "The blond lady." Agent and ad man smiled, made appropriate remarks while Bob scanned the note, recognized it as being in his own handwriting, failed to make it out, crammed it in his pocket.

"Mr. Anhalt," said Stuart, turning dark, large-pupiled eyes on his client, "is a very important man at Rutherford's: he has a corner office." A gentle, somewhat tired smile from Anhalt, who gave the conversation a turn and talked about his home in Darien, and the work he was doing on it, by himself. Thus they got through the round of drinks, then walked a few blocks to the restaurant.

Here Bob was infinitely relieved that Anhalt did not order poached egg on creamed spinach, corned beef hash, or something equally simple, wholesome, and disgusting, and tending to inhibit Bob's own wide-ranging tastes: Anhalt ordered duckling, Stuart had mutton chops, and Bob chose tripe and onions.

"Joe Tressling tells me that you're going to write something for the cheese show," said Anhalt, as they disarranged the pickle plate. Bob half-lifted his eyebrows, smiled. Stuart gazed broodingly into the innards of a sour tomato as if he might be saying to himself, "Ten percent of $17.72, Monegasque rights to a detective story."

"More cheese is being eaten today in the United States than twenty-five years ago," Anhalt continued. "Much, much more. . . . Is it the result of advertising? Such as the Aunt Carrie Hour? Has that changed public taste? Or— has public taste changed for, say, other reasons, and are we just riding the wave?"

"The man who could have answered that question," Bob said, "died the day before yesterday."

Anhalt let out his breath. "How do you know he could have?"

"He said so."

Anhalt, who'd had a half-eaten dilled cucumber in his hand, carefully laid it in the ash-tray, and leaned forward. "What else did he say? Old Martens, I mean. You *do* mean Old Martens, don't you?"

Bob said that was right, and added, with unintentional untruthfulness, that he'd been offered a thousand dollars for that information, and had turned it down. Before he could correct himself, Anhalt, customary faint pink face gone almost red, and Stuart Emmanuel, eyes glittering hugely, said with one voice, *"Who offered—?"*

"What comes out of a chimney?"

Stuart, recovering first (Anhalt continued to stare, said nothing, while the color receded), said, "Bob, this is not a joke. That is the reason we have this appointment. An awful lot of money is involved—for you, for me, for Phil Anhalt, for, well, for everybody. For just everybody. So—"

It slipped out. "For T. Pettys Shadwell?" Bob asked.

The effect, as they used to say in pre-atomic days, was electrical. Stuart made a noise, between a moan and a hiss, rather like a man who, having trustingly lowered his breeches, sits all unawares upon an icicle. He clutched Bob's hand. "You didn't godforbid *sign* anything?" he wailed. Anhalt, who had gone red before, went white this time around, but still retained diffidence enough to place his hand merely upon Bob's jacket cuff.

"He's a cad!" he said, in trembling tones. "A swine, Mr. Rosen!"

" 'The most despicable of living men'," quoted Mr. Rosen. ("Exactly," said Anhalt.)

"Bob, you didn't *sign* anything, godforbid?"

"No. No. No. But I feel as if I've had all the mystery I intend to have. And unless I get Information, why, gents, I shan't undo one button." The waiter arrived with the food and, according to the rules and customs of the Waiters' Union, gave everybody the wrong orders. When this was straightened out, Stuart said, confidently, "Why, of course, Bob: Information: Why, certainly. There is nothing to conceal. Not from *you*," he said, chuckling. "Go ahead, start eating. I'll eat and talk, you just eat and listen."

And so, as he tucked away the tripe and onions, Bob heard Stuart recount, through a slight barrier of masticated mutton-chop, a most astonishing tale. In every generation (Stuart said) there were leaders of fashion, arbiters of style. At Nero's court, Petronius. In Regency England, Beau Brummel. At present and for some time past, everyone knew about the Paris designers and their influence. And in the literary field ("Ahah!" muttered Bob, staring darkly at his forkful of stewed ox-paunch)—in the literary field, said Stuart, swallowing in haste for greater clarity, they all knew what effect a review by any one of A Certain Few Names, on the front page of the Sunday Times book section, could have upon the work of even an absolute unknown.

"It will sky-rocket it to Fame and Fortune with the speed of light," said Stuart.

"Come to the point." But Stuart, now grinding away on a chunk of grilled sheep, could only gurgle, wave his fork, and raise his eyebrows. Anhalt stopped his moody task of reducing the duckling to a mass of orange-flavored fibres, and turned to take the words, as it were, from Stuart's mutton-filled mouth.

"The point, Mr. Rosen, is that poor old Martens went up and down Madison Avenue for years claiming he had found a way of predicting fashions and styles, and nobody believed him. Frankly, *I* didn't. But I do now. What caused me to change my mind was this: When I heard, day before yesterday, that he had died so suddenly, I had a feeling that I *had* something of his, something that he'd left for me to look at once, something I'd taken just to get rid of him.

And, oh, perhaps I was feeling a bit guilty, certainly a bit sorry, so I asked my secretary to get it for me. Well, you know, with the J. Oscar Rutherford people, as with Nature, nothing is ever lost—" Phillips Anhalt smiled his rather shy, rather sweet and slightly baffled smile—"so she got it for me and I took a look at it. . . . I was . . ." he paused, hesitated for *mot juste.*

Stuart, with a masterful swallow, leaped into the breach, claymore in hand. "He was flabbergasted!"

Astounded, amended Anhalt. He was astounded.

There, in an envelope addressed to Peter Martens, and postmarked November 10, 1945, was a color snapshot of a young man wearing a fancy weskit.

"Now, you know, Mr. Rosen, no one in 1945 was wearing fancy weskits. They didn't come in till some years later. How did Martens *know* they were going to come in? And there was another snapshot of a young man in a charcoal suit and a pink shirt. Nobody was wearing that outfit in '45 . . . I checked the records, you see, and the old gentleman had left the things for me in December of that year. I'm ashamed to say that I had the receptionist put him off when he called again . . . But just think of it: fancy weskits, charcoal suits, pink shirts, in 1945." He brooded. Bob asked if there was anything about gray flannel suits in the envelope, and Anhalt smiled a faint and fleeting smile.

"Ah, Bob, now, Bob," Stuart pursed his mouth in mild (and greasy) reproof. "You still don't seem to realize that this is S*E*R*I*O*U*S*."

"Indeed it is," said P. Anhalt. "As soon as I told Mac about it, do you know what he said, Stu? He said, 'Phil, don't spare the horses.' " And they nodded soberly, as those who have received wisdom from on high.

"Who," Bob asked, "is Mac?"

Shocked looks. Mac, he was told, the older men speaking both tandem and *au pair*, was Robert R. Mac Ian, head of the happy J. Oscar Rutherford corporate family.

"Of course, Phil," Stuart observed, picking slyly at his baked potato, "I won't ask why it took you till this morning to get in touch with me. With some other outfit, I might maybe suspect that they were trying to see what they could locate for themselves without having to cut our boy, here, in for a slice of the pie. He being the old man's confidante and moral heir, anyway, so to speak." (Bob stared at this description, said nothing. Let the thing develop as far at it would by itself, he reflected.) "But not the Rutherford outfit. It's too big, too ethical, for things like that." Anhalt didn't answer.

After a second, Stuart went on, "Yes, Bob, this is really something big. If the late old Mr. Martens' ideas can be successfully developed—and I'm sure Phil, here will not expect you to divulge until we are ready to talk Terms— they will be really invaluable to people like manufacturers, fashion editors, designers, merchants, and, last but not least—advertising men. Fortunes can literally be made, and saved. No wonder that a dirty dog like this guy Shadwell is trying to horn in on it. Why, listen—but I'm afraid we'll have to terminate this enchanting conversation. Bob has to go home and get the material in order—" (What material? Bob wondered. Oh, well, so far: $40 from Shadwell and a free lunch from Anhalt.)—"and you and I, Phil, will discuss those horses Mac said not to spare."

Anhalt nodded. It seemed obvious to Rosen that the ad man was unhappy, unhappy about having given Peter Martens the brush-off while he was alive, unhappy about being numbered among the vultures now that he was dead. And, so thinking, Bob realized with more than a touch of shame, that he himself was now numbered among the vultures; and he asked about funeral arrangements. But it seemed that the Masonic order was taking care of that: the late Peter Martens was already on his way back to his native town of Marietta, Ohio, where his lodge brothers would give him a formal farewell: aprons, sprigs of acacia, and all the ritual appurtenances. And Bob thought, why not? And was feeling somehow, very much relieved.

On the uptown bus which he had chosen over the swifter, hotter, dingier subway, he tried to collect his thoughts. What on earth could he ever hope to remember about a drunken conversation, which would make any sense to anybody, let alone be worth money? "The Sources of the Nile," the old man had said, glaring at him with bloody eye. Well, Shadwell knew the phrase, too. Maybe Shadwell knew what it meant, exactly what it meant, because he, Bob Rosen, sure as Hell didn't. But the phrase did catch at the imagination. Martens had spent years—who knew how many?—seeking the sources of his particular Nile, the great river of fashion, as Mungo Park, Livingstone, Speke, and other half-forgotten explorers, had spent years in search of theirs. They had all endured privation, anguish, rebuffs, hostility . . . and in the end, just as the quest had killed Mungo Park, Livingstone, Speke, the other quest had killed old Peter Martens.

But, aside from insisting that there *was* a source or sources, and that he knew *where*, what had Peter said? Why hadn't Bob stayed sober? Probably that fat blonde at the next table, she of the poisonously green drink and the rotten step-children, probably she retained more of the old man's tale, picked up by intertable osmosis, than did Bob himself.

And with that he heard the voice of the waiter at the bar that noon: *The lady left it . . . What lady? . . . The blond lady* . . . Bob scrabbled in his pocket and came up with the note. On the sweaty, crumpled bit of paper, scrawled in his own writing, or a cruel semblance of it, he read: *Ditx sags su Bimsoh oh—*

"What the *Hell!*" he muttered, and fell to, with furrowed face, to make out what evidently owed more to Bushmill's than to Everhard Faber. At length he decided that the note read, *Peter says, see Bensons on Purchase Place, the Bronx, if I don't believe him. Peter says, write it down.*

"It must mean something," he said, half-aloud, staring absently from Fifth Avenue to Central Park, as the bus roared and rattled between opulence and greenery. "It has to mean something."

"Well, what a shame," said Mr. Benson. "But how nice it was of you to come and tell us." His wavy-gray hair was cut evenly around in soupbowl style, and as there was no white skin at the back of his neck, had evidently been so cut for some time. "Would you like some iced tea?"

"Still, he Went Quickly," said Mrs. Benson, who, at the business of being a woman, was in rather a large way of business. "I don't think there's any iced tea, Daddy. When I have to go, that's the way I want to go. Lemonade, maybe?"

"There isn't any lemonade if what Kitty was drinking was the last of the lemonade. The Masons give you a nice funeral. A real nice funeral. I used to think about joining up, but I never seem to get around to it. I think there's some gin. Isn't there some gin, Mommy? How about a nice cool glass of gin-and-cider, Bob? Kit will make us some, by and by."

Bob said, softly, that that sounded nice. He sat half-sunken in a canvas chair in the large, cool living-room. A quarter of an hour ago, having found out with little difficulty *which* house on Purchase Place was the Bensons', he had approached with something close to fear and trembling. Certainly, he had been sweating in profusion. The not-too-recently painted wooden house was just a blind, he told himself. Inside there would be banks of noiseless machines into which cards were fed and from which tapes rolled in smooth continuity. And a large, broad-shouldered young man whose hair was cut so close to the skull that the scars underneath were plain to see, this young man would bar Bob's way and, with cold, calm, confidence, say, "Yes?"

"Er, um, Mr. Martens told me to see Mr. Benson."

"There is no Mr. Martens connected with our organization and Mr. Benson had gone to Washington. I'm afraid you can't come in: everything here is Classified."

And Bob would slink away, feeling Shoulders' scornful glance in the small of his shrinking, sweaty back.

But it hadn't been like that at all. Not anything like that at all.

Mr. Benson waved an envelope at Bob. "Here's a connivo, if you like," he said. "Fooled I don't know how many honest collectors, and dealers, too: Prince Abu-Somebody flies over here from Pseudo-Arabia without an expense account. Gets in with some crooked dealers, *I* could name them, but I won't, prints off this *en—tire* issue of airmails, precancelled. Made a mint. Flies back to Pseudo-Arabia, *whomp!* they cut off his head!" And he chuckled richly at the thought of this prompt and summary vengeance. Plainly, in Mr. Benson's eyes, it had been done in the name of philatelic ethics; no considerations of dynastic intrigues among the petrol pashas entered his mind.

"Kitty, are you going to make us some cold drinks?" Mrs. B. inquired. "Poor old Pete, he used to be here for Sunday dinner on and off, oh, for just years. Is that Bentley coming?"

Bob just sat and sucked in the coolness and the calm and stared at Kitty. Kitty had a tiny stencil cut in the design of a star and she was carefully lacquering her toenails with it. He could hardly believe she was for real. "Ethereal" was the word for her beauty, and "ethereal" was the only word for it. Long, long hair of an indescribable gold fell over her heart-shaped face as she bent forward towards each perfectly formed toe. And she was wearing a dress like that of a child in a Kate Greenaway book.

"Oh, Bentley," said B., Senior. "What do you think has happened? Uncle Peter Martens passed away, all of a sudden, day before yesterday, and this gentleman is a friend of his and came to tell us about it; isn't that thoughtful?"

Bentley said, *"Ahhh."* Bentley was a mid-teener who wore jeans cut off at the knees and sneakers with the toes, insteps, and heels removed. He was naked to the waist and across his suntanned and hairless chest, in a neat curve commencing just over his left nipple and terminating just under his right nipple, was the word *VIPERS* stenciled in red paint.

"*Ahhh,*" said Bentley Benson. "Any pepsies?"

"Well, I'd asked you to bring some," his mother said, mildly. "Make a nice, big pitcher of gin-and-cider, Bentley, please, but only a *little* gin for yourself, in a separate glass, remember, now." Bentley said, "*Ahhh,*" and departed, scratching on his chest right over the bright, red *S*.

Bob's relaxed gaze took in, one by one, the pictures in the mantelpiece. He sat up a bit, pointed. "Who is that?" he asked. The young man looked something like Bentley and something like Bentley's father.

"That's my oldest boy, Barton, Junior," said Mother B. "You see that nice vest he's wearing? Well, right after the War, Bart, he was in the Navy then, picked up a piece of lovely brocade over in Japan, and he sent it back home. I thought of making a nice bed-jacket out of it, but there wasn't enough material. So I made it into a nice vest, instead. Poor old Uncle Peter, he liked that vest, took a picture of Bart in it. Well, what do you know, a few years later fancy vests became quite popular, and, of course, by that time Bart was tired of his ("Of course," Bob murmured), so he sold it to a college boy who had a summer job at Little and Harpey's. Got $25 for it, and we all went out to dinner down town that night."

Kitty delicately stenciled another star on her toenails.

"I see," Bob said. After a moment, "Little and Harpey's?" he repeated.

Yes, that same. The publishers. Bart, and his younger brother Alton, were publishers' readers. Alt had been with Little and Harpey but was now with Scribbley's Sons; Bart had worked for Scribbley's at one time, too. "They've been with *all* the biggest publishing houses," their mother said, proudly. "Oh, *they* aren't any of your stick-in-the-muds, no sirree." Her hands had been fiddling with a piece of bright cloth, and then, suddenly, cloth and hands went up to her head, her fingers flashed, and—complete, perfect—she was wearing an intricately folded turban.

Bentley came in carrying a pitcher of drink in one hand and five glasses—one to each finger—in the other. "I told you to mix yours separately, I think," his mother said. Taking no notice of her youngest's *Ahhh,* she turned to Bob. "I have a whole basket of these pieces of madras," she said, "some silk, some cotton . . . and it's been on my mind all day. Now, if I just remember the way those old women from the West Indies used to tie them on their heads when I was girl . . . and now, sure enough, it just came back to me! How does it look?" she asked.

"Looks very nice, Mommy," said Bart, Sr. And added, "I bet it would cover up the curlers better than those babushkas the women wear, you know?"

Bob Rosen bet it would, too.

So here it was and this was it. The sources of the Nile. How old Peter Martens had discovered it, Bob did not know. By and by, he supposed, he would find out. How did they *do* it, was it that they had a *panache*—? or was it a "wild talent," like telepathy, second sight, and calling dice or balls? He did not know.

"Bart said he was reading a real nice manuscript that came in just the other day," observed Mrs. Benson, dreamily, over her glass. "About South America. He says he thinks that South America has been neglected, and that there is going to be a revival of interest in non-fiction about South America."

"No more Bushmen?" Barton, Sr., asked.

"No, Bart says he thinks the public is getting tired of Bushmen. He says he only gives Bushmen another three months and then—poo—you won't be able to *give* the books away." Bob asked what Alton thought. "Well, Alton is reading fiction now, you know. He thinks the public is getting tired of novels about murder and sex and funny war experiences. Alt thinks they're about ready for some novels about ministers. He said to one of the writers that Scribbley's publishes, 'Why don't you do a novel about a minister?' he said. And the man said he thought it was a good idea."

There was a long, comfortable silence.

There was no doubt about it. *How* the Bensons did it, Bob still didn't know. But they did do it. With absolute unconsciousness and with absolute accuracy, they were able to predict future trends in fashion. It was marvelous. It was uncanny. It—

Kitty lifted her lovely head and looked at Bob through the long, silken skein of hair, then brushed it aside. "Do you ever have any money?" she asked. It was like the sound of small silver bells, her voice. Where, compared to this, were the flat Long Island vocables of, say, Noreen? Nowhere at all.

"Why, Kitty Benson, what a question," her mother said, reaching out her glass for Bentley to refill. "Poor Peter Martens, just to think—a little more, Bentley, don't think you're going to drink what's left, young man."

"Because if you ever have any money," said the voice like the Horns of Elfland. "We could go out somewhere together. Some boys don't ever have any money," it concluded, with infinitely loving melancholy.

"I'm going to have some money," Bob said at once. "Absolutely. Uh— when could—"

She smiled an absolute enchantment of a smile. "Not tonight," she said, "because I have a date. And not tomorrow night, because I have a date. But the day after tomorrow night, because then I don't have a date."

A little voice in one corner of Bob's mind said, "This girl has a brain about the size of a small split pea; you know that, don't you?" And another voice, much less little, in the opposite corner, shrieked, "Who *cares*? Who *cares*?" Furthermore, Noreen had made a faint but definite beginning on an extra chin, and her bosom tended (unless artfully and artificially supported) to droop. Neither was true of Kitty at all, at all.

"The day after tomorrow night, then," he said. "It's a date."

All that night he wrestled with his angel. "You can't expose these people to the sordid glare of modern commerce," the angel said, throwing him with a half-nelson. "They'd wither and die. Look at the dodo—look at the buffalo. Will you *look*?" "*You* look," growled Bob, breaking the hold, and seizing the angel in a scissors-lock. "I'm not going to let any damned account executives get their chicken-plucking hands on the Bensons. It'll all be done through me, see? Through *me!*" And with that he pinned the angel's shoulders to the mat. "And besides," he said, clenching his teeth, "I need the money . . ."

Next morning he called up his agent. "Here's just a few samples to toss Mr. Phillips Anhalt's way," he said grandiosely. "Write 'em down. Soupbowl haircuts for men. *That's* what I said. They can get a sunlamp treatment for the backs of their necks in the barber-shops. Listen. Women will stencil stars on their toe-nails with nail polish. Kate Greenaway style dresses for women are going to come in. Huh? Well, you bet your butt that Anhalt will know what Kate Greenaway means. Also, what smart women will wear will be madras kerchiefs tied up in the old West Indian way. This is very complicated, so I guess they'll have to be pre-folded and pre-stitched. Silks and cottons. . . . You writing this down? Okay.

" 'Teen-agers will wear, summer-time, I mean, they'll wear shorts made out of cut-down blue jeans. And sandals made out of cut-down sneakers. No shirts or undershirts—barechested, and—What? *NO*, for cry-sake, just the *boys!*"

And he gave Stuart the rest of it, books and all, and he demanded and got an advance. Next day Stuart reported that Anhalt reported that Mac Ian was quite excited. Mac had said—did Bob know what Phil said Mac said? Well, Mac said, "Let's not spoil the ship for a penny's worth of tar, Phil."

Bob demanded and received another advance. When Noreen called, he was brusque.

The late morning of his date-day he called to confirm it. That is, he tried to. The operator said that she was sorry, but that number had been disconnected. He made it up to the Bronx by taxi. The house was empty. It was not only empty of people, it was empty of everything. The wallpaper had been left, but that was all.

Many years earlier, about the time of his first cigarette, Bob had been led by a friend in the dead of night (say, half-past ten) along a quiet suburban street, pledged to confidence by the most frightful vows. Propped against the wall of a garage was a ladder—it did not go all the way to the roof: Bob and friend had pulled themselves up with effort which, in another context, would have won the full approval of their gym teacher. The roof made an excellent post to observe the going-to-bed preparations of a young woman who had seemingly never learned that window shades could be pulled down. Suddenly lights went on in another house, illuminating the roof of the garage; the young woman had seen the two and yelled; and Bob, holding onto the parapet with sweating hands and reaching for the ladder with sweating feet, had discovered that the ladder was no longer there. . . .

He felt the same way now.

Besides feeling stunned, incredulous, and panicky, he also felt annoyed. This was because he acutely realized that he was acting out an old moving picture scene. The scene would have been close to the (film) realities had he been wearing a tattered uniform, and in a way he wanted to giggle, and in a way he wanted to cry. Only through obligation to the script did he carry the farce farther: wandering in and out of empty rooms, calling out names, asking if anyone was there.

No one was. And there was no notes or messages, not even *Croatan* carved on a doorpost. Once, in the gathering shadows, he thought he heard a noise, and he whirled around, half-expecting to see an enfeebled Mr. Benson with a bacon-fat lamp in one hand, or an elderly Negro, perhaps, who would say, tearfully, "Marse Bob, dem Yan-kees done burn all de cotton..." But there was nothing.

He trod the stairs to the next house and addressed inquiries to an old lady in a rocking-chair. "Well, I'm sure that *I* don't know," she said, in a paper-thin and fretful voice. "I saw them, all dressed up, getting into the car, and I said, 'Why, where are you all *going,* Hazel?' ("Hazel?" "Hazel Benson. I thought you said you *knew* them, young man?" "Oh, yes. Yes, of course. Please go on.") Well, I said, 'Where are you all *going,* Hazel?' And she said, 'It's time for a change, Mrs. Machen.' And they all laughed and they waved and they drove away. And then some men came and packed everything up and took it away in trucks. Well 'Where did they all *go?*' I asked them. 'Where did they all *go?*' But do you think they'd have the common decency to *tell* me, after I've lived here for fifty-four years? Not-a-word. Oh—"

Feeling himself infinitely cunning, Bob said, offhandedly, "Yes, I know just the outfit you mean. O'Brien Movers."

"I do *not* mean O'Brien Movers. Whatever gave you such an idea? It was the Seven Sebastian Sisters."

And this was the most that Bob Rosen could learn. Inquiries at other houses either drew blanks or produced such probably significant items as, "Kitty said, 'Here are your curlers, because I won't need them anymore' "; "Yes, just the other day I was talking to Bart, Senior, and he said, 'You know, you don't realize that you're in a rut until you have to look up to see the sky.' Well, those Bensons always talked a little crazy, and so I thought nothing of it, until—"; and, "I said to Bentley, 'Vipe, how about tomorrow we go over to Williamsbridge and pass the chicks there in review?' and he said, 'No, Vipe, I can't make the scene tomorrow, my ancients put another poster on the bill-board.' So I said, 'Ay-las,' and next thing I know—"

"His who did what?"

"Fellow, you don't wot this Viper talk one note, do you? His *family,* see, they had made other plans. They really cut loose, didn't they?"

They really did. So there Bob was, neat and trim and sweet-smelling, and nowhere to go, and with a pocketful of money. He looked around the tree-lined street and two blocks away, on the corner, he saw a neon sign. *Harry's,* it flashed (green). *Bar and Grill* (red).

"Where's Harry?" he asked the middle-aged woman behind the bar.

"Lodge meeting," she said. "He'll be back soon. They aren't doing any labor tonight, just business. Waddle ya have?"

"A ball of Bushmill," he said. He wondered where he had heard that, last. It was cool in the bar. And then he remembered, and then he shuddered.

"Oh, that's bad," Stuart Emmanuel moaned. "That sounds very bad... And you shouldn't've gone to the moving van people yourself. Now you probably muddied the waters."

Bob hung his head. His efforts to extract information from the Seven Sebastian Sisters—apparently they were septuplets, and all had gray mustaches—had certainly failed wretchedly. And he kept seeing Kitty Benson's face, framed in her golden hair like a sun-lit nimbus, kept hearing Kitty Benson's golden voice.

"Well," Stuart said, "I'll do my damndest." And no doubt he did, but it wasn't enough. He was forced to come clean with Anhalt. And Anhalt, after puttering around, his sweet smile more baffled than ever, told Mac everything. Mac put the entire *force majeure* of the T. Oscar Rutherford organization behind the search. And they came up with two items.

Item. The Seven Sebastian Sisters had no other address than the one on Purchase Place, and all the furniture was in their fireproof warehouse, with two years' storage paid in advance.

Item. The owner of the house on Purchase Place said, "I told them I'd had an offer to buy the house, but I wouldn't, if they'd agree to a rent increase. And the next thing I knew, the keys came in the mail."

Little and Harpey, as well as Scribbley's Sons, reported only that Alt and Bart, Junior, had said that they were leaving, but hadn't said where they were going.

"Maybe they've gone on a trip somewhere," Stuart suggested. "Maybe they'll come back before long. Anhalt has ears in all the publishing houses, maybe he'll hear something."

But before Anhalt heard anything, Mac decided that there was no longer anything to hear. "I wash my hands of it all," he declared. "It's a wild goose chase. Where did you ever pick up this crackpot idea in the first place?" And Phillips Anhalt's smile faded away. Weeks passed, and months.

But Bob Rosen has never abandoned hope. He has checked with the Board of Education about Bentley's records, to see if they know anything about a transcript or transfer. He has haunted Nassau Street, bothering—in particular—dealers specializing in Pseudo-Arabian air mail issues, in hopes that Mr. Benson has made his whereabouts known to them. He has hocked his watch to buy hamburgers and pizzas for the Vipers, and innumerable Scotches on innumerable rocks for the trim young men and the girls fresh out of Bennington who staff the offices of our leading publishers. He—

In short, he has taken up the search of Peter Martens (Old Pete, Sneaky Pete). He is looking for the sources of the Nile. Has he *ever* found *anything?* Well, yes, as a matter of fact, he has.

The strange nature of cyclical coincidences has been summed up, somewhere, in the classical remark that one can go for years without seeing a one-legged man wearing a baseball cap; and then, in a single afternoon, one will see three of them. So it happened with Bob Rosen.

One day, feeling dull and heavy, and finding that the elfin notes of Kitty Benson's voice seemed to be growing fainter in his mind, Bob called up her old landlord.

"No," said the old landlord, "I never heard another word from them. And I'll tell you who else I never heard from, either. The fellow who offered to buy the house. He never came around and when I called his office, he just laughed at me. Fine way to do business."

"What's his name?" Bob asked, listlessly.

"Funny name," said the old landlord. "E. Peters Shadwall? Something like that. The Hell with him, anyway."

Bob tore his rooms apart looking for the card with the perforated top edge which Shadwell had—it seemed so very long ago—torn off his little book and given him. Also, it struck him, neither could he find the piece of paper on which he had scribbled Old Martens' last message, with the Bensons' name and street on it. He fumbled through the Yellow Book, but couldn't seem to locate the proper category for the mantisman's business. And he gave up on the regular directory, what with Shad, Shadd, -wel, -well, -welle, etc.

He would, he decided, go and ask Stuart Emmanuel. The dapper little agent had taken the loss of the Bensons so hard ("It was a beauty of a deal," he'd all but wept) that he might also advance a small sum of money for the sake of the Quest. Bob was in the upper East 40s when he passed a bar where he had once taken Noreen for cocktails—a mistake, for it had advanced her already expensive tastes another notch—and this reminded him that he had not heard from her in some time. He was trying to calculate just how much time, and if he ought to do something about it, when he saw the third one-legged man in the baseball cap.

That is to say, speaking nonmetaphorically, he had turned to cross a street in the middle of a block, and was halted by the absence of any gap between the two vehicles (part of a traffic jam caused by a long-unclosed incision in the street) directly in front of him. Reading from right to left, the vehicles consisted of an Eleanor-blue truck reading *Grandma Goldberg's Yum-Yum Borsht,* and an Obscene-pink Jaguar containing T. Pettys Shadwell and Noreen.

It was the Moment of the Shock of Recognition. He understood everything.

Without his making a sound, they turned together and saw him, mouth open, everything written on his face. And they knew that he knew.

"Why, Bob," said Noreen. "Ah, Rosen," said Shadwell.

"I'm sorry that we weren't able to have you at the *wedding*," she said. "But everything happened so *quickly*. Pete just swept me off my feet."

Bob said, "I'll bet."

She said, "Don't be bitter"—seeing that he was, and enjoying it. Horns sounded, voices cursed, but the line of cars didn't move.

"You did it," Bob said, coming close. Shadwell's hands left the wheel and came together at his chest, fingers down. "*You* saw that crisp green money he left and you saw his card and got in touch with him and *you* came in and took the note and—*Where are they?*" he shouted, taking hold of the small car and shaking it. "I don't give a damn about the money, just tell me where they are! Just let me see the girl!"

But T. Pettys Shadwell just laughed and laughed, his voice like the whisper of the wind in the dry leaves. "Why, *Bob,*" said Noreen, bugging her eyes and flashing her large, coarse gems, and giving the scene all she had, "why, Bob, was there a *girl*? You never told *me.*"

Bob abandoned his anger, disclaimed all interest in the commercial aspect of the Bensons, offered to execute bonds and sign papers in blood, if only he were allowed to see Kitty. Shadwell, fingering his tiny carat of a mustache, shrugged. "Write the girl a letter," he said, smirking. "I assure you, all mail will be forwarded." And then the traffic jam broke and the Jag zoomed off, Noreen's scarlet lips pursed in blowing a kiss.

"Write?" Why, bless you, of course Bob wrote. Every day and often twice a day for weeks. But never a reply did he get. And on realizing that his letters probably went no farther than Noreen (Mrs. T. Pettys) Shadwell, who doubtless gloated and sneered in the midst of her luxury, he fell into despair, and ceased. Where is Kitty of the heart-shaped face, Kitty of the light-gold hair, Kitty of the elfin voice? Where are her mother and father and her three brothers? Where now are the sources of the Nile? Ah, where?

So there you are. One can hardly suppose that Shadwell has perforce kidnapped the entire Benson family, but the fact is that they have disappeared almost entirely without trace, and the slight trace which remains leads directly to and only to the door of T. Pettys Shadwell Associates, Market Research Advisors. Has he whisked them all away to some sylvan retreat in the remote recesses of the Great Smoky Mountains? Are they even now pursuing their prophetic ways in one of the ever-burgeoning, endlessly proliferating suburbs of the City of the Angels? Or has he, with genius diabolical, located them so near to hand that far-sighted vision must needs forever miss them?

In deepest Brooklyn, perhaps, amongst whose labyrinthine ways an army of surveyors could scarce find their own stakes?—or in fathomless Queens, red brick and yellow brick, world without end, where the questing heart grows sick and faint?

Rosen does not know, but he has not ceased to care. He writes to live, but he lives to look, now selling, now searching, famine succeeding feast, but hope never failing.

Phillips Anhalt, however, has not continued so successfully. He has not Bob's hopes. Anhalt continues, it is true, with the T. Oscar Rutherford people, but no longer has his corner office, or any private office at all. Anhalt failed: Anhalt now has a desk in the bullpen with the other failures and the new apprentices.

And while Bob ceaselessly searches the streets—for who knows in which place he may find the springs bubbling and welling?—and while Anhalt drinks bitter tea and toils like a slave in a salt mine, that swine, that cad, that most despicable of living men, T. Pettys Shadwell, has three full floors in a new building of steel, aluminum, and blue-green glass a block from the Cathedral; he has a box at the Met, a house in Bucks County, a place on the Vineyard, an apartment in Beekman Place, a Caddy, a Bentley, *two* Jaguars, a yacht that sleeps ten, and one of the choicest small (but ever-growing) collection of Renoirs in private hands today. . . .

The Affair at Lahore Cantonment

INTRODUCTION BY EILEEN GUNN

Its twists and turns, its nested stories, its suggestion of other tales that never quite cross the path of the narration, all mark "The Affair at Lahore Cantonment" as a Davidsonian fabulation. It begins quite wonderfully, with a cool dawn, the promise of a hot day, a sudden plunge into bitter cold, then a damp plateau of thermal misery—all in the space of five sentences.

The layers of narration interact to yield a short, sharp meditation on the decline of empire. At the very heart of the piece is a theme to which Avram returned a number of times: the odd and not necessarily requited attachments formed by big, brawling soldiers to their smaller, meeker buddies.

The story's chilly glimpse of postwar London harkens back to a winter visit Avram made there in the early 1950s. A letter from that trip natters on cheerfully about the December weather: "California is California, . . . nothing but month after month of dreary, monotonous sunshine. Hey, look at that delightful drizzle!" Avram describes an improbable encounter with a pink-cheeked English lad:

"Will you give us a thruppence for the sweets?" he asks. Poor kid. Probably hasn't had a piece of candy in a coon's age. Everything is rationed over here.

"Which one of these are thruppence?" I ask him.

"That one there," he says.

"Isn't that what they call a florin?" They have more coins over here than Carter has liver pills.

"Ooo, you don't want to go calling it a florin, mister. Only foreigners call them that." Good thing to know.

. . . A couple years from now and most likely he'll be a Resident

Magistrate in Southern Somaliland, calmly picking off man-eating ti-gers while the anguished villagers beat their drums.

In some peculiar fashion, "The Affair at Lahore Cantonment" echos the letter's juxtaposition of Avram's experience and Kipling's Anglo-India.

First published in Ellery Queen's Mystery Magazine, *in June of 1961, "The Affair at Lahore Cantonment" received the Edgar Award from the Mystery Writers of America for best short story of the year. Oddly for a celebrated story, it has never before been collected.*

THE AFFAIR AT LAHORE CANTONMENT

IT IS SOME TIME before dawn, in the late spring, as I write this. The seagulls have more than an hour before it will be their moment to fly in from the river, screeing and crying, and then fly back. After them, the pigeons will murmur, and it will be day, perhaps a hot, sticky day. Right now the air is deliciously cool, but I find myself shivering. I find myself imagining the cold, the bitter cold, of that morning when Death came in full panoply, like one dressed for dinner. That morning so very long ago . . .

In the winter of 1946–7 it was cold enough to suit me, and more, although the thermometer was well above what I used to consider a cold winter at home. But I was then in England, and the wet and the chill never seemed to leave me. The cottage where I was staying had the most marvelous picturesque fire-places—it had them in every single room, in fact. But coal was rationed and firewood seemed not only unavailable, it seemed unheard of. There was an antique electric heater, but it emitted only a dull coppery glow which died out a few inches away. The only gas fire was, naturally enough, in the kitchen, a cramped and tiny room, where it was impossible to write.

And it was in order to write that I was in England. In the mornings I visited the private library, fortunately unbombed, where lay a mass of material unavailable in America. Afternoons I did the actual writing. In the early evenings I listened to the Third Program while I looked over what I had written, and revised it.

Late evenings? It was, as I say, cold. Raw and damp. I could retire to bed with a brace of hot water bottles and read. I could go to the movies. I could go to the local, see if they had any spirits left, or, failing that—and it usually failed—have a mug of cider. Beer, I don't care for. The local was named . . . well, I won't say exactly what it was named. It may have been called The Green Man. Or The Grapes. Or The Something Arms. A certain measure of reticence is, I think, called for, although by now the last of the principals in the story must surely be dead. But for those who are insatiably curious there are always the newspaper files to check.

But be all that as it may. It was eight o'clock at night. The Marx Brothers were playing at the cinema, but I had seen this one twice before the War and twice during the War. My two hot water bottles gaped pinkly, ready to preserve my feet from frostbite if I cared to retire early to bed. I would have, but it happened that the only reading matter was a large and illustrated work on Etruscan tombs.

So the local won. It was really no contest.

It was warm there, and noisy and smoky and sociable. True, almost none of the sociability was directed my way, but as long as I wasn't openly being hated, I didn't care. Besides, we were all in luck: there *was* whiskey on hand. Gin, too. I drank slowly of the stuff that keeps the bare knees of Scotland warm and watched the people at their quaint native rituals—darts, football pools, even skittles.

A large, rather loutish-looking man at my right, who had made somewhat of a point of ignoring me, said suddenly, "Ah, Gaffer's heard there's gin!" A sort of ripple ran through the crowded room, and I turned around to look.

A man and a woman had come in. A little husk of a shriveled old man, wrapped almost to the tip of his rufous nose. An old woman, evidently his wife, was with him, and she helped undo the cocoon of overcoat, pullover, and muffler that, once removed, seemed to reduce him by half. They were obviously known and liked.

"Hello, Gaffer," the people greeted him. "Hello, Ma."

"I don't know if I'll be able to come fetch him when it's his going-home time," she said.

"I can manage meself, Missus," the old man said querulously.

"If I don't turn up, some of you give him a hand and see he has all his buttons buttoned. One gin and two ales, Alfred—no more, mind!" And with a brisk, keen look all around she was off.

She seemed the younger of the two, but it may not have been a matter of years. Thin, she was, white-haired and wrinkled; but there was no pink or gray softness about her. Her black eyes snapped as she looked around. Her back was straight. There was something not quite local in the accents of her speech— a certain lilting quality.

The old man was given a seat at a table near me and the fellow who had first announced the old man's entrance now said, "Got your pension today, eh, Gaffer? Stand us a drink, there's a good fellow."

The old man stared at a palmful of change, then stirred it with a twisted finger. "My missus hasn't given me but enough for the gin and the two ales," he said.

"Ah, Tom's only having his games with you, Gaffer," someone said. "He does with everyone. Pay no mind." And they resumed their conversation where they'd left off, the chief topic of the night being that the English wife of an American serviceman stationed in the county had given birth to triplets. "Ah, those Yanks," they said indulgently.

" 'Ah, those Yanks,' " Tom mimicked. His spectacles were mended on the bridge with tape. "They get roaring drunk on the best whiskey that you and me can't find and couldn't afford to buy it if we could; they smash up cars like they cost nothing—you and me couldn't buy them if we saved forever. Curse and brawl like proper savages, they do."

There was an embarrassed silence. Someone said, "Now, Tom—" Someone looked at me, and away, quickly. And someone muttered, rather weakly, about there being "good and bad in all nations." I said nothing, telling myself that there was no point in getting into a quarrel with a middle-aged man whose grievances doubtless would be as great if all Americans, civil and military, vanished overnight from the United Kingdom.

To my surprise, and to everyone else's, it was the Gaffer who spoke up against the charge.

"You don't know what you're talking about, laddie-boy," he said to Tom, who must have been fifty, at least. " 'Tisn't that they're Yanks at all. 'Tis that they're soldiers, and in a strange land. That's a wicked life for a man. I've seen it meself. I could tell you a story—"

"Sweet Fanny Adams, no, don't!" Tom said loudly—an outburst which did nothing to increase his popularity. "I heard 'em all, millions of times. The old garrison at Lahore and the Pay-thans and the Af-gains and the Tarradiddles, mountain guns and mules, and, oh, the whole bloody parade. Give us a rest, Gaffer!"

He could have killed the old man with a slap of his hand, I suppose, the Gaffer looked that feeble. But he couldn't shut the old man up, now he'd had his sip of gin.

"No, you don't want to hear naught about it, but I'll tell it anyway. Me, that was fighting for the flag before you was born." For a moment his faded blue eyes seemed puzzled. "Oh, but I have seen terrible things," he said in a voice altogether different from his vigorously annoyed tone of a second before. "And the most terrible thing of all—to see my friend die before my eyes, and he died hard, and not to be able to do aught to help him." His words died off with a slow quiver.

Tom wasn't giving up that easily. "What's the football news?" he asked at large. No one answered.

"And not just the fighting in the Hills," the Gaffer went on. "What was that all for? India? They're giving India away now. No—other things . . . My *best* friend."

"How about a game of darts?" Tom urged, gesturing toward the back room, through the open door of which we could see the darts board and a frieze of old pictures which dated back six reigns or more. I'd often meant to examine them with attention, but never had.

". . . and it's all true, for I've got cuttin's to prove it. Young chap from newspaper was there and saw it and wrote it all up. Oh, it was terrible!" Tears welled to the reddened edges of his eyes. "But it had to be."

"Anyone for *darts?*"

Someone said, "Shut up, Tom. Go on, Gaffer."

And this was many years ago.

As you went along the Mall in Lahore (which was the local section of the Grand Trunk Road from Calcutta to Peshawur), you passed the museum and the cathedral and the Gardens and Government House and the Punjab Club. And you kept on passing, because you were an enlisted man and the Club was for officers and civilians of high rank. And then for three dusty miles there was nothing to speak of (natives hardly counted), and then there was the Cantonment, and in the Cantonment was the garrison.

"Head-bloody-quarters of the Third bloody Division of the Northern bloody Army," said the Docker. He spat into the dust. "And you can 'ave it all for one bloody yard of the Commercial Road of a Saturday night," he said. "Or *any* bloody night, for that matter!"

But his friend, the Mouse, knew nothing of the glories of the Commercial Road. He had taken the Queen's shilling in the market town that all his life he had regarded as if it were London, Baghdad, and Babylon. Lahore? He would have 'listed to go serve in Kamtchatka, if it had only got him away from his brute of a father, a drunken farm-laborer in a dirty smock. How, he often wondered, had he got the courage to take the step at all?

"It frightens me sometimes, Docker," he confessed. "It's all so strange and different."

The Docker gave him a look on which his habitual sneer was half overcome by affection. "Don't you 'ave no bloody fear while *I'm* wiv you!" And he touched him, very lightly, on the shoulder. The Docker was tall and strong, with straight black hair and sallow skin and a mouth that was quick to anger and quick to foul words even without anger, and a mind that was quick to take offense and slow—very slow—to forgive.

Sergeant-Major had shouted, "I'll teach you to look at me!" and had kicked him hard. That night in the lanes on the other side of the little bazaar, past the tank and the place where the hafiz taught, someone hit Sergeant-Major with a piece of iron, thrown with main force. Split his scalp open. Who? No one ever knew. When Sergeant-Major came off sick-list and went round telling about it, spreading his hair with his thick fingers to show the long and ugly wound with its black scab, the Docker passed by, walking proper slow. And Sergeant-Major looked up, suddenly, as if he recognized the footfalls, and there was a look passed between them that had murder in it. But nothing was said, nothing at all.

And no one kicked the Docker after that, and when it became known that he was the pal of the little private everyone called the Mouse, because of his coloring and his timid ways, why, no one kicked the Mouse either, after that.

"See that blackie there, Docker?" the Mouse demanded. "See that white bit of string round his waist and over? He's what they call a braymin. Like our parson back 'ome—only, fancy a parson with not more clothes on than that!"

A mild interest stirred the big soldier's face. "Knew a parson give me sixpence once, when I was a nipper," he said. "Only I 'ad to come to church and let 'im christen me, like, afore 'e'd leave me 'ave it. Nice old chap. Bit dotty."

The crowd was thick on the road, but somehow there was always space where the soldiers walked. They passed a blind Jew from Peshawur, with a gray lambskin cap on his head, playing music on the harmonium. It wasn't like any music the Mouse had ever heard, but it stirred him all the same. The Docker grandly threw a few pice in the cup and his little friend admired the gesture.

"That lane there—" the mouse drew close, dropped his voice— "they say there's women there. They say some of'm won't look at sojers. But they say that some of'm will."

The Docker set his cap acock on his head. "Let's 'ave a look, then, kiddy," he said. "And see which ones will." But they never did—at least, not that day. Because they met Lance-Corporal Owen going to the bazaar and with him were three young ladies, with ruffles and fancy hats and parasols. They were going to the bazaar to help Lance-Corporal Owen buy gifts to send home to his mother and sisters. And this was quite a coincidence, because when the Docker heard it he at once explained that he and the Mouse were bound on the same errand.

"Only they say the best prices are at the places where they don't speak English. And Alf, 'ere, and me, we don't know none of this Punjabee-talk, y'see."

And because the young ladies—two of whom were named Cruceiro and one De Silva, and they were cousins—said that they knew a few words and would be pleased to help Lance-Corporal Owen's friends, and because Owen was very decent about it all—and why not, seeing that he had three of them?—they all walked off, three pairs of them. The Mouse had the youngest Miss Cruceiro on his arm, and the Docker had Miss De Silva. Perhaps Owen wasn't quite so pleased with this arrangement, but he smiled.

That was how it began, many years ago.

Harry Owen was a proper figure of a man: broad shoulders, narrow waist, chestnut-colored hair, eyes as bright blue as could be. Always smiling and showing his good, white teeth. Not many men had teeth that good. Even the wives of the officers didn't feel themselves too proud to say, "Good morning, Owen." It was as if there was a sun inside of him, shining all the time.

The three of them became friends. The *six* of them. The Docker and Leah De Silva, Harry and Margaret Cruceiro, and the Mouse and Lucy Cruceiro. To be sure, Lucy was rather dim and didn't say much, but that suited her escort well enough: he had little to say to her. But he would have felt all sorts of things bubbling up inside of him—if he had been walking with Miss De Silva.

But that, he knew, was impossible. Miss De Silva was so clever, so handsome, so self-assured; he would have been tongued-tied beside her. Besides, she walked with the Docker. And so, for all that she was pleasant to the Mouse, he was too shy to do much more than nod.

Later on he was to think that if the Docker had known that Leah De Silva was not really English, and that she and her cousins and all the others of their class were not regarded by the soldiery as . . . well . . .

But he did not know. Chasteness was not a highly prized attribute in Cat's-meat Court where the Docker's wild, slum-arab childhood had been largely spent—indeed, it was a quality almost completely unknown. He had no experience of respectable girls, neither half-caste nor quarter-caste nor simon-pure English. The daughters of the officers lived in a world sealed off from him, and the few daughters of NCOs almost as much so.

To men like Lance-Corporal Owen, Eurasian girls may have seemed to lack that certain quality which spelled Rude Hands Off, which the English girls at home had had. But the Docker knew nothing of afternoon teas and tiny sandwiches, of strict papas and watchful mamas, of prim and chaperoned walks in country towns. For him the Victorian Age had never existed, raised as he had been in a world little changed from the fierce and savage Eighteenth Century.

But this did not bring him to take liberties now. On the contrary. To the Docker a railroad telegrapher (for such was Mr. De Silva, burly and black-mustached) was a member of a learned profession. He little noticed that the ever-blooming Mrs. De Silva wore no corsets and let her younger children run about the house naked. And little cared. He knew that there were girls to be had for a thrupney-bit and there were girls who were not. All the latter were respectable. No cottage in Kensington could have been more respectable, in the Docker's eyes, than the old house where the De Silvas lived, three or four generations of them, in dark and not always orderly rooms smelling of incense and odd sorts of cooking. That the girls were not exactly bleached-white in complexion was nothing to him; the Docker was dark himself. When Mr. and Mrs. De Silva boasted of their ancestry—of Portuguese generals and high-ranking officials of the old East India Company—the Docker felt no desire to doubt. He felt humble.

Miss Leah De Silva was quiet and ladylike enough when talking to the Docker. But she could be fierce and sudden when someone in her family did anything she thought not right. Perhaps her parents had been something less than keen as mustard about the Docker. He was only a corporal. Did they feel that their daughter should look higher? A sentence like a shower of swords from Leah, in a language which had once been Portuguese, silenced them.

One afternoon, when the barracks were almost deserted, the Docker summoned Owen and the Mouse to consult with. He produced a bottle and offered it.

"And risk my stripe? Thanks, my boy, but no thanks," said Owen. The Mouse took a small sip. The Docker's manner was very odd, he thought. He was proud and he was abashed; he was happy and he was uneasy.

" 'Ere's the thing," he said. "I mean to marry Miss De Silva." And he gave them a challenging look.

"Good!" said the Mouse.

"I know she'll 'ave me," the Docker went on. "But . . . well . . . there's Susanna."

"Oh, ah," agreed Owen. "There's Susanna."

Susanna was a girl who had a little house of her own, often visited by soldiers, one of whom had been the Docker. Her mother was a woman of some tribe so very deep in the Hills that they were neither Hindu nor Moslem. Heaven only knew how she had come to Lahore, or where she had gone after leaving it—for leave it she did, after her baby was born; and Heaven, presumably, knew who the father had been.

Susanna had been raised and educated by the Scottish Mission and had once been employed in the tracts department of its Printing Establishment. The officials of the Mission had been willing to forgive Susanna once, then twice—

they had even been willing to forgive Susanna a third time—but not to retain her in the Printing Establishment. Whereupon Susanna had renounced the Church of Scotland and all its works, and had gone altogether to the bad.

"I'm going to break off wiv 'er," said the Docker determinedly. "I shan't give 'er no present, neither—no money, I mean. I know it's the custom, but if I'm going to be married I shall need all the money I've got."

"That's rather hard on Susanna," said Owen.

"Can't be 'elped," said the Docker briefly. "Now I'm going to write 'er a letter." He wanted assistance, but he also was strong for his own style. The letter, in its third and least-smudged version, was brief.

> *Dear Friend,*
>
> *It's been a great lark but now it's all over, for I am getting married to someone else. Best not to see each other again. Keep merry and bright.*
>
> > *Respectfully,*

"That'll do it," the Docker said, with satisfaction. "Here's two annas—give 'em to a bearer, one of you, and send the letter off directly. I'm going to start tidying up meself and me kit, as I mean to speak to Mr. De Silva tonight."

But he never spoke to Mr. De Silva that night. Sergeant-Major came striding in, big as Kachen-junga, and swollen with violent satisfaction, and found the bottle in with the Docker's gear. The Docker drew three weeks, and was lucky not to lose his stripes.

There was a note waiting for him when he came out.

> *Dear Docker,*
>
> *I hope you will take it in good part but Miss De Silva and I are going to be married Sunday next. Perhaps it was not quite the thing for me to do—to speak during your absence—but Love knows no laws as the poet says and we do both hope you will be our friend,*
>
> > *Sincerely,*
> > *Harry Owen*

For a long time the Docker just sat and stared. Then he said to the Mouse, "Well, if it must be. I should 'ave known a girl of 'er quality wouldn't ever marry a brute like me."

"Ah, but Docker," the Mouse said. Then in a rush of words: "It isn't that at all! Don't you see what it was? The note you meant for Susanna—Owen sent it off to Miss De Silva instead! And then went and proposed 'imself! And it must've been 'im who peached that you 'ad the bottle."

The Docker's face went dark, but his voice kept soft. "Oh," he said, "that was how it was." And said nothing more. That night he got drunk, wildly, savagely drunk, wrecked twenty stalls in the little bazaar, half killed two Sikhs who tried to stop him, and coming into the sleeping barracks as silently as the dust, took and loaded his rifle and shot Harry Owen through the head . . .

"Yarn, yarn, yarn!" said Tom. "I don't believe you was ever in India in your life!"

The Gaffer, who had been sipping his beer silently, fired up.

"Ho, don't you! One of you fetch that pict're—the one directly under the old king's—"

He gestured toward the rear room. In very short time someone was back and handed over an old cardboard-backed photograph. It was badly faded, but it showed plainly enough three soldiers posed in front of a painted backdrop. They wore ornate and tight-fitting uniforms and had funny, jaunty little caps perched to one side of their heads.

"That 'un's me," said the Gaffer, pointing his twisted old finger. The faces all looked alike, but the one in the middle was that of the shorrest.

When it was passed to me I turned it over. The back was ornately printed with the studio's name and sure enough, it was in Lahore—a fact I pointed out, not directly to Tom, but in his general direction; and in one corner, somehow bare of curlicues, was written in faded ink a date in the late '80s, and three names: *Lance-Corporal Harry Owen, Corporal Daniel Devore, Private Alfred Graham.*

". . . young chap from newspaper was talking about it to the Padre Sahib," the Gaffer was saying. "Earnest young fellow, 'ad spectacles, young's 'e was. 'But a thing like that, sir,' says 'e, 'so unlike a British soldier—what could've made him do a thing like that?' And the Chaplain looks at 'im and sighs and says, 'Single men in barracks don't turn into plaster saints.' The writing-wallah thought this over a bit, then, 'No,' 'c says, 'I suppose not,' and wrote it down in 'is notebook."

"Well," Tom said grudgingly, "so you've been to India. But that doesn't prove the rest of the story."

"It's true, I tell you. I've got cuttin's to prove it. *Civil And Military Gazette* of Lahore."

Tom began singing:

> "All this happened in Darby
> (I never was known to lie.)
> And if you'd'a' been there in Darby
> You'd'u' seen it, the same as I."

Someone laughed. Tears started in the old man's weak blue eyes, and threatened to overflow the reddened rims. "I've got cuttin's."

Tom said, "Yes, you've always got cuttin's. But nobody does see 'em but you."

"You come 'ome with me," the Gaffer said, pushing his nobby old hands against the table top and making to rise. "You come 'ome with me. The cuttin's are in my old trunk and you ask my missus—for she keeps the keys—you just ask my missus."

"What!" cried Tom. "Me ask your missus for anything? Why, I'd as soon ask a lion or a tiger at Whipsnade Zoo for a bit o' their meat, as ask your missus for anything. She's a Tartar, *she* is!"

The Gaffer's mind had evidently dropped the burden of the conversation. He began to nod and smile as if Tom had paid him a very acceptable compliment. But he seemed to recall the object of Tom's remarks, rather than their tone.

"Oh, she was a lovely creature," he said softly. "Most beautiful girl you ever saw. And it was me that she married, after all, y'see. Not either of them two others, but *me*, that they called the Mouse!" And he chuckled. It was not a nice chuckle, and as I looked up, sharply, I caught his eye, and there was something sly and very ugly in it.

I went cold. In one second I was all but certain of two things. "Gaffer," I said, trying to sound casual. "What was your wife's maiden name?"

The Gaffer seemed deep in thought, but he answered, as casually as I'd asked, "Her name? Her name was Leah De Silva. Part British, part Portugee, and part—but who cares about that? Not I. I married her in church, I did."

"And how," I asked, "do you pronounce D-e-v-o-r-e?"

The dim eyes wavered. "Worked in the West India Docks, was why we called him the Docker," said the old man. "But his Christian name, it was Dan'l Deever."

"Yes," I said. "Of course it was. And it wasn't Harry Owen who peached about the whiskey bottle in Dan'l's gear, so as to get him in the guardhouse— and it wasn't Harry Owen who sent the note to the wrong young lady—was it? It was someone who knew what Harry would do if he had the chance. Someone who knew that the Docker would certainly kill Harry, if told the right set of lies. And he did, didn't he? And then the way was all clear and open for you, wasn't it?"

For just a second there was fear in Gaffer Graham's face. And there was defiance, too. And triumph. Then, swiftly, all were gone, and only the muddled memories of old age were left.

"It was cold," he whimpered. "It was bitter cold when they hanged Danny Deever in the morning. There was that young chap from the newspaper, that wrote about it. Funny name 'e 'ad—somethin' like Kipling—Ruddy Kipling, 'twas."

"Yes," I said, "something like that."

Afterword to "The Affair at Lahore Cantonment"

BY EILEEN GUNN

You may not be surprised to hear that, after rising to the bait Avram left for the "insatiably curious," I failed to find any sources that mention a historic referent for Kipling's poem "Danny Deever." Rudyard Kipling, of course, lived in Lahore as a young man and, as the story implies, wrote for the Civil and Military Gazette: *the scenario proposed in the story would not have been impossible. The poem was first published in* The Scots Observer *in 1890. It consists of four stanzas in drumroll cadences, a series of questions and responses between a sergeant and enlisted men who have been called out in files to witness a hanging.*

Each stanza ends with four lines in Cockney dialect that describe the effect of the hanging on the young recruits, and closes with a phrase (slightly different for each stanza) about "hangin' Danny Deever in the mornin'." The focus is entirely on the reactions of the men to witnessing a fellow-soldier being hanged, and we never find out anything about Danny Deever himself, other than he was convicted of shooting a sleeping comrade.

Reading "Danny Deever" again after reading "The Affair at Lahore Cantonment" adds an additional ironic patina to the poem that I think Kipling himself would have relished. It's in Barrack-Room Ballads; *you'll just have to look it up.*

Revolver

INTRODUCTION BY BILL PRONZINI

When "Revolver" was first published in Ellery Queen's Mystery Magazine *in 1962, editor Frederic Dannay blurbed it in part as "a kind of roundelay in prose, and a bitter, ironic slice of life—in the raw." A perfectly apt description as far as it goes. But it neglects to mention another vital element of the story: its understated and mordant wit.*

Humor plays a role in all of Avram's crime fiction, just as it does in his science fiction and fantasy tales; it was a central facet of his mind-set and his prose style. In some stories the humor is broad, farcical, laugh-out-loud funny. In others, such as "Revolver," it is subtle, and because of its subtlety, even more caustic. Read carefully his descriptions of Mr. Edward Mason, slumlord; of the tenants who inhabit Mason's old brownstone houses; of the other denizens of the inner-city neighborhood in which the brownstones stand a-moldering. The descriptions won't generate laughter, but they will produce wry smiles—and at the same time make you feel just a little uncomfortable. This kind of humor was an Avram specialty, the quiet kind with an edge and an attitude.

"Revolver" is one of several stories in the Avram oeuvre, both mysteries and fantasies, that remind me of another writer whose work I admire: Gerald Kersh. Each was his own person and his own writer, but it seems to me they shared a similar, slightly skewed worldview, a similar passion for oddball characters and situations; and that the humor which infuses their work is similarly acidulous and knife-edged. I wonder if Avram knew Kersh. If he did, I think they must have enjoyed each other's company. I wonder, too, what a Davidson-Kersh collaboration might have been like. Something pretty wonderful, to be sure. Something to create both a smile and a faint but pervasive unease, and to linger long in the memory. Something like "Revolver," perhaps . . .

REVOLVER

THERE WAS A MR. Edward Mason who dealt in real estate. His kind of real estate consisted mainly of old brownstone houses into which Mr. Mason crammed a maximum number of tenants by turning each room into a single apartment. Legally this constituted "increasing available residence space" or some similar phrase. As a result of this deed of civic good, Mr. Mason was enabled to get tax rebates, rent increases which were geometrically rather than arithmetically calculated, and a warm glow around his heart.

Mr. Mason's tenants were a select group, hand-picked; one might say—to use a phrase favored in other facets of the real estate profession—that his holdings were "restricted." He didn't care for tenants who had steady employment. You might think this was odd of him, but that would be because you didn't know the philanthropic cast of Mr. Mason's mind. He favored the lame, the halt, and the blind; he preferred the old and the feeble; he had no scruples, far from it, against mothers without marriage licenses.

And his kindheartedness was rewarded. For, after all, employment, no matter how steady, can sometimes be terminated. And then rent cannot be paid. A landlord who can't collect rent is a landlord who can't meet his own expenses—in short, a landlord who is bound to go out of business. In which case it follows that he is a landlord who can no longer practice philanthropy.

Therefore, Mr. Mason would be obliged to evict such a tenant in order to protect his other tenants.

But, owing to his care, foresight, and selectivity, he had no such tenants. Not any more. No, sir. All his tenants at the time our account begins were in receipt of a steady income not derived from employment. Welfare checks come in regularly, and so do old-age assistance checks, state aid checks, and several other variety of checks more or less unknown to the average citizen (and may he never have to know of them from the recipients' point of view—that is our prayer for him), the average citizen whose tax dollar supplies said checks.

Then, too, people who earn their own income are inclined to take a high-handed attitude toward landlords. They seem to think that the real estate investor has nothing better to do with his income than to lavish it on fancy repairs to his property. But a tenant whose soul has been purified by long years as the recipient of public charity is a tenant who is less troublesome, whose tastes are less finicking, who is in no position to carry on about such *rēs naturae* as rats, mice, roaches, crumbling plaster, leaky pipes, insufficient heat, dirt, rot, and the like.

Is it not odd, then, that after a term of years of being favored by the philanthropic attentions of Mr. Mason and similarly minded entrepreneurs, the neighborhood was said to have "gone down"? It could not really be, could it, that garbage, for instance, was collected less frequently than in other sections of town? Or that holes in streets and sidewalks were not repaired as quickly as in "better" neighborhoods? Surely it was a mere coincidence that these things were so—if, indeed, they were so at all.

And anyway, didn't the City make up for it by providing more protection? Weren't patrol cars seen on the streets thereabouts more often than elsewhere? Weren't policemen usually seen on the streets in congenial groups of three? To say nothing of plainclothesmen.

This being the case, it was disconcerting for Mr. Mason to acknowledge that crime seemed to be on the increase in the neighborhood where he practiced his multifold benevolences. But no other conclusion seemed possible. Stores were held up, apartments burglarized, cars broken into, purses snatched, people mugged—

It was almost enough to destroy one's faith in human nature.

Finally, there was no other choice but for Mr. Mason to secure a revolver, and a license for same. Being a respectable citizen, a taxpayer, and one with a legitimate reason to go armed—the necessity to protect himself and the collection of his tenants' rents—he had no difficulty in obtaining either . . .

Among Mr. Mason's tenants was a Mrs. Richards. She was quite insistent, whenever the matter was raised (though it was never raised by Mr. Mason, who was totally indifferent to such items), that "Mrs." was no mere courtesy title. She had, indeed, been married to Mr. Richards and she had a snapshot of Mr. Richards to prove it. The wedding may have occurred in North Carolina, or perhaps in South Carolina. Nor did she recall the town or country where the happy event took place: Mr. Richards (she *did* remember that his given name was Charley) had been a traveling man. Also, it was a long time ago.

Mrs. Richards may have been a bit feeble-minded, but she possessed other qualities, such as a warm, loving, and open—very open—heart. She had two children by the evanescent Mr. Richards, and two children by two other gentlemen, with whom she had been scrupulous not to commit bigamy; and was currently awaiting the birth in about six months of her fifth child, the father of whom she thought was most probably a young man named Curtis.

Current social welfare policy held that it would be destructive to the family unit to suggest that Mrs. Richards, now or at any time, place her children in a day nursery and go out and labor for her (and their) bread. Consequently, she was supplied with a monthly check made up with city, state, and federal taxes. It cannot be said that the amount of the check was lavish, but Mrs. Richards did not demand very much and was easily satisfied. She had never been trained in any craft, trade, or profession, and if anyone was crude or unkind enough to suggest that she had enough skill required to manipulate a scrub-brush and-bucket, she would point out that when she did this her back hurt her.

The state of the floor of her "apartment," on the day when Mr. Mason came to call, at an hour nicely calculated with reference to the mail schedule, indicated that Mrs. Richards had not risked backache lately.

After an exchange of greetings, Mr. Mason said, "If you've cashed your check, I've got the receipt made out."

"I don't believe it's come," she said placidly. This was her routine reply. It was her belief that eventually it might be believed, although it never had been; nor was it now.

"If you spend the rent money on something else," Mr. Mason said, "I'll have to go down to The Welfare and have them close your case." This was his routine reply.

Curtis, in a peremptory tone, said, "Give the man his money." The prospect of approaching fatherhood had raised in him no tender sentiment; in fact, it raised no sentiment at all other than an increasing daily restlessness and a conviction that it was time for him to move on.

Without so much as a sigh Mrs. Richards now produced an envelope from her bosom and examined it closely. "I guess maybe it might be this one," she said. "I haven't opened it."

Curtis, quite tired of every routine gambit of his lady-love, now said, quite testily, "*Give* the *man* his *money!*" He wanted cigarettes and he wanted whiskey and he knew that neither of these could be had until the check was cashed. "If I got to *hit* you—"

Mrs. Richards endorsed the check with her landlord's pen, and Mr. Mason began to count out her change. A new consideration now entered Curtis' mind—previously occupied only by the desire for cigarettes, whiskey, and moving on; it entered with such extreme suddenness that it gave him no time to reflect on it. He observed that Mr. Mason had a revolver in a shoulder holster inside his coat and he observed that Mr. Mason's wallet was quite engorged with money.

Curtis was not naturally malevolent, but he was naturally impulsive. He whipped Mr. Mason's revolver from its holster, struck Mr. Mason heavily on the side of the head with it, and seized his wallet.

Mr. Mason went down, but he went down slowly. He thought he was shouting for help, but the noise coming out of his mouth was no louder than a mew. He was on his hands and knees by the time Curtis reached the door, and then he slid to one side and lay silent.

Mrs. Richards sat for a moment in her chair. New situations were things she was not well equipped to cope with. After the sound of Curtis' feet on the stairs ceased, she continued to sit for some time, looking at Mr. Mason.

Presently a thought entered her mind. The familiar-looking piece of paper on the dirty table was a receipt for her rent. The money scattered around was the money Mr. Mason had been counting out to cash her check. His practice was to count it out twice and then deduct the amount of the rent.

Mrs. Richards slowly gathered up the money, slowly counted it, moving her lips. It was all there.

And so was the receipt.

Mrs. Richards nodded. She now had the receipt for her rent *and* the money. True, she no longer had Curtis, but, then, she knew he was bound to move along sooner or later. Men always did.

She hid the rent money in one of the holes with which the walls of the "apartment" were plentifully supplied, and then reflected on what she had better do next.

All things considered, she decided it was best to start screaming.

Curtis went down the stairs rapidly, but once in the street he had sense enough to walk at a normal pace. Running men were apt to attract the attention of the police.

Three blocks away was a saloon he favored with his trade. He entered by the back door, causing a buzzer to sound. He tried to slip quickly into the Men's Room, but wasn't quite quick enough to escape the attention of the bartender-proprietor, an irascible West Indian called Jumby, and no great friend of Curtis'.

"Another customer for the toilet trade," said Jumby, so loudly that he could be heard through the closed door. "I'd make more money if I gave the drinks away free and charged admission to the water closet!"

Curtis ignored this familiar complaint, and emptied the wallet of its money, dropping the empty leather case into the trash container which stood, full of used paper towels, alongside the sink. Then he left.

Police cars sped by him, their sirens screaming.

Vague thoughts of cigarettes and whiskey still floated in Curtis' mind, but the desire to move on was by now uppermost. It was with some relief, therefore, that he saw a young man sitting in an open convertible. The convertible was elegantly fitted out, and so was the young man. His name was William.

"You've been talking about going to California, William," Curtis said.

"I have *also* been talking," William said with precision, "about finding some congenial person with *money* to share the *expenses* of going to California."

Curtis said, "I hit the numbers. I got money enough to take care of all the expenses. Don't that make me congenial?"

"Very *much* so," said William, opening the door. Curtis started to slide in, but William stopped him with a long, impeccably groomed hand, which touched him lightly. "Curtis," he said in low but firm tones, "if you have something *on* you, I really must *insist* that you get *rid* of it first. Suppose I meet you here in an *hour*? That will also enable me to *pack*."

"One hour," Curtis said.

He went into another bar, obtained cigarettes and whiskey. At the bar was a man generally, if not quite popularly, known as The Rock.

"How you doing, Rock?" Curtis inquired.

The Rock said nothing.

"Got some business to talk over with you," Curtis went on.

The Rock continued to say nothing.

"Like to take in a movie?" Curtis asked.

The Rock finished his drink, set down the glass, looked at Curtis. Curtis put down money, left the bar, The Rock behind him. He bought two tickets at the movie theater and they went in. The house was almost empty.

After a minute or two Curtis whispered, "Fifty dollars buys a gun. I got it on me."

The Rock took out a handkerchief, spread it in his lap, counted money into it, passed it to Curtis. After a moment Curtis passed the handkerchief back. The Rock soon left, but Curtis stayed on. He still had the better part of an hour to kill.

The Rock took a bus and traveled a mile. He walked a few blocks on a side street and entered a house which, like most of its fellows, bore a sign that it has been selected for something euphemistically called "Urban Renewal," and that further renting of rooms was illegal. Most of the windows were already marked with large X signs.

On the second floor The Rock disturbed a teenage boy and girl in close, though wordless, conversation. The boy looked up in some annoyance, but after a quick glance decided to say nothing. The girl clutched his arm until the intruder passed.

The door on the third floor was locked, but The Rock pushed hard, once, and it yielded. The room was ornately furnished, and the dressing table was crowded with perfumes and cosmetics and a large doll; but seated on the bed was a man.

"It ain't you," the man said. He was red-eyed drunk.

"It ain't me," The Rock agreed.

"It's Humpty Slade," said the man on the bed. "*He* don't pay for her rent. *He* don't buy her no clothes. *He* don't feed her. *I* do."

The Rock nodded his massive head.

"Everybody knows that," The Rock said. He took a handkerchief out of his pocket, laid it on the bed, opened its folds. "Seventy-five dollars," he said.

A quick turnover and a modest profit—that was The Rock's policy.

The boy and girl, now seated on the stairs, shrank to one side as he came down. They did not look up. It was not very comfortable there in that all but abandoned house; but it was private—as private as you can get when you have no place of your own to go.

Upstairs, on the bed, the waiting man stared at the revolver with his red, red eyes . . .

After a while the boy and the girl sauntered down into the street and went separate ways in search of something to eat. But after supper they met again in the same hallway.

Scarcely had they taken their places when they were disturbed. A man and woman came up, talking loudly. They paused at the sight of the younger pair in the dim light of the single bulb, and for a moment the two couples looked at one another. The older woman was handsome, flamboyantly dressed and made up. Her companion was large and on the ugly side, his looks not improved by a crooked shoulder which jutted back on one side.

"What are you kids doing here?" he demanded. "Go on, get out—"

"Oh, now, Humphrey," the woman pleaded. "You leave them alone. They ain't hurting nobody."

"Okay, sugar," the big man said submissively. They continued up the stairs. The boy and girl listened as they fumbled at the door. Then the woman's voice went high and shrill with fear, screaming, *"No—no—no—"*

At the loud sound of the revolver the boy and girl leaped to their feet. Something fell past them, and landed below with a thud.

"You'd point a gun at *me?*" a man's voice growled. Then there was the noise of a blow.

"My woman—!"

"You'd take a shot at *me?*"

The sound of fist on flesh, again and again. The boy and girl crept down the stairs.

"No, Humpty, don't hit me any more! I'm sorry, Humpty! I didn't mean it! I was—oh, please, Humpty! *Please?*"

"Don't hit him any more, honey. He was drunk. Honey—"

The boy and girl stopped at the bottom floor for only a moment. Then they were gone . . .

Curtis paused, uncertain. He was sure that it was dangerous for him to remain on the street, but he didn't know where to go. That little rat, William, had failed to reappear. There were planes flying, and trains and buses running, but even if he decided what to take he would still have to decide *which* airfield, *which* station, *which* terminal. The problems seemed to proliferate each time he thought about them.

He would have a drink to help him consider.

There wasn't really any hurry.

That dirty rat, William!

The Sepoy Lords were holding an informal meeting—a caucus, as it were.

Someone has remarked that the throne of Russia was neither hereditary, nor elective, but occupative. The same might be said of office in the Sepoy Lords.

The scene was a friendly neighborhood rooftop.

"So you think you're going to be Warlord?" a boy named Buzz demanded.

"That's right," said the one called Sonny.

The quorum, including several Sepoy Ladies, listened with interest.

"*I* don't think you're going to be Warlord," said Buzz.

"I *know* I am," said Sonny.

"What makes you so sure?" inquired Buzz.

"This," Sonny said, simply, reaching into his pocket, and taking something out.

Sudden intakes of breath, eyes lighting up, members crowding around, loud comments of admiration. "Sonny got a *piece!*" "*Look* at that piece Sonny's got!"

The President of the Sepoy Lords, one Big Arthur, who had until now remained above the battle, asked, "Where'd you get it, Son'."

Sonny smirked, cocked his head. "*She* knows where I got it," he said. His girl, Myra, smiled knowingly.

Buzz said only one word, but he said it weakly. He now had no case, and he knew it.

The new Warlord sighted wickedly down the revolver. "*First* thing I'm going to do," he announced; "there's one old cat I am going to *burn*. He said something about my old lady, and that is something I don't take from *any*body, let alone from one of those dirty old Ermine Kings."

Diplomatically, no one commented on the personal aspect of his grievance, all being well aware how easy it was to say something about Sonny's old lady, and being equally aware that the old lady's avenging offspring now held a revolver in his hand. But the general aspect of the challenge was something else.

"Those Ermine Kings better watch out, is all!" a Sepoy Lady declared. There was a murmur of assent.

Big Arthur now deemed it time to interpose his authority. "Oh, yeah, sure," he said. " 'They better watch out!'—how come? Because we got one piece?"

Warlord Sonny observed a semantic inconsistency. With eyes narrowed he said, "What do you mean, 'we'? 'We' haven't got *any*thing. *I'm* the one who's got the piece, and *no*body is going to tell me what to do with my personal property—see?" He addressed this caveat to the exuberant Sepoy Lady, but no one misunderstood him—least of all, Big Arthur.

Allowing time for the message to sink in, Sonny then said, "Big Arthur is right. I mean, one ain't enough. We need money to get more. How? I got a plan. Listen—"

They listened. They agreed. They laughed their satisfaction.

"Now," Sonny concluded, "let's get going."

He watched as most of them filed through the door. He started after them, then stopped. *Was* stopped. Big Arthur seized his wrist with one hand and grabbed the revolver with the other.

Sonny, crying, "Gimme that back!" leaped for it. But Big Arthur, taking hold of Sonny's jacket with his free hand, slapped him—hard—back against the door.

"You got the wrong idea, Son'," Big Arthur said. "You seem to think that *you* are the President around here. That's *wrong*. Now, if you really think you are man enough, you can try to get this piece away from me. You want to try?"

For a while Sonny had been somebody. Now he was nobody again. He knew that he would never in a million years take the revolver away from Big Arthur, never burn that one old cat from the Ermine Kings who had said something about his old lady. Tears of pain and humiliation welled in his eyes.

"Cheer up," Big Arthur said. "We're going to see how your plan works out. And it better work out *good*. Now get down those stairs with the other members, Mr. Sonny Richards."

Head down, Sonny stumbled through the door. Myra started to slip through after him, but Big Arthur detained her. "Not so quick, chick," he said. "Let's move along together. You and me are going to get better acquainted." For just a second Myra hesitated. Then she giggled.

"*Much* better acquainted," Big Arthur said.

Feeling neither strain nor pain, Curtis glided out of the bar. The late afternoon spread invitingly before him. He was supposed to meet somebody and go somewhere . . . William . . .

There, slowly passing by in his fancy convertible, was the man himself. With great good humor Curtis cried, "William!" and started toward him.

William himself saw things from a different angle. Curtis, to be sure, was *rough*, but what had really set William against going to California with him was the fact that he had observed Curtis that way. He, William, wanted nothing to do at any time with people who carried guns. And, anyway, he wasn't quite ready to leave for California—something had come up.

What came up at that moment was Curtis, roaring (so it seemed) with rage, and loping forward with murder in his eye.

William gave a squeak of fright. The convertible leaped ahead, crashing into the car in front. And still Curtis came on—

Screaming, "Keep away from me, Curtis!" William jumped out of the car and started to run. Someone grabbed him. "Don't stop me—he's got a gun—Cur*tis!*" he yelled.

But they wouldn't let go. It was the police, wouldn't you know it, grim-faced men in plain clothes; of all the cars to crash into—

One of them finished frisking Curtis. "Nope, no gun," he said. "This one ain't dangerous. *You*." He turned to William. "What do you mean by saying he had a gun?"

William lost his head and started to babble, and before he could move, the men were searching *him*. And the *car*. They found his cigarette case stuffed with sticks of tea, and they found the shoebox full of it, too.

"Pot," said one of them, sniffing. "Real Mexican stuff. Convertible, hey? You won't need a convertible for a long time, fellow."

William burst into tears. The mascara ran down his face and he looked so grotesque that even the grim faces of the detectives had to relax into smiles.

"What about this one, Leo," one of them asked, jerking his thumb. "He's clean."

But Leo was dubious. "There must be some connection, or the pretty one wouldn't of been so scared," he said. A thought occurred to him. "What did he call him? What did you say his name was? Curtis?"

The other detective snapped his fingers. "Curtis. Yeah. A question, Curtis: You in the apartment of a Mrs. Selena Richards today?"

"*Never* heard of her," said Curtis, sobering rapidly. Move on, that's what he should have done—move on.

Mrs. Richards was entertaining company. The baby was awake—had been awake, in fact, since those chest-deep, ear-splitting screams earlier in the afternoon—and the girls had come home from school. She had sent them down to the store for cold cuts and sliced bread; they hadn't eaten more than half of it on the way back, and Mrs. Richards and the neighbors were dining off the other half. There was also some wine they had all chipped in to buy. Excitement didn't come very often, and it was a shame to let it go to waste.

"Didn't that man *bleed!*" a neighbor exclaimed. "All over your floor, Selena!"

"All over *his* floor, you mean—*he* owns this building."

After the whoops of laughter died down, someone thought of asking where Mrs. Richards' oldest child was.

"I don't know where Sonny is," she said, placid as ever. "He takes after his daddy. His daddy always was a traveling sort of man." She felt in her bosom for the money she had placed there—the money she had taken from the hole in the wall after the police and ambulance left. Yes, it was safely there.

All in all, she thought, it had been quite a day. Curtis gone, but he was on the point of becoming troublesome, anyway. Excitement—a *lot* of excitement. Company in, hanging on her every word. The receipt for the rent, *plus* the rent itself. Yes, a lucky day. Later on she would see what the date was, and tomorrow she would play that number.

If luck was coming to you, nothing could keep it away.

They had taken three stitches in Mr. Mason's scalp, and taped and bandaged it.

"You want us to call you a taxi?" the hospital attendant asked.

"No," Mr. Mason said. "I don't have any money to waste on taxis. The bus is still running, isn't it?"

"There's a charge of three dollars," the attendant said.

Mr. Mason snorted. "I don't have three cents. I'll have to borrow bus fare from some storekeeper, I guess. That dirty—he took everything I had. Right in broad daylight. I don't know what we pay taxes for."

"I guess we pay them to reward certain people for turning decent buildings into flophouses," the attendant said. He was old and crusty and due to retire soon, and didn't give a damn for anybody.

Mr. Mason narrowed his eyes and looked at him. "Nobody has the right to tell me what to do with my personal property," he said meanly.

The attendant shrugged. "That's your personal property, too," he said, pointing. "Take it with you; we don't want it."

It was the empty shoulder holster.

On leaving the hospital Mr. Mason headed first for a store, but not to borrow bus fare. He bought a book of blank receipts. He still had most of his rents to collect, and he intended to collect every single one of them. It hardly paid a person to be decent, these days, he reflected irritably. One thing was sure: nobody else had better tangle with him—not today.

He headed for the first house on his round, and it was there, in the hallway, that the Sepoy Lords caught up with him.

The Tail-Tied Kings

INTRODUCTION BY FREDERIK POHL

Avram Davidson was one of a kind. He was physically gentle, intellectually ferocious, and disturbingly erudite. He was also markedly Jewish. When I say "markedly," the word should be understood in the context of my own lapsed-Protestant relationship with Jewish people: most of the science-fiction fans and writers I grew up with were Jews, so were the fifty percent of my Brooklyn neighbors who weren't Catholic, so, at the time I first met Avram, was my wife. In my experience, however, few of them took the matter very seriously. They might remember to be choosy about their diet when it wasn't too inconvenient, and most of them thought seders were a lot of fun (for that matter, so did I), but that was about it. Avram was different.

I had not appreciated quite how *different until the day when, while Avram was supervising some friends' children in a swimming pool, one of the kids got into trouble and had to be taken to a hospital. The nearest hospital was ten miles away. It was the Sabbath. And Avram was the only adult around. So he took the child to the emergency room in a car, because that was permissible as a matter of saving life, but there was no such justification for riding back. In Avram's view the only lawful way to return was to walk. So he did. Ten long miles of it.*

Avram was good, civilized company; his opinions were always strongly held but his sense of humor was reliably meliorating. It was good fun to argue with him. Good exercise, too; half an hour with Avram toned you up for days of disagreement with lesser mortals.

And, of course, as a writer Avram was a pure wonder. His densely textured and beautifully phrased prose was a delight to read, and a pleasure to publish. Well, you can see the part about why it was a delight to read for yourself, because this book is full of some of the best of his stories. But I doubt that unless you've had the actual experience you can quite understand how pleasing it was to find,

~~among the bushels of hopelessly inept manuscripts that every editor has to pick~~
through in order to find the ones worth putting into print, one of Avram's little
gems.

"The Tail-Tied Kings" is one of my personal favorite Davidsons—partly
because of its own considerable merits, partly because it was one of the ones that
I was lucky enough to publish in Galaxy, partly because of an event that occurred shortly after its publication, thirty years ago or so.

I was visiting the Milford Science Fiction Writers Workshop (so long ago
that the workshop was actually still held in Milford, Pennsylvania). So was
Avram, and during a break in the proceedings he came up to me and, amiably
but forcefully, grabbed my lapel. "Why did you change my title to 'The Tail-
Tied Kings?' " he demanded.

I answered promptly, "Because I didn't think the title you had on it would
make anyone want to read the story. In fact, it was so uncompelling I don't
even remember what it was. What was it?"

He reflected for a belligerent moment, then shrugged. "I don't remember
it either," he said.

So I figured I won that one. I don't recall winning many others.

THE TAIL-TIED KINGS

He brought them water, one by one.

"The water is sweet, One-eye," said a Mother. "Very sweet."

"Many bring Us water," a second Mother said, "but the water you bring is sweet."

"Because his breath is sweet," said a third Mother.

The One-Eye paused, about to leave. "I would tell you of a good thing," a Father said, "which none others know, only We. I may tell him, softly, in his ear, may I not?"

In his corner, Keeper stirred. A Mother and a Father raised their voices. "It is colder now," They said. "Outside: frost. A white thing on the ground, and burns. We have heard. Frost." Keeper grunted, did not move. "Colder, less food, less water, We have heard, but for Us always food, always water, water, food, food . . ." They went on. Keeper did not move.

"Come closer," said the Father, softly. "I will tell you of a good thing, while Keeper sleeps." The Father's voice was deep and rich. "Come to my mouth. A secret thing. One-Eye."

"I may not come, Father," said the One-Eye, uncertainly. "Only to bring water."

"You may come," said a Mother. Her voice was like milk, her voice was good. "Your breath is sweet. Come, listen. Come."

Another Father said, "You will be cold, alone. Come among Us and be warm." The One-Eye moved his head from side to side, and he muttered.

"There is food here and you will eat," the other Father said. The One-Eye moved a few steps, then hesitated.

"Come and mate with me," said the milk-voiced Mother. "It is my time. Come."

The One-Eye perceived that it was indeed her time and he darted forward, but the Keeper blocked his way.

"Go, bring water for Them to drink," said Keeper. He was huge.

"He has water for Us now," a Mother said, plaintively. "Stupid Keeper. We are thirsty. Why do you stop him?"

A Father said, "He has water in his mouth which he has brought for Us. Step aside and let him pass. Oh, it is an ugly, stupid Keeper!"

"I have water in my mouth which I have brought for Them," the One-Eye said. "Step aside and—" He stopped, as they burst into jeers and titters.

The Keeper was not even angry. "There was nothing in your mouth but a lie. Now go."

Too late, the One-Eye perceived his mistake. "I may sleep," he muttered.

"Sleep, then. But go." Keeper bared his teeth. The One-Eye shrank back, and turned and slunk away. Behind him he heard the Mother in her milk-voice say, "It was a stupid One-Eye, Father."

"And now," the Father said. The One-Eye heard their mating as he went.

Sometimes he had tried to run away, but everywhere there were others who stopped him. "It is a One-Eye, and too far away. Go to your place, One-Eye. Go to your duty, bring water for the Mothers and Fathers, take Their food to the Keeper, go back, go back, One-Eye, go back," they cried, surrounding him, driving him from the way he would go.

"I will not be a One-Eye any longer," he protested.

They jeered and mocked. "Will you grow another eye, then? Back, back: it is The Race which orders you!" And they had nipped him and forced him back.

Once, he had said, "I will see the goldshining!"

There was an old one who said, "Return, then, One-Eye and I will show you the goldshining on the way." And the old one lifted a round thing and it glittered gold. He cried out with surprise and pleasure.

Then, "I thought it would be bigger," he said.

"Return, One-Eye, or you will be killed," the old one said. "Outside is not for you. Return . . . Not that way! That way is a death thing. Mark it well. *This* way. Go. And be quick—there may be dogs."

There was sometimes a new one to instruct, blood wet in the socket, at the place of water, to drink his fill and then fill his mouth and go to the Fathers and Mothers, not to swallow a drop, to learn the long way and the turnings, down and down in the darkness, past the Keeper, mouth to mouth to the Fathers and Mothers. Again and again.

"Why are *They* bound?" a new one asked.

"Why are *we* half-blinded? It is The Race which orders. It is The Race which collects the food that other One-Eyes bring to Keeper, and he stores it and feeds Them."

"Why?"

They paused, water dripping from above into the pool. *Why?* To eat and drink must be or else death. But why does The Race order Fathers and Mothers to be bound so that they cannot find their own food and water? "I am only a stupid One-Eye. But I think the Fathers and Mothers would tell me . . . There was mention of a secret thing . . . The Keeper would not let me listen after that . . ."

"That is a big Keeper, and his teeth are sharp!"

Water fell in gouts from overhead and splashed into the pool. They filled their mouths and started down. When he had emptied the last drop in his mouth he whispered, "Mother, I would hear the secret thing."

She stiffened. Then she clutched at him. The other Fathers and Mothers ceased speaking and moving. At the entrance the Keeper sat up. "What is it?" he called. There was alarm in his voice, and it quavered.

"A strange sound," said a Father. "Keeper, listen!" Then—"Slaves?" he whispered.

The Keeper moved his head from side to side. The Fathers and Mothers were all quite still. "I hear nothing," Keeper said, uncertainly.

"Keeper, you are old, your senses are dulled," the deep-voiced Father said. "We say there is a strange noise! There is danger! Go and see—go now!"

The Keeper became agitated. "I may not leave," he protested. "It is The Race which orders me to stay here—"

Fathers and Mothers together cried out at him. "The Race! The Race! We are The Race! Go and find out the danger to Us!"

"The One-Eye—where is the One-Eye? I will send him!" But they cried that the One-Eye had left (as, indeed, one of them had), and so, finally, gibbering and muttering, he lumbered up the passageway.

As soon as he had left, the milk-voiced Mother began to caress and stroke the One-Eye, saying that he was clever and good, that his breath was sweet, that—

"There is no time for that, Mother," she was interrupted. "Tell him the secret. Quick! Quick!"

"Before you were made a One-Eye and were set apart to serve Us, with whom did you first mate?" she asked.

"With the sisters in my own litter, of course."

"Of course . . . for they were nearest. And after that, with the mother of your own litter. Your sire was perhaps an older brother. After that you would have mated with daughters, with aunts . . ."

"Of course."

The Mother asked if he did not know that this incessant inbreeding could eventually weaken The Race.

"I did not know."

She lifted her head, listened. "The stupid Keeper is not returning yet. Good . . . It is so, One-Eye. Blindness, deafness, deformation, aborting, madness, still-births. All these occur from time to time in every litter. And when flaw mates with flaw and no new blood enters the line, The Race weakens. Is it not so, Fathers and Mothers?"

They answered, "Mother, it is so."

The One-Eye asked, "Is this, then, the secret? A Father told me that the secret was a good thing, and this is a bad thing."

Be silent, They told him, and listen.

In her milk-rich voice the Mother went on, "But We are not born of the same litter, We are not sib, not even near kin. From time to time there is a choosing made of the strongest and cleverest of many litters. And out of these further selections. And then a final choosing—eight, perhaps, or ten, or twelve.

With two, or at most, three males to be Fathers, and the rest females. And these, the chosen of the best of the young, are taken to a place very far from the outside, very safe from danger, and a Keeper set to guard them, and One-Eyes set apart to bring them food and water . . ."

A Father continued the story. "It is of Ourselves that We are talking. They bound Us together, tied Us tightly with many knots, tail to tail together, so that it was impossible to run away. We had no need to face danger above, no need to forage. We had only to eat, to drink, to grow strong—and you see that we are far larger than you—and to mate. All this as The Race has ordered."

"I see . . . I did not know. This is a good thing, yes. It is wise."

The Mothers and Fathers cried out at this. "It is not good!" They declared. "It is not wise! It is not right! To bind Us together when We were young and unknowing was well, yes. But to keep Us bound now is not well. We, too, would walk freely about! We would see the goldshining and the slaves, not to stay bound in the dimness here!"

"One-Eye!" They cried. "You were set apart to serve Us—"

"Yes," he muttered. "I will bring water."

But this was not what They wanted of him. "One-Eye," They whispered, "good, handsome, clever, young, sweet-breathed One-Eye. Set Us free! Unloose the knots! We cannot reach them, you can reach them—"

He protested. "I dare not!"

Their voices rose angrily. "You must! It is The Race which orders! We would rule and We will rule and you will rule with Us!"

". . . mate with Us!" In his ear, a Mother's voice. He shivered.

Again, they spoke in whispers, hissing. "See, One-Eye, you must know where there are death places and food set out which must not be eaten. Bring such food here, set it down. We will know. We will see that Keeper eats it, when he returns. Then, One-Eye, then—"

Suddenly, silence.

All heads were raised.

A Father's deep voice was shrill with fear. "That is smoke!"

But another Father said, "The Race will see that no harm comes to Us." And the others all repeated his assurance. They moved to and fro, in Their odd, circumscribed way, a few paces to each side, and around, and over each other, and back. They were waiting.

It seemed to the One-Eye that the smoke grew thicker. And a Mother said, "While We wait, let Us listen for Keeper and for the steps of those The Race will send to rescue Us. Meanwhile, you, One-Eye, try the knots. Test the knots, see if you can set Us free."

"What is this talk of 'try' and 'test' and 'see'?" a Father then demanded. "He has only to act and it is done! Have We not discussed this amongst Ourselves, always, always? Are We not agreed?"

A second Mother said, "It is so. The One-Eye has freedom, full freedom of movement, while We have not; he can reach the knots and We can not. Come, One-Eye. Act. And while you set Us free, We will listen, and when We are free, We will not need to wait longer for Keeper and the others. Why do they not come?" she concluded, querulous and uncertain.

And they cried to him to untie Them, set Them free, and great things would be his with Them; and, "If not," They shrilled, "We will kill you!"

They pushed him off and ordered him to begin. The smell of the smoke was strong.

Presently he said, "I can do nothing. The knots are too tight."

"We will kill you!" they clamored. "It is not so! We are agreed it is not!" And again and again he tried, but could do nothing.

"Listen, Mothers and Fathers," the milk-voiced one said. "There is no time. No one comes. The Race has abandoned Us. There must be danger to them; rather than risk, they will let Us die and then they will make another choosing for new Mothers and Fathers."

Silence. They listened, strained, snuffed the heavy air.

Then, screaming, terrified, the others leaped up, fell back, tumbling over each other. A Mother's voice—soft, warm, rich, sweet—spoke. "There is one thing alone. Since the knots will not loose, they must be severed. One-Eye! Your teeth. Quickly! Now!"

The others crouched and cringed, panting. The One-Eye sank his teeth into the living knot, and, instantly a Father screamed and lunged forward, cried stop.

"That is pain!" he whimpered. "I have not felt pain before, I cannot bear it. Keeper will come, the others will save Us, The Race—"

And none would listen to the Mother.

"Mother, I am afraid," the One-Eye said. "The smoke is thicker."

"Go, then, save yourself," she said.

"I will not leave without you."

"I? I am part of the whole. Go. Save yourself."

But still he would not, and again he crept up to her.

They came at last to the end of the passage. They could not count the full number of the dead. The smoke was gone now. The Mother clung to him with her fore limbs. Her hind limbs dragged. She was weak, weak from the unaccustomed labor of walking, weak from the trail of thick, red blood she left behind from the wound which set her free.

"Is this outside?" she asked.

"I think so. Yes, it must be. See! Overhead—the goldshining! The rest I do not know," the One-Eye answered.

"So that is the goldshining. I have heard—Yes, and the rest, I have heard, too. Those are the houses of the slaves and there are the fields the slaves tend, and from which they make the food which they store up for Us. Come help me, for I must go slowly; and we will find a place for Us. We will mate, for We are now The Race." Her voice was like milk. "And our numbers will not end."

He said, "Yes, Mother. Our numbers will not end."

With his single eye he scanned Outside—the Upper World of the slaves who thought themselves masters, who, with trap and terrier and ferret and poison and smoke, warred incessantly against The Race. Did they think that even this great slaughter was victory? If so, they were deceived. It had only been a skirmish.

The slaves were slaves still; the tail-tied ones were kings.

"Come, Mother," he said. And, slowly and painfully, and with absolute certainty, he and his new mate set out to take possession of the world.

The Price of a Charm; or, The Lineaments of Gratified Desire

INTRODUCTION BY HENRY WESSELLS

Astronomers had speculated about the existence of Pluto long before the planet was discovered in 1930: Even while it remained unseen, its influence on comets could be observed. "The Price of a Charm; or The Lineaments of Gratified Desire" is the story of one of the key events of the twentieth century, and it is all the more powerful for being extremely subtle. It is the account of a meeting between Old Steven, a maker of charms for success in the hunt or in love, and a younger man, Gabriel (or Gavrilo), who is a . . . fanatic. This brief, shattering tale (first published as "Price of a Charm" in 1963) is right at the core of an issue that is very much in the public eye (again) as I write this in 1996. The story will always be unsettling and timely, whatever the headlines may read.

The paradox of Avram Davidson's writing is that the unspoken, unwritten words matter as much as those actually on the page. In "There Beneath the Silky-Tree and Whelmed in Deeper Gulphs Than Me," there is a wonderful description of Jack Limekiller's first response to the peculiar economy of British Hidalgo:

> *. . . and he had the flashing thought that somehow he might help fill those holes; he was a while in finding out that this amounted to hoping to fill the holes in a piece of lace: the holes were part of the pattern.*

This is also a description of Avram's writing. His strategy of narration by omission is nowhere so clear as in this story (only "Naples" comes close). Avram doesn't use the overheated rhetoric of the horror writer; his omissions have nothing in common with latter-day minimalists whose world is narrow and monotone. What Avram writes is enough: he demands of us that we make

~~connections he himself made, so that we reach the point where we know why~~ his one or two clues are sufficient to evoke the entire history of Europe. I am not writing an explanation of this story, so I too must omit two or three words that Avram chose to leave out; for explanations, see my comprehensive survey, "A Preliminary Annotated Checklist of the Writings of Avram Davidson" in the Bulletin of Bibliography (vol. 53, issues 1 & 2 [1996]).

THE PRICE OF A CHARM; OR, THE LINEAMENTS OF GRATIFIED DESIRE

THE MOUNTAIN AIR WAS clear and sweet, scented with wild herbs, and although the young man had come quite a distance, he was not at all tired. The cottage—it was really little more than a hut—was just as it had been described to him; clearly, many people in the district had had occasion to visit it.

At one side a tiny spring poured over a lip of rock and crossed the path beneath a rough culvert. At the other side was a row of beehives. A goat and her kid grazed nearby, and a small black sow ate from a heap of acorns with a meditative air.

A man with white hair got up from the bench and held out his hand. "A guest," he said. "A stranger. No matter—a guest, all the same. Everyone who passes by is my guest, and the toll I charge is that I make them drink with me."

He laughed; his laugh was infectious, and the young man laughed too— though his sallow, sullen face was not that of one who laughed often.

The hand he shook was hard and callused. "I am called Old Stevan," the peasant said. "It used to be Black Stevan, but that was a long time ago. Even my mustache is white now—" he stroked its length affectionately—"except for here, in the middle. I am always smoking tobacco. Smoking and drinking, who can live without them?"

He excused himself, and returned almost at once with bottle, two glasses, and cigarettes.

"I do not usually—" the young visitor began, with a frown which seemed familiar to his face.

"If you do not smoke, you do not smoke. But I allow only Moslems to refuse a drink. One drink—a mere formality."

They had one drink for formality, a second drink for friendship, and a third drink to show that they did not deny the Trinity.

Stevan wiped his mustache between his index finger and thumb, thrust in a cigarette, lit it, and smiled contentedly.

"A good thing, matches," he said. "When I was a boy we had to use tinderboxes. How the world does change! You came for a charm?"

The young man seemed relieved now that the preliminaries of his visit were over. "I did," he said.

"Your name?"

"Gavrillo."

Old Stevan repeated it, nodding, blowing out smoke. "I am, of course, well-known for my charms," he said complacently. "I refer to those I make, not those with which Providence endowed me—although there was a time . . . Well, well. My hair was black in those days. I can make quite a number of charms, although some of them are not in demand any longer. I don't remember the last time I supplied one to keep a woman safe from Turks. Before you were born, I'm sure. On the other hand, charms to help barren women conceive are as much called for as ever."

Gavrillo said, scowling, that he was not married.

"My charges are really quite reasonable, too. I can guarantee you perfect protection against ghosts, vampires, werewolves, and the evil spirits of the hills and forests—their cloven hoofs and blood-red nails—"

"I am not afraid of those. I have my crucifix." His hand went to the neck of his open shirt.

"Very well," Old Stevan said equitably. "I've nothing to say against that. I also prepare an excellent charm for success in the hunt . . ."

"Ah."

"And an equally excellent one for success in love."

"Yes."

Old Stevan nodded benignly. "That's it, then, is it? The love charm?"

Gavrillo hesitated, then scowled again.

"Which one means more to you? Or, putting it another way, at which are you more proficient? Take the charm for the other."

The young man threw out his hands. "I am good at neither! And it is important to me that I must excel in one of them."

Stevan lit another cigarette. "Why only one? Take both. The price—"

But Gavrillo shook his head. "It's not the price." He looked out on the wide-spread scene, the deep and dark-green valleys with their forest of oak and beech and pine, the mountains blue with distance, the silvery river. "It's not the price," he repeated.

"As far as you can see on all sides," the old man said quietly; "in fact, farther, my reputation is known. People have come to me from across the frontier. If it is not the price, take both." He saw Gavrillo shake his head, but continued to speak. "The hunt. A day like today. You take your gun and go off in the woods with a few friends. The road is dusty, but in the woods, in the shade, it is cool. Your friends want to go to the right, but you, you have the charm, you know that the way to turn is to the left. They may protest, but you are so confident that they follow. Presently you see something out of the corner of your eye. The others have not noticed it at all, or perhaps assume it is the branch of a dead tree. But you know better. Your eye is clear, you turn swiftly, your arm and hand are quick as never before, the bird flushes, you fire! There it is, at your feet—a fine woodcock. Eh?"

Gavrillo nodded, eyes gleaming.

"Or it might be a red doe, or a roebuck. A fine stag! You can hardly count all the points! Everyone admires you . . . Perhaps in the winter the peasants come to you. 'Master, a wolf. No one is such a hunter as you are. Come, save our flocks.' They have not even seen the beast when your shot brings it down. You wait while they fetch it. They drag the creature along, shouting your praise: 'Only one shot, and at that distance, too!' they cry, and kiss your hand. 'Brave one, hero,' they call you."

A dreamy smile played on Gavrillo's face, and he slowly, slowly nodded.

Old Stevan waited a few moments; but when his visitor said no word, he went on. "Then there is love. What can compare to that? A man who does not enjoy the love of women is only half alive—if even so much. No doubt there is a young woman on whom you have looked, often, with longing, but who never returns that look. She has long black hair. How it glistens, how it gleams! Her lips are soft and red, and sometimes she wets them with her red little tongue. Inside her bodice the young breasts grow, ripe and sweet as fruit . . ."

The young man's eyes seemed glazed. He did not stop the slow nodding of his head.

"You return, the love charm is in your pocket, against your heart, *here*. There is a dance, you join in, so does she. Presently you come face to face. She looks at you—as if she has never seen you before. How wide her eyes grow! Her mouth opens. Her teeth are small and white. You smile at her and instantly she smiles back, then looks away, shyly—but only for an instant—and you dance together.

"Soon the stars come out and the moon rises. The old women are drowsing, the old men are drunk. You take her hand in yours and the two of you slip away. The moment you stop, she throws her arms around you and puts her mouth up to be kissed. The night is warm, the grass is soft. The night is dark and deep, and love is sweet."

Gavrillo made a sound between a sigh and a groan. Slowly he reached into his pocket, took out his purse, and began to slide its contents into his hand.

"You have made up your mind?" the old man asked. "Which is it to be, then?" There was no answer. Something caught the old man's eye. "This one is a foreign coin," he said, touching it with his finger. "But never mind, I will take it: it is gold."

Gavrillo's eyes fell to his hand. He picked up the coin, and an odd look came at once over his face. The dreamy, undecided expression vanished immediately. His eyelids became slits, his lips turned down in an ugly fashion, something like a sneer.

After a moment the old man said, "You have made up your mind?"

"Yes," Gavrillo said. "I have made up my mind." . . .

There was only an old woman before him at the ticket window. He had crossed the river just a few minutes before. The contents of his small suitcase had not engaged the attention of the customs officials for long; and from there it was only a short walk to the railroad station.

The old woman went away, and Gavrillo stepped up to the window. On the wall of the tiny office, facing him, were two framed photographs, side by side. The likeness of the older man was the same one that had been on the coin which had caught Old Stevan's attention; but Gavrillo knew the younger man's face, too—knew it very well, indeed. Once again the odd, ugly, strangely determined expression crossed his face.

The station agent looked up. "Yes, sir," he said. "Where to?"

"One ticket, one way." Gavrillo kept looking at the faces in the photographs.

"Very well, sir, a one-way ticket—but where to? Trieste, Vienna?" He was a self-important little man, and his tone grew a trifle sarcastic. "Paris? Berlin? St. Petersburg?"

Slowly Gavrillo's eyes left the picture. He did not seem to have noticed the sarcasm.

"No," he said. "Just to Sarajevo."

Sacheverell

INTRODUCTION BY SPIDER ROBINSON

I discovered Avram Davidson the summer I invented masturbation.

(That's right: I invented masturbation. It was 1963; I must ask you to take my word that absolutely the only hints offered to even inquisitive Catholic teenagers in that era were that a behavior called "touching oneself impurely" existed and that those who practiced it were both depraved and doomed. Armed solely with these clues, I intuited the region of the body that must be involved, constructed experiments, and in due time invented the wheel. What matter if I was not the first? Elisha Gray's invention of the telephone is no less admirable merely because A. G. Bell beat him to the Patent Office by twenty-four hours. I was quite proud of my invention, and all my memories of the summer of 1963 are [vividly] colored by it.)

A week later, in fact, when I brought home the Ace paperback edition of The Best from Fantasy & Science Fiction: 14th Series *and read its first story—* "Sacheverell"*—I was feeling so (I won't even pretend to apologize for this one) cocky that for a glorious moment or two I actually believed I had invented Avram, too. Like the stoned character in John Brunner's* Stand on Zanzibar, *gaping at the TV news and saying, "Christ, what an imagination I've got!" I had the solipsistic sensation that I had somehow caused Avram to appear in the Universe, out of an artistic necessity. Please, laugh with me at this youthful arrogance of mine, that I thought I had the power to invent an Avram David- son. Even God only managed that once.*

Fortunately, it was not necessary to invent him, only to discover him. And then to bicycle to the public library, ask why there were no Davidson titles on the shelves, and correct that condition. (I was vaguely aware that there were magazines that published sf, but they weren't offered for sale anywhere within bike range of my house.)

That particular anthology was truly excellent—I mean, it included Ze-lazny's "A Rose for Ecclesiastes," alright? Yet to this day, the story that lingers longest and deepest in my mind from that book is the first one: "Sacheverell." The second thing I asked the librarian was to order anything she could get with "Best from Fantasy and Science Fiction" in the title, and in time I hunted down all the worthy predecessors of and successors to that volume . . . but out of all that excellent sf, it's "Sacheverell" I can still quote large portions of from memory.

I marveled at it, at the time. I had just reached the age at which I was beginning to see how writers worked at least some of their magic, to spot a few of the more common professional tricks—but "Sacheverell" defeated me. I understood why my mother liked it, when I showed it to her—but I couldn't quite figure out why I found it so memorable. I tried, that summer, to understand the source of the story's power, to explain to myself its impact on me . . . with such poor success that I'm still at it thirty-three years later, sitting here typing this. Avram worked that trick often: effortlessly pushed buttons nobody else has been able to locate. A very hard writer to reverse-engineer . . . and therefore an immortal.

Here's my current best take on the source of "Sacheverell" 's intense, lay-ered emotional impact: maybe Avram captured, in an absolute minimum of words, what it is like to be a youth bright enough to read science fiction for pleasure.

Even masturbation doesn't help . . . enough. You need friends.

SACHEVERELL

THE FRONT WINDOWS OF the room were boarded up, and inside it was dark and cold and smelled very bad. There was a stained mattress on which a man wrapped in a blanket lay snoring, a chair with no back, a table which held the remains of a bag of hamburgers, several punched beer cans, and a penny candle which cast shadows all around.

There was a scuffling sound in the shadows, then a tiny rattling chattering noise, then a thin and tiny voice said, tentatively, "You must be very *cold*, George . . ." No reply. "Because I know *I'm* very cold . . ." the voice faded out. After a moment it said, "He's still asleep. A man needs his rest. It's very *hard* . . ." The voice seemed to be listening for something, seemed not to hear it; after an instant, in a different tone, said, "All right."

"*Hmm?*" it asked the silence. The chattering broke out again for just a second, then the voice said, "Good afternoon, Princess. Good afternoon, Madame. And General—how very nice to see *you*. I wish to invite you to a tea-party. We will use the best set of doll dishes and if anyone wishes to partake of something *strong*er, I believe the Professor—" the voice faltered, continued, "—has a drop of the oh-be-joyful in a bottle on the sideboard. And now pray take seats."

The wind sounded outside; when it died away, leaving the candleflame dancing, there was a humming noise which rose and fell like a moan, then ended abruptly on a sort of click. The voice resumed, wavering at first, "Coko and Moko? No—I'm very sorry, I really can't invite them, they're very stupid, they don't know how to behave and they can't even talk . . ."

The man on the stained mattress woke in a convulsive movement that brought him sitting up with a cry. He threw his head to the right and left and grimaced and struck at the air.

"Did you have a bad *dream*, George?" the voice asked, uncertainly.

George said, "*Uhn!*" thrusting at his eyes with the cushions of his palms. He dropped his hands, cleared his throat and spat, thickly. Then he reached out and grabbed the slack of a chain lying on the floor, one end fastened to a tableleg, and began to pull it in. The chain resisted, he tugged, something

THE AVRAM DAVIDSON TREASURY

~~fell and squeaked, and George, continuing to pull, hauled in his prize and~~
seized it.

"Sacheverell—"

"I hope you didn't have a bad *dream*, George—"

"Sacheverell—was anybody here? You lie to me and—"

"No, George, honest! Nobody was here, George!"

"You lie to me and I'll kill you!"

"I wouldn't lie to you, George. I know it's wicked to lie."

George glared at him out of his reddened eyes, took a firmer grip with both hands, and squeezed. Sacheverell cried out, thrust his face at George's wrist. His teeth clicked on air, George released him, abruptly, and he scuttled away. George smeared at his trouser-leg with his sleeve, made a noise of disgust. "Look what you done, you filthy little ape!" he shouted.

Sacheverell whimpered in the shadows. "I can't help it, George. I haven't got any sphincter muscle, and you *scared* me, you *hurt* me . . ."

George groaned, huddled in under his blanket. "A million dollars on the end of this chain," he said; "and Om living in this hole, here. Like a wino, like a smokey, like a *bum!*" He struck the floor with his fist. "It don't make sense!" he cried, shifting around till he was on all fours, then pushing himself erect. Wrapping the blanket around his shoulders, he shambled quickly to the door, checked the bolt, then examined in turn the boarded-up front windows and the catch on the barred and frost-rimmed back window. Then he did something in a corner, cursing and sighing.

Under the table Sacheverell tugged on his chain ineffectually. "I don't *like* it here, George," he said. "It's cold and it's dirty and *I'm* dirty and cold, too, and I'm hungry. It's all dark here and nobody ever comes here and I don't like it, George, I don't like it here one bit. I wish I was back with the Professor again. I was very *happy* then. The Professor was nice to me and so was the Princess and Madame Opal and the General. They were the only ones in on the secret, until *you* found out."

George swung around and looked at him. One eye sparked in the candle-light.

"We used to have tea-parties and Madame Opal always brought chocolates when she came, even when she came alone, and she read love stories to me out of a magazine book with pictures and they were all true. Why can't I be back with the Professor again?"

George swallowed, and opened his mouth with a little smacking sound. "Professor Whitman died of a heart-attack," he said.

Sacheverell looked at him, head cocked. "An attack . . ."

"So he's *dead!* So forget about him!" the words tore out of the man's mouth. He padded across the room. Sacheverell retreated to the end of his chain.

"I don't know what the hell Om gunna *do* . . . In a few weeks now, they'll tear this rotten building down. Maybe," he said, slyly, putting his foot down on the chain, "I'll sell you to a zoo. Where you belong." He bent, grunting, and picked up the chain.

Sacheverell's teeth began to chatter. "I *don't!*" he shrilled. "I *don't* belong in a zoo! The little people they have there are *stupid*—they don't know how to *behave,* and they can't even *talk!*"

George closed one eye, nodded; slowly, very slowly, drew in the chain. "Come on," he said. "Level with me. Professor Whitman had a nice little act, there. How come he quit and took off and came here?" Slowly he drew in the chain. Sacheverell trembled, but did not resist.

"We were going to go to a laboratory in a college," he said. "He told me. It was a waste to keep me doing silly tricks with Coko and Moko, when I was so smart. He should have done it before, he said."

George's mouth turned up on one side, creasing the stubble. "Naa, Sacheverell," he said. "That don't make sense. You know what they do to monkeys in them labs? They cut 'em up. That's all. I *know.* I went to one and I asked. They pay about fifteen bucks and then they cut 'em up." He made a scissors out of his fingers and went *k'khkhkhkh* . . . Sacheverell shuddered. George set his foot on the chain again and took hold of him by the neck. He poked him in the stomach with his finger, stiff. It had grown colder, the man's breath shown misty in the tainted air. He poked again. Sacheverell made a sick noise, struggled. "Come on," George said. "Level with me. There's a million dollars inside of you, you dirty little ape. There's *gotta* be. Only I don't know *how.* So you tell me."

Sacheverell whimpered. "I don't *know,* George. I don't *know.*"

The man scowled, then grinned slyly. "That's what *you* say. I'm not so sure. You think I don't know that if They found out, They'd take you away from me? Sure. A million bucks . . . how come I'm being followed, if They don't know? First a guy with a beard, then a kid in a red snow-suit. *I* seen them together. Listen, you frigging little jocko, you better *think,* I'm telling you—you better think hard!" He poked again with his stiff and dirty finger. And again. "I always knew, see, I always *knew* that there was a million bucks waiting for me somewhere, if I only kept my eyes open. What the hell is a guy like me doing unloading crates in the fruit market, when I got plans for a million? And then—" His voice sank and his eyes narrowed. "—this Professor Whitman come along and put up at the Eagle Hotel. I caught his act in the sticks once, I been around. *First* I thought he was practicing ventriloquism, *then* I found out about *you—you* was the other voice in his room! And that's when I—"

Abruptly he stopped. The outside door opened with a rusty squeal and footfalls sounded in the hall. Someone knocked. Someone tried the knob. Someone said, "Sacheverell? Sacheverell?" and George clamped his hairy, filthy hand over the captive's mouth. Sacheverell jerked and twitched and rolled his eyes. The voice made a disappointed noise, the footfalls moved uncertainly, started to retreat. And then Sacheverell kicked out at George's crotch. The man grunted, cursed, lost his grip—

"Help!" Sacheverell cried. *"Help! Help! Save me!"*

Fists beat on the door, the glass in the back window crashed and fell to the floor, a wizened old-man's face peered through the opening, withdrew. George ran to the door, then turned to chase Sacheverell, who fled, shrieking hysterically. A tiny figure in a red snow-suit squeezed through the bars of the back window and ran to pull the bolt on the door. Someone in boots and a plaid jacket and a woolen watch-cap burst in, melting snow glittering on a big black beard.

"Save me!" Sacheverell screamed, dashing from side to side. "He attacked Professor Whitman and knocked him down *and he didn't get up again*—"

George stooped, picking up the chair, but the red snow-suit got between his legs and he stumbled. The chair was jerked from his hands, he came up with his fists clenched and the bearded person struck down with the chair. It caught him across the bridge of the nose with a crunching noise, he fell, turned over, stayed down. Silence.

Sacheverell hiccupped. Then he said, "Why are you wearing *men's* clothing, Princess Zaga?"

"A bearded *man* attracts quite enough attention, thank you," the Princess said, disengaging the chain. "No need to advertise ... Let's get out of here." She picked him up and the three of them went out into the black, deserted street, boarded-shut windows staring blindly. The snow fell thickly, drifting into the ravaged hall and into the room where George's blood, in a small pool, had already begun to freeze.

"There's our car, Sacheverell," said the man in the red snow-suit, thrusting a cigar into his child-size, jaded old face. "What a time—"

"I assume you are still with the carnival, General Pinkey?"

"No, kiddy. The new owners wouldn't reckernize the union, so we quit and retired on Social Security in Sarasota. You'll like it there. Not that the unions are much better, mind you: Bismarkian devices to dissuade the working classes from industrial government on a truly Marxian, Socialist-Labor basis. We got a television set, kiddy."

"And look who's waiting for you—" Princess Zaga opened the station wagon and handed Sacheverell inside. There, in the back seat, was the hugest, the vastest, the fattest woman in the world.

"Princess Opal!" Sacheverell cried, leaping into her arms—and was buried in the wide expanse of her bosom and bathed in her warm Gothick tears. She called him her Precious and her Little Boy and her very own Peter Pan.

"It was Madame Opal who planned this all," Princess Zaga remarked, starting the car and driving off. General Pinkey lit his cigar and opened a copy of *The Weekly People*.

"Yes, I did, yes, I did," Mme. Opal murmured, kissing and hugging Sacheverell. "Oh, how neglected you are! Oh, how thin! We'll have a tea-party, just like we used to, the very best doll dishes; we'll see you eat nice and we'll wash you and comb you and put ribbons around your neck."

Sacheverell began to weep. "Oh, it was *awful* with George," he said.

"Never mind, never mind, he didn't know any better," Mme. Opal said, soothingly.

"The hell he didn't!" snapped Princess Zaga.

"Predatory capitalism," General Pinkey began.

"Never mind, never mind, forget about it, darling, it was only a bad dream ..."

Sacheverell dried his tears on Mme. Opal's enormous spangled-velvet bosom. "George was very *mean* to me," he said. "He treated me *very* mean. But worst of all, you know, Madame Opal, he *lied* to me—he lied to me all the time, and I almost believed him—that was the most horrible part of all: I almost believed that I was a monkey."

The House the Blakeneys Built

INTRODUCTION BY URSULA K. LE GUIN

Science fiction often paints a hopeful history of colonists and castaways on far planets. They not only survive, they thrive in their isolation; they keep all their skills, they remember how to operate the sawmill, how to program the computer, how to maintain liberty and justice for all. And when the Federation finds them after five hundred years, they talk just the way the Feds talk.

Avram didn't share the rationalist's faith that reason, once established, will prevail. I doubt he believed that reason had ever been established anywhere for more than about five minutes. In the incredibly fertile darkness of his imagination, rational behavior is the gleam of a flashlight for a moment in a midnight thunderstorm in a tropical forest.

The Blakeneys could well be a Heinlein survivalist scenario five centuries later, the offspring of a couple of masterful polygamist studs, the children of Reason.

This profoundly disturbing story comes on as light as a meringue. Avram's ear for weird ways of talking was wonderful, and his Blakeneys are very funny, mumbling on and going "Rower, rower." It's hard not to start talking like them, funnyfunny, a hey. But Avram's ear was also for the precise meanings of words; he wrote with a very rare accuracy of usage. Late in the story we realize that the Blakeneys have no plural for the word house. "Houses?"—"No such word, hey." And the whole story lies in that reply.

The funnyfunniest thing about them, to me, is that they don't have cows. They have freemartins. I suspect Avram of throwing this in to see if anybody knew what a freemartin is, and if so, if they'd wonder how the Blakeney cattle reproduce. A hey.

THE HOUSE THE BLAKENEYS BUILT

FOUR PEOPLE COMING DOWN the Forest Road, a hey," Old Big Mary said.

Young Red Tom understood her at once. "Not ours."

Things grew very quiet in the long kitchenroom. Old Whitey Bill shifted in his chairseat. "Those have's to be Runaway Little Bob's and that Thin Jinnie's," he said. "Help me up, some."

"No," Old Big Mary said. "They're not."

"Has to be." Old Whitey Bill shuffled up, leaning on his canestick. "Has to be. Whose elses could they be. Always said, me, she ran after him."

Young Whitey Bill put another chunk of burnwood on the burning. "Rowwer, rowwer," he muttered. Then everyone was talking at once, crowding up to the windowlooks. Then everybody stopped the talking. The big foodpots bubbled. Young Big Mary mumbletalked excitedly. Then her words came out clearsound.

"Look to here—look to here—I say, me, they aren't Blakeneys."

Old Little Mary, coming down from the spindleroom, called out, "People! People! Three and four of them down the Forest Road and I don't know them and, oh, they funnywalk!"

"Four strange people!"

"Not Blakeneys!"

"Stop sillytalking! Has to be! Who elses?"

"But not Blakeneys!"

"Not from The House, look to, look to! People—not from The House!"

"Runaway Bob and that Thin Jinnie?"

"No, can't be. No old ones."

"Children? Childrenchildren?"

All who hadn't been lookseeing before came now, all who were at The House, that is—running from the cowroom and the horseroom and dairyroom, ironroom, schoolroom, even from the sickroom.

"Four people! Not Blakeneys, some say!"

"Blakeneys or not Blakeneys, not from The House!"

Robert Hayakawa and his wife Shulamith came out of the forest, Ezra and

Mikicho with them. "Well, as I said," Robert observed, in his slow careful way, "a road may end nowhere, going in one direction, but it's not likely it will end nowhere, going in the other."

Shulamith sighed. She was heavy with child. "Tilled fields. I'm glad of that. There was no sign of them anywhere else on the planet. This must be a new settlement. But we've been all over that—" She stopped abruptly, so did they all.

Ezra pointed. "A house—"

"It's more like a, well, what would you say?" Mikicho moved her mouth, groping for a word. "A . . . a *castle*? Robert?"

Very softly, Robert said, "It's not new, whatever it is. It is very much not new, don't you see, Shulamith. *What*—?"

She had given a little cry of alarm, or perhaps just surprise. All four turned to see what had surprised her. A man was running over the field towards them. He stopped, stumbling, as they all turned to him. Then he started again, a curious shambling walk. They could see his mouth moving after a while. He pointed to the four, waved his hand, waggled his head.

"Hey," they could hear him saying. "A hey, a hey. Hey. Look to. Mum. Mum mum mum. Oh, hey . . ."

He had a florid face, a round face that bulged over the eyes, and they were prominent and blue eyes. His nose was an eagle's nose, sharp and hooked, and his mouth was loose and trembling. "Oh, hey, you must be, mum, his name, what? And she run off to follow him? Longlong. Jinnie! Thin Jinnie! Childrenchildren, a hey?" Behind him in the field two animals paused before a plow, switching their tails.

"Mikicho, look," said Ezra. "Those must be cows."

The man had stopped about ten feet away. He was dressed in loose, coarse cloth. Again he waggled his head. "Cows, no. Oh, no, mum mum, freemartins, elses. Not cows." Something occurred to him, almost staggering in its astonishment. "A hey, you won't know me! Won't know me!" He laughed. "Oh. What a thing. Strange Blakeneys. Old Red Tom, I say, me."

Gravely, they introduced themselves. He frowned, his slack mouth moving. "Don't know them name," he said, after a moment. "No, a mum. Make them up, like children, in the woods. Longlong. Oh, I, now! Runaway Little Bob. Yes, that name! Your fatherfather. Dead, a hey?"

Very politely, very wearily, feeling—now that he had stopped—the fatigue of the long, long walk, Robert Hayakawa said, "I'm afraid I don't know him. We are not, I think, who you seem to think we are . . . might we go on to the house, do you know?" His wife murmured her agreement, and leaned against him.

Old Red Tom, who had been gaping, seemed suddenly to catch at a word. "The House! A hey, yes. Go on to The House. Good now. Mum."

They started off, more slowly than before, and Old Red Tom, having unhitched his freemartins, followed behind, from time to time calling something unintelligible. "A funny fellow," said Ezra.

"He talks so *oddly*," Mikicho said. And Shulamith said that all she wanted was to sit down. Then—

"Oh, look," she said. *"Look!"*

"They have all come to greet us," her husband observed.

And so they had.

Nothing like this event had ever occurred in the history of the Blakeneys. But they were not found wanting. They brought the strangers into The House, gave them the softest chairseats, nearest to the burning; gave them cookingmilk and cheesemeats and tatoplants. Fatigue descended on the newcomers in a rush; they ate and drank somewhat, then they sank back, silent.

But the people of the house were not silent, far from it. Most of them who had been away had now come back, they milled around, some gulping eats, others craning and staring, most talking and talking and talking—few of them mumbletalking, now that the initial excitement had ebbed a bit. To the new-comers, eyes now opening with effort, now closing, despite, the people of the house seemed like figures from one of those halls of mirrors they had read about in social histories: the same faces, clothes . . . but, ah, indeed, not the same dimensions. Everywhere—florid complexions, bulging blue eyes, protruding bones at the forehead, hooked thin noses, flabby mouths.

Blakeneys.

Thin Blakeneys, big Blakeneys, little Blakeneys, old ones, young ones, male and female. There seemed to be one standard model from which the others had been stretched or compressed, but it was difficult to conjecture what this exact standard was.

"Starside, then," Young Big Mary said—and said again and again, clear-sound. "No elses live to Blakeneyworld. Starside, Starside, a hey, Starside. Same as Captains."

Young Whitey Bill pointed with a stick of burnwood at Shulamith. "Baby grows," he said. "Rower, rower. Baby soon."

With a great effort, Robert roused himself. "Yes. She's going to have a baby very soon. We will be glad of your help."

Old Whitey Bill came for another look to, hobbling on his canestick. "We descend," he said, putting his face very close to Robert's, "we descend from the Captains. Hasn't heard of them, you? Elses not heard? Funny. Funnyfunny. We descend, look to. From the Captains. Captain Tom Blakeney. And his wives. Captain Bill Blakeney. And his wives. Brothers, they. Jinnie, Mary, Captain Tom's wives. Other Mary, Captain Bob's wife. Had another wife, but we don't remember it, us, her name. They lived, look to. Starside. You, too? Mum, you? A hey, Starside?"

Robert nodded. "When?" he asked. "When did they come from Starside? The brothers."

Night had fallen, but no lights were lit. Only the dancing flames, steadily fed, of the burning, with chunks and chunks of fat and greasy burnwood, flickered and illuminated the great room. "Ah, when," said Old Red Tom, thrusting up to the chairseat. "When we children, old Blakeneys say, a hey, five hundredyear. Longlong."

Old Little Mary said, suddenly, "They funnywalk. They funnytalk. But, oh, they funnylook, too!"

"A baby. A baby. Grows a baby, soon."

And two or three little baby Blakeneys, like shrunken versions of their elders, gobbled and giggled and asked to see the Starside baby. The big ones laughed, told them, soon.

"Five hundred . . ." Hayakawa drowsed. He snapped awake. "The four of us," he said, "were heading in our boat for the Moons of Lor. Have you—no, I see, you never have. It's a short trip, really. But something happened to us, I don't know . . . how to explain it . . . we ran into something . . . something that wasn't there. A warp? A hole? That's silly, I know, but—it was as though we felt the boat *drop*, somehow. And then, after that, our instruments didn't work and we saw we had no celestial references . . . not a star we knew. What's that phrase, 'A new Heaven and a new Earth?' We were just able to reach her. Blakeneyworld, as you call it."

Sparks snapped and flew. Someone said, "Sleepytime." And then all the Blakeneys went away and then Hayakawa slept.

It was washtime when the four woke up, and all the Blakeneys around The House, big and little, were off scrubbing themselves and their clothes. "I guess that food on the table is for us," Ezra said. "I will assume it is for us. Say grace, Robert. I'm hungry."

Afterwards they got up and looked around. The room was big and the far end so dark, even with sunshine pouring in through the open shutters, that they could hardly make out the painting on the wall. The paint was peeling, anyway, and a crack like a flash of lightning ran through it; plaster or something of the sort had been slapped onto it, but this had mostly fallen out, its only lasting effect being to deface the painting further.

"Do you suppose that the two big figures could be the Captains?" Mikicho asked, for Robert had told them what Old Whitey Bill had said.

"I would guess so. They look grim and purposeful . . . When was the persecution of the polygamists, anybody know?"

Current social histories had little to say about that period, but the four finally agreed it had been during the Refinishing Era, and that this had been about six hundred years ago. "Could this house be that old?" Shulamith asked. "Parts of it, I suppose, could be. I'll tell you what I think, *I* think that those two Captains set out like ancient patriarchs with their wives and their families and their flocks and so on, heading for somewhere where they wouldn't be persecuted. And then they hit—well, whatever it was that *we* hit. And wound up here. Like us."

Mikicho said, in a small, small voice, "And perhaps it will be another six hundred years before anyone else comes here. Oh, we're here for good and forever. That's sure."

They walked on, silent and unsure, through endless corridors and endless rooms. Some were clean enough, others were clogged with dust and rubbish, some had fallen into ruin, some were being used for barns and stables, and in one was a warm forge.

"Well," Robert said at last, "we must make the best of it. We cannot change the configurations of the universe."

Following the sounds they presently heard brought them to the washroom, slippery, warm, steamy, noisy.

Once again they were surrounded by the antic Blakeney face and form in its many permutations. "Washtime, washtime!" their hosts shouted, showing them where to put their clothes, fingering the garments curiously, helping them to soap, explaining which of the pools were fed by hot springs, which by warm and cold, giving them towels, assisting Shulamith carefully.

"Your world house, you, a hey," began a be-soaped Blakeney to Ezra; "bigger than this? No."

Ezra agreed, "No."

"Your—Blakeneys? No. Mum, mum. Hey. Family? Smaller, a hey?"

"Oh, much smaller."

The Blakeney nodded. Then he offered to scrub Ezra's back if Ezra would scrub his.

The hours passed, and the days. There seemed no government, no rules, only ways and habits and practices. Those who felt so inclined, worked. Those who didn't . . . didn't. No one suggested the newcomers do anything, no one prevented from doing anything. It was perhaps a week later that Robert and Ezra invited themselves on a trip along the shore of the bay. Two healthy horses pulled a rickety wagon.

The driver's name was Young Little Bob. "Gots to fix a floorwalk," he said. "In the, a hey, in the sickroom. Needs boards. Lots at the riverwater."

The sun was warm. The House now and again vanished behind trees or hills, now and again, as the road curved with the bay, came into view, looming over everything.

"We've got to find something for ourselves to *do*," Ezra said. "These people may be all one big happy family, they better be, the only family on the whole planet all this time. But if I spend any much more time with them I think I'll become as dippy as they are."

Robert said, deprecatingly, that the Blakeneys weren't *very* dippy. "Besides," he pointed out, "sooner or later our children are going to have to intermarry with them, and—"

"Our children can intermarry with each other—"

"Our grandchildren, then. I'm afraid we haven't the ancient skills necessary to be pioneers, otherwise we might go . . . just anywhere. There is, after all, lots of room. But in a few hundred years, perhaps less, our descendants would be just as inbred and, well, odd. This way, at least, there's a chance. Hybrid vigor, and all that."

They forded the river at a point just directly opposite The House. A thin plume of smoke rose from one of its great, gaunt chimneys. The wagon turned up an overgrown path which followed up the river. "Lots of boards," said Young Little Bob. "Mum mum mum."

There were lot of boards, just as he said, weathered a silver gray. They were piled under the roof of a great open shed. At the edge of it a huge wheel turned and turned in the water. It, like the roof, was made of some dull and unrusted metal. But only the wheel turned. The other machinery was dusty.

"Millstones," Ezra said. "And saws. Lathes. And . . . all sorts of things. Why do they—Bob? Young Little Bob, I mean—why do you grind your grain by hand?"

The driver shrugged. "Have's to make flour, a hey. Bread."

Obviously, none of the machinery was in running order. It was soon obvious that no living Blakeney knew how to mend this, although (said Young Little Bob) there were those who could remember when things were otherwise: Old Big Mary, Old Little Mary, Old Whitey Bill—

Hayakawa, with a polite gesture, turned away from the recitation. "Ezra . . . I think we might be able to fix all this. Get it in running order. *That* would be something to do, wouldn't it? Something well worth doing. It would make a big difference."

Ezra said that it would make all the difference.

Shulamith's child, a girl, was born on the edge of a summer evening when the sun streaked the sky with rose, crimson, magenta, lime, and purple. "We'll name her *Hope,*" she said.

"Tongs to make tongs," Mikicho called the work of repair. She saw the restoration of the water-power as the beginning of a process which must eventually result in their being spaceborne again. Robert and Ezra did not encourage her in this. It was a long labor of work. They pored and sifted through The House from its crumbling top to its vast, vast colonnaded cellar, finding much that was of use to them, much which—though of no use—was interesting and intriguing—and much which was not only long past use but whose very usage could now be no more than a matter of conjecture. They found tools, metal which could be forged into tools, they found a whole library of books and they found the Blakeney-made press on which the books had been printed; the most recent was a treatise on the diseases of cattle, its date little more than a hundred years earlier. Decay had come quickly.

None of the Blakeneys were of much use in the matter of repairs. They were willing enough to lift and move—until the novelty wore off; then they were only in the way. The nearest to an exception was Big Fat Red Bob, the blacksmith; and, as his usual work was limited to sharpening plowshares, even he was not of much use. Robert and Ezra worked from sunrise to late afternoon. They would have worked longer, but as soon as the first chill hit the air, whatever Blakeneys were on hand began to get restless.

"Have's to get back, now, a hey. Have's to start back."

"Why?" Ezra had asked, at first. "There are no harmful animals on Blakeneyworld, are there?"

It was nothing that any of them could put into words, either clearsound or mumbletalk. They had no tradition of things that go bump in the night, but nothing could persuade them to spend a minute of the night outside the thick walls of The House. Robert and Ezra found it easier to yield, return with them. There were so many false starts, the machinery beginning to function and then breaking down, that no celebration took place to mark any particular day as the successful one. The nearest thing to it was the batch of cakes that Old Big Mary baked from the first millground flour.

"Like longlong times," she said, contentedly, licking crumbs from her toothless chops. She looked at the newcomers, made a face for their baby. A thought occurred to her, and, after a moment or two, she expressed it. "Not ours," she said. "Not ours, you. Elses. But I rather have's you here than that Runaway Little Bob back, or that Thin Jinnie . . . Yes, I rathers."

There was only one serviceable axe, so no timber was cut. But Ezra found a cove where driftwood limbs and entire trees were continually piling up; and the sawmill didn't lack for wood to feed it. "Makes a lot of boards, a hey," Young Little Bob said one day.

"We're building a house," Robert explained.

The wagoner looked across the bay at the mighty towers and turrets, the great gables and long walls. From the distance no breach was noticeable, although two of the chimneys could be seen to slant slightly. "Lots to build," he said. "A hey, whole roof on north end wing, mum mum, bad, it's bad, hey."

"No, we're building our own house."

He looked at them, surprised. "Wants to build another room? Easier, I say, me, clean up a no-one's room. Oh, a hey, lots of them!"

Robert let the matter drop, then, but it could not be dropped forever, so one night after eats he began to explain. "We are very grateful for your help to us," he said, "strangers as we are to you and to your ways. Perhaps it is because we *are* strange that we feel we want to have our own house to live in."

The Blakeneys were, for Blakeneys, quiet. They were also uncomprehending.

"It's the way we've been used to living. On many of the other worlds people do live, many families—and the families are all smaller than this, than yours, than the Blakeneys, I mean—many in one big house. But not on the world we lived in. There, every family has its own house, you see. We've been used to that. Now, at first, all five of us will live in the new house we're going to build near the mill. But as soon as we can we'll build a second new one. Then each family will have its own . . ."

He stopped, looked helplessly at his wife and friends. He began again, in the face of blank nonunderstanding, "We hope you'll help us. We'll trade our services for your supplies. You give us food and cloth, we'll grind your flour and saw your wood. We can help you fix your furniture, your looms, your broken floors and walls and roofs. And eventually—"

But he never got to explain about eventually. It was more than he could do to explain about the new house. No Blakeneys came to the house-raising. Robert and Ezra fixed up a capstan and hoist, block-and-tackle, managed—with the help of the two women—to get their small house built. But nobody of the Blakeneys ever came any more with grain to be ground, and when Robert and Ezra went to see them they saw that the newly-sawn planks and the lathe-turned wood still lay where it had been left.

"The food we took with us is gone," Robert said. "We have to have more. I'm sorry you feel this way. Please understand, it is not that we don't like you. It's just that we have to live our own way. In our own houses."

The silence was broken by a baby Blakeney. "What's 'houses'?," he asked.

He was shushed. "No such word, hey," he was told, too.

Robert went on, "We're going to ask you to lend us things. We want enough grain and tatoplants and such to last till we can get our own crops in, and enough milk-cattle and draft-animals until we can breed some of our own. Will you do that for us?"

Except for Young Whitey Bill, crouched by the burning, who mumble-talked with "Rower, rower, rower," they still kept silence. Popping blue eyes stared, faces were perhaps more florid than usual, large, slack mouths trembled beneath long hook-noses.

"We're wasting time," Ezra said.

Robert sighed. "Well, we have no other choice, friends . . . Blakeneys . . . We're going to have to take what we need, then. But we'll pay you back, as soon as we can, two for one. And anytime you want our help or service, you can have it. We'll be friends again. We *must* be friends. There are so many, many ways we can help one another to live better—and we are all there are, really, of humanity, on all this planet. We—"

Ezra nudged him, half-pulled him away. They took a wagon and a team of horses, a dray and a yoke of freemartins, loaded up with food. They took cows and ewes, a yearling bull and a shearling ram, a few bolts of cloth, and seed. No one prevented them, or tried to interfere, as they drove away. Robert turned and looked behind at the silent people. But then, head sunk, he watched only the bay road ahead of him, looking aside neither to the water or the woods.

"It's good that they can see us here," he said, later on that day. "It's bound to make them think, and, sooner or later, they'll come around."

They came sooner than he thought.

"I'm so glad to see you, friends!" Robert came running out to greet them. They seized and bound him with unaccustomed hands. Then, paying no attention to his anguished cries of "Why? Why?" they rushed into the new house and dragged out Shulamith and Mikicho and the baby. They drove the animals from their stalls, but took nothing else. The stove was now the major object of interest. First they knocked it over, then they scattered the burning coals all about, then they lit brands of burnwood and scrambled around with them. In a short while the building was all afire.

The Blakeneys seemed possessed. Faces red, eyes almost popping from their heads, they mumbled-shouted and raved. When Ezra, who had been working in the shed came running, fighting, they bore him to the ground and beat him with pieces of wood. He did not get up when they were through; it seemed apparent that he never would. Mikicho began a long and endless scream.

Robert stopped struggling for a moment. Caught off-guard, his captors loosened their hold—he broke away from their hands and his bonds, and, crying, "The tools! The tools!", dashed into the burning fire. The blazing roof fell in upon him with a great crash. No sound came from him, nor from Shulamith, who fainted. The baby began a thin, reedy wail.

Working as quickly as they could, in their frenzy, the Blakeneys added to the lumber and waste and scraps around the machinery in the shed, soon had it all ablaze.

The fire could be seen all the way back.

"Wasn't right, wasn't right," Young Red Bob said, over and over again.

"A bad thing," Old Little Mary agreed.

Young Big Mary carried the baby. Shulamith and Mikicho were led, dragging, along. "Little baby, a hey, a hey," she crooned.

Old Whitey Bill was dubious. "Be bad blood," he said. "The elses women grow more babies. A mum mum," he mused. "Teach them better. Not to funnywalk, such." He nodded and mumbled, peered out of the window-look, his loose mouth widening with satisfaction. "Wasn't right," he said. "Wasn't *right*. Another house. Can't be another *house*, a second, a third. Hey, a hey! Never was elses but The House. Never be again. No."

He looked around, his gaze encompassing the cracked walls, sinking floors, sagging roof. A faint smell of smoke was in the air. "The House," he said, contentedly. "The House."

The Goobers

INTRODUCTION BY JAMES GUNN

Avram Davidson had an eye for the curious and the obscure. Not for the sort of absurdity that appears nowadays under the heading of "News of the Weird," but those oddities of human behavior that get fossilized in language or in myth. Every now and then a postcard would materialize on my desk, dropped, as it were, from some invisible observer, with a report from Avram about some strangeness he had come across.

"Do you know," one said, "that Gunn is the horse of MacDonald?" I think it was MacDonald; it could have been some other Scottish name.

That sensitivity to language was evident from his first published story, "My Boy Friend's Name Is Jello," and it was evident in everything he wrote, including the story at hand, "The Goobers." "The Goobers" is unusual, however, in that it is narrated by a language-challenged boy and cannot display Avram's customary virtuosity. But Avram was the master of his trade, and he could adapt his vocabulary when the story called for it—he could sound like a country boy.

The story was unusual, too, in being published in a place different from his favorite science fiction and fantasy magazines, particularly the magazine he edited for a time, Fantasy & Science Fiction. Swank was one of those men's magazines that flourished for a season after the success of Playboy. But "Goobers" was typically Avram in its sly introduction of the fantastic into the everyday, and the startling impact of the figurative become literal.

THE GOOBERS

WHEN I WAS A boy I lived for a while after my folks both died with my grandfather and he was one of the meanest, nastiest old men you'd ever want to know, only you wouldn't've wanted to've known him. He had a little old house that there was nothing in the least cute or quaint about and it smelled of kerosene and bacon grease and moldy old walls and dirty clothes. He must've had one of the largest collections of tin cans filled up with bacon grease around there in those parts. I suppose he was afraid there might be a shortage of this vital commodity some day and he was sure as Hell going to be prepared for it.

The dirty old kitchen had two stoves, one wood and one kerosene, and although the thicket out behind the house had enough dead brush and timber in it to heat the place for years he was too damned lazy to swing an axe. Same thing with the clothes. Rather than pay a woman to do a laundry or perish forbid he should actually do it himself, he just let the clothes accumulate and then he'd go through it and use the least dirty ones all over again. Finally every so often it would get so bad that none of the other kids wanted to sit next to me and the teacher'd talk to the neighbors and then one or the other of them who happened to have a gasoline power washing-machine of the old-fashioned sort would come by with one of her kids and a wagon and a couple of bushel baskets.

"I don't know how you let things get into such a condition, Mr. Harkness," she'd say, wrinkling up her nose and breathing through her mouth. "You load these things up and I'll wash'm for you, for pity's sake, before they *fester* on you! You'll both wind up in the *pest* house before you know it. Mercy!"

And the old turd would hobble around trying to look debilitated when actually he was as limber as a blacksnake when he wanted to be, frowning and making motions at me to get busy and trot the clothes out, and all the while he'd be whining things like, "I sure do thank you, Miz Wallaby . . ." or whatever in the Hell her name was, "I don't know what we'd do without our neighbors, as the Good Book says. I'm just a poor sick old man and this Boy is too much for me, it's not right I should have such a burden thrust upon me in the decline of my life, I haven't got the strength for it, no I haven't ma'am, he'll be the death of me I predict, for he won't work and he won't listen and he won't obey," and so on and so forth.

Then, once she was out of sight and hearing, he'd sit back in his easy chair that had the bottom sprung out of it and he'd smirk and laugh and carry on about how he'd sure gotten the best of that deal, all right.

"Just set and wait long enough and let the word get around and sure enough, Boy, some damn fool will turn up and do the work! Well, I'm willing. Let'm. Good for their souls." And he'd cackle and hee-haw and dribble Apple Twist tobacco juice onto his dirty old moustache.

He had no shame and he had no pride. Send me begging for food. He'd do that, although he had money for the bootlegger. And he'd send me to steal, too. "Don't tell me you don't want to, Boy. It's the easiest thing there is. You got that big old hole in your overcoat pocket, alls you got to do, Boy, is just drop in a can of pork'n-beans or a box a sardines, let 'm fall into the lining, then just walk out as easy as you please with your two hands in plain sight, Boy, your two hands in plain sight. So don't tell me you don't *want* to, Boy. You want to *eat*, don't you?"

He had it all figured out. It was a perfectly good sort of thing to steal from the A & P, because the A & P was a monopoly. And it was a perfectly good thing to steal from Ah Quong, because Ah Quong was a Chinaman. "Live on a fish-head and handful of rice a day, Boy, and that's the reason us Americans can't compete with 'm."

He talked this way all around town and one day when I was "shopping" in the E Light Grocery Store, old Ah Quong waved me over. I was so afraid, I almost messed myself. I was sure old Ah Quong was going to brain me with a hatchet, having caught on to me, but all he did was to hand me a package. "You give you gland-fodda," he said. I took it and all but ran.

What was there inside of it but a bag of fish-heads and a bag of rice.

You think he was ashamed?

"By grannies, Boy," he said, running his tongue over his gummy old mouth, "we'll make chowder. Nothing makes a better chowder than fish-heads. Rice is nice, too. Rice is a thing that settles mighty easy on the stomach."

He claimed he'd been wounded in the Spanish and American War but was cheated out of a pension by the politicians. He claimed he'd been to the Yukon for gold. He claimed he'd been a railroad engineer and he claimed this and that and the other thing, but as I got older I come to realize that they were all lies, just lies. He'd rather work hard at a lie than tell the easy truth. But I was a while in catching on to this.

When I say he was mean, I mean he was *mean*. I don't mean he'd ever actually beat me. He wanted to for sure, he'd almost tremble with eagerness to do it sometimes, pulling at his belt and yelling and swearing. But he was too afraid to, because even though I was only about ten years old I was mighty big for my age and getting bigger all the time, and I had all my teeth, too. He knew that in a few years I'd be big enough to take him on and stamp all over him.

So he'd threaten. Mean, nasty threats. "Won't go to get an old man's medicine just because it's mizzling a few drops," he'd yell—meaning, Won't go pick up my booze when it's raining fit to drown kittens. "I've had enough.

Boy, hear me now! I've had *enough!* I'm turning you over to the Authorities! The County can take care of you from now on! We'll see how you like it in the orphanage asylum from now on! Water mush three meals a day and the cat-o'-nine-tails if you look down your nose at it. I'm going now, I'm going *now*, do you hear me? To tell'm to come pick you up...."

He bundled himself up and skettered out, rain and all. Of course he was just going to get his pint of moon, but I didn't know that. I spent that night moving from one hiding spot to another, my teeth chattering. And finally fell asleep under the bed.

It was after the Authorities started never coming that he began with other threats. "Boy, I don't know what I'm going to do with you. Yes, I *do* know. I'm going to sell you, Boy—*I'm going to sell you to the Goobers!*"

Well, I didn't know if the Goobers lived in the next township or if they were the name of a foreign power. All I knew was, they weren't good. If they'd've been good my grandfather would sure've never've mentioned them. Nobody ever heard him threaten to put me with some family which would dress me right and keep me clean and feed me decent, that's for sure. He'd even threatened once to feed me to the hogs—not *our* hogs, we never kept hogs, it would've been too much of a work to slop them—but there were plenty of hogs kept in the town—and everybody knew that hogs have been known to eat children, though of course not of my size and age, just babies, but I didn't know that then.

"What're Goobers?" I asked after a little while. Maybe they could've been a kind of animal, I thought, but in a minute I realized no they couldn't, animals couldn't *buy* anything, they had to be people. Maybe the Goobers was their name—like we were the Harknesses.

"You'll wish you never come to know," was his answer. He made his mean little eyes all small, then he opened them so wide that the whites showed all around and the red under lids. "That's what you'll wish! When I sell you to the Goobers! Which I'll do by the Ever-Living Lord of Heaven and Earth...." He never went to church or said a prayer, mind you and he didn't finish, just sucked in his scabby lower lip and nodded at me.

Maybe they were another kind of Authorities. State, maybe, instead of County. Mr. Smith, Chief Goober of the State...? And of course his helpers. Anyway, whatever it was they might want to buy me for, it couldn't be good. I knew that. But I wanted to know more. So I asked Rodney Sloat. He wasn't a friend of mine, I had no friends, but he was a non-enemy at least, and he was known to read books.

"Rodney, is there any such a thing as Goobers?"

He nodded his head. "They live in holes in the ground," he said.

It must've been about ten years ago that all of a sudden it came to me that what he must've been thinking of was, of course, *gophers*—and I spilled my coffee all over myself and scalded my legs. All that time it was a mystery what he had in mind. But right just then, when he told me they lived in holes in the ground, it never occurred to me that this was the thing he meant. *They lived in holes in the ground!* Oh, this was worse than anything ever imagined.

The old dog saw how he'd gotten to me, and it was like the smell of blood.

He never let up. It was, Do this, Do that, Don't you dast do this or that, or I'll sell you to the Goobers, sure as I'm alive. . . . And I went about in fear of my life, almost, because although he'd never said that the Goobers would kill me—or even harm me—why, how did I know they wouldn't? *They lived in holes in the ground,* didn't they?

The old man didn't have any friends any more than I had friends, but he had cronies, which was more than I had. One of them was a big ruined old hulk of a man with a long fat face all sunken in the middle and white stubble on it, but two little clumps of black eyebrow like curled-up caterpillars. And his name was Barlow Brook. Never just Barlow and never Brook or Mr. Brook.

I broke a plate.

"Got the dropsy," said Barlow Brook.

Grandfather went into his song and dance. "Barlow Brook, the Boy is a torment to me by day and by night."

"Take the hide off of him."

"I swear, Boy, my patience is running out. There's a show-down coming, do you hear me, Boy? It's coming to that. I won't whip you like Barlow Brook says, nooo. I'm too soft-hearted for that. But I warn you, Boy, and I call Barlow Brook to my witness, unless you mend your ways and mighty quick, I will *sell* you to the Goobers."

Barlow Brook hooked open the door of the cold old dusty wood stove with his foot and spit into it. "George Wolf used to talk about the Goobers." He reached himself a hunk of bread and one of our six hundred cans of bacon grease and smeared it on with his fingers and gobbled at it.

"George Wolf," said my grandfather. "He was a bad one."

"Bad as they come. Used to talk about the Goobers. Remember that girl at George Wolf's?"

"Sassy girl?"

"Sassy as they come. You can't make me, used to say. You ain't my father, used to say. Ain't even married to my mother. Try to catch her, he would. Couldn't do it. Take care, he'd tell her. The Goobers will get hold of you one a these days." Bread crumbs, greasy bread crumbs, coming out of his mouth, but I never missed a word, thick as he was speaking, about the sassy girl at George Wolf's.

Barlow Brook washed down his dinner from the smoky-looking bottle, didn't wipe it or his mouth either.

"She says to him, there ain't no such of a thing as any Goobers. Goobers is peanuts, she says to him. George Wolf, he told her. That's *why* they call'm Goobers, he says, they *look* like that. Only not so small. Not near so small. Got wrinkled old shells on. Dirty yellow colored. Even sometimes a couple of hairs. Watch out, sassy. They'll git ahold of you. George Wolf."

Barlow Brook put his moldering shoes up to the kerosene stove.

"You hear, now, Boy," said my grandfather, smirking at me.

I swallowed. I asked what, what happened to the sassy girl at George Wolf's. A quick, secret look passed between those two evil old men. *Something* had happened to her, I knew that. I know it now. And I've got my own idea as to what. But, then . . . When Barlow Brook said, "Came and *got her*," I had no idea except for sure that the Goobers were the *they*.

You can be sure that I did my best not to break any more plates. I fetched and I carried. When my grandfather said "Come here, Boy," I came a running. But he was a bully, and there is no satisfying of bullies. He knew I was in mortal terror of being sold to the Goobers and he never let up. There were hickory trees back in the thicket and one day he sent me to get some nuts. I didn't mind at all and I went quick.

And I came back quick. There was a bad family by the name of Warbank lived outside of town, so bad that even my grandfather didn't want anything to do with them. They were meaner than he was and they had a bunch of big yellow dogs meaner than they were. When I got to the hickory trees with my bucket, there was Ding Warbank and Cut Warbank with their own buckets, and their dogs.

"You get the Hell out of here," said Ding.

"It ain' your thicket," I said.

"Get him," said Cut. The dogs came after me and I ran. One of them got hold of my pants and it came away in his teeth. Behind me, Cut called them back.

"We better not see you here again," yelled Ding.

My grandfather took on fierce. No trashy Warbanks, he yelled, were going to tell him he couldn't have nuts from "his own" thicket.

"You go on back there," he ordered. "Go on, now."

I didn't move.

"Go *on*, I tell you! Go on, go on, go on! You want me to sell you to the Goobers?"

Oh, I was afraid of that, all right. I was afraid of the Goobers. But I'd never really seen any. And I *had* seen those Warbanks' yellow dogs, felt their white shiny teeth pulling that bite out of my pants legs. And I wouldn't go.

He yelled and he raged. Then, all of a sudden, he quit. "All right, Boy," he said. "All right, then. I am through warning you. In one hour's time, as I live and as my name's Dade Harkness, in one hour's time I swear that I will sell you to the Goobers. Now git out my sight—but don't you leave the yard!"

What he figured on, I guess, was that the Warbanks would be gone by then and I'd rush out and get his old hickory nuts and then he'd pardon me . . . for the time being.

I stumbled away. "It's four o'clock," he yelled after me. "They'll be here at five. Don't bother packing—you won't need nothing!"

An hour like that, I never want to pass again. I hid here and hid there, till I was sweaty and dirty as never before. But I didn't trust any place. By and by I got so thirsty that I had to come out and get to the pump. I could hear the old man muttering to himself.

His warning about not leaving the yard didn't matter to me worth a poke of peas—he, well, what could he've done to me for disobeying? Sell me to the Goobers? He was going to do that anyway. . . he said. Of course, he'd said it before and he'd changed his mind before, too. I knew only one thing for sure, and that was that I couldn't stand any more of it. Anything was likely to be better.

I'd never been to George Wolf's place, but I knew where it was, and it wasn't all that far away. About a mile or so off, on the old dirt road along the creek. It was an ugly old shack, never had a lick of paint on it, I guess, though I barely noted that any more than I did the broken windows or the roof falling in on one side and the weeds and underbrush choking up the front yard.

If George Wolf had been the original local acquaintance of the Goobers, then the Goobers couldn't've lived too far away from his place. That was the way my thoughts were running—and I was running, too—right into the woods and down the hill and almost into the swamp that stopped me going further.

"Goobers!" I yelled. "Goobers! You old Goobers! You hear me?" I screamed.

There was nothing but the echo of my voice. It was darkish there, and clammy, and it smelled bad and I was hot and cold and sweaty and I took a big breath and went on yelling again.

"I don't care if he sells me! I don't care if you buy me! He isn't going to go on scaring me like this! You want to buy me? You just come on and do it!"

Something was buzzing when I stopped again. Maybe just a dragon fly. Something moved in the gray underbrush. Maybe just the wind. I could see a hole in the ground not far off. Maybe it was just a plain, ordinary hole. But I didn't wait to find out about any of this. I turned and ran and stumbled away.

Where? Why, where but back to the old man's house, back to the only sort of home I knew. I didn't know what was going to happen, but I knew it was going to happen there. It had to.

I slowed down to a soft walk before I got to the yard. Probably he didn't even know I'd gone, didn't think I'd've dared to. And I could still hear him muttering to himself for a while. Then, suddenly, he stopped.

So did I. Stopped breathing, I mean. I guess. The bell in the old church was striking, and while I'd missed the start, there was no need for me to count the chimes. It only struck the hours. So it had to be five o'clock.

I darted a quick look at the vines hiding his chair from where I was standing. Chair, no, I couldn't see it. But I could see *him*—see his head, anyway, for he'd gotten up, sort of and had poked his face forward. It had gone the most horrible ugly sort of putty color. His eyes had a glaze over them like cold fried eggs. I had to turn to see what he was looking at, though of course I knew.

There were the Goobers, coming up the back path.

They were under my height. There were three of them and they had dirty yellow-colored wrinkled old shells on, with even a few hairs. And dirt was clinging to them.

"Where Boy?" asked the first.

"Here Boy," said the second.

"You sell Boy?" asked the third.

They walked up and squeezed my arms and felt my legs. They pulled on my nose and grabbed hold of my tongue. They spun me around and thumped me on the back. Then they quit.

"No," said the first.

"No good," said the second.

"No buy Boy," said the third.

They turned around and walked off. I watched them go, not even turning around when I heard my grandfather keel over and thump the porch floor.

After that, of course, I made his life a living Hell until I ran off two years later at the age of twelve, and there wasn't a damned thing the old bastard could do about it.

The Power of Every Root

INTRODUCTION BY THOMAS M. DISCH

In 1964, having been an official SF writer for all of two years, I set off for Mexico to write my first novel. There I moved into the shell lately emptied by my sometime editor at F&SF, *Avram Davidson. I had never met Avram, but having inherited his home, garden, landlady, and friends in Mexico City, I came to feel a peculiar intimacy, quite as though I were leading his life as much as my own, a sense that would be heightened when, later, I learned in a letter from Avram that a young woman who'd been his traveling companion in Belize had run off with Tony, a dashing young con man whom I'd earlier befriended at a beach on the Pacific coast, where he was selling solid gold watches to gas station attendants.*

Like Avram, I fell in love with the raffishness of the Mexico that opened its doors and its cantinas to visiting gringos. Unlike Avram, I never became so well assimilated that I could make that love yield an homage as affectionate and closely observed as "The Power of Every Root." Reading it again, now that my expatriate days are over (and Avram's, too), I can smell all the spices and fetors of the marketplace he inventories so lovingly in this tale—and remember the heady freedoms of being a penny-a-word writer living high off the hog in a lush garden between two great volcanoes.

CARLOS RODRIGUEZ NUÑEZ, A police officer of the municipality of
Santo Tomas, sat in the private waiting room of Dr. Olivera considering his
situation. Perhaps he ought not to be there at all.

Not the private waiting room in particular: it was usually empty except
during the week following major fiestas, when it was likely to be much occupied by the younger sons of prosperous families who had (the younger sons)
visited the Federal Capital, touring the libraries and theaters and museums and
other buildings of the national patrimony . . . but never, never *las casitas*. The
reason, therefore, why they were here?

"A strain, Sir Doctor. Without doubt, nothing more than a strain . . . ! Woe
of me, Sir Doctor! What an enormous needle! Surely—just for a tiny, little
strain?"

The physician would smile benignly, speak soothingly, continue charging
his syringe with penicillin.

None of this was applicable to the police officer Carlos. In fact, it was not
applicable to the younger sons of the *non*-prosperous families, who—for one
thing—could only afford to visit the District Capital (or, at most, the State
one) on fiestas; and—for another—did not take their subsequent difficulties to
a physician: they took them to the *curandero*. Carlos now wondered if he
should not do the same. No . . . No . . . The social status of a government employee, a civil servant, might be imperiled by visiting a native herbalist and
wizard. Besides, the physician's public waiting room was just that: public. Let
him be seen there, word would get around, Don Juan Antonio would ask
questions. Don Juan Antonio was *jefe de policia*, and it seemed to Carlos that
his superior's manner to him of late had lacked cordiality. But, then, it seemed
to Carlos that everybody's attitude toward him of late lacked cordiality. He
could not understand why this should be. He was a very gentle policeman; he
took only the customary little bites of graft; he did not hit drunks hard; he
gave cigarettes to prisoners. Often.

Why, therefore, people should—suddenly, sometimes only for matters of
a few seconds—change, become hideous, diabolical, when they looked at him,
he could not know. Their faces would swell, become even more horrible than

those of the masked *moros* or the judases in the fiesta parades had seemed to him as a child. The air would become hot; voices would croak and mutter ugly things; he had difficulty breathing, sometimes. And his head—

A large, tinted oval photograph of old Doña Caridad, Dr. Olivera's mother, glared at him from the wall. Her lips writhed. She scowled. Carlos got up hastily. Doña Caridad's unexpected and totally unprovoked hostility was more than he could stand. He had his hand out to open the outer door when the inner door opened and the physician himself stood there—momentarily surprised, immediately afterwards urbane as always. Bowing him in. Doña Caridad was as immovable and expressionless as before.

There was a formal exchange of courtesies. Then silence. Dr. Olivera gestured toward a publication on his desk. "I have just been reading," he said, "in the medical journal. About eggs. Modern science has discovered so much about eggs." Carlos nodded. Dr. Olivera placed his fingertips together. He sighed. Then he got up and, with a sympathetic expression, gestured for Carlos to drop his trousers.

"Ah, no, Sir Medico," the officer said hastily. "No, no, it isn't anything like that." Dr. Olivera's mouth sagged. He seemed to hesitate between annoyance and confusion. Carlos breathed in, noisily, then said, all in a rush, "My head is bursting, I have dizziness and pains, my eyes swell, my chest burns, my heart also, and—and—" He paused. He couldn't tell about the way people's faces changed. Or about, just now, for example, Doña Caridad. Dr. Olivera might not be trusted to keep confidence. Carlos choked and tried to swallow.

The physician's expression had grown increasingly reassured and confident. He pursed his lips and nodded. "Does the stomach work?" he inquired. "Frequently? Sufficiently frequently?"

Carlos wanted to tell him that it did, but his throat still was not in order, and all that came out was an uncertain croak. By the time he succeeded in swallowing, the *señor medico* was speaking again.

"Ninety percent of the infirmities of the corpus," he said, making serious, impressive sounds with his nose, "are due to the stomach's functioning with insufficient frequency. Thus the corpus and its system become poisoned. Sir Police Officer—poisoned! We inquire as to the results—We find—" he shook his head rapidly from side to side and he threw up his hands "—that pains are encountered. They are encountered not only in the stomach, but in," he enumerated on his fingers, "the head. The chest. The eyes. The liver and kidneys. The urological system. The upper back. The lower back. The legs. The entire corpus, sir, becomes debilitated." He lowered his voice, leaned forward, half-whispered, half-hissed, "*One lacks capacity . . .*" He closed his eyes, compressed his lips, and leaned back, fluttering his nostrils and giving short little up-and-down nods of his head. His eyes flew open, and he raised his brows. "*Eh?*"

Carlos said, "Doctor, I am thirty years old, I have always until now been in perfect health, able, for example, to lift a railroad tie. My wife is very content. Whenever I ask her, she says, *¿Como no?* And afterwards she says, *¡Ay, bueno!*

I do *not* lack—" A baby cried in the public waiting room. Dr. Olivera got up and took out his pen.

"I will give you a prescription for an excellent medication," he said, making a fine flourish and heading the paper with a large, ornate, *Sr. C. Rodriguez N.* He wrote several lines, signed it, blotted it, handed it over. "One before each alimentation for four days, or until the stomach begins to function frequently . . . Do you wish the medicine from me, or from the *farmacia?*"

Discouraged, but still polite, Carlos said, "From you, Doctor. And . . . Your honorarium?"

Dr. Olivera said, deprecatingly, "With the medication . . . ten pesos. For you, as a civil servant. Thank you . . . ah! And also: avoid eggs. Eggs are difficult to digest—they have very, very large molecules."

Carlos left via the private waiting room. Doña Caridad looked away, contemptuously. Outside, those coarse fellows, woodcutters, the cousins Eugenio and Onofrio Cruz, nudged one another, sneered. Carlos looked away.

He crossed the plaza, vaguely aware of its smells of grilling, crisp pork *carnitas,* ripe fruit, wood smoke. His head and eyes and throat were misbehaving again. He remembered that the *Forestal* authorities had forbidden woodcutting for a month as a conservation measure and that he had meant to look out for possible violations. A toothless old Indian woman with bare, gray feet, padded by, mumbling a piece of fried fish. Her face twisted, became huge, hideous. He shut his eyes, stumbled. After a moment he felt better and went on up the steps of the covered market and into the *excusado.* As always he received mild pleasure from not having to pay the twenty centavos charge. He closed the door of the booth, dropped the pills in the bowl, flushed it. So. Saved twenty centavos, spent—wasted—ten pesos. On the wall was a new crop of graffiti. *A harlot is the mother of Carlos Rodriguez N.* read one. Ordinarily he would have read it without malice, even admiring the neat moderation of the insult—by crediting him with two family names, albeit reducing one to the formal initial, the writer had avoided accusing him of illegitimacy. Or he might have remarked to himself the effects of enforcing the lowered compulsory school entrance age: the obscenities were increasingly being written lower and lower on the walls.

But now—now—

Incoherent with rage, he rushed, shouting, outside. And almost ran into his superior, Don Juan Antonio, the chief of police. Who looked at him with the peculiar look so familiar nowadays, asked, "Why are you shouting?" And sniffed his breath.

Accepting this additional insult, Carlos muttered something about boys begging in the market. Don Juan Antonio brushed this aside, gestured toward the other end of the plaza. "Twenty auto-buses of students from the high schools and colleges of the State Capital are stopping over here before they continue on to the National Youth Convention. Must I direct traffic myself while you are chasing beggar boys?"

"Ah, no, *señor jefe!*" Carlos walked hastily to where the yellow buses were slowly filing into the plaza and began directing them to the somewhat restricted

~~place available for parking—the rest of the space being already occupied by~~ vendors of black pottery marked with crude fish, brown pottery painted with the most popular women's names, parrot chicks, Tabasco bananas, brightly colored cane-bottom chairs, pineapples sliced open to reveal the sweet contents, shoes, rubber-tire-soled sandals, holy pictures and candles, *rebozos, mantillas,* pear-shaped lumps of farm butter, grilled strips of beef, a hundred varieties of beans, a thousand varieties of chili peppers, work shirts, bright skirts, plastic tablecloths, patriotic pictures, knitted caps, sombreros: the infinite variety of the Latin American marketplace—he called out to the bus driver, banging his hand on the bus to indicate that the vehicle should come back a little bit more . . . a little bit more . . . a little bit—

Crash!

He had backed the bus right into the new automobile belonging to Don Pacifico, the *presidente municipal!* The driver jumped out and cursed; the mayor jumped out and shouted; the students descended; the population assembled; the police chief came running and bellowing; Señorita Filomena—the mayor's aged and virginal aunt—screamed and pressed her withered hands to her withered chest; her numerous great-nephews and great-nieces began to cry—Carlos mumbled, made awkward gestures, and that ox, the stationmaster, a man who notoriously lacked education, and was given to loud public criticism of the police: he laughed.

The crowd became a mob, a hostile mob, the people of which continuously split in two in order to frighten and confuse the miserable police officer with their double shapes and now dreadful faces. It was horrible.

Lupe's body, one was always aware, was altogether independent of Lupe's dress. It did not depend upon it for support, nor did it quarrel or struggle to escape from it, but, firm and smooth and pleasant, it announced both its presence and its autonomy and, like the dress itself, was always bright and clean and sweet. Others might doubt the fidelity of a comely wife, but not Carlos.

Lupe was the best thing about the *ranchito* Rodriguez, but there were other good things about it—everything, in fact, about it was good. The large brown adobe bricks of the walls were well-made, well-cured, well-set in their places; the tiles of the roof neither cracked nor leaked nor slipped. *Pajaritos* hopped about from perch to perch in their wooden cages, chirping and singing, outdone in their bright colors only by the dozens of flowering plants set in little pots or cans. Carlos and Lupe never had to buy corn to make *nixtamal,* the dough for tortillas or tamales; they grew their own, and this supplied them as well with husks to wrap and boil the tamales in, and when the cobs had dried they made good fuel. There was an apple tree and a great tall old piñole which supplied them with blue-gray nuts whose kernels were as sweet as the apples. The goat had always fodder enough, the pig was fine and fat, and half a dozen hens relieved them of any need to depend upon the chancy eggs of the market women. Not the least of the *ranchito*'s many amenities was its stand of fleshy maguey cactus whose nectar gave an *aguamiel* from which, mixed with the older and stronger *madre de pulque,* came the delicious and finished milk-colored drink which made it unnecessary for either Carlos or Lupe to patronize the bare and shabby, sour-smelling, fly-ridden *pulquerias.*

True, there were no children, but they had only been married two years. It was Carlos's experienced observation that it sometimes took longer than that before children started arriving, and that once they did start, they generally continued in sufficient quantity.

The *ranchito* was good; it was very, very good—but there was all the difference in the world between being a civil servant with a country place and being a peasant. Lupe's figure, with its small but lovely curves, would become stooped and stringy and prematurely old. Carlos would wear the patched, baggy cottons of the *campesino* instead of his neat gabardines. That is, if he merely lost his job. What costume they wore, those unfortunates in the Misericordia, the great walled hospital for the mentally infirm, he did not know.

This institution, long since secularized, had been originally of religious foundation, and Carlos, remembering that, considered the possibility of discussing his problem with the local priest. He did not consider it long. True, Carlos was a believer, and wore no less than two medals on a golden chain against his strong chest. He never went to church: also true. For one thing, it was not very male to go to church. That was for women. And old men. For another, it was regarded that servants of the secular state should neither persecute nor patronize religious functions. Also, the priest, that amiable and gregarious man, might accidently let slip a wrong word in a wrong ear. Of course it was not to be thought for a moment that he would betray the seal of the confessional. But this—this horror of Carlos's days of late—this was no matter to confess. It was not a sin, it was a misfortune. He could seek the *cura's* friendly counsel no more. That worthy man mingled much with the *caciques*, those of political importance. A single sympathetic reference to "poor Carlos," and "poor Carlos" might find himself displaced in office by a *cacique's* nephew, cousin, brother-in-law—the precise degree of relationship hardly mattered.

Not with Don Juan Antonio's warning words still in his ears.

"One more mistake, young one! Just one more—!"

Carlos blinked. He hadn't realized he'd come so far from town. Behind and to his left was the Holy Mountain, the high hill on which had stood the pyramid in pagan times, from which now sounded the discordant bells of the little church. Behind and to his right was the concrete circle of the bullring. Ahead, the footpath he had for some reason been following broke into a fork. The one to the right led to the little house of his maternal aunt Maria Pilar, a woman of strong personality, who inclined to take advantage of his infrequent visits by asking him to mend her roof or say the rosary or perhaps both. He did not desire to see *Tia* Maria Pilar. Certainly not now. Why, then, was he here?

The path to the left, where did it lead? Eventually to the tiny hamlet of San Juan Bautista. Before that? It paralleled the railroad tracks a long while. It provided access to a well. A small river frequented by washer-women and occasional gringo artists. Various tracts of woodland. Cornfields. And the isolated house of Ysidro Chache, the *curandero*.

Carlos took off his cap and wiped his forehead. Cautiously, he looked from form side to side. Casually, very casually. Far, far off, a tiny figure toiled across the fields leading a laden burro. It was entirely possible that the burro carried a combustible—charcoal, made from illegally cut wood. Or, more simply, the wood itself. Those fellows were so bold! But it was too far away, and besides, that whole matter would wait for another time. What was immediately of concern was that no one, apparently, was observing him, Carlos.

He replaced his cap. Then, still casual—bold, in fact—he turned and took the path to the left.

Ysidro Chache was a wiry, ugly little man with one bad eye, the subject of occasional and uneasy low-toned talk. Could he see out of it, or not? Some held that he could, that, indeed, he could turn his eyes in different directions at once, like a mule. It was also remarked how popular, despite his ugliness, Ysidro Chache was among women. Not ugly ones alone, either. True, he was male. He was very male. In fact, a certain Mama Rosa, shameless, had been heard to say, "Don Ysidro is a bull, and the other men are merely oxen! And he is generous, too . . ."

But the other men had a different explanation. "It is his charms, his love-potions," was the whispered consensus. Often, after such a conversation, more than one man, himself loudly and boastfully male in his *cantina* conversation, would sneak off to the lone small house in the countryside where the healer lived by himself with no steady company except a parrot reputed to be older than the Conquest and to speak all languages; as well as an odd-looking dog which could speak none. Someone, once, had been absurd enough to maintain that this dog came from a breed of barkless ones—but it was known that the man's father had been a foreigner (a Turk, or a Lutheran, or a gringo, or a Jew), and this had added to the absurdity of his contention.

It stood to obvious reason that Ysidro Chache's magic had deprived the dog of his bark in order to demonstrate how clearly he had no need of it to warn him. It was not even fierce! What ordinary person in the world would keep a dog for any other purposes? It was enough to make one shiver!

The path cut into the shoulder of a sloping hill and passed, slowly, by still sturdy though much overgrown stone walls, from the sunlight into the shadow. It was cool in the woods. Perhaps it was no more silent here, perhaps only suddenly it seemed so. Almost, he could wish for the thudding sound of an illicit axe and its flat echo. But he heard none. Only the stealthy movement of something in the underbrush. Then, suddenly, he was at the house. The ancient parrot muttered something, the dog looked up, then down, indifferently. The police officer approached, slowly, announced himself without confidence. No one answered. From somewhere came the sound of a high, weak voice chanting or crooning. The parrot scowled, suddenly became two scowling parrots, but this lasted for only an eye-blink. Carlos was encouraged rather than otherwise . . . it did seem as though the potent influence of the *curandero* and his house was itself sufficient to diminish whatever was wrong with him. He announced himself again and pushed open the door.

The house was dim (naturally, properly) and smelled (not at all dimly) of wood smoke, herbs, rum, and a number of other things, including—recognized at once although for the first time—Ysidro Chache himself.

Who was squatting on the floor, singing his strange song, scattering his colored seeds from a painted gourd onto the floor and examining the pattern in the single thin shaft of sunlight, then scooping up the seeds to cast them down again. Abruptly his song ceased. "*Abuelita* Ana must die," he said, matter-of-factly. His voice no longer high and weak, but deep and strong.

Carlos tensed. Was the *curandero* intending—Then he remembered who *Abuelita* Ana was, and relaxed. "She has been dying for as long as I can remember her," he said. Grandma Ana, with her twenty layers of garments, her tray of pills and salves and lotions and elixirs, palms and beads and holy pictures, her good luck charms and her patent medicines with the likenesses and signatures of grave and bearded Spanish doctors . . . and most of all, her long and thick and filthy yellow-gray and black fingernails.

Ysidro Chache nodded. "I have been keeping her alive," he said. "But I can't do it any longer. Perhaps today . . . Perhaps tomorrow . . ." He shrugged. "Who knows?"

"And how are you, Sir Healer?"

"I? I am very well. The Lord and the saints love me." He snickered.

Remembering that he was a policeman and that the good offices of a policeman were not despised, Carlos said, "No one has been bothering you, I hope."

The medicine man opened his good and bad eyes very wide. "Bothering *me*? Who would dare?" he said, "but someone has been bothering *you*."

Carlos Rodriguez Nuñez stared. He sighed, and his sigh broke into a sob. With his voice not always under control, he told the healer of his troubles . . . the ugly voices heard, the ugly faces seen, the pains of body and head, dizziness, doubling of vision, unfriendliness and enmity of people, and—finally—fear that he might lose his job.

Or worse.

The *curandero*'s expression, as he listened and nodded was not totally dissimilar from that of Doctor Olivera. "*Pues* . . . I don't think we have to deal here with the results of impiety," he said slowly, with a reflective air. "You're not a hunter or a woodcutter; you'd have little occasion to offend the Deer people or the Small People . . . even if you had, this is not the way in which they generally take revenge. I say, *generally*. But—for the moment—this is something we'll leave to one side.

"What then? The Evil Eye? One hears a lot of nonsense about it. As a matter of fact, grown men are very rarely the victims of the Evil Eye: it is the children whom one must look out for . . ."

He discussed various possibilities, including malfunctioning of the stomach, or its functioning with insufficient frequency, a difficulty for which he, Ysidro Chache, had many excellent herbs. "But—" the policeman protested, "it is not that. I assure you."

Chache shrugged. "What do you suspect, yourself, then?"

In a low, low voice, Carlos murmured, "Witchcraft. Or, poison."

Chache nodded, slowly, sadly. "Eighty percent of the infirmities of the corpus," he admitted, "proceed from one or the other of these two causes."

"But who—? But why—?"

"Don't speak like an idiot!" the medicine man snapped. "You are a police officer, you have a hundred thousand enemies, and each one has a hundred thousand reasons. *Why* is a little consequence; as for *who*, while it would be helpful if we knew and could lay a counter-curse, it is not essential. We do *not* know *who*, we only know *you*, and it is with *you* that we must concern ourselves."

Humbly, Carlos muttered, "I know. I know."

He watched while Chache cast the seeds again, made him a *guardero* out of shells and stones and tufts of bright red wool, censed him with aromatic gum and fumed him with choking herbs, and performed the other rituals of the healer's arts, concluding his instructions with a warning to be exceedingly careful of what he ate and drank.

The officer threw up his head and hands in despair. "A man with a thousand eyes could be taken off guard for long enough—If I turn my head in the cantina for a second, someone could drop a pinch of something into my food or drink—"

"Then eat only food of your wife's preparing, and as for drink, I will give you a little charm which will protect you for either rum or aguardiente."

Vague about the amount of his *honorario*, Chache would say only that the cost of the first visit was twenty pesos, including the two charms. He directed that the next visit be in three days. Carlos walked away feeling partly reassured and partly re-afraid. The smell of the magic infumations was still in his nostrils, but, gradually, in the vanishing day, it was succeeded by others. A haze hung over everything. Despite official exhortations in the name of science and patriotism, the ignorant small farmers, and the people of the Indian *ejidos,* whose lands ringed around the municipality had begun the annual practice of burning their fields and thickets to prepare for the corn crop. It was perhaps not the best season, this one chosen by the *Forestal,* to have forbidden illicit wood cutting and burning; it would be difficult to distinguish one smoke from another at any distance—or, at night, one fire from another. It was a season when the land seemed to have reverted, in a way, to pagan times; there was fire all around, and always fire, and not infrequently some confused and terrified animal would find itself cut off, surrounded, and would burn to death. But these offenses against, say, the Deer People, Carlos left to the offending Indios, and to the *curandero.*

Another and lighter haze hung over the town and its immediate environs. It was present twice daily, at early morning and at dusk: the haze of wood and charcoal fires which bore the faint but distinctive odor of tortillas, reminiscent of their faint but distinctive flavor, toasting on griddles. And the *pat-pat-pat* of the hands of the women making them.

Carlos had come to prefer the darkness. In it he could see no hostile, no distorted faces. Seeing fewer objects, he would be disturbed by fewer objects malevolently doubling themselves. If only at such times his irregular pains and distress would diminish as well . . . They seemed to, a little. But a little was not enough. Perhaps the things the *curandero* Ysidro Chache had done would diminish them much. Hastily, furtively, in the gathering darkness, Carlos fell to his knees and said a short, quick prayer to *La Guadalupana.*

It was in his mind that his wife's full name was, after all, Maria de Guadalupe.

"*Tu cafe*," she said, pouring it as soon as he entered; hot and strong and sweet. "*¿Tu quieres una torta?*"

He proceeded cautiously with his supper at first. But although his sense of taste was distorted, imparting a faintly odd flavor to the food, it seemed that tonight his throat at least would give him no difficulty. Afterwards, as she finished washing the dishes, he approached and embraced her, one arm around her waist, one hand on her breast, and thoughtfully and gently took her ear between his teeth. She said, "*¿Como no?*" as usual.

But afterward she did not, as usual, say, "*¡Ay, bueno!*"

And afterward, also, in the bitterness of failure and the fatigue of despair, turning his thoughts to other things, he had his idea.

Surely, if he were to pull off a great coup—arrest someone besides a troublesome *borracho* for a change, for example—surely this would restore his so-greatly fallen credit with the police department, to wit, Don Juan Antonio. At least so he reasoned. He had the vague notion that the plan was not perfect, that, if he considered it carefully, he might find flaws in it. But he didn't wish to consider it that carefully; the effort was too great; there were too many voices muttering ugly things and distracting and bothering him, and besides, if he were to decide against the plan, he would have no reason for getting up. His pains were worse, and he knew he could not get back to sleep again. Therefore he should get up, and if he got up, there was nothing to do but leave the house.

And therefore he might as well try to carry out his plan.

He rose and dressed, buckled on his gun-belt, reassured himself of his flashlight, and went outside.

Dawn was yet not even a promise on the horizon. The stars were great white blazes in the black sky. He searched for Venus, hugest of all, remembering stories of how important she had been in the old religion, before the Conquest—but either she had not yet risen to be the morning star, or he was looking in the wrong place, or some tree or hill obscured her—

He did not need his flashlight yet, knowing the way hereabouts as well as he did his own house, or his own wife. He knew the very tree stump which, suddenly, unkindly . . . but, somehow, not unexpectedly . . . began to croak, "*Carlo' el loco. Carlo' el loco.* Soon you will be encountered in the Misericordia. *¡Ja ja! ¡Loco Carlo'!*"

The officer drew his gun, then thrust it back. A bullet was undoubtedly of no use. "Wait," he said. "As soon as it is day and I have finished with my other duty, I will return and cut you up and pour *petroleo* on you and burn you up. Wait."

The tree trunk fell silent at once and tried to hide itself in the blackness. But Carlo knew very well where it was, and passed on, giving many grim nods as he thought of it. He strained his ears but heard nothing of what he hoped he might. Doubtless the malefactors had done their original work kilometers away, back in the wooded slopes of the mountains. Deer poachers worked the same territory, usually in pairs, one to hold the bright light to attract and fascinate the animal, and one to shoot it as it stood exposed. One man could carry half a deer easily enough. Such poachers needed neither roads nor paths either coming or going; it was useless to attempt to catch them.

Not so, however, with the woodcutters, those thieves of natural resources and national patrimony, denuding the forested hills and leaving them a prey to erosion! The more he thought of them, the more he realized the iniquity of their crimes. Moreover, look what great rogues they were even when in town— Consider how those cousins Eugenio and Onofrio Cruz (a choice pair!) had sneered and gibbered at him only the day before, in the plaza. In fact, on reflection, not only yesterday, either. And why? For no reason. So, clearly, Carlos's previous attitude had been wrong. Woodcutters were not mere poor devils toiling hard to earn their bread, and currently forbidden even to toil by *burócratas* intent on their own devious ends; merely to confront the axe-men and issue warnings was not enough. The darkness of the woods became over-shot with red, scarlet and crimson. They needed to be taught one good lesson, once and for all. *Ladrones. Hijos de putas.*

But even two men could not carry on their backs enough wood from forest to town to make it worth the effort. A woodcutter required a horse, or a mule, or, at very least, a burro. Which confined him largely to paved or at any rate beaten thoroughfares. There were at least twenty such on this side of the town, but the nearer they approached to town the more they combined, so that, for the practical purposes of the moment, there were only five to be considered. The San Benito road led into the main highway too far south; daylight would find them in the open. The road of the old convent led past a checkpoint. A third was too long and winding; a fourth had in recent months become identical with one of the local creeks. Carlos was not very strong on arithmetic, but he felt fairly certain that this left but one road. To his surprise, he realized that he had, presumably while calculating, reached just that one. It now remained to consider exactly, or even approximately, where on that road might be the best place for his *emboscada*. Too close to the woods, the criminals might escape back into them. Too near the town, they might find refuge in house or patio. An ideal situation would be a place where the road was not only sunken but surrounded by walls on either side, not too near and not too far. Such a situation was not only ideal, it was actual, and it contained, moreover, a niche in which had once reposed an image of La Guadalupana before the Republic was secularized. Carlos snickered, thinking of the astonishment of the rogues as he sprang out upon them from that niche, pistol in hand!

He was still snickering when something seized hold of his foot and sent him sprawling.

The fall jarred his back and all his other bones. It sickened him, and all his quiescent pains flared up. Voices hooted and gibbered and mocked; faces made horns and spat at him. He lay there in the road, fighting for breath and for reason, sobbing. By and by he was able to breathe. The darkness was only darkness once again. He groped about, his fingers recoiled from what they found, then groped again and found the flashlight. He gave a long, high cry of anguish and of terror at what the yellow beam disclosed lying there in the road: the body of a man lying on its back in a pool of blood. It had shirt and pants and hands and feet, all as a man should.

But where a man's head should be, it had no head.

Slowly, slowly, the sky lightened. Mist mingled with the smoke and obscured the sun. Carlos Rodriguez N., with burning and smarting eyes, paced back and forth in the road. He had been doing so for an hour, two hours, three—who knows how long? He dared not sleep. Suppose someone were to steal the body? He had not dared return to town and report the killing, for the same reason. He had been sustained in his vigil by the certain knowledge that daylight would bring people out on the road, and that he could send one of them into town with his message—preferably one of a group of mature and respectable *ciudadanos* whose testimony about the body would be incontrovertible. But as it happened, the first ones along the road were a pair of boys taking four cows out to pasture.

Or one boy taking two cows. It was no longer possible for Carlos to be sure if he were seeing single or double. One boy and two cows. Two boys and four cows. One body with no head. Two bodies with no heads. The sky was gray and cold and the treacherous sun feared to show itself. Eventually he was satisfied there were two boys, for one of them agreed to run back with the message and Carlos could see him running at the same time he could see the other boy drive the cows off the road so as to get them past the body. Life or death, the cows must eat. The boys were out of sight, the cattle, too, and someone was shouting, still shouting, had been shouting forever. With a shock, he recognized his own voice, and fell silent.

Flies began to settle on the blood and on the body. Very soberly, very tiredly, Carlos observed the corpse. He did not recognize it. It looked neither familiar nor strange; it looked merely at rest, with no more problems. It didn't even seem so odd any more—one had heard before of murderers removing the heads of their victims in order to destroy or at least delay identification . . . Rest. And no problems. How long would it take the boy to get back to town?— and how long for Don Juan Antonio to arrive? And then? And what then? Would he commend Carlos? Curse him? Discharge him? Arrest him? Commit him?

The man's arms and legs began to tremble. He tried to repress the tremors, failed, seated himself on a stone, placed his back against the side of the roadside wall, placed his revolver in his lap, and without volition or premonition immediately fell asleep. His head jerked back and he jumped forward and upward with a cry of alarm, thrusting his hands forth to catch the revolver. He did not catch it, neither did he see it fall, neither could he find it. His shout and motion startled the flies and they rose from the drying blood with an ugly, thrumming buzz. Carlos pitched forward onto his hands and knees, stared stupidly at the dark pool with its blue lights. The blood was still there.

But the body was gone.

Everything whirled around and around, and Carlos whirled with it, staggering along the road with arms outstretched to keep from falling. He had slept, he had slept, after the hours of keeping awake to guard the body in the darkness, he had fallen asleep in the earliest daylight! Now he was worse off than ever, for now Don Juan Antonio knew there was a body—and how would Carlos be able to account for its loss? Weeping, sobbing, cursing, stumbling along, he knew that he could account for that no more than for the loss of his revolver. He was certainly doomed.

Unless—Unless—he provided another body, so no one would know the difference.

Below him he saw the railroad tracks. Half-sliding, he descended the slope and ran along the rails. He knew who had, who *must* have done this to him! Who else but the woodcutters, those thieves and sons of harlots? Why else but to take revenge upon him for his intended capture?—and to prevent his ever doing so! But he would show them, now and forever. They had incited the entire *poblacion* against him, but he would show them . . . He came to a switch and just a short distance away was the equipment shed of the maintenance crew, with its weathered inscription: *This Edifice And Its Entire Contents Is The Property Of The Republic.* With his shoulder skewed around he burst it open, seized up the first grass-machete he saw, and rushed out again. He had time? Would he be in time? Would Don Juan Antonio have been awake? Been elsewhere? How soon would he start out? Carlos prayed for time to stand in between Don Juan Antonio and the barbarous plot of the woodcutters.

And luck was with him. The mists parted as he came back over the slope and there down below was a man leading a burro laden with wood. Cautiously and carefully, so shrewdly that he was obliged to smile to himself and to stifle his own laughter, Carlos approached bent over and on crouching knees. The burro approached, the burro passed, Carlos rose to his feet and darted forward on his toes. The machete swung. The body fell, spouting blood. Carlos kicked the fallen head like a football, watched it drop into the underbrush. He threw the body over his shoulder and ran and ran and ran and ran.

"Carlos," said Don Juan Antonio. "Carlos! Do you hear me? Stop that! Stop that and listen to me! Do you hear—"

"No use, *jefe*," said his assistant, Raimundo Cepeda. "It's the shock—the shock. He won't come out of it for a while."

Don Juan Antonio wiped his face with an impeccably ironed and cologne-scented handkerchief. "Not he alone . . . I am also in such a situation. Dreadful. Horrible. People do not realize—"

"Poor young man," sighed the elderly jailor, Uncle Hector, shaking his head. "Only consider—"

Don Juan Antonio nodded vigorously. "By all means let us consider. And let us consider the whole case. Thus I reconstruct it:

"We have the precious pair, the coarsely handsome cousins Eugenio and Onofrio Cruz. Ostensibly and even occasionally woodcutters. On the side— drunkards, when they had the money; thieves . . . and worse . . . when they had the chance. Partners against the rest of the world, fighting often between them- selves. Last night they go out to cut wood, illegally. And on the way back a quarrel breaks out. Who knows why? For that matter, perhaps Eugenio merely decided on the spur of the moment to kill Onofrio. At any rate, he *does* kill him, with a blow of his axe. Then, to conceal the identity of the corpus, with the same axe he decapitates it. And returns to his hut, carrying the head. Also, the defunct's wallet.

"Once there, the thought occurs to him that he should not have left the body. With daylight coming, it will soon be found. So he prepares a pile or pyre of wood. With all the burning of fields and thickets, one more smoke will hardly be observed. Should anyone smell anything, they will assume it to be a trapped deer. And he goes back to gain the body. But meanwhile the police have not been idle. Officer Carlos Rodriguez Nuñez is not only up and around, but he has also located the corpus and is guarding it. Eugenio conceals himself. By and by the sun begins to rise, the little brothers Santa Anna approach, and Carlos sends one of them with a message to me. But the child is, after all, only a child; he doesn't go to the right place, wanders around, time is lost. Meanwhile Carlos, content that all will soon be well, sits down and falls asleep. Erroneously," he added, with emphasis, "but—understandably. Understandably.

"Out from his place of concealment creeps the criminal murderer Eugenio Cruz. He steals both Carlos's service revolver *and* the corpus, loads it on the horse which he had brought with him and also concealed at a distance, returns to his hut. There he decides that he has not enough wood to incinerate the victim. So he conceals the corpus inside the hut and goes out for more wood. Meanwhile the unfortunate and valiant Carlos awakens, discovers his loss. By dint of the faculty of ratiocination so highly developed in our police, he deduces who the killer must be and where he must have gone. He tracks him down, securing, along the way, a machete. He confronts the arch-criminal. He kills him. Again, I must say: erroneously. And again I must say: understandably. Doubtless the murderer Cruz would have attempted to escape.

"At any rate, this second slaying is witnessed by the much respected citizen and veteran of the Revolution, Simon-Macabeo Lopez—"

The much respected citizen and veteran of the Revolution, Simon-Macabeo Lopez, snapped his sole remaining arm into a salute, and nodded solemnly.

"—who had risen early in order to go and cultivate the piece of land granted him by the grateful Republic. Veteran Lopez immediately and properly proceeds to inform me, arriving at the same time as the little brother Santa Anna. The police at once move to investigate, and we find—that which we found. A body here, a body there, here a head, and there a head, Carlos in a state of incoherent shock. So. Thus my reconstruction. What do you think of it?"

There was a silence. At length the assistant head of the police said, "Masterful. Masterful."

"Thank you."

"It is such a reconstruction, so neat, so lucid, so full of clarity, as is usually to be met with only in the pages of criminal literature. But . . . *señor jefe* . . . it is not the truth. No, I must say, it is not the truth."

Don Juan Antonio snapped, "Why not?"

Cepeda sighed, gestured to the unfortunate Rodriguez. "Because, *señor jefe*, you know and I know and almost everybody in town knows why. That bitch, that strumpet, Lupe de Rodriguez, was cuckolding poor Carlos with the cousins Eugenio and Onofrio Cruz, too. One man was not enough for her. And Carlos was blind to all."

"Truth," said the jailor, sighing.

"Truth," said the veteran, nodding.

"Truth," said the other policemen, shaking their heads, sadly.

Don Juan Antonio glared. Then his expression relaxed, and he lowered his head. "It is the truth," he said, at last. "Ay, Carlos! ¡Woe of me! ¡Hombre! The husband is always the last to learn. For weeks, now, I have scarcely been able to look him in the face. Why, the very honor of the police was imperiled. How the railroad men were laughing at us. Mother!

"So, my poor Carlos—You finally found out, eh? *Nevertheless!*" Don Juan Antonio all but shouted at the others. "It is my reconstruction which must stand, do you agree? Carlos has suffered enough, and moreover, there is the honor of the police."

"Oh, agreed, agreed, *señor jefe,*" the other officers exclaimed, hastily and heartily.

"We may depend upon the discretion of the Veteran Lopez, I assume?"

The old man placed his hand over his heart and bowed. "Securely," he said. "What Carlos did may have been, in some sense, technically illegal; I am no scholar, no lawyer. But it was natural. It was male."

"It was male, it was very male," the others all agreed.

Don Juan Antonio bent over, took the weeping Carlos by the shoulder, and tried to reassure him. But Carlos gave no sign of having heard, much less understood. He wept, he babbled, he struck out at things invisible, now and then he gave stifled little cries of alarm and fright and scuttled backwards across the floor. The chief and the others exchanged looks and comments of dismay. "This commences to appear as more than temporary shock," he said. "If he continues like this, he may finally be encountered in the Misericordia, may God forbid. You, Gerardo," he directed the youngest officer, "go and solicit Dr. Olivera to appear as soon as convenient. He understands the techniques of modern science . . . Take no care, Carlos!" he said, encouragingly. "We shall soon have you perfectly well . . . Now . . . There was something in my mind . . . Ah, Cepeda."

"Yes, Sir Chief?"

"You said, ' . . . with Eugenio and Onofrio Cruz, too.' *Too.* Who else? Eh? What other man or men—I insist that you advise me of their names!"

Rather reluctantly, the assistant said, "Well . . . sir . . . I know of only one other. Ysidor Chache. The *curandero.*"

Astounded, first, then outraged, then determined, Don Juan Antonio arose to his full height. "The *curandero,* eh. That mountebank. That whore-monger. That charlatan." He reached over and took up his cap. "Come. We will pay a call upon this relic of the past. Let us inform him that the police have teeth. Eh?"

The jailor, old Hector, shook his head vigorously. The even older veteran of the Revolution put out his hand. "No, no, *patron,*" he said, imploringly. "Do not go. He is dangerous. He is very dangerous. He knows all the spirits and the demons of the woods. He can put a fearful curse upon you. No, no, no—"

"What!" cried Don Juan Antonio, scornfully. "Do you think for a moment that I put stock in such superstition?" He stood brave and erect, not moving from his place.

Old Hector said, "Ah, *patron.* It is not only that. I, after all, I, too, am a civil servant. I do not—But, sir, consider. The *curandero* knows the power of every root and herb and leaf and grass. He is familiar with each mushroom and toadstool. Consider, consider—a single pinch in food or drink (and what man has a thousand eyes?)—Consider the result of such poison! Sterility, impotence, abortion, distortion of vision, paralysis of the throat, imaginary voices, dizziness, pain, swelling of the eyes, burning of the chest and heart, hallucinations, wasting away, insanity, and who knows what else? No, *patron,* no, no."

"He traffics with the devil," old Lopez muttered, nodding.

"Hm, well," said Don Juan Antonio. "This commences to sound like a matter for the priest, then, would you say?"

"Securely, the priest! If not, indeed, the bishop!"

Instantly the chief of police returned his cap to its place. "Obviously, then, it would be unfitting for a servant of the secular Republic to mix in such a matter. I thank you for calling this to my attention. We shall not dignify the old fraud with our presence."

His eye at that moment was looking out the window. He seemed startled. "Speaking of the—Heh-hem. Did I not mention the good priest? Look." The good priest was indeed at that moment crossing the plaza, his technically illegal cassock covered by an unobjectionable overcoat for most of its length. Preceding him was his sacristan, bearing the small case in which, all knew, were carried the vessels for the administering of last sacrament.

"Hector—do me the favor, go and enquire, who has died?—and then go and see what is keeping the doctor. ¡Ay, Carlos, hombre!"

Hector trotted out. A moment later he returned close enough to call a name before proceeding to the physician's office.

"What did he say?" Don Juan Antonio inquired. "Who?"

"Sir, *Abuelita* Ana. You know, the—"

"What?" Don Juan Antonio was surprised. "*Grandmother* Ana? Who would have expected it? She had been dying as long as I can remember her. Well, well, well . . ." His mouth still astonished, he lifted his right hand and slowly crossed himself.

THE SEVENTIES

Selectra Six-Ten

INTRODUCTION BY ED FERMAN

I had the good fortune to know Avram best during the eventful years from 1962 to 1964. The events included his marriage to Grania, a move from New York to Milford, PA (I drove him and his cats down to Pennsylvania, a ride full of laughs and ripe smells), and another move to Mexico.

These were the years when he took a detour from his writing to edit F&SF. What initially impressed his young assistant (me) was his witty and scholarly story introductions. But what has stayed with me the most is the remarkable care and sensitivity with which he handled each submission, perhaps the result of the fact that he had not always been treated with courtesy as a writer.

In 1964 Avram resigned as editor to return to full-time writing. My father wrote to him that "you've done an extraordinarily fine job under very trying circumstances" (i.e., being mostly over one thousand miles from the office without even a phone close at hand), and Avram replied:

> Thank you for your kind and complimentary letter about your satisfaction with my work as editor. I have not done as well as I wished to, but I think that I did as well as a part-time and absent person of my habits could. It was an honor and a pleasure to have this work. I appreciate the fact that you at all times treated me like a gentleman. Needless to say that I wish my successors, and The Magazine under their hands, all possible success. Meanwhile, I forge ahead on my writing and hope to have time for short stories before the end of the year . . .

After I succeeded Avram as editor, he sent me a story that I loved, but I asked for some minor changes. Avram made them and returned the piece to his agent, who promptly sold it to another market. Avram sent me "Selectra Six-Ten" as a replacement; I loved it even more and it appeared in F&SF's October 1970 issue.

SELECTRA SIX-TEN

His Honor the Ed., F&SF
Dear Ed:
Well, whilst sorry that you didn't feel BELINDA
BEESWAX didn't exactly and immediately leap up and
wrap her warm, white (or, in this case, <u>cold</u>) arms
around you, so to speak, nevertheless I am bound to
admit that your suggestions for its revision don't
altogether seem difficult or unreasonable. Though,
mind you, it is against my moral principles to admit
this to any editor. Even you. However. This once.
I'll do, I think I shd be able to do the rewrites
quite soonly, and whip them off to you with the
speed of light. At least, the speed of whatever dim
light it is which filters through the window of our
local Post Office and its 87,000 friendly branches
throughout the country.
By the way, excuse absence of mrag, or even marger
Oh you would you. Take that. And THAT.
AND THSTHATHAT. har har, he laughed harshly. The
lack of m a r g i n s. There. I have just gotten a
new tripewriter; viz an Selectra Six-Ten, with
Automated Carriage
Return
Return
Return
hahahaHA! I can't resist it, just impress the tab
and without sweat or indeed evidence of
labor of any swort, or sort, whatsoever,
ZING.
RETURN! You will excsuse me, won't you? There I
knew you would. A wild lad, Master Edward, I sez

to the Gaffer, I sez, but lor blesse zur its just
hanimal sperrits, at art h's a good lad, I sez.
WELL. Enough of this lollygagging and skylarking
Ferman. I am a WORKING WROTER and so to business.
Although, mind ewe, with this Device it seems more
like play. It hums and clicks and buzzes whilst
I am congor even cog cog cog got it now? gooood.
cogitating. very helpful to thought. Soothing. So.
WHERE we was. Yus. BELINDA BEESWAX. Soonly. I
haven't forgotten that advance I got six years ago
when my wife had the grout. Anxious to please.
(Tugs forelock. Exit, pursued by a
Your Seruant to Command,
Avram

Eddy dear;
I mean, of course, Mr. Ferman Sir. Or is it now
Squire Ferman, with you off in the moors and crags
of Cornwall Connecticut. Sounds very Jamaica Inn,
Daphne Du Maurieresque. I can see you on wild and
stormy nights, muffled to your purple ears in your
cloak and shawl, going out on the rocky headlands
with False Lights to decoy the Fall River Line
vessels, or even the Late After-Theater Special of
the New York, New Haven, and Hartburn, onto
the Rocks. And the angry rocks they gored her
sides/Like the horns of an angry bull. Zounds they
don't indite Poerty like that anymore. I mean,
I don't have to tell you, ethn ethic pride, all
very well, _enthic_? e t h n i c, there, THAT wasn't
hard, was it deary? Noooo. Now you can ahve a piece
of treacle. Where was I. I mean, my grandfather
was a was a, well, acttually, no, he WAS n 't a Big
Rabbi In The Old Country, he drove a laundry wagon
in Yonkers, N.Y., but what Imeantosayis: ''Over the
rocks and the foaming brine/They burned the wreck
of the _Palatine_ ''—can ALAN GUINZBURG write poetry
like that? No. Fair is fair.
Zippetty-ping. Kerriage Return. Automatic. Whheee!
After all Ed I have known you a very long time,
that time your old girl friend, the one you hired to
read Manuscripts, you remember? Nuf sed. And I know
you have only my own welfare at heart. Right? Right.
So you wouldn't be angry when I explain that Igot
the idea, whilst triping on my new tripewriter, that
if I carried out your nifty keen suggestions for

the rewrite of my BELINDA BEESWAX story, that would
drolly enough convert it into a Crime Story, as well
as F and SF. Just for the fun of it, then, I
couldn't resist sharyimg or even s h a r i n g, my
amusement at this droll conceit with Santiago
Ap Popkin, the editor over at QUENTIN QUEELEY's
MYSTERY MUSEUM. But evidentially I wasn't as clear
in my explanations as I should have been. Fingers
just ran away with themselves, laughing and
giggling over their shoulders (well, knuckles. be
pedantic), down the pike. ANYhow, Caligula Fitz-
Bumpkin somehow misunderstood. He is <u>not</u>, I mean we
must simply <u>Face</u> these things, and Seneca Mac Zipnick
is just NOT/very <u>bright</u>. He, do you know what
simpleton did? this will hand yez a real alugh,*Ed:
Guy sent a check. Thought I was offering the story
to <u>him</u>. Boob. A doltish fellowe, Constantine O'Kaplan.
But, well, Ed, put yourself in my position. Could I
embarass the boy? Bring a blush to those downy
cheeks? Nohohohoho.
Well Ed it's just one of those things that we have
to face as we go through life: and the fact that
QQMM happens to pay four or is it five times what
F&SF pays, has got simply nothing to do with it.
Avile canard, and that's that.
However, I have not forgotten that advance
the time I was in Debtors Prison. And I will,
I <u>will</u>, promise you now NOW, I''l sit down at my
merry chuckling Selectra Six-Ten, and write
you a real sockadaol sok?dolager of a Science
Fiction story. VISCIOUS TERRESTRIAL BIPED
xxxxxxxxxxxxxxxXXXXXXXXXXX ZZZZZZZzzzznnngfhfghhhBZZZ
blurtle blep ha ha, well, perhaps not quite
along t<u>hose</u> lines. Zo. So
''Forgiven''?
Thine ever so
Avram

Dear Ed:
Well, you mehk me sheahme, mahn, the way you have
forgiven me for that peculiar contretemps anent
BELINDA BEESWAX's going to the QUENTIN QUEELEY's
MYSTERY MUSEUM people instead. That yuck, Gerardo A

*or ''laugh'', as some have it.—Ibid.

Klutskas. ~~Anyway, I have really been sticking to~~
my last, tappetty-tapp. ''Tap''. ZWWWWEEPPP! Cling.
It's a veritable psychodrama of Semi-Outer Space.
XXXXXXXXnnnnnggggg llullrp prurp plup ZZZZBBGGGgnn
INTELLIGENT NONCHITINOUS BIPED ATTEND ATTEND ATTEND
ATTEND haha it's always fun and games with this new
Selectra Six-Ten, clicketty-cluch, hmble-hmble-
hmble-hmble. Just you should drip by you the mouth,
so enclosed is a couple pp of the first draft.
draught. drocht Spell it can't, not for sour owl
stools, but leave us remember the circumstances
under which it grew to maturity. More to be piddled
than centered. You like, huh? Huh? Huh. Thass whut
I thought. XXXxxZZZZzzzzxxxxngngngn clurkle cluhnkle
NOCHITINOUS BIFRU BIFURCATE ATTEND ATTEND ATTEND.
Agreat line, hey? Arrests you with its like
remorseless sweep, doesn't it? Well well,
back to the saline cavern
Love and kisses,
Avram

Dear ED:
See, I knew you would enjoy LOADSTAR EXPRESS.
Even the first draft gripped you like ursus
somethingorothera, didn't it? Yes. True, it was
rather rough. Amorphous, as you might say. But I
was going to take care of that anyway. Yesyes I
had that rough spot, pp 3-to-4 well in mind.
I admit that I hsdn't a hadn't exactly planned to do
it the way you tentatively suggest. But. Since you
do. It would be as well that way as any other.
Blush, chuckle. Not exactly what one would formerly
have considered for the pp of a family, or even
a Family Magazine. Tempura o mores, what? However.
WHY N T? XXXXXxxxx--ZZZZZzzzz bgbgbgbngngngn
bluggabluggablugga TATATA TA TA AT ATT AT ATTEND
ATTEND ATTEND TERRESTRIOUS BIFURCATE NONCHERIDER-
MATIC XXXNN FASCIST AGGRESSIVE BIPED goddam Must
quit reading alla them student Undrground Wellhung
Classified Revolt Papers. To work work WORK toil
''With fingers weary and worn, with eyelids heavy and
red/ Awoman sat in unwomanly rags, mumbling a crust
of bread.'' Can Laurence Ferlinghetti write lines
like that? Can Richard Gumbeiner? It is to laugh.
Anon, sir, anon. We Never Forget. Advances
advanced to us in our hour od Need, earned eternal

gratichude. clicketty-clunck.
Industrously, <u>Avram</u>

Dear Edward:
Wow<u>Wow</u>WOW! WOW-WOW/WOWW'. !gotcha at alst)) Ignore.
Confused by Joy. BUNNYBOY. B U N N Y B O Y, hippetty
goddam <u>HOP</u>, B*U*N*N*N*Y*B*O*Y* M*A*G*A*Z*I*N*E*.
You got that? Educational & Literary Compendium?
With the big tzitzkas? Tha-hats the one. <u>Bunnyboy</u>
Magazine has bumped a burse of bold, gumped a
gurse of XXXXXXX xHa xHa xHa bgnbgn of gold,
dumped a purse of gold in my lap. I kid y ou not.
NOT NOT. ''Not.'' He adumbrated hilarriously.
EXPLOITIVE DIOXIDIFEROUS BIPEDS ah cummon now,
cumMON. Shhest, I hardly know what to say, and this
Selectra Six-Ten, elecrtified wit and terror, never
but <u>never</u> a case of The DULL LINE LABOURS, AND
THE WHEEL TURNS SLOW, goes faster than my MIND, my
mind is BLOWN, out through both ears, walls all
plastered with brain tissue.
Carriage return. When in doubt. Carstairs Macanley,
formerly of <u>Midland Review</u>, to which I sold,
years ago—but you don't want to hear about that,
anyway he is now and has been for some time past
Fiction Editor of <u>B</u>unnyboy. So whilst making with
the clicketty-clack and addressing the MS of
LOADSTAR EXPRESS, I H happened to be thinking of
him, and just for kicks, you know, Ed, I mean, YOU.
Know <u>me</u>. Ed. Just abig, overgrown kid. So just for
k.i.c.k.s., I absentmindedly addressed it to him.
Laughed like a son of a gun' when I found out what
I'd done. And had already stamped the manila!
''Well . . .'' (I figured) ''I'll send it to good old
Ed at F&SF soons as Carstairs Macanley returns it.
Just to let him see what <u>I</u>'m doing these days.
Ed, you have never wished me nothing but good, Ed,
from the very first day we met, Ed, and I know that
the last thing on your pure, sweet mind, i would be
that I return the money to Bunyboy, and, besides, I
am almost 100% sure it's already in type: and we
could hardly expect them to yank it. You're a pro
yourself, Ed. But don't think for aminute, Eddy,
that I've got abig head and/or have forgotten that
advance you so, well, <u>tenderly</u> is really the only—
And, Ed, any time you're out on the West Coast,
just any time at <u>all</u>, night or day, give me a ring,

~~and we'll go out for dinner somewhere.~~ ''A Hot bird
and a cold bottle'', eh Ed? Hows that b grabg bgrarg
XXXxx TREACHEROUS BgN BgN bGN TERCH XXXXXzzZZZ bgn
bgn bgn TREACHEROUS AMBULATORY TERRESTRIAL AGGRES-
SIVE BIPED ATTEND ATTNEDNA Attn bgna bgn cluck.
Please excuse my high spirits, my head is just
buzzing and clicking right now, Inever SAW such a
C*E*C*K in my L I F E L I F E in my life. Hey, Ed,
I could offer to rewrite the story for Bunnyboy
leaving out the parts you suggested, but I don't
think it would be right to deprive you of the
pleasure of seiing them in print. Wait for the
story. I''ll do you something else sometime.
Right now I'm going out and buy the biggest can of
typewriter cleaning fluid anybody ever saw WE
EXSALIVATE ON YOUR PROFFERED BRIBES EXPLOITIVE
TERCHEOROSE TERRESTRIAL BIPED AGGRESSIVE NONCHERO-
DERMATOID BIPED LANDING YOUR PLANETARY-RAPING PROBE
MODULEWS ON THE SACRED CHITIN OF OUR MOTHER-
WORLD FASCISTICLY TERMED ''MOOM'' XXXZZZZBGN BGN BGN
BGN BGN BGN IGNORING OUR JUST LONG-REPRESSED PLEAS
FOR YOUR ATTEND ATTE ND ATTEnD OHmigod
ed oh ed my god i i oh
e
d
e
d
o
bgna bgna bgna bgna bgna bgna bgna bgna bgna bgna
bpur bpur bpur bpur bpur bpur bpur bpur bpur BURP

Goslin Day

INTRODUCTION BY JACK DANN

When Grania Davis told me she was editing a comprehensive volume of Avram's best stories, I made a case for including "Goslin Day." For my money, this is one of Avram's very best stories, a story that has been unfortunately overshadowed by the charming and more famous "The Golem." Avram's "The Golem" is more accessible, more mainstream, if you will, but "Goslin Day" is perhaps the best example of his stylistic brilliance. It's a tour de force of stylistic pyrotechnics. It's sheer poetry. And, like "The Golem," it goes to the very root of Avram's Orthodox Jewish concerns.

Even as Avram's literary playfulness threatens to overwhelm this rich loaf of a story, Avram shows himself to be in absolute control. Here is a seamless example of style and content informing each other. In the few pages that follow, you'll discover one of Avram's most completely realized worlds, a world bursting with nervous movement, a world of deadly goslin spooks and night-spirits, a world conjured out of the ancient arts of Kabbalah, out of numerology, gematria, noutricon, anagrams, and acrostics.

In Yiddish, gozlin *means thief or swindler. Avram gives us "goslins": the thieves that lie within us all, the swindlers that at any time can come "leaping through the vimveil to nimblesnitch, torment, buffet, burden, uglylook, poke, makestumble, maltreat . . ."*

Here are the monsters that stare back at us from dusty mirrors.

Here is the world that inheres inside the world.

Here we are.

God bless you Avram. Nobody could do this better than you!

GOSLIN DAY

IT WAS A GOSLIN day, no doubt about it, of course it can happen that goslin things can occur, say, once a day for many days. But *this* day was a *goslin* day. From the hour when, properly speaking, the ass brays in his stall, but here instead the kat kvells on the rooftop—to the hour when the cock crows on his roost, but here instead the garbageman bangs on his can—even that early, Faroly realized that it was going to be a goslin day (night? let be night: *It was evening and* [after that] *it was morning: one day.* Yes or no?). In the warbled agony of the shriekscream Faroly had recognized an element present which was more than the usual ketzelkat expression of its painpleasure syndrome. In the agglutinative obscenities which interrupted the bangcrashes of the yuckels emptying eggshells orangerinds coffeegrounds there was (this morning, different from all other mornings) something unlike their mere usual brute pleasure in waking the dead. Faroly sighed. His wife and child were still asleep. He saw the dimlight already creeping in, sat up, reached for the glass and saucer and poured water over his nails, began to whisper his preliminary prayers, already concentrating on his Intention in the name *Unity*: but aware, aware, aware, the hotsticky feeling in the air, the swimmy looks in the dusty corners of windows, mirrors; something a tension, here a twitch and there a twitch. Notgood notgood.

In short: a goslin day.

Faroly decided to seek an expert opinion, went to Crown Heights to consult the kabbalist, Kaplánovics.

Rabbaness Kaplánovics was at the stove, schauming off the soup with an enormous spoon, gestured with a free elbow toward an inner room. There sat the sage, the sharp one, the teacher of our teachers, on his head his beaver hat neatly brushed, on his feet and legs his boots brightly polished, in between his garments well and clean without a fleck or stain as befits a disciple of the wise. He and Faroly shook hands, greeted, blessed the Name. Kaplánovics pushed across several sheets of paper covered with an exquisitely neat calligraphy.

"Already there," the kabbalist said. "I have been through everything three times, twice. The *NY Times,* the *Morgen Dzshornal,* I. F. Stone, Dow-Jones, the *Daph-Yomi,* your name-Text, the weather report, Psalm of the Day. Everything is worked out, by numerology, analogy, gemátria, noutricon, anagrams, allegory, procession and precession. So.

"Of course today as any everyday we must await the coming of the Messiah: 'await'—*expect? today?* not today. Today he wouldn't come. Considerations for atmospheric changes, or changes for atmospheric considerations, *not—bad. Not—bad.* Someone gives you an offer for a good airconditioner, cheap, you could think about it. Read seven capitals of psalms between afternoon and evening prayers. One sequence is enough. The day is favorable for decisions on growth stocks, but avoid closed-end mutual funds. On the corner by the beygal store is an old woman with a pyshka, collecting dowries for orphan girls in Jerusalem: the money, she never sends, this is *her* sin, it's no concern of yours: give her eighteen cents, a very auspicious number: merit, cheaply bought (she has sugar diabetes and the daughter last week gave birth to a weak-headed child by a schwartzer), what else?" They examined the columns of characters.

"Ahah. Ohoh. If you get a chance to buy your house, don't buy it, the Regime will condemn it for a freeway, where are they all *going* so fast?—every man who has two legs thinks he needs three automobiles—besides—where did I write it? oh yes. There. The neighborhood is going to change very soon and if you stay you will be killed in three years and two months, or three months and two years, depending on which system of gemátria is used in calculating. You have to warn your brother-in-law his sons should each commence bethinking a marriagematch. Otherwise they will be going to cinemas and watching televisions and putting arms around girls, won't have the proper intentions for their nighttime prayers, won't even read the protective psalms selected by the greatgrandson of the Baalshemtov: and with what results, my dear man? Nocturnal emissions and perhaps worse; is it for nothing that The Chapters of the Principles caution us, 'At age eighteen to the marriage canopy and the performance of good deeds,' hm?"

Faroly cleared his throat. "Something else is on your mind," said the kabbalist. "Speak. Speak." Faroly confessed his concern about goslins. Kaplánovics exclaimed, struck the table. "Goslins! you wanted to talk about goslins? It's already gone past the hour to say the Shema, and I certainly didn't have in mind when I said it to commence constructing a kaméa." He clicked his tongue in annoyance. "Am I omniscient?" he demanded. "Why didn't you let me know you were coming? Man walks in off the street, expects to find—"

But it did not take long to soothe and smooth him—Who is strong? he who can control his own passion.

And now to first things first, or, in this case, last things first, for it was the most recent manifestation of goslinness which Faroly wished to talk about. The kabbalist listened politely but did not seem in agreement with nor impressed by his guest's recitation of the signs by which a goslin day might make itself known. " 'Show simônim,' " he murmured, with a polite nod. "This one loses an object, that one finds it, let the claimant come and 'show simônim,' let him cite the signs by which his knowledge is demonstrated, and, hence, his ownership . . ." but this was mere polite fumfutting, and Faroly knew that the other knew that both knew it.

. . .

On Lexington a blackavised goslin slipped out from a nexus of cracked mirrors reflecting dust at each other in a disused nightclub, snatched a purse from a young woman emerging from a ribs joint; in Bay Ridge another, palepink and blond, snatched a purse from an *old* woman right in front of Suomi Evangelical Lutheran. Both goslins flickersnickered and were sharply gone. In Tottenville, a third one materialized in the bedroom of an honest young woman still half asleep in bed just a second before her husband came back from the nightshift in Elizabeth, New Jersey; uttered a goslin cry and jumped out the window holding his shirt. Naturally the husband never believed her—would *you*? Two more slipped in and out of a crucial street corner on the troubled border-marches of Italian Harlem, pausing only just long enough to exchange excla-mations of *guineabastard!/goddamnigger!* and goslin looks out of the corners of their goslin eyes. Goslin cabdrivers curseshouted at hotsticky pregnant women dumb enough to try and cross at pedestrian crossings. The foul air grew fouler, thicker, hotter, tenser, muggier, murkier: and the goslins, smelling it from afar, came leapsniffing through the vimveil to nimblesnitch, torment, buffet, burden, uglylook, poke, makestumble, maltreat, and quickshmiggy back again to gezzle guzzle goslinland.

The kabbalist had grown warm in discussion, eagerly inscribed circles in the air with downhooked thumb apart from fist, " ' . . . they have the forms of men and also they have the lusts of men,' " he quoted.

"You are telling me what every schoolchild knows," protested Faroly. "But from *which* of the other three of the four worlds of Emanation, Creation, Formation, and Effectation—from *which* do they come? And why more often, and more and more often, and more and more and more often, and—"

Face wrinkled to emphasize the gesture of waving these words away, Kaplánovics said, "If Yesod goes, how can Hod remain? if there is no Malchuth, how can there be Quether? Thus one throws away with the hand the entire configuration of Adam Qadmon, the Tree of Life, the Ancient of Days. Men tamper with the very vessels themselves, as if they don't know what happened with the Bursting of the Vessels before, as though the Husks, the Shards, even a single shattered Cortex, doesn't still plague and vex and afflict us to this day. They look down into the Abyss, and they say, 'This is high,' and they look up to an Eminence and they say, 'This is low.' . . . And not thus alone! And not thus alone! Not just with complex deenim, as, for example, those concerning the fluxes of women—no! no! but the simplest of the simple of the Six Hundred and Thirteen Commandments: to place a parapet around a roof to keep some-one from falling off and be killed. What can be simpler? What can be more obvious? What can be easier?

"—but do they do it? What, was it only three weeks ago, or four? a Puer-torican boy didn't fall off the roof of an apartment house near here? Dead, perished. Go talk to the wall. Men don't want to know. Talk to them *Ethics*, talk to them *Brotherhood*, talk to them *Ecumenical Dialogue*, talk to them any kind of nonsenseness: they'll listen. But talk to them, It's written, textually, in the Torah, to build a parapet around your rooftop to prevent blood being shed—no: to this they won't listen. They would neither hear nor understand. They don't know *Torah*, don't know *Text*, don't know *parapet, roof*—this they never heard of either—"

He paused. "Come tomorrow and I'll have prepared for you a kaméa against goslins." He seemed suddenly weary.

Faroly got up. Sighed. "And tomorrow will you also have prepared a kaméa against goslins for everyone else?"

Kaplánovics didn't raise his eyes. "Don't blame the rat," he said. "Blame the rat-hole."

Downstairs Faroly noticed a boy in a green and white skullcap, knotted crispadin coming up from inside under his shirt to dangle over his pants. "Let me try a sortilegy," he thought to himself. "Perhaps it will give me some remez, or hint . . ." Aloud, he asked, "Youngling, tell me, what text did you learn today in school?"

The boy stopped twisting one of his stroobley earlocks, and turned up his phlegm-green eyes. " 'Three things take a man out of this world,' " he yawned. " 'Drinking in the morning, napping in the noon, and putting a girl on a wine-barrel to find out if she's a virgin.' "

Faroly clicked his tongue, fumbled for a handkerchief to wipe his heat-prickled face. "You are mixing up the texts," he said.

The boy raised his eyebrows, pursed his lips, stuck out his lower jaw. "Oh indeed. You ask me a question, then you give me an answer. How do you know I'm mixing up the texts? Maybe I cited a text which you never heard before. What are you, the Vilna Gaon?"

"Brazen face—look, look, how you've gotten your crispadin all snarled," Faroly said, slightly amused, fingering the cinctures passed through one belt-loop—then, feeling his own horrified amazement and, somehow, *knowing . . . knowing . . .* as one *knows* the refrigerator is going to stop humming one half second before it does stop, yet—"What is this? What is this? The cords of your crispadin are tied in *pairs?*"

The filthgreen eyes slid to their corners, still holding Faroly's. "Hear, O Israel," chanted the child; "the Lord our God, the Lord is Two."

The man's voice came out agonyshrill. "Dualist. Heresiarch. Sectary. Ah. Ah ah *ah—goslin!*"

"Take ya hands outa my pants!" shrieked the pseudochild, and, with a cry of almost totally authentic fear, fled. Faroly, seeing people stop, faces changing, flung up his arms and ran for his life. The goslin-child, wailing and slobbering, trampled up steps into an empty hallway where the prismatic edge of a broken windowpane caught the sunlight and winkyflashed rainbow changes. The goslin stretched thin as a shadow and vanished into the bright edge of the shard.

Exhausted, all but prostrated by the heat, overcome with humiliation, shame, tormented with fear and confusion, Faroly stumbled through the door of his home. His wife stood there, looking at him. He held to the doorpost, too weary even to raise his hand to kiss the mazuzah, waiting for her to exclaim at his appearance. But she said nothing. He opened his mouth, heard his voice click in his throat. "Solomon," his wife said. He moved slowly into the room. "Solomon," she said.

"Listen—"

"Solomon, we were in the park, and at first it was so hot, then we sat under a tree and it was so *cool*—"

"Listen . . ."

". . . I think I must have fallen asleep . . . Solomon, you're so quiet . . . Now you're home, I can give the Heshy his bath. Look at him, Solomon! Look, look!"

Already things were beginning to get better. "*And the High Priest shall pray for the peace of himself and his house. Tanya Rabbanan:—and his house.* This means, his wife. He who has no wife, has no home." Small sighs, stifled sobs, little breaks of breath, Faroly moved forward into the apartment. Windows and mirrors were still, dark, quiet. The goslin day was almost over. She had the baby ready for the bath. Faroly moved his eyes, squinting against the last sunlight, to look at the flesh of his first-born, unique son, his Kaddish. What child was this, sallow, squinting back, scrannel, preternaturally sly—? Faroly heard his own voice screaming screaming changeling! changeling!

—Goslin!

Polly Charms, the Sleeping Woman
INTRODUCTION BY GENE WOLFE

This is, as you will already have guessed, Avram Davidson's variation on the ever-popular sleeping beauty theme.

Ever popular because it is ever fertile, never more so than here. Nor will you, I think, find any variant quite so difficult to harvest as this. It is elfinfield, to be reaped only by the seventh son of a seventh son, wielding a silver sickle by moonlight. Don't worry, I am here to help you.

But first let me recommend three more-recent variations on the same theme: Briar Rose, by Jane Yolen; "Summer Wind," by Nancy Kress; and "Waking the Prince," by Kathe Koja. You can read all three, I promise you, and this story as well, without ever reading the same story twice.

In the high and far off times before women warred upon men, the tale of the sleeping beauty was told at firesides so that young women might know they slept but might someday be awakened, and so that young men might know young women sleep, and that gallantry and chivalry are needed, not threats or force. Perhaps the best way to explain the sleeping beauty story is to say that it is the other side of the story about the frog who is kissed.

The frog story is about men, and so lapses only too readily into comedy. The sleeping beauty story is about women, and so flashes with new colors in each new hand; for men are always much the same, but every woman is a new woman with a new man.

You will not have to be told that in "Polly Charms, the Sleeping Woman" Davidson is burlesquing the detective story. He pokes so much broad fun at it that no one could miss that. Very possibly, however, you must be told that nothing could be more like Davidson than to burlesque the detective story in a real detective story, or to omit the scene in which Doctor Engelbert Eszterhazy collects Frow Grigou, Dougherty, Commissioner Lobats, and (one rather hopes) Ignats Louis and Explains Everything.

Davidson was never one to explain everything.

No more am I. But to his multitude of clues I will add two additional hints. The first is that the Ancients knew that it was possible to torture the dead by burning the hair of the corpse. The second is that the worst crime is not murder. And the third (Did you really expect me to tell you everything when I numbered them?) is that you may wish to consider the fifty daughters of Endymion and the Moon.

POLLY CHARMS, THE SLEEPING WOMAN

VISITORS TO THE GREAT city of Bella, capital of the Triune Monarchy of Scythia-Pannonia-Transbalkania, have many famous and memorable sights to see, and will find many guides to show them. Assuming such a visitor to be so limited, unfortunately, in his time as to be able to see but three of these sights, and assuming the guide to be of any experience at all, there are three which will under any circumstances however hasty be shown.

One, of course, is the great Private Park, and, of course, the greatest thing about it is that it is no longer private: the first thing which the King-Emperor Ignats Louis having done, upon succeeding the reclusive Mazzimilian the Mad on the throne, being to throw open the Private Park to the public. The park is a marvel of landscape architecture, although this is perhaps caviare to the general. The general prefer to flock there to what is, after all, the largest merry-go-round in the world. And, next to that, the general prefer to stand and watch the vehicles on the New Model Road, which Ignats Louis, with great foresight, established for the exclusive use of what are now coming to be know as "motor-cars," in order (as The Presence sagely said), "In order that they may experiment without frightening the horses or being frightened by them." In a surprisingly brief period of time it became traditional for all owners of "motor-cars," between the hours of three and four in the afternoon, to make at least three complete circuits of the New Model Road. (The order that all such vehicles, whether propelled by steam, electricity, naphtha, or other means, be hauled to and from the Road by horsepower, is no longer enforced.)

The second sight which it would certainly be impossible to leave Bella without having seen is the Italian Bridge. Although this is no longer the only bridge which crosses, at Bella, the blue and beautiful Ister, the gracious parabolas of its eleven arches are always sure to lift the heart; the legend that it was designed by Leonardo da Vinci remains unproven. But of course it is neither the architecture nor the legend which brings most visitors, it is the site, midway across, marked by a marble plaque [*From This Point On The Italian Bridge* / *The Pre-Triune-Monarchial Poet* / IZKO VARNA / *Having Been Spurned By The Beautiful Dancer, Gretchelle* / LEAPED TO HIS DOOM / *Leaving Behind A Copy Of His Famously Heart-Rending Poem* / FAREWELL, O BELLA / *A*

Clever Play Upon Words Which Will Not / Escape The Learned] usually accompanied by some floral tribute or other. The late well-known character, Frow Poppoff, for many years made a modest living by selling small bundles of posies to visitors for this very purpose; often, when trade was slow, the worthy Poppoff would recite Varna's famous poem, with gestures.

The third of the sights not to be missed is at Number 33, Turkling Street; one refers of course, to The Spot Where The Turkling Faltered And Turned Back. (The well-known witticism, that the Turkling faltered and turned back because he could not get his horse past the push-carts, refers to an earlier period, when the street was an adjunct to the salt-fish, comb, and bobbin open-air market. This has long since passed. Nor is to be thought that the fiercest action of the Eleventh Turkish War took place under the bulging windows of Number 33, for the site at that time lay half a furlong beyond the old city wall. The "Turkling" in question was, of course, the infamous Murad the Unspeakable, also called Murad the Midget. It was certainly here that the Turkish tide turned back. According to the Ottoman Chronicle, "Crying, 'Accursed be those who add gods to God!' the valiant Prince Murad spurred on his charger, but, alas, fell therefrom and broke his pellucid neck. . . ." The Glagolitic Annals insist that his actual words were, "Who ordered this stupid charge? He should be impaled!"—at which moment he himself was fatally pierced by the crossbow bolt of one of the valiant Illyrian Mercenaries. But the point is perhaps no longer important.

A uniformed guard with a drawn sword paces up and down by the granite slab set level with the pavement which marks the place where Murad fell, and it is natural that visitors take it for granted that the guard is a municipal functionary. Actually, he is not. A law passed during the Pacification of 1858 has limited private guards with drawn swords under the following terms: The employer of such a guard must have at least sixteen quarterings of nobility, not less than five registered degrees in the learned sciences, and a minimum of one hundred thousand ducats deposited in the Imperial Two Percent Gold Bond Funds.

Throughout the entire Triune Monarchy of Scythia-Pannonia-Transbalkania, only one person has ever qualified under this law: and that one is, of course, the unquestionably great and justly famous Engelbert Eszterhazy, Doctor of Jurisprudence, Doctor of Medicine, Doctor of Philosophy, Doctor of Literature, Doctor of Science, *et sic cetera;* and the guard is his own private guard and patrols in front of his own private home, Number 33, Turkling Street.

One afternoon in the middle late autumn, a heavyset man wearing the heavy gray suit and high-crowned gray derby hat which were almost the uniform of the plain-clothes division of the Municipal Police approached the guard and raised his eyebrows. The guard responded by raising his sword in salute. The caller nodded, and, opening the door, entered Number 33. There was none of this petty-bourgeois business of knocking, or of doorbells. Inside the lower hall, the day porter, Lemkotch, arose from his chair and bowed.

"Sir Inspector."

"Ask Dr. Eszterhazy if he can see me."

"My master is expecting the Sir Inspector. Please to go right up. I will tell the housekeeper that she may bring the coffee."

The caller, who had expelled a slight sough of surprise at hearing the first sentence, displayed a slight smile at hearing the last. "Tell me, Lemkotch, does your master know absolutely everything?"

The stalwart, grizzle-haired servant paused a moment, then said, casually, "Oh yes, Sir Inspector. Everything." He bowed again, and departed on his errand.

The caller trod heavily upon the runner of the staircase, of a dull, ox-blood color which seemed to glow in the gaslight. It had been pieced together from a once-priceless Ispahani carpet which had suffered damages during the Great Fire of '93 and had been presented by an informal syndicate of the poorer Armenian merchants.

"This is for remembrance," the spokesman said.

And Eszterhazy's reply was, "It is better than rue."

He said now, "You are welcome, Commissioner Lobats. You are not, as you know, invariably welcome, because sometimes you bring zigs when I am engaged in zags. But this business of the young Englishwoman, Polly Charms, promises to be of at least mild interest."

Lobats blinked, gave a respectful glance at the signed cabinet photograph of The Presence in a silver frame, considered a few conversational openings, decided, finally, on a third.

"Your porter is well-trained in simple honesty," he said. "He greets me simply as 'Sir Inspector,' with none of this 'High-born Officer,' with the slight sneer and the half-concealed leer which I get from the servants in some houses . . . I needn't say which. Everyone knows that my father is a butcher, and that *his* father carried carcasses in the Ox Market."

Eszterhazy waved a dismissal of the matter. "All servants are snobs," he said. "Never mind. Remember what one of Bonaparte's marshals said to that hangover from the Old Regime who told him, 'You have no ancestors.' 'Look at *me*,' he said; '*I* am an ancestor.' "

Lobats's heavy lips slowly and silently repeated the phrase. He nodded, took a small notebook from his pocket, and wrote it down. Then his head snapped up. "Say . . . Doctor. Explain how you knew that I was coming about this Polly Charms. . . ." His eyes rested upon another framed picture, but this one he recognized as a caricature by the famous newspaper artist, Klunck: a figure preternaturally tall and thin, with a nose like a needle and the brows bulging on either side like a house-frow's market-bag. And he wondered, almost bitterly, how Eszterhazy could refrain from rage at having seen it—much less, framing it and displaying it for all to see.

"Well. Karrol-Francos," Eszterhazy began, almost indulgently, "you see, I get my newspapers almost damp from the press. This means that the early afternoon edition of the *Intelligencer* got here at eleven o'clock. Naturally, one does not look for a learned summary of the significance of the new price of silver in the *Intelligencer,* nor for an editorial about the Bulgarian troop movements. One does not read it to be enlightened, one reads it to be entertained.

On hearing about this—this exhibition, shall we call it—upon the arrival of the *Intelligencer* I turned at once to the half-page of 'Tiny Topics' . . . you see . . ."

Lobats nodded. He, too, no matter what he had heard or had not heard, also turned at once to the half-page of "Tiny Topics," as soon as he had the day's copy of the *Intelligencer* to hand. And, even though he had already turned to it once, and already read it twice, he not only turned to see it in the copy which Eszterhazy now spread out over his desk, he took out his magnifying glass. (Lobats was too shy to wear spectacles, coming of a social class which looked upon them as a sign of weakness, or of swank.)

NEW INTERESTING LITTLE SCIENTIFIC EXHIBIT

We found our curiosity well repaid for having visited a little scientific exhibit at the old Goldbeaters' Arcade where we saw the already famous Mis Polly Charms, the young Englishwoman who fell into a deep sleep over thirty years ago and has not since awakened. In fact, she slept entirely the raging cannot-shot of the Siege of Paris. The beautiful tragic English-woman, Mis Polly Charms, has not seemingly aged a day and in her condition of deep mesmerism she is said to be able to understand questions put to her by means of the principle of animal magnetism and to answer the questions put to her without waking up; also for a small sum in addition to the small price of admission she sings a deeply affecting song in French.

Lobats tapped the page with a thick and hairy finger. "I'll tell you what, Doctor," he said, gravely. "I believe that this bit here—where is it?—what rotten ink and type these cheap papers use nowadays . . . move my glass . . . ah, ah, oh here it is, this bit where it says, '*In fact she slept entirely the raging cannot-shot of the Siege of Paris,*' I believe that is what is called a misprint and that it ought to read instead . . . oh . . . something like this: '*In fact, she slept entirely* through *the raging* cannon-*shot of the Siege of Paris,*' or something like that. Eh?"

Eszterhazy looked up. His gray eyes sparkled. "Why, I believe that you are quite right, Karrol-Francos," he said. "I am proud of you."

Commissioner Lobats blushed, and he struggled with an embarrassed smile.

"So. Upon reading this, I looked to see the time, I calculated that the *Intelligencer* would reach you by twenty minutes after eleven, that you would have read the item by eleven-thirty, and that you would be here at ten minutes of twelve. Do you think it is a case of abduction, then?"

Lobats shook his head. "Why should I try to fool *you?* You know as well as I do, better than I do, that I'm a fool for all sorts of circus acts, sideshows, mountebanks, scientific exhibitions, odd bits, funny animals, house-hauntings, and all such—"

Eszterhazy snapped his fingers, twice. In a moment his manservant was at his side with hat, coat, gloves, and walking stick. No one else in the entire Triune Monarchy (or, for that matter, elsewhere) had for manservant one of the wild tribe of Mountain Tsiganes; no one else, in fact, would even have thought of it. How came those flashing eyes, that floating hair, that so-untamed countenance, that air of savage freedom, here and now to be silently holding out coat, hat, gloves, and walking stick? Who knows?

"Thank you, Herrekk," said Eszterhazy. Only he and Herrekk knew.

"I will tell you, Commissioner," Eszterhazy said, *"so am I!"*

"Well, Doctor," the Commissioner said, *"I thought as much."*

Chuckling together, they went down the stairs.

At least one of the goldbeaters was still at work in the old Arcade, as a rhythmical thumping sound testified, but for the most part they had moved on to the New. Some of the former workshops were used as warehouses of sundry sorts; here was a fortune-teller, slightly disguised as a couturière; there was a corn-doctor, with two plaster casts in his window showing BEFORE and AFTER, with BEFORE resembling the hoof of a gouty ogre, while AFTER would have been worthy of a prima ballerina. And finally, under a cheaply painted and already flaking wooden board reading **The Miniature Hall of Science,** was a sort of imitation theater entrance. Where the posters would have been were bills in Gothic, Avar, Glagolitic (Slovatchko), Romanou, and even—despite the old proverb, "There are a hundred ways of wasting paint, and the first way is to paint a sign in Vlox"—Vlox. The percentage of literacy among the Vloxfolk may not have been high, but someone was certainly taking no chances.

The someone was certainly not the down-at-heels fellow with a homemade crutch who, pointing the crutch at this last bill, enquired, "Do you know what you'd get if you crossed a pig with a Vloxfellow?" And, answering his own question, replied, "A dirty pig." And waited for the laugh.

"Be off with you," said Lobats, curtly. The loafer slunk away.

There was even a bill in French.

POLLY CHARMS	SLEEPING BEAUTY
SLEEPING WOMAN	30 YEARS SLUMBER 30
ANSWERS QUESTIONS!	ENGLISHWOMAN!!!!
MOST REMARKABLE!	VERY UNUSUAL SIGHT!

DOES SHE ANSWER FROM THE WORLD OF THE
LIVING OF THE DEAD????? COME! AND! SEE!!!

And so on. And so on.

The fat old woman at the ticket window, with dyed hair and wearing the traditional red velveteen dress split under the arms, smiled fawningly at them.

"Permit," said Lobats, putting out his hand.

Nodding rapidly, she reached up to where a multitude of papers hung from a wire on clothespins, took one down, examined it, returned it, took another down, gave it a peep, nodded even more rapidly, and handed it out the window.

"Very well, Frow Grigou," said Lobats, handing it back. "Two tickets, please," putting coins on the counter.

Frow Grigou, instead of nodding her head, now began to shake it rapidly, and pushed the money back, smiling archly. "Guests, the High-born Gentlemen, our guests, oh no no *oh* no—"

Lobats turned as red as Frow Grigou's dress. "*Tickets!*" he growled. "Take the money. Take the—"

She took it this time, and hastily, extending the tickets, her head now rocking slowly from side to side, still smiling archly, but now with a puzzled note added, as though the insistence on paying for admission were some bit of odd behavior, which required the indulgence of the tolerant. "Always glad to see," she gobbled, her voice dying away behind them as they walked the short, dusty hall, ". . . High-born Gents . . . law-abiding . . . delighted . . ."

Only one of the five or six functioning gas jets inside the Exhibition Room had a mantle, and at least two of the others suffered a malfunction which caused them to bob up and down whenever a dray went by in the street; the light was therefore both inadequate and uncertain. And a soft voice now came from out of the dimness, saying, "*Billet? Billet?*"

Nature had formed the man who now came forward to look noble, but something else had re-formed him to look furtive. His head was large, his features basically handsome, with long and white side whiskers neatly trimmed so that not a hair straggled, but the head itself was completely hairless, with not even a fringe. The head was canted to one side, and the man looked at them out of the corner of one faded-blue eye as he took the tickets. Eszterhazy, almost as though automatically, and rather slowly, reached over and placed the tips of his fingers upon the man's head and ran them lightly over the surface . . . for just a moment . . .

Then he pulled them away, as though they had been burned.

"A phrenologist," the man murmured in English, indulgently, almost contemptuously.

"Among other things," said Eszterhazy, also in English.

A horrid change came over the man's face; his haggard and quasi-noble features dissolved into a flux of tics and grimaces. Once or twice his mouth opened and closed. Then, "*Come right in, gentlemen, the exhibition will commence almost any moment now,*" he said, unevenly, in a mixture of terrible French and broken German. And, ". . . *one of the most remarkable phenomena of the age,*" he whispered, again in English. Then he seemed to fall in upon himself, his head bowed down, his shoulders hunched, and he turned away from them in a curious twisting motion.

Lobats looked with a quizzical face to Eszterhazy and observed with astonishment and concern that his companion was—even in that dim and fitful light—gone pale and drawn, jaw thrust outwards and downward in a grimace which might have been—had it been someone else, anyone else—fright . . .

But, in a moment, face and man were the same as before, save that the man had swiftly taken out a silken pocket handkerchief, wiped his face, and as swiftly returned it. And before Lobats had time to say one word, a thin and almost eerie sound announced a gramophone had added its "note scientific" to the atmosphere. It took a few seconds, during which a group of newcomers, evidently mostly clerks and such who were taking advantage of their luncheon-time, entered the room . . . it took a few seconds for one to recognize, over the sudden clatter and chatter, that the gramophone was offering a song in French.

Strange and curious were the words, and curious and strange the voice.

> *Curieux scrutateur de la nature entière,*
> *J'ay connu du grand tout le principe et la fin.*
> *J'ay vu l'or en puissance au fond de sa minière,*
> *J'ay saisi sa matière et surpris son levain.**

Few of those present, clearly, understood the words, yet all were somehow moved. Obscure the burden, the message unclear; the voice seemed moreover odd, unearthly, and grotesque through the transposition of the primitive machine: yet the effect was as beautiful as it was uncanny.

> *J'expliquay par quel art l'âme aux flancs d'une mère,*
> *Fait sa maison, l'emporte, et comment un pépin*
> *Mis contre un grain de blé, sous l'humide poussière,*
> *L'un plante et l'autre cep, sont le pain et le vin.*

Lobats dug his companion in the ribs gently and in a hoarse whisper asked, "What is it?"

"It is one of the occult, or alchemical, sonnets of the Count of Saint-Germain . . . if he was . . . who lived at least two hundred years . . . if he did," Eszterhazy said, low-voiced.

Once more the voice—high and clear as that of a child, strong as that of a man—took up the refrain.

> *Rien n'était, Dieu voulut, rien devint quelque chose,*
> *J'en doutais, je cherchay sur quoi l'universe pose,*
> *Rien gardait l'équilibre et servait de soutien.*

The Commissioner uttered an exclamation. "Now I know! I remember hearing—was years ago—an Italian singer—"

"—Yes—"

"He was a . . . a . . . a whatchemaycallit . . . one of *them*—"

"A castrato. Yes . . ."

Once more, and for the last time, the voice, between that of men and women, soared up, magnificent, despite all distortion, from the great, curling cornucopia of the gramophone horn.

*From *Poëmes Philosophiques sur l'Homme*, Paris, 1795, quoted in *The Count of Saint Germain*, by Isabel Cooper-Ashley, Steiner, Blauvelt: New York, 1970.

Enfin, avec les poids de l'éloge et du blâme,
Je pesay l'éternel, il appela mon âme,
Je mourus, j'adoray, je ne savais plus rien . . .

The moment's silence which followed the end of the song was broken by another and more earthly voice, and one well-enough known to both Eszterhazy and Lobats. It was that of one Dougherty, a supposed political exile of many years' residence in Bella. From time to time one came upon him in unfashionable coffeehouses, or establishments where stronger drink was served. Sometimes the man was writing something; sometimes he explained that it was part of a book which he was writing, and sometimes he explained nothing, but scrawled slowly away in a dreamy fashion. At other times he had no paper in front of him, only a glass, into or beyond which he stared slackly. This man Dougherty was tall and he was stooped and he wore thick eyeglasses and now and then he silently moved his lips—lips surprisingly fresh and full in that ruined gray countenance. Officially he described himself as "Translator, Interpreter, and Guide," and he was evidently acting now in the first and second of these capacities.

"Gentlemen," he began (and he used the English word), "Gentlemen . . . Mr. Murgatroyd, the entrepreneur of this scientific exhibition has asked me to thank those of you who have honored him with your patronage, and to express his regret that he does not speak with fluency the languages of the Triune Monarchy, whose warm and frequent hospitality . . ." Here he paused, and seemed to sag a bit, as though bowed beneath the weight of all the nonsense and humbug which convention required him to be saying—and which he had been saying, in one way or another, over and over, for decades. Indeed, he frankly sighed, put his hand to his forehead, then straightened, and took in his hand something which the entrepreneur had given: it seemed to be a pamphlet, or booklet.

"Mmmm . . . yes . . . Some interesting facts, taken from a voluminous work written on the subject of the mysterious sleeping woman, Polly Charms, by a member of the French Academy and the Sorbonne. The subject of this scientific exhibition, the ever-young Englishwoman, Miss Mary Charms, called Polly, was born in—"

His remarks, which had sunk to a monotone, were interrupted by several exclamations of annoyance, amidst which one voice now made itself heard, and distinctly: "Come on, now, Dear Sir ["Lijberherra"—sarcastically], save all this muckdirt ["Schejssdrekka"] for those there *gentlemen* who've got the whole afternoon at their leisure: come on, let's see . . ."

Lobats coughed sufficiently to draw attention. The voice hesitated, then went on, though in tones somewhat less rough and menacing, to say that they were working-people, didn't have much time, had paid to see this here Miss Sharms, and wanted to see her or their money back, so, "Save the French Sorbonne for the dessert course, for them as can wait, and let's get on with it."

Dougherty shrugged, leaned over and spoke to Murgatroyd, who also shrugged, then gestured to Frow Grigou, who did not bother to shrug, but, indicating by a flurry of nods and smirks that she was only too happy to oblige and merely wondered that anyone should think otherwise, trotted swiftly to the side of the room and pulled at a semi-visible cord. The filthy old curtain, bearing the just-visible name of a firm of patent-medicine makers long bankrupt, began—with a series of jerks and starts in keeping with the hiccuppy gaslights—to go up.

And Mr. Murgatroyd, not even waiting for the process to be complete, moved forward and with a smack of his lips began to speak, and then to speak in English, and went on speaking, leaving to Dougherty to catch up, or not, with the translation and interpretation.

"It was just thirty years ago, my lords and ladies and gentlemen, just exactly thirty years ago to this very day—" But his glib patter, obviously long and often repeated, plus the fact of the term **30 Years** appearing in faded letters on several of the bills posted outside, made it at once obvious that the "thirty years" was a phrase by now ritualized and symbolic. Perhaps he, or perhaps another, had endowed Polly Charms with thirty years' slumber at the very beginning of the show's career; or, perhaps, and the thought made one shudder, Murgatroyd had been saying "30 years" for far longer than any period of only thirty years. "That young Miss Mary Charms, called Polly, at the age of fifteen years, accompanied by her mother and several other loved ones . . ."

He trailed off into silence, having been pushed aside by several of those honoring him with their patronage as they shoved up to see; in the silence, Dougherty proceeded with his translations . . . which may or may not have been listened to by any.

Eszterhazy realized that he had been expecting, for some reason, to see either a coffin or something very much like it. What he actually saw was something resembling an infant's crib, though of course much larger, and, at very first glimpse, it seemed to be filled with a mass of—

". . . Professor Leonardo de Entwhistle, the noted mesmerologist," Murgatroyd's voice suddenly was heard again, after the first burst of exclamations had subsided. His eyes shifted and met Eszterhazy's. The Englishman's eyes at once closed, opened, closed, opened, and, as it were desperately, looked away. Where Eszterhazy looked was into the crib, and what he saw it was almost filled with was, or seemed to be, hair . . . long and lustrous golden-brown hair. Coils and braids of it. Immense tresses of it. Masses and masses of it. Here and there ribbons had been affixed to it. And still it went on.

And, almost buried in it, slightly raised by a pillow at the head of the crib was another head, a human head, the head of, and indeed of, a female in early womanhood.

"Can we touch it—uh, *her?*"

Murgatroyd muttered.

"One at a time, and gently," said Dougherty. "Gently . . . *gently!*"

Fingers were applied, some hesitantly. A palm was applied to the side of the face. Another was raised and moving down, though not, by the looks of it, or by the owner's looks, to the face; at this point Lobats grunted and grabbed the man's wrist. Not gently. The man growled that he was just going to—but the disclaimer fell off into a snarl, and the gesture was not repeated. Someone managed to find a hand and lifted it up, with a triumphant air, as though no one had ever seen a hand before.

And Eszterhazy now said, "All right. *Enough* . . ." He moved up; the crowd moved back. He took out the stethoscope. The crowd said *Ahhh.*

"That's the philosopher," someone said to someone else. Who said, "*Oh* yes," although what quality either one attached to the term perhaps neither understood precisely.

God only knew where the girl's garment had been made, or when, or by whom; indeed, it seemed to have been made over many times, and to consist of sundry strata, so to speak. Now and again it had occurred to Whomever that the girl was supposed to be sleeping, and so the semblance of a nightgown had been fashioned. Several times. And on several other occasions the theatrical elements of it all had overcome, and attempts had been made to provide the sort of dress which a chanteuse might have been wearing . . . wearing, that is, in some provincial music hall where the dressmakers had odd and old-fashioned ideas of what a chanteuse might like to wear . . . and the chanteuses, for that matter, even odder ones.

There was silk and there was cotton and there was muslin, lace, artificial flowers, ruches, embroidered gores, gussets, embroidered yokes—

The girl's eyes were almost entirely closed. One lid was just barely raised, and a thin line gleamed, at a certain angle, underneath. Sleepers of that age do not flush, always, as children often do, in sleep. There was color in the face, though not much. The lips were the tint of a pink. A small gold ring showed in one ear; the other ear was concealed by the hair.

"*The hair,*" said Murgatroyd, "*the hair has never stopped growing!*" A kind of delight seemed to seize him as he said it.

Eszterhazy's look brought silence. And another flurry of tics. Several times he moved the stethoscope. Then the silence was broken. "A wax doll, isn't it, Professor? Isn't—"

Eszterhazy shook his head. "The heartbeat is perceptible," he said. "Though very, very faint." The crowd sighed. He removed the ear-pieces and passed the instrument to Commissioner Lobats, who, looking immensely proud and twice as important, attached himself to it—not without difficulty. After some moments, he—very slowly—nodded twice. The crowd sighed again.

"Questions? Has anyone a question to ask of Polly Charms, the Sleeping Woman?—ah, one moment please. It is time for her daily nourishment." Murgatroyd, with a practiced flourish, produced two bottles, a glass, and a very tarnished, very battered, but unquestionably silver, spoon. "All attempts to make the mysterious and lovely Miss Mary partake of solid sustenance have failed. Nor will her system accept even gruel. Accordingly, and on the advice of her physicians—of the foremost physicians in Christendom—" Here he turned and beckoned to a member of the audience, an elderly dandy, audibly recognized by several as a ribbon clerk in a nearby retail emporium. "I should like to ask of you the favor, sir, to taste and smell of this and to give us your honest and unbought opinion as to its nature."

The man simpered, sniffed, sipped. Smacked his lips. "Ah. Why that's Tokai. Bull's-blood Tokai." And he made as though to take more. Laughs and guffaws and jests. The contents of the other bottle were declared to be water. The girl's manager then ceremonially mixed the glass half-full of wine and half of water. He might have been an alchemist, proving an elixir. "Come on, now, come on. Some of you are in a hurry, you say . . . Questions?"

Snickers, jokes, people being pushed forward, people holding back. Then the ribbon clerk, glancing at his watch, a-dangle and a-bangle with fobs and seals, said, "Very well. One question and then I must go. Gracious Lady: Who is Frantchek? And where?"

Murgatroyd held the spoon to her lips, and, indeed so gently, raised her head a trifle. "Just a spoonful. Polly. A nice spoon of something good. To please Father Murgatroyd." The slick and hairless head bent over, indeed like that of a father cosseting an ill child. Slowly and slightly the lips parted. The spoon clinked against the even rows of teeth. Withdrew.

"*Very* well, Polly. You're a *good* girl. Father Murgatroyd is very *pleased* with you. And now, if you please, an answer to the question. 'Who is Frantchek? And where?' "

The lips parted once again. A faint, a very faint sigh was heard. And then, in the voice of a girl in her middle teens imitating one much younger, in tones artificial and stilted, Polly Charms spoke.

"*Why, Brother, I am in America. With Uncle.*"

All turned to the old dandy, who had been standing, one hand on hip, with an expression of one who expects to be fooled. But who won't be, even if he is. Because of expecting it. This expression quite fell away. He gaped.

"Well, Maurits. And what about that?" they pressed him.

"Why . . . why . . . Why, Frantchek *is* my brother. He run off, oh, five-and-twenty-year ago. We none of us had a word of him—"

"And the uncle? In America?"

Old Maurits slowly nodded, dumbfounded. "I *did* have an uncle, in America. Maybe still do. *I* don't know—" With a jerk away from the hand on his shoulder, he stumbled out, face in his hands.

Comment was uncertain. One said, "Well, that didn't really prove nothing. . . . Still . . ."

And another one—probably the same who had loudly demanded the biographical details be omitted, now said, loudly, "Well, Miss, *I* think you're a fake, a clever fake. Wha-at? Why, half the people in the Empire have a brother named Frantchek, and an uncle in America! Now, just you answer *this* question. What's this in my own closed hand, here in this coat pocket?"

Another spoonful of wine and water.

Another expectant silence, this time with the questioner openly sneering. Another answer.

"*The pearl-handled knife which you stole at the bath-house . . .*"

And now see the fellow, face mottled, furious, starting toward the sleeping woman, hand moving up and out of the pocket. And see Lobats lunge, hear a sudden and sick cry of pain. See a something fall to the ground. And watch the man, now suddenly pale, as Lobats says, "Get out! Or—!" Watch him get . . . holding one hand with the other. And see the others stoop and gape.

"A pearl-handled knife!"

"Jesus, Mary, and—"

"—known him for years, he ain't no good—"

And now someone, first clutching his head in his hands, and then leaning forward, then drawing back and staring, glaring all round, face twisted with half shame and half defiance: "Listen . . . listen. . . . Say—I want to *know*. Is my wife . . . is she all that she should be—to me—*is she*—" He doesn't finish, nobody dares to laugh. They can hear him breathing heavily through heavily distended nostrils.

Another spoonful. Another pause.

"Better than she should be . . . though little you deserve it . . ."

The man will not face anyone. He leans to one side, head bent, breathing *very* heavily.

And soon the last question has been asked, and the wine is all gone.—Or, perhaps, it is the other way around.

And, as Murgatroyd goes to put down the spoon, and the audience is suddenly uncertain, suddenly everyone looks at someone whom nobody has looked at before. Who says, "And so, Professors, what about the French song?" A spruce, elderly gent, shiny red cheeks, garments cut in the fifth year of the Reign, looking for all the world like a minor notary from one of the remoter suburbs ("Ten tramways and a fiacre ride away," as the saying goes) where each family still has its own cow, and probably up to the center of the city for his annual trip to have his licensure renewed; wanting a bit of fun along with it, and, not daring to tell the old lady ("Tanta Minna," probably) that he has had it at any place more risky, has been having it at a "scientific exhibition."

"Wasn't there supposed to be a French song?" he asks calmly.

Murgatroyd, at a murmur from Dougherty, produces a wooden tray lined with worn green velveteen and covertly places in it a single half-ducat, which he watches rather anxiously. "For a very slight additional charge," he says, starting the rounds, "a beautiful song in the French language will be sung by the lovely and mysterious Polly Charms, the—"

Spectators show signs of departing . . . or, at any rate, of drawing away from the collection tray. A single piece of gold spins through the air, all a-glitter, falls right upon the half-ducat with a pure ringing sound. Mr. Murgatroyd looks up, almost wildly, sees Eszterhazy looking at him. Who says, "Get on with it."

Murgatroyd makes the money vanish. He leans over the sleeping woman, takes up her right hand, and slowly caresses it. "Will you sing us a song, Polly dear?" he asks. Almost, one might think, anxiously.

"That sweet French song taught you by Madame, in the old days . . . Eh?" And, no song being forthcoming, he clears his throat and quaveringly begins, " '*Je vous envoye un bouquet* . . .', Eh, Polly?"

Eszterhazy, watching, sees a slight tremor in the pale, pale throat. A slight rise in the slight bosom, covered in its bedizened robe. The mouth opens. An indrawn breath is clearly heard. And then she sings. Polly Charms, the Sleeping Lady, sings.

Je vous envoye un bouquet de ma main
Que j'ai ourdy de ces fleurs epanies:
Qui ne les eust à ce vespre cuillies,
Flaques à terre elles cherroient demain.

No one had asked Dougherty to translate the previous French song, sung by the eunuch singer (surely one of the very last) on the gramophone; nor had he done so; nor did anyone ask him to translate now. Yet, and without his gray face changing at all, his gray lips moved, and he began, " 'I send you now a sheaf of fairest flowers / Which my hand picked; yet are they so full blown, / Had no one plucked them they had died alone, / Fallen to earth before tomorrow's hours.' "*

Still, Murgatroyd caressed the pallid hand. And again, the eerie and infantile voice sang out.

Cela vous soit un exemple certain
Que voz beautés, bien qu'elles soient fleuries,
En peu de tems cherront toutes flétries,
Et periront, comme ces fleurs, soudain.

" 'Then let this be a portent in your bowers,' " Dougherty went on. " 'Though all your beauteous loveliness is grown, / In a brief while it falls to earth o'erthrown, / Like withered blossoms, stripped of all their powers . . .' "

Quietness.

A dray rumbles by in the street. The gas lights bob up and down. Breaths are let out, throats cleared. Feet shuffle.

"Well, now," says old Uncle Oskar, "that was very nice, I am sure." Smiling benignly, he walks over, and, into the now empty collection plate he drops a large old five-kopperka piece. Nodding and beaming, he departs. It has been worth every kopperka of it to him, the entire performance. Tonight, over the potato dumplings with sour-crout and garlic wurst, he will tell Tanta Minna all about it. In fact, if he is alive and she is alive, ten years from now, he will still be telling about it; and she, Tanta Minna, will still be as astonished as ever, punctuating each pause with *Jesus, Mary, and Joseph!* or, alternately, *Oh, thou dear Cross!*

Some follow after, some still remain.

"The performance is over," says Eszterhazy.

Lobats: "*Over.* Good afternoon to you."

And Frow Grigou calls after them, anxious as ever, "There is another performance at half-past five, Dear Sirs, and also at eight and at ten!"

*From Ronsard, *Poems of Love*, selected and edited by Grahame Castor and Terence Cave, Manchester University Press, 1975.

Lobats looks at Eszterhazy, as though to say, *What now?* And Eszterhazy looks at Murgatroyd. "I am a Doctor of Medicine and a Titular Court Physician," he says; "and I should like your permission to make an examination of—" he gestures. Dougherty, without looking anywhere in particular, at once begins to translate Eszterhazy's English into Avar, then slowly seems to feel that this is, perhaps, not exactly what is wanted at the moment, and his voice dies away.

Murgatroyd licks his lips, the lower parts of his moustache. Almost, he licks the tip of his nose. "Oh no," he says. "Oh no . . ."

"And this," Eszterhazy says, calmly, "is a Commissioner of Police."

Murgatroyd looks at the Commissioner of Police, who looks back; he looks at Dougherty, who looks away; then he looks for Frow Grigou.

But Frow Grigou has gone, quite gone.

Excerpts from the Day-Book of Dr. Eszterhazy:

> . . . Query Reuters for the precise date of the death by apoplexy of ENTWHISTLE, LEONARD (see Private Encyclopedia), British mesmerist and mountebank, supposedly in the midst of an exhibition or performance . . .
>
> . . . no signs of any callosities whatever on the soles of the female's feet, or heels . . . degeneration of the muscular tissue, such as is found among the long-senile, was not present, however . . .
>
> Murgatroyd declared, though reluctantly, that passage of waste materials was infrequent, and cleanly . . .
>
> Murgatroyd was almost violent in reply to the tentative suggestion of Lobats that an attempt, by mesmerism, to bring the young woman out of this supposed-mesmeric trance be attempted. MEMO: To re-read story by American writer E. A. Poe, "The Case of Monsieur Waldemar." In this tale, a presumed account of facts, a dying man is placed under mesmeric trance of long duration (exact duration not recalled); removal of trance state or condition discloses that "Waldemar" has actually been dead, body at once lapsing into decay. Cannot state at present if the story is entirely fictitious or not; another story by same writer (Marie Roget?) known to be demi-factual.
>
> Obvious: welfare of young woman, Charms, is first consideration.
>
> Suggestions: Consider question of use of galvanic batteries, but only if—

For some seconds the sound of running feet had echoed in the narrow street below. A voice, hoarse and labored . . . Then the night porter, Emmerman, entered. He was always brief. "Goldbeaters' Arcade on fire, master," he said now. Adding, as Eszterhazy, with an exclamation, ran for his medical bag, "Commissioner Lobats has sent word." The Tsigane had appeared, as though rising from out of the floor (where, indeed, on the threshold of his master's bedroom door he always slept), but Eszterhazy, waving aside the coat and hat, said two words: *"The steam—"* He followed the silently running Herrekk through the apartment and down the back steps to the mews, where the run-about was kept, and they leaped on it. Schwebel, the retired railroad engineer who maintained the machine, had been charged to see that a head of steam was always kept up, and he had never failed. With a sketch of a salute, he threw open the stable door. With a low hiss, the machine, Eszterhazy at the tiller, rolled out into the night. Herrekk had already begun to toll the great bronze handbell to warn all passersby out of the way.

Lobats had said that he was "a fool for all sorts of circus acts, sideshows, mountebanks, scientific exhibitions, odd bits, funny animals, house-hauntings ...." He might have added: "and fires."

Three fire engines of the newest sort, each drawn troika-fashion by three great horses of matching colors, had come one after another to The Street of the Defeat of Bonaparte (universally called Bonaparte Street), as near as they could maneuver, and made much with hoses into the Arcade. But the watchmen of the neighborhood, many of whom had been employed there before the modern fire department came into being, had set up their bucket brigade and were still passing the old but functioning leather containers from hand to hand. A sudden breeze now whipped up the flames and sparks and sent them flying overhead, straight up and aloft into the black sky—at the same time clearing the passageway of the Arcade from all but the smell of smoke.

Off in a corner, her red velveteen dress flying loose about her fat body, Frow Grigou crouched, hand to mouth, mouth which screamed incessantly, "*Ruined! Ruined! The curtains, the bad gas jets! The bad gas jets, the curtains! Ruined! Ruined! Ruined!*"

All at once the firehoses heaved, writhed, gushed forth in a potent flow. The smoke turned back and clouds of steam arose. Eszterhazy felt himself choking, felt himself being carried away in the powerful arms of Herrekk, the Mountain Tsigane. In a moment he cried, "I am all right! Set me down." He saw himself looking into the anxious face of Lobats, who, seeing Eszterhazy on his feet and evidently recovered, gestured silently to two bodies on the pavement in Bonaparte Street.

Murgatroyd. And Polly Charms.

[Later, Lobats was to ask, "What was it that you found out when you put your fingers on the Englishman's head?" And Eszterhazy was to answer, "More than I will ever speak of to anyone."]

Eszterhazy flung himself down beside them. But although he cursed aloud the absence of his galvanic batteries, and although he plied all the means at his behalf—the cordials, the injections, the ammoniated salts—he could bring no breath or motion to either of them.

Slowly, Lobats crossed himself. Ponderously, he said, "Ah, they're both in a better world now. She, poor little thing, her life, if you call that long sleep a life—And he, bad chap though I suppose he must've been in lots of ways, maybe in most—but surely he expiated his sins in dragging her almost to safety, trying to save her life at the risk of his own when her very hair was on fire—"

And indeed, most of the incredible mass of hair had burned away—those massive tresses which Murgatroyd (for who else?) must have daily and nightly spent hours in brushing and combing and plaiting and braiding . . . one must hope, at least lovingly . . . that incredible profusion of light-brown hair, unbound for the night, had indeed burned away but for a light scantling, like that of a crop-headed boy. And this shown in the dim and flaring lights, all a-glitter with moisture, shining with the drops of the water which had extinguished its fire. The girl's face as calm now as ever. The lips of the color of a pink were again so slightly parted. But whatever she might once have had to tell would now forever be unknown.

And as for Murgatroyd, Death had at least and at last released him from all need of concealment and fear. The furtive look was quite gone now. The face seemed now entirely noble.

"I suppose you might say that he'd exploited her, kept her in that state of bondage—but at least he risked his life to save hers—"

One of the watchmen standing by now stepped a pace forward and respectfully gestured a salute. "Beg the Sir High Police Commissioner a pardon," he said now. "However, as it is not so."

"What is not so?" Lobats was annoyed.

The watchman, still respectful, but quite firm: "Why, as the poor gentleman tried, dying, to save the poor missy. But it wasn't so, Sir High Commissioner and Professor Doctor. It was as one might say the opposite way. 'Twas *she* as was trying to get *him* out. *Oh*yes, Sirs. We heard of him screaming, oh Jesus, Mary, and Joseph, how he screamed! We couldn't get in to them. We looks around and we looks back and there she comes, she come out of the flames, sometimes carrying him and sometimes she dragged at him and then her pretty hair went all ablaze and they two fell almost at our feet and we doused them with water. . . . Y'see," he concluded, his eloquence exhausted.

"Ah, stop your damned lies, man!" said Lobats.

Eszterhazy, shaking his head, murmured, "See, then, how swiftly the process of myth-making and legendry begins . . . *Oh! God!*" Shocked, speechless, he responded to Lobats only with a gesture. Still on his knees, Eszterhazy pointed wordlessly to the feet of Polly Charms, the Sleeping Woman. The feet were small and slight. They were, as always, naked, bare. And Lobats, following the slight gesture, saw with a shock that even experience had not prepared him for that the bare feet of the dead girl were deeply scratched, and torn and red with blood.

The Final Adventure of Harlan in Avramland by his friend, Harlan Ellison

I loved him most because he redeemed me from almost a decade of ridicule, and he did it all-knowing. It wasn't an accident; he knew what he was doing; and I was his pal from that moment to this, even though he's gone.

I was a hyperkinetic fan when I was a teenager. Loud, and whacky, and far too cocky for my own good. So smartalecky that I made instant enemies, just because of the brashness, just because of the ebullient manner. That I had a good heart, and meant no harm . . . well, that didn't much serve to beat the bull dog, as they say. I rubbed people the wrong way. Not at all the urbane, suave, and charming self I present today, midway in my sixties.

And it came to pass that one of those who found my manner rankling, even pawky, set about humiliating me . . . lynching me with my own hubris.

It was something like 1952. We all wanted to sell our first story. Me, Bob Silverberg, Terry Carr, Lee Hoffman, Joel Nydahl, Bill Venable, every fan in the game. We hungered to follow Bob Tucker and Bob Bloch and Arthur Clarke and John Brunner, and all those other one-time fans who had crossed over into the Golden Land of Professionalism. I was in high school in Cleveland. And I was writing stories that Algis Budrys was reading with dismay, as he tried by mail and occasional personal contact to turn me into something like a writer.

But I kept getting rejections. Not just from Campbell at (what was then, still) Astounding, and Horace Gold at Galaxy, but from everyone. I was an amateur, a callow callow amateur, and the best I could get was a scribbled note of pity from dear, now-gone Bea Mahaffey at Other Worlds. And at The Magazine of Fantasy and Science Fiction the world-famous and incredibly astute Anthony Boucher was returning my pathetic efforts with little 4×5 bounce notes that read (as did one dated Sep 14 51)

Harlan Ellison———THE BEER CAMPAIGN———Sorry, but—
nice idea . . . but once you've stated it, that's all.
You haven't developed it into a story.

AB

Come by the house some time. I'll show you the original. And its many companions.

Of all the markets available to writers in the genre in 1952, the most prestigious—if you had any literary aspirations at all—was F&SF. Boucher and McComas. Oh, be still my heart! But I kept being bounced. And out there somewhere . . . probably still alive and still smirking . . . someone who had it in for that smartmouth kid was setting me up.

I sent a story to Mr. Boucher. I think it was called "Monkey Business." Can't tell you if it had any merit or not, because I don't even have a copy of it. Maybe someone out there has a copy, but I don't. And I waited for the word. All drool and expectation, dumb kid, waiting for what I knew in my heart had to be another of the many many rejections.

And one day there came an envelope from wherever it was in California that Tony Boucher edited the magazine (did I mention I was in East High School in Cleveland?). And it was in that dove-gray typewriter face that Mr. Boucher used in his letters, the typeface I knew so well by then.

And I opened the envelope when I got home from school, and it wasn't a rejection note. It was an acceptance. Tony Boucher was buying "Monkey Business" and he said he was pleased to be able to make another First Sale author, like Richard Matheson and Charles Beaumont and Daniel Keyes and Walter Miller and so many others.

I'll spare you. I called Bob Silverberg first, because, well, never mind why *because. Just because. And he was cool, but pleased for me. I'd beaten him to publication, it appeared, by a hair, because Bob was on the edge of professional status himself. And then I called everyone in the known universe.*

Well, it was a hoax, of course. Someone had gotten hold of a sheet of official F&SF stationary, and s/he had done a very good job—or at least a serviceable job—of emulating Tony's way with the typewriter, even to the strikeovers, and had sent it on to hang me out to dry. And I'd done the rest. To a fare-thee-well.

I spent the next ten years trying to sell to F&SF, even after Mick McComas and Tony were gone, and I couldn't even sell a story to the magazine when my own agent, Robert P. Mills, one of the finest men who ever lived, was the editor. Nope. No way.

And then Avram became editor. In 1962 he bought my short fantasy "Paulie Charmed the Sleeping Woman"—yes, I know what you're startledly thinking—yes, of course, he was running a pun on my title with his own—yes, he did it on purpose—we were joshing pals, remember—and he published it in the August 1962 issue. And when he sent me an advance copy of the issue (I was living in Los Angeles by that time), he wrote me a note and it said, "Remember 'Monkey Business'? This should damp the sound, bad cess to them; and may they choke on their laughter."

I have appeared in Fantasy & Science Fiction *close on a hundred times. Some of my best work over more than three and a half decades. But no triumph in those pages was ever as sweet to me as the one put in print by my now-gone friend, Avram, who was brilliant beyond the telling; funny and witty and acerbic and cranky beyond the believing; who once purposely dropped and broke my Olympia typewriter on purpose, when I was on a stepladder handing it down to him prior to our trip to the WorldCon in Pittsburgh in 1960, because it was a German-made machine, and Avram took the Holocaust very seriously and wouldn't go anywhere near a German-made product. But he rode all the way from Manhattan where we lived at that time, to Pittsburgh, with the top down on my Austin-Healy, wearing a jaunty sporting cap, singing at the top of his voice.*

He is gone, and I miss him. And that. Is that.

My last adventure, this one, in Avramland.

And Don't Forget the One Red Rose

INTRODUCTION BY RICHARD A. LUPOFF

In a perfect world, Avram Davidson would be revered as one of the great writers of his generation. You can name your own list of the others. Updike, Mailer, Heller, Atwood, and perhaps a few more, might share Avram's pedestal. But instead, he is known to a small circle of readers and admirers, and we are sometimes inclined to ask if it is the rest of the world that is crazy . . . or ourselves.

In fact, Avram suffered two misfortunes which robbed him, in his lifetime, of the critical and financial rewards that his works clearly merited. He was a natural short story writer who lived and worked in the age of the novel, and he selected for his realm of imagination the world of science fiction.

His stories, complex and lovingly crafted miniatures, were relegated to the category of minor works, ancillary to the one true form for worthwhile fiction, the novel. Avram's manuscripts weighed in at an ounce or two. The serious literati (and, for the most part, the moguls of publishing) preferred works that were measured by the pound.

And as for Avram's selection of science fiction as his major area of creation, one fears that he was ensnared, as so many other authors have been, into mistaking one of science fiction's periodic flirtations with "maturity" for true love. Alas, when the field reverted to its usual hodgepodge of crude narrative and cliché themes, Avram was left, a wounded giant, brought down by a keening troop of Lilliputians.

Avram's fine story "And Don't Forget the One Red Rose" is alone a greater achievement than the entire bloated accumulation of ponderous fantasy novels that cross my desk each month. I see in it a literary tradition that bears comparison to the best stories of Lord Dunsany, Ambrose Bierce, John Collier, and Stanley Ellin. That Avram was able to place the story with Playboy magazine rather than one of the penny-a-word pulps is at least a small consolation to me.

AND DON'T FORGET THE ONE RED ROSE

CHARLEY BARTON WAS THE staff of an East New York establishment that supplied used gas stoves on a wholesale basis. He received deliveries at the back door, dollied them inside, took them apart, cleaned them (and cleaned them and cleaned them and cleaned them) till they sparkled as much as their generally run-down nature would allow, fitted on missing parts and set them up in the front of the place, where they might be chaffered over by prospective buyers.

He never handled sales. These were taken care of by his employer, a thick-set and neckless individual who was there only part of the time. When not fawning upon the proprietors of retail used-appliance stores, he was being bru-tal to Charley. This man's name was Matt Mungo, and he arrived in neat, middle-class clothes from what he referred to as his "other place," never further described to Charley, who did not venture to be curious.

Charley doubted, however, that Mungo did—indeed, he was certain that Mungo did not—display to employees and patrons of his other place the in-sulting manner and methods he used in the stove warehouse.

Besides calling Charley many offensive names in many offensive ways, Mungo had the habit of shoving him, poking him, and generally pushing him around. Did Charley, goaded beyond patience, pause or turn to complain, Mungo, pretending great surprise, would demand, "What?, *What?*"—and, be-fore Charley could formulate his protest, he would swiftly thrust stiff thick fingers into Charley's side or stomach and dart away to a distance, whence he would loudly and abusively call attention to work he desired done, and which Charley would certainly have done anyway in the natural course of things.

Charley lived on the second floor of an old and unpicturesque building a few blocks from the warehouse. On the first floor lived two old women who dressed in black, who had no English and went often to church. On the top floor lived an Asian man about whom Charley knew nothing. That is he knew nothing until one evening when, returning from work and full of muscular aches and pains and resentments, he saw this man trying to fit a card into the frame of the name plate over the man's doorbell in the downstairs entrance.

The frame was bent, the card resisted, Charley pulled out a rather long knife and jimmied the ancient and warped piece of metal, the card slipped in. And the Asian man said, "Thank you, so."

"Oh, that's all right," and Charley looked to see what the name might be. But the card said only BOOK STORE. "Funny place for a store," Charley said. "But maybe you expect to do most of your business by mail, I guess."

"No, oh," the Asian man said. And with a slight bow, a slight smile and a slight gesture, he urged Charley to precede him up the stairs in the dark and smelly hall. About halfway up the first flight, the Asian man said, "I extend you to enjoy a cup of tea and a tobacco cigarette whilst in my so newly opened sales place."

"Why, sure," said Charley, instantly. "Why, thank you very much." Social invitations came seldom to him and, to tell the truth, he was rather ugly, slow and stupid—facts that were often pointed out by Mungo. He now asked, "Are you Chinese or Japanese?"

"No," said his neighbor. And he said nothing else until they were on the top floor, when, after unlocking the door and slipping in his hand to flip on the light switch, he gestured to his downstairs co-resident to enter, with the word "Do."

It was certainly unlike any of the bookstores to which Charley was accustomed . . . in that he was accustomed to them at all. Instead of open shelves, there were cabinets against the walls, and there were a number of wooden chests as well. Mr. Book Store did not blow upon embers to make the tea, he poured it already sweetened, from a Thermos bottle into a plastic cup, and the cigarette was a regular American cigarette. When tea and tobacco had been consumed, he began to open the chests and the cabinets. First he took out a very, very tiny book in a very, very strange looking language. "I never saw paper like that before," Charley said.

"It is factually palm leaf. A Bhuddist litany. Soot is employed, instead of ink, in marking the text. Is it not precious?"

Charley nodded and politely asked, "How much does it cost?"

The bookman examined an odd-looking tag. "The price of it," he said, "is a bar of silver the weight of a new-born child." He removed it gently from Charley's hand, replaced it in the pigeon-hole in the cabinet, closed the cabinet, lifted the carven lid of an aromatic chest and took out something larger, much larger, and wrapped in cloth of tissue of gold. "Edition of great illustrated work on the breeding of elephants in captivity, on yellow paper smoored with alum in wavy pattern; most rare; agreed?"

For one thing, Charley hardly felt in a position to disagree and for another, he was greatly surprised and titillated by the next illustration. "Hey, look at what that one is *doing!*" he exclaimed.

The bookman looked. A faint, indulgent smile creased his ivory face. "Droll," he commented. He moved to take it back.

"How much does *this* one cost?"

The dealer scrutinized the tag. "The price of this one," he said, "is set down as 'A pair of white parrots, an embroidered robe of purple, sixty-seven

~~fine inlaid vessels of beaten gold, one hundred platters of silver filigree work~~
and ten catties of cardamoms.' " He removed the book, rewrapped it and restored it to its place in the chest.

"Did you bring them all from your own country, then?"

"All," said the Asian man, nodding. "Treasures of my ancestors, broughten
across the ice-fraught Himalayan passes upon the backs of yaks. Perilous journey." He gestured. "All which remains, tangibly, of ancient familial culture."

Charley made a sympathetic squint and said, "Say, that's too bad. Say! *I*
remember now! In the newspapers! Tibetan refugees—you must of fled from
the approaching Chinese Communists!"

The bookman shook his head. "Factually, not. Non-Tibetan. Flight was
from approaching forces of rapacious Dhu thA Hmy'egh, wicked and dissident
vassal of the king of Bhutan. As way to Bhutan proper was not available, escape
was into India." He considered, withdrew another item from another chest.

"Well, you speak very good English."

"Instructed in tutorial fashion by late the Oliver Blunt-Piggot, disgarbed
shaman of a Christian fane in Poona." He lifted the heavy board cover of a
very heavy volume.

"When was this?"

"Ago." He set down the cover, slowly turned the huge, thick pages. "Perceive, barbarians in native costume, bringing tribute." Charley had definite
ideas as to what was polite, expected. He might not be able to, could hardly
expect to buy. But it was only decent to act as though he could. Only thus
could he show interest. And so, again, ask he did.

Again, the bookman's pale slim fingers sought the tag. "Ah, mm. The price
of this one is one mummified simurgh enwrapped in six bolts of pale brocade,
an hundred measures of finest musk in boxes of granulated goldwork and a
viper of Persia pickled in Venetian treacle." He replaced the pages, set back the
cover and set to rewrapping.

Charley, after some thought, asked if all the books had prices like that.
"Akk, yes. All these books have such prices, which are the carefully calculated
evaluations established by my ancestors in the High Vale of Lhom-bhya—
formerly the Crossroads of the World, before the earthquake buried most of
the passes, thus diverting trade to Lhasa, Samarkand and such places. So."

A question that had gradually been taking the shape of a wrinkle now
found verbal expression. "But couldn't you just sell them for *money*?"

The bookman touched the tip of his nose with the tip of his middle finger.
"For money? Let me have thought.... Ah! Here is *The Book of Macaws,
Egrets and Francolins,* in the Five Colors, for only eighty-three gold mohurs
from the mint of Baber Mogul and one silver dirhem of Aaron the Righ-
teous.... You call him Aaron the Righteous? Not. Pardon. Harun al-Rashid.
A bargain."

Charley shook his head. "No, I mean, just ordinary money."

The bookdealer bowed and shook his own head. "Neighboring sir," he
said, "I have not twenty-seven times risked my life nor suffered pangs and
pains innumerable, merely to sell for ordinary money these treasures handed
down from my progenitors, nor ignore their noble standards of value. Oh,

nay." And he restored to its container *The Book of Macaws, Egrets and Francolins. In the Five Colors.*

A certain stubbornness crept over Charley. "Well, then, what is the cheapest one you've got, then?" he demanded.

The scion of the High Vale of Lhom-bhya shrugged, fingered his lower lip, looked here and there, uttered a slight and soft exclamation and took from the last cabinet in the far corner an immense scroll. It had rollers of chalcedony with ivory finials and a case of scented samal-wood lacquered in vermillion and picked with gold; its cord weights were of banded agate.

"This is a mere diversion for the idle moments of a prince. In abridged form, its title reads, *Book of Precious Secrets on How to Make Silver and Gold from Dust, Dung and Bran; Also How to Obtain the Affections; Plus One Hundred and Thirty-Eight Attitudes for Carnal Conjuction and Sixty Recipes for Substances Guaranteed to Maintain the Stance as Well as Tasting Good: by a Sage.*" He opened the scroll and slowly began to unwind it over the length of the table.

The pictures were of the most exquisitely detailed workmanship and brilliant of color on which crushed gold quartz had been sprinkled while the glorious pigments were as yet still wet. Charley's heart gave a great bound, then sank. "No, I said the *cheapest* one—"

His host stifled a very slight yawn. "This is the cheapest," he said, indifferent, almost. "What is cheaper than lust or of less value than alchemy or aphrodisiacs? The price . . . the price," he said, examining the tag, which was of ebony inlaid with jasper. "The price is the crushed head of a sandal merchant of Babylon, with a red, red rose between his teeth: a trifle. The precise utility of that escapes me, but it is of no matter. My only task is to obtain the price as established—that and, of course, to act as your host until the stars turn pale."

Charley rose. "I guess I'll be going, anyway," he said. "I certainly want to thank you for showing me all this. Maybe I'll be back tomorrow for something, if they haven't all been sold by then." His heart knew what his heart desired, his head knew the impossibility of any of it, but his lips at least maintained a proper politeness even at the last.

He went down the stairs, his mind filled with odd thoughts, half enjoyable, half despairing. Heavy footsteps sounded coming up; who was it but Mungo. "I thought you said you lived on the *second* floor," he said. "No use lying to *me*; come on, dumbell, I need you. Earn your goddamn money for a change. My funking car's got a flat; *move* it, I tell you, spithead; when I say move it, you *move* it!" And he jabbed his thick, stiff fingers into Charley's kidneys and, ignoring his employee's cry of pain, half guided, half goaded him along the empty block lined with closed warehouses where, indeed, an automobile stood, somewhat sagging to one side.

"Get the goddamn jack up; what're you dreaming about? Quit stumbling over your goddamn feet, for cry-sake; you think I got nothing better to do? You think I do nothing but sell greasy stoves to greaseballs? *Move* it, nipplehead! I want you to know that I also own the biggest goddamn shoe store in Babylon, Long Island. Pick up that tire iron!"

Crazy Old Lady

INTRODUCTION BY ETHAN DAVIDSON

When I was fourteen, I lived with my father, Avram Davidson, in the town of Richmond, California. I picked up his copy of Ellery Queen, *and read the Edgar-nominated story "Crazy Old Lady." As was often the case when I read his stories, I didn't quite understand the ending, so he explained it to me.*

At that time, Richmond was a boring, lower-middle-class suburb. Avram shared a house with a blind man.

Avram liked to move every few months, and I became accustomed to living with all sorts of people. Most of these people had something unusual about them. In this case, it was a physical disability. Others had psychological problems. One was even a crazy old lady. Even when he lived alone, he sometimes brought in homeless derelicts or confused young people. Avram was sometimes irritable. But he often also displayed quite a bit of compassion.

Eighteen years have passed. The number of people who are poor, elderly, and live in bad neighborhoods has increased tremendously. Richmond today is a violent, crime-infested slum town. Toward the end of his life, Avram found himself living in another slum. This one was in Bremerton, Washington. He was robbed in his home by two men who must have seen him as eccentric and very vulnerable, much like the woman in this story.

The story provides no real answers. It does provide a vivid and insightful description of the problem. This, it seems to me, can only help. As Avram might have said, "Could it hoyt?"

CRAZY OLD LADY

BEFORE SHE BECAME THE Crazy Old Lady she had been merely the Old Lady and before that Old Lady Nelson and before that (long long before that) she had been Mrs. Nelson. At one time there had also been a Mr. Nelson, but all that was left of him were the war souvenirs lined up on the cluttered mantelpiece which was never dusted now—the model battleship, the enemy helmet, the enemy grenade, the enemy knife, and some odd bits and pieces that had been enemy badges and buttons.

The enemy had seemed a lot farther away in those days.

But the shopping had been a lot closer.

Of course it was still the same in miles—well, blocks, really—it just seemed like miles now. It had been such a nice walk, such a few blocks' walk, under the pleasant old trees, past the pleasant old family homes, and down to the pleasant old family stores. Now not much was left of the way it had been.

For one thing, the trees had not had sense enough to adjust to changing times. Their branches had interfered with the electric power lines and their roots had interfered with the sewer lines and their trunks had interfered with the sidewalks.

So most of the old trees had been cut down.

That was quite a shock and no one had prepared the Old Lady for it. One day the old trees had been there as always and then the next day there were only stumps and branches, bruised twigs and leaves and sawdust. And the next day not even that.

A lot of the old family homes had been, so to speak, cut down too, and most of those that had not been cut down had been cut up and converted into multiple dwelling units. It is odd that somehow families do not seem to feel the same about dwelling units as they do about homes.

And as for the pleasant old family stores, what had happened to them? Mr. Berman said, "There's hardly anything I sell today that they don't sell for less in the supermarket, Mrs. Nelson. The kids don't come in the way they used to with a note from their parents, they just come in to steal. I used to think my boy would take over when I'm gone but he came back from Vietnam in a box, so what's the use of talking."

Where there had been a lot of storefronts with either changing displays, which were interesting, or the same familiar old displays, which were comforting, now the storefronts were all boarded over.

The supermarket was where there hadn't been a supermarket—strange that it wasn't built where all the boarded-up stores were; strange that the pleasant old empty lot with its wild flowers had to give way to the supermarket, and now the children played in the street instead.

But that was the way it was. Prices may have been cheaper in the supermarket in the long run, but the prices had to be paid in cash and there were no deliveries, no monthly bills, no friendly delivery boy who thanked you for a fresh-baked cookie.

Often after Mr. Nelson passed away, the delivery boy—or was it his brother?—would mow the small lawn for a quarter. Now no one would mow the small lawn for a quarter or even for two quarters. No boys were interested in collecting empty bottles for the deposits, the way they used to be. Strange, if they were poor, why they would prefer to smash the bottles on the sidewalk and against the lampposts. The yard was a thicket now and not even a clean thicket.

"What is the world coming to?" the Old Lady used to ask.

By and by she stopped asking and started screeching. "Don't think I don't see you there!" she would screech. That was around the time they started calling her the Crazy Old Lady. She said the bigger boys had thrown rocks at her and the bigger boys denied this and the police said they could do nothing.

It wasn't the police who laughed when she took to wearing the military helmet whenever she did her shopping. She had to go out to do her shopping because it was a thing of the past to phone the store and say, "Now before I even ask about Esther and the new baby, don't let me forget the quarter pound of sweet butter for my pastry crust." Sometimes she would forget and call the old number which now belonged to some other people and after a while they weren't nice about it, not nice at all.

There were, of course, still some other old ladies and old gentlemen around in the old neighborhood, although she didn't at first think of them as old. "Now my Grandmother Delehanty, she was old and she had seen the soldiers marching off to remember the Maine and she never forgot anyone's birthday to the last day she lived, but I don't suppose you would remember her."

"Listen to the Crazy Old Lady talking to herself," some girls would say very loud and not nicely at all.

"There, never mind, Mrs. Nelson, pay no attention and we'll pretend we didn't notice, shhh," Mrs. Swift would say, hobbling up.

"Why, Mrs. Swift. Your arm! Your poor arm. What happened?"

"Let's just walk along together and I'll tell you when they aren't listening."

Mrs. Swift, what a fine-looking woman she had been in her time! Why would anyone want to knock her down so badly that she broke her arm?

"My grocery money was in my purse. I don't know what to do. I can't afford to live anywhere else."

"Oh dear, oh dear."

CRAZY OLD LADY | 305

It just went to prove how necessary it was to wear the war helmet. If Mr. Schultz had been wearing one, would they have been able to fracture his skull?

They who?

"Why don't you catch them? What are the police for?"

The policemen said that the descriptions would fit half of the hoodlums in the neighborhood. "More than half," they said. The policemen said that about the one who killed Mr. Schultz. The policemen said that about the ones who had just grabbed her and pulled the war helmet off her head and then shoved her and had hardly bothered to run away very fast, just half looking back and half laughing. "You got off lucky," the policeman said to her. "Don't go out at night if you can help it."

"It was broad daylight!" she screeched.

And then someone threw a rock through her window. No, it wasn't a rock, it was the war helmet, her husband's souvenir from the mantelpiece. How hard they must have worked to dent it and bash it and cave it in so that no one could wear it now. And what was she to do about protection now when she had to go out for the quarter pound of bacon and the box of oatmeal and the three eggs? Where were the police?

"Sorry, lady, sorry," the policemen said. "You can't carry no knife this size. It's against the law." The knife was her husband's war souvenir of the enemy, but the police took it away from her anyway.

She wanted to tell Mrs. Swift—what a fine-looking woman she was in her time—and she called out, "Oh, Mrs. Swift," but her voice didn't carry. No one heard her over the street noises and the noises of all the radios and record players from every window and all the television sets on full blast. How fast the man was running when he grabbed Mrs. Swift's purse as though he had practised and practised, and he knocked her down as before and kicked her as she started to get up and then he ran away laughing and laughing with the purse held high up, shielding his face.

What could she do then? No helmet. No knife. And she had to go out shopping. She couldn't carry much at one time. She looked for the old coat with the inside pocket so she could keep the money in that, but somehow she couldn't find it and so she had to carry a purse after all.

Carrying the purse with the few dollars in it when the man came running up. She could hear him running and she started screeching when he grabbed her purse, just as she knew he would some day, and he tugged hard and the string broke. The Crazy Old Lady, had she thought tying something with a string to her scrawny old arm would help?

Then something fell to the sidewalk and jangled, a metal ring or pin, and he ran off laughing and faster than she could ever run, the purse held high to shield his face from passers-by as the Crazy Old Lady screeched after him. And he must have got almost half a block away when the enemy grenade went off.

It was well known, of course, that she was crazy, and really they take good care of her where she is, and anyway she can do her little bit of shopping in the canteen, as they call it, and nobody bothers her now at all.

"Hark! Was That the Squeal of an Angry Thoat?"
INTRODUCTION BY MIKE RESNICK

Avram Davidson was a wise, humorous, gentle, and knowing man. I would have thought (and still believe) that if he were to start counting his friends he'd run snack-dab into Eternity before he finished. So to find that I was on a list of "special friends" was not only a surprise, but more of an honor than I think you can imagine.

My very last conversation with Avram was the day I bought the reprint rights to the following story for an anthology I was editing (Inside the Funhouse if you can find it, and I'll lay plenty of eight-to-five that you can't).

"Hark! Was That the Squeal of an Angry Thoat?" is relatively minor Davidson, if such a thing can be said to exist. Yet if you take a good hard look at it, it is absolutely stunning in its complexity, not unlike Avram himself.

The use of language is unique. It might drive an unimaginative high school English teacher straight up a wall, but Avram, like the immortal Walt Kelly before him, refused to be hemmed in by standard sentences and punctuation. Check the end of the very first paragraph; you'll see what I mean. More to the point, you'll see, quite clearly, what Avram means.

Then there are the in-jokes. Calvin M. Knox was a pseudonym of the youthful Robert Silverberg—and Wendell Garrett is a very thinly disguised version of science fiction writer and bon vivant Randall Garrett, Silverberg's sometime collaborator in the early days of his career.

In fact, the entire cast of mildly warped characters acting in concert for no particularly valid reason is reminiscent of many of the conceits of R. A. Lafferty, though with Avram's unique backspin on the notion.

I could go on and on, but why bother? Avram does it so much better.

Enjoy.

"HARK! WAS THAT THE SQUEAL OF AN ANGRY THOAT?"

A T A TIME SUBSEQUENTLY I was still living back East, we were so many of us then Living Back East, and I was still living on the seventh floor of a seven-floor walk-up in Greenwich Village. Edward lived down the hall: Fox-fire Edward. Fiduciary Debenture III lived downstairs. Gabriel Courland lived around the corner in the hay-loft of the Old De Witt Clinton Livery Stable, a location ideally suited and situate—he said—to pour boiling oil down upon unwelcome visitors: bill collectors, indignant fathers of daughters, people with Great Ideas For Stories ("All you got to do is write it down and we'll split the money, I'd do it myself if I had the time."), editors with deadlines, men come to turn off the electricity (the gas) (the water) (the whale-oil)—

"Doesn't it *smell* a little in here, Gabe?" asked Edward.

"It smells a *lot*—but look! Look!" Here he'd point to the neat trap-door through which hay had once been hauled (and maybe smuggled bombazine and who knows what, poled up Minetta Stream, midnights so long long ago). "You can pour boiling *oil* down on people!"

Edward gives me to understand that Gabe never actually *did* pour boiling oil or even *un*boiling oil, down on people; although occasionally, Edward said, G. would allow trickles of water to defoliate the importunate, as who? put it. Someone else.

Fiduciary Debenture III lived downstairs, and across the narrow street dwelt Wendell Garrett, in the parlor of a once-huge apartment deftly cut up and furnished by his Great-aunt Ella, relict of his Great-uncle Pat Garrett, yes! The very same Sheriff Pat Garrett Who; Aunt Ella was in the Canary Islands at the time, teaching (I understand) the two-step to the wives of the Spanish officials, to whom, in that not-exactly-then-in-the-beating-heart-of-things archipelago, it—the two-step—represented Modern Culture, if not Flaming Youth in Revolt, and one of the few (very few) occupations or occasions for which their husbands would let them out of the patio.

"The Moors may have been driven out of Spain," Aunt Ella had said, or, rather, written; "but they haven't been driven out of the Spaniards. For God's sake, Wendell, see to it that Mary Teresa empties the pan under the ice-box."

Mary Teresa was the, so to speak, concièrge, and refused to allow an electric, gas, or even kerosene fridge to be installed in her own kitchen: slightly larger than a commemorative stamp. This devotion to tradition was much appreciated by the sole remaining Iceman in The Village, whose clientèle by that time consisted of several fish markets and a dozen or so other ladies of the same age and model as Mary Teresa; the Iceman was related by ties of spiritual consanguinity to all the prominent mafiosi—a godfather to godfathers, so to speak—and this in turn enabled her to do as she liked and had been accustomed to do, in a manner which would be tolerated in no one else, nowhere else.

Wendell lived rent-free in the former parlor of the house in return for his acting as an Influence upon Mary Teresa and curbing in some few important particulars her turn-of-the-century vigor.

When asked where he lived, he would say, bland as butter, "In a parlor house."

Round the corner in a decayed Federalist Row located behind an equally decayed non-Federalist row (Whig, perhaps, or, as Wendell once suggested, brushing himself, Free Soil), lived the retired Australian sanitary scientist and engineer called Humpty Dumpty. He had indeed once had a lot of cards printed:

Sir Humphrey Dunston
Remittance Man
Privies Done Cheap Retail and to the Trade

But, he had observed, these last phrases had been subject to most gross interpretations by members of one of the Village's non-ethnic minorities; so the only card still in evidence was tacked to his greasy front door. Humpty patronized the Ice-man, too, Sangiaccomo Bartoldi, but not for ice: Jockum retained the antique art of needling beer, an alchemy otherwise fallen into desuetude since the repeal of the 18th (or Noble Experiment) Amendment, and which—Humpty Dumpty said—alone could raise American lager to the kick of its Australian counterpart ("Bandicoot's Ballocks," or something like that).

If you stood on what had once been the Widow's Walk atop the only one of the Federalists which still had one, you could toss a rubber ball through the back window of the Death House and into the Muniments Room of Calvin M. Knox. This great granite sarcophagus of a building had once, it was said, carried across the front of it the advice that THE WAGES OF SIN IS DEATH: but only the last of those words remained. Mary Teresa, that repository of local arcane information, sometimes claimed that "The Patriot Boys" had torn off the others to hurl them at the Invalid Corps of the Union Army during what she termed "the Rebellion"—not, indeed, the entire Civil War, but that part of it fought thereabouts and called by others The Draft Riots. Not, of course, by Mary Teresa.

Nor, in fact, did she ever use the name Invalid Corps of the Union Army. She called them "the Prodissint Bastids."

"I understand that this used to be a House for Fallen Women," Fiduciary Debenture III had once said to Calvin Knox.

"Yes," said C. Knox, gloomily, "and if you're not careful, you're going to fall through the very same place in the floor, too. It quivers when my cat walks across it." It was in consequence of this statutory infirmity of part of the front floor that the back chamber was called the Muniments Room and was heaped high with pulp magazines in neat piles, each bearing some such style and label as (it might be) *Influences of Ned Buntline on Doc Savage,* or *Foreshadowings of Doc Savage in Ned Buntline,* or *Seabury Quinn Type Stories Not Written By Seabury Quinn,* and *J. Sheridan Le Fanu Plot Structures Exemplified in Spicy Detective Stories.*

And, as Mary Teresa so often put it, ecKt, ecKt, ecKt.

"I have reduced," C. Knox said, entirely without boastfulness, "the Basic Short Story to its essential salts."

The last, the very very last of the Hokey Pokey Women practiced in the basement. Edward often patronized her.

Wendell at that time was devoting less time to writing fiction than to his great project of reconciling the Indo-European Exarchate with the Dravidian Rite of the Sanscrit Church (Lapsed Branch) in Exile. Bengali archimandrites in cruciform dhoties and deaconesses in the Proscribed Saffron Sari fluttered round about his doors like exotic butterflies—*could* chrismation be administered in ghee?—*was* the bed of nails a legitimate form of penance?—their collective presence a great perturbation to Mary Teresa, who referred to the entire *kehilla* as Them Gypsies. The only thing which indeed prevented her taking her broom to the lot of them was that a genuine Monsignor of the True Church as recognized by the Police Department had chanced by: whereat the whole ecclesia had knelt as one and collectively kissed his brogans.

"Ah well, nobody is all bad," was her philosophic comment, as she resheathed her besom and, clearing her nasal passages, skillfully swamped a fly in the gutter.

It was to this picturesque scene, as yet unstirred by Beat, Hippy, Freak, Funk, RadLib or LibRad influences (and, indeed, only still faintly tinctured by the froth of the waves which once had beaten ceaselessly upon the Seacoasts of Bohemia) that there came one day clad only in his harness and his sword that strange brave man known, very simply, as John Carter of Mars.

Some few of the readership may have figured out, all by themselves, that Fiduciary Debenture III (who lived downstairs) was not *really* named Fiduciary Debenture III. His *real* name was in fact A. Cicero Guggenhimer, Jr. He was not related to the *the* Guggenhimers. In fact I do not know, even, if there are, or were, any *the* Guggenhimers. The people who peddled lace, smolt copper, leisurely migrated between the State of Colorado, the US Senate, and the Venetian Litoral, now and then pausing to found an art museum or transport a monastary to a choicer location, are *Guggenheims.* With *ei.* Without *er.* However, A. Cicero's grandmother was the last surviving granddaughter of old John Jacob You-Know-*Who,* and she had left A.C. her half of Manhattan Island, plus the bed of the East River, which Yon Yockoob had bought cheap in between grifting furs from the Redskins and whisking from the Knickerbockers (who had guffawed in Hudson Dutch when thinking how *they* were taking

~~*him* in) those hay meadows and swamp-lots on which now stands *the* most~~
valuable real estatery in the world.

Bar none.

Hence the A.

As for the Cicero, he always claimed his grandmother got it out of a dream-
book.

It may not be generally known that every, but I spit you not, *every* commercial vessel which plies or "stands" up and down the East River pays through
the hawse-hole for the privilege: because if not, trolls will come up and *eat*
them. Naturally, when you got this kind of money, no matter how tied up in
trusts and annuities and danegeld it may be, estates mean nothing, penthouses
mean nothing, fancy cars and yachts mean nothing: so naturally you come to
live in Greenwich Village, where everything is so, well, Interesting.

People would snort when I told them that Edward and I lived on the
seventh story of a seven-story walk-up: but we did. On the ground floor was
the Dante Alighieri Association, the door of which in those days opened only
wide enough to admit one small man with well-shined shoes at a time: doubtless
to discuss Canto II, or whichever. As to its subsequent career as a coffee-house,
of this I know nothing, I say nothing, I've heard nothing, wild horses would
drag nothing out of me, so don't even ask.

"Seven stories and no *e*levator?" people would exclaim rolling eyes and
clutching chests. "That's *got* to be il*l*egal!'

"It does got," I would agree. "But it didn't used to got.' Furthermore it
was made of cast-iron and not wood, and was not mouldering at all: it was
indeed a tenement house, probably one of the last of the Old Law or the first
of the New Law tenements, but it was a tenement house in good condition, I
should only be in half such good condition at the same age. I was younger in
them days and had more than my memories, and thought nothing of charging
up or down the full seven story mountain, heigh ho. Maurice with his Biblical
beard used to pass by with his arms full of publications from the four or five
quarters of the earth, the sales of which, such as they were, sustained him in
scraps of food and the rent on the dozens if not scores of public coin lockers
in which he stored the paper memorabilia of decades:

Eheu, Maurice, Maurice! Where are you now?

You were ahead of your time, as well as the wrong age and appearance,
these were your only faults: had you lived today, had you been younger, were
your beard not white nor your locks long, had you the proper academical
affiliations an academician of the academicians (they should plotz), or a friend
or a protegé of a bevy of academicians and critticks see how fast the Guggen-
futzes (they should plotz) would bestow upon you Foundlingship after Foundlingship, weevils should only eat their navels: may you, o contrare, O Rare
Maurice, flourish in eternal life.

Amidst the Crash of Matter.

And the Wrack of Worlds.

G. (for Gabriel) Courland . . . the Moriarity Expert? The same. Whom
else? G. Courland was then much exercised (if that is not too vigorous a word)

in the matter of his trousers, yea cuffs? nea cuffs? He wanted no cuffs, his tailors want cuffs. "But they *trip* when you run fast," he would explain. This cut neither ice nor worsted with Morris, Max, and Rocco. "So don't *run* fast," they said.

All very well for *them:* staid old cockers with their wild, wild youths be-hind them. Gabriel G. was at that time running (there! that *verb* again!) a sort of Consolation Service. For listless wives. And the energy displayed by (now and then, though only now and then) some of them husbands on learning All, would, if devoted on behalf of their wives, have left them (the wives) quite listful. And McCourland *ohn* a Consolation Service.

In Bleecker Street the Open Air Market how it flourished! Greens galore. Greens (as Butch Gyrene he put it) up the ass. Flowers in bloom, too. Nearbye, the old-established markets, all the names ending in vowels. Wendell Garrett, scarlet vest well-filled, cap of maintenance on his audacious head, would stroll in and out, tweaking the poultry. "Have you any," this he would ask of the Sons of Sicily and the Abruzzi, you or me they would *kill:* "Have you any *guinea* fowl?"

Dandelion greens, fresh-made latticini, lovely reeky old pastafazool, no, had some other name, *cheese*, hm, mm, ah! Provalon'! *Smekk* Mussels in icy pools with water always a drip-drip-drip-a-drip, pizza—you let the word pass you by without your lips trembling, your nostrils pirouetting and corvetting, your salivary glands drooling and your eyes rolling? You must be dead, *dead....*

Or else, for your sins and your bad karma, you have known nothing but *Protestant* pizza, may God help you. *Not* baked in a stone oven according to the Rules of the Council of Trent. *Not* with the filling so firmly bonded to the crust—and the crust brown and crisp and bubbly round the rim, Marón!, that wild horses could not part filling from crust: *No!* What do you know of pizza, you with your heritage of Drive-ins, and McDonald's, and the Methodist Church, pizza, you think *that* is pizza, that franchised flop, comes frozen, is thawed, is redone in an ordinary metal quick-a-buck oven, with the cheese from Baptist cows, the tomatoes by Mary Worth, the filling rolling back from off the crust limper than a deacon's dick: *this* you call *pizza?*

Marón.

As for the fruit bread for the Feast of St. Joseph—

"Whats a matta you no shame?" screamed Philomena Rappini, of the Fresh Home-Made Sausage Today Market. "Put a some clothes on! You some kine comuniss? Marón, I no look!" But between her fingers, plump and be-ringed, ahaah, oh ho: she *did* look! And why not? So there he was, dark and well-thewed and imperially slim.

(Well-hung, too.)

"Your pardon, Matron, and a daughter to a Jeddak of Jeddaks I perceive you must be by your grace and slender high-arched feet: may I place my sword in pawn? A message to Ed Burroughs? Magnetic telegraph message to muh nevvew Ed Burroughs? Jest tell him it's Uncle John. John Cyarter.

"Of Mars."

As to how he had gotten here, *here,* I mean *there,* in The Village, across the countless leagues and aeons and ions of interstellar freezing space, who knows? Who knows, in fact, what song the sirens sang? Who gives a shit?

When one tired of the coffee-house scene in The Village, there was always The Museum. And by "The Museum" neither I nor any denizen of the Old Village Scene as it then obtained meant one of the sundry establishments displaying genuine old art or artifacts or modern exempla of the Dribble, Splotch, Drool, or Ejaculate, School(s): no. We meant *The* Museum, there on Great Jones Street, *Bar*num's Museum. A mere shadow of itself, you say? May be. May have *been.* Old William Phineas, Jr. himself was then alive, great-nephew to the Yankee Showman himself. Billy Finn. The most recently painted sign was the one reading: *Veterans of the World War, One-Half Price*—and to this had been added by pen a new *s* after *War,* plus the words, in between lines, *And of the Korean Conflict.* These letters had a pronounced wobble, so indicative of the State of the Nation as well as of old Bill Barnum's hand not being quite so firm as it once was. Inside? Jumbo's hay-rack. A corset belonging to one of the Dolly Sisters. Anna Held's bath-tub plus one of her milk bills for same. Genuine rhinestone replica of the famed Bicycle Set which Diamond Jim had given Lillian Russell. William Jennings Bryan's hat. Calvin *Cooli*dge's hat. Old Cool Cal. The oldest wombat in the world, right this way, folks.

And so on.

Across the street the incredible wooden Scotchman, no mere Indian being good enough, was the emblematic figure in front of the establishment of MENDEL MOSSMAN, SNUFF AND SEGARS, *also Plug, Cut-Plug, Apple Twist and Pigtail Twist.* Also (though not openly designated as such, of course), behind the third mahogany door with opaque crystal glass window from the left, an entrance to a station of the Secret Subway System.

Officially, no, it was not officially *called* the Secret Subway System; officially it was called Wall Street, Pine Street, Bowling Green and Boulevard Line. The Boulevard, ask any old-timer in them days, was *upper* Broadway. Ask any one or more old-timer as to at what point "upper" Broadway begins: watch them flail at each other with their walking-sticks and ear-trumpets.

There is a Secret Station in the State Bank Notes Registry Room of the old Counting House (Where no state bank notes have been registered since about 1883, owing to a confiscatory Federal Tax on the process).

There is a Secret Station in the marble men's room of the *original* Yale Club.

There is one beneath Trinity Church and one behind the North River Office of the State Canal Authority and one next to the Proving Room (Muskets) of the Mercantile Zouaves and Armory.

There are a few others. Find out for yourself . . . if you can.

The fare is and has been and always will be, one silver dollar each way. *Or.* For a six-day ticket good for round trips, one half-eagle (a five-dollar gold piece, to the ignorant).

The ticket agents are the color of those fungi which grow in the basements of old wood-and-stone houses on Benefit Street in Providence, Rhode Island

and Providence Plantations. It is intimated that these agents once held offices of responsibility above grounds, but Blotted Their Copy Books.

One of them is named Crater.

Crater, if you just think about it a moment, is very much like Carter.

La Belle Belinda lived upstairs over Mossman's, which she insisted had the loveliest smell in the world.

And there are those who say that this distinction belonged to The Fair Belinda herself.

The Sodality of the Decent Dress (a branch of the Legion of Utmost Purity) had just let out into the street after its monthly meeting at Our Lady of Leghorn, and was threatening to cut up rough with John Carter: just then Gabriel C., Wendell G., Edward and myself chanced by; we caught his arcane references at once—although, of course, we did not believe a word of them, still, it was a madness which we not only recognized but respected—and, under pretense of assisting the man to send his message, we spirited him away; after having first clothed his virility under Wendell's naval cloak.

We told the man that it had belonged to the Commanding Officer of the Confederate Ram *Pamunkey*. A faint mist of tears rose in his sparkling eyes, and his protests died away on his lips. His finely-chiseled lips.

"They're after me, boys, you know," he said, simply. "But they mustn't find me. Not until I've obtained a replacement for the wore-out part of the oxygen machine. All Mars depends on that, you know."

Exchanging significant glances, we assured him that we did indeed know.

We further assured him that we would with despatch arrange for sleeping silks and furs; meanwhile he consented to doss down for a much-needed nap on Gabriel's Murphy bed (for once, not occupied by a listing wife). Edward agreed to stand by. Just In Case.

There we left him, his strong chest rhythmically rising and falling, and stepped down to the courtyard, where we exchanged a few more significant glances, also shaking our lips and pursing our heads. We were thus occupied when Mary Teresa passed by, holding Kevin Mathew Aloysius, her great-grand-nephew, in a grip which would have baffled Houdini.

"Stop tellin them lies," she was adjuring him, "or yez'll burn in Hell witt the Prodissint Bastidds."

"No I won't either, because I'm still below the age of reason, nyaa, and anyway, I did *too* seen it, Aunty Mary T'resa, it was all tall as the second-floor window and it looked in at me but I made the sign of the cross, I blessed myself, so it went away," said Kevin Mathew Aloysius, rubbing some more snot on his sleeve.

Wendell, august and benevolent, asked, "What was it that you saw, my man?"

Kevin Mathew Aloysius looked at him, his eyes the same color as the stuff bubbling from his nostrils. "A mawnster," he said. "A real mawnster, cross my heart and hope to die. It was green, Mr. Garrett. And it had four arms. And tux growing out of its mouth."

Did some faint echo, some dim adumbration or vibration of this reach the sleeping man? Edward said some had. Edward said that the sleeping man stirred, half-roused himself, flung out an arm, and, before falling back into deep slumber, cried out:

"Hark! Was that the squeal of an angry thoat? Or the sound of a hunting banth in the hills? *Slave! My harness—and my sword!*"

Manatee Gal, Won't You Come Out Tonight
INTRODUCTION BY PETER S. BEAGLE

When I began corresponding with Avram, he was living in Belize, still British Honduras in those days. I mention this because Belize—under the alias of "British Hidalgo"—is not merely the setting for Avram's stories about Jack Limekiller, but is in fact the real protagonist of these tales. We never learn much more about Limekiller than that he is Canadian, pushing thirty: an amiable, adaptable man who, longing for adventure and a new life in tropical waters, sold his car, bought a small sailboat, and now lives aboard it, mostly in the Port Cockatoo harbor, in company with his first mate—a tailless, off-white cat. He seems a pleasant sort, and can play a bit of banjo.

But British Hidalgo we know; or at least Avram persuades us that we do. Long before "Manatee Gal, Won't You Come Out Tonight" has rambled peaceably to its terrifying conclusion, we have come to believe in our own long acquaintance with the steamy, fly-ridden beauty of land and water, of the parrot-bright sky, the patient bush always waiting to take over, and the seductive imminence of what Avram calls its "timeless tropical forever." It's an ingratiating place, British Hidalgo, and a sleepily dangerous one.

I've never known a writer who so clearly understood the relationship between the rhythms and usages of a language or a dialect and the daily rhythms of its speakers' lives. In the same placidly deliberate way that the inhabitants of British Hidalgo move through their days and tell their stories, so "Manatee Gal" at first seems to be meandering around all manner of irrelevant switchbacks and detours. Only in Avram's own sweet, sinister while do we come— far too late for our comfort—to the realization that those were not digressions at all, but coils. . . .

THE CUPID CLUB WAS the only waterhole on the Port Cockatoo waterfront. To be sure, there were two or three liquor booths back in the part where the tiny town ebbed away into the bush. But they were closed for siesta, certainly. And they sold nothing but watered rum and warm soft-drinks and loose cigarettes. Also, they were away from the breezes off the Bay which kept away the flies. In British Hidalgo gnats were flies, mosquitoes were flies, sandflies—worst of all—were flies—*flies* were also flies: and if anyone were inclined to question this nomenclature, there was the unquestionable fact that mosquito itself was merely Spanish for little fly.

It was not really cool in the Cupid Club (Alfonso Key, prop., LICENSED TO SELL WINE, SPIRITS, BEER, ALE, CYDER AND PERRY). But it was certainly less hot than outside. Outside the sun burned the Bay, turning it into molten sparkles. Limekiller's boat stood at mooring, by very slightly raising his head he could see her, and every so often he did raise it. There wasn't much aboard to tempt thieves, and there weren't many thieves in Port Cockatoo, anyway. On the other hand, what was aboard the *Sacarissa* he could not very well spare; and it only took one thief, after all. So every now and then he did raise his head and make sure that no small boat was out by his own. No skiff or dory.

Probably the only thief in town was taking his own siesta.

"Nutmeg P'int," said Alfonso Key. "You been to Nutmeg P'int?"

"Been there."

Every place needs another place to make light fun of. In King Town, the old colonial capital, it was Port Cockatoo. Limekiller wondered what it was they made fun of, down at Nutmeg Point.

"What brings it into your mind, Alfonso?" he asked, taking his eyes from the boat. All clear. Briefly he met his own face in the mirror. Wasn't much of a face, in his own opinion. Someone had once called him "Young Count Tolstoy." Wasn't much point in shaving, anyway.

Key shrugged. "Sometimes somebody goes down there, goes up the river, along the old bush trails, buys carn. About now, you know, mon, carn bring good price, up in King Town."

Limekiller knew that. He often did think about that. He could quote the prices Brad Welcome paid for corn: white corn, yellow corn, cracked and ground. "I know," he said. "In King Town they have a lot of money and only a little corn. Along Nutmeg River they have a lot of corn and only a little money. Someone who brings down money from the Town can buy corn along the Nutmeg. Too bad I didn't think of that before I left."

Key allowed himself a small sigh. He knew that it wasn't any lack of thought, and that Limekiller had had no money before he left, or, likely, he wouldn't have left. "May-be they trust you down along the Nutmeg. They trust old Bob Blaine. Year after year he go up the Nutmeg, he go up and down the bush trail, he buy carn on credit, bring it bock up to King *Town.*"

Off in the shadow at the other end of the barroom someone began to sing, softly.

> *W'ol' Bob Blaine, he done gone.*
> *W'ol' Bob Blaine, he done gone.*
> *Ahl, ahl me money gone—*
> *Gone to Spahnish Hidalgo. . . .*

In King Town, Old Bob Blaine had sold the corn, season after season. Old Bob Blaine had bought salt, he had bought shotgun shells, canned milk, white flour, cotton cloth from the Turkish merchants. Fish hooks, sweet candy, rubber boots, kerosene, lamp *chim*ney. Old Bob Blaine had returned and paid for corn in kind—not, to be sure, immediately after selling the corn. Things did not move that swiftly even today, in British Hidalgo, and certainly had not Back When. Old Bob Blaine returned with the merchandise on his next buying trip. It was more convenient, he did not have to make so many trips up and down the mangrove coast. By and by it must almost have seemed that he was paying in advance, when he came, buying corn down along the Nutmeg River, the boundary between the Colony of British Hidalgo and the country which the Colony still called Spanish Hidalgo, though it had not been Spain's for a century and a half.

"Yes mon," Alfonso Key agreed. "Only, that one last time, he *not* come bock. They say he buy one marine engine yard, down in Republican waters."

"I heard," Limekiller said, "that he bought a garage down there."

The soft voice from the back of the bar said, "No, mon. Twas a coconut walk he bought. Yes, mon."

Jack wondered why people, foreign people, usually, sometimes complained that it was difficult to get information in British Hidalgo. In his experience, information was the easiest thing in the world, there—all the information you wanted. In fact, sometimes you could get more than you wanted. Sometimes, of course, it was contradictory. Sometimes it was outright wrong. But that, of course, was another matter.

"Anybody else ever take up the trade down there?" Even if the information, the answer, if there was an answer, even if it were negative, what difference would it make?

"No," said Key. "No-body. May-be you try, eh, Jock? May-be they trust you."

There was no reason why the small cultivators, slashing their small corn-fields by main force out of the almighty bush and then burning the slash and then planting corn in the ashes, so to speak—maybe they would trust him, even though there was no reason *why* they should trust him. Still. . . . Who knows. . . . They might. They just might. Well. . . . some of them just might. For a moment a brief hope rose in his mind.

"Naaa. . . . I haven't even got any crocus sacks." There wasn't much point in any of it after all. Not if he'd have to tote the corn wrapped up in his shirt. The jute sacks were fifty cents apiece in local currency; they were as good as money, sometimes even better than money.

Key, who had been watching rather unsleepingly as these thoughts were passing through Jack's mind, slowly sank back in his chair. "Ah," he said, very softly. "You haven't got any crocus sack."

"Een de w'ol' days," the voice from the back said, "every good 'oman, she di know which bush yerb good fah wyes, fah kid-ney, which bush yerb good fah heart, which bush yerb good fah fever. But ahl of dem good w'ol' 'omen, new, dey dead, you see. Yes mon. Ahl poss ahway. No-body know bush med-icine nowadays. Only *bush-doc-tor*. And dey very few, sah, very few."

"What you say, Captain Cudgel, you not bush *doc*-tor you w'own self? Nah true, Captain?"

Slowly, almost reluctantly, the old man answered. "Well sah. Me know few teeng. Fah true. Me know few teeng. Not like in w'ol' days. In wo'ol' days, me dive fah conch. Yes mon. Fetch up plan-ty conch. De sahlt wah-tah hort me wyes, take bush-yerb fah cure dem. But nomah. No, mon. Me no dive no mah. Ahl de time, me wyes hort, stay out of strahng sun now. . . . Yes mon. . . ."

Limekiller yawned, politely, behind his hand. To make conversation, he repeated something he had heard. "They say some of the old-time people used to get herbs down at Cape Manatee."

Alfonso Key flashed him a look. The old man said, a different note sud-denly in his voice, different from the melancholy one of a moment before, "Mon-ah-*tee*. Mon-ah-*tee* is hahf-*mon*, you know, sah. Fah true. Yes sah, mon-ah-*tee* is hahf-*mon*. Which reason de lah w'only allow you to tehk one mon-ah-*tee* a year."

Covertly, Jack felt his beer. Sure enough, it was warm. Key said, "Yes, but who even bother nowadays? The leather is so tough you can't even sole a boot with it. And you dasn't bring the meat up to the Central Market in King *Town*, you *know*."

The last thing on Limekiller's mind was to apply for a license to shoot manatee, even if the limit were one a week. "How come?" he asked. "How come you're not?" King Town. King Town was the reason that he was down in Port Cockatoo. There was no money to be made here, now. But there was none to be lost here, either. His creditors were all in King Town, though if they wanted to, they could reach him even down here. But it would hardly be worth anyone's while to fee a lawyer to come down and feed him during the court session. Mainly, though, it was a matter of, Out of sight, somewhat out of mind. And, anyway—who knows? The Micawber Principle was weaker down here than up in the capital. But still and all: something might turn up.

"Because, they say it is because Manatee have teats like a woman."

"One time, you know, one time dere is a mahn who mehk mellow wit ah mon-ah-tee, yes sah. And hahv pickney by mon-ah-tee." It did seem that the old man had begun to say something more, but someone else said, *"Ha-ha-ha!"* And the same someone else next said, in a sharp, all-but-demanding voice, "Shoe *shine?* Shoe *shine?*"

"I don't have those kind of shoes," Limekiller told the boy.

"Suede *brush?* Suede *brush?*"

Still no business being forthcoming, the bootblack withdrew, muttering.

Softly, the owner of the Cupid Club murmured, "That is one bod bob-boon."

Limekiller waited, then he said, "I'd like to hear more about that, Captain Cudgel. . . ."

But the story of the man who "made mellow" with a manatee and fathered a child upon her would have to wait, it seemed, upon another occasion. Old Captain Cudgel had departed, via the back door. Jack decided to do the same, via the front.

The sun, having vexed the Atlantic coast most of the morning and afternoon, was now on its equal way towards the Pacific. The Bay of Hidalgo stretched away on all sides, out to the faint white line which marked the barrier reef, the great coral wall which had for so long safeguarded this small, almost forgotten nation for the British Crown and the Protestant Religion. To the south, faint and high and blue against the lighter blue of the sky, however faint, darker: Pico Guapo, in the Republic of Hidalgo. Faint, also, though recurrent, was Limekiller's thought that he might, just might, try his luck down there. His papers were in order. Port Cockatoo was a Port of Entry and of Exit. The wind was free.

But from day to day, from one hot day to another hot day, he kept putting the decision off.

He nodded politely to the District Commissioner and the District Medical Officer and was nodded to, politely, in return. A way down the front street strolled white-haired Mr. Stuart, who had come out here in The Year Thirty-Nine, to help the war effort, and had been here ever since: too far for nodding. Coming from the market shed where she had been buying the latest eggs and ground-victuals was good Miss Gwen; if she saw him she would insist on giving him his supper at her boarding-house on credit: her suppers (her breakfasts and lunches as well) were just fine. But he had debts enough already. So, with a sigh, and a fond recollection of her fried fish, her country-style chicken, and her candied breadfruit, he sidled down the little lane, and he avoided Miss Gwen.

One side of the lane was the one-story white-painted wooden building with the sign DENDRY WASHBURN, LICENSED TO SELL DRUGS AND POISONS, the other side of the lane was the one-story white-painted wooden building where Captain Cumberbatch kept shop. The lane itself was paved with the crushed decomposed coral called pipeshank—and, indeed, the stuff did look like so much busted-up clay pipe stems. At the end of the lane was a small wharf and a flight of steps, at the bottom of the steps was his skiff.

He poled out to his boat, where he was greeted by his first mate, Skippy, an off-white cat with no tail. Skippy was very neat, and always used the ashes of the caboose: and if Jack didn't remember to sweep them *out* of the caboose as soon as they had cooled, and off to one side, why, that was his own care-lessness, and no fault of Skippy's.

"All clear?" he asked the small tiger, as it rubbed against his leg. The small tiger growled something which might have been "Portuguese man o'war off the starboard bow at three bells," or "Musket-men to the futtock-shrouds," or perhaps only, "Where in the Hell have *you* been, all day, you creep?"

"Tell you what, Skip," as he tied the skiff, untied the *Sacarissa,* and, taking up the boat's pole, leaned against her in a yo-heave-ho manner; "let's us bugger off from this teeming tropical metropolis and go timely down the coast . . . say, to off Crocodile Creek, lovely name, proof there really is no Chamber of Commerce in these parts . . . then take the dawn tide and drop a line or two for some grunts or jacks or who knows what . . . sawfish, maybe . . . maybe . . . *some*thing to go with the rice-and-beans tomorrow. . . . Corn what we catch but can't eat," he grunted, leaned, hastily released his weight and grabbed the pole up from the sucking bottom, dropped it on deck, and made swift shift to raise sail; *slap/slap/* . . . and then he took the tiller.

"And *thennn* . . . Oh, shite and onions, *I* don't know. Out to the Welsh-man's Cayes, maybe."

"Harebrained idea if ever I heard one," the first mate growled, trying to take Jack by the left great-toe. "Why don't you cut your hair and shave that beard and get a job and get drunk, like any decent, civilized son of a bitch would do?"

The white buildings and red roofs and tall palms wavering along the front street, the small boats riding and reflecting, the green mass of the bush behind: all contributed to give Port Cockatoo and environs the look and feel of a South Sea Island. Or, looked at from the viewpoint of another culture, the District Medical Officer (who was due for a retirement which he would not spend in his natal country), said that Port Cockatoo was *"gemütlich."* It was certainly a quiet and a gentle and undemanding sort of place.

But, somehow, it did not seem the totally ideal place for a man not yet thirty, with debts, with energy, with uncertainties, and with a thirty-foot boat.

A bright star slowly detached itself from the darkening land and swam up and up and then stopped and swayed a bit. This was the immense kerosene lamp which was nightly swung to the top of the great flagpole in the Police yard: it could be seen, the local Baymen assured J. Limekiller, as far out as Serpent Caye. . . . Serpent Caye, the impression was, lay hard upon the very verge of the known and habitable earth, beyond which the River Ocean prob-ably poured its stream into The Abyss.

Taking the hint, Limekiller took his own kerosene lamp, by no means immense, lit it, and set it firmly between two chocks of wood. Technically, there should have been two lamps and of different colors. But the local vessels seldom showed any lights at all. "He see me forst, he blow he conch-*shell;* me see *he* forst, me blow *my* conch-shell." And if neither saw the other. "Well, we suppose to meet each othah . . ." And if they didn't? Well, there was Divine Profidence—hardly any lives were lost from such misadventures: unless, of course, someone was drunk.

The dimlight lingered and lingered to the west, and then the stars started to come out. It was time, Limekiller thought, to stop for the night.

He was eating his rice and beans and looking at the chart when he heard a voice nearby saying, "Sheep a-high!"

Startled, but by no means alarmed, he called out, "Come aboard!"

What came aboard first was a basket, then a man. A man of no great singularity of appearance, save that he was lacking one eye. "Me name," said the man, "is John Samuel, barn in dis very Colony, me friend, and hence ah subject of de Queen, God bless hah." Mr. Samuel was evidently a White Creole, a member of a class never very large, and steadily dwindling away: sometimes by way of absorbtion into the non-White majority, sometimes by way of emigration, and sometimes just by way of Death the Leveler. "I tehks de libahty of bringing you some of de forst fruits of de sile," said John S.

"Say, mighty thoughtful of you, Mr. Samuel, care for some rice and beans?—My name's Jack Limekiller."

"—to weet, sour*sop,* bread*fruit,* oh-*ronge,* coco*nut*—what I care for, Mr. Limekiller, is some *rum. Rum* is what I has come to beg of you. De hond of mon, sah, has yet to perfect any medicine de superior of *rum.*"

Jack groped in the cubbyhold. "What about all those bush medicines down at Cape Manatee?" he asked, grunting. There was supposed to be a small bottle, a *chaparita,* as they called it. Where—Oh. It must be. . . . No. Then it must be. . . .

Mr. Samuel rubbed the grey bristles on his strong jaw. "I does gront you, sah, de vertue of de country yerba. But you must steep de *yerba* een de *rum,* sah. Yes mon."

Jack's fingers finally found the bottle and his one glass and his one cup and poured. Mr. Samuel said nothing until he had downed his, and then gave a sigh of satisfaction. Jack, who had found a mawmee-apple in the basket of fruit, nodded as he peeled it. The flesh was tawny, and reminded him of wintergreen.

After a moment, he decided that he didn't want to finish his rum, and, with a questioning look, passed it over to his guest. It was pleasant there on the open deck, the breeze faint but sufficient, and comparatively few flies of any sort had cared to make the voyage from shore. The boat swayed gently, there was no surf to speak of, the waves of the Atlantic having spent themselves, miles out, upon the reef; and only a few loose items of gear knocked softly as the vessel rose and fell upon the soft bosom of the inner bay.

"Well sah," said Mr. Samuel, with a slight smack of his lips, "I weesh to acknowledge your generosity. I ahsked you to wahk weet me wan mile, and you wahk weet me twain." Something splashed in the water, and he looked out, sharply.

"Shark?"

"No, mon. Too far een-shore." His eyes gazed out where there was nothing to be seen.

"Porpoise, maybe. Turtle. Or a sting-ray . . ."

After a moment, Samuel said, "Suppose to be ah tortle." He turned back and gave Limekiller a long, steady look.

Moved by some sudden devil, Limekiller said, "I hope, Mr. Samuel, that you are not about to tell me about some Indian caves or ruins, full of gold, back in the bush, which you are willing to go shares on with me and all I have to do is put up the money—because, you see, Mr. Samuel, I haven't got any money." And added, "Besides, they tell me it's illegal and that all those things belong to the Queen."

Solemnly, Samuel said, "God save de Queen." Then his eyes somehow seemed to become wider, and his mouth as well, and a sound like hissing steam escaped him, and he sat on the coaming and shook with almost-silent laughter. Then he said, "I sees dot you hahs been ahproached ahlready. No sah. No such teeng. My proposition eenclude only two quality: Expedition. Discretion." And he proceeded to explain that what he meant was that Jack should, at regular intervals, bring him supplies in small quantities and that he would advance the money for this and pay a small amount for the service. Delivery was to be made at night. And nothing was to be said about it, back at Port Cockatoo, or anywhere else.

Evidently Jack Limekiller wasn't the only one who had creditors.

"Anything else, Mr. Samuel?"

Samuel gave a deep sigh. "Ah, mon, I would like to sogjest dat you breeng me out ah woman . . . but best no. Best not . . . not yet . . . Oh, mon, I om so lustful, ahlone out here, eef you tie ah rottlesnake down fah me I weel freeg eet!"

"Well, Mr. Samuel, the fact is, I will not tie a rattlesnake down for you, or up for you, for any purpose at all. However, I will keep my eyes open for a board with a knot-hole in it."

Samuel guffawed. Then he got up, his machete slap-flapping against his side, and, with a few more words, clambered down into his dory—no plankboat, in these waters, but a dug-out—and began to paddle. Bayman, bushman, the machete was almost an article of clothing, though there was nothing to chop out here on the gentle waters of the bay. There was a splash, out there in the darkness, and a cry—Samuel's voice—

"Are you all right out there?" Limekiller called.

"Yes mon. . . ." faintly. "Fine . . . bloddy Oxville tortle. . . ."

Limekiller fell easily asleep. Presently he dreamed of seeing a large Hawksbill turtle languidly pursuing John Samuel, who languidly evaded the pursuit. Later, he awoke, knowing that he knew what had awakened him, but for the moment unable to name it. The awakeners soon enough identified themselves. Manatees. Sea-cows. The most harmless creatures God ever made. He drowsed off again, but again and again he lightly awoke and always he could hear them sighing and sounding.

. . .

Early up, he dropped his line, made a small fire in the sheet-iron caboose set in its box of sand, and put on the pot of rice and beans to cook in coconut oil. The head and tail of the first fish went into a second pot, the top of the double boiler, to make fish-tea, as the chowder was called; when they were done, he gave them to Skippy. He fried the fillets with sliced breadfruit, which had as near no taste of its own as made no matter, but was a great extender of tastes. The second fish he cut and corned—that is, he spread coarse salt on it: there was nothing else to do to preserve it in this hot climate, without ice, and where the art of smoking fish was not known. And more than those two he did not bother to take, he had no license for commercial fishing, could not sell a catch in the market, and the "sport" of taking fish he could neither eat nor sell, and would have to throw back, was a pleasure which eluded his understanding.

It promised to be a hot day and it kept its promise, and he told himself, as he often did on hot, hot days, that it beat shoveling snow in Toronto.

He observed a vacant mooring towards the south of town, recollected that it always had been vacant, and so, for no better reason than that, he tied up to it. Half of the remainder of his catch came ashore with him. This was too far south for any plank houses or tin roofs. Port Cockatoo at both ends straggled out into "trash houses," as they were called—sides of wild cane allowing the cooling breezes to pass, and largely keeping out the brute sun; roofs of thatch, usually of the bay or cohune palm. The people were poorer here than elsewhere in this town where no one at all by North American standards was rich, but "trash" had no reference to that: *Loppings, twigs, and leaves of trees, bruised sugar cane, corn husks, etc.,* his dictionary explained.

An old, old woman in the ankle-length skirts and the kerchief of her generation stood in the doorway of her little house and looked, first at him, then at his catch. And kept on looking at it. All the coastal people of Hidalgo were fascinated by fish: rice and beans was the staple dish, but fish was the roast beef, the steak, the chicken, of this small, small country which had never been rich and was now—with the growing depletion of its mahogany and rosewood—even poorer than ever. Moved, not so much by conscious consideration of this as by a sudden impulse, he held up his hand and what it was holding. "Care for some corned fish, Grandy?"

Automatically, she reached out her tiny, dark hand, all twisted and withered, and took it. Her lips moved. She looked from the fish to him and from him to the fish; asked, doubtfully, "How much I have for you?"—meaning, how much did she owe him.

"Your prayers," he said, equally on impulse.

Her head flew up and she looked at him full in the face, then. "T'ank you, Buckra," she said. "And I weel do so. I weel pray for you." And she went back into her trash house.

Up the dusty, palm-lined path a ways, just before it branched into the cemetery road and the front street, he encountered Mr. Stuart—white-haired, learned, benevolent, deaf, and vague—and wearing what was surely the very last sola topee in everyday use in the Western Hemisphere (and perhaps, what with one thing and another, in the Eastern, as well).

"Did you hear the baboons last night?" asked Mr. Stuart.

~~Jack knew that "baboons," hereabouts, were howler-monkeys. Even their~~ daytime noises, a hollow and repetitive *Rrrr-Rrrr-Rrrr,* sounded uncanny enough; as for their night-time wailings—

"I was anchored offshore, down the coast, last night," he explained. "All I heard were the manatees."

Mr. Stuart looked at him with faint, grey eyes, smoothed his long moustache. "Ah, *those* poor chaps," he said. "They've slipped back down the scale . . . much *too* far down, I expect, for any quick return. Tried to help them, you know. Tried the Herodotus method. Carthaginians. Mute trade, you know. Set out some bright red cloth, put trade-goods on, went away. Returned. Things were knocked about, as though animals had been at them. *Some* of the items were gone, though. But nothing left in return. Too bad, oh yes, too bad . . ." His voice died away into a low moan, and he shook his ancient head. In another moment, before Jack could say anything, or even think of anything to say, Mr. Stuart had flashed him a smile of pure friendliness, and was gone. A bunch of flowers was in one hand, and the path he took was the cemetery road. He had gone to visit one of "the great company of the dead, which increase around us as we grow older."

From this mute offering, laid also upon the earth, nothing would be expected in return. There are those whom we do not see and whom we do not desire that they should ever show themselves at all.

The shop of Captain Cumberbatch was open. The rules as to what stores or offices were open and closed at which times were exactly the opposite of the laws of the Medes and the Persians. The time to go shopping was when one saw the shop open. Any shop. They opened, closed, opened, closed . . . And as to why stores with a staff of only one closed so often, why, they closed not only to allow the proprietor to siesta, they also closed to allow him to eat. It was no part of the national culture for Ma to send Pa's "tea" for Pa to eat behind the counter: Pa came home. Period. And as for establishments with a staff of more than one, why could the staff not have taken turns? Answer: De baas, of whatsoever race, creed, or color, might trust an employee with his life, but he would never trust his employee with his cash or stock, never, never, never.

Captain Cumberbatch had for many years puffed up and down the coast in his tiny packet-and-passenger boat, bringing cargo merchandise for the shopkeepers of Port Caroline, Port Cockatoo, and—very, very semi-occasionally—anywhere else as chartered. But some years ago he had swallowed the anchor and set up business as shopkeeper in Port Cockatoo. And one day an epiphany of sorts had occurred: Captain Cumberbatch had asked himself why he should bring cargo for others to sell and/or why he should pay others to bring cargo for he himself to sell. Why should he not bring his own cargo and sell it himself?

The scheme was brilliant as it was unprecedented. And indeed it had but one discernable flaw: Whilst Captain Cumberbatch was at sea, he could not tend shop to sell what he had shipped. And while he was tending his shop he could not put to sea to replenish stock. And, tossing ceasely from the one horn of this dilemma to the other, he often thought resentfully of the difficulties of competing with such peoples as the Chinas, Turks, and 'Paniards, who—most unfairly—were able to trust the members of their own families to mind the store.

Be all this as it may, the shop of Captain Cumberbatch was at this very moment open, and the captain himself was leaning upon his counter and smoking a pipe.

"Marneen, Jock. Hoew de day?"

"Bless God."

"Forever and ever, ehhh-men."

A certain amount of tinned corned-beef and corned-beef hash, of white sugar (it was nearer grey), of bread (it was dead white, as unsuitable an item of diet as could be designed for the country and the country would have rioted at the thought of being asked to eat dark), salt, lamp-oil, tea, tinned milk, cheese, were packed and passed across the worn counter; a certain amount of national currency made the same trip in reverse.

As for the prime purchaser of the items, Limekiller said nothing. That was part of the Discretion.

Outside again, he scanned the somnolent street for any signs that anyone might have—somehow—arrived in town who might want to charter a boat for . . . well, for anything. Short of smuggling, there was scarcely a purpose for which he would have not chartered the *Sacarissa*. It was not that he had an invincible repugnance to the midnight trade, there might well be places and times where he would have considered it. But Government, in British Hidalgo (here, as elsewhere in what was left of the Empire, the definite article was conspicuously absent: "Government will do this," they said—or, often as not, "Government will not do this") had not vexed him in any way and he saw no reason to vex it. And, furthermore, he had heard many reports of the accommodations at the Queen's Hotel, as the King Town "gaol" was called: and they were uniformly unfavorable.

But the front street was looking the same as ever, and, exemplifying, as ever, the observation of The Preacher, that there was no new thing under the sun. So, with only the smallest of sighs, he had started for the Cupid Club, when the clop-clop of hooves made him look up. Coming along the street was the horse-drawn equivalent of a pick-up truck. The back was open, and contained a few well-filled crocus sacks and some sawn timber; the front was roofed, but open at the sides; and for passengers it had a white-haired woman and a middle-aged man. It drew to a stop.

"Well, young man. And who are *you?*" the woman asked. Some elements of the soft local accent overlaid her speech, but underneath was something else, something equally soft, but different. Her "Man" was not *mon*, it was *mayun*, and her "you" was more like *yieww*.

He took off his hat. "Jack Limekiller is my name, ma'am."

"Put it right back on, Mr. Limekiller. I do appreciate the gesture, but it has already been gestured, now. Draft-dodger, are you?"

That was a common guess. Any North American who didn't fit into an old and familiar category—tourist, sport fisherman, sport huntsman, missionary, businessman—was assumed to be either a draft-dodger or a trafficker in "weed" ... or maybe both. "No, ma'am. I've served my time, and, anyway, I'm a Canadian, and we don't have a draft."

"Well," she said, "doesn't matter even if you are, I don't *cay*-uh. Now, sir, I am Amelia Lebedee. And this is my nephew, Tom McFee." Tom smiled a faint and abstract smile, shook hands. He was sun-dark and had a slim moustache and he wore a felt hat which had perhaps been crisper than it was now. Jack had not seen many men like Tom McFee in Canada, but he had seen many men like Tom McFee in the United States. Tom McFee sold crab in Baltimore. Tom McFee managed the smaller cotton gin in a two-gin town in Alabama. Tom McFee was foreman at the shrimp-packing plant in one of the Florida Parishes in Louisiana. And Tom McFee was railroad freight agent in whatever dusty town in Texas it was that advertised itself as "Blue Vetch Seed Capital of the World."

"We are carrying you off to Shiloh for lunch," said Amelia, and a handsome old woman she was, and sat up straight at the reins. "So you just climb up in. Tom will carry you back later, when he goes for some more of this wood. Land! You'd think it was *teak*, they cut it so slow. Instead of pine."

Limekiller had no notion who or what or where Shiloh was, although it clearly could not be very far, and he could think of no reason why he should not go there. So in he climbed.

"Yes," said Amelia Lebedee, "the war wiped us out completely. So we came down here and we planted sugar, yes, we planted sugar and we made sugar for, oh, most eighty years. But we didn't move with the times, and so that's all over with now. We plant most anything *but* sugar nowadays. And when we see a new and a civilized face, we plant them down at the table." By this time the wagon was out of town. The bush to either side of the road looked like just bush-type bush to Jack. But to Mrs. Lebedee each acre had an identity of its own. "That was the Cullen's place," she'd say. And, "The Robinsons' lived there. Beautiful horses, they had. Nobody has horses anymore, just us. Yonder used to be the Simmonses. Part of the house is still standing, but, land!—you cain't see it from the road anymore. They've gone back. Most everybody has gone back, who hasn't died off ..." For a while she said nothing. The road gradually grew narrower, and all three of them began thoughtfully to slap at "flies."

A bridge now appeared and they rattled across it, a dark-green stream rushing below. There was a glimpse of an old grey house in the archaic, universal-tropical style, and then the bush closed in again. "And *they*-uh," Miss Amelia gestured, backwards, "is Texas. Oh, what a fine place that was, in its day! Nobody lives there, now. Old Captain Rutherford, the original settler, he was with Hood. *Gen*eral Hood, I mean."

It all flashed on Jack at once, and it all came clear, and he wondered that it had not been clear from the beginning. They were now passing through the site of the old Confederate colony. There had been such in Venezuela, in Colombia, even in Brazil; for all he knew, there might still be. But this one here in Hidalgo, it had not been wiped out in a year or two, like the Mormon colonies in Mexico—there had been no Revolution here, no gringo-hating Villistas—it had just ebbed away. Tiny little old B.H., "a country," as someone (who?) had said, "which you can put your arms around," had put its arms around the Rebel refugees . . . its thin, green arms . . . and it had let them clear the bush and build their houses . . . and it had waited. . . . and waited. . . . and, as, one by one, the Southern American families had "died out" or "gone back," why, as easy as easy, the bush had slipped back. And, for the present, it seemed like it was going to stay back. It had, after all, closed in after the Old Empire Mayans had so mysteriously left, and that was a thousand years ago. What was a hundred years, to the bush?

The house at Shiloh was small and neat and trim and freshly painted, and one end of the veranda was undergoing repairs. There had been no nonsense, down here, of reproducing any of the ten thousand imitations of Mount Vernon. A neatly-mowed lawn surrounded the house; in a moment, as the wagon made its last circuit, Jack saw that the lawnmowers were a small herd of cattle. A line of cedars accompanied the road, and Miss Amelia pointed to a gap in the line. "That tree that was there," she said, calmly, "was the one that fell on my husband and on John Samuel. It had been obviously weakened in the hurricane, you know, and they went over to see how badly—that was a mistake. John Samuel lost his left eye and my husband lost his life."

Discretion . . . Would it be indiscreet to ask—? He asked.

"How long ago was this, Miss Amelia?" All respectable women down here were "Miss," followed by the first name, regardless of marital state.

"It was ten years ago, come September," she said. "Let's go in out of the sun, now, and Tom will take care of the horse."

In out of the sun was cool and neat and, though shady, the living room-dining room was as bright as fresh paint and flowered wall-paper—the only wall-paper he had seen in the colony—could make it. There were flowers in vases, too, fresh flowers, not the widely-popular plastic ones. Somehow the Bayfolk did not make much of flowers.

For lunch there was heart-of-palm, something not often had, for a palm had to die to provide it, and palms were not idly cut down: there was the vegetable pear, or chayote, here called cho-cho; venison chops, tomato with okra; there was cashew wine, made from the fruit of which the Northern Lands know only the seed, which they ignorantly call "nut." And, even, there was coffee, not powdered ick, not grown-in-Brazil-shipped-to-the-United-States-roasted-ground-canned-shipped-to-Hidalgo-coffee, but actual local coffee. Here, where coffee grew with no more care than weeds, hardly anyone except the Indians bothered to grow it, and what *they* grew, *they* used.

"Yes," Miss Amelia said, "it can be a very good life here. It is necessary to work, of course, but the work is well-rewarded, oh, not in terms of large sums of money, but in so many other ways. But it's coming to an end. There is just no way that working this good land can bring you all the riches you see in the moving pictures. And that is what they all want, and dream of, all the young people. And there is just no way they are going to get it."

Tom McFee made one of his rare comments. "*I* don't dream of any white Christmas," he said. "I am staying here, where it is always green. I told Malcolm Stuart that."

Limekiller said, "I was just talking to him this morning, myself. But I couldn't understand what he was talking about . . . something about trying to trade with the manatees. . . ."

The Shiloh people, clearly, had no trouble understanding what Stuart had been talking about; they did not even think it was particularly bizarre. "Ah, those poor folks down at Mantee," said Amelia Lebedee; "—now, mind you, I mean *Mantee*, Cape Mantee, I am *not* referring to the people up on Man*a*tee River and the Lagoons, who are just as civilized as you and I: I mean *Cape* Mantee, which is its correct name, you know—"

"Where the medicine herbs grew?"

"Why, yes, Mr. Limekiller. Where they grew. As I suppose they still do. No one really knows, of course, *what* still grows down at Cape Mantee, though Nature, I suppose, would not change her ways. It was the hurricanes, you see. The War Year hurricanes. Until then, you know, Government had kept a road open, and once a month a police constable would ride down and, well, at least, take a look around. Not that any of the people there would ever bring any of their troubles to the police. They were . . . well, how should I put it? Tom, how would *you* put it?"

Tom thought a long moment. "Simple. They were always simple."

What he meant by "simple," it developed, was simple-minded. His aunt did not entirely agree with that. They gave that impression, the Mantee people, she said, but that was only because their ways were so different. "There is a story," she said, slowly, and, it seemed to Jack Limekiller, rather reluctantly, "that a British man-of-war took a Spanish slave-ship. I don't know when this would have been, it was well before we came down and settled here. Well before The War. Our own War, I mean. It was a small Spanish slaver and there weren't many captives in her. As I understand it, between the time that Britain abolished slavery and the dreadful Atlantic slave-trade finally disappeared, if slavers were taken anywhere near Africa, the British would bring the captives either to Saint Helena or Sierra Leone, and liberate them there. But this one was taken fairly near the American coast. I suppose she was heading for Cuba. So the British ship brought them *here*. To British Hidalgo. And the people were released down at Cape Mantee, and told they could settle there and no one would 'vex' them, as they say here."

Where the slaves had come from, originally, she did not know, but she thought the tradition was that they had come from somewhere well back in the African interior. Over the course of the many subsequent years, some had trickled into the more settled parts of the old colony. "But some of them just stayed down there," she said. "Keeping up their own ways."

"Too much intermarrying," Tom offered.

"So the Bayfolk say. The Bayfolk were always, *I* think, rather afraid of them. None of them would ever go there alone. And, after the hurricanes, when the road went out, and the police just couldn't get there, none of the Bayfolk would go there at *all*. By sea, I mean. You must remember, Mr. Limekiller, that in the 1940s this little colony was very much as it was in the 1840s. There were no airplanes. There wasn't one single highway. When I say there used to be a road to Mantee, you mustn't think it was a road such as we've got between Port Cockatoo and Shiloh."

Limekiller, thinking of the dirt road between Port Cockatoo and Shiloh, tried to think what the one between Port Cockatoo and the region behind Cape Mantee must have been like. Evidently a trail, nothing more, down which an occasional man on a mule might make his way, boiling the potato-like fruit of the breadnut tree for his food and feeding his mule the leaves: a trail that had to be "chopped," had to be "cleaned" by machete-work, at least twice a year, to keep the all-consuming bush from closing over it the way the flesh closes over a cut. An occasional trader, an occasional buyer or gatherer of chicle or herbs or hides, an occasional missioner or medical officer, at infrequent intervals would pass along this corridor in the eternal jungle.

And then came a hurricane, smashing flat everything in its path. And the trail vanished. And the trail was never re-cut. British Hidalgo had probably never been high on any list of colonial priorities at the best of times. During the War of 1939–1945, they may have forgotten all about it in London. Many of Hidalgo's able-bodied men were off on distant fronts. An equal number had gone off to cut the remaining forests of the Isle of Britain, to supply anyway a fraction of the wood which was then impossible to import. Nothing could be spared for Mantee and its people; in King Town, Mantee was deemed as distant as King Town was in London. The p.c. never went there again. No missioner ever returned. Neither had a medical officer or nurse. Nor any trader. No one. Except for Malcolm Stuart . . .

"He did try. Of course, he had his own concerns. During the War he had his war work. Afterwards, he took up a block of land a few miles back from here, and he had his hands full with that. And then, after, oh, I don't remember how many years of stories, stories,—there is no television here, you know, and few people have time for books—stories about the Mantee people, well, he decided he had to go have a look, see for himself, you know."

Were the Mantee people really eating raw meat and raw fish? He would bring them matches. Had they actually reverted to the use of stone for tools? He would bring them matches, axes, knives. And . . . as for the rest of it. . . . the rest of the rather awful and certainly very odd stories. . . . he would see for himself.

But he had seen nothing. There had been nothing to see. That is, nothing which he could be sure he had seen. Perhaps he had thought that he had seen some few things which he had not cared to mention to Jack, but had spoken of to the Shiloh people.

They, however, were not about to speak of it to Jack.

"Adventure," said Amelia Lebedee, dismissing the matter of Mantee with a sigh. "Nobody wants the adventure of cutting bush to plant yams. They want the adventure of night clubs and large automobiles. They see it in the moving pictures. And you, Mr. Limekiller, what is it that *you* want?—coming, having come, from the land of night clubs and large automobiles . . ."

The truth was simple. "I wanted the adventure of sailing a boat with white sails through tropic seas," he said. "I saw it in the moving pictures. I never had a night club but I had a large automobile, and I sold it and came down here and bought the boat. And, well, here I am."

They had talked right through the siesta time. Tom McFee was ready, now, to return for the few more planks which the sawmill might—or might not—have managed to produce since the morning. It was time to stand up now and to make thanks and say goodbye. "Yes," said Amelia Lebedee, pensively. "Here we are. Here we all are. We are all here. And some of us are more content being here than others."

Half-past three at the Cupid Club. On Limekiller's table, the usual single bottle of beer. Also, the three chaparitas of rum which he had bought—but they were in a paper bag, lest the sight of them, plus the fact that he could invite no one to drink of them, give rise to talk that he was "mean." Behind the bar, Alfonso Key. In the dark, dark back, slowly sipping a lemonade (all soft drinks were "lemonade"—coke was lemonade, strawberry pop was lemonade, ginger stout was lemonade. . . . sometimes, though not often, for reasons inexplicable, there was also lemon-flavored lemonade)—in the dark rear part of the room, resting his perpetually sore eyes, was old Captain Cudgel.

"Well, how you spend the night, Jock?" Alfonso ready for a tale of amour, ready with a quip, a joke.

"Oh, just quietly. Except for the manatees." Limekiller, saying this, had a sudden feeling that he had said all this before, been all this before, was caught on the moebius strip which life in picturesque Port Cockatoo had already become, caught, caught, never would be released. *Adventure!* Hah!

At this point, however, a slightly different note, a slightly different comment from the old, old man.

"Een Eedalgo," he said, dolefully, "de monatee hahv no leg, mon. Becahs Eedalgo ees a smahl coun-*tree,* ahn every-teeng smahl. Every-teeng *weak.* Now, een Ahfrica, mon, de monatee *does* hahv leg."

Key said, incredulous, but still respectful, "What you tell we, Captain Cudgel? *What?*" His last word, pronounced in the local manner of using it as a particular indication of skepticism, of criticism, of denial, seemed to have at least three *T*s at the end of it; he repeated: "Wha*ttt?*"

"Yes, mon. Yes sah. Een Ahfrica, de monatee hahv *leg,* mon. Eet be ah poerful beast, een Ahfrica, come up on de *lond,* mon."

"I tell you. *Me* di hear eet befoah. Een Ahfrica," he repeated, doggedly, "de monatee hahv leg, de monatee be ah poerful beast, come up on de *lond,* mon, no lahf, mon—"

"Me no di lahf, sah—"

"—de w'ol' people, dey tell me so, fah true."

Alfonso Key gave his head a single shake, gave a single click of his tongue, gave Jack a single look.

Far down the street, the bell of the Church of Saint Benedict the Moor sounded. Whatever time it was marking had nothing to do with Greenwich Meridian Time or any variation thereof.

The weak, feeble old voice resumed the thread of conversation. "Me grahndy di tell me dot she grahndy di tell *she*. Motta hav foct, eet me grahndy di give me me name, b'y. Cudgel. Ahfrica name. Fah true. Fah true."

A slight sound of surprise broke Limekiller's silence. He said, "Excuse me, Captain. Could it have been 'Cudjoe'. . . . maybe?"

For a while he thought that the question had either not been heard or had, perhaps, been resented. Then the old man said, "Eet could be so. Sah, eet might be so. Lahng, lahng time ah-*go*. . . . Me Christian name, Pe-tah. Me w'ol' grahndy she say, "Pickney: you hahv ah Christian name, Pe-tah. But me give you Ahfrica name, too. Cahdjo. No fah-get, pickney? Time poss, time poss, de people dey ahl cahl me 'Cudgel,' you see, sah. So me fah-get . . . Sah, hoew you know dees teeng, sah?"

Limekiller said that he thought he had read it in a book. The old captain repeated the word, lengthening it in his local speech. "Ah boook, sah. To t'eenk ahv dot. Een ah boook. Me w'own name een ah boook." By and by he departed as silently as always.

In the dusk a white cloth waved behind the thin line of white beach. He took off his shirt and waved back. Then he transferred the groceries into the skiff and, as soon as it was dark and he had lit and securely fixed his lamp, set about rowing ashore. By and by a voice called out, "Mon, where de Hell you gweyn? You keep on to de right, you gweyn wine up een *Sponeesh* Hidalgo: Mah to de lef, mon: mah to de *lef!*" And with such assistances, soon enough the skiff softly scraped the beach.

Mr. John Samuel's greeting was, "You bring de rum?" The rum put in his hand, he took up one of the sacks, gestured Limekiller towards the other. "Les go timely, noew," he said. For a moment, in what was left of the dimmest dimlight, Jack thought the man was going to walk straight into an enormous tree: instead, he walked across the enormous roots and behind the tree. Limekiller followed the faint white patch of shirt bobbing in front of him. Sometimes the ground was firm, sometimes it went squilchy, sometimes it was simply running water—shallow, fortunately—sometimes it felt like gravel. The bush noises were still fairly soft. A rustle. He hoped it was only a wish-willy lizard, or a bamboo-chicken—an iguana—and not a yellow-jaw, that snake of which it was said. . . . but this was no time to remember scare stories about snakes.

Without warning—although what sort of warning there could have been was a stupid question, anyway—there they were. Gertrude Stein, returning to her old home town after an absence of almost forty years, and finding the old home itself demolished, had observed (with a lot more objectivity than she was usually credited with) that there was no *there*, there. The *there*, here, was simply a clearing, with a very small fire, and a *ramada*: four poles holding up a low thatched roof. John Samuel let his sack drop. "Ahnd noew," he said, portentously, "let us broach de rum."

After the chaparita had been not only broached but drained, for the second time that day Limekiller dined ashore. The cooking was done on a raised fire-hearth of clay-and-sticks, and what was cooked was a breadfruit, simply strewn, when done, with sugar; and a gibnut. To say that the gibnut, or paca, is a rodent, is perhaps—though accurate—unfair: it is larger than a rabbit, and it eats well. After that Samuel made black tea and laced it with more rum. After that he gave a vast belch and a vast sigh. "Can you play de bon-*joe?*" he next asked.

"Well. . . . I have been known to try. . . ."

The lamp flared and smoked. Samuel adjusted it . . . somewhat . . . He got up and took a bulky object down from a peg on one of the roof-poles. It was a sheet of thick plastic, laced with raw-hide thongs, which he laboriously un-knotted. Inside that was a deerskin. And inside *that*, an ordinary banjo-case, which contained an ordinary, if rather old and worn, banjo.

"Mehk I hear ah sahng. . . . ah sahng ahv *you* country."

What song should he make him hear? No particularly Canadian song brought itself to mind. Ah well, he would dip down below the border just a bit. . . . His fingers strummed idly on the strings. The words grew, the tune grew, he lifted up what some (if not very many) had considered a not-bad-baritone, and began to sing and play.

> *Manatee gal, ain't you coming out tonight,*
> *Coming out tonight, coming out tonight?*
> *Oh, Manatee gal, ain't you coming out tonight,*
> *To dance by the light of the—*

An enormous hand suddenly covered his own and pressed it down. The tune subsided into a jumble of chords, and an echo, and a silence.

"Mon, mon, you not do me right. I no di say, "Mehk I hear a sahng ahv *you* country?" Samuel, on his knees, breathed heavily. His breath was heavy with rum and his voice was heavy with reproof . . . and with a something else for which Limekiller had no immediate name. But, friendly it was not.

Puzzled more than apologetic, Jack said, "Well, it *is* a North American song, anyway. It was an old Erie Canal song. It—Oh. I'll be damned. Only it's supposed to go, '*Buffalo gal, ain't you coming out tonight,*' and I dunno what made me change it, what difference does it make?"

"What different? What different it mehk? Ah, Christ me King! You lee' buckra b'y, you not know w'ehnnah-teeng?"

It was all too much for Limekiller. The last thing he wanted was anything resembling an argument, here in the deep, dark bush, with an all-but-stranger. Samuel having lifted his heavy hand from the instrument, Limekiller, moved by a sudden spirit, began,

> *Amazing grace, how sweet the sound,*
> *To save a wretch like me.*

With a rough catch of his breath, Samuel muttered, "Yes. Yes. Dot ees good. Go on, b'y. No stop."

I once was halt, but now can walk:
Was blind, but now I see . . .

He sang the beautiful old hymn to the end: and, by that time, if not over-powered by Grace, John Samuel—having evidently broached the second and the third chaparita—was certainly overpowered: and it did not look as though the dinner-guest was going to get any kind of guided tour back to the shore and the skiff. He sighed and he looked around him. A bed rack had roughly been fixed up, and its lashings were covered with a few deer hides and an old Indian blanket. Samuel not responding to any shakings or urgings, Limekiller, with a shrug and a "Well what the Hell," covered him with the blanket as he lay upon the ground. Then, having rolled up the sacks the supplies had come in and propped them under his head, Limekiller disposed himself for slumber on the hides. Some lines were running through his head and he paused a moment to consider what they were. What they were, they were, *From ghoulies and ghosties, long-leggedy feasties, and bugges that go* boomp *in the night, Good Lord, deliver us.* With an almost absolute certainty that this was not the Authorized Version or Text, he heard himself give a grottle and a snore and knew he was fallen asleep.

He awoke to slap heartily at some flies, and the sound perhaps awoke the host, who was heard to mutter and mumble. Limekiller leaned over. "What did you say?"

The lines said, Limekiller learned that he had heard them before.

"Eef you tie ah rottlesnake doewn fah me, I weel freeg eet."

"I yield," said Limekiller, "to any man so much hornier than myself. Pro-duce the snake, sir, and I will consider the rest of the matter."

The red eye of the expiring fire winked at him. It was still winking at him when he awoke from a horrid nightmare of screams and thrashings-about, in the course of which he had evidently fallen or had thrown himself from the bed-rack to the far side. Furthermore, he must have knocked against one of the roof-poles in doing so, because a good deal of the thatch had landed on top of him. He threw it off, and, getting up, began to apologize.

"Sorry if I woke you, Mr. Samuel. I don't know what—" There was no answer, and looking around in the faint light of the fire, he saw no one.

"Mr. Samuel? Mr. *Samuel?* John? Oh, hey, *Johhhn . . . !?*"

No answer. If the man had merely gone out to "ease himself," as the Bayfolk delicately put it, he would have surely been near enough to answer. No one in the colony engaged in strolling in the bush at night for fun. "Son of a bitch," he muttered. He felt for and found his matches, struck one, found the lamp, lit it, looked around.

There was still no sign of John Samuel, but what there were signs of was some sort of horrid violence. Hastily he ran his hands over himself, but, despite his fall, despite part of the roof having fallen on him, he found no trace of blood.

All the blood which lay around, then, must have been—could only have been—John Samuel's blood.

And the screaming and the sounds of something—or somethings—heavily

~~thrashing around, they had not been in any dream.~~ They had been the sounds of truth.

And as for what else he saw, as he walked, delicate as Agag, around the perimeter of the clearing, he preferred not to speculate.

There was a shotgun and there were shells. He put the shells into the chambers and he stood up, weapon in his hand, all the rest of the night.

"Now, if it took you perhaps less than an hour to reach the shore, and if you left immediately, how it is that you were so long in arriving at Port?" the District Commissioner asked. He asked politely, but he did ask. He asked a great many questions, for, in addition to his other duties, he was the Examining Magistrate.

"Didn't you observe the wind, D.C.? Ask anyone who was out on the water yesterday. I spent most of the day tacking—"

Corporal Huggin said, softly, from the wheel, "That would be correct, Mr. Blossom."

They were in the police boat, the *George* . . . once, Jack had said to P. C. Ed Huggin, "For George VI, I suppose?" and Ed, toiling over the balky and antique engine, his clear tan skin smudged with grease, had scowled, and said, "More for bloody George III, you ask *me.* . . ." At earliest daylight, yesterday, Limekiller, red-eyed and twitching, had briefly cast around in the bush near the camp, decided that, ignorant of bush-lore as he was, having not even a compass, let alone a pair of boots or a snake-bite kit, it would have been insane to attempt any explorations. He found his way along the path, found his skiff still tied up, and had rowed to his boat. Unfavorable winds had destroyed his hope of being of getting back to Port Cockatoo in minimum time: it had been night when he arrived.

The police had listened to his story, had summoned Mr. Florian Blossom, the District Commissioner; all had agreed that "No purpose would be served by attempting anything until next morning." They had taken his story down, word by word, and by hand—if there was an official stenographer anywhere in the country, Limekiller had yet to hear of it—and by longhand, too; and in their own accustomed style and method, too, so that he was officially recorded as having said things such as: *Awakened by loud sounds of distress, I arose and hailed the man known to me as John Samuel. Upon receiving no response,* etcetera.

After Jack had signed the statement, and stood up, thinking to return to his boat, the District Commissioner said, "I believe that they can accommodate you with a bed in the Unmarried Police Constables' Quarters, Mr. Limekiller. Just for the night."

He looked at the official. A slight shiver ran up and down him. "Do you mean that I am a prisoner?"

"Certainly not, Mr. Limekiller. No such thing."

"You know, if I had wanted to, I could have been in Republican waters by now."

Mr. Blossom's politeness never flagged. "We realize it and we take it into consideration, Mr. Limekiller. But if we are all of us here together it will make an early start in the morning more efficacious."

Anyway, Jack was able to shower, and Ed Huggin loaned him clean clothes. Of course they had not gotten an early start in the morning. Only fishermen and sand-boatmen got early starts. Her Majesty's Government moved at its accustomed pace. In the police launch, besides Limekiller, was P. C. Huggin, D. C. Blossom, a very small and very black and very wiry man called Harlow the Hunter, Police-Sergeant Ruiz, and white-haired Dr. Rafael, the District Medical Officer.

"I wouldn't have been able to come at all, you know," he said to Limekiller, "except my assistant has returned from his holidays a day earlier. Oh, there is so much to see in this colony! Fascinating, fascinating!"

D. C. Blossom smiled. "Doctor Rafael is a famous antiquarian, you know, Mr. Limekiller. It was he who discovered the grave-*stone* of my three or four times great-grand-sir and-grandy."

Sounds of surprise and interest—polite on Limekiller's part, gravestones perhaps not being what he would have most wished to think of—genuine on the part of everyone else, ancestral stones not being numerous in British Hidalgo.

"Yes, yes," Dr. Rafael agreed. "Two years ago I was on *my* holidays, and I went out to St. Saviour's Caye ... well, to what is left of St. Saviour's Caye after the last few hurricanes. You can imagine what is left of the old settlement. Oh, the Caye is dead, it is like a skeleton, bleached and bare!" Limekiller felt he could slightly gladly have tipped the medico over the side and watched the bubbles; but, unaware, on the man went. "—so, difficult though it was making my old map agree with the present outlines, still, I did find the site of the old burial-ground, and I cast about and I prodded with my iron rod, and I felt stone underneath the sand, and I dug!"

More sounds of excited interest. Digging in the sand on the bit of ravished sand and coral where the ancient settlement had been—but was no more—was certainly of more interest than digging for yams on the fertile soil of the mainland. And, even though they already knew that it was not a chest of gold, still, they listened and they murmured *oh* and *ah*. "The letters were still very clear, I had no difficulty reading them. *Sacred to the memory of Ferdinando Rousseau, a native of Guernsey, and of Marianna his Wife, a native of Mandingo, in Africa.* Plus a poem in three stanzas, of which I have deposited a copy in the National Archives, and of course I have a copy myself and a third copy I offered to old Mr. Ferdinand Rousseau in King Town—"

Smiling, Mr. Blossom asked, "And what he tell you, then, Doctor?"

Dr. Rafael's smile was a trifle rueful. "He said, 'Let the dead bury their dead'—" The others all laughed. Mr. Ferdinand Rousseau was evidently known to all of them. "—and he declined to take it. Well, I was aware that Mr. Blossom's mother was a cousin of Mr. Rousseau's mother—" ("Double-cousin," said Mr. Blossom.)

Said Mr. Blossom, "And the doctor has even been there, too, to that country. I don't mean Guernsey; in Africa, I mean; not true, Doctor?"

Up ahead, where the coast thrust itself out into the blue, blue Bay, Jack thought he saw the three isolated palms which were his landmark. But there was no hurry. He found himself unwilling to hurry anything at all.

Doctor Rafael, in whose voice only the slightest trace of alien accent still lingered, said that after leaving Vienna, he had gone to London, in London he had been offered and had accepted work in a British West African colonial medical service. "I was just a bit surprised that the old grave-stone referred to Mandingo as a country, there is no such country on the maps today, but there are such a people."

"What they like, Doc-tah? What they like, thees people who dey mehk some ahv Mr. Blossom ahn-*ces*-tah?"

There was another chuckle. This one had slight overtones.

The DMO's round, pink face furrowed in concentration among memories a quarter of a century old. "Why," he said, "they are like elephants. They never forget."

There was a burst of laughter. Mr. Blossom laughed loudest of them all. Twenty-five years earlier he would have asked about Guernsey; today....

Harlow the Hunter, his question answered, gestured towards the shore. A slight swell had come up, the blue was flecked, with bits of white. "W'over dere, suppose to be wan ahv w'ol' Bob Blaine cahmp, in de w'ol' days."

"Filthy fellow," Dr. Rafael said, suddenly, concisely.

"Yes sah," Harlow agreed. "He was ah lewd fellow, fah true, fah true. What he use to say, he use to say, 'Eef you tie ah rottle-snehk doewn fah me, I weel freeg eet....'"

Mr. Blossom leaned forward. "Something the matter, Mr. Limekiller?"

Mr. Limekiller did not at that moment feel like talking. Instead, he lifted his hand and pointed towards the headland with the three isolated palms.

"Cape Man'tee, Mr. Limekiller? What about it?"

Jack cleared his throat. "I thought that was farther down the coast... according to my chart..."

Ed Huggin snorted. "Chart! Washington chart copies London chart and London chart I think must copy the original chart made by old Captain Cook. *Chart!*" He snorted again.

Mr. Florian Blossom asked, softly, "Do you recognize your landfall, Mr. Limekiller? I suppose it would not be at the cape itself, which is pure mangrove bog and does not fit the description which you gave us...."

Mr. Limekiller's eyes hugged the coast. Suppose he couldn't *find* the god-damned place? Police and Government wouldn't like that at all. Every ounce of fuel had to be accounted for. Chasing the wild goose was not approved. He might find an extension of his stay refused when next he went applying for it. He might even find himself officially listed as a Proscribed Person, trans.: haul-ass, Jack, and don't try coming back. And he realized that he did not want that at all, at all. The whole coast looked the same to him, all of a sudden. And then, all of a sudden, it didn't... somehow. There was something about that solid-seeming mass of bush—

"I think there may be a creek. Right there."

Harlow nodded. "Yes mon. Is a creek. Right dere."

And right there, at the mouth of the creek—in this instance, meaning, not a stream, but an inlet—Limekiller recognized the huge tree. And Harlow the Hunter recognized something else. "Dot mark suppose to be where Mr. Limekiller drah up the skiff."

"Best we ahl put boots *on*," said Sergeant Ruiz, who had said not a word until now. They all put boots on. Harlow shouldered an axe. Ruiz and Huggin took up machetes. Dr. Rafael had, besides his medical bag, a bundle of what appeared to be plastic sheets and crocus sacks. "You doesn't mind to cahry ah shovel, Mr. Jock?" Jack decided that he could think of a number of things he had rather carry: but he took the thing. And Mr. Blossom carefully picked up an enormous camera, with tripod. The Governments of His and/or Her Majesties had never been known for throwing money around in these parts; the camera could hardly have dated back to George III but was certainly earlier than the latter part of the reign of George V.

"You must lead us, Mr. Limekiller." The District Commissioner was not grim. He was not smiling. He was grave.

Limekiller nodded. Climbed over the sprawling trunk of the tree. Suddenly remembered that it had been night when he had first come this way, that it had been from the other direction that he had made his way the next morning, hesitated. And then Harlow the Hunter spoke up.

"Eef you pleases, Mistah Blossom. I believes I knows dees pahth bet-tah."

And, at any rate, he knew it well enough to lead them there in less time, surely, than Jack Limekiller could have.

Blood was no longer fresh and red, but a hundred swarms of flies suddenly rose to show where the blood had been. Doctor Rafael snipped leaves, scooped up soil, deposited his take in containers.

And in regard to other evidence, whatever it was evidence of, for one thing, Mr. Blossom handed the camera over to Police-Corporal Huggin, who set up his measuring tape, first along one deep depression and photographed it; then along another . . . another . . . another . . .

"Mountain-cow," said the District Commissioner. He did not sound utterly persuaded.

Harlow shook his head. "No, Mistah Florian. No sah. No, no."

"Well, if not a tapir: what?"

Harlow shrugged.

Something heavy had been dragged through the bush. And it had been dragged by something heavier . . . something much, much heavier . . . It was horridly hot in the bush, and every kind of "fly" seemed to be ready and waiting for them: sand-fly, bottle fly, doctor-fly. They made unavoidable noise, but whenever they stopped, the silence closed in on them. No wild parrot shrieked. No "baboons" rottled or growled. No warree grunted or squealed. Just the waiting silence of the bush. Not friendly. Not hostile. Just indifferent.

And when they came to the little river (afterwards, Jack could not even find it on the maps) and scanned the opposite bank and saw nothing, the District Commissioner said, "Well, Harlow. What you think?"

The wiry little man looked up and around. After a moment he nodded, plunged into the bush. A faint sound, as of someone—or of something?—Then

Ed Huggin pointed. Limekiller would never even have noticed that particular tree was there; indeed, he was able to pick it out now only because a small figure was slowly but surely climbing it. The tree was tall, and it leaned at an angle—old enough to have experienced the brute force of a hurricane, strong enough to have survived, though bent.

Harlow called something Jack did not understand, but he followed the others, splashing down the shallows of the river. The river slowly became a swamp. Harlow was suddenly next to them. "Eet not fah," he muttered.

Nor was it.

What there was of it.

An eye in the monstrously swollen head winked at them. Then an insect leisurely crawled out, flapped its horridly-damp wings in the hot and humid air, and sluggishly flew off. There was no wink. There was no eye.

"Mr. Limekiller," said District Commissioner Blossom, "I will now ask you if you identify this body as that of the man known to you as John Samuel."

"It's him. Yes sir."

But was as though the commissioner had been holding his breath and had now released it. "Well, well," he said. "And he was supposed to have gone to Jamaica and died there. I never heard he'd come back. Well, he is dead now, for true."

But little Doctor Rafael shook his snowy head. "He is certainly dead. And he is certainly not John Samuel."

"Why—" Limekiller swallowed bile, pointed. "Look. The eye is missing. John Samuel lost that eye when the tree fell—"

"Ah, yes, young man. John Samuel did. *But not that eye.*"

The bush was not so silent now. Every time the masses and masses of flies were waved away, they rose, buzzing, into the heavy, squalid air. Buzzing, hovered. Buzzing, returned.

"Then who in thee Hell—?"

Harlow wiped his face on his sleeve. "Well, sah. I cahn tell you. Lord hahv mercy on heem. Eet ees Bob Blaine."

There was a long outdrawn *ahhh* from the others. Then Ed Huggin said, "But Bob Blaine had both his eyes."

Harlow stopped, picked a stone from the river bed, with dripping hand threw it into the bush. . . . one would have said, at random. With an ugly croak, a buzzard burst up and away. Then Harlow said something, as true—and as dreadful—as it was unarguable. "He not hahv either of them, noew."

By what misadventure and in what place Bob Blaine had lost one eye whilst alive and after decamping from his native land, no one knew: and perhaps it did not matter. He had trusted on "discretion" not to reveal his hideout, there at the site of his old bush-camp. But he had not trusted to it *one hundred percent.* Suppose that Limekiller were deceitfully or accidently, to let drop the fact that a man was camping out there. A man with only one eye. What was the man's name? John Samuel. What? John *Samuel.* . . . Ah. Then John Samuel had not, after all, died in Jamaica, according to report. Report had been known to be wrong before. John Samuel alive, then. No big thing. Nobody then would have been moved to go down there to check up.—Nobody, now, knew why Bob Blaine had returned. Perhaps he had made things too hot for himself, down in "republican waters"—where hot water could be so very much hotter than back here. Perhaps some day a report would drift back up, and it might be a true report or it might be false or it might be a mixture of both.

As for the report, the official, Government one, on the circumstances surrounding the death or Roberto Blaine, a.k.a. Bob Blaine . . . as for Limekiller's statement and the statements of the District Commissioner and the District Medical Officer and the autopsy and the photographs: why, that had all been neatly transcribed and neatly (and literally) laced with red tape, and forwarded up the coast to King Town. And as to what happened to it there—

"What do you think they will do *about it, Doctor?*"

Rafael's rooms were larger, perhaps, than a bachelor needed. But they were the official quarters for the DMO, and so the DMO lived in them. The wide floors gleamed with polish. The spotless walls showed, here a shield, there a paddle, a harpoon with barbed head, the carapace of a huge turtle, a few paintings. The symmetry and conventionality of it all was slightly marred by the bookcases which were everywhere, against every wall, adjacent to desk and chairs. And all were full, crammed, overflowing.

Doctor Rafael shrugged. "Perhaps the woodlice will eat the papers," he said. "Or the roaches, or the wee-wee-ants. The mildew. The damp. Hurricane . . . This is not a climate which helps preserve the history of men. I work hard to keep my own books and papers from going that way. But I am not Government, and Government lacks time and money and personnel, and . . . perhaps, also. . . . Government has so many, many things pressing upon it. . . . Perhaps, too, Government lacks interest."

"What were those tracks, Doctor Rafael?"

Doctor Rafael shrugged.

"You do know, don't you?"

Doctor Rafael grimaced.

"Have you seen them, or anything like them, before?"

Doctor Rafael, very slowly, very slowly, nodded.

"Well . . . for God's sake . . . can you even give me a, well, a *hint?* I mean: that was a rather rotten experience for me, you know. And—"

The sunlight, kept at bay outside, broke in through a crack in the jalousies, sun making the scant white hair for an instant ablaze: like the brow of Moses. Doctor Rafael got up and busied himself with the fresh lime and the sweetened lime juice and the gin and ice. He was rapt in this task, like an ancient apothecary mingling strange unguents and syrups. Then he gave one of the gimlets to his guest and from one he took a long, long pull.

"You see. I have two years to go before my retirement. The pension, well, it is not spectacular, but I have no complaint. I will be able to rest. Not for an hour, or an evening . . . an evening! only on my holidays, once a year, do I even have an evening all my own!—Well. You may imagine how I look forward. And I am not going to risk premature and enforced retirement by presenting Government with an impossible situation. One which wouldn't be its fault, anyway. By insisting on impossible things. By demonstrating—"

He finished his drink. He gave Jack a long, shrewd look.

"So I have nothing more to say . . . about *that*. If they want to believe, up in King Town, that the abominable Bob Blaine was mauled by a crocodile, let them. If they prefer to make it a jaguar or even a tapir, why, that is fine with Robert Rafael, M.D., DMO. It might be, probably, the first time in history that anybody anywhere was killed by a tapir, but that is not my affair. The matter is, so far as I am concerned, so far—in fact—as *you* and I are concerned—over.

"Do you understand?"

Limekiller nodded. At once the older man's manner changed. "I have many, many books, as you can see. Maybe some of them would be of interest to you. Pick any one you like. Pick one at random." So saying, he took a book from his desk and put it in Jack's hands. It was just a book-looking book. It was, in fact, volume ii of the Everyman edition of Plutarch's Lives. There was a wide card, of the kind on which medical notes or records are sometimes made, and so Jack Limekiller opened the book at that place.

seasons, as the gods sent them, seemed natural to him. The Greeks that inhabited Asia were very much pleased to see the great lords and governors of Persia, with all the pride, cruelty, and

"Well, now, what the Hell," he muttered. The card slipped, he clutched. He glanced at it. He put down vol. ii of the Lives and he sat back and read the notes on the card.

It is in the nature of things [they began] for men, in a new country and faced with new things, to name them after old, familiar things. Even when resemblance unlikely. Example: *Mountain-cow* for tapir. ('Tapir' from Tupi Indian *tapira*, big beast.) Example: Mawmee-*apple* not apple at all. Ex.: *Sea-cow* for manatee. Early British settlers not entomologists. Quest.: Whence word *manatee*? From Carib? Perhaps. After the British, what other people came to this corner of the world? Ans.: Black people. Calabars, Ashantee, Mantee, Mandingo. Re last two names. Related peoples. Named after totemic animal. *Also,* not likely? *likely*—named unfamiliar animals after familiar (i.e. familiar in Africa) animals. Mantee, Mandee-hippo. Refer legend

Limekiller's mouth fell open.

"Oh, my God!" he groaned. In his ear now, he heard the old, old, quavering voice of Captain Cudgel (once Cudjoe): "*Mon, een Ahfrica, de mon-ah-tee hahv leg, I tell you. Een Ahfrica eet be ah poerful beast, come up on de lond, I tell you. . . . de w'ol' people, dey tell me so, fah true. . . .*"

He heard the old voice, repeating the old words, no longer even half-understood: but, in some measure, at least half-true.

Refer legend of were-animals, universal. Were-wolf, were-tiger, were-shark, were-dolphin. Quest.: Were-manatee?

"Mon-ah-tee ees hahlf ah mon. . . . hahv teats like a womahn . . . Dere ees wahn mon, mehk mellow weet mon-ah-tee, hahv pickney by mon-ah-tee . . ."

And he heard another voice saying, not only once, saying, *"Mon, eef you tie ah rottlesnake doewn fah me, I weel freeg eet. . . ."*

He thought of the wretched captives in the Spanish slaveship, set free to fend for themselves in a bush by far wilder than the one left behind. Few, to begin with, fewer as time went on; marrying and intermarrying, no new blood, no new thoughts. And, finally, the one road in to them, destroyed. Left alone. Left quite alone. Or . . . almost . . .

He shuddered.

How desperate for refuge must Blaine have been, to have sought to hide himself anywhere near Cape Mantee—

And what miserable happenstance had brought he himself, Jack Limekiller, to improvise on that old song that dreadful night?—And what had he called up out of the darkness . . . out of the bush . . . out of the mindless present which was the past and future and the timeless tropical forever . . . ?

There was something pressing gently against his finger, something on the other side of the card. He turned it over. A clipping from a magazine had been roughly pasted there.

Valentry has pointed out that, despite a seeming resemblance to such aquatic mammals as seals and walrus, the manatee is actually more closely related anatomically to the elephant.

. . . out of the bush . . . out of the darkness . . . out of the mindless present which was also the past and the timeless tropical forever . . .

"They are like elephants. They never forget."

"Ukh." he said, through clenched teeth. "My God. Uff. Jesus. . . ."

The card was suddenly, swiftly, snatched from his hands. He looked up, still in a state of shock, to see Doctor Rafael tearing it into pieces.

"Doña Sana!"

A moment. Then the housekeeper, old, all in white. "Doctór?"

"Burn this."

A moment passed. Just the two of them again. Then Rafael, in a tone which was nothing but kindly, said, "Jack, you are still young and you are still healthy. My advice to you: Go away. Go to a cooler climate. One with cooler ways and cooler memories." The old woman called something from the back of the house. The old man sighed. "It is the summons to supper," he said. "Not only must I eat in haste because I have my clinic in less than half-an-hour, but suddenly-invited guests make Dona 'Saña very nervous. Good night, then, Jack."

Jack had had two gin drinks. He felt that he needed two more. At least two more. Or, if not gin, rum. Beer would not do. He wanted to pull the blanket of booze over him, awfully, awfully quickly. He had this in his mind as though it were a vow as he walked up the front street towards the Cupid Club.

Someone hailed him, someone out of the gathering dusk.

~~"Jock! Hey, mon Jock! Hey, b'y! Where you gweyn so fahst? Bide, b'y,~~ bide a bit!"

The voice was familiar. It was that of Harry Hazeed, his principal creditor in King Town. Ah, well. He had had his chance, Limekiller had. He could have gone on down the coast, down into the republican waters, where the Queen's writ runneth not. Now it was too late.

"Oh, hello, Harry," he said, dully.

Hazeed took him by the hand. Took him by both hands. "Mon, show me where is your boat? She serviceable? She is? Good: Mon, you don't hear de news: Welcome's warehouse take fire and born up! Yes, mon. Ahl de carn in King *Town* born up! No carn ah-tahl: No tortilla, no empinada, no tamale, no carn-*cake!* Oh, mon, how de people going to punish! Soon as I hear de news, I drah me money from de bonk, I buy ahl de crocus sock I can find, I jump on de pocket-*boat*—and here I am, oh, mon, I pray fah you. . . . I pray I fine you!"

Limekiller shook his head. It had been one daze, one shock after another. The only thing clear was that Harry Hazeed didn't seem angry. "You no understond?" Hazeed cried. "Mon! We going take your boat, we going doewn to Nutmeg P'int, we going to buy carn, mon! We going to buy ahl de carn dere is to buy! Nevah mine dat lee' bit money you di owe me, b'y! We going make plenty money, mon! And we going make de cultivators plenty money, too! What you theenk of eet, Jock, me b'y? Eh? Hey? What you theenk?"

Jack put his forefinger in his mouth, held it up. The wind was in the right quarter. The wind would, if it held up, and, somehow, it felt like a wind which would hold up, the wind would carry them straight and clear to Nutmeg Point: the clear, clean wind in the clear and starry night.

Softly, he said—and, old Hazeed leaning closer to make the words out, Limekiller said them again, louder, "I think it's great. Just great. I think it's great."

Afterword to "Manatee Gal, Won't You Come Out Tonight"

BY LUCIVS SHEPARD

The literature of the expatriate has a proud tradition in English and American literature, marked by names such as Conrad, Lowry, Kipling, Bowles, Greene, and Stone, and by some of the best novels produced in the language, novels such as Under the Volcano, Lord Jim, *and* The Sheltering Sky. *Its classic themes are loneliness, man's folly, and the inimical nature and mysterious laws of a place not one's own. But more pertinently, in every instance the literature is marked by a writer's fascination with the place in which he—and his protagonist—have chosen to live, and with his love for that place, even though he may depict it as vile and treacherous and sad.*

In his story "Manatee Gal," Avram Davidson engaged the classic themes with the quirky eloquence for which he became known, incorporating as well many tropes of the great adventure stories—: embracing all his characters, whether villain or naïf or boor, with a kind of splendid, generous crankiness that makes plain his affection for the setting of the story—British Honduras, or Belize. The sense of place he gives us in this and in all the Limekiller stories is pungent, lustrous, sensual in every regard, a feast for eye and nose, ear and palette, and though Jack Limekiller is a wonderfully drawn character, it is ultimately Belize that is the dominant character of the tale, with its dancing butterflies and magical lizards and mystical coves, all illuminated by the exotic precision of the speech of its citizenry, which Avram rendered in such loving detail. It, Belize, is a great character, as palpably individual as Conrad's Borneo and Stone's Vietnam, and I only wish Avram had done more of these stories, or had expanded his territory to include the surrounding region. Had he done so, I believe his name would have been more widely known while he was alive—as it most certainly will now that he has passed away—and we might have seen something even more remarkable from his pen, for I believe he had barely scratched the surface of what he had to tell us about this beautiful, devious, and subtle stretch of beach and jungle and cay.

Sad to say, Avram's Belize no longer exists, as it is currently being inundated in a wave of American and British commercialism, which may one day soon transform it into something grotesquely Cancun-esque. But that, of course, speaks to the other virtue of the expatriate writer: his ability to preserve a corner of the world and of time for our enduring pleasure. So here, in all its pervasive sweetness and Gauguin-like brightness, embellished by colorful bromeliads and majestic garobos and trees older than most nations, is a real place and time now elevated to the realm of the fantastic and the legendary, caught at the moment when its innocence was just about to be swept away, a place in which every oddly shaped rock had a story attached to it and the lore of jungle and sea was a vital element of people's lives, and bandits who robbed chicleros *had not yet been replaced by Colombian cowboys with aluminunm suitcases and small black guns.*

When I was starting out as a writer, I wrote Avram a letter telling him that I had recently finished a couple of stories set in Central America, and that I was a bit concerned that, because of the Limekiller stories, people were going to think I was stealing his act, and that I hoped he didn't think so. It was a terribly naive letter, one of those you wish to God you hadn't mailed the second you drop it through the slot. A couple of weeks later I received a reply wherein Avram, utilizing that generous crankiness of which I've spoken, informed me that "yes, you are absolutely right. The Caribbean littoral is my exclusive preserve. No one could possibly illuminate it as well as I . . ." Of course I knew he was kidding.

Now, having just reread the story you have read, I'm not so sure.

Naples

Introduction by William Gibson

I once told Avram Davidson that I was very busy, finishing a first novel. "But you mustn't do that," he wrote back, "you'll be letting down the side." Eventually I found myself writing a second novel. I told Avram. He sighed. "But I've told you that you mustn't do that."

He was a very droll man, was Avram, and one who knew a thing about the perils of literature, and a thing about the giving of encouragement.

I miss him. I missed him quite sharply, and unexpectedly, one afternoon this past winter, when I was forestalling the completion of yet another novel with an A-to-Z reading of a facsimile edition of the Lexicon Balatronicum, 1811, *otherwise known as* A Dictionary of Buckish Slang, University Wit, and Pickpocket Eloquence. *Deep in the W's, my day a dead loss, I had just discovered the following entry:*

WOLF IN THE BREAST. An extraordinary mode of imposition, sometimes practised in the country by strolling women, who have the knack of counterfeiting extreme pain, pretending to have a small animal called a wolf in their breasts, which is continually gnawing them.

Now the truly stunning peculiarity of that, its sheer lack of context, is quite phenomenal. Extraordinary mode of imposition. Strolling women. Counterfeiting pain. Wolf in the breast. And the instant of my missing Avram, and very precisely Avram, was the instant of my running down the full and lifetime list of my available human resources, frantic for someone to whom to take this mystery, this marvel, this extraordinary mode of imposition, and finding that, of course, there was Avram, and only Avram. Avram who could at the very least have invented a context for a small animal called a wolf, or who might even have known, somehow, through the vast and trackless courses of a life-time's reading and remembering, what it possibly was that these strolling women were about.

And remembering that Mr. Davidson, the sum of however many whole Borgesian libraries stored so casually in his head, was no longer available for consultation.

But still. That same Mr. Davidson had himself let down the side, and most handsomely, very many times, and one of these was with the story you are about to read, which won the World Fantasy Award, and well it should have done, and many others he wrote as well, had such things existed when he wrote them.

"Naples" is a story that knows something of the wolf in all our breasts, something of addiction and quite possibly of love, and of that coin in which the very oldest things are trafficked.

A wonderful, grim, dark thing.

NAPLES

IT IS A CURIOUS thing, the reason of it being not certainly known to me—though I conjecture it might be poverty—why, when all the other monarchs of Europe were still building palaces in marble and granite, the kings of that anomalous and ill-fated kingdom called Of Naples and the Two Sicilies chose to build theirs in red brick. However, choose it they did: These last of the Italian Bourbons have long since lost their last thrones, no *castrato* singers sing for them from behind screens to lighten their well-deserved melancholy anymore, and their descendants now earn their livings in such occupations as gentlemen-salesclerks in fashionable jewelry stores—not, perhaps, entirely removed from all memory of the glory that once (such as it was) was theirs. But the red-brick *palazzi* are still there, they still line a part of the waterfront of Naples, and—some of them, at least—are still doing duty as seats of governance. (Elsewhere, for reasons equally a mystery to me, unless there is indeed some connection between red bricks and poverty, buildings in the same style and of the same material usually indicate that within them the Little Sisters of the Poor, or some similar religious group, perform their selfless duties on behalf of the sick, the aged, and the otherwise bereft and afflicted; and which is the nobler function and whose the greater reward are questions that will not long detain us.)

Some twenty years ago or so, a man neither young nor old nor ugly nor comely, neither obviously rich nor equally poor, made his way from the docks past the red-brick *palazzi* and into the lower town of ancient and teeming Naples. He observed incuriously that the streets, instead of swarming with the short and swarthy, as foreign legend implies, swarmed instead with the tall and pale. But the expectations of tradition were served in other ways: by multitudes of donkey carts, by women dressed and draped in black, by many many beggars, and by other signs of deep and evident poverty. Almost at once a young man approached him with a murmured offer of service; the young man clutched the upturned collar of his jacket round about his throat, and, as the day was not even cool, let alone cold, it might have been assumed that the reason for the young man's gesture was that he probably did not wish to reveal the absence of a shirt. It was not altogether certain that the young man had no shirt at all, probably he had a shirt and probably this was its day to be washed and probably it was even now hanging from a line stretched across an alley where the sun did not enter in sufficient strength to dry it quickly.

There were many such alleys and many such lines, and, it is to be feared, many such shirts. There were also many such men, not all of them young; and if a count had been made, it might have been found that there were not enough shirts to go around.

Naples.

The traveler continued, with frequent pauses and considerings, to make his way slowly from the port area and slowly up the steep hill. Now and then he frowned slightly and now and then he slightly smiled. Long ago some humble hero or heroine discovered that if the hard wheat of the peninsula, subject to mold and rust and rot if stored in the ear, be ground into flour and mixed with water into a paste and extruded under pressure in the form of long strips, and dried, it would never rot at all and would keep as near forever as the hunger of the people would allow it. And when boiled it formed a food nutritious as bread and far more durable, and, when combined with such elements as oil or tomato or meat or cheese and perhaps the leaves of the bay and the basil, be good food indeed. However, the passage of time failed to bring these added ingredients within the means and reach of all. So, to vary in some measure at least the monotony of the plain pasta, it was made in the widest conceivable variety of shapes: thin strips and thick strips, ribbons broad and narrow, hollow tubes long and hollow tubes bent like elbows, bows and shells and stars and wheels and rosettes and what-have-you. And, if you have nothing, it is anyway some relief to eat your plain pasta in a different design . . . when you have, of course, pasta to eat.

At least every other doorway in the narrow streets and the narrower alleys kept a shop, and many of the shops sold pasta: for the further sake of variety the pasta was not merely stacked up in packages, it was also—the straight kinds—splayed about as though the stalks held flowers at their upper ends. And when the traveler saw these he faintly smiled. The young man who paced him step for step also looked at these modest displays. But he never smiled at them. In fact, although he continued his soft murmurs, he never smiled at all.

Most of these ways seemed hardly wide enough for outside displays, but such there were; there were second-hand clothes and fewer by far displays of some few new clothes; there were whole cheeses, although none hereabouts were seen to buy them whole, and perhaps not very many very often bought them by the slice or crumbling piece. And there were small fish, alive, alive-o, and larger fish in dim slabs that had not been alive in a long time, dry and hard and strong-smelling and salty, redolent of distant and storm-tossed seas. Tomatoes and peppers lay about in baskets. Oil was poured in careful drops into tiny bottles. There were also olives in many colors. Pictures of saints were sold, and the same shops sold, too, odd little emblematic images in coral and silver and—this was surely strange in such a scene of poverty—even gold: behind the narrow windows of narrow shops, crosses, too, yes, and beads: the universal signia of that religion. . . . But what were these horns? What were these tiny hands, fingers tucked into a fist with the thumb protruding between first and second fingers?

Best not to ask, you would empty the street in a trice. Everybody in Naples knows, no one in Naples would speak of it above a whisper . . . to a stranger, not at all. Speak not the word, lest it come to pass. Look not overlong at anyone in these streets, particularly not at the children they produce in such numbers of abundance. Who knows if your eye be not evil?

The eye of the traveler passed over the swarming and ragged *bambini* without stopping, and in the same manner he glanced at the scrannel cats and the charcoal braziers fanned by the toiling housewives: When one's home is but one room, one may well prefer the street as a kitchen.

When one has that which to cook, and fuel with which to cook it.

At length the passageway widened into a sort of a *piazza*. At one end was a church, on either side were the blank walls of some *palazzo* a good deal more antique than the brick ones down below: perhaps from the days of Spanish viceroys, perhaps from the days of King Robert. Who knows. There were anyway no more shops, no stalls, no wide-open-to-the-street one-room "houses" . . . and, for once, no masses of people . . . no beggars, even . . . there was even a sort of alley that seemingly went nowhere and that, surprisingly, held no one. And the traveler, who had so far only from time to time looked out from the corners of his eyes at the young man cleaving close to him as a shadow does, and who had made no reply at all to the soft murmurs with which the young man (ever clutching his jacket round about his naked throat) continually offered his services as "guide"; now for the first time, the traveler stopped, gave a direct look fleeting-swift, jerked his head toward the tiny passageway, and stepped inside.

The shirtless one's head went up and he looked at the heavens; his head went down and he looked at the filthy worn stones beneath. His shoulders moved in something too slight for a shrug and his unclothed throat uttered something too soft for a sigh.

He followed.

The traveler turned, without looking into the other's eyes, whispered a few short words into the other's ears.

The face of the young man, which had been stiff, expressionless, now went limp. Surprise showed most briefly. His brows moved once or twice.

—But yes—he said.—Surely—he said.

And he said, with a half bow and a small movement of his arm—I pray, follow. Very near—he said.

Neither one paused at the church.

And now the streets became, all of them, alleys. The alleys became mere slits. The shops grew infrequent, their store ever more meager. The lines of clothes dripping and drying overhead seemed to bear little relation to what human beings wore. What actually dangled and flapped in the occasional gusts of flat, warm, and stinking air may once have been clothing. Might once more, with infinite diligence and infinite skill, with scissors and needle and thread, be reconstituted into clothing once again. But for the present, one must either deny the rags that name, or else assume that behind the walls, the scabby walls, peeling walls, broken walls, filthy damp and dripping-ichorous walls, there dwelled some race of goblins whose limbs required garb of different drape.

The traveler began to lag somewhat behind.

How often, now, how carefully, almost how fearfully, the youngman guide turned his head to make sure the other was still with him. Had not stepped upon some ancient obscenely greasy flagstone fixed upon a pivot and gone silently screaming down into God knows what. Had not been slip-noosed, perhaps, as some giant hare, hoisted swiftly up above the flapping rags . . . Rags? Signal flags? What strange fleet might have its brass-bound spy-glasses focused hither? Or perhaps it was fear and caution lest the other's fear and caution might simply cause him to turn and flee. In which case the youngman guide would flee after him, though from no greater fear than loss of the fee.

When one has no shirt, what greater fear?

Turned and into a courtyard entered through a worm-eaten door whose worms had last dined centuries ago, perhaps, and left the rest of the wood as inedible. A courtyard as dim, as dank as the antechamber to an Etruscan Hell. Courtyard as it might be the outer lobby of some tumulus, some tomb, not yet quite filled although long awaiting its last occupant. Shadow. Stench. The tatters hung up here could never be clothing again, should they in this foul damp ever indeed dry. At best they might serve to mop some ugly doorstep, did anyone within the yard have yet pride enough for such. And yet, if not, why were they hanging, wet from washing? Perhaps some last unstifled gesture of respectability. Who knows.

Naples.

Around a corner in the courtyard a door, and through the door a passage-way and at the end of that a flight of stairs and at the end of the flight of stairs a doorway that no longer framed a door. A thing, something that was less than a blanket, was hung. The youngman paused and rapped and murmured. Something made a sound within. Something dragged itself across the floor within. Something seemed simultaneously to pull the hanging aside and to wrap itself behind the hanging.

At the opposite side to the door a man sat upon a bed. The man would seemingly have been the better for having been in the bed and not merely on it. On the cracked and riven and flaking, sodden walls some pictures, cut from magazines. Two American Presidents. Two Popes. And one Russian leader. And two saints. Comparisons are odious. Of those whose likenesses were on that filthy fearful wall it might be said they had in common anyway that all were dead.

—Good day—the youngman guide said.

—Good day—the man on the bed said. After a moment. He might, though, have been excused for not having said it at all.

—This gentleman is a foreigner—

The man on the bed said nothing. His sunken eyes merely looked.

—And he would like, ahem, ha, he would like to buy—

—But I have nothing to sell—

How dry, how faint, his voice.

—Some little something. Some certain article. An item—

—But nothing. I have nothing. We have nothing here—

His hand made a brief gesture, fell still.

A very small degree of impatience seemed to come over the face of the older visitor. The younger visitor, observing this, as he observed everything, took another step closer to the bed.—The gentleman is a foreigner—he repeated, as one who speaks to a rather stupid child.

The man on the bed looked around. His stooped shoulders, all dirty bones, shrugged, stooped more.—He may be a foreigner twice over, and what is it to me—he said, low-voiced, seemingly indifferent.

—He is a foreigner. He has, fool, son of a jackal, son of a strumpet, he has money—the youngman turned, abruptly, to the traveler. Said—Show him—

The traveler hesitated, looked all about. His mouth moved. So, too, his nose. His hands, no.

—You will have to show, you know. Can you pay without showing—

The traveler suddenly took a wallet from an inner pocket of his coat, abruptly opened it, and abruptly thrust it in again, placed his back not quite against the noisome wall, crossed his arms over his chest.

Slowly, slowly, the man on the bed slid his feet to the floor.

—Wait outside—he said.—Halfway down—he added.

On the half landing they waited. Listened. Heard.

Dragging, dragging footsteps. A voice they had not heard before.—*NoNO*—A voice as it might be from behind the curtain or the blanket or the what-was-it in place of the door. The faint sounds of some faint and grisly struggle. Voices but no further words. Gasps, only.

Something began to wail, in a horrid broken voice. Then, outside the door-frame, at the head of the stairs, the man, tottering against the wall. Extending toward them his hands, together, as though enclosing something within.

—Be quick—he said. Panting.

And, all the while, the dreadful wail went on from behind him.

The youngman sprang up the stairs, his left hand reaching forward. Behind his back his right hand formed a fist with its thumb thrust out between first and second fingers; then both his hands swept up and met both hands of the other. The youngman, face twisted, twisting, darted down the steps to the half landing.

—The money—

Again, hands met. The traveler thrust his deep into his bosom, kept one there, withdrew the other. Withdrew his wallet, fumbled.

—Not here, not here, you know—the youngman warned.—The police, you know—

One look the older man flung about him.—Oh no. Oh God, not here—he said.—On the ship—

The youngman nodded. Roughly divided the money, tossed half of it up and behind without looking back. He did not come close to the older man as they hurried down the stairs.

Above, the wailing ceased. That other voice spoke, in a manner not to be described, voice changing register on every other word, almost.

—Curse the day my daughter's daughter gave you birth. May you burn, son of a *strega* and son of a strumpet, burn one hundred thousand years in Purgatory without remission—

The voice broke, cracked wordlessly a moment. Resumed.

—One dozen times I have been ready to die, and you, witch's bastard, you have stolen my death away and you have sold my death to strangers, may you burst, may you burn—

Again the voice broke, again began to wail.

The two men reached the bottom of the stained stairs, and parted, the younger one outdistancing the other and this time never looking back.

Above, faintly, in a tone very faintly surprised, the man who had been on the bed spoke.

—Die? Why should you die when I must eat?—

Naples.

THE EIGHTIES AND NINETIES

Full Chicken Richness

INTRODUCTION BY GARDNER DOZOIS

As editor of Asimov's Science Fiction, *and as an anthologist, I had occasion to work with Avram Davidson on several different occasions. He was not always an easy man to work with (our proofreaders always* hated *proofing a manuscript of Avram's, for instance, because so much of the text was so eccentric, and Avram would insist that all of it was* stet—*even an obscure spelling or usage from some even more obscure source which, of course, could not be found in any of the standard references . . . and, of course, he usually turned out to be* right, *which they found even more annoying), and on occasion he could be quite difficult. But I was one of the editors who thought that his stories were worth every bit of the aggravation you sometimes had to put up with in order to obtain them— for Avram was one of the most eloquent and individual voices in science fiction and fantasy, and there were few writers in any literary field who could match his wit, his erudition, or the stylish elegance of his prose.*

Avram had a strong presence in the pages of Asimov's *over the years, making a string of twenty-four sales to the magazine that started under former editor George Scithers and continued for more than ten years to Avram's death, and even a bit beyond; we have published two posthumous stories by Avram, and we still have one of his stories in inventory as I write this. During the same period, he was appearing regularly in* The Magazine of Fantasy & Science Fiction, Amazing, *and other markets. Avram was never prolific, by genre standards, but throughout most of his long career he managed to continue to turn out a small but steady stream of high-quality short fiction, stories that earned him the Hugo Award, the World Fantasy Award (including the prestigious Life Achievement Award), and the Edgar Award . . . making him one of the few writers ever to win all three. (Although Avram was at his best at short story length—his short work has been collected in many volumes, including* The Best of Avram Davidson, Or All the Seas with Oysters, What Strange Seas and Shores, *and* Collected Fantasies—*his novels still contain much that is brilliant, engrossing, and fascinating, especially the underrated* Masters of the Maze, Rork!, Rogue Dragon, *and* The Phoenix and the Mirror.) *And unlike many another aging Grandmaster, his later work was as strong or stronger than ever; his recent series of stories about the bizarre exploits of Dr. Engelbert Eszterhazy (collected in the World Fantasy Award–winning* The Adventures of Doctor Eszterhazy) *and the lush, strange, and vivid adventures of Jack Limekiller (as yet uncollected, alas—publishers take note!) must surely rank among the best short fantasies written by* anyone *in the last fifteen years . . . and that includes those by writers with much greater critical reputations than Avram, who make far larger amounts of money than Avram ever did.*

At his best, Avram Davidson may have been one of the great short story writers of our times, in or out of the fantasy/science fiction genre. He was probably the equal, at the very least, of, say, Saki, and perhaps even of John Collier— although, unlike them, you will find no stories of Avram's being taught in college textbooks. That's as may be. What I think is incontestable, though, is that Avram was certainly one of the great Uniques, an absolutely individual voice and perspective and mind; nobody other than Avram could possibly have written any of Avram's stories, nor could you have possibly mistaken a line of Avram's prose for the prose of any other writer. This is something rare and valuable in a day when some people are trying to force fiction to be as bland and interchangeable and "marketable" as possible. Avram fit no molds, and can not be replaced. The only comfort we can take from his death is that his work *survives, and will be there to speak to us in that unique, instantly recognizable, quirky, intensely flavored voice every time we open the page and read.*

So open the page and read the sly, witty, and elegant story that follows, which features—among many other delights—what is very probably the single silliest use for a time-machine in the entire history of time-travel stories. . . .

FULL CHICKEN RICHNESS

LA BUNNE BURGER WAS said to have the best hamburger on The Street; the only trouble with that was that Fred Hopkins didn't care much for hamburger. However there were other factors to consider, such as these: other items on La Bunne's menu were probably just a bit better than comparable items composed elsewhere on The Street, they sold for just a bit less than, etc. etc., and also Fred Hopkins found the company just a bit more interesting than elsewhere, etc. What else? It was nearer to his studio loft than any eating-place else. Any place else save for a small place called The Old Moulmein Pagoda, the proprietor of which appeared to speak very fluent Cantonese for a Burman, and the Old Moulmein Pagoda was not open until late afternoon. *Late* afternoon.

Late morning was more Fred's style.

He was likely to find there, at any given time of late morning, a number of regulars, such as: well, there was Tilly, formerly Ottilie, with red cheeks, her white hair looking windblown even on windless days; Tilly had her own little routine, which consisted of ordering coffee and toast; with the toast came a small plastic container of jelly, and this she spread on one of the slices of toast. That eaten, she would hesitantly ask Rudolfo if she might have more jelly . . . adding, that she would pay for it. Rudolfo would hand her one or two or three more, she would tentatively offer him a palm of pennies and nickels and he would politely decline them. Fred was much moved by this little drama, but after the twelfth and succedant repetitions it left him motionless. (Once he was to encounter Tillie in a disused doorway downtown standing next to a hat with money while she played—and played beautifully—endless Strauss waltzes on that rather un-Strauss-like-instrument, the harmonica.)

Also unusually present in La Bunne Burger in the 40 minutes before the noon rush were Volodya and Carl. They were a sort of twosome there: that is, they were certainly not a twosome elsewhere. Carl was tall and had long blond hair and a long blond beard and was already at his place along the counter when Volodya walked in. Carl never said anything to Volodya, Volodya always said anything to Carl. Volodya was wide and gnarly and had small pale eyes like those of a malevolent pig. Among the things he called Carl were *Popa!*

Moskuev! Smaravatchnik!—meaning (Fred Hopkins found out by and by) Priest! Inhabitant of Moscow! and One Who, For Immoral Purposes, Pretends to be a Chimney Sweep! Fred by and by tried to dissuade Volodya of this curious delusion: "He's a Minnesota Swede," Fred explained. But Volodya would have none of it. *"He's A Rahshian Artoducks priest!"* was his explosive come-back—and he went on to denounce the last Czar of Russia as having been in the pay of the freemasons. Carl always said nothing, munched away as droplets of egg congealed on his beard.

And there was, in La Bunne Burger, often, breaking fast on a single sausage and a cup of tea, a little old oriental man, dressed as though for the winters of Manchuria; once Fred had, speaking slowly and clearly, asked him please to pass the ketchup: "Say, I ain't deef," said the l.o.o.m., in tones the purest American Gothic.

Fred himself was not in the least eccentric, he was an *artist*, not even starving, though . . . being unfashionably representational . . . not really prospering, either. His agent said that this last was his, Fred's, own fault. "Paint doctors' wives!" his agent insisted. "If you would only paint portraits for doctors' wives, I could get you lots of commissions. Old buildings," the agent said, disdainfully. "Old buildings, old buildings." But the muse kisseth where she listeth and if anything is not on the list, too bad: Fred had nothing against doctors' wives; merely, he preferred to paint pictures of old buildings. Now and then he drove around looking for old buildings he hadn't painted pictures of and he photographed them and put the photos up by his canvas to help when he painted at home: this of course caused him to be regarded with scorn by purists who painted only from the model or the imagination; why either should be less or more scornable, they disdained to say.

Whom else was F. Hopkins likely to see in La Bunne Burger over his late breakfast or his brunch? Proprietors of nearby businesses, for example, he was likely to see there; mamma no longer brought pappa's dinner wrapped in a towel to keep hot. Abelardo was sometimes there. Also Fred might see tourists or new emigrés or visiting entrepreneurs of alien status, come to taste the exotic tuna fish sandwich on toast, the picturesque macaroni and cheese, the curious cold turkey, and, of course, often, often, often the native La Bunne De Luxe Special . . . said to be the best hamburger on The Street. Abelardo had long looked familiar; Abelardo had in fact looked familiar from tbe first. Abelardo always came in from the kitchen and Abelardo always went back out through the kitchen, and yet Abelardo did not work in the kitchen. Evidently Abelardo delivered. Something.

Once, carrying a plate of . . . something . . . odd and fragrant, Rudolfo rested it a moment on the counter near Fred while he gathered cutlery; in response to Fred's look of curiosity and approbation, at once said. "Not on the menu. Only I give some to Abelardo, because our family come from the same country;" off he went.

Later: "You're not from Mexico, Rudolfo."

"No. South America." Rudolfo departs with glasses.

Later: "Which country in South America you from, Rudolfo?"

"Depend who you ask." Exit, Rudolfo, for napkins.

Fred Hopkins, idly observing paint on two of his own fingers, idly wondered that—a disputed boundary being clearly involved—Rudolfo was not out leading marches and demonstrations, or (at *least!*) with drippy brushes slapping up grafitti exhorting the reader to *Remember the 12th of January* . . . the *3rd of April* . . . the *24th of October* . . . and so on through the existing political calendar of Ibero-America . . . Clearly, Rudolfo was an anachronism. Perhaps he secretly served some fallen sovereign; a pseudo-crypto-Emperor of Brazil. Perhaps.

Though probably not likely.

One day, the hour being later than usual and the counter crowded, Fred's eyes wandered around in search of a seat; met those of Abelardo who, wordlessly, invited him to sit in the empty place at the two-person table. Which Fred did. And, so doing, realized why the man had always seemed familiar. Now, suppose you are a foreigner living in a small city or medium town in Latin America, as Fred Hopkins had once been, and it doesn't really matter which city or town or even which country . . . doesn't really matter for *this* purpose . . . and you are going slightly out your *mind* trying to get your electricity (*la luz*) turned on and eventually you notice that there are a few large stones never moved from the side of a certain street and gradually notice that there is often the same man sitting on one of the boulders and that this man wears very dusty clothes which do not match and a hat rather odd for the locale (say, a beret) and that he also wears glasses and that the lens of one is opaque or dark and that this man often gives a small wave of his hand to return the greetings of passersby but otherwise he merely sits and looks. You at length have occasion to ask him something, say, At what hour does the Municipal Palace open? And not only does the man politely inform you, he politely engages you in conversation and before long he is giving you a fascinating discourse on an aspect of history, religion, economics, or folklore, an aspect of which you had been completely ignorant. Subsequent enquiry discloses that the man is, say, a Don Eliseo, who had attended the National University for nine years but took no degree, that he is an *idiosyncratico*, and comes from a family *muy honorado*—so much *honorado*, in fact, that merely having been observed in polite discourse with him results in your electricity being *connectido muy pronto*. You have many discourses with Don Eliseo and eventually he shows you his project, temporarily in abeyance, to perfect the best tortilla making-and-baking machine in the world: there is some minor problem, such as the difficulty of scraping every third tortilla off the ceiling, but any day now Don Eliseo will get this licked; and, in the meanwhile and forever after, his house is your house.

This was why Abelardo had seemed familiar from the start, and if Abelardo was not Eliseo's brother than he was certainly his nephew or his cousin . . . in the spirit, anyway.

Out of a polite desire that Fred Hopkins not be bored while waiting to be served, Abelardo discussed various things with him—that is, for the most part, Abelardo discussed. Fred listened. La Bunne Burger was very busy.

"Now, the real weakness of the Jesuits in Paraguay," Abelardo explained.

"Now, in western South America," said Abelardo, "North American cor-

porations are disliked less for their vices than for their virtues. Bribery, favor-
itism, we can understand these things, we live with them. But an absolute
insistence that one must arrive in one's office day after day at one invariable
hour and that frequent prolonged telephone conversations from one's office to
one's home and family is unfavored, this is against our conception of personal
and domestic usement," Abelardo explained.

He assured Fred Hopkins that the Regent Isabella's greatest error, "though
she made several," was in having married a Frenchman. "The Frankish temperament is not the Latin temperament," Abelardo declared.

Fred's food eventually arrived; Abelardo informed him that although individual enterprise and planned economy were all very well in their own ways,
"one ignores the law of supply and demand at peril. I have been often in businesses, so I know, you see." Said Abelardo.

Abelardo did not indeed wear eyeglasses with one dark or opaque lens,
but one of his eyes was artificial. He had gold in his smile—that is, in his teeth—
and his white coverall was much washed but never much ironed. By and by,
with polite words and thanks for the pleasure of Fred's company, Abelardo
vanished into the kitchen; when Fred strolled up for his bill, he was informed
it had already been paid. This rather surprised Fred. So did the fact, conveyed
to him by the clock, that the noon rush was over. Had *been* over.

"Abelardo seems like—Abelardo is a very nice guy."

Rudolfo's face, hands, and body made brief but persuasive signal that it
went without saying that Abelardo was indeed a very nice guy. "But I don't
know how he stay in business," said Rudolfo, picking up a pile of dishes and
walking them off to the kitchen.

Fred had no reason to remain to discuss this, as it was an unknown to him
how anybody stayed in business. Merely he was well aware how week after
week the price of paints and brushes and canvases went up, up, up, while the
price of his artwork stayed the same, same, same. Well, his agent, though
wrong, was right. No one to blame but himself; he could have stayed in advertising, he might be an account executive by now. Or—Walking along The
Street, he felt a wry smile accompany memory of another of Abelardo's comments: "Advertisage is like courtship, always involve some measure of deceit."

This made him quickstep a bit back to the studio to get in some more
painting, for—he felt—tonight might be a good one for what one might call
courtship; "exploitation," some would doubtless call it: though why? if ladies
("women!") did not like to come back to his loft studio and see his painting,
why did they do so? And if they did not genuinely desire to remain for a while
of varying length, who could make them? Did any one of them really desire
to admire his art, was there no pretense on the part of any of them? Why was
he not the exploited one? You women are all alike, you only have one thing
on your mind, all you think of is your own pleasure . . . Oh well. Hell. Back
to work.—It was true that you could not sleep with an old building, but then
they never argued with you, either. And as for "some measure of deceit," boy
did that work both ways! Two weeks before, he'd come upon a harmonious
and almost untouched, though tiny, commercial block in an area in between
the factories and the farms, as yet undestroyed by the people curiously called

"developers"; he'd taken lots of color snaps of it from all angles, and he wanted to do at least two large paintings, maybe two small ones as well. The date, 1895, was up there in front. The front was false, but in the harmony was truth.

A day that found him just a bit tired of the items staple in breakfast found him ordering a cup of the soup du jour for starters. "How you like the soup?"—Rudolfo.

Fred gave his head a silent shake. How. It had gone down without exciting dismay. "Truthful with you. Had better, had worse. Hm. What was it. Well, I was thinking of something else. Uh—chicken vegetable with rice? Right? Right. Yours or Campbell's?"

Neither.

"Half mine, half Abelardo's."

"I *beg* your pardon."

But Rudolfo had never heard the rude English story about the pint of half-and-half, neither did Fred tell it to him. Rudolfo said, "I make a stock with the bones after making chickens sandwiches and I mix it with this." He produced a large, a very large can, pushed it over to Fred. The label said, *FULL CHICKEN RICHNESS Chicken-Type Soup.*

"Whah-haht?" asked Fred, half-laughing. He read on. *Ingredients: Water, Other Poultry and Poultry Parts, Dehydrated Vegetables, Chickens and Chicken Parts, seasoning* . . . the list dribbled off into the usual list of chemicals. The label also said, *Canned for Restaurant and Institutional Usement.*

"Too big for a family," Rudolfo observed. "Well, not bad, I think, too. Help me keep the price down. Every little bit help, you know."

"Oh. Sure. No, not bad. But I wonder about that label." Rudolfo shrugged about that label. The Government, he said, wasn't going to worry about some little *chico* outfit way down from the outskirt of town. Fred chuckled at the bland non-identification of "Other Poultry"—Rudolfo said that turkey was still cheaper than chicken—"But I don't put it down, 'chicken soup,' I put it down, 'soup du jour'; anybody *ask*, I say, "Oh, *you* know, chicken and rice and vegetable and, oh, stuff like that; *try* it, you don't like it I don't charge you.' Fair enough?—Yes," he expanded. "Abelardo, he is no businessman. He is a *filosofo*. His mind is always in the skies. I tell him, I could use more soup—twice, maybe even three times as many cans. What he cares. 'Ai! Supply and demand!' he says. Then he tells me about the old Dutch explorers, things like that. —Hey! I ever tell you about the time he make his own automobile? ("Abelar-do did?") Sure! Abelardo did. He took a part from one car, a part from another, he takes parts not even from cars, *I* don't know what they from—"

Fred thought of Don Eliseo and the more perfect tortilla making-and-baking machine. "—well, it work! Finally! Yes! It start off, *yooom!* like a rocket! Sixty-three mile an hour! But oh boy when he try to slow it down! It stop! He start it again. Sixty-three mile an hour! No other rate of speed, well, what can you do with such a car? So he forget about it and he invent something else, who knows what; then he go into the soup business. —Yes, sir! You ready to order?" Rudolfo moved on.

So did Fred. The paintings of the buildings 1895 were set aside for a while so that he could take a lot of pictures of a turn-of-the-century family home scheduled for destruction real soon. *This Site Will be Improved With a Modern Office Building*, what the hell did they mean by *Improved*? Alice came up and looked at the sketches of the family home, and at finished work. "I like them," she said. "I like you." She stayed. Everything fine. Then, one day, there was the other key on the table. On the note: *There is nothing wrong*, it said. *Just time to go now. Love*. No name. Fred sighed. Went on painting.

One morning late there was Abelardo in the Bunne. He nodded, smiled a small smile. By and by, some coffee down. Fred said, "Say, where do you buy your chickens?" Abelardo, ready to inform, though not yet ready to talk, took a card from his wallet.

> E. J. Binder Prime Poultry Farm
> also
> Game Birds Dressed To Order
> 1330 Valley Rd by the Big Oak

While Fred was still reading this, Abelardo passed him over another card, this one for the Full Chicken Richness Canned Soup Company. "You must visit me," he said. "Most time I am home."

Fred hadn't really cared where the chickens were bought, but now the devil entered into him. First he told Abelardo the story about the man who sold rabbit pie. Asked, wasn't there anyway maybe some horsemeat in the rabbit pie, said it was fifty-fifty: one rabbit, one horse. Abelardo reflected, then issued another small smile, a rather more painful one. Fred asked, "What about the turkey-meat in your chicken-type soup? I mean, uh, rather, the 'Other Poultry Parts?' "

Abelardo squinted. "Only the breast," he said. "The rest not good enough. —For the *soup*, I mean. The rest, I sell to some mink ranchers."

"How's business?"

Abelardo shrugged. He looked a bit peaked. "Supply," he said. "Demand," he said. Then he sighed, stirred, rose. "You must visit me. Any time. Please," he said.

Abelardo wasn't there in the La Bunne Burger next late morning, but someone else was. Miles Marton, call him The Last of the Old-Time Land Agents, call him something less nice: there he was. "Been waiting," Miles Marton said. "Remember time I toll you bout ol stage-coach buildin? You never came. It comin down tomorrow. Ranch houses. Want to take its pitcher? Last chance, today. Make me a nice little paintin of it, price is right, I buy it. Bye now."

Down Fred went. Heartbreaking to think its weathered timbers, its mellowed red brick chimney and stone fireplace, were coming down; but Fred Hopkins was very glad he'd had the favor of a notice. Coming down, too, the huge trees with the guinea-fowl in them. *Lots* of photographs. Be a good painting. At least one. Driving back, lo! a sign saying E. J. BINDER PRIME POULTRY FARM; absolutely by a big oak. Still, Fred probably wouldn't have stopped if there hadn't been someone by the gate. Binder, maybe. Sure enough. Binder. "Say, do you know a South American named Abelardo?"

No problem. "Sure I do. Used to be a pretty good customer, too. Buy oh I forget how many chickens a week. Don't buy many nowdays. He send you here? Be glad to oblige you." Binder was an oldish man, highly sun-speckled.

"You supply his turkeys and turkey-parts, too?" The devil still inside Fred Hopkins.

Old Binder snorted. " 'Turkeys,' no we don't handle turkeys, no sir, why chickens are enough trouble, cost of feeding going up, and—No, 'guinea-fowl,' no we never did. Just chickens and of course your cornish."

Still civil, E. J. Binder gave vague directions toward what he believed, he said, was the general location of Mr. Abelardo's place. Fred didn't find it right off, but he found it. As no one appeared in response to his calling and honking, he got out and knocked. Nothing. *Pues*, "My house is your house," okay: in he went through the first door. Well, it wasn't a *large* cannery, but it was a *cannery*. Fred started talking to himself: solitary artists often do. "Way I figure it, Abelardo," he said, "is that you have been operating with that 'small measure of deceit in advertising, as you so aptly put it. *I* think that in your own naive way you have believed that so long as you called the product 'Chicken-Type Soup' and included *some* chicken, well, it was all right. Okay, your guilty secret is safe with me; where are you?" The place was immaculate, except for. Except for a pile of . . . well . . . shit . . . right in the middle of an aisle. It was as neat as a pile of shit can be. Chicken-shits? Pigeon-poops? Turkey-trots? ¿*Quien sabe*?

At the end of the aisle was another door and behind that door was a small apartment and in a large chair in the small apartment lay sprawled Abelardo, dead drunk on mescal, *muzhik*-grade vodka, and sneaky pet . . . according to the evidence. Alcoholism is not an especially Latin American trait? Who said the poor guy was an alcoholic? Maybe this was the first time he'd ever been stewed in his *life*. Maybe the eternally perplexing matter of supply and demand had finally unmanned him.

Maybe.

At the other end of *that* room was *another* door and behind that other door was *another* room. And in that *other* room was. . . .

. . . something else. . . .

That other room was partly crammed with an insane assortment of machinery and allied equipment, compared to which Don Eliseo's more perfect make-and-bake tortilla engine, with its affinities to the perpetual motion invention of one's choice, was simplicity. The thing stood naked for Fred's eyes, but his eyes told him very little: wires snaked all around, that much he could say. There was a not-quite-click, a large television screen flickered on. *No.* Whatever it was at the room's end, sitting flush to the floor with a low, chicken-wire fence around it, it was not television, not even if Abelardo had started from scratch as though there had been no television before. The quality of the "image" was entirely different, for one thing; and the color, for another, was *wrong* . . . and wrong in the way that no TV color he had ever seen had been wrong. He reached to touch the screen, there *was* no "screen," it was as though his hand met a surface of unyielding gelatin. The non-screen, well, what the hell, *call* it a screen, was rather large, but not gigantically so. He was looking at a savannah somewhere, and among the trees were palms and he could not identify the others. A surf pounded not far off, but he could not hear it. There was no sound. He saw birds flying in and out of the trees. Looking back, he saw something else. A trail of broken bread through the room, right up to the, mmm, screen. A silent breeze now and then rifled grass, and something moved in the grass to one side. He stepped back, slightly. What the hell could it *mean?* Then the something which was in the grass to one side stepped, stiff-legged, into full view, and there was another odd, small sound as the thing—it was a bird—lurched through the screen and began to gobble bread. Hopkins watched, dry-mouthed. Crumb by crumb it ate. Then there was no more bread. It doddled up to the low fence, doddled back. It approached the screen, it brushed the screen, there was a Rube Goldberg series of motions in the external equipment, a sheet of chicken wire slid noisily down to the floor. The bird had been trapped.

Fred got down and peered into the past till his eyes and neck grew sore, but he could not see one more bird like it. He began to laugh and cry simultaneously. Then he stood up. "Inevitable," he croaked, throwing out his arms. "Inevitable! Demand exceeded supply!"

The bird looked up at him with imbecile, incurious eyes, and opened its incredible beak. "*Doh*-do," it said, halfway between a gobble and a coo. "*Doh*-do. *Doh*-do."

Afterword to "Full Chicken Richness"

BY GARDNER DOZOIS

And, now that I can say this without ruining the ending, I should also point out that this is one of only two science fiction stories I can think of where the plot centers around dodoes. The identity of the other story—not by Avram—I leave as an exercise for the reader.

The Hills Behind Hollywood High

Introduction by Grania Davis

Hollywood was my hometown, and Hollywood Boulevard was my Main Street. I graduated from Hollywood High. Hollywood was a company town, and the big film and TV studios were The Company.

Avram Davidson lived in Hollywood during the placid 1950s. He worked as a night clerk in a cheap hotel off Vine Street, to support his writing habit. Every night he saw the has-beens and the rejects, the character actors and the genuine characters. From our shared experiences, this story was born, about the sacrifices that go on behind the scenes.

I collaborated with Avram Davidson on four short stories, and on the last novel published during his lifetime, Marco Polo and the Sleeping Beauty. We were working on a dark fantasy novel, Boss in the Wall, just before he passed on.

I've been asked how I could possibly imitate Avram Davidson's style. The answer is easy. Nobody can imitate Avram Davidson's style. All I could do was create a framework for his glittering prose, like a jeweler setting gems. There are many Avram Davidson gems in this droll story.

THE HILLS BEHIND HOLLYWOOD HIGH

BY AVRAM DAVIDSON AND GRANIA DAVIS

THAT THERE *ARE* HILLS behind Hollywood—that is, behind Hollywood Boulevard and Hollywood High School—is perhaps not universally known. Smog often hides them, and tourists have no reason to look for, let alone explore, them. They remain unnoticed by the valley commuters who flood past them twice daily. Fish, it is said, do not see the water in which they swim, nor birds observe the winds which bear them.

In the late thirties, according to Life magazine, that omniscient observer of the world scene, the students of Hollywood High School were the most beautiful in the world, being the issue of beautiful young men and women who had come to Hollywood in the twenties seeking movie stardom and, although they had failed—*because* they had failed—stayed on in Hollywood doing Something Else, anything else.

Success would have removed them to Beverly Hills or Brentwood—failure prevented their return to Cowpat, Kansas; Absalom, Alabama; or Pretty Bird, Idaho. ("Diddunt *make* it in thuh pitchers, huh, Jeff? Huh, Jean? Huh huh haw!") So there they stayed, frying hamburgers on Hollywood Boulevard, pumping gas or sacking groceries on Vine. Marcelling waves or setting perms on Cahuenga, clipping hedges or mowing lawns on Selma. Or, if exceptionally lucky, working in studio jobs on the other side of the cameras.

Hollywood was their hometown now, just as Cowpat, Absalom, or Pretty Bird had been. No more profitable maybe, but lots more interesting. And the beautiful failures met and married other beautiful failures—and together begat beautiful babies, who their parents hoped *would* Make It In The Movies. Make It Big.

"*What?* Television, what is *that?*"

It was in the mid-fifties. The huge red juggernaut trolley cars still rolled down the alley right of way. Vibi's restaurant still advertised *Breakfast Served 24 Hours a Day,* but did not advertise the answer to the old-timers' eternal question: Was "Vibi" Vilma Bankey or was she not, and if not, who *was* she? Because the old-timers knew she was *some* movie star from the old days.

As to who was the little old lady in the short black velvet tunic and the sandals cross-strapped halfway up her shrunk shanks, nobody had an answer, or knew why she carried a cane-length silver wand: an ancient fairy in the ancient meaning of the word, she stepped her light-fantastic way and bothered no one.

Dorothy, Angela, and Luanne giggled when they saw her—but only after she had moved well on—as they giggled in confused respect when passing the old dark house smothered in foliage, which was the home of the ninety-odd-year-old widow of L. Frank Baum, the original *Wizard of Oz*. The original house where he had dreamed his strange—and strangely profitable—dreams.

Sometimes the three girls went to buy snacks at the all-night Ranch Market on Vine, and sometimes they went there just to stare at the odd types who went there to stare at the other odd types. Once they heard a squat woman who looked as though Central Casting had selected her as a Ma Kettle stand-in say to her equally typical Farmer-Husband: "Land sakes, Pa, what is *this?*"—holding up the scaly green fruit of the cherimoya-tree—and Pa had said: "Looks like a armadillo egg to me, Ma!"

Past the Hollywood Hotel, which presumably dated from the Spanish *Conquista,* and near Grauman's Chinese Theatre, built like an oriental shrine with hand-and-foot-prints of the famous set into cement out front for the faithful pilgrims to worship, was the business place of Angelo, the dwarf news-vendor. Sometimes they would see Angelo darting across Hollywood Boulevard to pick up a bundle of papers while he meanwhile waved a large white sheet of cardboard as a signal to drivers that he was not merely a driven leaf. Angelo had been in the movies, too.

Side by side, waving and squealing, Dorothy, Angela, and Luanne had seen *Robert Cummings* ride past in an open car with his family, and *Robert Cummings* had waved back and smiled widely—but did not squeal.

More than once they had clutched each other to see, walking on the sidewalk, just like anybody else, the movie-villainous *Porter Hall,* not looking the least villainous, looking dapper and rosy-cheeked—and *Porter Hall* had tipped his dapper hat and said: "Hello, lovely ladies!"

Lovely ladies!

As for names even more (well . . . much more) glamorous than Robert Cummings, or Porter Hall—well, Dorothy, Angela, and Luanne seldom saw *them* . . . in the flesh. Very seldom, though, at great and rare intervals, some of the Very Biggest Stars could be seen cruising majestically along at less than top speed. Showing the flag, as it were. Tryone. Lana. Lauren and Bogie. Bette. Ava. Joan. Clark.

In a Company Town, people naturally hope to get jobs with The Company. In Hollywood there is no one company—there is The Industry. So, although none of their parents had ever become even minor stars, it remained the natural hope of Dorothy, Luanne, and Angela that she . . . and she . . . and she . . . would nevertheless become Major Ones.

Outsiders, had they ever penetrated the neighborhood of squat, scaly palm trees and pseudo-Spanish stucco houses in the Hollywood Foothills, where the smog meets the ocean breezes, might have seen merely three perfectly ordinary teen-age girls—wearing fluffy bouffant felt skirts and fluffy bouffant hairdos, or pedal pushers and pageboys. One with large dark eyes and a slight, skimpy figure (Dorothy), one a tall and narrow blonde with a face marked chiefly by freckles and zits (Angela), one with a lovely complexion and a lavish bosom, but stocky hips and legs (Luanne).

To themselves, however, they were far from ordinary. They were *Daughters of Hollywood*. Moviedom was their birthright; obstacles in the form of imperfectly good looks were merely temporary. Things to be overcome. They were still at Hollywood High School, yes, but they merely endured the boring academic routine (really! classes in *English!* Like they were some kind of *foreigners!*). They saved all enthusiasm for their drama courses.

If there were diets, Luanne dieted them. If there were complexion creams, Angela creamed her complexion with them. If there were exercises, all three exercised them—Luanne for hips and legs, Angela and Dorothy for bosoms.

And—did it *help?*

Well.

Luanne at least obtained a one-shot modeling job, with her picture cut off above the hips.

Angela did get, once, an extra part in a scene at a youth rally. (Politics? Circa 1953? Bless your Adam's apple, *no!* The youths rallied for—in the film— a newer and larger football stadium.)

These opportunities never knocked again; even *so*—

But Dorothy got . . . nothing at all.

Sigh

The last straw was the sign in the storefront window: *Now Signing Up! For Open-Air Spectacular! WANTED. One Hundred Teen-Aged GIRLS! GIRLS! GIRLS!* In she went. Surely, if a hundred were wanted, she—

"No."

"But why *not?*"

The woman at the table heaped with application forms said, "Because, honey, *who* goes to *see* these things? Men." She pronounced this last word as though she were pronouncing "pubic lice." And went on to explain, "My dear, the average American man has never been *weaned*. If a girl is not prominent in the mammary section, if she doesn't have what is called 'a full figure,' though one might ask, 'full of *what?*'—well, Mr. Average American John hasn't gotten his money's worth, the *fool!*"

Perhaps she should have stayed? Only perhaps not.

What she *did* do, after getting the hell out, was to walk fast. Next to walk rapidly, and next to run. Then to stumble, then to halt. And then to start weeping. She didn't burst into tears, she just wept.

And cried.

At that moment, Dorothy caught sight of her slender, tiny self reflected in a store window. Even amidst her grief and woe she realized that, if her life had been a movie, someone would have come up behind her and asked, "Why are you crying?"

At that moment someone came up behind her and asked, "Why are you crying?"

The moment was one of genuine thrill. Mingled with its pleasure, however, was an element of alarm. The voice wasn't that of a wholesome, handsome American Boy with a mouthful of large white teeth set in a cornflakes smile; *no:* it definitely had a Foreign Accent.

Dorothy looked up. Was the man who had spoken—*was* he tall, dark, and handsome? Truth to say—not altogether. He was rather short. He was kind of dark; sallow, one might say. He had large and shining eyes. Now there was nothing wrong with all of this, or with any of this. Dorothy had long ago learned that even the most wholesome-looking of American Boys was not above urging her into some rotten old Nash or Chevy or Studebaker, stinking of grease, and then trying to Get Fresh with her. She gave a cautious sniff: no auto grease. However: something else. What? Something odd. But something not unpleasant.

"Why are you crying?" the man repeated. Impossible to guess his age.

"It's my figure," she said mournfully. "It's too thin and skimpy."

This was the strange man's signal to say, "Nonsense, there's nothing wrong with your figure; it's all in your mind, you have a *lovely* figure." Which would be her signal to slip away and get going. Men and boys had lied to her before, and with what result? (Never mind.)

What the strange man did say was, "Hmm, yes, that is certainly true. It *is* too thin and skimpy. About that you should something do."

So right. "I need to see a doctor," she whimpered.

"*I* am a doctor," said the stranger. In his hand he held a small, wet-glistening bottle of a brown liquid, which he shifted to draw a wallet out, and out of the wallet a card. He handed the card to her. It read:

Songhabhongbhong Van Leeuwenhoek
Dr. Philosof. Batavia.

The word *Batavia* had been crossed out with a thin-point fountain pen and the word *Djakarta* written above. The word *Djakarta* had been scratched out with a thick-point fountain pen and the word *Hollywood* written beneath. In pencil.

"I have only come down to buy this bottle of celery tonic at the deli store. Of course you are familiar with it, an American drink. I wish to have it with my *Reistafel.* How. 'Rice Table,' you would say. It is a mixed dish, such as me, self. Part Nederlandse, part Indonesian. Are you fond of?"

Dorothy had no idea if she was fond, or not fond of. She had a certain feeling that this doctor with the funny name was weird. *Weird.* But still there was the chance that he might be able to help her. If anything, it increased the chance, for everything normal had certainly failed.

"Is your office near here?" she asked.

It wasn't like other doctors' offices, for sure. It had funny things in it: skulls, stuffed things, carved things, things in bottles. *Other* doctors didn't give her a spicy meal. Was she fond of? Or not? Well, it was different.

So—"What kind of medicine do you think will help me?"

The doctor, who had been eyeing her intently, seemed surprised by the question. "What? Ah, the medicine. Oh, to sure be. Hmm!"

He got up and opened a few drawers, then took out a funny-looking bottle with a funny-looking powder in it. "In my native island Sumatra," he explained, "I was very interested in natural history and botany, zoology and pharmacology, also hunting and fishing. And so therefore. But. Details."

She eyed the powder. "Do I take it by the spoonful? Or in a capsule, Doctor?"

He was again staring at her with his odd and shining eyes. "Take—Oh, but first I must you examine," said he.

Well, what he did with Dorothy before, during, and after the examination was certainly no worse than what had been done with her by others, not that most of them had been doctors, though *this* doctor used his *fingers* fairly freely. It was . . . well . . . *int*eresting. And the couch was nicer than the back seat of a tatty old jalopy, and the spices and incense certainly smelled lots better than auto grease.

"Gnumph," he said, after helping her on with her clothes. "You seem in excellent physical condition, exception of thin, skimpy figure, of course. The medicine substance; it is a glandular one which I prepared myself from—but details you would not be fond. I will dilute with water," he said, moving to the sink. But nothing came from the faucet save a wheeze, a grind, and a trickle of rust.

"Ah, I had forgotten. Repairs; they had informed me. No water for a while. So. Another liquid. Not alcoholic. What? Ho!" He took up the small bottle of celery tonic. It was still half full, and he pulled the odd stopper out of the odd bottle and emptied the carbonated beverage into it. Swirled it several times. Handed it to her.

Well! This certainly beat paying a drugstore, and it was better than an injection! She closed her eyes and swallowed. And swallowed. How did it taste? A little like celery and no worse than she had expected. *Much* easier than *ex*ercises! "How much do I owe you?" she asked.

Once again the liquid look. "Owe? Oh. Please pay me with the pleasure of listening with me some of my maternally native music. Here is one gramophone. I shall play some gamalan."

After quite some of this unusual music the doctor asked how she felt. She said she felt sort of funny; he said he would examine her again. She said she would go to the bathroom first; and then, removing her shoes and holding them in her hands, she silently left the premises of Songhabhongbhong Van Leeuwenhoek, Dr. Philosof, and went home.

After a night of odd and restless dreaming, in which she seemed to be rather high up in a greenish place with lots of grass and trees and some rather, well, *funny*-peculiar people, Dorothy awoke with a faint sick-headache. Was it—? No, it wasn't; wrong time of the month, for one thing, and it really didn't feel like that anyway. She drifted back to sleep, this time with no dreams, and awoke again. As she stirred in her bed the thought came that she *did* feel heavier than usual. The medicine! Had it begun to work so soon? She hurried to the bathroom and hopped onto the scales. As she looked down she realized two things: For one, she *had* certainly gained weight! And, for another, her feet were covered with dark hair.

"Oh, my *God!*" she whimpered and, slipping off her nightie, she turned to face the full-length mirror.

It wasn't just her feet.

It was all of her.

As far as she could see, and even in the mirror she couldn't see all of her— she had turned into a gorilla.

It was certainly better than turning into a giant cockroach. But that was all she could think of in its favor.

The pounding on the door had been going on for a long time. Of course it was impossible to let anyone see her—and what good luck that her father had gotten one of the irregularly occurring jobs which kept the household going, and was away helping build sets on location somewhere. She'd better speak through the door. But someone was speaking through the door to *her!*

"I know you're in there, hairy!" the voice was shouting. *Hairy!* Then ... then they already *knew!* How—? Who—?

She peered through a gap in her bedroom curtain, being careful not to move it, but in vain! Though she scuttled away in terror, whoever was outside began tapping, rapping on the bedroom window. Suddenly she remembered whom she'd seen. Not "hairy"! The man was shouting for "Harry," her father!

Dorothy's mother, smelling of whisky and perfume, had vanished from their lives some years ago—but she had left debts. Lots of debts. Dad had borrowed to pay the debts, then he borrowed to pay the money he had borrowed.

The whole thing had spiraled and doubled and tripled, and then fallen into the hands of the Greater Los Angeles Punitive Collection Agency. In fact, as she tiptoed into the living room she saw that another of the familiar cards had been slipped under the door. Bang! Bang! Bang! *"I know you're in there, Harry! Better open up and let me talk, Harry! We can't wait forever, Harry!"*

On the card was printed the name of Hubbard E. Glutt, District Agent. Mr. Glutt wasn't an entire stranger. He wore a once-white shirt and a once-gray suit, both with ingrown ketchup stains, and he had *extremely* hairy nostrils. It could not be said, even with the best of intentions, that he was a very nice man. His breath smelled, too.

"Go away, please go away," Dorothy said through the door. She was thankful to note that her voice was unchanged. She wasn't thankful for much else. "My dad's not in—"

"I don't care who's not in," yelped Mr. Glutt. "Ya gunna pay sompthing?"

"But I have no money!"

Mr. Glutt made a noise between a grunt and a snarl. "Same old story: 'My dad's not in and I have no money.' Huh? Still not in? Well, I gotta sudgestion."

Here his voice sank and grew even nastier. "Lem*me* in, and I'll tell ya how we can, mmm, take mebbe twenty dollas affa the bill, liddle gurl, huh, huh, huh. . . ."

Dorothy could stand it no longer. She jerked the door open and pulled Mr. Glutt inside. The scream had not even reached his throat when Dorothy's new-formed fangs sank into it.

As though in a blur, she dragged the suddenly inert body into the breakfast nook. And feasted on it.

Moments passed.

The blur vanished. Oh God, what had she done? Killed and partially eaten someone, was what. But how? Gorillas don't eat people, gorillas eat bananas . . . *don't* they?

Therefore she wasn't even a gorilla. She was some sort of monster—like a werewolf? A were-gorilla? Trembling with shock and horror and fear, she stared at her image in the big front hall mirror . . . and gave a squeal of terrified loathing. The hair that covered her was now darker and coarser, and her facial features had coarsened, too. Her fingernails had become talons, although fragments of the Pearly Peach nail polish still remained. And examining her mouth as the squeal died away, she saw that it was full of yellow fangs. She began to sob.

How could something like this have *hap*pened to her? That's what girls always asked when they found themselves unwantedly pregnant—as if they didn't *know* how! But this was worse than pregnancy, a million times worse . . . and besides, pregnancy had a well-known cause, and she really couldn't imagine what had caused *this*.

Then a sudden thought came, echoing like a clap of thunder, illuminated as by a flash of lightning: that . . . that weird glandular-extract *medi*cine which she had taken only yesterday! To make her figure fuller. Well, fuller it certainly was! But oh, at what a price! There was nothing to do but call the doctor and have him come over, and give her something to undo its effects. Only—only— would he make house calls? Well, she'd just have to see.

Only alas, she could not see. The most searching examination of the L.A. phone books, all several of them, failed to show any listing for a Doctor Van Leeuwenhoek . . . however spelled. Nor could she remember a phone in his small apartment. She was afraid to go out as she was now, at least by day. At night? Maybe. If anybody found out about what she'd done to Mr. Glutt they'd have her jailed . . . or even killed . . . or put in a mental home. She'd have to conceal the body, run away and hide in the woods of Griffith Park, high in the Hollywood Hills, where she would roam and kill like a wild beast . . . until she was finally discovered and slain with a silver bullet.

At this thought she gave another tearful squeal.

Weeping, Dorothy cleaned the blood off the Spanish-style tiles in the entry hall and kitchen with her O-Cello sponge mop, and methodically put the remains of the collection agent in a large plastic bag, which she placed in the refrigerator to eat later. Oh, how lucky that her father wouldn't be home for another week! She had until then to decide what to do. Well, at least she had enough food.

Although, between weeping and listening to Jack Benny, the Whistler, and Stella Dallas on the radio, and watching Uncle Milton Berle and Kukla, Fran, and Ollie cavort on their prized new television set, she grew hungry again—she realized that she had no appetite at all for the rest of Mr. Hubbard E. Glutt. Evidently she had partially devoured him out of mere rage and shock. Listlessly, Dorothy ate some lasagna instead.

And so passed the remainder of the week inside the psuedo-Spanish house in the Hollywood foothills. A few times Angela or Luanne or other friends, and twice religious representatives of two different exclusive Truths, came to the door (besides phone calls)—Dorothy said (over the phone and through the door) that she had a highly contagious flu. She gave the same excuse to the newsboy, the Avon Lady, and the highly confused Welcome Wagon Woman.

As the week's end approached with no thoughts except flight into the hills, etc., her mood became almost frantic. Then one glorious morning she woke to find the hair vanished, her body lighter, and her teeth and nails returned to normal. She hastened to replace the Pearly Peach Polish.

But . . . wasn't there something *else* she had to do? The answer came at the week's absolute end, with her body again distressingly short and thin—but human. Clicking her tongue reproachfully at her forgetfulness, she dressed quickly and toted Mr. Hubbard E. Glutt's very chilled remains in their plastic sack, and deposited them fairly late at night in a public trash bin.

Dad Harry returned on schedule, sunburned and exhausted, and demanding fried chicken and beer. Then he went to bed, and Dorothy, again in her padded bra, tight sweater, bouffant skirt, and (very) high heels, went back to school. She felt relieved, she felt worried. A visit to the place where Doctor Funny Name lived disclosed empty windows and a FOR RENT sign: Would the horrible condition recur? Oh, how she hoped not! Better to remain thin and skimpy all the days of her life—and never get into the movies at all!

Luanne and Angela were happy to see her again. They chattered away about the trifling things which had happened at Hollywood High during her absence, and now and again Dorothy squealed with interest which was only sometimes simulated. Would it happen again?

Early one night, about a month later, feeling vaguely ill at ease, she went for a stroll. The malaise increased; she thought a trip to a ladies room would help, but the one in the park was now closed. There was nothing to do but go behind a bush; and it was there, as she adjusted her dress, that she felt her hands again come in contact with—a shaggy pelt. She let out a squeal of anguish. And fainted.

It was a lucky thing that her Dad was once again away, this time on his monthly week-long visit to his girl friend in the unfashionable section of Malibu, the girl friend's mother then making *her* monthly visit to her other daughter in Chula Vista.

Now it was impossible for Dorothy to fit into her clothes, so she made a bundle and dropped them into a debris receptacle as she passed it by. How to get home? Slinking was the only way, but as she sought out the most dimly lit streets, she only seemed to get further from home rather than nearer. And, oh!

~~*Was* she suddenly hungry! She fought and fought against the desire for im-~~
mediate food, but her stomach growled menacingly. Well, she knew how waste-
ful the average American family was. So of a sudden she lifted up the lid of a
garbage can near a private home, with intent to delve into its contents.

No sooner had she lifted off the lid and bent over to examine what was
inside, than there appeared suddenly, out of the *chiaroscuro*, the figure of a
well-nourished early middle-aged man with a small moustache. He had a large
brown-paper bag in his hands which looked like garbage for disposal; astonishment was simultaneous. Dorothy squealed and dropped the lid with a clatter.
The man said, "Gevalt!" and dropped the brown-paper bag, then recovered it
almost immediately. Dorothy would have fled, but there was a high fence behind her. In theory she could have turned upon him with tooth and fang and
claw, but unlike Mr. Glutt, this man offered no gross importunity. And beneath
the astonishment he seemed to have rather a kindly face.

"For a moment you had me fooled," said he. "A better-looking gorilla suit
I never seen. What, you're embarrassed. Someone should see you rifling the
garbage can, you should have what to eat?"

He shook his head from side to side, uttered a heavy sigh which seemed
not devoid of sympathy.

"I'm not wearing a gorilla suit!" exclaimed Dorothy.

This time the shake of the head was skeptical. "Listen," said the man. "That
L.A. has one weird what you might call ecology, this I know: possums, coyotes,
escaped pythons, the weird pets some people keep because from human beings
they don't find empathy: okay. But go*ril*las? No. Also, gorillas don't talk. They
make clicking noises is what, with an occasional guttural growl, or a squeal.
Say. That was some squeal you gave just now. Give it again."

Dorothy, partly because of relief at finding the man neither hostile nor
terrified, partly because of pride that *any*thing she could do should meet with
approbation, obliged.

"Not bad. Not. Bad. At. All. I like it. I like it. Listen, why don't we do
this? Come into the house, we'll have a little something to eat. I'm batching it
right now; you like deli stuffed cabbage? Warming up now on the stove. Miffanwy ran away on me; luck with women I have yet to find, but hope I haven't
given up yet, springs eternal in the human breast." Gently he urged Dorothy
forward towards the house.

"Sandra hocked me a tchainik by day and by night, Shelley would gritchet
me in kishkas until I could spit blood, I took up with Miffanwy. We'll eat a
little something, we'll talk a little business—no commitments on either side.
What we'll eat is anyway better than what's in the garbage can, although gour-
met cooking isn't my line—listen, you wanna know something about shiksas?
They never hock you a tchainik, they never gritchet you in kishkas, they don't
kvetch in public places till you could drop dead from the shame; no. All they
do is cheat. Watch out for the step."

Dorothy had seen better kitchens and she had seen worse. However,
kitchen decor wasn't uppermost in her mind; what was uppermost was friendly
human contact; also food. The man of the house ("Alfy is the name") filled
her plate with stuffed-cabbage rolls and plied her with tangerines, asked if she

preferred milk or cream soda and set out some Danish, pointed to a bowl of cut-up raw vegetables and pointed out that it kept away the dread scurvy, offered her a choice of seeded rye, pumpernickel, and egg-bread.

"Where there is no food, there is no religion. Where there is no religion, there is no food. So my first father-in-law used to say. What a gonnif. Eat, my shaggy friend. Eat, eat."

After quite some time, during which they both ate heartily and, truth to tell, noisily, Alfy gave grateful eructation. Gave a sudden exclamation. "Almost missed the news on the video! Finally I broke down and bought one. Many a movie big shot it will wipe out of business, they say, but me it wouldn't wipe out. Pardon my back," he said, as he turned to watch the small screen.

Dorothy gladly did so, for quite apart from her contentment in the immediate situation, she was also pleased to watch what many still called "video," which was not yet to be found in every room of every house, rather like an ashtray.

Neither black and white screen nor sound adjusted immediately, and Alfy adjusted the rabbit-ear antennas; at length a voice was heard to say: ". . . meanwhile, search continues for the so-called Monster of the Hollywood Hills."

"I'll give them yet a Monster of the Hollywood Hills," growled Alfy. "What are they trying to do with my property values? Communists! Holdupnikkes! Shut up, Alfy," he advised himself.

Two men, besides the television news personality, sat before a background of greatly enlarged photographs and plaster casts.

"Well, Dr. William Wumple of the University of Southern Los Angeles Department of Primate Sciences, and Superintendent Oscar Opdegroof of the County Police Bureau of Forensic Zoology, won't you tell us what your opinion is about all this?"

Professor Wumple said, "These photographs and plaster casts are of the foot-and-knuckle prints of the increasingly rare Sumatran mountain gorilla of Sumatra, and—"

"I grant you, Professor Wumple," said Superintendent Opdegroof, "that there is certainly a resemblance. But the increasingly rare Sumatran mountain gorilla, a native of Sumatra in Indonesia, is vegetarian in its habitat. There is, as you know, no record of an increasingly rare Sumatran mountain gorilla, which inhabits the East Indies or Sumatra, ever having killed and eaten part of a credit bureau representative and concealed his bones in a plastic bag. The diet of this otherwise harmless creature is mostly the stalk of the wild celery plant which grows profusely on every wild mountain slope of the archipelago of Sumatra."

"Depraved appetite," said Professor Wumple, "may be found in any species. I refresh your memory with the fact that pachyderms are also herbivorous, and yet there is the classical case of the elephant named Bubi which fatally trampled and ate a young woman named Anna O. in the Zurich Zoo, who had heedlessly fed him leftover kümmelbrot from the table of her employer, a dealer in low-priced watch cases named Schultz."

The television news personality opened his mouth, but it and the rest of him dwindled and vanished as Alfy switched off the set. "Look, so now to

~~business. Um, what did you say your name was, unwilling though I am to force~~ you out of your chosen anonymity? *Dorothy?* A girl in a gorilla suit, this I never encountered before," he said, surprised; but rallied quickly. "My mother, she should rest in peace, told me that in her own younger days, if a woman so much as smoked a cigarette in the public street, she might as well have gone to Atlantic City with a traveling salesman. But now we live in an enlightened era. Lemme hear you squeal."

"Squeal?" asked Dorothy, somewhat lethargic from food and rest.

Alfy nodded. "Yeah, squeal. Use your imagination. Say you're strolling through your native jungle and you see, like, reclining under a tree and fast asleep because she's lost from her expedition—what then, a bewdyful young woman. You never seen nothing like this in your *life* before! So naturally, you give a squeal of astonishment. Lemme hear."

Dorothy, with only the slightest of thoughtful pauses, gave a squeal. Of, she hoped, astonishment.

"Bewdyful," said Alfy.

Dorothy gave him a doubtful look. "No," he said. "I mean it, I swear it. By my second mother-in-law's grave, she should soon be inside of it. Hypocrisy is alien to my nature, even though I never finished high school, but was cast out in the midst of the teeming thoroughfares, what I mean *jungles,* which are the streets of our large cities. But of this I needn't bore you, Dotty.—Now use your imagination again. You and this lovely young woman are going along a jungle trail in search of the mysterious Lost Temple of Gold. Her boy friend, the head of the expedition, gets knocked on the head by a falling coconut, and as he sinks to the ground, simultaneously you—and you alone—become aware that an unfriendly tribe of rotten natives are slinking through the underbrush to attack: lemme hear you convey this information to your lovely human new-found lady friend with a series of intelligent squeals."

Dorothy did her best to oblige, and in the unpremeditated fervor of her performance, began to use gestures. Alfy was immensely pleased. "We'll dub it, we'll dub it!" he cried.

She was so excited that she found herself jumping up and down and scratching her pelt.

Alfy, watching her benignly, became concerned. "Even through your gorilla suit you're sweating," he said, "let me get you some ice cubes for your cold drink." Running water over the old-fashioned all-metal tray, he turned and asked, "Why not take off your costume, you'll be more comfortable, Dotty?"

Even as she opened her mouth to repeat that she wore no costume, Dorothy observed a strange woman come running across the dimly lit dining room adjoining the kitchen; and as she ran, thus she screamed:

"I'll *give* you 'take off your costume,' I'll *give* you Dotty, I'll *give* you Shelley, I'll *give* you Miffanwy—"

"Sandra, if you hock me a tchainik, I'll—"

Dorothy reacted to Sandra with as little instinctive affection as she had to Hubbard E. Glutt; raising herself on her toes, extending her arms high and her hands out, her talons clawing and her fangs showing, she began to utter squeals of pure rage.

Sandra never for a moment showed the slightest sign of believing that she was confronted by someone in a gorilla suit; Sandra turned and fled, giving shriek after shriek of terror, horror and fright.

Dorothy pursued her down the street, sometimes erect, sometimes bounding along on all fours; till the lights of an oncoming car caused her to shinny up the nearest deciduous tree, whence she dropped upon a housetop, thence to another tree, and thence to another housetop. Until eventually she realized that she was absolutely lost.

Inadvertently scattering the inhabitants of a hobo jungle, she moodily drank their bitter black coffee and spent the night on a musty mattress in a culvert near their fire. The illustrated magazines of a certain type which those lonely and semihermitical men used to while away the hours of their solitude, she merely fed into the flames in disgust.

Much of the next day Dorothy spent in a eucalyptus grove destined soon to be "developed" into total destruction. She gave a lot of thought to her condition. It was no doubt the celery tonic in which the incompetent quack-doctor Songhabhongbhong Van Leeuwenhoek had administered the so-called glandular extract—containing as the soft drink must have done, certain elements very similar to the wild celery stalks eaten by the increasingly rare mountain gorilla of Sumatra—which had caused this change to come upon her. Of this she was certain.

Since it wasn't concurrent with her monthly cycle, and seemed not even to be identical with the full moon, she wondered if its occurrence might have something to do with her sign: Aries on the cusp. Vaguely she remembered hearing of a certain economically priced astrologer mentioned by her mother before she left to become an Avon Lady in Anaheim—or so her father said; perhaps (Dorothy now wondered for the first time) he had been shielding some less respectable occupation.

Her thoughts were interrupted with the utmost suddenness by the appearance in the grove of a simianlike creature who appeared equally startled. For a long moment both stood still, each staring at the other. Was this another increasingly rare Sumatran mountain gorilla? Another victim of the celery and hormone tonic?—No. It appeared to be a man in a flea-bitten gorilla suit! And it held a bottle of something wrapped in a brown paper bag.

"Listen," it said. (Or, though the voice was slightly slurred, it was a masculine voice—said *he*.) "In times past, honey, when I was a well-known star of stage and screen, I drank nothing but the best Madeira, with a preference for *sercial,* but when you're down it's all over with the imported vintages. Any kind of sneaky pete will do. Go on, my dear. Go on and take a hit." His sunken snout came so near to her face that she sensed it wasn't his first drink of the day.

The well-known former star of stage and screen took the bottle and slid the top of it up high enough so that he could uncap it and drink of its contents,

~~and yet quickly slide it back down inside of~~ the paper bag; for many people might object to someone blatantly imbibing alcohol in public—even in a eucalyptus grove which had formerly served as the site of a hobo jungle—for to do so is against the law.

Next, and though he had gallantly offered her a hit, he proceeded to do the following: turning slightly at an angle away from Dorothy, he fumbled his paw into his pelt and produced a second bottle, a smaller one with clear liquid in it; of this he swiftly drank and swiftly disposed it once again in a pocket of some sort; and next he took a much longer tug of the cheap wine. *Then* he offered it to her again, and as she hesitated, thinking of a tactful refusal, he said, "It's only polite to offer, but to insist would be most *im*polite.—And jerked it away.

His voice had become increasingly slurred, and as he lurched off down the road, Dorothy considered the possibility that the clear liquid was vodka. It was only because he half-turned his head, and inclined it as though in invitation for her to accompany him, that she followed. Grotesquery prefers company, and she thought that she might as well go along—because she wasn't sure what else to do. So follow she did.

Now and then some of the passersby looked at them, but nobody looked twice. Not only was this Hollywood, but this was the famous "Gower St. Gulch," as outsiders in the know called it. To those on the inside it was merely "The Gully."

To outsiders *not* in the know it might have seemed as if preparations were being made for the annual cattle drive to Dodge City, so numerous were the men in cowboy outfits. There was a slight stir in their ranks, seemingly caused by a dark man wearing a soiled khaki shirt and faded dungarees, moccasins and a pair of reddened eyes, who was standing on the sidewalk and shouting:

"Slant-eyed folks and Mexicans and Very Light Colored People, keep the hell outa the gully!" he yelled, in particular directing his cries to several people in war paint and feathers. "Leave the depiction of Native American Indian roles to jen-u-wine Native American Indians!—You, *you*, Marcus Garvey Doothit, professional named Marco Thunderhorse, I'm addressing myself ta *you*, don't gi' *me* no bull about yer Grandmother bein' a full-blooded Cherokee Injin!"

M. G. Doothit, a.k.a. Marco Thunderhorse, gave a scornful pout and said, "All I have to say to *you*, Amos Littlebird, is that sticks and stones and arrows and musket balls may break my bones, but ethnic epithets merely reflect upon those who hurl them."

Scarcely had all this faded behind them when Dorothy and her lurching companion encountered a scowling young man bearing a sign which read: SO-CALLED "SCIENCE FICTION" MOVIES/STOP LIBELOUS PORTRAYALS OF SO-CALLED "MAD SCIENTISTS," SCIENCE IS THE HOPE OF THE PEOPLE!

It was not yet the 1960s, but the winds were full of straws.

By and by they came to a high wire fence surrounding a barrackslike compound; and here the senior simian figure paused to drain both of his bottles and hurl them away. Then he approached the gate in, for the first time, a fairly good simulation of an apelike lope. A gray-haired man stepped out of a booth, beaming.

"Gee, good *morn*ing, Mr. Bartlett Bosworth," he exclaimed. "Only last night I was saying to my wife, 'Guess who I saw at AESSP this A.M., sugar?' And she says, 'Who?' And I told her, 'Remember Bart Bosworth who played Greeta Garbo's boy friend and also he played Mree Dressler's grown-up handsome son?' And she says 'Sure! What's he doing *now?*' And I told her, 'He's imitating a gorilla for Alf Smatz, King of the D-Movies,' and she says, 'Oh gee, what a shame,' and—"

Thickly, from behind his gorilla mask, Bart Bosworth said, "Both of you just take your pity and divide it in two and then you can both shove it." And he lurched on through the gate.

The gray-haired man, no longer beaming, pointed to Dorothy and asked, "Who's this?"

"Who's it look like? Myrna *Loy?* My understudy."

The gateman turned his attention to other arrivals. Ahead of them was a sign reading: ALFRED EMMANUEL SMITH-SMATZ PRODUCTIONS. POPULAR ENTERTAINMENT AT POPULAR PRICES. The way seemed endless, but Bartlett Bosworth evidently knew his way.

By and by they came upon a clearing in a jungle. Scarcely had Dorothy time to express surprise in a single squeal, when Bart Bosworth, uttering a huge and hideous hiccup, fell full length upon the synthetic turf and began to snore.

This dull and repetitive sound was interrupted by a short, sharp slap: a man in a long-considered-obsolete uniform of a moving-picture director (including turned-around cap), had occasioned this by striking his forehead with the flat of his hand. "Again!" he cried. "Again! Drunk yesterday, drunk the day before—get him up! Hot coffee, bennies if anybody's got any, an ice pack. But get him *up*, get him *sober!*"

Although a shriveled-looking chap with the air of a superannuated yesman turned round and round like a dervish, shrilling: "Right, Chief! Yes, Chief! How coffee! Benzedrine! A nice pack!" others were not convinced.

"It's no use, Mr. Smatz," said the script girl.

"Wouldn't help, Alfy," called down the cameraman.

"We couldn't get him sober yesterday and we couldn't keep him sober the day before," declared a blond, youngish-looking fellow in short khaki pants and shirt, and a pith helmet.

And in a high, petulant voice, a bosomy blonde youngish-looking woman dressed similarly announced that she was "fed up with alla this stuff"—actually, she didn't say *stuff*—and in another minute would go sit in her dressing room.

"Get somebody else," advised somebody else, "for the ape part."

The man with the turned-around cap gave, through his megaphone, an anguished howl. "Even in a low-budget film no one could afford to maintain a shikker gorilla on the payroll!—Also," he said, giving the youngish-looking woman a baleful stare, "histrionics in high places I'm not appreciative of; also, furthermore, in low-budget films high places ain't so damn high.—*What*, 'Get

somebody else?' *Who*, 'Get somebody else?' *Where*, 'Get somebody else for
the ape part?' Ape-part-playing is a dying art, gorilla suits cost a fortune—and
if I had a fortune would I be making D-films? No," he answered.

Then an odd expression came over his face. One hand he cupped around
his ear; the other hand he used to shade his eyes. "Wait. Listen. Look. Just
before shikker here, he plotzed, didn't I hear like a high-pitched squeal which
clearly indicated astonishment and alarm? Sure I did. So. Okay. Who
squealed?"

Voices were heard denying that he or she or they had squealed. Ears were
cupped and eyes were shaded. . . . It was very soon indeed that fingers were
pointed. Dorothy, realizing that concealment was useless, shyly stepped forward.

Alfred Emmanuel Smith-Smatz—"Alfy" (for it was he) clapped both
hands together. *"Dotty!"* he exclaimed. "Not only did you chase away Sandra,
that yenta; early this morning I get a phone call from my thirty-year-old step-
son Sammy, the schmuck: 'Mommy is so terrified she swears she'll never leave
Desert Hot Springs again'—but you are *still* giving out the intelligent squeals,
with *expression!* Bartlett Bosworth never got no expression in his squeals; that's
the way it is with them silent screen stars: squeak, yes; squeal, no. Are you a
quick study, Dotty? Yeah? Good! So take a quick sixty seconds to study the
next scene. . . . You got it? Yeahh! Yeay! Lights! Camera! Dolly in on Dotty,
this great little gorilla lady! ACTION! Let'm roll!"

The rest is Film History, even if much of it must be concealed from the fans
and the gossip columns and the world at large. To be sure, Alfy Smatz ("King
of the D-films") was a bit put out at first when he learned that Dorothy
couldn't play gorilla roles week after week; but only during those weeks when
the moon is full in central Sumatra.

But the month has, after all, more than one week. The first week Dorothy,
in her own natural form (with artfully padded hips and bosom) plays the heroine in a science fiction film as the daughter of (despite feeble social protest)
the mad scientist. The second week Dorothy is kidnapped from various wagon
trains and restored to various wagon trains by, alternatively, Marco Thunderhorse and Amos Littlebird. The third week Dorothy is, first, threatened by
love-starved Arabs, and second, saved from same by the noble efforts of either
Marco or Amos in djellabas.—But the *fourth* week in the AESSP shooting
schedule: *Ahah!*

In the fourth week of every month Dorothy stars in one STARRING
JEANNIE OF THE JUNGLE, THE WORLD'S MOST LOVABLE LITTLE
GORILLA film after another after another after another. These movies have
wowed the fans in every drive-in in North America, and break records in every
box office from Tampa to Tahiti; and, boy! How the money rolls in!

Dorothy has paid off her father's debts and retired him on a personal
pension, with modest privileges at the gaming tables in the poker palaces of
Gardena.

Every now and then she and her blond, youngish-looking leading man of
the moment get into her lemon-yellow Pighafetti-Zoom convertible to visit

Luanne and Angela. They are green with envy. Again and again, separately and together, Luanne and Angela wonder. What is the secret of Dorothy's success? It isn't looks. It isn't figure. What? What? What?

It's showbiz, is what.

Dr. Songhabhongbhong Van Leeuwenhoek has never been heard from again.

Serves him right.

The Slovo Stove

INTRODUCTION BY MICHAEL SWANWICK

"The Slovo Stove" is probably the definitive statement on a process central to the American immigrant experience—the loss of ethnicity. I once wrote Avram to praise this story and mentioned that my wife, Marianne Porter, who is of Ruthenian extraction, had been able to learn almost nothing about her heritage. He wrote back:

> *As for the already dead and gone Czechoslovakian Republic of my youth. Local attitudes in Yonkers went like this: "What about the Czechs?" "The Czechs . . . The Czechs are all right. They have funny names but basically they are all right." "And the Slovacks?" "Well . . . the Slovacks . . . they work hard . . . but on Saturday night they get drunk and beat up their wives and kids, the Slovacks . . . they don't wear hats . . . they wear caps!" "And the Carpatho-Ruthenians?" Answer: "Ha ha ha ha ha ha ha!" I never heard anybody mention them without laughing. To this day I don't know what is or is supposed to be so damned funny about the Carpath-Russian-Ruthenians. NO idea.*

Which was how Avram wrote casually—with erudition, street smarts, and enormous humor. If, by the way, you have a loved one who "doesn't read science fiction," but appreciates the fine literary craftsmanship of (say) Updike, Cheever, or Raymond Carver, here is a story you can urge upon him or her with confidence. Because Avram was—is—their peer. In craft, in heart, in experience, his best are the equal of theirs. He was, like them, a great American short story writer.

As to why this fact was never acknowledged in his lifetime, I simply cannot say. NO idea.

THE SLOVO STOVE

IT WOULD HAVE BEEN a little bit hard for Fred Silberman to have said a completely good word for his hometown; "a bunch of boors and bigots," he once described it; and life had carried him many leagues away. However. In Parlour's Ferry lived Silberman's sole surviving aunt, Tanta Pesha; and of Tanta Pesha (actually a great-aunt by marriage) Silberman had only good memories. Thinking very well of himself for doing so, he paid her a visit; as reward—or punishment—he was recognized on the street and almost immediately offered a very good job. Rather ruefully, he accepted, and before he quite knew what was happening, found himself almost a member of the establishment in the town where he had once felt himself almost an outcast.

Okay, he had a new job in a new business; what was next? A new place to live, that was what next. He knew that if he said to his old aunt, "Tanta, I'm going to live at the Hotel"—Parlour's Ferry had one, count them, *one*—she would say, "That's nice." *Or,* if he were to say, "Tanta, I'm going to live with you," she would say, "That's nice." However. He rather thought that a roomy apartment with a view of the River was what he wanted. Fred developed a picture of it in his mind and, walking along a once long-familiar street, was scarcely surprised to see it there on the other side: the apartment *house,* that is. He hadn't been imagining, he had been remembering, and there was the landlady, sweeping the steps, just as he had last seen her, fifteen years ago, in 1935. He crossed over. She looked up.

"Mrs. Keeley, do you have an apartment to rent? My name is Fred Silberman."

"Oh," she said. "*Oh.* You must be old Jake Silberman's grandson. I reckernize the face."

"Great-nephew."

"I reckernize the face."

The rent was seventy-five dollars a month, the painters would come right in, and Mrs. Keeley was very glad to have Nice People living there. Which was very interesting, because the last time Silberman had entered the house (Peter Touey, who used to live upstairs, had said, "Come on over after school; I got a book with war pictures in it") Mrs. Keeley had barred the way: "*You* don't live here," said she. Well, Times had changed. Had times changed? *Something* had certainly changed.

The building where the new job would be lay behind where the old livery stable had been; Silberman had of course already seen it, but he thought he would go and see it again. The wonderful dignified old blue-gray thick flagstones still paved most of the sidewalks on these unfashionable streets, where modernity in the form of dirty cracked concrete had yet to intrude; admiring them, he heard someone call, "Freddy! Freddy?" and, turning in surprise, almost at once recognized an old schoolmate.

"Aren't you Freddy Silberman? I'm Wesley Brakk. We still live here." They rambled on a while, mentioned where each had been in the War, catalogued some common friends, then Wesley said, "Well, come on into the house, we're holding my father's *gromzil,*" or so it sounded; "you don't know what that means, do you? See, my father passed away it's been three years and three months, so for three days we have like open house, it's a Slovo and Huzzuk custom, and everybody has to come in and eat and drink." So they went in.

There were a lot of people in the big old-fashioned kitchen at the end of the hall; the air was filled with savory smells, the stove was covered with pots— *big* pots, too. One of the older women asked something in a foreign language; im*med*iately a younger man snapped, "Oh for Crise sake! Speak United States!" He had a dark and glowering face. His name, Fred learned, was *Nick.* And he was a relative.

"This is beef stomach stuffed with salami and hard-boiled eggs," said a woman. "Watch out, I'll pick away the string."

"You gonna *eat* that stuff?" asked Nick. "*You* don't hafta eat that stuff; I'll getcha a hamburger from Ma's Lunch."

Ma's Lunch! And its french-fried grease! And *Ma,* with frowsy pores that tainted the ambient air. "Thanks, Nick, this is fine," said Fred.

Nick shrugged. And the talk flowed on.

By and by a sudden silence fell and there was a tiny sound from forward in the house. "Aintcha gonna feed the *baby,* f'Crise sake?" cried Nick. His wife struggled to rise from a chair crowded behind the table, but "old Mrs. Brakk," who was either Wes's mother or Wes's aunt, gestured her not to; "*I* will do," said she. And produced a baby bottle and a saucepan and filled the pan at the sink. There was a movement as though to take one of the heavy cook pots off the stove to make room to warm the bottle, but the dowager Mrs. Brakk said a word or two, and this was not done. Perhaps only Fred noticed that she moved toward a small pile of baby clothes and diapers in a niche, as though she wanted to bring them with her, but Fred noticed also that her hands were full. So he picked them up and indicated that he would follow.

"Thank you, gentleman," she said. She gave him, next, an odd glance, almost as though she had a secret, of which she was very well aware and he was utterly ignorant. Odd, yes; what was it? Oh well.

In her room, "You never see a Slovo stove," Mrs. Brakk said. It was not a question. It was a fact. Until that moment he had never *heard* of a Slovo stove. Now he gave it a glance, but it was not interesting, so he looked away; then he looked back down at it. Resting on a piece of wood, just an ordinary

piece of wood, was a sort of rack cut from a large tin can, evidently not itself
brought from Europe by whichever Slovo brought the stove. On top of the
rack was something black, about the length and width of a book, but thinner.
Stone? Tentatively he touched a finger to it. Stone . . . or some stonelike com-
position. It felt faintly greasy.

"You got to put the black one on first," Mrs. Brakk said. However glossy
black the old woman's hair, wrinkled was her dark face. She put on the saucepan of water and put the baby's nursing bottle in the pan. "Then the pot and
water. *Then* you slide, underneath, the blue one." This, "the blue one," was
about the size and thickness of a magazine, and a faint pale blue. Both blue and
black pieces showed fracture marks. As she slid "the blue one" into the rack,
Mrs. Brakk said, "Used to be *bigger*. Both. *Oh* yeah. Used to could cook a
whole meal. Now, only room for a liddle sorcepan; sometimes I make a tea
when too tired to go in kitchen."

Fred had the impression that the black piece was faintly warm; moving his
finger to the lower piece (a few empty inches were between the two), he found
that definitely this was cool. And the old woman took up the awakening child
and, beaming down, began a series of exotic endearments: "*Yes,* my package;
yes, my ruby stone; *yes,* my little honey bowl—" A slight vapor seemed to
arise from the pan, and old Mrs. Brakk passed into her native language as she
crooned on; absolutely, *steam* was coming from the pan. Suddenly Silberman
was on his knees, peering at and into the "stove." Moistening a fingertip as he
had seen his mother and aunts do with hot irons a million times, he applied it
to "the blue piece," below. Mrs. Brakk gave a snort of laughter. The blue piece
was still cool. Then he wet the fingertip again and, *very* gingerly, tested the
upper "black piece." It was merely warm. *Barely* warm. The *pan? Very* warm.
But the steam continued to rise, and the air above pan and bottle was . . .
well . . . *hot.* Why not?

She said, "You could put, between, some fingers," and, coming over, baby
pressed between one arm and bosom, placed the fingers of her free hand in
between the upper and lower pieces. He followed her example. It was not hot
at all in between; it was not even particularly warm.

Silberman peered here and there, saw nothing more, nothing (certainly) to
account for . . . well . . . *anything.* . . . She, looking at his face, burst out laughing, removed the lower slab of stone (if it was stone), and set it down, seemingly, just anywhere. Then she took the bottle, shook a few drops onto her
wrist and a few drops onto Fred *Silberman's* wrist—oh, it was *warm* all right.
And as she fed the baby, calling the grandchild her necklace, her jewel ring,
her lovely little sugar bump, he was suddenly aware of two things: one, the
bedroom smelled rather like Tanta Pesha's: airless, and echoing faintly with a
cuisine owing nothing to either franchised foods or Fanny Farmer's cookbook
(even less to *Ma's Lunch!*); two, that his heart was beating very, very fast. He
began to speak, heard himself stutter.

"Buh-buh-but h-h-how does it wuh-work? *work?* How—" Old Grandmother Brakk smiled what he would come to think of as her usual faint smile;
shrugged. "How do boy and girl love? How does bird fly? How water turn
to snow and snow turn to water? How?"

Silberman stuttered, waved his arms and hands; was almost at once in the kitchen; so were two newcomers. He realized that he had long ago seen them a hundred times. And did not know their names, and never had.

"Mr. Grahdy and Mrs. Grahdy," Wesley said. Wes seemed just a bit restless. Mrs. Grahdy had an air of, no other words would do, faded elegance. Mr. Grahdy had an upswept moustache and a grizzled Vandyke beard; he looked as though he had once been a dandy. Not precisely pointing his finger at Fred, but inclining it in Fred's general direction, Mr. Grahdy said, "How I remember your grandfather well! ["Great-uncle."] His horse and wagon! He bought scraps metal and old newspaper. Sometimes sold eggs."

Fred remembered it well, eggs and all. Any other time he would have willingly enough discussed local history and the primeval Silbermans; not now. Gesturing the way he had come, he said, loudly, excitedly, "I never saw anything *like* it before! How does it work, how does it *work?* The—the"—*what* had the old one called it?—*"the Slovo stove?"*

What happened next was more than a surprise; it was an astonishment. The Grahdy couple burst out laughing, and so did the white-haired man in the far corner of the kitchen. *He* called out something in his own language, evidently a question, and even as he spoke he went on chuckling. Mr. and Mrs. Grahdy laughed even harder. One of the Brakk family women tittered. Two of them wore embarrassed smiles. Another let her mouth fall open and her face go blank, and she looked at the ceiling: originally of stamped tin, it had been painted and repainted so many times that the design was almost obscured. There was a hulking man sitting, stooped (had not Fred seen *him,* long ago, with his own horse and wagon—hired, likely, by the day, from the old livery stable— calling out *Ice! Ice!* in the summer, and *Coal! Coal!* in the winter?); he, the tip of his tongue protruding, lowered his head and rolled his eyes around from one person to another. Wesley looked at Silberman expressionlessly. And Nick, his dark face a-smolder, absolutely glared at him. In front of all this, totally unexpected, totally mysterious, Fred felt his excitement flicker and subside.

At length Mr. Grahdy wiped his eyes and said something, was it the same something, was it a different something? was it in Slovo, was it in Huzzuk? was there a difference, what was the difference? Merry and cheerful, he looked at Fred. Who, having understood nothing, said nothing.

"You don't understand our language, gentleman?"

"No."

"Your grandfather understood our language."

"Yes, but he didn't teach me." Actually, Uncle Jake *had* taught him a few words, but Silberman, on the point of remembering anyway one or two of them, and quoting, decided suddenly not to. Uncle Jake had been of a rather wry and quizzical humor; who knew if the words really meant what Uncle Jake had said they did?

Wes's sister (cousin?) said, perhaps out of politeness, perhaps out of a wish to change the subject, perhaps for some other reason—she said, "Mrs. Grahdy is famous for her reciting. Maybe we can persuade Mrs. Grahdy to recite?"

Mrs. Grahdy was persuaded. First she stood up. She put on a silly face. She put her finger in her mouth. She was a little girl. Her voice was a mimic's voice. She became, successively: hopeful, coy, foolish, lachrymose, cheerful. From the company: a few chuckles, a few titters. Then she stopped playing with her skirts, and, other expressions leaving her face, the corners of her mouth turned down and she looked around the room at everyone. Some exclamations of, supposedly, praise were heard, and a scattered clapping of hands; Mrs. Grahdy silenced all this in a moment. For a second she stood there, poker-faced, stiff. Then she began a rapid recitation in what was obviously verse. Her face was exalted, tragic, outraged, severe: *lots* of things! *How* her arms and hands moved! *How* she peered and scouted! *How* she climbed mountains, swung swords. A voice in Fred's ear said, half whispering, "This is a patriotic poem." Mrs. Grahdy planted the flag on, so to speak, Iwo Jima. Loud cries from the others. *Much* applause. The patriotic poem was evidently over. The down-turned mouth was now revealed to be, not the mask of Tragedy, but the disciplined expression of one too polite to grin or smirk at her own success.

After a moment she turned to Silberman. "I know that not one word did you understand, but did the ear inform you the verses were alexandrines?"

He was hardly expecting this, scarcely he knew an alexandrine from an artichoke: and yet. Not pausing to examine his memory or to analyze the reply, he said, "Once I heard a recording of Sarah Bernhardt—" and could have kicked himself; surely she would feel he was taking the mickey out of her? Not at all. All phony "expression" gone, she made him a small curtsy. It was a perfectly done thing, in its little way a very sophisticated thing, an acknowledgment of an acceptable compliment, an exchange between equals. It made him thoughtful.

Grahdy: "So you didn't understand what this Mr. Kabbaltz has asked?"—gesturing to the white-haired man in the far corner. Fred shook his head; if the question dealt with iambic pentameter, he would *plotz*. "This Mr. Kabbaltz has asked, the Slovo stove, you know, 'Did it even get warm yet?' *Hoo, hoo, hoo!*" laughed Mr. Grahdy, Mrs. Grahdy, Mr. Kabbaltz. *Hoo, hoo, hoo!*

Fred decided that ignorance was bliss; he turned his attention to the steaming bowl set before him as the people of the house dished out more food. Soup? Stew? *Pottage?* He would ask no more questions for the moment. But could he go wrong if he praised the victuals? "Very good. This is very good." He had said, evidently, the right thing. And in the right tone.—It *was* very good.

Mr. Grahdy again: "Your great-grandfather never send you to the Huzzuk-Slovo Center to learn language?"

"No, sir. Not there."

"Then where he did send you?"

"To the Hebrew School, as they called it. To learn the prayers. And the Psalms." Instantly again he saw those massive ancient great thick black letters marching across the page. *Page* after page. A fraction of a second less instantly Mr. Grahdy made the not quite pointing gesture, and declaimed. And paused. And demanded, "What is the second line? Eh?"

Silberman: "Mr. Grahdy, I didn't even understand the *first* line."

Surprise. "What? Not? But it is a *Psalm*." He pronounced the *p* and he pronounced the *l*. "Of course in Latin. So—?"

"They didn't teach us in Latin."

More surprise. Then, a shake of the head. Silberman thought to cite a Psalm in Hebrew, reviewed the words in his mind, was overcome with doubt. *Was* that a line from a Psalm?—and not, say, the blessing upon seeing an elephant? . . . or something? The Hebrew teacher, a half-mad failed rabbinical student, had not been a man quick with an explanation. "Read," he used to say. "Read."

More food was set out: meat, in pastry crust. Then (Mr. Grahdy): "When you will be here tomorrow? Perhaps I shall bring my *violin*"—he pronounced it vee-o-leen—"and play something."

"That would be nice"—Fred, noncommittally; and turning again to the food of the memorial feast, "Delicious!" said Fred.

"Is it warm yet?"—Mr. Grahdy. *Hoo, hoo, hoo!*—*Mr.* Grahdy, *Mrs.* Grahdy, Mr. Kabbaltz. People entered, talked, ate, left. Someone: "You're old Jake Silberman's grandson?" "Great-nephew." By and by Fred looked up: Mr. Kabbaltz and the Grahdys were gone. For a moment he heard them just outside the door. Laughing. Footfalls. The gate closed; nobody seemed left but family members. And Fred. Silence. Someone said, "Well, there go the Zunks." Someone else: "Don't call them that. Call them Huzzuks."

Wesley suddenly leaped up, almost toppling his chair. Began to bang his head against the wall. "I can take Chinks!" *Bang.* "I can take Japs!" *Bang.* "I can take Wops, Wasps, Heebs, and Micks!" *Bang. Bang. Bang.*

"Wesley—"

"Wes—"

"Wassyli—"

"Was—"

"I can take Spics and Niggers." *Bang! Bang!* "I can*not* take—*Zunks!*" *Bang!* Abruptly, he sat down, and held his head.

In Fred's mind: *Question:* So what's a Zunk? *Answer:* A deprecated Huzzuk.

Wes began again. "They can talk Latin. We can hardly grunt. They recite poems. We can barely tell a dirty joke. They have violinists. We are lucky if we got fiddlers. Why did God punish us poor Slovo slobs by putting us in the same country with them, over there in Europe? Why are we still respectful to them, over here in America? Why? Somebody please tell me. *Why?*"

A sister, or maybe a sister-in-law, said, somewhat slowly, "Well . . . they are better educated—"

This set Wes off again. "In *their* dialect, *they* had books, magazines, newspapers. All *we* had was the catechism and the missal, in ours. *They*—"

"*We* had a newspaper. Didn't Papa's brother used to send it to us . . . sometimes? *We*—"

Wesley brushed the invisible ethnic newspaper aside. "The *Patriótsk?* The *Patriótsk.* Came out once a month. One sheet of paper, printed on four pages. What was in it? The new laws, the price of pigs, *some* obituaries, *no* births, and the Saints' Days in both Church calendars: that's *all. Finish.* The *Patriótsk!*" Evidently the invisible newspaper had climbed on the table again, for Wesley swept it off again, and then he trampled on it. Heavily.

"Hey, look at the time. I got to be going. I sure want to thank you for that delicious—"

"We are giving you some to take with you, home," said an aunt. Or was it a niece?

"Oh, I—"

"It's the *cus*tom. And you *liked.*"

"Oh, sure. But my new apartment isn't ready yet, and my aunt is strictly kosher." They didn't say anything ecumenical, neither did they tell him that the Law of Moses was dead and reprobate; they began to put fruit into a paper bag. A *large* paper bag.

But Wes, taking head from hand, was not finished yet. "Why? *Why?* Will someone tell me *why?*"

Someone, surely a sister, too straight-faced to be serious, said, "They are so beautiful; they ride red horses." Wes almost screamed. When had she ever seen a Huzzuk on a horse? When had she ever seen a *red* horse? Nick's wife told Silberman that it was a saying. A proverb.

"Anyway, *you* know, some people say it wasn't the *horse* that was red, but, uh, the things on the horse? What the horse, like, *wore?*" Nick, who had been reading the funny papers with a very unfunny expression, now fired up. Who *gave* a damn? he demanded. Quit *talk*ing about all them old European things, he demanded. Fred announced his thanks for the fruit. Wes asked Nick if he wasn't *in*terested in his rich Old World heritage; Nick, upon whom subtlety was wasted, shouted that *no,* he *was*n't; Wes ceased being subtle and shouted back; Fred Silberman said that he really had to be going. And started out.

Someone came out into the hall and walked along with him: old Mrs. Brakk . . . being very polite, he thought. A dim light was on in her room. She stopped. He paused to say good night. The look she now gave him, had she been forty years younger, would have been an invitation which he knew could not be what she now meant; *what* was it she now meant?

"You want to come in," she said. "You want to see how it works." She moved inside the room. Silberman followed, beginning to breathe heavily, beginning to feel the earlier excitement. He had forgotten! How could he have forgotten?

"First you put on the black piece, up on here." The book-sized slab slid into its place on the rack. The infant sighed in sleep. "*Yes,* my rope of pearls," she said softly. "Next, you put on the sorcepan with the water in it. Now, I make just a bowl of tea, for me. And so . . . *next* . . . you put in the blue piece," about the size of a magazine, "down . . . *there.* See? This is what we call the Slovo stove. And so now it gets warm. . . ."

What had the old Huzzuks, those quasi-countrymen of the old Slovos, what had they *meant,* "Is it even warm yet?" Silberman forgot the question as he watched the vapors rise, felt the air warm, above; felt the unwarmed space between the two "pieces," the thicker fragment of black stone (if it *was* stone) and the thin fragment of pale blue; saw, astonishingly soon, the size of crabs' eyes, the tiny bubbles form; and, finally, the rolling boil. He was still dazed when she made the tea; he hadn't remembered setting down the bag of fruit, but now he picked it up, set a soft thank-you and good-night, left the house.

He could hear them still shouting in the kitchen.

. . .

"That's nice," said Tanta Pesha when he gave her the fruit.

"Tanta, what is it with the Huzzuks and the Slovos?"

Out came the bananas. "The Huzzuks?" She washed the bananas, dried them with a paper towel, dropped it in the garbage. "The Huzzuks. They are all right." Out came the oranges.

"Well, what about the Slovos?"

She washed the oranges. "The Slovos?" She dried the oranges with a paper towel, dropped it in the garbage. "The Slovos? They are very clean. You could eat off their floors. On Saturday night they get drunk," and he waited for more, but no more came: Tanta Pesha was washing the apples. This done, she was overcome by a scruple. "Used to," she said. "Now? I don't know. Since I moved away." How long had she and Uncle Jake lived near the Huzzuks' and Slovos' neighborhood? She began to dry the apples with a paper towel. How long? Forty years, she said.

"Forty years? Forty-two? Let be: forty."

Had she ever heard of the Slovo stove? No . . . she never had.

"Well. Why don't—how come they don't *like* each other?"

Tanta Pesha looked at him a moment. "They *don't?*" she said. She dropped the paper towel in the garbage. Then she put the fruit into a very large bowl and, standing back, looked at it. "That's nice," she said.

The next morning, early, Silberman drove down to the City and made arrangements to be moved, and drove back to "the Ferry." He went to take a look at his apartment-to-be: lo! the painters were actually painting in it. Mrs. Keeley stopped sweeping, to assure him that everything would be ready in a day or two. "Well, a *cup* la days," she amended. "You won't be sorry; this is always been a very nice block, more'n I can say for *some* parts a town, the Element that's moving in nowadays. I give you a very nice icebox, Mr. Silberman."

"Say, thanks, Mrs. Keeley; I really appreciate that. Say, Mrs. Keeley, what's the difference between the Huzzuks and the Slovos?"

Mrs. Keeley shrugged and pursed her lips. "Well, they mostly don't live right around *here*. Mostly they live down around, oh, Tompkins . . . Gerry . . . De Witt. . . . Mostly around there." She adjusted her hairnet.

"But—is there a difference between them? I mean, there's got to be; some are called Huzzuks and some are called Slovos. So there must be a—"

Mrs. Keeley said, well, frankly, she never took no interest in the matter. "Monsignor, up at St. Carol's, that big church on the hill, *he* used ta be a Hozzok, rest his soul. What they tell *me*. Now, your Bosnians, as they call 'um, they mostly live around on Greenville Street, Ashby, St. Lo. The *Lemk*os, whatever the hell *they* are, excuse my French, you find *them* mostly in them liddle streets along by the Creek . . . Ivy, Sumac, Willow, Lily, Rose. Well . . . *use* to. Nowadays . . . nowadays people are moving around, moving *around*," she said, rather fretfully, "and I wish they would-int. I wish people they would stay *put*. So, as t'them people that you ast me about, Hozzoks and Slobos, mostly you find them down around on Tompkins . . . Gerry . . . De Witt . . .

them streets there. What time is it? Is my program coming on?" She went into
her apartment and closed the door behind her. A second later he heard a radio
increased in volume. He wandered out into the street.

The streets.

The streets had certainly been wide enough when Uncle Jake's had not
been almost the only horse-and-wagon plying for trade along them. But that
had been a long time ago. The streets had been full of children then, oh what
a merry cheerful sight: you think so? To Fred Silberman as a small child this
had been Indian Country, full of hostiles. Oh well. Then, during the Depression, there had been a considerable depopulation. Stores had emptied, and
stayed empty, and one of the public schools, "Number Seven," had even closed.
However. In the year or two before the War several empty factories had been
reopened as Defense Plants, and many new faces had appeared on the streets.
Southern Blacks. Island Tans. Mountain Whites. Then Fred had gone off into
the Army, and . . . really . . . had only now come back. Coming back out of his
revery, he found himself in a time warp.

Gone were the four-story tenements, block after block of them; he was in
a neighborhood of wooden houses, *old* wooden houses, old wooden fences,
old wooden trees. Right across the street was a store building, a sagging rec-
tangle of boards. Seemingly *just* as he remembered it, even to the raised letters
on the glass storefront: SAL DA T A. Untouched by any recent paint was a sign,
Mat. Grahdy, Meats, Groceries. He went in, knowing that a bell would tinkle,
so of course one *did.*

The showcase on one side was large enough to show lots and lots of meats;
what it showed now were some scrawny pieces of pig, a hunk of headcheese,
a hunk of Swiss cheese, a tray of lilac-colored sausages, and (in a puddle of
congealing blood) half of a head of something, cut longitudinally and looking
incredibly anatomical. The store seemed vast, and was vastly empty; the smell
proclaimed that Coolidge was President; the floor was splintery and clean.
Looking up from something on the counter, Mr. Grahdy gazed with absolute
amazement. Was he merely amazed that Fred Silberman was coming into his
store?—that someone who *looked* like Fred Silberman was coming into his
store?—or, simply, that someone, *any*one, was coming into his store?

Then he smiled. Dipped his head to one side. They shook hands. Fred
asked for some small item. Grahdy shrugged one shoulder. Fred asked for a
different small item. Another shrug. Fred tried to think of some other small
item, opened his mouth to name something, said, "Uh—" and named nothing.
Grahdy laughed, finger-brushed his long moustaches: *Right! Left!*

"Rice?" he asked. "Sugar? Potatoes?" It was Silberman's turn to laugh.
The elder man joined in. A cut of headcheese was his next suggestion; "and a
cut of Swiss? a sliced roll? I give mustard for nothing." Somehow they wound
up sharing the sandwich. Fred, observing an opened book on a newspaper there
atop the counter, asked Mr. Grahdy What was he reading?

The book was turned around. But it was Greek to Fred. "Schiller," said
the grocer, turning pages. "Heine. You can read in the original?" He widened
his eyes at Fred's headshake. "What great pleasure you are missing. So. But . . .

Lermontov? Pushkin? What? '*Nope*'?" A look of mild surprise. And mild reproof. A sigh. "So. No wonder you have Slovo friends!" The front of his very clean, very threadbare apron moved in merriment.

This was it. The opening. "*Mr.* Grahdy—" Mr. Grahdy bowed slightly. His horse, his carriage, were at Fred Silberman's disposal. "Mr. Grahdy . . . what *is* it with you . . . with you people . . . your people . . . and the Slovo people? Could you tell me that? I would like to know. I would really like to *know*."

Mr. Grahdy stroked his smile, moustachioes, Vandyke, and all. He looked (Silberman suddenly thought), he would have looked, much like the Kaiser . . . if the Kaiser had ever looked much like having a sense of humor. "Well, I shall tell you. In our old kingdom there back in Europe. In one province lived mainly Huzzuk only. In one province lived mainly Slovo only. In our own province lived we both. How shall I explain? To say that the Slovo were our serfs? Not exact. To say they were our tenants, our servants? Mm . . . but . . . well . . . Our thralls? You *see*. The kings, they were of foreign origin, a dynasty. We were their feudalists. We Huzzuk. And the Slovo, the *Slovo*, they were *our* feudalists!" His smile indicated not so much satisfaction with the subordinate position of the Slovo as satisfaction with his explanation. And, as Silberman stood leaning against the counter digesting this, the old grocer added to it.

The Slovo were not, hm, bad people. They were simple. Very simple people. Had come into Europe long ago following behind the Magyar and the Avar. Had been granted permission to settle down in "empty land" belonging to the Huzzuk. Had become Christianized. Civilized. Gave up their old language. Adopted the language of the Huzzuk. Which they spoke badly. *Very* badly.—Here, with many chuckles, Grahdy gave examples of the comical Slovo dialect, of which exemplar Fred of course understood nothing whatsoever.

He did take advantage of the old man's laughing himself into a coughing fit and then into smiling silence. "What about their *stove,* Mr. Grahdy? What's with the Slovo *stove*? What *is* it, what *is* it, how does it *work*?" And here Mr. Grahdy threw back his head and laughed and laughed and coughed and coughed and laughed and coughed and laughed.

It took quite a while for him to recover. And after he had been slapped on the back and had sipped a glass of water and sucked a Life Saver and assured Fred (with many mimes and gestures) that he was now all right, Grahdy spoke in a weakened voice, incomprehensibly; then, rather more clearly, though very husky: "*Did it get warm yet?*" he asked.

Silberman jumped away from the counter. "But what do you *mean* by that? You said it last night and so did Mr. What's-His-Name with the thick white hair and you both laughed and laughed *then*—"

"The woman in the story. The Slovo woman in the story. The famous story anecdote. You know."

But finally Fred got his point across that no, he did *not* know. Grahdy was amused at this. At this, next, Grahdy was incredulous. And finally, persuaded that indeed, famous or never so famous, the story anecdote was absolutely unknown to F. Silberman—"Your great-grandfather did not ever told you? No? *No?*"—Grahdy was absolutely delighted. *God* knows when he had last had an absolutely fresh audience. . . .

A Slovo woman had newly emigrated to the United States. Came to stay with relatives. By and by someone asked that a pot of water be put on for tea. "I will do it," said the greenhorn woman. Did she know how to do it? Of course, of course! What did they think? Of course she knew how! "Shouldn't someone go and show her?" Nonsense; not necessary! Off she went, from the front room into the kitchen to put the water on for the tea. So they talked and they waited and they waited and they waited, and still no call from the kitchen. Had she gone out the back door? So someone went in to see. They found her standing by the stove and looking at it. (Grahdy indicated her perplexed look.) *"Was the water hot yet?"* Here Grahdy indicated that the great punch line was coming; here Grahdy put hands on hips and an expression of annoyance and bewilderment on face.

" 'Was the water hot yet?' "

" *'Hot? Hot? It didn't even get warm!'* "

Neither did Silberman. What the hell. But the story anecdote was not over. The punch line was followed by an explanation. (a) The Slovo greenhorn woman knew nothing about a gas range. (b) The Slovo greenhorn woman assumed that the gas range was, simply, a Slovo stove, American style. (c) So she, seeing that the grate—which to her was, of course, "the black part"— seeing this already in place, she put water in the pot and set it on top. (d) Leaning against the gas stove there happened to be the grease tray, usually placed of course underneath the burners to catch spatters and drips; it had just been cleaned, was why it was where it was. It was enameled, and a pale blue. (e) So, assuming that this was "the blue part," she had slid it into place, underneath the burners. (f) Had *not* turned on the gas, (g) had *not* struck a match, (h) had just waited for this American gas stove to behave like a *Slovo* stove—

—and here came the question and answer together again, as inexorable as Greek tragedy and by now almost as familiar as Weber and Fields or Abbott and Costello:

" *'Was the water hot yet?'* "

" *'Hot? Hot? It didn't even get warm!'* "

This was, evidently, and by now Fred had had lots of evidence, the hottest item there had ever been in Huzzuk humor in the history of the *world:* Joe Miller, Baron Munchausen, Charlie Chaplin, step *way* back. Get ready for something *really* funny: the anecdote story of the greenhorn who thought that by sliding the grease tray underneath the gas burners, and by doing nothing else, she could produce heat!

Hot-cha!

*Yock*etty-*bop*-cha!

Why this venerable race joke, certainly worth a chuckle when fresh and crisp, still guffawed its way down the corridors of time, required more consideration than Fred was then prepared to give. But it was a lot, *lot* easier to understand why the Slovos, who had been listening to it for . . . *how* long? forty years? *eighty* years? . . . were beginning to get kind of restless. And—

"And how does it *work,* Mr. Grahdy? I mean . . . scientifically?"

The one-shoulder shrug. "Who knows, my dear young gentleman? Consider the electrical properties of the amber, a great curiosity in the former age; but today, merely we flick a switch."

The local public library was not changed much since Andrew Carnegie had helped endow it; there was nothing in the catalogue under either *Huzzuk, Slovo,* or *Stove* which provided even faint enlightenment. The encyclopedia ran to information about the former dynasty and its innumerable dull rulers; also *The Huzzukya areas have become moderately industrialized* and *The interests of the Slovoya areas remain largely agrarian* and *Exports include duck down, hog bristles, coarse grades of goat hair and wool.* Goody.

In the Reference Room the little librarian with the big eyeglasses listened to his request; said, in her old-time professionally hush-hush voice, "I think there is a pamphlet" . . . and there certainly *was* a pamphlet; it was bound in, and bound in tightly, with a bunch of other pamphlets on a bunch of other subjects. The nameless author-publisher ("Published by the Author") had disguised the fact of not having much to say by saying it in rather large type. Leaning on the volume with both hands to keep it open, Silberman learned that "the Slovoi themselves no longer admit to know just where was or even approximately their ancestral 'Old Home' or 'Old Place' near 'The Big Water.' The latter has been suggested for Caspian Sea or Aral Sea, even fantastically has been suggested 'Lake Baikal.' In Parlour's Ferry are found Huzzuki in many Middle Class professional commercial role and has been correctly suggested Slovoi fulfill labor tasks with commendable toil and honesty." There was nothing about stoves, and Fred felt that unless he wanted eventually to sell photographs of his wrists to Charles Atlas, he might as well let go of the bound volume of pamphlets; he did, and it closed like a bear trap.

The pamphlet probably contained the text of a paper done for a pre-WWI class in Night School, the Author of which, intoxicated by getting a fairly good grade, had rushed it off to a job printer; it was suggested in Fred's mind that he was probably (*probably?*) a Huzzuk.

Back at Fred's new apartment-to-be, lo! the painters were no longer painting; the painters were no longer, in fact, there; and neither was the painting finished. Only, in the middle of the drainboard of the kitchen sink sat a white bread and sardine sandwich with a single symmetrical bite missing out of it. Another unsolved mystery of the sea; or had it come there by a fortuitous concourse of the atoms: why not? Down went Fred and rang Mrs. Keeley's bell. By and by the door opened a crack long enough to transmit heavy breathing and the odor of gin and onions; almost at once the door closed shut again and by and by the volume of the radio went up. Mrs. Keeley was not one of your *picky* listeners out there in Radioland who require very fine tuning, and Silberman was unable to say if she was listening to an old recording of the Tasty Yeast Jesters or maybe one of a love song by President Harding. He went away.

A côte chez Brakk, an aunt said, as he came in, "I saved you some fruit stew," and also Wes poured him something powerful-looking. Evidently the conventicle/potlatch was still going on, with Fred's presence still acceptable.

Although—A newspaper was lowered; behind it was *Nick*. "Don't make the Old Lady show ya that jee-dee *stove* no more," he said. "She's all wore out."

Fred said, easily, "Okay, Nick.—Who else has got one?" he asked the world at large. There was a thinking pause. Wes said, No one that *he* knew of.

"It's the last of the Mohicans," Wes said.

Nick slapped down the paper. "She better get *rid*da it. Y'hear me? I'm gonna smash it up, I'm gonna throw it offa the bridge; I don' wanna even *hear* about it—no wonder they make funna us all the time!" No one said a word, so Nick said a word, a short and blunt one; and then, as though shocked himself, slammed out of the room. In a moment a car drove rapidly away. Wes was expressionless and, seemingly, emotionless.

Fred sampled the fruit stew. Was it the same as stewed fruit? no it *wasn't*. Good, though. As soon as his spoon scraped the bottom, a bowl of something else was set down beside him. And a plate of something else. "Here is beaten-up bean soup with buttermilk and vinegar. This is lamb fritters with fresh dill." Golly, they sounded odd! Golly, they were good!

In a corner across the room an old man and an old woman discordantly sang-sung religious texts from, shared between them, an old wide book in Old Wide Huzzuk or something of the sort. "That's supposed to benefit the soul of the late deceased," said a very young man with a very large and shiny face, in a tentatively contentious tone.

"College boy," said Wes. "Could it hurt?"

Fred Silberman put down his spoon. (Eating fritters with a *spoon?* Sure. Why not? Hurts *you?*) "Listen, where was 'the Old Home Place by the Big Water'?" he asked.

The college boy instantly answered, "Gitche Gumee."

Wes said, with a shrug of his own, far heavier than Mat. Grahdy's, "Who the hell knows? Whoever *knew?* You think they had *maps* in those days? I suppose that one year the crops failed and there was no nourishment in the goat turds, so they all hit the road. *West.* And once they crossed a couple mountains and a couple of rivers, not only didn't they know where they *were,* they didn't even know where they'd *been.*"

Fred said, "Listen. Listen. Nick isn't here, the Huzzuks aren't here, nobody is here but us chickens, *cut*-cut-cut-*cut,* God should strike me dead if I laugh at you: *Where did the stoves come from? The* Slovo *stoves?*"

"Who the hell knows?"

"Well, did they have them when they *left* . . . wherever it was? Lake Ontario, or the Yellow Sea? Did they . . . ?"

Wes just sighed. But his, probably, sister took to answering the question, and the further questions, and, when she didn't know, asked her elders and translated the answers. According to old stories, yes, they *did* have the stoves before they left the Old Place. The black parts they came from the mountain and the blue parts they came from the Big Water. From the *inside* of the mountain, what mountain, nobody knows what mountain, and from the bottom of the Big Water. How did they get the *idea?* Well, Father *Yock*im said that the angels gave it to them. Father *Yock*im said! That's not what the *old* people use

to say . . . what *did* the old people used to say? The old people used to say it
was the little black and white gods but Father Yockim he thought people would
think that meant like devils or something, so he changed it and—Well, there
aren't any little black and white *gods,* for God's sake!—Oh, you're so smart,
you think you—

"Maybe they were from outer space," said Silberman, to his own surprise
as much as anyone else's.

Silence the most profound. Then the "college boy," probably either a
nephew or a cousin, said, slowly, "Maybe they *were.*" Another silence. Then
they were all off again.

The trouble all began with Count Cazmar. Count Cazmar had, like, a
monopoly on all the firewood from the forest. The king gave it to him. Yes,
but the king didn't just "give" it to him; he had to *pay* the king. Okay, so he
had to *pay* the king. So anybody wanted firewood *they* had to *pay* Count
Cazmar. Then he got sore because the Slovo people weren't buying enough
firewood, see, because he *still* had to pay the king. Which king? Who the hell
knows which king? Who the hell cares? None of them were any damn good
anyway. What, old King Joseph wasn't any good, the one who let Yashta
Yushta out of the dungeon? Listen, will you for*get* about old King Joseph and
get on with the story!

So Count Cazmar sent out all the blacksmiths to go from house to house
with their great big sledgehammers to smash up all the Slovo stoves to force
the Slovos to buy more firewood and—What? Yeah, that's how Gramma's
stove is, like, broken. They *all* got, like, broken. Of *course* you could still use
them. But dumb Count Cazmar *he* dint know that. So, what finely happen,
what finely happen, everybody had to pay a firewood tax irregardless of how
much they used or not. So lotta the Slovo people they figured, ya gotta pay
for it anyway? so might as well *use* it. See? Lotta them figure, ya gotta pay for
it anyway, so might as well use it. And so, lotta them quit usin' their Slovo
stoves. Y'see.

"That's your superior Huzzuk civilization for you," Wes said. Just then
the deacon and deaconess in the corner, or whatever they were, lifted their
cracked old voices and finished their chant; and everybody said something
loudly and they all stamped their feet. "Here, Fred," said Wes, "have some
more—have another glass o' mulberry beer." And promptly an aunt set two
more bowls down in front of Fred. "In this one is chopped spleen stew with
crack buckwheats. And in udder one is cow snout cooked under onions. Wait.
I give you pepper."

Eventually Silberman got moved into his new apartment and eventually
Silberman got moved into his new job; his new job required (among other
things . . . among *many* other things) a trip to the diemakers, a trip to the prin-
ters, a trip to the suppliers: *how* convenient that all three were located in a new
or newish commercial and industrial complex way out on the outskirts of. As
he drove, by and by such landmarks as an aqueduct, a cemetery, an old brick
foundry, reminded him that, more or less where the commercial and industrial
complex now was, was where old Applebaum used to be. Lo! it seemed: still

was! Shabby, but still reading M. APPLEBAUM CASH AND CARRY WHOLESALE GROCERIES. The complicated commerces and industries perhaps didn't *like* shabby Old Applebaum's holding out in their midst? Tough. Let them go back where they came from.

Afterwards, business finished elsewhere, thither: "Freddy. Hel*lo*."

"Hello, Mr. Applebaum. How are *you?*"

"How should I be? Every week seems like another family grocery bites the dust. Nu. I own a little swamp in Florida and maybe I will close up the gesheft and go live on a houseboat with hot and cold running crocodiles. Ah-ah, here comes an old customer with his ten dollars' worth of business if we are both lucky; Mat. Grahdy."

Sure enough. Beat *him* to the punch. "Hey, Mr. Grahdy, did it get hot yet?"

Grahdy *laughed* and laughed; then gave the counterword: "It didn't even get *warm!* Ho ho ho ho." He gestured to another man. "This is Petey Plazzek, he is a half-breeth. Hey, Petey, did it get hot yet? Ho ho ho ho!—Mosek!"—this to Old Applebaum. "A little sugar I need, a little semolina I need, a little cake flour, licorice candy, marshmallow crackers." M. Applebaum said he could give him a good buy on crackers today. They went inside together.

Petey Plazzek, a worn-looking man in a worn-looking lumber jacket, came right to the point. "If you're driving by the *bus dee*po, you could give me a ride."

"Sure. Get in." Off they went. Silberman's glance observed no Iroquois cheekbones. "Excuse me, but what did he mean, 'A half-breed'? No offense—"

"Naa, naa. Half Huzzuk, half Slovo."

A touch of the excitement. "Well, uh, Mr. Plazzek—"

"Petey. Just Petey."

"Well, uh, Petey, how many people have one of those old Slovo stoves anymore?"

"Nobody. Them stoves are all a thing o' the past nowadays. Watch out for that truck."

"How come, Petey? How come they are?"

Petey rubbed his nose, sighed very deeply. "Well. *You* know. Some greenhorn would come to America—as we used to say, 'He had six goats and he sold five to get the steamship ticket and he gave one to the priest to pray for a good journey.' I'm talking about a *Slovo* now. Huzzuk, that's another thing altogether. So the poor Slovo was wearing high boots with his pants tucked innem and a shirt smock and a sheepskin coat and a fur hat. This was before Ellis Island. Castle *Gar*den in those days. *He* didn't have a steamer trunk, *he* didn't have a grip, he only had a sort of knapsack; so what was *in* it? A clean smock shirt and some clean foot rags, because they didn't use socks, and a little iron pot and some hardtack-type bread and those two stove parts, the black part and the, uh, the, uh—"

"The *blue* part."

"—the *blue* part, right. Watch out for that Chevy. Well, he'd get a job doing the lowest-paid dirtiest work and he'd rent a shack that subsequently you wouldn't dast keep a *dog* in it, y'understand what I'm telling you, young

fellow? ~~Lights, he had no lights, he didn't even have no *lamp,* just a tin can~~
with some pork fat and a piece of rag for a wick. And he'd pick up an old brick
here and an old brick there and set up his Slovo stove and cook buckwheat in
his little iron pot and he'd sleep on the floor in his sheepskin coat."

But by and by things would get better; this was *America,* the land of opportunity. So as soon as he started making a little money he brought his wife
over and they moved into a room, a real room, and he'd buy a coal-oil lamp
and a pair of shoes for each of them, but, um, people would still laugh attem,
partickley the *Zunks* would still be laughing at them because of still using the
Slovo *stove,* y'see. So by and by they'd buy a *wood* stove. Or a *coal* stove. And
they'd get the gaslight turned on. And they'd even remember not t' blow it
out."

"Yes, but, Petey. The wood and coal cost *money.* And the Slovo stove was
free. So—"

Petey sighed again. "Well. To tell you the truth. It could *cook:* sure. Didn't
give out much *heat,* otherwise. Boil up a lotta water, place'd get *steamy.*"

Fred Silberman cried, "Steam heat! Steam *heat!*"

Petey looked startled, then—for the first time—interested. Then the interest ebbed away. He sighed. "None of them people were plumbers. *They* never
thought of nothing like that, and neither did anybody else. The Slovo stove,
what it come to mean, it come to mean *poverty,* see? It come to mean *ridi*cule.
And so as soon as they quit being dirt-poor, well, that was *that.*"

Fred asked, eagerly, "But aren't there still a lot of them in the attics?
Well . . . *some* of them? In the *cellars?*"

Petey's breath hissed. "Where you *going?* You going to the *bus dee*po, y'
shoulda turned *leff!* Oh. Circling the block. Naa . . . they juss, uh, thrown'm
away. Watch out for that van."

The new job and its new responsibilities occupied and preoccupied most of
Silberman's time, but one afternoon as he was checking an invoice with the
heating contractor fitting up the plant, lo! the old matter came abruptly to his
mind.

"Sudden thought?" said Mr. McMurtry.

"Uh. Yuh. You ever hear of a . . . Slovo stove?"

Promptly: "No. *Should* I have?"

Suppose Fred were to *tell* him. What then? Luddite activity on the part of
McMurtry? "Let me ask you a make-believe question, Mac—"

"Fire when ready."

So . . . haltingly, ignorantly . . . Fred (naming no names, no ethnic groups)
described matters as well as he could, winding up: "So could you think, Mac,
of any scientific explanation as to how such a thing could, or might, maybe,
work? At all?"

Mac's brow furrowed, rolling the hairs of his conjoined eyebrows: a *very*
odd effect. "Well, obviously the liquid in the container acts as a sort of non-
contiguous catalyst, and this amplifies the vortex of the force field created by
the juxtaposition of the pizmire and the placebo"—well of *course* McMurtry

did not say *that:* but that was what it sounded like to Silberman. And so McMurtry might just as well have said it.

McMurtry said one last word or two. "If these things weren't make-believe it would be interesting to examine them. Even a couple of little pieces might do. What can be analyzed could maybe be duplicated."

Once things got going well at work, Fred thought he would go and ask old Mrs. Brakk . . . go and ask old Mrs. Brakk *what?* Would she let the sole extant Slovo stove be examined by an expert? be looked at in a lab? be scraped to provide samples for electronic microscopic analysis?

???

He might suggest that, if she didn't trust *him,* it might be done through a Brakk Family Trust . . . or something . . . to be set up for that purpose. Via Wes . . . and, say, *Nick. . . .*

Sure he might.

But he waited too long.

Silberman of course knew nothing; how could he have known? The people of the house had just learned themselves. All *he* knew, arriving early one night, was that, as he came up to the house, a tumult began within. Lots of people were yelling. And as he came into the Brakk kitchen, Nick was yelling alone.

"We're Americans, ain't we?" he yelled. "So let's *live* like Americans; bad enough so the Huzzuks make fun of us, I'm *tired* of all them Old Country ways, what next, what else? Fur hats? Boots? A goat in the yard?" He addressed his wife. "A hundred times I told your old lady, 'Throw it away, throw the damned thing a*way*, I-am-*tired* they making fun of us, Mamma, you hear?' But she didn't. She didn't. So *I, did.*" He stopped, breathing hard. "And that's all. . . ."

A sick feeling crept into Silberman's chest.

"*Where* did you throw it? *Where?* It wasn't *yours!*"—his wife. Nick pressed his lips together. His wife clapped her hand to her head. "He always used to say, 'I'll throw it off the bridge, I'll throw it off the bridge!' *That's* where! Oh, you hoo-*dlóm!*" For a moment his eyes blazed at her. Then he shrugged, lit a cigarette, and began to smoke with an air of elaborately immense unconcern.

Old Mrs. Brakk sat with her faint smile a moment more. Then she began to speak in her native language. Her voice fell into a chant, then her voice broke, then she lifted her apron to her eyes.

"She says, 'All she had to remind her of the old home country. All she wanted to do was sometimes warm the baby's bottle or sometimes make herself a bowl of tea in her own room if she was tired. She's an old lady and she worked hard and she never wanted to bother nobody—' "

Nick threw his cigarette with force onto the linoleum and, heedless of shrieks, stamped on it heavily. Then he was suddenly calm. "All *right*. Listen. Tomorrow I'll buy you a little electric stove, a, a whadda they call it? *A hot plate!* Tomorrow for your own room I'll buy y'a hot plate. O*kay?*"

The effect was great; Nick had never been known—voluntarily—to buy *any*thing for *any*one.

Old Mrs. Brakk exclaimed, in English, "You *will?*"

He gave a solemn nod. "I swear to God." He crossed his heart. "Tomorrow. The best money can buy. Mamma can come with me," he added. His wife kissed him. His older brother-in-law patted him on the back. The old woman began to smile again.

Silberman felt his heart pounding at twice its regular rate. He dared say nothing. Then, by and by, Nick strolling out into the yard and lighting up another cigarette, he strolled out after him.

"Nick."

"Yeah."

"I'm going to ask you something. Don't get mad."

"Gaw head."

"You really threw the stove parts off the bridge?"

"Yeah. Well . . . the *pieces.*"

"Pieces?"

Nick yawned. Nodded. "I took the damn thing to the shop. Where I work. *You* know." Fred knew. "An I runnum through the crusher. And what was *left* . . . I puttum in a bag. An I threw it offa the bridge." He wasn't angry *or* regretful. He let fall his cigarette, stomped it, went back into the house. Fred heard him working the television.

The shop. Sneaky as could be, Fred lurked and skulked and peeked. The light was on, the door was open. Had Nick left them so? No matter; surely *some* crumbles of blue, of black, would be left, and he would zip in, scoop them off the floor by the crusher, and—A long shadow oozed across the floor. The janitor, humping his broom. A real, old-time Slovo, immense moustache and all, of the real, old-time Slovo sort; in a minute he was gone. Fred zipped, all right. But he didn't scoop; there was nothing to scoop. *No* crumbles. There wasn't even *dust.* Tanta Pesha was not physically present but her voice sounded in her great-nephew's ears: *The Slovos? They are very clean . . . you could eat off their floors. . . .*

He drove his car up and down the silent streets. Shouted aloud, "I don't *believe* it! The greatest discovery in thermodynamics since the discovery of *fire!* And it's *gone.* It's *gone!* It can't be gone! It can't be—"

In the days that followed, in the weeks and months, he knocked on doors, he advertised, he offered rewards. Pleaded. Begged. That incredible discovery, mysteriously having come to earth who knew how and who knew how many thousands of years ago or how many thousands of miles away.

It was *gone.*

Fred threw himself into his work. Developed, locally, an active social life. Womanized. Thought of marriage. *Changed.* Other things changed too. Wes Brakk abruptly moved to Idaho, why Idaho? Of all places. "Because he said it was as far away from the Huzzuks as he could get and still wear shoes." Oh. And the rest of the Brakk family, plus Nick—*led* by Nick—almost as suddenly moved to Brownsville, Texas. Why Brownsville, *Texas?* "To get away from the cold." Others might move to Florida, California, Arizona, to get away from the cold: the rest of the Brakk family (plus Nick) moved to *Brownsville, Texas,* to get away from the cold.

It seemed, somehow, a very Slovo sort of thing to do.

They were ripping up Statesman Street again and Fred had to detour. *Had* he to drive along Tompkins, Gerry, and De Witt streets? For one reason or another, he did drive along there: *my,* the neighborhood had changed! The new neighbors glanced at him with unneighborly glances. There was Grahdy's store. But one whole once-glass pane was missing, boarded up. He stopped. Went in. There was Mr. Grahdy, part of his face bandaged, the other part bruised and discolored. His violin was in his hand. He nodded his jaunty nod. "Would you enjoy to hear a little Paganini?" he asked. Began to play.

Silberman felt that he was present at almost the last scene of a very antick drama. Old Mat. Grahdy, with his wife's alexandrines, his violin, Heine, Schiller, Lermontov, Pushkin, Paganini, and the Latin *Psal*ms—how long could he last? If he didn't starve to death in his almost empty store, how long before they killed him?

The old man let the violin fall to his side. For an odd, long moment he gazed at Silberman with a very level gaze. Then a smile twitched onto his swollen, battered face. He shrugged one shoulder. He began to laugh. *"It didn't even get warm,"* he chuckled.

Two Short-Shorts: "The Last Wizard" and "Revenge of the Cat-Lady"

INTRODUCTION BY F. M. BUSBY

With publication of "My Boy Friend's Name Is Jello" in an early 1954 issue of F&SF, Avram Davidson served notice that a new and unique viewpoint had joined the sf and fantasy fields. Over the years he made good on that notice. His stories and novels covered a wide range of themes and treatments, but always they had two features in common: a rare degree of erudition, and the evident fact that no one else could have written them.

It was on the final day of PittCon, the eighteenth World sf Convention at Pittsburgh, PA, that Elinor and I first met Avram. In those days the pros for some reason tended to hide out from the vast (three-figure!) Worldcon crowds; I forget who tipped us off where to find him, but there we went and there he was, being witty and affable as might be expected. With a train to catch, we had to leave much sooner than we wanted to.

Next meeting, I think, was at the 1962 Westercon, in Los Angeles. Avram and Grania were expecting—and late that year Avram wrote a wonderful new-father testimonial for our local group's fanzine, Cry.

Well, it go along and it go along: the stories, the letters, the books. All to be remembered warmly—but with regret that we'll never know where The Phoenix and the Mirror, for instance, eventually wound up. And that we can't ever ask him.

But now here's a book to remind us, to symbolize all the goodies Avram did give us. "The Last Wizard" and "Revenge of the Cat-Lady" are, I submit, fine examples of his craft.

FOR THE HUNDREDTH TIME Bilgulis looked with despair at the paper and pencil in front of him. Then he gave a short nod, got up, left his little room, and went two houses up the street, up the stairs, and knocked on the door.

Presently the door opened and high up on the face which looked out at him were a pair of very pale gray-green eyes, otherwise bloodshot and bulging.

Bilgulis said, "I want you teach me how to make spell. I pay you."

The eyes blinked rapidly, the face retreated, the door opened wider, Bilgulis entered, and the door closed. The man said, "So you know, eh. How did you know?"

"I see you through window, Professor," Bilgulis said. "All the time you read great big books."

" 'Professor,' yes, they call me that. None of them know. Only you have guessed. After all this time. I, the greatest of the adepts, the last of the wizards— and now you shall be my adept. A tradition four thousand, three hundred and sixty-one years old would have died with me. But now it will not. Sit there. Take reed pen, papyrus, cuttlefish ink, spit three times in bottle."

Laboriously Bilgulis complied. The room was small, crowded, and contained many odd things, including smells. "We will commence, of course," the Professor said, "with some simple spells. To turn an usurer into a green fungus: *Dippa dabba ruthu thuthu*—write, write!—*enlis thu.* You have written? So. And to obtain the love of the most beautiful woman in the world: *Coney honey antimony funny cunny crux.* Those two will do for now. Return tomorrow at the same hour. Go."

Bilgulis left. Waiting beside his door was a man with a thick briefcase and a thin smile. "Mr. Bilgulis, I am from the Friendly Finance Company and in regard to the payment which you—"

"*Dippa dabba ruthu thuthu enlis thu,*" said Bilgulis. The man turned into a green fungus which settled in a hall corner and was slowly eaten by the roaches. Bilgulis sat down at his table, looked at the paper and pencil, and gave a deep sigh.

"Too much time this take," he muttered. "Why I no wash socks, clean

toilet, make a big pot cheap beans with pig's tail for eat? No," he said determinedly and once more bent over the paper and pencil.

By and by there was a knock on his door. Answering it he saw before him
the most beautiful woman in the world. "I followed you," she said. "I don't
know what's happening . . ."

"Coney honey antimony," said Bilgulis, *"funny cunny crux."*

She sank to her knees and embraced his legs. "I love you. I'll do anything
you want."

Bilgulis nodded. "Wash socks, clean toilet," he said. "And cook big pot
cheap beans with pig's tail for eat." He heard domestic sounds begin as he
seated himself at the table and slowly, gently beat his head. After a moment he
rose and left the house again.

Up the street a small crowd was dispersing and among the people he recognized his friend, Labbonna. "Listen, Labbonna," he said.

Labbonna peered at him through dirty, mended eyeglasses. "You see excitement?" he asked, eager to tell.

"I no see."

Labbonna drew himself up and gestured. "You know Professor live there?
He just now go crazy," he said, rolling his eyes and dribbling and flapping his
arms in vivid imitation. "Call ambulance but he drop down dead. Too bad,
hey?"

"Too bad." Bilgulis sighed.

"Read too much big book."

Bilgulis cleared his throat, looking embarrassed. "Listen, Labbonna—"

"What you want?"

"How long you in country?"

"Torty year."

"You speak good English."

"Citizen."

Bilgulis nodded. He drew a pencil and piece of paper from his pocket.
"Listen, Labbonna. Do me big help. How you make spell in English, *Please
send me your free offer?* One 'f' or two?"

REVENGE OF THE CAT-LADY

IN A SAD-SMELLING HOUSE on a weedy back street, Beulah Gurnsey sat watching a TV program. She was sitting in a sagging armchair whose upholstery had gone slick. Her face was sallow and its contours had long since slipped, and her eyes were large behind her eyeglasses. In the house next door three Oriental refugee children peered openmouthed from a window at the children of a darker and more abundant people playing in the street. These latter had not yet made up their minds about those former. They had long since made up their minds about Beulah Gurnsey, who nowadays tended not to go out very often. On the TV screen two women faced each other against the background of a house interior, to furnish which would have taken several years of Beulah's income. These women often spoke about their being poor, but not right now.

"I feel so *sorry* about Loretta," said one of them, right now. "It's such a shock for her, her daughter Kimberly not being able to graduate because of that terrible scandal, when, after all, she was only an innocent victim of Brett Brock's malice."

"Yes, I feel terribly sorry for her, too," said the other woman in the television. "And just when she was recovering from her—"

"Huh!" said Beulah Gurnsey. "You feel sorry for *her,* that brazen thing; what about *me?*"

The television lady with the frosted hair sort of wet her lips with the tip of her tongue, and said to the real-blonde television lady, "Uh, well, yes, what *about* Beulah Gurnsey?"

A sort of sarcastic smile on her face, the blonde one asked, "Well, what *about* her? *She's* nothing special. Why is she any better than anyone else?"

In the kitchen the icebox made that funny sound that meant it was going to die again, and so Beulah would have to eat the lunch leftovers for supper or else they would be no good by tomorrow. "Oh, you rotten thing!" she exclaimed.

"Oh, well, *you* know," said the frosty-haired one, "she came from such a good family once upon a time and now look at the awful element moving into her neighborhood; besides which she hasn't got any money and she hasn't the first idea where to go look for any."

"Oh *no?*"—*such* sarcasm!

"No!" cried Beulah, striking the worn-through cloth on the arm of the chair. "No, she hasn't! So you just shut up—"

"And the few old-timers who are left around where she still lives, never coming to see her for years on end and looking at her house when they go by and talking about her and saying *you*-know-what . . . and besides that, as I say, she hasn't got any money. Well, that's what it is to be poor, as well we know; let me give you some fresh tea in that nice bone china cup, dear. We can't afford anything better, because we're poor."

Blondie in the television let Frosty pour, but then she said, after a single sip, "Well, why doesn't she just go right down to J. Saul Sloane and ask *him* what *about* her late brother Clarence's bearer bonds that he has?"

Beulah Gurnsey stretched neck up straight and peered all around the room. "*I* don't know anything about any bearer bonds of my late brother Clarence's that J. Saul Sloane has!"

Frosty in the television put her head slightly to one side, said, "You see, she doesn't *know* anything about that. Isn't the receipt for that inside the big paperweight on her late brother's desk? *She* doesn't know about that—"

Blondie smirked. Anyone could see what *she* was. "*Weh*-ll," said she, with a toss of her head, "you can just bet that J. Saul *Sloane* knows about that. So—" But Beulah Gurnsey turned the set off before that one could say another word. Then she went into the closet and got out her ugliest black velvet hat and put it on with firm little jerks. Then she went into Clarence's bedroom, everything just as he had left it: there was the big paperweight on his desk. She pulled with her fingers, she pushed with her fingers—lo! part of the bottom came sliding out. Just like Clarence. *Who* always had to have the nicest lamb chop? Clarence! Beulah didn't exactly remember the last time she had had a lamb chop. There was the receipt. Secretive. Sly. Clarence.

She picked up the shopping bag with the neatly folded newspapers in it; *people* didn't have to think she didn't have a house to shop for.

Out she went.

The two children on the street had already grown bored with trying to bait the three at the window; on seeing her, they slid simultaneously across her path, their faces gone rubbery but not quite blank. She leaned over toward them and opened her eyes wide as she could and crossed them and with a quick movement of her tongue slid her false uppers almost entirely out between her lips, then immediately slipped them in again. The children fled, mouths open to express a silent horror. "Don't you *dare* eat *my* cats!" she shouted at the suddenly empty window, shaking her fist. Beulah didn't exactly remember the last time she had had a cat.

J. Saul Sloane. Insurance. Real Estate. Usury. Unscrupulous Bilking of Widows, Orphans, and Legatees.

In she went.

That was a sight to see. Oh, that would have made your heart feel *good*. *Oh,* how he looked up when she just marched in as bold as you please. *She* knew about his filthy rotten low vile immoral life. His putty mouth opening in his putty face under his putty nose as he saw her just march in and wave that receipt so he could see it and recognize it, and *then* what did he say? *Ha!*

"Miss Beulah. Miss Beulah. I can explain. I was just keeping them for you. I—"

She said, "Hand them over. Ev-er-y-single-*one*-of-them, J. Saul Sloane." Which he did. And she gave him one look. Out of his safe. In the manila envelope. Did she think to check them to see if they were all of them there? Oh, you just bet. And left him his old paper and said not one word more.

Out she went.

County First National Bank and Trust Company.

"Now, Miss Gurnsey, we are really very sorry, but another extension would be out of the—Oh."

"Oh." *Ha!* Took the wind out of *his* sails!

Herman Heinrichs and Sons. Fine Meats. The young heinie, well, one of the young heinies, drew a sour face when he saw her. "No, I don't have any bones for your dog today," he said. Beulah Gurnsey didn't exactly remember the last time she had had a dog. A legal fiction; *never* mind.

Ignoring the young one, she turned to the old one, who was *there* today, for a change; "Heinie," she said, firmly, "I want six of your best, biggest, nice rib lamb chops, and don't you trim an ounce off them and don't you break a single bone: *you* know how I like them."

"Yes, Miss Kurnssey," he said, obediently. And after, he asked, "Shoult I but dem on your pill, Miss Kurnssey?"

Oh, how the young one yelped! "Grossdaddy, we don't *carry* any more bills," he cried.

Beulah paid him no mind. "*I*. Shall pay. *Cash. Thank* you, Heinie."

Simmons Electrical. It always took Hi Simmons a week to stand up, he was so tall. "Beulah Gurnsey," said he, now, "that was a good enough and cheap enough used icebox when I sold it to you and I have worked many a miracle with it for you and for the old times in Old Granger Grammar School, but I am not Frankenstein and cannot hang it up in a tower in a lightning storm to revive it again; therefore—" He was all stood up.

"I want a nice new one."

"You can have a nice new one for $300."

"I want a nice new one for $500."

"You shall have it. Though there's got to be a catch."

"Yes. The catch is that the men who bring the new one take away the old one. *You* pay the dump fee. *Good*-bye, Hiram-firam."

Back home she simply sat in her chair awhile. A long while. Then she got up and unwrapped the lamb chops and she salted them and peppered them and garlic'd them and onioned them and thymed them and put them in the broiler and turned it on, and then she washed her hands. The fat would bubble and crisp and they would grow nice and brown on the outside and yet be pink and juicy on the inside and she would hold each one by its bone-handle and eat it while she watched television.

Speaking of *which*.

7:30 2 WHERE IT'S AT. Featured: *Treasure in Your Attic and Basement.*
8:00 13 MOVIE ★½ *Revenge of the Cat-Lady* (1953) Percy Wilkins, Velda Snow. An insane spinster terrorizes her neighborhood with the aid of a strange old family amulet. (2 hrs. 5 mins.)

Good, good. Those looked very good. Beulah Gurnsey sat back in her armchair.

What *was* the treasure in her attic and in her basement? Well, she would find out. The television would let her know.

And tomorrow she must certainly get a cat.

Cats.

She leaned forward and turned on the television.

While You're Up

INTRODUCTION BY FORREST J. ACKERMAN

AVRAM THE MARVA

I'm an Esperantist and, as a recognizer of the "universalanguage" Esperanto, when I look at author Davidson's first name it reverses itself and practically suggests "marvelous." In any language, Avram was marvelous.

My auctorial specialty is the short-short story. I have had the world's shortest published, "Cosmic Report Card: Earth." You may guess the one failing letter of the alphabet that the flying saucer sociologists give Earth.

I've collaborated on short stories with Catherine L. Moore, Robert W. Lowndes, Theodore Sturgeon, and A. E. van Vogt, among others. Why didn't it occur to me while there was still time to ask Avram if he'd consider collaborating with me on a sequel to "Cosmic Report Card"? After all, I sold it five times for a total of five hundred dollars and it's been translated into eight languages.

But enough of my ambling along in this preamble, this is a collection of Davidson stories, not Ackermanuscripts. I'm delighted that the word "friend" was found after my name in Avram's address book and therefore I was contacted to write an introduction to "While You're Up."

I had only finished the first sentence when I realized something was wrong, inexplicably anachronistic. Undoubtedly you will too when you wonder why anyone would include Maxfield Parrish as a compatriot (dare I, with a bow to Avram, say compaintriot?) of da Vinci and Rembrandt?

Warm wine?

Crystal bowls for divining—not balls?

Aprons outlawed?

Handkerchiefs archaic?

What's going on here?

And when Sexton—But, no, I'll leave you to read the shock yourself.

Avram, you **marva** *rascal, you've done it again!*

WHILE YOU'RE UP

THE SCENE MIGHT HAVE been painted by Maxfield Parrish, perhaps the best of painters during that rich, lost era that also gave the world Leonardo and Rembrandt. While the latter two have their spokesmen, nay, their devotees, even they would have to concede that neither ever painted so blue a sky, and that there are those who deny that such blue skies ever indeed existed is (as Sexton often explained) beside the point. "They ought to have existed," Tony said now to the few friends, to Mother Ruth—his wife of many years—all sitting in the large front room to which his preeminence and seniority entitled him. "They *ought* to have existed, for, as we see now, sometimes they almost do—and—look! a cloud!"

Mother Ruth, who had certainly seen clouds from this room before, merely smiled and murmured something soft and inaudible; the others craned and clearly spoke of their delight and good fortune. All, except of course, for Samjo, who continued sitting with his mouth open. Tony Sexton more than once had said, though—they could all well remember—"Don't ever underestimate Samjo. He sees more than you think, and he adds things up, too."

"The wine should be warm enough to drink in a few minutes," Sexton said now. "We brought it up from the cellar several hours ago."

Barnes, from his chair with the wooden arms, declared, hands sweeping the air, "Good friends, a good view, good thoughts, and—good wine, too." Overfamiliarity may have perhaps tarnished the quotation, but Barnes's enthusiasm was always contagious.

Maria said, "This moment, with the view and the blue and the cloud and, shortly, the wine—will be a moment that I shall always remember." She peered forward, probably seeking to look into Mother Ruth's eyes, for such was Maria's habit; when she said something worthy, she felt, of notice, she sought someone's eyes and, as it were, sought to bring forth an evident approval: a smile, a nod, an expression of the face, a gesture. But this time it was not forthcoming. Perhaps Maria, for all she knew, was just a bit annoyed.

Perhaps Tony understood all this, for he smiled his famous Sexton smile, and said, "Mother Ruth often looks into her apron as the ancient sibyls did into their crystal bowls." For it was true, Mother Ruth dared to wear the antique apron, so long outlawed; and almost it did seem to make her look like something from antique eras.

Barnes picked up the metaphor and asked—Barnes often asked very odd questions—"Father, were those crystal bowls empty when the sybils looked into them, or did they contain something, a . . . a liquid, perhaps?"

Tony Sexton very slightly pursed his lips. "Wine, I suppose, would have been too precious for such a use; water would always be in short supply. What, then? A thick soup would surely have interfered with the visioning, so—broth perhaps?"

Barnes in a moment went bright: A new concept! Then the brightness went. "One never knows when you are making a joke," he muttered.

"I wanted to have a few friends over," Sexton said, lightly leaving the subject. "Wine and five glasses waiting, a day with a lot of blue, and, if we were lucky . . . and I felt we would be lucky . . . even a cloud. A day to be remembered."

Murmurs from all assured him that the day would surely be remembered. With an effect most odd, Sexton's face turned gray, and his body seemed to fall in upon itself. For a second only, his face—like a dim, thin, crusted mask—rested on what seemed a pile of ashes; then it, too, dissolved.

The reaction of the others was varied. Maria started to rise, fell back, composed herself, looked about with a rueful air. Mother Ruth sagged. "Oh, Tony, Tony," she said, her voice very small. Barnes exclaimed loudly, beat his hands upon the costly arms of his chair. "He didn't *renew!*" cried Barnes. "Time and time again, I asked, I begged—much good that will do now," he said, deeply annoyed. He bent over, removed from the still settling pile the small tag of malleable substance, read aloud, "Your warranty expires on or about the hour of noon on the 23rd of April, 2323." Several voices declared that Tony Sexton had timed it just about right—leave it to Sexton! they said.

Maria now rose all the way. "I think," she said, "that now is *just* the time to drink that container of wine Sexton was saving; he'd want that, wouldn't he?"

"Bound to!" exclaimed Barnes. "Absolutely!"

Mother Ruth looked up from her lap. "Maria, dear. While you're up. *Would* you mind also bringing back with you the dustpan *and* the broom? Thank you, dear."

Samjo had as usual seemed to have been thinking of nothing at all; as often, this semblance was deceptive. He had been wiping, first his eyes, then his nose, with an article of cloth quite as archaic as Mother Ruth's apron. Then he spoke. "Only four glasses now, Maria," said he.

Who could help chuckling?

The Spook-Box of Theobald Delafont De Brooks

INTRODUCTION BY ALGIS BUDRYS

"The Spook-Box of Theobald Delafont De Brooks," Avram's last story published before his death, came to me via a literary agent. But when it was published, he wrote to Kandis Elliot, my Production Manager and, in this case, illustrator, to say how much he liked the illustrations, and could he have them? What I don't think he knew was that Kandis composed them on her computer, so it was no trouble at all to run off a complete set and send them to him. But he was dead by then.

Avram and I go back a long way. At one point, when we were both selling men's hairy-chested "true" adventures, we even were collaborators, in the sense that we often talked about it, and fully intended to do it. The problem became that Avram's stories were true, whereas mine were "true," and we finally decided against it. But when he published Masters of the Maze, *about a hack who wrote "true" adventure stories, he mentioned my invariable working title: "Love-Starved Arabs Raped Me Often." And when I became editor-in-chief of Regency Books, I published an excellent collection—*Crimes and Chaos—*of Avram's true adventure tales.*

We went back further than that. Both of us were living in New York City, and I often wound up in his place on 110th Street. We had something—exactly what is difficult to pin down—that drew us together. It turned out, among other things, that his father had had a chicken farm a few miles up the road from my father's chicken farm, but that would hardly account for even a part of it, because we never came in contact during that period. But whatever it was, it endured; he and I would trade letters pretty steadily from about 1955 to his death (and he always included my wife in his greetings). I was immensely flattered; here was one of the finest wordsmiths in the English language, with a first-class mind behind all that, and first-class creativity, and he deigned to speak to me as "Uncle Ajay."

I wish he still did. I saw him at all the Norwescons I attended, and I did not think he would be gone so soon. I did not realize that Jahweh would dare to take him away from an Earth he made special.

THE SPOOK-BOX OF THEOBALD DELAFONT DE BROOKS

I**T WAS MORE THAN** his theory, it was the very foundation of his belief, that if you were legally entitled to use a name containing the names of two very well-known people, then . . . sooner or later . . . it would result in some very good pieces of business getting thrown your way. It hadn't happened yet . . . well . . . not *very* good pieces of business. He collected rents on a number of properties, collected them for the owners, that is, and he sold the insurance policies to the same properties. He alas did not hold a power of attorney for any of the properties. Not as yet. And he had managed to keep an apartment in one of the properties vacant for so long that old Miss Whittier had forgotten it was even rentable. And then—

"Eighty-five West Elm really needs a night watchman, Miss Whittier," he said.

"It *does?*" her voice had already begun to flutter.

"Yes, it does. But it isn't going to get it. Tell you what I am going to do, Miss Whittier—"

"Ye-es?"

"*I*. Am going to give up the place I now have. And *I*. Will move in there. Will," and here he named a sum about the third of his present rent, a rent which he was increasingly finding it inconvenient to pay, "—will that be all right, Miss Whittier?"

Miss Whittier would have undergone a slow course of the water torture rather than admit she really no longer had a good notion of what would be all right for the place (or any other place). "Oh . . . why I suppose . . ." Some last vestige of business sense entered Miss Whittier's aged mind. "Wasn't that about what those nice Van Dynes used to pay?" *Was* it necessary for him to remind her that the Van Dynes (they had been dead for decades) had actually occupied another apartment in another building? Theobald Delafont De Brooks didn't think it was.

He squinted a moment, deep in thought, then: "Oh, I have to hand it to you, Miss Whittier. For a minute there *I* had a hard time remembering just what the Van Dynes used to pay. Little bit less, Miss Whittier. Little bit less, they paid."

Another flutter. "Well, then, is that quite fair to *you* . . . Mr. De Brooks? To pay more than—"

But Mr. De Brooks begged her not to think about him. "The main thing, you see, is to have somebody living in that apartment. Apartment stays vacant, no curtains, no screens, no shades in the windows: gives the place a bad name."

Miss Whittier was never moved to ask how long the apartment in question had stayed vacant, or anything else pertaining to its possible bad name. "Why . . . then . . . I'm sure it will be just fine. *Thank* you—"

Very politely he brushed away her thanks. "Anybody wants anything, for example, at night: there I am. Never go out at night anymore. Except," he did want to be honest with her, his face said, "Thanksgiving. *Got* to." He breathed the magic words, *Family Dinner.*

Ever squeeze a drop of lemon on a live oyster? Remember what happened? That, more or less, is what happened to Miss Whittier. "Well, of *course*—why, oh, *cer*tainly, Mr. De Brooks! The very idea! that you for one moment or any reason shouldn't *think* of going—!"

"Don't like to leave the place alone, you see." Do *you* see? He hadn't even moved into the place yet, Thanksgiving was months away, already the owner was begging him not to give it a second thought.

The prophets, where are they? And your fathers, do they live forever?

And, bringing it up to date, do your owners live forever, either? It would have been almost as easy as for him to have gotten the apartment rent-free. But a man had to look at the future. Were he to have done so, and the cold eye of an executor or a cost-accountant looked at that No Rent arrangement—and not by any means could De Brooks have pretended he had acted as janitor—superintendent—engineer, so as to have justified the rentlessness: No. Whereas this way, if it were even mentioned, "Well, the late Miss Whittier very much wanted someone whom she knew very well to live in that apartment and, as she put it, 'Keep an eye on things . . .' " What could the heir . . . the banker . . . the whoever . . . say? At most, a slight grunt, and at worst, some small amount of time later, a civil letter on crisp paper to the effect that his services were no longer . . . but that was likely enough in any event. No camp lasts forever.

So *there* was one piece of good, if not very, very good, piece of business.

And although he did not know it, yet he—having a sixth or/and a seventh sense for such things—would have been not at all surprised to learn that a Certain Connection of Miss Whittier had, oh, some several years ago, at her own expense, obtained an independent genealogical report; from which we will cite just a bit, as follows:

The family line or lines of Mr. Theobald Delafont De Brooks himself are certainly traceable to 1820, and probably to 1800. Possibly as far back as 1787. There were quite a number of De Brookses in New York, and only one known progenitor, the Jacobus Aurelius De Broogh who had arrived from Bergen-op-Zoom in the Netherlands in 1643 and on whose great success in the Indian trade the De Brooks family fortunes were founded . . . so that a distant relationship to both Presidents is certainly probable, though now impossible either to prove or disprove. A further search, though perhaps more productive, would be much more expensive.

And at the words *more expensive,* the Certain Connection (certain . . . and suspicious) drew in her horns, bore the costs in silence, and never, ever said another word. Just as well.

Visitors and possible clients, gazing at the two large framed photographs, invariably asked on their first visit, "Are you related to *both* presidents?" and Theobald Delafont De Brooks would say, with a smile, "Shirt-tail cousins, you might say—" Adding, "We were the poor relations." And . . . *invariably?* . . . well . . . just in case the visitors and possible clients didn't ask, TDD would somehow always manage to get in an early reference to *Cousin Theo* and to *Cousin Grosvenor,* would laugh and add, "They stopped sending us the Christmas turkey after My Folks supported the other candidates." Who could fail to enjoy that not-quite-a-story? and who could fail to get the not-quite-point?— *High Family Connections* . . . and . . . *Fearlessly Independent People.* . . .

But . . . really . . . *were* they? . . . *weren't* they? Mr. Quincy De Brooks was once semi-publicly asked this outright; rather smoothly said, "If they didn't have a lot of enemies, then we are probably not related;" rather smoothly passed on before further question time. Still—how could one but wonder? What names to be announced by trumpets! *Theobald De Brooks, President of the United States!* and *Grosvenor Delafont De Brooks, President of the United States!* Dead now, long dead, both of them, of course—but what about the descendants?

Q. Do you ever see anything of any of them, Del?

A. Nope. *Nope.* They don't push it. And *we* don't push it.

This was perhaps wise of Mr. Theobald Delafont De Brooks who had, anyway, a few other stories to tell. Not many.

Story Number One. When TDD's grandfather was a student in the seventh grade at the old Governor Daniel Tompkins School (long obliterated), who should make a visit to said school but old T. D. himself: see an officious principal shove Del's grandfather forward, *Mr. President, here is a namesake of yours!* Well, you don't get to be President by asking *too* many dumb questions and so all that old T. D. said was, "I believe we may be related, then." "I believe we may, sir." Old T. D. grinned, made feint of offering the boy a cigar, and, amidst the genial laughter, briskly shook hands with him, and passed on along.

Story Number Two. Del's father did have the courage to send a letter beginning *Dear Cousin Grosvenor* congratulating GDD on his first election: back came another letter, from the same mold and form as all replies to all such letters, but beginning—mind you, mind you—*Dear Cousin Delafont.* Explain *that,* would you. They knew—almost spooky, as you might say.

In neither case: *No* invitation to come boating or swimming at Muskrat Sump. *No* invitation to go golfing or riding at Parkill Ridge.

Oh well. Take what you can get. Hope for the Big Chance. Keep your powder dry. And—say?—don't knock it. On the strength of the Story Number One, Theobald De Brooks the distant, floated into a job offered by an uncle of the boy standing next to him during the handshake. And on the strength of the letter (framed) D. James De Brooks floated into a job given *him* by the local Commiteeman: not much of a job, but it kept them in groceries and off Relief. *See?*

Maybe at one time they *had* been the poor relations. But for a long, *long* time, they hadn't even been that. Had Del's dad been merely boasting, swaggering, in giving his son the names, the given names, of both the presidential De Brookses? Or had he merely given what he had to give—

Were there any other family anecdotes? There were no other family anecdotes. Were there, then, any family traditions . . . ? any, even, family words or phrases, such as almost every family has? Well . . . this expression: *More money than six patroons*. . . . Theo. Del. De Brooks's grandfather sometimes used to say that. And, actually, for quite a while, the grandson had taken it for granted that a patroon must be a rich Irishman! Later he learned, long later, that a patroon had been a Hudson Valley landowner, a sort of squire, with a land-grant from the old Dutch or English governments. And *this* expression: did someone say, Say, guess what I found? a family answer was, *the spook box!* No explanation came with that. And *this* expression (and a little bit more): If the family was having a hot-dog roast or toasting marshmallows in the backyard (the barbecue had yet to cross the Mississippi) and the fire didn't at first or at second burn too well, see Grandpa De B. grub for a cigar-or cigarette-butt or even a pinch of pipe-tobacco, stamp his foot, and say, with an air of mock solemnity something that sounded like Skah-*ootch!* and cast the bit of tobacco on the fire. And the fire did always seem to burn better. Once: Theo. Del De B.: "Grandpa, what does Skah-*ootch* mean?" Grandpa (once) "That's what the pow-wow man used to say." "Grandpa, who was the—" Mrs. De Brooks: "Pa, you are going to *burn* that frankfurter!" A low-scale squabble, but after that it (the trick) was seldom done. A few times, if an electric light flickered or the old vacuum-tube radio misbehaved, the boy did actually stamp his foot and cry "the magic word" and sometimes it did work. But his Mother didn't like feet being stamped in the house. So he quit doing it.

And the funny old yellow brick "from the old house in the Bowery"? Vanished. Dusty old thing. Forget it.

And don't think, either, that it was all peaches and cream and little anecdotes (even what little there were of them), having a famous Name. Names. For one thing: If you're so much, whutta ya doin' *here*? If your name is De Brooks, why ain't chew rich? *How* often, merely to answer, What's your name? was to collect a sneer, a scowl, a jeer, jibe, explicit insult, sometimes—more than once—a poke in the ribs? Often. There was an army sergeant who had made his life a living hell, and—Ya don't *like* it? Write t' GDD! Well . . . doubtless there had been people who had hated George Washington . . . Millard Fillmore, for that matter.

Once, Theo (actually, he had more often been called Baldy) did put the question to his old man. "How come all we've got are the names?"

At once he saw that his father well knew the meaning of the question and only pretended his, "Huh? Whuddaya mean?"

"*They're* famous. We're not famous. They got *money*. We haven't got no—any—money. They're up on *top*. We're down at the *bottom*. *How . . . come . . . ?*

A weary expression. A sigh. "I dunno, Theo. I just don't know. How'd *I* know? Maybe one of us married the servant girl. Maybe one of us was a horse thief. Maybe we're illegitimate, or something. And I'll tell ya somethin' else, sonny. My great-great-grandmother? She was a cousin to Commodore Aurelius Vandervelt. And it never even got none of us a job shovelin' coal on the old East Coast Steam Boat Line. They say that once she went to the Old Man's wife's funeral. And at the, ah, reception? *They* wouldn't even give her a glass of *sherry*. Said, 'No, this is just for the family.' And so she just turned around and went home. Big people don't like little people, and if they got the same name? seems like they like 'em even less. The, uh, *names?* Well . . . hold onto 'em. Who knows. . . ."

And, before turning back to his newspaper, he added, "You're entitled to *them, anyway.*"

So.

There had in those days been someone, at least *someone,* to whom the matter *had* meant something; his high school teacher, the virginal Miss Vark: "Are you planning to go to college, Theobald?"

"No money."

And Miss Vark had explained to him that there was a certain scholarship, he had long ago forgotten its name, "for the benefit of native-born American boys being of Holland Dutch descent." "I *think*," said Miss Vark, "that the part about the being of Dutch descent . . . which I am, too, Theobald . . . may actually be of more importance than the actual grades." Poor Miss Vark. Ancestry was no dowry. And, rather to his own surprise, there really was such a scholarship: that year there were three openings, and they all went to native-born American boys being of Holland Dutch descent, all of them having names like Vanderdam, Vanderzam, Vanderbam, and all of them of a more recent and perhaps more vigorous immigration, by way of Grand Rapids, Michigan. But good Miss Vark didn't stop there. *He* was fazed, but *she* wasn't. Her face an unaccustomed pink, she said to him, "I am going to write to Sophronia Vandervelt De Brooks," no need to explain who *she* was, you'd have to be illiterate never to have read about her; half way between the two lines of Presidential De Brookses—very famous . . . *very* charitable And so, he hadn't meant to, he'd known better than to mention it to any of the kids, he told her of the great-great-grandmother who'd been Commodore Vandervelt's cousin. He left out about the snub and the sherry.

Miss Vark felt sure that this would clinch it . . . and *what* was the lady's maiden name? Dad De Brooks put his poor old head in his hands at the question, and said, "Jesus." It took a personal visit from Miss Vark to persuade him to look into the matter; in his Sunday suit he traveled via two changes on the subway to find his only living great-uncle, who gave to the question the same pious reply. Great-uncle Greeley, however, was game. And took Dad De

Brooks, via trolley-car, to the uttermost end of the wilderness, where miraculously there still survived, God knows how, an aged lady cousin, in an ancient cottage smelling of kerosene. She didn't even remember her cousin's great-nephew but she remembered the incident. "They wouldn't even give her *a glass of sherry!*" she exclaimed, as vivid to her as though it were yesterday. She went on to say a few vivid things about Old Aureeley Chaw-Tobacco (as she called him). None of them to his credit: but—*what was the lady's maiden name?*

Long, long the ancient creature sat, from time to time murmuring *Now, don't mix me up*—and then—like a tongue of fire at Pentecost—"Phoebe Fisher! That's what it is! Phoebe Fisher! From Fishkill, New York!" The fire died down, leaving only age and suspicion: "Why do ye want ta know, Greeley?"

"Delly here, wants t'send his boy to the academy, and he hopes Soprony De Brooks'll give'm some money, they bein' distant double-cousins, as y'might—"

"She'll never do it! She'll give him nothing! Not a thrip, not a fip, not a shinplaster! All them old family connections?—*not-worth-a-continental!*" Very, very suddenly she stopped. Looked Del in the eye. Very slowly got up, fumbled through the Family Bible, extracted an envelope crumbling with age, and drew forth a splendidly engraved and antique five-dollar bill, so archaic that it was blue and not green. "I send this to your boy," said she. "Tell him that Millie Totten sends it."

"Say, guess what I got, Theo?"

"The *spook* box?"

The five-dollar bill looked so odd that they bore it to the bank with trepidation. "Is this worth anything?" "It's worth five *dollars,*" said the cashier, cheerfully. "Real old-timer. Want it changed?"

It was a nine-days wonder; and, after much talk, bought Theo a pair of shoes. He needed them. Badly.

Primed with the name of Phoebe Fisher De Brooks of Fishkill, New York, and with whatever other information Miss Vark was able to find on her own researches—there was after all a rather large gap between Jacobus Aurelius De Broogh and John Quincy A. De Brooks, whose services with *the* Army of *the* Potomac had anyway earned him an honorable mustering-out—off the letter went. To be followed, in no haste, by one from Sophronia Vandervelt De Brooks's secretary. To the effect that there were so many demands upon her employer's means and so many commitments had already been made that Miss De Brooks was absolutely unable to be of assistance even in regard to distant family ties, and that she hoped that Theobald would meet with all the success to which his merits might entitle him.

"Well, such a disappointment," Miss Vark observed. "Though rather a nice letter in its way, all the same."

Delafont James De Brooks said, "The old lady was right. Not worth a continental."

· · ·

When you're on your own, and having nothing else to do in particular, you might as well sell insurance. In doing so, Theo left the Old neighborhood and moved into a rather better one where, anyway, there were no more—well, very few—insults. In fact, people . . . some people . . . seemed rather impressed by the double-barreled, the ancient and honorable name(s). One thing led to another. By and by he opened his own office, added the words *Real Estate* to his sign and calling card. In order to do that he'd had to pass an exam, yet nothing but the assistance of the sign painter and the printer was required to add the words *Business and Financial Management*. Sometimes (often) he much felt that he was god-awful tired of the names and all, and that maybe he'd just change it to, say, Higgins . . . or, for that matter, to his mother's maiden name of Puckleman; the Pucklemans were cheerful outgoing urban yeomen, brewery deliverymen who had never looked a glass of sherry in the eye; asked, where had they come from? cried, *Off the pickle-boat!* and farther than that, did not and could not have cared less. But . . . somehow . . . Theobald Delafont *Puckle*man? And if it came to changing first and middle names as well, well really, there were just too many choices. So he held to his, such as it was, heritage.

Someone in his family, perhaps a grandmother still reluctant to accept that marriage into a glorious name had brought her no further to glory than a rather shabby house on a rather shabby street, had begun, long and long ago, an attempt to keep a scrap-book about people with The Name; but the effort did not persist—how could it?—no library in the world could have kept up with it. But some loose pages persisted here and there throughout the house: in the kind of old cardboard cartons which continue on in the cellar of almost every house, a nuisance, but no one wants to throw them away . . . in the backmost part of a closet . . . in the bottoms of drawers, along with an old shirtwaist, an old pair of longjohns, a fountain pen which had been awaiting a bladder transplant since 1920 . . . and some of these must have followed (*must* have followed, for surely he would not have wanted to bother taking them) TDD from place to place in his various moves; most of them did not interest him any longer.

Now and then one would surface, a page from the extinct scrapbook, that is, would surface, like an old piece of shrapnel or a fragment of bone from a tooth which was no longer there. These had become familiar to him in his long and lonely hours waiting for The Chance which never came, and when, unaccountably, one would rise and appear again, he would read it again, although he may have read it a dozen times before . . . Theobald De Brooks, Jr. had perhaps shot a rare antelope somewhere in Manchuria, say . . . James Q. De Brooks's yacht had been overdue but all's well that ends well . . . Grosvenor D. K. De Brooks III had been appointed to an office and the newspaper wondered if this newly-begun career would culminate in the presidency . . . just as certain cardinals were considered papable, so certain De Brookses were considered presidentiable (but no one had ever proposed appointing Theobald Delafont D. to any office, however minor). Interest in these appointees persisted, then flickered, then went out: twenty years later another one would come into focus . . . for a while. But no reporter or feature writer or political leader ever focused, however briefly, on Theobald Delafont De Brooks, because *nobody even knew he was there*. Nobody watched him during the long grey years while he grew more and more solitary and his wraith of a business just about sufficed to bring his two good suits to the dry-cleaners a few times a year and his six good white shirts to the French Laundry down the block.

At perhaps somewhat shorter intervals the classical old De Brooks homes at Muskrat Sump or Parkill Ridge were always good for a story; same, dim and thin as old tissue-paper by now, the faded dream that a Someone would appear, "Say, I'm Jim K. De Brooks! Mother and Dad think it's about time you paid us a visit . . . I've got the car outside." Through the years (decades) *the car* changed: it was a Stutz . . . a Star . . . a Caddy . . . a Kaiser . . . Edsel . . . Jag . . . but . . . somehow . . . it never really Got Outside. *Here.*

There was one old newspaper story in particular; unlike others, which tended to be cyclical, it seemed to have appeared in print only once: and the scissors had missed the date: it was worn, torn, and faded: its headline was, MISSING TREASURE OF THE PATRIOT PATROON. A patroon, remember, was a sort of squire who held an old land grant from the Dutch or English governments; this particular patroon was Wouter Cornelius De Brooks, and he was a *patriot* because, unlike anyway *some* other patroons he remained steadfast to the Continental Cause, whose ultimate victory he did not live to see. The list of the treasure itself was so detailed that it must have been read even by King George while he helped himself to his breakfast beer and beef. And, except for 75 silver Pieces of Eight Royals, it was all in gold: escudos, guineas, louis d'or, doubloons. The Patriot Patroon, one season during the War of the Revolution, had in the presence of witnesses packed the treasure into a traveling-chest made of cedarwood and black bull's-hide and set off in his very own sloop from De Brooks Castle high above the lordly Hudson with the expressed intention of making his way to Philadelphia via the kills, creeks, rivers, and bays which lay outside of British Occupation, and, once arrived, to put said treasure at the disposal of the Patriot Government. One month later he turned up in York, Pennsylvania, "tired, hungry, muddy, bloody, and exceedingly confused." He had nothing with him save the clothes on his poor old back, and died a few weeks later, without ever having disclosed where he had been, what he had done, or what had happened to the carefully-listed Treasure. A contemporary source (said the old newspaper clipping) had darkly suggested that "the poor old man" (the Patriot was then fifty-five in age) "had somehow been waylaid by the British or the Tories and feloniously robbed." Three generations later some sad, sour Whig (this was *not* in the article, but TDD had found it in a letter at the Historical Society) commented, with who knows what mad motive, that "Neeley De Brooks had really intended to send it by ship to be banked in France, but was made drunk and lost it at the craps"; fie upon the fellow who said so.

And, "is this all there is?" Theo asked the faded, quiet lady at the Historical Society. She thought for a moment. "Well, there is this," she said, removing a manila envelope from a file. Within lay something between translucent sheets; removed, *this* appeared to be a page from an old, *old* letter, so stained with time and water and *God*-knows what, that only a few words were, theoretically,

legible. And Theo could not have read even them, had not the letter-page been
accompanied by a conjectural reading of those words, typed on even-now-
yellowing paper by an old-time typewriter. As follows:

```
. . . . . . cadet of [the] fam[ly?] . . . . . . . . . . . addlepa[te?] or
drunkar[d?] . . . . . . . . . strong[ly] defen[ded?] himself, but
cou[ld?] or [wou?]ld produ[ce?] no [evi?]dence . . . . . . . . but
never shewed any Signs of [ac?]crued Wealth, so . . . . . . . . .
alOthoug[?] tis true that a Fool and his money are soon . . . . . .
```

Also in the old-fashioned typewriting:

```
This paper was certainly manufactured between 1820 and
1829 or 30, but the Penmanship is of the late 18th century,
Mr. Stuyvesant believes it relates somehow to the Patriot Pa-
troon.—G. D.
```

"Mr. Stuyvesant, of course, has been dead for some years," said the faded,
quiet lady; "and so has Mr. Gilbert Dawes, our former Director. Our budget,"
she concluded, "does not allow us to submit the paper to any of the later
scientific tests."

That was *that*.

And, last and last of all, was *this*, from a letter of Phillip Hone, Mayor of
a then-much-smaller New York City, both in population and in area, say a
million years ago, give or take a quarter of a million; addressed to a Mr. Gan-
sevoort, Officer aboard the Ship *Nepera*, care of the Office of the Seamens'
Chapel, Honolulu, Sandwich Islands: skip most of it; stop at this: *"Yesterday
was the funeral of Aurelius De Brooke, son of the Patroon, last of the old Indian
Traders, of whom I recall my Gt. Aunt Maria used to say, That he knew more
of the ways of the Pow-whaw Men than was lawful for a Christian to know, I
cd not go, having a bad cold."*

Did the old Patroon learn how to cast the always at least semisacred tobacco into a not very flourishing fire and cry Skah-*ootch?*

Useless to ask. Useless even to wonder.

And, just as no young and handsome and famously-De Brooks-grinning
distant cousin had ever appeared to invite poor Theo to tennis and tea, just so
no unknown figure had ever appeared out of the dusk to hand him the map
and the key to the traveling-chest made of cedar and black bull's-hide.

And the years rolled on and he had rolled on with them, explaining endlessly to anyone who would listen why their family *needed* that extra protection
which only the Special Indemnity Policy offered; and to collect the rents for
Miss Whittier and a few other ancients who still thought that he went annually
to Parkill Ridge or Muskrat Sump for Thanksgiving Dinner to be made privy
to the secrets of America's almost-royal family. Whereas actually he went over
to his mother's folks, where he was loudly and cheerfully greeted as *Pres-i-*

dent-De-Brooks! (once: then the annual joke was over), and cheerfully squeezed into a place at the crowded table where the only political philosophy expressed was that fingers were made before forks; and lavishly poured many glasses of whatever beer the Pucklemans were currently contracted to deliver

Once, out of the mists, an elderly man in a high-crowned fedora such as Warren G. Harding might have worn at the Convention of 1912 (the sweat-band was *very* sweaty, though; even its sweat-stains) and a once-elegant suit with matching vest—that is, the spots on it matched those on the jacket and pants—had visited TDD in his office. The visitor glanced carefully at him, glanced carefully at the two framed photographs, made him a ponderous nod. "Yep!" said he. "You're a De Brooks for sure!" His faded blue eyes had a sort of film over them and there were little traces of yellow gum at the corners and his complexion was as grey as his suit.

"I . . . am . . . a Hammerson! Augustus Hammerson, Minister of Marine under John Adams? [Was *this* the face to launch a thousand ships and—] Great-uncle, four times removed, in the di-rect line!" And he leaned back, awaiting the effect. "Can call me Gus," he said.

"Gus," said Theo, obediently. And, after a moment, added, "Well. well. well."

"Wrong side of the *tracks!*" exclaimed his visitor, suddenly and bitterly. "Won't even give me the time of day!—Suppose it's sort of the same with you, I guess," he concluded, in a not-quite questioning tone. "All of those fancy-dancy De Brookses, hand in glove with the Big Bankers, hey."

Theo said, slowly, "Well. . . ."

And Gus Hammerson, after expressing his own grievances, which were many, went on to invite TDD to attend an informal get-together of a group of Real Americans interested in purifying the political system and restoring things the way they used to be and the way they ought to be: " 'No Irish need apply,' " said he. And gave another ponderous nod. "Apply our united *strength*," said he. "Get some of those good political plums for our*selves!*" said he. And, after some more such talk, asked TDD if he had a cigar, then borrowed a dollar to get one, then took his leave, still nodding deeply.

TDD, after a lifetime of ungratified hopes and increasingly entrenched disappointments, was no longer really sure of what he really wanted. But he was sure that it was not to become a part of a would-be cabal of unpensioned former railroad telegraphers, retired secretaries of down at the heel institutions, bankrupted salesmen of the bonds of obscure municipalities: seeking to revive the ghost of the Know Nothings and secure for themselves a share of the openings for U.S. vice-consulates and inspectorates of intestate properties, to which their descents from militia officers of the War of 1812 obviously entitled them. He opened his office door to let a little air in, and wrote the dollar off as charity.

—Was *that* how he seemed to others? he wondered—and the wondering of it gave him a very sharp pain whenever he thought about it: and, after that, he thought about it often.

. . .

Not very many months after that Old Miss Whittier died, leaving him—surprisingly—a $1,000 Liberty Bond. Her nephew and niece, it was very plain,
deeply begrudged him this trifle; but, inasmuch as Miss Whittier's will had
specified that if any of the heirs contested the will, such contestants were to
receive the sum of $25 each and nothing more, decided to let him carry it away
as spoil. As then, one hoped they neither of them broke a leg in their haste,
sold all the Whittier properties to a syndicate with offices in Zurich and Hong
Kong. The syndics sent TDD a nicely-worded letter expressing appreciation
for his long services, for which their plans however. . . .

Having lost his apartment in Miss Whittier's West Elm building, and not
feeling quite ripe for yet another major move, Theobald Delafont De Brooks
sold some of the furniture, gave some away to an eleemosynary organization
whose bands had, now and then, briefly brightened his boyhood; and moved
a very few items (such as, for example, a folding screen and an army cot and
some blankets and sheets) into his office. He considered that what he would
henceforth save on house rent would, if he were lucky, outweigh the increasing
costs of dry-cleaning and finished shirts, and so on. It also came to pass that a
morning meal consisting of a little orange juice and a little vodka not only cost
less than a heavy greasy breakfast however traditional (and what had tradition
ever done for Theobald Delafont De Brooks?) but that he felt rather better
afterwards. Slowly going over these matters in his mind one night as preparation for unfolding the cot, he gazed—as one engaged in a religious ritual which
no longer greatly attached him but which was very much a part of his routine—
at the large framed oval photographs: President Theobald De Brooks, the Hero
of the Pampas War; President Grosvenor Delafont De Brooks, who presided
over the nation during more perilous times (happy era! whose major enemy
was *Spain!*)—

—came a knocking at the door—

"Come *in!*"

No one could have looked less like a raven than the decent-looking, tired-
looking woman who entered, a woman of about the same age as Theo. Woman
who at once saw the photographs, at once recognized them. Was at once impressed. Then, "Am I talking to Mr. De Brooks?"

"You certainly are." Well . . . he certainly *was. Wasn't* she? The woman
(really, he thought of her as "the lady") looked at him carefully. Her face,
somewhat faded, but fairly pleasant, asked a very over-familiar question.
"Shirt-tail cousins," said Theo. *Didn't* feel like rest of the routine at all, at all.
"What can I do for you, Mrs.—?" (Had to be *Mrs.*, she wore a wedding ring
and was not of the generation to be a *Ms.*)

"Thatcher. Ella Thatcher. Widow of Bob—Robert Thatcher—I married
my cousin, didn't even get to change my last name." (How brief, the dry, wry
smile, anticipating the oh *God* how foreseeable remark which she must have
heard a hundred thousand times: and weary of it as he of the one which
he—). They shook hands. "Mr. De Brooks, have you ever heard of . . .
Thatcher's Storage?" Her manner was a bit embarrassed, a bit defiant, a bit
irresolute, and . . . though rather less . . . a bit hopeful.

TDD was not very used to women (and certainly not respectable women) calling on him late at night; he was just a bit embarrassed, certainly more than a bit puzzled; politeness won, however. "That-cher's . . . Storage..? Yes! Browning Street! Isn't that—"

Ella Thatcher laughed briefly. "You've seen that old sign, the one painted on the side of the old Odeon Building by the railroad tracks. Why, that advertisement, it's been there since the Year of One! My goodness! We moved, the firm moved, as a matter of fact, in 1930. To 635 Oldham." She seemed rather pleased: however obsolete the sign, it had at least—

"Well, Mrs. Thatcher. I'll be glad to sell you some insurance, or—" He *would* be glad. He would be surprised, too.

Ella Thatcher again gave her short laugh. "We're going out of business. Did you ever hear of Mullet River, Florida? Just a wide place in the road, the town, can't even call it a town. I own a couple of little bungalows there, and that's where I'm going, just as soon as I wind things up here. Got my social security, going to catch and sell bait. Bob taught me how to load a hook and hold a net when we were just kids. I have a book about a hundred ways to cook fish. . . ."

"Sounds great." It *did*.

"Yes? Do you think so? Well, *I* think so, too. The place is just too far from the nearest fire hydrant, I couldn't *get* insurance . . . come on down, then, I'll rent you the bungalow out behind for almost nothing, just for the company. It's on, oh, a sort of canal. Quiet."

Quietly, " 'Why are you going out of business, Mrs. Thatcher?"

Mrs. Thatcher sighed. "Well, people just don't *store* things the way they used to. And . . . seems like the government, and the Unions, they are just making it harder and harder for a body to stay in business. Taxes, my God, the taxes! And . . . then . . . the place's got about seventeen mortgages on it, and my brother-in-law, he owns sixteen of them. You know how long we've been in business, Mr. De Brooks? No . . . I suppose not . . . I sort of thought, you being a real old family, you might have heard something. Well, the fact is, we don't *know* how long we've been in business! A lot of those old records, they were burned up, about the time of the Civil War. That's when the last Mr. Simkins, he married . . . his daughter married . . . my great-grandfather, he was named Robert Thatcher, too. Before that," her voice had taken on a slight sing-song rhythm, and TDD formed the notion that perhaps Mrs. Thatcher had recited this history many times. ". . . before thaaat, it was called The Great Repository. How's that for a name, The Great Repository? Anyway, to come to the point. Cleaning out the place, way down in the sub-basement, I come across this great big box—"

"A box?" TDD's heart gave a sudden thump.

"Great big box. My hunch, you know if you've been in the same business all your life, you sort of get hunches sometimes about things, and my hunch, is that inside the box there's maybe another box. Or something. And, on the *box*, it's painted with the word, the name, I mean. . . ."

"De Brooks."

The two of them had spoken the word simultaneously. They chuckled.

Then stopped. Was there, very suddenly, a slight but definite drop in the temperature?

"See, maybe you *do* know something about it. And besides the name there's a number, but the number doesn't *mean* anything—Well: maybe it meant something to Simkins, and maybe it meant something to The Great Repository. But it doesn't mean a thing to Thatcher's. I mean, it-is-*old* . . . the box."

TDD nodded. "And you want to clear it out . . . and close up, I see."

Mrs. Thatcher, speaking with rather more confidence, said that she had written to every De Brooks in the book. Maybe because it was because she had no more letterheads and didn't see any reason to *get* anymore and had just written in ink on plain paper and used just plain envelopes. . . . "Or maybe they just thought I was trying to *rook* them, I don't know. But, do you know what? *Not one of them answered*. Not a single *one*."

"I believe you," Theo said, with great sincerity.

"I never wrote *you*, Mr. De Brooks, because you, you're in a different phone book, here. Just, tonight, thinking it over, I did remember that I did once see your name when I was driving past. So . . . well . . . so . . . Here I *am*."

Very quietly, Theobald Delafont De Brooks asked, "What's the bill?"

Ella Thatcher took a piece of paper from her purse, started to look at it, started to speak, then looked at it again, and then read aloud, "Three thousand, five hundred and thirty-five dollars and thirty-five cents." And she looked at TDD, slightly diffident, slightly embarrassed, slightly defiant, and withal: somewhat hopeful.

It flashed across TDD's mind that, on something which had been in storage so long that no one knew how long it had been in storage, and the very records of which had been burned over a hundred years ago that the bill as announced could represent nothing but a pious hope; he said, "Will you take a $1,000 Liberty Bond in full settlement?" Surprise and delight moved across Ella Thatcher's face, and so, in a second, did a slight shadow.

"—that will cover moving it over here . . . and we won't need to mention a thing to your brother-in-law—"

In an instant they were shaking hands.

In twenty minutes they were in a bar for which *dim, drab, sleazy* were inadequate qualifiers. "Red." (Mrs. Thatcher speaking.) "Red. Want to help us move a *box*?"

"Gimme twenny dollars," said Red, "and I'll move the Moon."

The warehouse truck was old, it was, for a truck still in service, very old. But it, with the dolly, Red, Ella Thatcher, and TDD, made no hard task of transportation. By midnight they had moved it into TDD's office. Red received his $20, was *gone*, leaving only the thought of a thirst for beer.

"Does that do it?" asked Mrs. Thatcher.

"That does it," said TDD. He opened his (mostly-empty) old safe, removed the manila envelope, slid the bond out for swift inspection, handed it over.

"Lots of luck," said Ella.

"Lots of luck," said TDD.

And yet she did not move to go. He made no move to hasten her, eager though he was to be at work on the crate.

"Well . . ." she said. Gave her purse a nervous pat, as though perhaps a bit afraid she might lose it. "Well . . ." she said, again. "Honestly, I should have told you honestly before . . . although I *did* come across the thing just a month or so ago, well, I had *heard* of it before. Bob mentioned it. My father and my uncle and *their* father mentioned it. And I'll tell you what they called it." She stopped suddenly. He had felt his face change. She had seen it change.

"The spook box," he said.

Everybody has read of someone's jaw dropping. Hers now dropped.

After a moment it was back in place.

" 'Well, I've heard the expression, too. But I . . . we . . . never knew what it meant," he said. "What *does* it—?"

She had somewhat recovered. He saw her swallow. But she did not ask for a glass of water, or even if she might sit down. She was *game*. "Well, it was an old family story. I mean, *old*. It was a . . . 'now you see it and now you don't' sort of thing. Every now and then it would turn up. By the time it would take for someone to go and tell about it, by the time someone would come back, it was . . . well . . . *gone*. As though it had some kind of a hex on it."

Theo said, "Maybe he had cheated the pow-whaw man on a bale of furs, or something. Or maybe *his* father had. They didn't get rich buying dear and selling cheap, that's for sure. *Well*. Guess we'll never know."

She agreed that, probably, they never would. "But when I saw it and touched it myself, I knew that if there really had been a hex! on it, the hex was really off it now. Woman's intuition; I *really* have to go." And she really went.

Sometimes dreams come true. Among the (few) things which TDD had brought with him in his latest move was the old toolbox, its last remembered use being the dismantling of a hen-house: "It *smells*, is 'why,' " said Mrs. Delafont James De Brooks, nee Puckelman. The box was far more well-built than the hen-house had been, and it must have taken him an hour to get it open, his heart beating, beating, beating. *How* many years? Over three hundred years. *What* did he have to show for it? A lifetime of unrealized hopes. And many sly tricks, most of which never worked. *How* was he going to handle the matter? Some of the gold coins he would sell in Boston. Some he would sell in New York. Some in Philadelphia. Some in Baltimore. No dumping. And then he would catch a plane. Where to, a plane? Jamaica . . . Barbados . . . Curacao . . . and . . . Ella . . . ?

He never doubted for a minute what, exactly, was inside the box.

He was right.

Mrs. Thatcher was right, too.

The story of how the traveling-chest made of cedar-wood and black bull's-hide got packed into a snug box and how it found its way into The Great Repository and what had happened to the poor Old Patriot Patroon and why it had lain abandoned for almost two centuries would never, certainly, now be known. And as for the rich De Brookses, screw the rich De Brookses. They had had their chance. Chances.

And maybe the pow-whaw man *taught* the Patriot Patroon the hex.

The chest was easier to break into than the heavy outer box had been. The black bull's-hide crumbled easily. The cedar was sturdy, but the builders had not built it precisely snug, and the crowbar fitted between the gaps. Theo felt a slight difficulty in breathing; there was fortunately a bottle kept in case of emergencies; as he sipped, these words came into and ran through his mind: Seventy-five silver Pieces of Eight Royals, and the rest all in gold: gold escudos, golden guineas, golden louis, gold doubloons: every one of the rightful heritage of Theodore Delafont De Brooks.

And sometimes they don't.

The treasure chest of the Patriot Patroon contained not a brass farthing nor a pewter shilling nor two copper pence, and certainly neither silver nor gold. Witnesses had seen that it had once been packed with metal money. But Wouter Cornelius De Brooks had not been called the *Patriot* patroon for nothing; it was not in word alone that he had supported the Continental Congress: he had trusted in its currency as well; and sometime during that mysteriously missing month he had exchanged every single piece of hard money for paper money, and the fruits of this exchange filled the chest. How unpatriotic, then, how cruel, on the part of whoever it was who had first used the phrase, *Not worth a continental.*

The Continental Congress had been gallant.

But it had not stuck around to pay.

The ancient, the august, the almost-noble house of De Brooks, for reasons which Theobald Delafont had never known and would never know, had smitten him, innocent as he was, more than one blow: and this one more and greatest blow, it had waited more than two hundred years to smite.

The greatest.

But the last. Had he, though, been entirely innocent? Had he not wasted his life on a dead claim to a dead name? Was there not, waiting in the chest, one message of great worth? *Lay thy burden down,* it seemed to say. It had to say *something,* didn't it? He spent another while neatly dividing the old paper money into two equal portions, and in neatly wrapping and addressing them. One to Muskrat Sump. And one to Parkill Ridge. And in the upper left-hand corner of each he wrote, *Wouter Cornelius De Brooks.* It was morning by now, the post office would soon be open. And . . . then . . . ? Mullet River was so small that he could not even find it on the map in the Atlas.

But he could look for it, on or off the main-traveled roads. There was lots of time.

Yellow Rome; or, Vergil and the Vestal Virgin
INTRODUCTION BY DARRELL SCHWEITZER

"Yellow Rome," at first merely a pervasive image, suggesting the sunbaked brick, the searing sky, the soap-shy vulgus with their stained tunics, a condemned convict uncontrollably urinating; but in the hands of Avram Davidson it becomes something else, a resonant incantation. Yellow Rome! Teeming, filthy, and magnificent, where even a magus might lose himself.

In the hands of Avram Davidson, everything becomes something else. The Yellow Rome of Emperor Julius I is not that of history. Julius Caesar wasn't an emperor, for one thing. Every citizen most certainly did not carry knives as described here. In fact, the Julian law forbade them to. (This law coming to the attention of most readers—and most Romans—when repealed some four centuries later, as the center could not hold, mere anarchy was loosed upon the world, and the government told the provincials, "We cannot protect you. Go ahead and carry knives. Good luck!")

What we have here is ancient Rome seen through the filter of medieval remembrance, the setting of two exemplary Davidson novels, The Phoenix and the Mirror and Vergil in Averno, based on the curious legend that Vergil, the author of the Aeneid, was also a sorcerer. Davidson, the most playfully erudite of fantasy writers, brought the exploits of Vergil Magus irresistibly to life.

"Yellow Rome" is the opening chapter of the unpublished third Vergil Magus novel, The Scarlet Fig. It is Avram at his atmospheric and arcane best. Read it for the pleasure of Avram's presence and Avram's unique voice.

YELLOW ROME; OR, VERGIL AND THE VESTAL VIRGIN

IN ROME—YELLOW ROME! Yellow Rome!—a man was being led to public execution. Aristocrats might be quietly done-in in dungeons; this was no aristocrat. Some common thug, a street-robber by night, or a house-breaker; thick and shambling, ill-made and ill-looking, he had killed a cobbler's apprentice for a stiver—the smallest coin. The lictor went first, carrying the bundle of rods which might be used to flog the criminal (but wouldn't) wrapped around the single-edged axe which might be used to cut off his head (but wouldn't). It was a symbol only, and the lictor looked bored and disdainful. Then, arms bound behind him at the elbows, legs hobbled with ropes, the felon followed between two files of soldiers. Grasping him fast by a noose round his neck came the common hangman: one might have had them change clothes and places and scarcely told them apart.

"Well, 'one Vergil, a natural of Rome, and no mere denizen,' do they have anything to do with this in Naples ... I say nothing of the Bail of Brundisy ... ?" The wauling in my ear was Quint's, to be heard above the clamor of the throng. There was in his voice some light and affectionate taunt that I had not been born in the City itself but in a fœderate town in the Italies' south, well within the Empery, but nearer to where I now lived by the great Voe of Naples than to Yellow Rome itself. The so-well-paved Appian Way went straight and strait between Yellow Rome and Brundisy, but there branched off a branch of it for Naples. A young mage, not yet very well-established in his profession (or in public fame) did well to travel now and then to the Imperial capital, and gently press the thought that there was one (myself) useful to be friend of a friend (Quint) with a friend (the rich Etruscan) to the Court Imperial, to the Oliphaunt Throne ... not to be lightly named: whosoever sate upon it.

I pressed my bearded lips to Quint's smooth ear-hole, said loud and sharp, that we had throngs and thugs, all right: but neither one was anything to this particular display.

The throng howled, as the throng always would.

"Chin up, cock! Brave it out!"

"They'll stretch that short neck!"

"Hang the hangman! A louse for the hangman!"

"You'll scrag no more widdies nor prentices!"

"Up tails all!"

"Die! For a lousy stiver? *Die!*"

The wretch's face changed expression, but it changed slowly: now he had the sly look of a pig who had broken into a pea-patch, now he was pleased at the attention, now he scowled as some thick and gross insult struck home, now he looked desperately from side to side; always the hangy forced him on, as close to him as the butcher to the ox. All this passed before me and before Quint, and we stood and looked on; I was his guest, and he was the guest of Someone Important in Yellow Rome. Even a wizard, even if he did not want wealth, was willing to draw near to wealth, if he were young and new and scarcely known. And near to power, even if that sort of power he did not much want. Soon enough this procession would pass by, and then we would cross, cross safely on foot, for in Rome (and in Rome alone) no wheeled vehicle might pass through the streets in the day time.

In that case, in a sudden silence, what hooves were those, and what wheels? Quint, I saw, that Roman of Romans, knew at once: and would tell me soon enough . . . if I did not ask. The mob broke into noise again, its inalienable right, and though it was still shouting, it seemed to be shouting the same something, though not all at the same time. Half the yammering throng faced the nice little wagonette and its nice little mule, and the woman, half-veiled, who was in it. Her small slave-girl holding the sea-silk sunshade or ombello was beginning to be inattentive a bit and a bit the sunshade slipped.

And half the vulgus faced the procession and shouted and gestured, pointing, pointing—

The lictor had strode on, eyes down; and in fact by then he had gotten ahead of the procession and seemed rather to have forgotten it: lictors, too, have their secret private thoughts.

The soldiery slogged along in its fixed rhythms, paying no attention at all to the *thing* its ranks confined; probably thinking of the evening's rations: bread, salt, garlic, parsley, wine, perhaps a bit of dried meat or a bit of dried fish—tunny harpooned in the bloody trapping pens, for instance—and the anticipated meal with its, perhaps, treat, meant far more to them than any execution of a sentence of death (death, to an old soldier, was more boring than exciting).

The hangman, whose attention was so suddenly besought by many cries and movements, pressed on. I noticed that the hangman pressed on.

What Quint, with his pale thin face and dark thin hair, noticed, was not known to me.

Who made up the mob rabbling and howling? The meanest class of citizenry, whose leather badges with S P Q R stamped in gilt served to prove citizenship, made up the largest part. They had no money to buy anything and no mind to read anything, so a procession to the gibbet was an absolute gift for them.

Men, too, from all the peoples of the Empery were there: Franks with long hair and Celts with short and Ægyptians with none; pale Berbars from the

Solitudes of Syrtica and of As'hara, sand as high as mountains and hills of solid stone pierced with holes where the Troglodytes live; dark Numidians who had seen the Sphynges flying in their thousands to drink of the waters at the sources of the Nile—of all other waters drink they not, of the Waters of Ægypt drink they not—and Gauls with their bearded chops, the wailing of whose dead fills the islands and the highlands of the misty great green darkling Sea of Atlantis between shore to shore of whose vasty waters might no bird fly; and Æthiops with emeraulds in their ears. Many indeed could I see (though not *so* many) were aliens from outside the Empery, and even the Œconomium.

I was indifferent at seeing or smelling the so-called Foul or Infamous Crafts such as the knackers and the carriers of dogs'-dung for the tanneries, for I still had the muck of the farmyards and the fernbrooks on my legs and feet, and the odor of dead beasts and dung-heaps was fresher to my nose-holes than those of ambergrise and nard.

And here and there, as so often of late (and some said, more and more often, and they darkly mumbled their gums about laws graven on the Twelve Iron Tablets about the artificial production of monsters and other omens . . . no one of course was ever able to find such laws) here and there through the mass went wandering a satyr or a centaur of, say, the size of a goat-kid. There were no weanling Lapiths to be seen, however; and who would know one, had there been? memory of one Cluco, a night-soil-man little wittier than a wittold, in my home-hamlet in the Bail of Brundisy, who used to stop anyone too purblind to avoid him, and confide, "My granddam, now, she seen a Laypith, she seen 'un with a horn in the muddle o' his forrid: which be the reason, she bein' six months gorn wi' child, that I has six finger on my left 'and." What the logical, or even illogical connection between the two things were, no one was ever able to conjecture; certainly all local priests denied that ever there had been stories—"myths," you might call them—of monoceroid Lapiths; and neither was anyone, lay or cleric, able to credit Cluco's being able to invent such a story. But, however invented, tell it he did, decade after decade, to whoever could not trot faster than he could, and who—usually—was glad or let us say willing enough to avoid the presence of Cluco, polydactylous or not (for *rhododactylos* I assure you he wasn't, and neither was he rosy-scented) with the dole of a very small coin or a not-quite-so-small chunk of bread: at which see Cluco become unseen; this may or may not have been more profitable than the night-soil business, but was certainly much easier.

When I mention the size of a goat-kid I refer to the centaurs, for the satyrs were man-sized (as I could have told anyone), and very near each creature was someone (invariably a shill) mentioning confidentially the name of the thaumaturge who'd made it, in some such words as, "That 'un's the work of that same Septimus as keeps his crib atween Apollo's Court and the Steps of Woe."—why would anyone *want* a confected satyr or centaur? perhaps one of those newly-rich who kept a baby elephant in his atrium might want one, and for the same reason: show.

Thieves were there, in the vulgus; as they could not steal the golden spikes from the ridge-poles of the temples and the other public buildings, they cut the thongs of purses with their knives so much sharper than razors; sellers of snacks were there, for many a man had neither cook nor kitchen to dress a meal of victuals, and if he turned aside into a cheap eating-place he might miss something: but whether a rabbleman stewed hog-palates in vinegar or cut the thongs of purses or did, as was the right of citizens, nothing at all, something there had now changed and perhaps everything had changed. But the hangman wished to behave as though nothing had happened. The lictor, whose attention was now besought by many cries and movements, strode on, eyes down, and in fact by now he had gotten ahead of the procession. The hangman pressed on. A bit the woman's sunshade slipped and a bit the veil, revealing to me a face of such extraordinary loveliness and purity that my breath was stopped.

The word coming up from the populus now was *pardon:* the hangman would not stop for it; why should he? He received the deadman's clothes as a perquisite: even if they were rags (and they were not always rags) they had their value and their price as ingredients of the Black Rite; he got to receive everything which was, or at the time of prisonment had been, on the body of the dead-man-to-be; and he also received his fee for making the liveman's body dead by pushing it off the ladder at the gibbet and at once leaping onto his shoulders and jumping up and down on them—thus assuring that the caitiff's neck must break if it had not already been broken by the drop. Of these benefits the hangman would receive none at all in case of *pardon,* so why should he stop for it? and lastly, it would deprive him of all the pleasure of the death scene: the hangman, howl the mob as it would, would not stop. And who might stop him?

(The lictor, fasces bundled into his arms, was by now rather far ahead, stooped, aloof, deep in thought: of what, who could say? Perhaps that *time there was, ere Roma's woes began* . . . perhaps not.)

Who else? Himself, the August Caesar? Where was *he?* not here. From what other place, then, did the musty multitude seem to think that help might arise? The woman in the wagonette commenced to rise, in a slow and flowing motion like a hieratical dancer: though, perhaps actually not: only . . . somehow . . . it seemed so. The brute would not see her. I caught her eye, and again, that ambiguous impression, that impression deep yet perhaps false. Had I caught her eye at all? Erect, like a statue of the golden age, she seemed.

The lictor, perhaps grown somewhat aware of the hideous shriek and hum from that mass of men—here and there some women: not trulls alone: vendors of fragrant citrons, of pickled samphire for relish, of sieves and baskets in many sizes, fishwives going down to the river to renew supplies of mullet and sardines and dogfish with double-lobed livers; others—the lictor at once saw all. Quint, keenly enjoying everything, was telling me nothing; scarcely he raised a thin and hairy hand to brush the ever-deliquescent ointment from his bleary eyes— his physicians were generally agreed 'twas from an excess of some humor, but they never yet agreed on which humor, though there were not many, but prescribed this salve or that; they might as well, I thought, have told him to graze grass like an ox . . . whoever saw a blear-eyed ox? And, "Ow!" shouted the throng, and "Yow!" shouted the throng. "*Pardon! Pardon!*" it howled. And ever and again, "Uptails, all!" and "A louse for the hangman!"

The hangman may or may not have gotten a louse (close-pressed in that

stinking swarm, it would have been no surprise if he had) but what he very
quickly got was the lictor at his side; and the lictor said to him, more in astonishment than anger, "Where are you *going*, turd of a toad? Don't you *see* the
highborn Virgin lady? *Stop!*—Or I'll let the populus have you, and may they
eat your liver!"

The Vestal, meanwhile, remained standing in her wagon all but motionless,
the very image of aristocratic calm. Silence took a while. When things were
almost silent, the felon seemed to emerge from his daze. One could almost
read—no, one *could* read—the play of thoughts coursing over across his
sword-slashed and much-confused face. Where *was* he? What was *hap*pening?
Why had they *stop*ped? Why was everything *quiet?* Answer: they were arrived
and halted at the place of execution; any minute now he might have a small
and ill-tasting coin thrust into his mouth and feel nothing beneath his feet, and
a sharp brief pain in his neck. With a sound like the lowing of a yearling ox he
spread his hobbled legs, and pissed.

The swarm went wild with laughter. Only the lictor's leather face, the
Vestal's marmoreal countenance, did not change, for all that her little maid,
hand hiding mouth, seemed to whisper in her ear. At length silence was again
achieved, and in that silence—though the punks and pogues still rolled their
painted eyes and smirked at potential clients—the Vestal rose completely to
attention, put out her white arm and hand and in a lovely ringing tone declared,
"*I pardon that man.*" No one word more. And sat down. It had been a completely legal formula, sans emotion. "I divorce you; herewith your dowerfund."
"Slave, thou art henceforth free." "Bear witness: I sell this horse-stud for six
solids." *I pardon that man.* No one word more. And sat down.

The crowd went wild again. A soldier in a swift second slashed the bonds
about the elbows; another slightly stooped and severed those around the ankles.
For a second more the thug gaped. Then he started to run at a stumbling trot.
Many hands caught at him: he fought against them. Many cries of, "Not yet,
man!"

"Not yet! *Thank* the holy lady! Go and kiss the Virgin's foot! Thank her
for your life!"

But one might as well have spoken to a pig escaped from the shambles;
loose, was he? Then he meant to stay loose. And this meant to flee. For a full
minute (so I guessed) the absurd scene continued, the pardoned man butting
furiously against the arms and bodies which would have had him first do his
duty by giving thanks for that pardon; the crowd all of one mind now (the
whores most of all: could it have been they fancied a slight upon that one
quality which they universally lacked, and lacked, one might say, almost by
definition?), the crowd's sense of amour propre was seriously offended; while
the lictor covered his grim face with his free hand and gazed through his spread
and ringless fingers as though he could not believe his eyes—And then herself
the Vestal: something which might have been a mere flicker of rueful amusement passed over her fine face and was in an instant gone (more than Caesar's
wife must a Vestal Virgin be above suspicion, she must be above suspicion of
vulgar emotion). She raised her hand at an angle to her wrist, slightly pushed
it away from her; the other hand fluttered the colored leathers on the mule's

neck. The crowd released the fool felon and laughed to hear his running feet; at once made way for the Vestal's wee carriage, and saluted her with the utmost respect. Did the little maid murmur something, something, anything, with well-practised and almost motionless lips? did the sea-silk sunshade dip for a second a fraction of an inch in a particular direction? this was not certain.

Certain it was that a mule was not a horse, all horses were hysterical more or less, the most placid old cob was likely to behave like a northish bear-shirt if—if, whatever; this would differ from cob to cob—horse to horse. But mules were mysterious creatures, that this one was a small mule did not make its potential mystery any smaller; probably it had been bred for the service it now performed out of a pony-mare by one of the jack-donkeys of the northern lands, lighter in build and in size than the asses of the south, brought to Rome or its countryside for just this purpose. And in view of what was about to happen it was necessary to consider also the probable history of the street-bed. Quint might know just when the street had last been paved, I not. But in some short moment I envisioned the scene—a man engaged in ramming the gravel turning aside for a moment to go piss or to get a drink of water, another workman not waiting for his return or not even considering the matter of had the gravel been rammed sufficiently—and it had not—the second workman perhaps, then, mechanically setting down the pave-stone; the first workman returning and, likely even without so much as a shrug, picking up his implement and moving on a few feet to commence the work of ramming a bit further on. And then the passing of the years, the rains, many years of rains, the not-fully-packed gravel shifting, moving; then perhaps the fall of a heavier stone from an improperly-laded wagon passing by in the torchlight: the paving stone sustaining a crack not observed in the night, more years passing, the incessant traffic at last splitting the pave-stone. Somehow the inspectors had missed it . . . or, their reports ignored . . . the night-traffic cared nothing for any bad spot which their heavy wagons could lurch across . . . had, anyway, the drivers and teamsters, no time to spend on complaints: into the city by nightfall, in-cargo laded-off, out-cargo laded-on, out of the city by nightrise: so.

A horse, had it felt a sunken spot behind it . . . *if* it felt it . . . would either have strained forward or strained backward. An ass would have stopped. And stayed. Time to put something under the wheel. But the mule, even the small, supposedly sophisticated mule, reacted entirely differently. The mule was, after all, the Symbol of Unbridled Lust—though why this should be so when the mule was sterile, was hard to say: the mule (this particular one) had somehow missed the sunken spot. Now it somehow backed up a trifle. Now it felt it. *The wheel not right! The wheel sinking!* The entire universe of a sudden gone awry! The mule at once went insane: the mule screamed, rolled back its eyes, laid down its ears, made as if to stand on its hind legs—on its forelegs—to lie down and roll over—it was at once evident that there was nothing the mule might not do.

In a second the little slave girl had jumped out of the car to safety, held up her wrists, thin as carrots, at an absolutely useless angle for the Vestal to lean upon. The crowd gave a great groan. It was no slight thing to witness the fall of a Vestal Virgin. Should she be killed, for a space of time at least there would be only ~~*five* "sisters" to hold safe the hearths of Rome . . . who knew what~~ might happen during such an interregnum. Many in the crowd believed that seeing such a sight obliged one to fast: many even believed that whoso saw such would—must!—within the year surely die. From the crowd a great groan. Many rushed forward . . . I amongst them . . . some seized the mule . . . some seized the car . . . some seized hold of their knives, such as each man wore at his belt, or was no man: to cut reins, traces . . . one man alone seized the Vestal by the arm . . . by the upper and the lower arm . . . it lasted a second. The mule was suddenly calm and collected: panic? what panic? The car was suddenly steady and safe. The knives were all suddenly back in their belts, absit omen lest any delator or informer should occasion to ask, *How didst thou dare to bare thy knife unto the high-born Virgin Lady?* a man might well be well-dead before an explanation were forthcoming. A man might receive a most pressing intimation to slip the short sword between any twain ribs he preferred, thus to prevent his family from attainder and his property from escheatal. Might. Might not. A man might receive a silver pottle or an ember-scuttle enchased with gold, as reward. Might. Might not.

It was all so very suddenly done. So very suddenly her arm was free from my steadying hands. In a second's time; less than it took a drop of water to fall from the clock—And in that second, while a flame of fire seemed to run up both my hands and arms and through my heart and thence into my manly parts (Touched a Vestal! Touched the Virgin's naked arm!); in that second our eyes chanced to meet—then her eyes were gone—then she was gone herself—and three thoughts like three bolts of lightning, so swift that before one fades away the other flashes, passed across my mind.

What color are her eyes?
It is death, by the Tarpaean Rock, to have carnal congress with a Vestal.
Her virgin's vows expire in her forty-fifth year.

The woman's age then, I did not know. How old was I then, I will not say.

She was gone at once, long enough had she tarried at the sordid scene beneath the walls of saffron-colored stone, sallow where long suns had beat upon them; not swiftly yet very steadily the small carriage departed, the mule's ears aprick, heading back towards the Temple of Vesta up there beneath the Palatine. It might be that her six-hour watch approached, of guarding and tending the sacred fire. Or it might be that she sought rest and refreshment after the noise and dust and glare. Where had she been? Secluded though they generally were, the Vestals were allowed to take the air at intervals: perhaps to worship at another temple, perhaps to pray before two-faced Janus, he *with red mouth straining and with face all grim,* as the Oracles of Maro had it. Scraps of thought flitted through my mind. Only a Vestal Virgin might drive a wheeled vehicle through day-time Rome (but ah gods! the hideous rumbling noisy nights!). Should she be accused of inchastity, two defenses were open to her: she might draw off a ship foundered on some shoal in the Tiber . . . using only a single thread. The Tiber at Rome was full of shoals, but as this knowledge was elementary and universal, ships (as distinct from bumboats) seldom came as high as Rome. Or . . . she might instead carry water in a sieve. A brave option; small wonder they were seldom accused. Only a Vestal might pardon a man on the way to execution. No one might pardon a Vestal caught in flagrant delight, or convicted after trial—Meherc! that a priestess of fire should be tried by water!—she was buried alive in a tomb at once sealed shut and a grim byword pointed out her last and only choice: starve while the lamp burned, or drink the oil and live a while longer in the dark. Whichever, the glory of the world would soon enough pass, and with it, too: the beauty, the damps, the chills, the plots, the pests, the fevers, and the fleas, of eternal Rome. Of Yellow Rome. Yellow Rome.

As the great fire of the First Year of the Emperor Julius I was destined to occur, *dixit David cum Sybilla* (whoever "David" is), it was fortunate that it occurred whilst the Roy was completing the conquest of Gaul the Sur, for when word of the extent of the conflagration reached Himself the August Caesar as he was entering the great Port called Marsayle, he ordered that it never be fired but that every building faced with marble be taken apart and the facing be sent by galley-drawn barges to the Ost Port of Rome and thence by oxen-courted shallow-draft vessels up the Tiber. This nonpareil stayne was at once named the *Gallo Antico,* the Ancient Gaul; some take it from *giallo antico,* the old gayle, as one says, *the blaunche fever and the gayle:* or in that poetic line, *his face as gayle as Winter grass, sello beneath the snae.* Soon enow came marbe of tother hues, *rosso antico,* and the green one green as the pistuquimnut; the maid-pale-white, the black-as-night, the mottled and the creamy brown; other yet. Well might the Julio exult, *A hamlet of wooden huts and hovels so I found, and one of marmol structoes I am to leave behind.* As this was in effect the first great quantity of marmorstone seen in Mamma Roma, its popular name was quickly given and ever been left so.

"Good fortune to that man," I said, shaking my head as though to dispel the flimsies of bad dreams.

Quint made a scoffing sound, such as only the tutelage of the costliest of rhetors could have produced. "Did you *see* that animal face? He will be caught for another dirty crime and condemned again and this time surely hanged for it within the year—if not, indeed, the week—and should he encounter another Vestal?"

I asked if the Vestals always set the felon free. Quint considered. "First you must meet your felon face to face," he said, shrugging. Quint was a great shrugger. "Then—of the current Six, you mean?" Instantly it occurred to him that I would scarcely have meant the Six current in the reign of Tarquin the Proud or Judah King of the Jews, and he went on to capitulate them. "Clothilda pardons everyone. Volumnia pardons no one. Honoria, would you believe it, gravely casts dice to decide. Carries them with her in a monopede's shoe—a *monopede's* shoe!" (There would be no gain in asking how he knew it was the shoe of a monopede, for he might have given me some such answer as, "Everybody knows it," or, "Because there is only one"—in which case my respect for him would be diminished.)

"Aurelia pardons now and then.—the dice? They are the most ordinary dice; sort of spoils the story, doesn't it? Stories are often spoiled like that: tiresome." My respect for him increased. "Lenora, they say, never drives that way, so as not to have to choose." He quirked his mouth, hunched his shoulders, flung out his hand and fluttered his fingers, with what might just be perceived as a very slight emphasis of the digit of infamy. "Soft-hearted Lenora, eh?—but they are all brutes, these fellows. Kindness to them is cruelty to others."

And he told a recent report, not even to be designated as a rumor, that the man just freed had once been a provincial gladiator of the lowest sort, probably expelled for incompetence. "I shouldn't wonder," he said. "You saw that sword-scarred face. No brow. No chin. Some ancestral taint, I'd venture. They sell very good bread with opium seed over there."

My question almost burst forth. "But which one was *she?*" She was only one of six sacred women in the service of Vesta, the goddess of the hearth, without whom there could really be no home, and hence, no Rome: but which one was she? The bread *did* smell good; they say there is at least one bakeshop in the capital for every province in the Empery. One does not doubt.

Quint turned to me, immediately (he) a man of the most scornful urban world. "But my dear fellow, you know *nothing!*—mage though you are— Well . . . how could you, there in Naples? She is Claudia."

"And does she often spare?"

Quint started again his rigmarole, stopped. Sincerely he seemed in doubt. Then, somewhat surprised, said that he did not know. That the matter had never—in his presence—come up before. Then he fell silent, merely gestured to his important friend's litters (only two of many, of course) which were waiting for us: quite in the Roman fashion: not *too* very far from the appointed place. He certainly did not ask, "Handsome woman, is she not?" or "What did you think of her?" or, "Do you fancy her?" One simply never asked such questions about a Vestal Virgin. It was a long way up to the Tarpaean Rock when you had to climb.

But it was only a short way down when you were pushed.

There were nights when I slept like a farmer, and nights when I could not sleep, or slept but ill. That night I fell soon into slumber, for thank the gods, in that very quiet—and very, very rich—quarter of Rome, where Quint's Etruscan friend had one of his villas, there was neither wagon traffic nor roistering. Whence, then, came that noise, a mere murmur at first, then tumult and clamor? I must have left my bed the better to observe and to hearken—what, then, a horrid shock, to realize that my arms were bound behind me at the elbows and my feet confined by straps or ropes so that I might take no very long steps and certainly could not run. I turned to ask my terrified question of the man nearest to me, an intent and stinking fellow in a dirty tunicle; but this one held, looped around his hands and arms, a rope: and the rope was noosed round my neck! It did not choke me, not so long as I kept up with my keeper. "But what then?" I begged the fellow. "But what then?" The shun-soap made no answer, but steadily led me along, as a nacker leads the nag before stopping him, stunning him, stabbing him, skinning him, and then cutting him up: hooves, hide, and pizzle to the glue-maker, and the other parts to—Suddenly the sound of the vulgus ceased, then resumed in another note and another register.

Then ceased again.

A woman's voice, strong and level and chill. *"I pardon that man."* Our gazes met. She showed her shock. Her eyes were blue and clear.

It was yet dark when I woke, but Rome generally awoke in the yet dark; a few lamps had already been kindled in the corridor; I noticed this abstractedly as I rushed to Quint: but Quint was already rushing to me. We met in the lesser atrium with the dull red walls where a few servants passed hither and thither like wraiths, thin vapors rising from the vessels in their hands. The heavy master of the household had either not yet aroused, or was occupied elsewhere; had he been present, our own respective business, however much it agitated us, must needs wait: but present he was not. At first our confrontation was in silence, there were sighs and moanings inarticulate, but not words. Then Quint said, and his voice trembled, "I have had such a dream!"

"And I—"

"Dreams are best kept silent, except to a qualified interpreter—or to a closemost friend—"

"Yes. . . ."

"I am older, let me speak first," said Quint. I staying silent, he went on to speak his words, clutching my arm, my arms, as though he would draw me to him. "Did you notice?" he asked. "Did you notice that old pedlar-dame in yesterday's mob? selling baskets and sieves? She passed through my dream at an angle and then I saw the woman, I mean *the* woman . . . the real woman . . . I saw the woman holding the sieve . . . Claudia it was . . . it was Claudia . . . she held the sieve—*you know what that means*—and my heart went chill and swollen and I peered to see if the sieve did indeed hold the water, or if it had merely let it slip through and the mesh still wet. But she held it upside-down, she held it upside-*down!* What does *that* mean? And she looked at me and I saw that her eyes were very blue and very clear," his own eyes, I saw in the increasing light of early day, were very red, and quite without salve or ointment; "and she looked past *me* and she looked at *you* and her eyes went wide and I re-marked her voice, I shall always remember her voice: it was level and strong and clear, and she pointed her hand at you and she said, *'Thou art the man!'* And what *that* means, I dare not think: but I would that you would leave our Yellow Rome at once."

After I had spoken in turn, Quint leaned closer to me, and almost, somehow, I expected to see a thin cold breath from his mouth, like that from the basins of hot water for a quick early morning wash even now hurried past us by a few diligent slaves: but slavery makes for diligence . . . and makes it, much. Quint asked, "What is the meaning of this two-part dream? Does one part come from the Gate of Ivory and is false? does one part issue from the Gate of Horn and is it true? Is the whole dream one of evil omen? or of good? If we say, *Good,* in that she pardons you? of some sentence of death, it is sure, for if it were merely a matter of a fine . . . prison . . . the dungeon . . . or the scourge—" here I shuddered, he went on—"how many men yearly die beneath the lash, merely, the lash? how many in the dungeon, where even a reflection of a reflection of the light of the sun or the moon never shines? . . . let alone in the mere prison? where sometimes a gleam of sunlight creeps as it were uncertainly amongst the filthy littered rushes or the trampled straw . . . or now and then a beam of moonlight is reflected by a burnished mazer or a pewter plate polished like a mirror? For that matter," he babbled, as we stood, crouched, in the atrium, close together; "for that matter," he went on, "when a mere fine, merely the matter of a fine has broke a man's bench, his *bancus* become *ruptus,* his lands his fields his house his yards his loft his laboratory all his goods his gear his tools his attire and even the very dead embers of his hearth for potash, and even the broken pisspot in the corner of his house of office: all, all, sold to pay the fine—eh?—how many, sinking beneath shame and broken spirit, the fine like blazing fire consumes all means of earning food?"

Quint, beside himself, was now unwittingly imitating the gestures, the very vocal tricks, of any advocate seen and heard in Apollo's Court. He swept the air with his hands, he bulged his eyes, he stood on his tip-toes, he touched his ear-lobe with a finger. "But all of these *minor penalties,*" this was a new Quint to me and no longer the sophisticate, the man-about-Rome, the cynical; "and if the enemy of the enemies of mine enemy does not die of the stinking-pox, then let him live . . . let him live under these *minor penalties;* And these, allegedly the lesser of evils, the Vestal Virgin may not pardon: not a farthing, not a fig: not the theft of enough crushed walnut paste to cover the toenail of an infant child: *none!*"

To sum up: I, Vergil, once with brief: an advocate: 'twas very brief: eh? if the Vestal Virgin in this probably vatic dream—and every dream in one way or another must be vatic, must be prophetic, else why is a dream dreamed? if I, Vergil, am he whom the Vestal pardons, she can be pardoning me only from sentence of death. Not from charge of a crime meriting death, no, from *sentence* of death. And what can I, Vergil, have done or what would I *do,* to merit?

Dared I, would I dare? to love her—?

And as for the other dream, and her cry of, *"Thou art the man!"* if this was not accusative, then what was it? *Could* it be exculpatory? all things were, some barely, possible: but . . . he would believe that this the Virgin's exclamation was exculpatory? then he would believe anything . . . let him, if he would, believe—

But let him first flee. And if not to the end of the Empery, then at least from Yellow Rome. To be, at least, a while more, safe.

Where would he safest be? from the accusations of the vatic voice in a state of dream—? whither flees the frightened child? he flees to home.

And now and for a long time: *Naples was home.*

. . . whence he might, if he would, if he need, having taken stock, flee again . . .

But why *at once* . . . ? Why, because there was no set time indicated in these dreams. Who knows but what even now delators and informants were bespeaking those who bespoke the soldiery, *He laid his hands upon the Virgin's naked flesh,* and, *Act quickly, he may soon escape and flee* . . .

Also, *did* I wait, tarry? . . . opportunity . . . temptation . . . lust . . .
Thus: *at once.*

It is tiresome to say what everyone knows, in this case that some things are more quickly said than done. There was no ship at a wharf behind a signboard reading HOME, AT ONCE. We had to wait until Quint's friend, our host, was willing to see us. Then it was needful (he, Quint, thought) that I should leave the City by a round-about way and not by any of the broader streets, and essential (I thought) that Quint should not be seen with me; and I was a long time persuading him of this, and even I had a chore preventing him of this, and even I had a chore preventing him that he might not even, as he put it, "put bread in my wallet" for the journey, in my old doe-skin budget, *bread:* had I yielded at all, we would likely have wandered over half of Rome to find some particular bake-shop. With or without opium seed. Even, yes indeed! he might bethink him, *bread is not enough!* and insist he obtain me *cheese,* and *salame-sausage!*—at which, by the sod and staff! might I give myself up for lost—

I was therefore long in leaving, and I neither drew rein of my borrowed horse, a gentle stalwart grey with dappled haunches; his name alas I never learned, I called him *Thee* (the Etruscan . . . a bit mysterious, like most his kind; and like most his kind: rich . . . had many horses, asked no questions) nor looked back till I had reached the rise by the third milestone. Then I halted, and turned. No pursuit? None . . . though I was uneasy in recalling that a dream, like a curse, might sometimes wait as much as seven years for fulfillment. No sign of pursuit, nor yet I was not easy. Ease is not always to the wise; was I wise? Some knowledge had I gained, but had I gained wisdom?

And lifting my eyes from the Appian Road I saw in the setting sun the cloud of dust raised by the hooves of the beasts being driven into the city to be slaughtered early next morning for sale in the markets, and the dust was faintly yellow. I saw in the suddenly visible middle distance the gold-spiked roofs, and stonework in marble the color of the hair of a fair-haired woman, brickwork the shade of straw, tiles a tint between that of the lemon of Sicily and a bright marigold blowing in the wind. I saw the glittering roofs and glow-ing golden buildings of Rome. By the yellow Tiber in the yellow dusk I saw the city of Yellow Rome . . . of Yellow Rome. . . .

Yellow Rome.

I turned and urged on my horse. It was a long way to Naples.

Afterword to "Yellow Rome; or, Vergil and the Vestal Virgin"

BY RAY NELSON

All the Vergil Magus stories together are only the tip of an iceberg the size of a rather large universe, as I realized when Avram allowed me to browse the boxes containing the detailed notes on fact, myth, and fantasy upon which they rest. Here's a glimpse into the Vergil Magus Cosmos, a tiny bright diamond in which the infinite whole is reflected.

Afterword

NIGHT TRAVEL ON THE ORIENT EXPRESS, DESTINATION: AVRAM

RAY BRADBURY

There are several risks connected with writing an Afterword to another writer's works.

One, you may overpraise, in which case the reader turns off, saying: He can't be that good. The reader then approaches all the stories with a chip on his shoulder, daring the writer to be as fine as he has been told.

Two, you may underpraise. In an effort to be fair and unassuming, you may hold back. In which case the reader says: How peculiar. This critic seems dreadfully quiet. The stories that follow, then, can't really be worthwhile.

And so the book is shut.

I would like to balance myself somewhere between the two extremes.

Let me plunge right in, then, looking neither to right nor to left, ahead nor behind.

Avram Davidson, to me, combines many talents and attributes, including imagination, style, and, perhaps above all, wit.

Many of these stories are complete mysteries, puzzles. Avram Davidson starts us in a fog and lets us orient ourselves slowly. He tosses us bits of information. We do not know where we are, who the characters are, or what they are up to. Slowly we begin to find our way toward the light, with Mr. Davidson always a few quick steps ahead, calling us, as a good storyteller calls: This way, now this, over here, now up, now down, now to one side, come along!

And he knows exactly how much information to give us any one second. He knows how to pay out the rope, inch by inch. Too slow and we would fall asleep. Too fast and we would miss the point. His knack for a proper pace is that of a true teller of tales.

A teller of tales. The designation is almost an insult in our time. We have been sore put upon by your *New Yorker* slice-of-life writer and all of the other non-talents of our age appearing in magazine after magazine, so that when we come upon such as Avram Davidson we go into a mild shock of surprise. For this is what story writing once was, and can be again, if we leave it to more-capable hands.

Reading through his collection, a number of storytellers' names leaped to mind. I hope that Mr. Davidson will approve this list that tossed itself up, now here, now there: Rudyard Kipling, Saki, John Collier, G. K. Chesterton.

I could make the list longer, but those must do for now.

I can imagine nothing better than taking a long train journey, oh, let us say, on the old Orient Express with good food and good wine waiting in the diner, and seated across from me, the personification of their books, such as Mr. Kipling, Saki, Collier, Chesterton, and, holding his own, amid them all, Avram Davidson in high good humor.

I realize that is a rare fine company I have put him in, but I have always been one to stick my neck out through affection and admiration. If I would not say he measures completely to their height, I *do* say this: On such a train, on such a sweet night journey, these men would gladly listen to Avram Davidson and read and enjoy him. You would find his stories in their book bags, even as you would find theirs in his. If their abilities differ, as do tastes, we know they are good companions, and similar people who would travel well because of their knack for the agreeably strange, the small truth that becomes a lie or the lie suddenly revealed as truth.

I would gladly ride with these and stay up half the night training across Europe in the dark, and even keep my mouth shut, to hear their tales.

The shadow of Kafka might fall across their night-traveling talk, here or there.

And outside of Budapest, through some whim of impossible geography, Dickens' phantom signalman might flag the train to a ghost stop for some while.

Avram Davidson is not like any of these, and yet, as I have said, their night company was made for him. They would ask him in out of the corridor, even if he were simply passing, disguised as ticket agent, covered with strange punched-out confetti left over from most peculiar destinations.

There is a bit of the scalawag in Avram Davidson. He can be wrongheaded, but it is the sort of wrongheadedness we did not tolerate in Bernard Shaw so much as delight in. We enjoy an outrageous person, for so many puritan radicals among us wouldn't know how to radicalize a mole, much less outrage a snail. Davidson, no less than John Collier, is a maker of gyroscopes that by their very logic of manufacture *shouldn't* work but—lo! there above the abyss they *do* spin and hum.

A final warning, not repeated often enough: Collections of short stories, like vitamins, should be taken, one or two a night, just before sleep. It will be a temptation, but don't gorge yourself on this book. Easy does it, and much affection for this teller of tales Avram Davidson will be the healthy result.

At the end of a week of such nights, you will have developed a proper appetite for further journeys to that strange, wild country of Avram in all the years ahead.

—RAY BRADBURY
Los Angeles, California
November 18, Apollo Year Two.

Afterword

TURN OUT THE LIGHTS*

Harlan Ellison

(Harlan Ellison has written or edited seventy-three books; in his bibliography, more than seventeen-hundred stories, essays, articles, newspaper columns, motion pictures, and teleplays. Among his many awards and honors, he has won the World Fantasy Lifetime Achievement Award, the Mystery Writers of America Edgar Allan Poe award twice (he came in second on his third nomination), the Horror Writers of America Bram Stoker Award five times (including a Lifetime Achievement honor), the Nebula three times, the Hugo 8 ½ times, the Writers Guild of America Most Outstanding Teleplay Award for solo work an unprecedented four times, the Silver Pen for Journalism from PEN, and the universal opinion that he is the most contentious person now walking the Earth. He is still delighted to recall the day in 1962 when he finally managed to sell a short story to Avram Davidson at The Magazine of Fantasy & Science Fiction: *"Polly Charms the Sleeping Woman," which appeared in August of that year.* Slippage, *Ellison's latest story collection and seventieth book altogether, was published in Fall 1997.)*

On the day I sit down to write this note, ruminations meant to add a grace note to an event, a publication, a fervent wish, a vain hope I've harbored for thirty-eight years (since I sold my first story at the end of 1955)—I have just hung up the phone, having been informed that my pal, the most excellent and virtually unremembered master talent, the great Avram Davidson, has died.

And I am suddenly more concerned with stealing a moment here to honor him, than I am with blowing my own horn about how clever I was to have written "The Man Who Rowed Christopher Columbus Ashore." Because, you see, for all the hot air and Monday-morning-quarterback deconstructionist

*Excerpted from the Contributors' Notes in *The Best American Short Stories 1993, ed. Louise Endrich pp. 363–65.

horse puckey that writers and academics like to slather on the subject, there are only a couple of genuine Secrets about writing.

The first has to do with the *why*. And most of what is said and written is sententious claptrap, intended to buy us a shot at posterity by providing untenured educationists drivel for their treatises. Quentin Crisp once observed that "Artists in any medium are nothing more than a bunch of hooligans who cannot live within their income of admiration." Oh, how we want that assurance that once we're gone, no matter that we were as specialized a savory as Nathanael West or as common a confection as Clarence Budington Kelland, that we will be read fifty years hence. Because the *why* is as simply put as this: "I write only because I cannot stop." Don't credit that one to me, I'm not that smart. It was Heinrich Von Kleist. And he nailed it; what he suggests, in literary terms, is the equivalent of the answer to *most* of the stuff that we do: "It seemed like a good idea at the time."

But West is barely read today, not to mention Shirley Jackson (who was the inspiration for "The Man Who Rowed—"), or James Agee, or William March, or Jim Tully, or even John O'Hara or Zoë Oldenbourg. Or Avram Davidson, who was one of the most stylish, witty, erudite, and wildly imaginative writers of our time. Author of more than twenty-five books. Only one of them in print.

He died in a VA hospital's liaison "recuperation facility" called Resthaven; in Bremerton, Washington; all alone save for a compassionate nurse who knew his name as a superior fantasist; penniless, unknown to a nation of readers though he was working right up to the end; seventy years old and cranky as a screw being turned against its threads; a man who wrote like a wonky, puckish, amusing Henry James, sans the stick up his butt.

Avram dies, and like Kelland, who was as commercially successful in his time as Stephen King is in his, or Jackson, who was never higher than "midlist," gone is gone, and Posterity is busy figuring out who among today's Flavors-of-the-Month will bring in the most money by going "interactive."

On this day that I sit down to write my note to accompany (finally, after thirty-eight years of dreaming about it, lusting after it) my inclusion in *The Best American Short Stories*, all I can think about is Avram, and how he deserved many times to have been included here over the years, how he never got that notice, how posterity may have escaped him entirely, and I keep returning to this damned question of why we miss going to the movies, or attending a concert, or spending a quiet evening with a loved one, or taking that trip to the Great Barrier Reef . . . because we've got yet another deadline, yet another story to write, yet another idea burning to be slammed onto paper. It's far far less, I think, of Mario Vargas Llosa's "The writer is an exorcist of his own demons," than it is what Von Kleist and Quentin Crisp said.

I have a T-shirt that bears the message NOT TONIGHT, DEAR, I HAVE A DEADLINE.

Funny, till the last deadline comes, as it did for Avram. And then, like West or Tully or F. Van Wyck Mason, you're no-price. So what was it all about?

The secret is this: *anyone* can become a writer. If you look at the actual work of many of the creatures appearing on the bestseller lists, you know that things that flourish in petri dishes can become writers. The trick, the secret, is to *stay* a writer. To produce a body of work that you hope improves and changes with time and the accumulation of skill. To stay a writer day after year after story, till at last you get smart enough, or work long enough pulling the plow, to write something that gets included in *The Best American Short Stories,* a dream you know (in those cold moments when you can't lie to yourself) will always elude you, because there is no great bearded sentience in the universe, and "it ain't fair . . . I deserve it" doesn't mean shit, as David Webb Peoples said in his screenplay for *Unforgiven* (which should've won the Oscar for Best Original Screenplay). There is no god, or even upper-case God, wasting his, her, or its time mucking about in our daily affairs. There is only random chance and the cupidity of the uncaring cosmos.

Which is *exactly* what "The Man Who Rowed Christopher Columbus Ashore" is about. There is no pattern; no pantheon of busybody entities up there in the clouds ordaining our lives; no Grand Scheme. You can be walking down the street, slip and tear your Achilles tendon, and walk with a limp for the rest of your life, thereby killing your career as a ballet dancer, but forcing you to make a living at brain surgery, during which career you discover the cure for brain cancer. *That's* what the story is about. Don't listen to the bone-head deconstructionists when they start all that "basic Apollonian-Dionysian Conflict" hooey. The story is about nothing more difficult or loftier than the admonition that *you* are responsible, that posterity is a snare, that memory is short, and that life is an absolutely unriggable crap shoot, with the stickman a civil servant who works for some department as inept as you are. Some days he does something swell, some days he does something creepy, some days he does something crummy, and some days, well, he don't do nothin' at all.

Even if you're standing all alone in the middle of the Gobi Desert at high noon, and a Mosler safe falls out of the baggage compartment of a Concorde zipping by overhead at thirty-three thousand feet, and the great heavy thing falls right on top of you and squashes you to guava jelly . . . it was your fault. You're responsible. It was, after all, *you* who chose to stand in that spot, at that moment.

And it only took me fourteen years, from conception and the writing down of the first few lines of the story, to get smart enough to write the *complete* story, and do it properly. And I cannot tell you how goofily pleased I am to be here. It only took thirty-eight years, and I'm nuts with pleasure. I'm one of the lucky ones. Avram never made it.

Rest in peace, old pal.